RISE OF THE TERRAN EMPIRE

THE TECHNIC CIVILIZATION SAGA

BAEN BOOKS
❖BY❖
POUL ANDERSON

The Van Rijn Method
David Falkayn: Star Trader
Rise of the Terran Empire
Young Flandry (forthcoming)

To Outlive Eternity and Other Stories

Time Patrol

Hokas! Pokas! (with Gordon R. Dickson)
Hoka! Hoka! Hoka! (with Gordon R. Dickson)

RISE OF THE TERRAN EMPIRE

THE TECHNIC CIVILIZATION SAGA

POUL ANDERSON

RISE OF THE TERRAN EMPIRE

"Introduction" copyright © 2009 by Hank Davis. "A Chronology of Technic Civilization" by Sandra Miesel copyright © 2008 by Sandra Miesel.

A Baen Book

Baen Publishing Enterprises
P.O. Box 1403
Riverdale, NY 10471
www.baen.com

ISBN 13: 978-1-4391-3275-3

Cover art by Bob Eggleton

First Baen printing, June 2009

Distributed by Simon & Schuster
1230 Avenue of the Americas
New York, NY 10020

Library of Congress Cataloging-in-Publication Data

Anderson, Poul, 1926-2001.
  Rise of the Terran Empire / by Poul Anderson.
    p. cm.
  ISBN 978-1-4391-3275-3 (trade pbk.)
  1. Life on other planets—Fiction. 2. Human-alien encounters—Fiction. 3. Interplanetary voyages__Fiction. I. Title.
  PS3551.N378R57 2009
  813'.54--dc22
                                    2009011712

Printed in the United States of America

10 9 8 7 6 5 4 3 2 1

CONTENTS

DESCENT INTO EMPIRE

The third volume of the Technic Civilization saga is centered around a major faultline in the series' future history; "interesting times," as the famous Chinese curse phrases it. There is darkness, disaster, and tragedy. But there are also men and women fighting the darkness, enduring through tragedy, striving to bring light back to the human worlds.

The series was written by Poul Anderson, after all . . .

The Commonwealth was no utopia, but it had a measure of political freedom. The Polesotechnic League was no confederation of saints, but its members (for their own benefit, of course) were a counterforce to the power of the Confederation, insuring economic freedom.

It couldn't last, of course. Sooner or later, the center cannot hold. The traders might have acted against their "colleagues" who were engaging in outright piracy and pillage—but they didn't, and doomed the Polesotechnic League. Nor did they act against those who sold starships and high-tech weapons to barbarian planets, thereby dooming the Confederation.

That's the big picture. On a smaller scale, *Mirkheim*, the novel that leads off this volume, is a last hurrah for Nicholas Van Rijn, David Falkayn, Adzel, and Chee Lan. The old order is crumbling. As one of the Baburites says to David Falkayn during a tense situation, "You do not speak for the entire League. It no longer has a single voice."

Yet Van Rijn and his trader team persevere. Quoth Adzel, "Oh, I regret nothing . . . Let us savor this final adventure of ours for what it is." They'll tell sad stories of the deaths of kings some other time, after the hurly-burly's done.

Still, even though one danger is averted, the triumph is bittersweet, as the four go their separate ways, with Van Rijn musing (in his characteristic fractured Anglish), "I suppose will still be held solemn councils of the League for another century, till some Napoleon type without no sense of humor comes along and ends the farce."

As it happened, the Napoleon type was named Manuel, and he built an empire that would protect beleaguered Terra—Earth—from those extraterrestrial barbarians with starships and high-tech weapons. Empires can accomplish great things . . . and they can also commit even more terrible atrocities, sometimes at the same time. For its own protection, if not for less compelling reasons, the rising Terran Empire began annexing formerly independent star systems, whether they wanted to join the club or not.

And in the end, the Terran Empire contains the seeds of its own doom, a doom darker and more disastrous than was that of the smaller Commonwealth which it replaced. Its fall will be followed by the Long Night, which may engulf that sector of the Galaxy for thousands of years.

Yet there are those who fight to delay that inevitable fall, and make plans to shorten the Long Night's duration. Chief among them is Dominic Flandry, one of science fiction's most popular and beloved figures. He'll step onstage in the next volume, if the unfailingly patient reader will forgive my getting ahead of the story.

Once again, a word about the introductions to the stories. Poul Anderson did not, to my knowledge, do introductions to the two novels, but did introductions (and an afterword) to the two short stories set on Avalon when they appeared in *The Earth Book of Stormgate*. They were written as if by the Ythrian, Hloch of the Stormgate Choth. (For other details, see my introduction to *The Van Rijn Method*, the first volume in the Technic Civilization series.)

As for the two novelettes, "The Star Plunderer" had an introduction by Anderson on its first appearance in print, in *Planet Stories*. And in the case of "The Sargasso of Lost Starships," also from that grand old

Planet pulp and here appearing in book form for the first time, all the blame for that story's introduction is mine.

"Sargasso" is pure-quill pulp writing, both in the style and in the plot, which is much unlike anything else in the Technic Civilization saga. I thought of doing an introduction exploring that aspect, and yielded to the temptation. (That was nowhere as strong a temptation as Valduma was for Donovan, but I'm obviously a lesser man than him.) I hope that Poul Anderson would not too severely disapprove of what I've done. And you don't *have* to read it.

Finally, as with *The Van Rijn Method*, once again the e-book version of *Rise of the Terran Empire* has a bonus: another essay by Sandra Miesel, authority extraordinaire on the works of Poul Anderson. It will illuminate the intricacies of the novel *The People of the Wind* (contained herein) far more than I could ever do.

—Hank Davis, 2009

MIRKHEIM

❖Prologue❖

Y minus 500,000.

Once there had been a great proud star, bright as a hundred Sols. Through four hundred million years its blue-white fire burned steadily, defiance of the darkness around and challenge to those other suns whose distant brilliances crowded the sky. Orbiting it afar was a companion worthy of its majesty, a planet whose mass equaled fifteen hundred Earths, redly aglow with the heat of its own contraction. There may have been lesser worlds and moons as well; we cannot now say. We simply know that the giant stars rarely have attendants, so this one was due to a curious ordainment of God, or destiny, or chance.

The giants die young, as arrogantly as they have lived. A day came when the hydrogen fuel at the core was exhausted. Instead of swelling and reddening as a lesser sun would do in its old age, this fell in upon itself. Energies beyond imagination broke free; atoms crashed together to fuse in strange new elements; the star exploded. For a short while, in its fury, it shone well-nigh as radiant as its entire galaxy.

No ordinary world could have endured the storm of incandescence which then swept outward. Something the size of Earth must have perished entirely, the very iron of its core made vapor. Even the huge companion lost most of its mass, hydrogen and helium bursting forth into endlessness. But this drank so much energy that the metallic

1

heart of the globe was only turned molten. Across it seethed the matter cast out by the star in its death struggle.

More of that matter escaped into space. For tens of millennia the wrecks of sun and planet whirled in the middle of a nebula which, seen from afar, glowed like faerie lacework. But it dissipated and lost itself across light-years; darkness moved inward. The remnant of the planet congealed, barely aglimmer where its alloys cast back the gleam from distant constellations.

For half a million years, these ruins drifted alone through the deep.

Y minus 28.

The world men call Babur will never be a home to them. Leaving his spaceship, Benoni Strang grew violently aware of weight. Upon his bones lay half again the drag of the Hermes which had bred him or the Earth which had bred his race. Flesh strained against the burden of itself. The armor that kept him alive became a stone on either shoulder, either foot.

Nevertheless, though he could have activated his impeller and flitted from the airlock, he chose to stride along the gangway to the ground, like an arriving king.

At first he could barely see that beings awaited him. The sun Mogul was high in a murky purple heaven where red clouds roiled, and its radiance was more fierce than that of Maia or Sol; but it was tiny at its distance. Hoar soil gave back some light, as did an ice cliff a kilometer away and the liquid ammonia cataract toppling over its sheerness. Yet his vision did not reach to the horizon. He thought a grove of low trees with long black fronds stood at the edge of sight on his left, and that he could make out the glistening city he knew was to his right. However, this was as unsure as the greeting he would get. And every shape he discerned was so alien that when he glanced elsewhere he could not remember it. Here he must learn all over again how to use his eyes.

A hydrogen-helium atmosphere turned shrill the boom of the falls, the thump of boots on gangway and afterward their scrunch across sod. By contrast, his breath within the helmet, the slugging of blood in his ears, came to him like bass drumbeats. Sweat dampened his skin and reeked in his nostrils. He hardly noticed. He was too exultant at having arrived.

The blur before him gained form with each step he took, until it was a cluster of a dozen creatures. One of them moved to meet him. He cleared his throat and said awkwardly, through a speaker: "I am Benoni Strang. You wanted me to join you."

The Baburite carried a vocalizer, which changed hums and mumbles into Anglic words. "We required that for your sake as well as ours. If you are to maintain close relationships and do research on us, as we on you, then you must often come to the surface and interact directly with us. This visit will test your ability."

It had already been tested in the environmental chambers of the school that had trained him. Strang didn't say so. That might somehow give offense. Despite two decades of contact, trade which had culminated in exchanging spacecraft technology for heavy metals and a few other goods, humans knew little about Baburites. *We're absolutely ignorant of how much they know about us,* he recalled.

"I thank you," he said. "You'll have to be patient with me, I'm afraid, but eventually I should be in a position to reward your efforts."

"How?"

"Why, by finding new areas where we can do business to our mutual benefit." Strang did not admit his superiors had scant expectation of that. He had barely gotten this assignment, mainly to give him a few years' practical experience, he a young xenologist whose education had concentrated on subjovian planets.

He had uttered no hint of the ambition he nourished. The hour to do so would be when he had proof the scheme was possible—if it ever would be.

"After our experience on Suleiman," the native said, "we question what we may gain from the Polesotechnic League."

The flat artificial voice could convey none of the resentment. And did such an emotion lie behind it? Who could read the heart of a Baburite? It did not even have anything like a heart.

"The Solar Spice & Liquors Company is not the whole League," Strang answered. "Mine is entirely different from it. They've nothing in common but membership, and membership means less than it used to."

"This we will study," the being told him. "That is why we will cooperate with your scientific team. We mean to get as well as give knowledge, information we need before our civilization can claim a place by yours."

The dream in Strang flared upward.

Y minus 24.

Both moons of Hermes were aloft, Caduceus rising small but nearly full, the broad sickle of Sandalion sinking westward. High in the dusk, a pair of wings caught light from the newly set sun and shone gold. A tilirra sang amidst the foliage of a millionleaf, which rustled to a low breeze. At the bottom of the canyon it had cut for itself, the Palomino River rang with its haste; but that sound reached the heights as a murmur.

Sandra Tamarin and Peter Asmundsen came out of the mansion onto a terrace. Halting at the parapet, they looked down to where water gleamed through shadow, then around them to the forest which enclosed Windy Rim, and across to violet silhouettes of the Arcadian Hills. Their hands joined.

She said at last, "I wish you had not to go."

"Me too," he replied. "'Tis been a wonderful visit."

"Are you positive you can't handle the matter from here? We have complete equipment, communication, computation, data retrieval, everything."

"Ordinarily that would be fine. But in this case—well, my Traver employees do have legitimate grievances. In their place, belike I'd threaten a strike myself. If I can't avoid giving preferential promotions to Followers, at least I can try to hammer out a set of compensations for Travers, as might be extra vacations. Their leaders will be in more of a mood to compromise if I've taken the trouble to come meet them in person."

"I suppose you're right. You have a sense for such things." She sighed. "I wish I did."

He regarded her a while, and she him, before he said, "You do. More than you realize." Smiling: "You'd better—our probable next Grand Duchess."

"Do you believe so in truth?" On the instant, the question they had been thrusting aside throughout this holiday was with them. "I did once, oh, yes. Now I'm not sure. That's why I've, well, retreated here to my parents' home. Too many people made plain what they think of me after seeing the consequence of my own damn foolishness."

"Brake that nonsense," he said, perhaps more roughly than intended. "If your father had not those business interests that disqualify him, there'd be no doubt of his election. You're his daughter, the best possibility we own—equal to him, maybe better—and for precisely that reason, you're intelligent enough to know it. Are you telling me you've let a few prudes and snobs hurt you? Why, you should be bragging about Eric. Eventually your youngling will be the best Grand Duke Hermes ever had."

Her eyes went from his toward the darkling wilderness. He could barely hear her: "If he can curb the devil that's in him from *his* father."

Straightening, she met his gaze again and said aloud, "Oh, I've stopped being angry at Nick van Rijn. He was more honest with me, really, than I was with him or myself. And how could I regret having Eric? But of late—Pete, I'll admit to you, I wish Eric were legitimate. That his father were a man who could bide with us."

"Something of the kind might be arranged," he blurted. And then his tongue locked, and they stood long mute, two big blond humans who searched each other's faces through a twilight that half blinded them. The breeze lulled, the tilirra chanted, the river laughed on its way to the sea.

Y minus 18.

A ship hunted through space until she found the extinct supernova. Captain David Falkayn beheld the circling planetary core and saw that it was good. But its aspect was so forbidding that he christened it Mirkheim.

Soon afterward, he guided other ships there, with beings aboard who meant to wrest hope out of desolation. They knew the time granted them would be slight, so while they could they must labor hard and dare much.

Falkayn and his comrades did not linger. They had lives of their own to lead. From time to time they would come back, eager to learn how the work had gone; and always the toilers would bless them.

Y minus 12.

When he descended on Babur, Strang no longer walked, but traveled about at comparative ease, held in a harness atop a gravsled. The natives knew he could handle himself sufficiently well on their world to merit their respect. He had proved that over and over—occasionally at mortal risk, when the violent land suffered an outburst, a quake, or an avalanche. Today he sat in a chamber built of ice and talked for hour after hour with one he called Ronzal.

That was not the Baburite's true name. There was a set of vibrations which the computer in a vocalizer decided to render as "Ronzal." Conceivably it was not nomenclature at all. Strang had never found out for certain. Nonetheless, in the course of time he and the bearer had become friends, as nearly as was possible. And who could tell how near that was?

Which language they used during their discussion depended on what either wanted to say. Anglic or League Latin lent themselves best to some concepts, "Siseman" to others. (Those three syllables were another artifact of the vocalizer.) And still, every now and then they must grope about for a way to express what they meant. They were not even sure always what they thought. Though they had spent their careers patiently trying to build bridges across the differences of their brains and their histories, the endeavor was far from reaching an end.

Yet Ronzal could say what wakened trumpets in Strang: "The final opposition has yielded. The entire globe is meshed in the Imperial Band. Now we are ready to look outward."

At last, at last! But years lie ahead before we—Babur and I—can do more than look. Calm, Benoni, lad, calm. The human hauled back down his soaring thoughts. "Wonderful," he said. That was about as much enthusiasm as he saw any point in showing. The two races did not rejoice alike. "My colleagues and I have been expecting it, of course. You've rolled up victories till I was puzzled why any society

dared resist you. In fact, I'm just back from a conference with my"—
he hesitated—"my superiors." *They aren't really. No longer. As events
here gathered momentum, as it grew more and more likely that Babur
can in fact become the kind of instrument I foresaw, and I am now
their vital principal liaison with Babur; I have become their equal. In
the end, I am going to be their chieftain.*

*No matter now. No sense in boastfulness. It's a weary way yet till
I stand again on Hermes.*

"I'm authorized to begin talks about creating a space navy for
you," he said.

"We have considered among ourselves how that can be an
economic possibility," Ronzal responded. "How can we meet the cost?"

Fighting for coolness against the thrill that went through him,
Strang spoke with caution. "It may be our relationship is ready to go
beyond the immediate value-for-value we've exchanged hitherto.
Obviously you can't buy weapons development from us with the
resources you have to offer."

(Gold and silver, cheap on Babur because, at its temperatures,
solid mercury filled their industrial roles better. Plant secretions
which were convenient starting points for organo-halogen syntheses.
Some other materials that formed links in a chain of trades, from
planet to planet, till the traders finally got what they wanted.
Commerce between worlds so mutually foreign would always be
marginal at best.)

"Our races can exchange services as well as goods," Strang said.

Ronzal fell silent, doubtless pondering. How deeply dared it trust
monsters who breathed oxygen, drank liquid water, and radiated
oven-hotly from their armor? Strang sympathized. He had passed
through the same unsureness; he would never be quite at ease either.
As if to remind himself how out of place he was here, he squinted
through gloom at the Baburite.

When both stood erect, Ronzal's head reached the man's waist.
Behind an upright torso stretched a horizontal barrel, tailless,
mounted on eight short legs. It seemed to bear rows of gills. Actually
those were the opercula protecting tracheae which, given a dense
hydrogen atmosphere, aerated the body as efficiently as Strang's
lungs did his. From the torso sprang a pair of arms terminating in
lobsterlike claws; extending from the wrists above these were strong

tendrils to serve as fingers. The head consisted mostly of spongy snout, with four tiny eyes behind. The smooth skin was striped in orange, blue, black, and white. A filmy robe covered most of it.

The Baburite had no mouth. It ground up food with its claws and put this into a digestive pouch on the abdomen to be liquefied before the snout dipped down to absorb the nourishment. Hearing and smell centered in the tracheal organs. Speech arose from vibrating diaphragms on the sides of the head. The sexes were three, and individuals changed cyclically from one to the next according to patterns and circumstances which Strang had never managed to elucidate fully.

An untrained human would only have perceived grotesqueness. He, looking at the being in its own environment, saw dignity, power, and a curious beauty.

A humming behind the vocalizer asked, "Who of us will gain?"

"Both of us." Though Strang knew his words would have no meaning to the listener, he let them clang forth: "Security. Mastery. Glory. Justice."

Y minus 9.

Seen from an activated transparency in Nicholas van Rijn's penthouse atop the Winged Cross, Chicago Integrate was a godland of spires, towers, many-colored walls, crystalline vitryl, gracefully curving trafficways, flickering emblems, here and there a stretch of trees and greensward, the sky and the lake as aglitter with movement as the ground itself. Whenever they visited, the Falkayns never tired of that spectacle. To David it was comparatively fresh; he had spent most of his life off Earth. But Coya, who had been coming to see her grandfather since before she could walk, likewise found it always new. Today it beckoned their attention more than ever before: for they would soon be embarked on their first shared voyage beyond Sol's outermost comets.

The old man was giving them a small, strictly private farewell dinner. The live servitors whom he could afford didn't count, they were well trained in discretion, and he had sent both his current mistresses to his house in Djakarta to await his arrival in a day or so.

Knowing that van Rijn's idea of a small dinner took a couple of hours, from the first beluga caviar to the last magnificently decadent cheese, the Falkayns brought good appetites. A Mozart sonata lilted them welcome; tankards of beer stood beside icy muglets of akvavit and a dozen varieties of smoked seafood; incense from Tai-Tu drifted subtle on the air. Their host had in their honor put on better clothes than he usually wore, full-sleeved shirt, lace at his throat and wrists, iridescent vest, plum-colored trousers—though his feet were in straw slippers—and he seemed in boisterous good humor.

Then the phone chimed.

"*Wat drommel?*" van Rijn growled. "I told Mortensen no calls from anybody less rank than the angel Gabriel. That porridge brain he got is gone cold and pobbery with lumps in, ha?" His huge form slap-slapped across an expanse of trollcat rug to the instrument at the opposite end of the living room. "I give him his just deserts, *flambé,* by damn!" A hairy finger poked the accept button.

"Freelady Lennart is calling, sir," announced the figure in the screen. "You said you would speak to her whenever she answered your request for a conversation. Shall she be put through?"

Van Rijn hesitated. He tugged the goatee which, beneath waxed mustaches, ornamented his triple chin. His beady black eyes, close set under a sloping forehead on either side of a great hook nose, darted toward his guests. It was not really true what many asserted, that the owner of the Solar Spice & Liquors Company had a cryogenic computer as prosthesis for a soul. He rather doted on his favorite granddaughter, and her newly acquired husband had been his protégé before becoming his agent. "I know what she got to honk-honk about," he rumbled. "Grismal. Not for our happy fun gastogether."

"But you'd better grab the chance to contact her when it comes, right, Gunung Tuan?" Coya replied. "Go ahead. Davy and I will admire the view." She didn't suggest he take the call in a different room. That he could trust them as he did himself went without saying. As confidence dwindled in public institutions, those of the Solar Commonwealth and the Polesotechnic League alike, loyalties grew the more intensely personal.

Van Rijn sighed like a baby typhoon and settled himself into a chair, paunch resting majestically on lap. "I won't be long, no, I will currytail discussion," he promised. "That Lennart, she gives me indigestion, *ja,* she makes my ghastly juices boil. But we got this need for standing back to back, no matter how bony hers is. . . . Put her through," he told his chief secretary.

Falkayn and Coya took their drinks back to the transparency and looked out. But their glances soon strayed, for they found each other a sight more splendid than anything below or around them.

He might have been less in love than she, being eighteen years older and a wanderer who had known many women in many strange places. But in fact he felt that after all that time he had finally come to a haven he had always, unknowingly, been seeking. Coya Conyon, who proudly followed a custom growing in her generation and now called herself Coya Falkayn, was tall and slender in a scarlet slack-suit. Her dark hair fell straight to her shoulders, framing an oval face where the eyes were wide and gold-flecked green, the mouth wide and soft above a firm little chin, the nose snubbed like his own, the complexion sun-tinged ivory.

And she could not yet sate her gaze with him. He was tall, too; his gray outfit showed off an athletic build; his features were lean in the cheeks and high in the cheekbones, his eyes the blue and his hair the yellow common among the aristocratic families of Hermes. He also had the erect bearing of that class; but his lips denied their heritage, creasing too readily into laughter. Thus far he needed no meditechnic help to look younger than his forty-one years.

They touched tankards and smiled. Then van Rijn's bellow jerked their minds willy-nilly across the room.

"What you say?" The merchant reared where he sat. Black ringlets, the style of three decades ago, swirled about his beefy shoulders. Through Falkayn flitted recollection of a recent episode when a rival firm had mounted an elaborate espionage operation to find out if the old man was dyeing his hair or not. It might be a clue to whether age would soon diminish his rapacious capacities. The attempt had failed.

"You shouldn't make jokes, Lennart," van Rijn bawled on. "Is not your style. You, in a clown suit with a red balloon snoot and painted grin, you would still look like about to quote some minor Hebrew prophet on a bad day. Let's talk straight about how we organize to stop this pox-and-pestilence thing."

Across several thousand kilometers, Hanny Lennart's stare

drilled into his. She was a gaunt and sallow blonde, incongruously wearing a gilt-embroidered tunic. "You are the one acting the fool, Freeman van Rijn," she said. "I tell you quite plainly, the Home Companies will not oppose the Garver bill. And let me make a suggestion for your own good. The popular mood being what it is, you would be most ill-advised to turn your above-ground lobbyists and your undercover bribe artists loose against it. They would be bound to fail, and you would gain nothing except ill will."

"But—*Hel en verdoeming!* Can't you see what this will bring? If the unions get that kind of voice in management, it won't be the camel's nose in our tent. No, by damn, it will be the camel's bad breath and sandy footprints, and soon comes in the rest of him and you guess what he will do."

"Your fears are exaggerated," Lennart said. "They always have been."

"Never. Everything I warned against has been happening, year by year, clomp, clomp, clomp. Listen. A union is a profit-making organization same as a company, no matter how much wind it breaks about the siblinghood of workers. Hokay, no harm in that, as long as it stays honest greedy. But these days the unions are political organizations as well, tied in with government like Siamese twin octopuses. You let them steer those funds, and you are letting government itself into your business."

"That can be reciprocal," Lennart declared. "Frankly—speaking personally for a moment, not as a voice of the Home Companies— frankly, I think your view of government as a natural enemy of intelligent life, I think it belongs back in the Mesozoic era. If you want a clear-cut example of what it can lead to, look out beyond the Solar System; see what the Seven do, routinely, brutally, on world after world. Or don't you care?"

"The Seven themselves don't want open competition—"

"Freeman van Rijn, we are both busy. I've done you the courtesy of making this direct call, to tell you not to waste your efforts trying to persuade the Home Companies to oppose the Garver bill, so you may know we mean it. We're quite content to see the law pass; and we feel reasonably sure it will, in spite of anything you and your kind can do. Now shall you and I end this argument and get back to our proper concerns?"

Van Rijn turned puce. He gobbled a few words which she took for assent. "Goodbye, then," she said, and switched off. The vacant screen hummed.

After a minute, Falkayn approached him. "Uh, that seemed like bad news," he ventured.

Van Rijn slowly lessened his resemblance to a corked volcano. "Wicked news," he mumbled. "Unrighteous news. Nasty, sneaking, slimy news. We will pretend it was never spewed out."

Coya came to stand beside his chair and brush a hand across his mane. "No, talk about it, Gunung Tuan," she said quietly. "You'll feel better."

Between oaths and less comprehensible phrases in various languages, van Rijn conveyed his tidings. Edward Garver, Lunograd delegate in Parliament, had introduced a bill to put the administration of private pension funds credited to employees who were citizens of the Commonwealth, under control of their unions. In the case of Solar Spice & Liquors, that meant principally the United Technicians. The Home Companies had decided not to oppose passage of the measure. Rather, their representatives would work with the appropriate committees to perfect it for mutual satisfaction. This meant that the Polesotechnic League as a whole could take no action; the Home Companies and their satellites controlled too many votes on the Council. Besides, the Seven In Space would likely be indifferent, such a law affecting them only slightly. It was the independent outfits like van Rijn's, operating on an interstellar scale but with much of their market in the Commonwealth, which would find themselves hobbled as far as those monies were concerned.

"And when United Technicians say where we invest, United Technicians got that much extra power," the merchant finished. "Power not just in our affairs, but in finance, business, government— and government is getting more and more to be what runs the show. *Ach,* I do not envy the children you will have, you two."

"Don't you see any hope of heading this off?" Falkayn asked. "I know how often you've played skittles with whoever got underfoot. How about a public relations effort? Pressure on the right legislators; logrolling, oh, every trick you know so well . . ."

"I think no chance, with the big five against us," van Rijn said heavily. "Maybe I am wrong. But . . . *ja, ja,* I am thirty years your senior, Davy boy, and even if I got long-life chromosomes and lots of good antisenescence treatment, still, in the end a fellow gets tired. I will not do much."

He shook himself. "But hoy, what fumblydiddles is this I am making? We are supposed to have a happy evening and get drunk, before Coya ships out with your team and finds me lots of lovely new profits." He surged to his feet. "We need more drink here! Mars-dry we are. Where is that gluefoot butler? More beer, I say! More akvavit! More everything, by damn!"

Y minus 7.

The sun Elena was a dwarf, but the nearness of its planet Valya made its disc stand big and red-orange in an indigo heaven. At midmorning it would not set for almost forty hours. The ocean sheened calm as a lake. Land rolled away from it under a russet cover of shrubs and turf. Tiny, glittery flyers which were not insects rode a warm, faintly iron-tangy breeze.

Outside the headquarters building of the scientific base, Eric Tamarin-Asmundsen spoke his anger and his intent to the commander, Anna Karagatzis. Beside them, long-limbed, spindly, blue-furred, head like a teardrop with antennae, crouched the native they called Charlie.

"I tell you, you can do nothing there but waste your time," the woman said. "Do you think I haven't gone from protests to pleas to threats? And Wyler laughed at me—till he grew irritated and threatened me in turn if I didn't stop pestering him."

"I didn't know that!" Eric stiffened. Blood heated his face. He tried to calm himself. "A bluff. What would they dare do to any of us? What could they?"

"I'm not sure," Karagatzis sighed. "But I've been to their camp and seen how well armed they are. And we, what are we but a community of researchers and support personnel who've never been shot at in their lives? Stellar's men can do anything they want. And we're outside every civilized jurisdiction."

"Are we? The Commonwealth claims a right to punish misdeeds by its citizens wherever they are, not?"

"True. But I suspect many, perhaps all of this group have different citizenship. Besides, we'd get no police investigation here, across more than two hundred light-years."

"Hermes isn't so far."

Karagatzis gave him a probing look. He was large. His weather-browned features seemed older than his twenty-one standard years: broad, Roman-nosed, square-jawed, hazel-eyed, ordinarily rather pleasantly ugly but now taut with wrath. In the style of men on his home planet as well as Earth, he went beardless and cropped his black locks above the ears. His garb was plain coverall and boots; however, a shoulder patch bore the insigne of his ducal family.

"What could Hermes do?" Karagatzis wondered. "What would it? Valya is nothing to your people, I'm sure."

"Stellar Metals trades with us," he reminded her. "I don't think Wyler's bosses would thank him for provoking a good trading partner."

"Would one more set of outrages on one more backward world really annoy anybody? If you were back there, if you'd never served here, and heard the story, would you care that much? Be honest with yourself."

He drew breath. "Freelady, I am here. I must try. Not?"

"Well . . ." She reached a decision. "Very well, Lord Eric," she said carefully, addressing him as if she too had been born to the dialect of Anglic which they spoke on Hermes. "You may go and see if your influence can help the situation. Don't bluster, though. Don't commit us to something reckless. And don't make any promises to natives." Pain broke through her shell. "It's already hurt too much, having them come bewildered to us when they'd thought humans were their friends, and . . . and having to admit we can do zero."

Eric cast a glance down at Charlie. The autochthon had sought him out on his return. They had gotten acquainted when the Hermetian was doing field work in the mountains from which Charlie had since become a refugee. Taken aback, he could merely say, "I haven't built up this lad's hopes on purpose, Freelady."

Karagatzis gave him a bleak smile. "You haven't mine, at least."

"I oughtn't be gone long," Eric said. "Wish me luck. Goodbye." He strode quickly from her, Charlie beside him.

A few persons hailed them as they went. The greetings were not cheerful. Directly or indirectly, the invasion jarred on everybody's projects. More to the point, maybe, was the fact that these workers liked the Valyans. It was hard to stand helpless while the mountain folk were being robbed.

Helpless? he thought. *We'll see about that.* At the same time, the back of his mind told him that this had been going on for weeks. If it was possible to curb Stellar, wouldn't someone already have acted?

He and his partners had been on a different continent, mainly to observe dance rituals. Everywhere on the planet, choreography was an intimate, intricate part of life. To minimize the effect of their presence, they had parked their car well away from the site. The risk in thus cutting themselves off from radio contact had not seemed worth worrying about. But then he came back to a woe that he might have been able to prevent. . . .

Outside the base stood half a dozen knockdown shelters, their plastic garish against the soft reds and browns of vegetation. Karagatzis had told Eric how the Stellar Metals men had chased the few earlier independent gold miners—whose activities had been harmless, as small as their scale was—out of the mountains along with every native who resisted. The victims were waiting for the next supply ship to give them transportation.

Of the several men whom he saw sitting idle and embittered, one rose and approached him. Eric had met him before, Leandro Mendoza. "Hello, Freeman Tamarin-Asmundsen," he said without smiling.

For a split second, in his preoccupation, the Hermetian was startled. Who? Surnames were not ordinarily used in conversation with his class; he was "Lord Eric" when addressed formally, otherwise plain "Eric" or, to close comrades, "Gunner." He remembered that Mendoza was using Earth-style Anglic, and swore at himself. "Hail," he said as he came to a reluctant halt.

"Been away, have you?" Mendoza asked. "Just got the news, eh?"

"Yes. If you'll excuse me, I'm in haste."

"To see Sheldon Wyler? What do you think you can do?"

"I'll find out."

"Be careful you don't find out the hard way. We did."

"Uh, yes, I heard his razzos ordered you off your own digs, with guns to back them up. Where's your equipment?"

"Sold. No choice. We each had a nova's worth of investment in it, and not yet enough earned to pay for shipping it elsewhere. He bought us out at a price that leaves us only half ruined."

Eric scowled. "Was that wise? Haven't you compromised your case when you bring it to court? You will sue, of course."

Mendoza rattled forth a laugh. "In a Commonwealth court? If Stellar itself hasn't bought the judge, another company will have; and they swap favors. Our plea would be thrown out before we'd finished making it."

"I meant the Polesotechnic League. Its ethics tribunal."

"Are you joking?" After a few breaths, Mendoza added, "Well, run along if you want to. I appreciate your good intentions." Head drooping, he turned away.

Eric stalked on. "What did your other self say?" Charlie asked— a rough translation of his trilled question. Psychologists were still trying to understand the concept of you-and-me which lay beneath the upland language. And now, Eric thought, the whole upland culture was in danger of disruption by the operations in its country.

His own vocabulary was meager, the result of sessions with an inductive educator. "He is among those who were taking gold before the newcomers drove them off," he explained.

"Yes, ourselves know himselves well. They paid generously in tools and cloths for the right to dig a few holes. The newcomers pay nothing. What is much worse, they scatter the woods-cattle."

"The man who spoke to me did not expect my success."

"Do you?"

Eric didn't respond.

At the garage, he chose a car and motioned Charlie in ahead of him. The Valyan's antennae quivered. He had never flown before. Yet when the vehicle rose on silent negagravity, he regarded the land through the bubble canopy and said, "I can guide you. Steer yonder." He pointed north of east.

A human with a corresponding background could not have interpreted an aerial view so fast the first time, Eric thought. He had come here about a year ago prepared to feel a little patronizingly amicable toward beings whose most advanced society was in a bronze age. He had progressed to admiring them. Technologically they had nothing to teach a starfaring species. However, he wondered what eventual influence might come from their arts and their philosophies.

If their societies survived. The foundations of existence are often gruesomely vulnerable. As an immediate example, the uplanders got most of their food from leaf-eating beasts, not wild, not tame, but something which neither of those words quite fitted. By filling the choicest territory with seeking, gouging, roaring machines, the Stellar Metals expedition broke up the herds: and thus became akin to a plague of locusts on ancient Earth.

By all three blundering Fates, jagged through Eric, *why does gold have to be an important industrial resource?* The mature part of him said dryly: *Its conductivity, malleability, and relative chemical inertness.* He protested: *Why does an outsider corporation have to come plundering it here, when they could go to thousands of worlds that are barren?* The response came: *A rich deposit was noticed by a planetologist, and word got out, and a minor gold rush started, which the corporation heard about. The prospecting had already been done; and on Valya men need no expensive, time-consuming life support apparatus.*

Then why did the lode have to occur right where it is? That question had no answer.

The car flew rapidly over the coastal plain. Land wrinkled upward, turned into a range clad in trees. An ugly bare patch hove in view beside a lake. Charlie pointed, Eric descended.

On the ground, a pair of guards hurried to meet him as he emerged, a human and a Merseian. "What're you doing here?" the man snapped. "This is a no trespassing zone."

Eric bristled. "Who gave you property rights?"

"Never mind. We have them and we enforce them. Go."

"I want to see Sheldon Wyler."

"He's seen enough of you slopheads." The guard dropped hand to the blaster holstered at his waist. "Go, or do we have to get tough?"

"I don't believe he'd appreciate your assaulting the heir presumptive to the throne of Hermes," Eric said.

The mercenaries could not quite hide nervousness. The Grand Duchy was not many light-years hence, and it did possess a miniature navy. "All right, come along," said the human at length.

Crossing the dusty ground, Eric saw few workers. Most of them were out raping the forest. Stellar was not content to pick at veins and sift streams. It ripped the quartz from whole mountainsides, passed it through a mobile extractor, and left heaps of poisonous slag; it sent whole rivers through hydraulic separators, no matter how much swimming life was destroyed.

Inside a prefab cabin was a monastic office. Wyler sat behind the desk. He was bulky and heavy-featured, with a walrus mustache, and at first he was unexpectedly mild of manner. Dismissing the guards, he invited, "Have a chair. Smoke? These cigars are Earth-grown tobacco." Eric shook his head and lowered himself. "So you're going to be Grand Duke someday," Wyler continued. "I thought that job was elective."

"It is, but the eldest child is normally chosen."

"How come you're being a scientist here, then?"

"Preparation. A Grand Duke deals with nonhumans too. Uh, xenological experience—" Eric's voice trailed off. *Damn! The illwreaker's already put me on the defensive.*

"So you don't really speak for your world?"

"No, but—no—Well, I write home. In time I'll be going home."

Wyler nodded. "Sure, we'd like you to have a good opinion of us. How about hearing our side of the case?"

Eric leaned forward, fists on knees. "Freelady Karagatzis has, uh, told me what you told her. I know how you got your 'charter for exploration and development.' I know you claim real property is not a local institution, thus you violate no rights. And you say you'll be done in a year or two, pack up and leave. Yes. You needn't repeat to me."

"Then maybe you needn't repeat what your leader said."

"But care you not what you're *doing?*"

Wyler shrugged. "Every time a spaceship lands on a new planet, you get consequences. We knew nobody had objected to mining by free lances, though they had no charter—no legal standing. I was ready to bargain about compensation for the jumpies . . . the natives. But for that, I'd need the help of your experts. What I got was goddamn obstructionism."

"Yes, for there's no way to compensate for ruining a country. Argh, why go on?" Eric snarled. "You never cared. From the beginning, you intended being a gang of looters."

"That's for the courts to decide, wouldn't you say? Not that they'd try a suit, when no serious injury can be shown." Wyler put elbows on desk and bridged his fingers. "Frankly, you disappoint me. I'd hoped you wouldn't go through the same stale chatter. I can claim to be doing good too, you know. Industry needs gold. You'd put the convenience of a few thousand goddamn savages against the needs of billions of civilized beings."

"I—I—Very well." Eric lifted his head. "Let's talk plainly. You've made an enemy of me, and I have influence on Hermes. Want you to keep things that way, or not?"

"Naturally, Stellar Metals wants to be friends, if you'll allow. But as for your threat—I admit I'm no expert on your people. But I do seem to remember they've got their own discontented class. Will they really want to take on the troubles of a bunch of goddamn outsiders, long after these operations are over and done with? I doubt it. I think your mother has more sense."

In the end, Eric went bootless back to his car. It was the first absolute defeat he had ever known. As Karagatzis had warned, telling Charlie made it doubly painful.

Y minus 5.

That moon of Babur which humans had dubbed Ayisha was of approximately Lunar size. From a viewport in one of the colony domes, Benoni Strang looked out at dimly lit stone, ashen and crater-pocked. The sky was black and stars shone unwinking through airlessness. The planet hung gibbous, a great amber shield emblazoned with bands of cloud whose whiteness was softened by tints of ocher and cinnabar. Rearing above the near horizon, a skeletal test-pad support for spacecraft seemed like a siege tower raised against the universe.

Within the domes were more than warmth, Earth-normal weight, air that a man dared breathe. Strang stood on velvety grass, among flowering bushes. Behind him the park held a ball court, a swimming pool, fountains, tables where you could sit to dine on delicate food and drink choice wines. Elsewhere in the base were pleasure facilities of different kinds, ranging from a handicraft shop and an amateur theater to vices as elaborate as any in the known worlds. Folk here did not only need distraction from exacting work. They needed offsets for the fact that they would spend goodly portions of their lives on Ayisha and Babur and in ambient space; that they got no leaves of absence, were allowed no visitors, and had their outgoing mail censored. Those who eventually could endure it no longer, even with high pay accumulating at home, must submit to memory wipe before departing. The agreement was part of their contract, which colony police stood ready to enforce.

Strang's mind returned to early years, the toil and peril and austerity when men first carved for themselves a foothold in this waste; and he almost regretted them. He had been young then.

Though I was never especially merry as the young are supposed to be, he thought. *I was always too driven.*

"What're you brooding about?" asked Emma Reinhardt.

He turned his head and regarded her. She was a handsome woman from Germania, an assistant engineer, who might well become his next mistress; they had lately been much in each other's company.

"Oh," he said, "I was just thinking how far we've come since we began here, and what's left to do."

"Do you ever think about something besides your . . . your mission?" she asked.

"It's always demanded everything I had to give," he admitted.

She studied him in her turn. He was of medium height and slim, graceful of movement, his face rectangular in outline and evenly shaped, his hair and mustache sleek brown, his eyes gray-blue. In this leisure hour he wore an elegantly tailored slacksuit. "I sometimes wonder what'll become of you when this project is finished," she murmured.

"That won't be for quite a while," he said. "I'm presently estimating six standard years before we can make our first major move."

"Unless you're surprised."

"Yes, the unpredictable is practically the inevitable. Well, I trust that what we've built will be sound enough that it can adjust—and act."

"You misunderstand me," she said. "Of course you've got a lot of leadership ahead of you yet. But eventually matters will be out of your hands. Or at least many other hands will be there too. Then what?"

"Then, or actually before then, I'm going home."

"To Hermes?"

He nodded. "Yes. In a way, for me, this whole undertaking has been a means to that end. I've told you what I suffered there."

"Frankly, it hasn't seemed very terrible to me," she said. "So you were a Traver born, you couldn't vote, the aristocrats owned all the desirable land, and—Well, no doubt an ambitious boy felt frustrated. But you got offplanet, didn't you, and made your own career. Nobody tried to prevent you."

"What about those I left behind?"

"Yes, what about them? Are they really badly off?"

"They're underlings! Never mind how easy the conditions may seem, they're underlings. They've no say whatsoever in the public affairs of their planet. And the Kindred have no interest in progress, in development, in anything but hanging onto their precious feudal privileges. I tell you, the whole rotten system should have been blasted away a century ago. No, it should have been aborted at the start—" Strang curbed himself. "But you can't understand. You haven't experienced it."

Emma Reinhardt shivered a bit. She had glimpsed the fanatic.

Y minus 1.

Leonardo Rigassi, spaceship captain from Earth, was the man who tracked down the world for which several crews were searching. Astonished, he found that others were present before him. They called it Mirkheim.

Thereafter came the year which God, or destiny, or chance had ordained.

✤❚✤

Under a full moon, Delfinburg was making its slow way over the Philippine Sea. A thousand colors flared and jumped, voices resounded, flesh jostled flesh through the streets of the pleasure district. There were those who sought quieter recreation. Among places for them was the roof garden of Gondwana House. At the starboard edge of a leading pontoon, it offered a sweeping overlook of the ocean city on one side, of the ocean itself on another. By day the waters were often crowded with boats, but usually after dark you saw only the running lights of a few patrolling fish herders and, in tropical climes, pumpships urging minerals up from the bottom to keep the plankton beds nourished. They resembled fireflies that had wandered far from land.

The garden's own fluoros were dimmed tonight and the live orchestra muted. It played dance music of the Classical Revival, waltzes, mazurkas, tangos leading couples to hold each other close and glide softly. Flowers and shrubs surrounded the floor, setting fragrances of rose, jasmine, aurelia, livewell adrift on the mild air. Stars overhead seemed almost near enough to touch.

"I wish this could go on forever," Coya Falkayn murmured.

Her husband attempted a chuckle. "No, you don't, sweetheart. I never knew a girl who has less tolerance of monotony than you, or more talent for driving it off."

"Oh, I wish a lot of things would be eternal—but concurrently, you understand," she said. He could hear how she, too, strove for lightness. "Life should be a Cantorian aleph-one. An infinity of infinities to you, my dear mathematical hobblewit."

Instead, he thought, *we move through a single space-time on our single tracks, for a hundred years or thereabouts if we have the best antisenescence regimes available to us—or less, of course, if something happens to chop a particular world line short. I don't mind my own mortality too much, Coya; but how I resent yours!*

"Well," he told her, "I used to daydream about an infinity of women, all beautiful and accessible. But I found that you were plenty, and then some." He bent his head to lay his cheek along hers. Through a hint of perfume he drew in the clean odor of her hair. "Now come on, lass. Since we have to do things sequentially, let's concentrate on dancing."

She nodded. Though her movements continued deft, he felt no easing of the tension that had risen in her, and her fingers gripped his needlessly hard.

Therefore, at the end of the number he suggested, "Suppose we drink the next one out," and led her to an offside bar. When a champagne glass was in her hand, she said in turn, "I'd like to watch the sea for a while."

They found a private place by the outer rail. Vine-heavy trellises screened them from the dance floor and from any other pairs who might also have sought the peace that was here. Luna stood on the starboard quarter, casting a broad track and making the nearer wave crests sparkle; elsewhere the water was like fluid obsidian. Leaves shone wan among shadows. The deck underfoot carried a pulse of engines through feet and bones, as quiet as the pulse of blood in the heart, and a *hush-hush-hush* around the bows barely reached a keen hearing. A breeze carried the least touch of night chill.

Falkayn put forth his free hand to lift Coya's chin toward him. He smiled on the left side of his face. "Don't worry about me," he said. "You never did before."

"Oh, I did when I was a youngster," she answered. "I'd hear about the latest adventure of the fabulous *Muddlin' Through* team and go icy at the thought of what might have happened to you."

"I didn't notice you fretting after you'd joined us; and we hit a few turbulences then."

"That's it. I was there. Either we had nothing to fear or we were too busy to be frightened. I didn't have to stay home wondering if I'd ever see you again."

Her gaze went from his, skyward, until it reached the ghost-road of the Milky Way and came to rest on a white star within. "Each night I'll look at Deneb and wonder," she said.

"May I remind you," he answered as genially as he was able, "in that general neighborhood, besides Babur and Mirkheim, is Hermes? If I came from there once, I'll surely repeat."

"But if war does break out—"

"Why, my citizenship is still Hermetian, not Commonwealth. And I'm on a straightforward mission of inquiry and unofficial diplomacy, nothing else. The Baburites may not be the most accommodating race in the universe, but they're rational. They won't want to make enemies needlessly."

"If your task is that simple and safe, why must *you* go?"

Falkayn sighed. "You know why. Experience. For over thirty years, I've been dealing with nonhumans; and Adzel, Chee, and I make a damned efficient unit." He grinned anew. "Modesty is the second most overrated virtue in the canon. The first is sincerity, in case you're interested. But I'm dead serious about this. Gunung Tuan was right when he asked us to go. We'll have a better chance than anybody else of accomplishing something useful, or at least of bringing back some definite information. And you know all this, darling. If you wanted to raise objections, why wait till our last evening?"

She bit her lip. "I'm sorry. I thought I could keep my fears from showing . . . till you were gone."

"Look, I was being honest, too, when I said bad words on getting the job precisely when you can't come. I really meant it when I wished aloud you could. Would I do that if I anticipated any risk worth fussing about? The biggest unknown in the equation is simply how long we may be gone."

She nodded slowly. They had both stopped space roving when their Juanita was born, because it meant indefinite absences from Earth. An older, more hedonistic, less settled generation than Coya's had bred enough neurotics that she felt, and made her husband feel, children needed and deserved a solid home. And now she had another on the way.

"I still don't see why it has to be you," she said in a last hint of mutiny. "After three years in the Solar System—"

"You're a bit rusty, yes," he finished for her. "But you only had five years of trade pioneering with us. I had more than twenty. The tricks of the trade are practically stamped on my genes. When the old man asked, I couldn't well refuse."

Not when it was the very world of Mirkheim which caused me to betray his trust in me, eighteen years ago, went through his mind.

I've been forgiven, I'm van Rijn's crown prince, but I've never quite forgiven myself, and here is a chance to make amends.

Coya knew what he was thinking. She raised her head. "Aye, aye, sir. I apologize. If we do get a war, a lot of women will be much worse off than I am."

"Right," he replied soberly. "It's barely possible that my gang can contribute a smidgen toward keeping the peace."

"Meanwhile we have hours and hours left." She lifted her glass in the moonlight. Music rollicked forth afresh. "Our first duty is to this excellent champagne, wouldn't you say?"

"That's my girl talking." Falkayn smiled back at her. The rims clinked together.

When the two human members of the *Muddlin' Through* team retired, the two nonhumans went their separate ways. Chee Lan signed on as the xenobiologist of another trade pioneer crew. She didn't feel ready to settle down yet. Besides, she wanted to become indecently wealthy off her commissions, in order to indulge her every whim when at last she returned to that planet which astronomy designates as O_2 Eridani A II and the Anglic language calls Cynthia. She happened to be on Earth when the Mirkheim crisis developed, and this was probably what had crystallized Nicholas van Rijn's idea of reviving the threesome—though he must have consulted his company's registry first in hopes of learning that he could indeed contact her immediately.

"What?" she had spat when he phoned her at her lodge. "Me? To spy and wheedle—No, shut up, I realize you'll call it 'gathering intelligence' and 'attempting negotiations.' You waste syllables like a drunken lexicographer." She arched her back. "Do you seriously propose sending us to Babur . . . in the middle of a possible war? Those barrels of butter you eat every day must have gone to your head."

Van Rijn's image in the screen rolled eyes piously in the general direction of heaven. "Do not get excited, little fluffcat," urged his most unctuous voice. "Think on traveling once more with your closest friends. Think on helping prevent or stop trouble what gets people killed and maybe cuts into profits. Think on the glory you can win by a daring exploitation, to smear off on your children. Think—"

"I'll think on what good hard cash you offer," Chee interrupted. "Name a figure."

Van Rijn spread his hands in a gesture of horror. "You speak so crass in this terrible matter? What are you, anyways?"

"We know what I am. Now let's decide my price." Chee made herself comfortable on a cushion. In lieu of alcoholic refreshment, which did not affect her nervous system, she put a mildly narcotic cigarette in an interminable ivory holder and kindled it. This was going to take awhile.

With lamentation by him and scorn by her and much enjoyment on both sides, the fee was haggled out for a service which might be dangerous and certainly would not yield a monetary return. She insisted that Adzel be paid the same. Left to himself, the Wodenite was too diffident, and looking out for the big bumbler's interests could count as her good deed for the month. Van Rijn admitted what she had suspected, that Adzel had been recruited by a shameless appeal to his sense of duty.

He was still in the Andes Mountains, and did not intend to leave until the eve of departure. When that time came, Chee found from an update of the registry that he had taken a room in a cheap hotel in Terraport. She recognized its name from former days; it was the kind which had no facilities for approximating the home environment of a nonhuman. Well, she thought, Adzel didn't actually need two and a half standard gravities, thick hot air, the blinding light of an F_5 sun, and whatever other delights existed on the world men knew as Woden. He had managed without during the years aboard *Muddlin' Through,* not to speak of the Buddhist monastery where he had spent the past three as a lay brother. *No doubt he figures to give the money he's saving to the poor, or some cause similarly grubby,* she guessed, then caught a cab to the nearest airport and the next transoceanic flight from there.

En route, she drew stares. An extraterrestrial fellow passenger was still rather a rarity on Earth—even from Cynthia, whose most advanced culture was well into the spacefaring stage. She was used to that, and content to let people learn what a truly graceful species looked like. They saw a small being, ninety centimeters in length plus a bushy tail which added half again as much. Her legs were long in proportion, ending in five prehensile toes on each foot; her arms were equally long, the hands six-fingered. Her round head bore huge emerald eyes, pointed ears, a short muzzle with a broad nose, a delicate mouth with exceedingly sharp teeth framed in wiry whiskers. Silky fur covered her body save for the bare gray skin of hands and feet; it was pure white except where it formed a blue-gray mask around her eyes. She had once heard herself compared to a cross between an Angora cat, a monkey, a squirrel, and a raccoon, and idly wondered which of these were supposed to be on what side of the family. The speculation was natural, since she came of a bisexual, viviparous race like Adzel—homeothermic like his, too, though neither of them was strictly a mammal.

A little boy cried, "Ooh, kitty!" and wanted to pet her. She glanced from her printout of the London *Times* and said sweetly to the mother, "Why don't you eat your young?" Thereafter she was left in peace.

Arriving, she hailed another cab and gave it the hotel's address. The time here was after sundown and Adzel should be in. She hoped he wasn't meditating too deeply to notice a buzz at his door. Hearing the dry rustle of scales across scales, she knew he was uncoiling and about to admit her. Good. She'd be glad to see the old oaf again, she supposed.

The door opened. She looked up, and up. Adzel's head was more than two meters off the floor, on the top of a thick, serpentine neck and a horse-bulky torso which sprouted two correspondingly powerful arms with four-fingered hands. Rearward, his centauroid body stretched four and a half meters, including the crocodilian tail. His head was likewise faintly suggestive of a reptile: long snout, rubbery-lipped mouth, omnivore's teeth that had among them some alarming fangs, large amber-colored eyes protected by jutting brow ridges, bony ears. A serration of triangular plates ran from the top of his skull and down his spine to its end. One behind the torso had been surgically removed in order that comrades might safely ride on him. Scales shimmered over the whole frame, dark green above shading to gold on the belly.

"Chee Lan!" he boomed in Anglic. "What a splendid surprise. Come in, my dear, come in." Four cloven hoofs carrying a ton of mass made a drum-thunder as he moved aside for her. "I did not expect to greet you before we meet at the ship tomorrow," he went on. "I thought it best if I—"

"We shouldn't need much preliminary checkout, we three and Muddlehead," she agreed.

"—if I attempted—"

"Still, I figured we'd do well to compare notes in advance. You couldn't get Davy loose from his family with a crowbar before rendezvous time, but you and I don't have any current infatuations."

"I am attempting to—"

"Do you?"

"What? I am attempting to brief myself on the current situation." Adzel gestured at the room's video. A man was speaking:

"—review the background of the crisis. It goes back well beyond the discovery of Mirkheim this past year. In fact, that was a rediscovery. For about fifteen years before, the Supermetals consortium were in possession of the planet, mining its riches without ever letting it be known where the treasure they had to sell came from. They tried to give the impression that their source was a secret manufacturing process, beyond the reach of any known technology. This trick succeeded to a degree. But eventually various scientists concluded it was far more likely that the supermetals had been produced and concentrated by nature—"

"You've heard that!" Chee jerked her tail at the screen.

"Yes, of course, but I have hopes he will give me a comprehensive precis of current events," Adzel said. "Remember, for three years I have heard no newscast, read no secular literature besides planetological journals." Chee was glad to learn that he had not neglected his profession. It probably wouldn't be needed on this trip; but you were never sure, and in any event, his keeping abreast of scientific developments showed that he had not been completely spun off the wheel of his particular karma. "We got occasional visitors," the dragon continued, "but I avoided them as much as possible, fearing that my appearance might distract them from the serenity of the surroundings."

"Seeing your version of the lotus position certainly would," Chee snapped. "Listen, I can brief you better and faster than that klong."

"Would you like a spot of tea?" Adzel asked, pointing to a five-liter thermos. "I had it brewed at the place where I got supper. Here, this ashtray is clean." He set it on the floor and poured it full for Chee to lap. He himself hoisted the container to his mouth.

Meanwhile the lecturer skimmed over basic physics.

From the actinide series onward, the periodic table of the elements holds nothing but radioactives. In the biggest atoms, the mutual repulsion of protons is bound to overcome attractive forces within the nucleus. Beyond uranium, the rates of disintegration become great enough that early researchers on Earth found no such materials in nature. They had to produce neptunium and plutonium artificially. Later it was shown that micro-micro amounts of these two do occur in the rocks. But their presence is a mere technicality. Virtually all that there was in the beginning has vanished, broken down into simpler nuclei. And beyond plutonium, half-lives are generally so short that the most powerful and elaborate apparatus can barely make a quantity sufficient to register on ultrasensitive instruments; then the product is gone.

Yet theory indicated that an "island of stability" should exist, beginning at atomic number 114 and ending at 122: nine elements, most of whose isotopes are only weakly radioactive. To manufacture infinitesimal amounts of these was a laboratory triumph. Gigantic energy was required to fuse that many particles. Theory went on to hint at physical and chemical properties, whether of the materials themselves or of solid compounds of those that were volatile in isolation. These were an engineer's dream, in catalysts, conductors, components of alloys with supreme strength. Nobody saw any road to the realization of that dream . . . until a sudden thought occurred.

(It came first to David Falkayn, eighteen years ago. But the speaker was unaware of that. He simply recited the reasoning of later thinkers.)

We believe all matter began as a chaos of hydrogen, the smallest atom. Some of it was fused in the primordial fireball to form helium; more of this process happened later, in the enormous heat and pressure at the hearts of stars which condensed from that gas. And there the higher elements were built, step by step as atoms interacted. Scattering mass in their solar winds, or as dying red giants, or as novae and supernovae, the early generations of stars enriched with such nuclei the interstellar medium from which later generations of suns and planets would form. The carbon in our proteins, the calcium in our bones, the oxygen we breathe were forged in those ancient furnaces.

Had no extremely big stars ever formed, the series would have ended with iron. It is at the bottom of the energy curve; to join together still more protons and neutrons lies beyond the power of any steadily burning sun. But the monster stars do not die peacefully. They become supernovae, briefly shining on a scale comparable to an entire galaxy. In that moment of unimaginable violence, reactions otherwise impossible take place; and copper, gold, uranium, every element above iron comes into being, and is blown into space to enter the stuff of new stars, new worlds.

Among the substances thus created are the supermetals of the island of stability. Being as hard to make as they are, they occur only in a tiny proportion, so tiny that at first none were found in nature, not even after man broke free of the Solar System and began exploring his corner of the galaxy. Yet they should be there. The problem was to locate a measurable concentration of them.

Suppose a giant star had a giant planet, sufficiently massive that its core would survive the explosion. That was not impossible, though theory said it was improbable. The bursting sun would cast a torrent of elements across the core. Those with low volatility should condense, or even plate out. True, they would be a minute fraction of the total which the supernova vomited into space; but that fraction should equal billions of tons of valuable metals, and a lesser amount of immensely more precious supermetals. Given their comparatively slight radioactivity, a worthwhile proportion of the supermetals ought to last for several million years. . . .

"—evidently its first discoverers had run a mathematical analysis on a computer of the highest capabilities," the speaker said. "By using available data on present star distributions and orbits in this galactic vicinity, plus similar data for interstellar gas and dust, magnetic fields, et cetera, a sophisticated program could calculate the probability of there having been a supernova with a superjovian companion within the appropriate span of time and space, and show roughly where its remnants ought to be in this epoch. More accurately, the program computed out a space-time distribution of probabilities, which in turn yielded an optimal search pattern. The odds looked best in the general direction of Deneb, in a region at about half its distance.

"If scientists a year or two ago could make this deduction, then it was reasonable to believe that the Supermetals combine had made it earlier. Hence the treasure hoard *must* exist. Energetic seeking must eventually find it. Ships went eagerly forth.

"Captain Leonardo Rigassi of the European Exploratory Foundation succeeded.

"The secret was out. The beings who spoke for Supermetals now told quite openly how they had been working the planet, which they called Mirkheim. They had tried to get legal ownership. Immediately a stinging swarm of questions arose. First and fiercest is the question of who has jurisdiction, what government can rightly rule. The Supermetals operators have no government behind them, they are loners, and—"

"Will you shut that blatbox off?" Chee Lan demanded. "You can't help already knowing everything it can conceivably say."

"Forgive me, but that is a rather unhumble attitude," Adzel reproached her. Nevertheless he reached over and tapped the switchplate. For a moment, silence filled the shabby room.

Likewise did his bulk. In a gesture familiar of old, he settled down on the floor and curled the end of his tail to make a comfortable rest for Chee. She accepted it, taking her ashtray of tea along.

"For example," he said, "I was relieved to find that we—you, Davy, and I—have not yet been publicly identified as the original discoverers of Mirkheim, indeed, the bestowers of the name. Notoriety would be most distressing, would it not?"

"Oh, I've toyed with notions for cashing in on it, should that happen," Chee replied. "But with matters as crazily half-balanced as they are—yeh, no doubt it's just as well the Supermetals people have kept faith. I don't know how much longer they will. They've no obvious reason left to preserve our anonymity. I suppose they're doing it out of habit—not to give anything, not even a reminiscence, to the slimespawn who want to pluck them of their treasure."

"And their hopes," Adzel said low. "Do you think they can get a fair compensation?"

"From whichever government makes its claim stick, the Commonwealth or Babur? Ho, ho, ho. Commonwealth control means control by corporations out for nothing but a bonanza, and by politicians and bureaucrats who hate the Supermetals Company because it never truckled to them. Baburite possession means—who knows? Except that I can't imagine Babur giving two toots on a flute for the rights of a few oxygen breathers."

"Do you seriously believe Babur might get Mirkheim? The basis of its claim, the 'sphere of interest' principle, sounds preposterous."

"No more absurd than the Commonwealth's 'right of discovery.' I daresay a good brisk war will decide."

"Would they actually fight over a . . . a wretched lump of alloy?" Adzel asked, appalled.

"My friend, they'll have trouble avoiding a war, unless Babur is bluffing, which I doubt." Chee drew breath. It smelled of tea and of the Wodenite's warm, slightly acrid body odor. "You do understand why van Rijn is sending us there, don't you? Mainly for information—any information whatever, so he can plan what to do. Right now, everything is a-rattle. The Commonwealth government is blundering blind the same as everyone else, not knowing what to expect of creatures as alien as the Baburites. But also, if we possibly can, we should try to make, or at least suggest, a bargain. They're in a position to harm quite a chunk of Solar Spice & Liquors' holdings, its trade; and they do have a grudge against us in particular."

"Why?"

"You don't know? Well, about thirty years back, they tried to muscle in on a business that Solar had in a stuff called bluejack, on a planet in their neighborhood. For them, it was more lucrative than for us. Still, our factor there didn't see why we should tamely accept what amounted to straight robbery. He euchred them out of their gains by a clever trick, and made sure they could get no benefit from returning. That was the first aggressive move Babur made in space. They seem to think they're ready for the real action now. And cosmos knows the Commonwealth is ill-prepared."

"And so we fare forth again, we three and our ship, like our young days come back," Adzel sighed, "except that this time our mission is not into the hopeful yonder."

Still below the horizon, Maia, sun of Hermes, made the tops of steeples and towers in Starfall shine as if gilded. When it rose out of Daybreak Bay, its light struck westward over the Palomino River and straight along Olympic Avenue to Pilgrim Hill. There the brightness lost itself among trees, gardens, and buildings, the gray stone mass of the Old Keep, the fluid lines and many-paned walls of the New Keep, the austere erectness of Signal Station. A beam went past an upper balcony on the New Keep, through the French doors beyond, and across the bed of Sandra Tamarin-Asmundsen.

She woke from dreams. "Pete, darling," she whispered, reaching for him. Her eyes opened and she remembered she was alone. For an instant, emptiness possessed her.

But the accident that claimed Peter Asmundsen (big, boisterous, strong but fundamentally gentle man) lay more than four years in the past. Time had eased pain, time and the work of being Grand Duchess, head of a planet whereon dwelt fifty million willful people. She sat up and made herself take pleasure in cool air and soft light.

As usual, her alarm was not quite ready for her. She turned it off, rose, and strode out onto the balcony. A breeze from the dew and flowerbeds below caressed her bare skin. Nobody else seemed to be about, though her vision swept from the hilltop, down across the city to the bay and the Auroral Ocean beyond. A nidifex flew past, flutter of colorful wings and trill of song.

After a minute Sandra went back inside, switched her phone to television reception, and commenced her daily half hour of exercises. She had more faith in them than in antisenescence, though in her mid-fifties she was duly taking those treatments. Her big body had changed little since youth. On the broad, high-cheekboned face were not many wrinkles, those mostly crow's feet around the dark-browed green eyes. But her blond hair had gone silvery.

Automatically moving, she escaped boredom by holding her attention on an early newscast. The Mirkheim crisis came first.

"Rumors were widespread that Babur has issued a new declaration, a copy of which has reached Hermes. Spokesmen for the throne would neither confirm nor deny this, but promised a public statement soon.

"The basis of the rumor was the landing at Williams Field yesterday of a navy speedster known to have been stationed at Valya. I'll just give review to that situation. The Baburites have delivered their last three Anglic-language pronunciamentos to the primitive planet Valya, by a ship which has gone into orbit and radioed the message to the scientific outpost there, with a request that the content be distributed as widely as possible. So several governments, including ours, are keeping boats on the scene, and by agreement aren't allowing news services to do likewise. 'Tis the closest thing to contact that anybody has with that nonhuman race, and officials say they fear possible bad results of premature disclosures."

The rumors were true, though the reality wasn't worth overmuch excitement. "The Autarchy of United Babur," whatever that meant, had simply reiterated its claim. Because Mirkheim was located so near, as interstellar distances went, and because the supermetals were of incalculable strategic importance, Babur could not and would not tolerate possession of that globe by any power which had demonstrated hostility to Babur's legitimate activity in space. The sole novelty was that this time these powers were bluntly identified, the Solar Commonwealth and the Polesotechnic League. At the urging of her advisors, Sandra had withheld publication of the note until a committee of xenologists could have examined it for new implications. She doubted they'd find any.

"Yesterday also we received a tape of an address by Prime Minister Lapierre of the Solar Commonwealth at a convention of the Justice Party. He maintained that his government is willing to negotiate, but that Babur thus far has made none of the normal preliminary moves, such as arranging for exchange of ambassadors. At the same time, he said, the Commonwealth will under no circumstances yield to what he called 'naked aggression.' Somberly, he admitted that Babur does appear to have great naval strength. He recalled the concentration of warcraft which human officers were invited to observe, shortly after a Baburite ship, with stunning insolence, radioed that first claim to Mirkheim from orbit around Earth. He said that, while information is far from complete, the signs are that Babur has somehow—unnoticed over a long period—built a fleet still larger than what it revealed. Nevertheless, Lapierre insisted, the Commonwealth will stand firm, and if necessary will take, quote, 'forceful measures.'"

Sandra muttered an oath. This was ancient. The fastest hyperdrive vessel took worse than two weeks, Terrestrial calendar, to go from Earth's sun to Babur's, Mirkheim's, or Hermes'. Between any two of those systems out in this sector, travel time must still be reckoned in days. Societies could put themselves on collision courses for sheer lack of data. She wished bitterly that some faster-than-light equivalent of radio existed.

Although you could argue that because of isolation, the early colonists of Hermes had been free to develop a new kind of civilization which, on the whole, she found good. . . .

Not everybody did. The program gave a report, with visuals, of the latest Liberation Front rally. It had been held last night at a resort on the Longstrands. The intemperance of the orators and the size and enthusiasm of the crowd were worrying. If that many Travers would meet on a chilly seashore in person, how many more watched and cheered in their homes?

Items of less importance soon drove her to switch over to those memoranda which her staff had recorded for her while she slept. At once she slammed to full attention. Calisthenics forgotten, she crouched on the floor and stared at the image of her executive secretary.

"About midnight, a ship belonging to the Supermetals Company landed at Williams Field," his voice said. "The captain identified himself to the port authorities and got through to me at home. He urgently asked for a private interview with you, madam. I considered having you roused, but trust I did right in scheduling him for 0930, subject to your approval. Meanwhile, as a precaution, I had his crew ordered to stay on board their vessel.

"The commander's a Wodenite hight Nadi." Visuals showed the great shape striding among humans. "He heads the small defensive force which Supermetals maintains around Mirkheim. You'll belike recall how, having captured the ship of Leonardo Rigassi, the recent rediscoverer, Nadi soon ordered her released, because the secret was out and keeping prisoners would only brew ill will without much delaying the inevitable.

"Instead, he says, the outfit has decided to appeal to Hermes, that we establish a protectorate over Mirkheim. This is what he wants to discuss with you."

Sandra stiffened. *Isn't that a red-hot rivet dropped into my palm!* She forced herself to continue her gymnastics. They brought a measure of calm to which a cold shower added. She likewise took her time about braiding her hair and dressing. Her garments she made more formal than ordinarily, a gown whereon the only bright colors belonged to the Tamarin family shoulder patch. With leisured strides, she sought her breakfast room.

Her two younger children, the ones whom Pete had given her, were still abed. Eric was at the table, emptying his coffee cup in fierce draughts. The chamber was fragrant with cooking in the kitchen. The west wall was a vitryl pane whose view swept down that side of Pilgrim Hill, over the last buildings in Starfall, and on across intensely green farmland. Pale above the horizon floated the snowpeak of Cloudhelm.

Eric stood up at Sandra's entrance, as men did for women on Hermes. He was clad in crisp tunic and breeks, but looked as if he hadn't slept. Had he been out carousing? Her oldest son and probable heir was a steady enough fellow as a rule, but sometimes the blood of his father rose in him. *No,* she decided after scanning his features, *not this time.*

"Good morning, Mother," he blurted. "Listen, I heard about Nadi, I've been out and talked to him and his crew. . . . Will we grab the chance? It's going by almighty fast."

Sandra seated herself and tilted the coffeepot. "Come back down from the stratosphere," she advised.

"But we can *do* it!" Eric paced before her. His soles clacked on the parquet. "Babur, the Commonwealth, the League, they're dithering despite their brags, not? Each fears to commit itself. A single decisive move—"

The waiter appeared with laden trays. "Sit down and eat," Sandra said.

"But—look you, Mother, you know I hold no roots-in-air notion of us as an imperial power. We could never stand against any of the others. If we're there at Mirkheim, though, in possession, firmly allied with the original discoverers, who do own the clearest moral right, would the rest of them not hold back?"

"I can't tell. Moral rights seem of scant account these days. Do sit down. Your food will cool."

Eric obeyed. His right hand jerked through gestures while his left lay in a fist. "We're the natural arbiters. None need be afraid of us. We could see to it that everybody gets a fair share." Behind his homely visage was fire. "Only, damnation, first we've need to assert ourselves! Fast!"

"The Polesotechnic League has been suggested for the same role," Sandra reminded him.

"Them?" He chopped the air in contempt. "When they're too divided, too corrupt to control their own members according to the ethical rules in their own covenant—You jest, not?"

"I don't know," Sandra said heavily. "When I was young, the League was a force for peace because in the long run peace is more profitable than war. Now . . . sometimes I shudder. And sometimes I daydream that it can be reformed in time."

By men like Nicholas van Rijn, your father, Eric? she wondered. *Not that he would ever feel called on to carry out a holy mission. He'd simply want to preserve his independence, by whatever means will also shake more money out of the universe.*

Is it too late for that?

Through her mind passed a swift review of history, as familiar as her own life but skimmed over once again in the dun hope of finding some hope.

Given abundant nuclear energy, comparatively cheap and easily operated hyperdrive spacecraft, and related technological developments, interstellar trade was bound to burgeon. Theoretically, any habitable planet should be self-sufficient, able to synthesize whatever did not occur naturally. In practice, it was often more economical to import goods, especially in view of restrictions on industry to preserve the environment. Besides, the wealthier Technic civilization grew, the more it dealt in luxuries, arts, services, and other commodities which could not be duplicated at home.

Private enterprise, ranging over greater reaches of space than any government, frequently where no effective government whatsoever existed, and soon becoming richer than any state, took over most of the Technic economy. The companies formed the Polesotechnic

League as an association for mutual help and, to a degree, mutual discipline. The Pax Mercatoria spread among the stars.

When did it go bad? Did it succumb to the vices of its very virtues?

Often having to serve as their own magistrates, legislators, naval commanders, and being in any case usually rambunctious, acquisitive individualists with gigantic egos, the great merchants of the League began more and more to live like ancient kings. Abuses grew ever more common: coercion, venality, reckless exploitation. The sheer scale of operations and overwhelming rate of information flow made it apparently impossible to cope with much of this.

No, wait. The League might have brought itself back under control just the same—had not the attempt at control created two mighty factions which as the years went on grew ever more unlike.

There were the Home Companies, whose businesses were principally within the Solar System: Global Cybernetics, General Atomistics, Unity Communications, Terran Synthetics, Planetary Biologicals. Their relationship with the dominant unions—United Technicians, Service Industries Workers, the Commonwealth Scientific Association—grew steadily closer.

And there were the Seven In Space: Galactic Developments, XT Systems, Interstar Transport, Sanchez Engineering, Stellar Metals, Timebinders Insurance, Abdallah Enterprises—the corporate titans among the other suns.

The rest, such as Solar Spice & Liquors, remained precariously unallied, openly competitive. Most were essentially one-man or one-family fiefs. *Does any future lie in them? Aren't they mere fossils of an earlier, freer age? Oh, Nick, my poor devil. . . .*

"Let be the brattling philosophy, and let's get a Hermetian presence at Mirkheim," Eric said. "If naught else, think you what a bargaining lever that gives us against the Seven. Long enough have they been jacking us up. We needn't fear the Commonwealth making war on us. Public opinion wouldn't stand for humans fighting humans while Babur gloats in the background."

"I'm unsure of that. Nor am I sure Babur will sit passive. Frankly, that realm frightens me."

"Bluff."

"Count not on it. Everybody always supposed oxygen breathers and hydrogen breathers would never have any serious conflict because they want not the same real estate, and they're mutually too alien for strife over ideologies. That's why so little attention has been paid to Babur, why it's still so mysterious. But . . . what intelligence I can get shows me the Imperial Band of Sisema as a powerful aggressor that's taken over the whole planet and isn't sated yet. And Mirkheim is real estate that everybody wants."

Not simply out of greed, Sandra's mind went on. *Already the supermetals begin to revolutionize technology, in electronics, alloys, nuclear processes, I know not what else. Did Babur get a hold on the sole source, Babur could deny the stuff to mankind.*

"I agree we humans had best put our feuds aside for a spell," she said. "Maybe Hermes should cooperate with the Commonwealth."

"Maybe. But see you not, Mother, if we take charge first, we can set conditions for handing Mirkheim over and—Well, elsewise, if we stay put, we must needs take whatever somebody else chooses to dole out."

Not his spark of idealism but his angry impatience to act reminded Sandra of his father.

A Wodenite was not exactly inconspicuous among humans, and larynxes must be buzzing throughout Starfall. However, nobody else would listen to what she and Nadi said this morning.

The room where they met was intended for confidential conferences: long, darkly wood-paneled, its windows open on a lawn where a mastiff kept watch. She had made it her own with souvenirs of her youthful offplanet travels: pictures of exotic scenes, odd little bits of art, weapons intended for nonhuman hands racked on the wall. Entering some minutes in advance of appointment time, she found her eye falling on a battle-ax from Diomedes. Her spirit followed, back through years, to Nicholas van Rijn.

She had never loved the merchant. In many ways, even at that unfastidious stage of her life, she found him almost unendurably primitive. But that same raw vigor had saved both their lives on Diomedes. And she was looking for a man who would be a partner, neither domineering nor subservient toward her who was the likeliest successor to the throne of Hermes. (Duke Robert was then old and childless. His niece Sandra was a natural choice for the electors, since not much else could be said for any of the other possible Tamarins.) Nobody she had met on Hermes had greatly stirred her, which was one reason why she went touring. Whatever his flaws, van Rijn was not a man she could be casual about. No previous affair of hers had been as full of thunderstorms and earthquakes—nor of memories to laugh or exult at afterward. When a year had passed, she knew he wouldn't consider marriage, or anything else she might want that he didn't. Eric was in her womb, because at the time she had been an ardent eugenicist. Regardless, she left. Van Rijn made no effort to stop her.

Their parting was not altogether acrimonious, and they had exchanged a few business communications afterward whose tone was not unfriendly. As the years passed, she came to remember him in a more kindly fashion than at first—when she thought of him at all, which was seldom after she met Peter Asmundsen.

He was Hermetian, not of the Kindred but of respectable Follower family; he had organized and personally led enterprises on sister planets of the Maian System; various deeds had made him a popular hero. When he married Sandra Tamarin and legally adopted Eric, the scandal that had surrounded her return home was laid to rest. Not that it had been much of a scandal. Under the influence of League and Commonwealth, the Hermetian aristocracy had acquired an easygoing attitude toward personal matters. Nevertheless, probably her consort had had a great deal to do with her election to the throne after Duke Robert's death. And when Pete died—she didn't imagine she would ever want anybody else.

Then why am I thinking about Nick, when I should be thinking about what to do with Nadi?

Because of Eric, I suppose. Eric will inherit this world as I have helped shape it, for weal or woe. So will Joan and Sigurd, of course; but Eric may be saddled with the leadership of it.

If aught is left to lead.

She took a restless turn around the chamber, stopped at the ax and let her fingers curl around its haft. How she wished she could be out in this beautiful day, hunting, steeplechasing, skiing, sailing, driving her hovercycle at speeds which horrified her well-wishing subjects. Or she might visit the theatrical troupe she patronized; her fascination with drama was lifelong. Or—

The door opened. "Madame, Captain Nadi of the Supermetals Company," said the guard, and closed it when the huge body had passed through.

Sandra had never met a Wodenite before. Most of the dwellers on that planet were at a savage stage of technology, though they had apparently developed several intricate, subtle cultures. A few, in contact with Polesotechnic trading centers, had won scholarships or otherwise earned their way into space. Nadi gravely offered his hand, which engulfed Sandra's. The warmth of it surprised her; she had unconsciously expected a scaly being to be cool, as they were on Hermes or Earth.

"Welcome," she said a trifle uncertainly.

"Thank you, my lady." The Anglic was fluent, comprehensible though indescribably accented by the nonhuman conformation of the vocal tract. "I will endeavor not to take unduly much of your time. Yet I feel that what I have to relate is of the highest importance to your people also."

"Belike true. Ah . . . I'm sorry we've no suitable furniture here. Please make yourself comfortable as best you can."

"I can quite well stand indefinitely in this low gravity." The pull of Hermes was ninety-seven percent that of Earth. "I realize you humans sit by choice."

"I will. First, though, care you for a smoke? Not? Mind you if I light up? Good." Sandra took a cigar from a humidor, struck fire to it, and lowered herself into an heirloom armchair. Its carven massiveness was somehow reassuring. The tobacco soothed her palate.

"I will go directly to the point," Nadi rumbled. "Do you know how and why I departed from Mirkheim?"

Sandra nodded. She had spent an hour after breakfast getting informed. "You propose that we of Hermes act unilaterally, making ours the government in possession."

"By the express wish of the original discoverers and rightful owners, my lady. Naturally, we understand you will have to grant access to others. But you can regulate this so that each group will get a proper share, including ours."

"If the great powers will let us."

"They may be happy to have you present them with such a formula. Please believe me, this is not a sudden counsel of desperation on our part. We knew from the beginning that our monopoly would be short-lived, and studied possible tactics to use after the news was out. David Falkayn himself suggested Hermes as the eventual caretaker. True, he was only thinking of the Commonwealth versus the League as rivals for Mirkheim. He did not foresee Babur's entry. However, we have decided his idea remains the best we have."

"David—the hero of the Shenna affair? Said you his name?"

"You do not know? I took for granted the story would be widespread by now." Nadi stood awhile silent. It was almost as if Sandra could see gears turning ponderously in his head. At length:

"Well, I will no longer be betraying a trust if I tell you, and it may be that you will understand our position better if you know of its origins."

She settled back in her chair. He was right. If nothing else, a background explanation would give her nerves time to ease, her brain time to rally. "Go on," she invited.

"Eighteen standard years ago," Nadi said, "David Falkayn, as you doubtless recall, was still a trade pioneer of the Solar Spice & Liquors Company. Together with his partners, he went in secret, deliberately seeking a world like Mirkheim. Analysis of astronomical data showed him that possibly one existed, and approximately where it would be if it did. He found it, too.

"Instead of notifying his employer, as a trade pioneer is supposed to do whenever he finds a promising new territory, Falkayn went elsewhere. He went to well-chosen leaders among the backward peoples, the poor peoples, the humble peoples whose neglect and abuse by the League had roused his indignation. He it was who got them to form a consortium for the purpose of mining and selling the wealth of Mirkheim, that the gain might go to their folk."

Sandra nodded. Since Rigassi's expedition, spokesmen for Supermetals had pleaded their cause in those terms. She remembered one man who had addressed an audience in Starfall:

". . . How will planets like Woden, Ikrananka, Ivanhoe, Vanessa—how will the inhabitants of planets like these reach the stars? How will they come to share in the technology that eases labor, preserves health, prevents famine, educates, gives mastery over an indifferent nature? They have hardly anything to market—a spice, a fur, a style of artwork, possibly a few natural resources like oils or easily available minerals. They cannot earn enough thus to buy spaceships, power plants, automatons, research laboratories, schools.

The League has no interest in subsidizing them. Public and private charities already face more demands than they can handle. Must whole races then spend millennia full of preventable anguish, in order to develop for themselves everything that has long existed elsewhere?

"And what of colonies planted by humans or Cynthians or other spacefaring species? Not the prosperous, successful colonies like Hermes; the gaunt ones, the outlying ones, whose settlers have little except the pride of independence. They can modify their harsh environments if they can buy the means. Else they risk final extinction.

"The Supermetals Company was organized by trustworthy dwellers on such worlds. The profit to be won on a comparatively minor capital investment was fantastic. But would the magnates of the League respect their property rights? Would governments leave them in sovereign peace? The prize was too great for that—"

"Ah . . . my lady?" came Nadi's voice.

She started back out of her recollection. "I beg your pardon," she said. "My mind wandered."

"I fear I have bored you."

"Not, not. Far from it. In fact, later I'd like to hear details of the tricks you used to keep your holdings hidden. Evasive maneuvers when scouts trailed your ships, precautions against bribery, kidnap, extortion—'Tis amazing you lasted as long as you did."

"We saw the end was near when Falkayn's employer, Nicholas van Rijn, deduced that the supermetals must come from a world of Mirkheim's type, and used the same method of search to find it. . . . Did I distress you?"

"No. You, you surprised me. Van Rijn? When?"

"Ten standard years ago. Falkayn and Falkayn's future wife persuaded him to maintain silence. In fact, he very kindly helped our agents keep the issue confused, to delay the eventual rediscovery."

"Mmm, yes, Nick would have gotten fun out of doing that." Sandra leaned forward. "Well. This is fascinating, but 'tis past. As you remarked, I knew most of it beforehand, and we can fill in the details later. If you and I stay in touch. I sympathize with you, but you realize my first duty is to Hermes. What can our people gain at Mirkheim that's worth the cost and hazard?"

The giant being looked helpless and alone. "We beg for your

assistance. In return for keeping us in business, you will become sharers in the wealth."

"And targets for everybody who wants that same share, or more." Sandra drew hard on her cigar. "Maybe you're not aware, Captain Nadi, I am no absolute ruler. The Grand Duke or Duchess is elected from the Tamarin family, which may not belong to any domain, by the presidents of the domains of Hermes. My powers are strictly limited."

"I understand, my lady. But I am told you can call a legislative assembly, electronically, on an hour's notice. I am told that your leaders, living on a world which still has a frontier of wilderness, are used to making quick decisions.

"My lady, your intervention could prevent whole armadas from clashing. But very little time remains for you to take action. If you do not move soon, then best you never move."

Sandra's pulse accelerated. *By cosmos, he's right as far as he goes,* she thought admidst the bloodbeat, *he and Eric and . . . no few others, I'm sure. The gamble isn't too much if we're careful, if we keep a line of retreat open. I'll need more information, more opinions, of course, before I can even raise the presidents and lay a recommendation before them. But at this moment I think we have a chance.*

Yes, we! I've been soberly hard-working too bloody damn long; and I am commander-in-chief of the navy. If Hermes sends an expedition, I'm going to lead it.

✧ III ✧

The Council of the Polesotechnic League met in Lunograd to consider the Mirkheim situation. Hastily convened, it did not include a representative of every member. Several heads of independent businesses could not be reached in time or could not leave their work on notice that short. However, between them the Home Companies and the Seven In Space almost made up a quorum, and speakers for enough of the unallied organizations arrived, or were already on hand, to complete it.

After the first twenty-four hours of deadlock, Nicholas van Rijn invited two delegates to his suite in the Hotel Universe. They accepted, which they would scarcely have done for any other independent. Van Rijn's enterprise was sufficiently large and spread its tentacles sufficiently wide to make him powerful. Many observers found it hard to believe that, even with modern data and logic systems, one man could stay on top of it without having to incorporate like the giants. He was the natural leader of those outfits which had entered into no close-knitting agreements such as bound together the Seven In Space or the five Home Companies.

For their parts, Bayard Story seemed to be the guiding genius of the first group and Hanny Lennart of the second.

It was close to Lunar midnight. From the main room of the suite, the view through a transparency was awesome. Buildings stood well apart and were not high. They must stay below the forcefields which kept air in this bubble and the ozone layer beneath. But between them were parks wherein the low gravity let trees soar and arch like the fountains, amidst fiercely colored great blossoms. Lamps, on posts formed to resemble vines, glowed everywhere. They did not haze view of the stark crater floor beyond the fields, of Plato's ringwall shouldering in cliffs and steeps over the near horizon, or of the sky. Against infinite darkness, stars shone in their myriads, keen, jewel-hued, unwinking; the Milky Way was a quicksilver river; Earth's heart-snaring loveliness hung blue and white in the south. Confronting that sight, the opulence of the chamber seemed tawdry.

Lennart and Story arrived together. Van Rijn skipped across the floor to let them in. He had left unused the unit that could have supplied Terrestrial weight. "Ho, ho, you been confabulating before you come here, *nie?*" he bawled as the door opened. "No, don't deny, don't tell lies to a poor old lonely fat man who got one foot in the gravy. Come drink his liquor instead."

Story swept a glance across him and said genially, "For as far back as I've heard about you, Freeman van Rijn, and that's farther than I could wish, people tell how you've been lamenting your age and feebleness. I'd give long odds that you still have twenty years or more of devilment left."

"*Ja,* I look healthy, me, built like a brick wedding cake. But low gee helps more than you think, you two what could be my son and daughter except I always had better taste in women. How I long for to retire, forsake the bumps and inanities of this wicked world, wash my soul clean of sin till it squeaks."

"In order to make room for new and bigger sins?"

"Please stop that nonsense," Lennart interrupted. "This is supposed to be a serious discussion."

"If you insist, Freelady," Story said. "Myself, I feel ready for a little fun. Might as well take it, too. The Council is an exercise in futility. I wonder why I bothered to come."

The others regarded him narrowly for a moment, as if they also wondered. They had never met him before this occasion; they had only known—as a result of routine information gathering—that for the past ten years his name had been on the list of directors of Galactic Developments, in that corporation's headquarters on Germania. Evidently he was so rich and influential that he could kill publicity about himself and operate almost invisibly.

He was a rather handsome man, medium-sized, slender, his features regular in a tanned rectangular face, eyes blue-gray, hair and mustache smooth brown with a sprinkling of white. An elastic gait indicated that he used his muscles a good deal, perhaps under intermittently severe conditions. His soft speech held a trace of non-Terrestrial accent, though it was too far eroded by time to be identifiable. An expensive slacksuit in subdued greens fitted him as if grown from his body. Beside him, dark-clad Lennart looked dowdy and haggard. Beside either of them, van Rijn was outrageous in his favorite clothes of snuff-stained ruffled blouse and a sarong wrapped around his Jovian equator.

"Eat, drink, smoke," the host urged, waving at a well-stocked portable bar, trays of intricate canapés, boxes of cigars and cigarettes. He himself held a churchwarden pipe which had seen years of service and grown fouler for each day of them. "I wanted we should talk here, not on a circuit with seals, so we could relax, act honest, not have to resent what anybody maybe says."

Story nodded and took Scotch whisky in the civilized manner, neat with a water chaser. Van Rijn refilled a tumbler of Genever gin, adding a dash of what he called *angst en onrust* bitters. They settled down in loungers. Lennart sat upright on a sofa opposite, accepting nothing.

"Well," she said. "What do you have in mind?"

"We should see if we can compromise, or if not that, map out our areas of disagreement. Right?" Story supplied.

"Also horse-trade information," van Rijn said.

"That can be a mighty valuable commodity, especially when it's in short supply," Story observed.

"I hope you realize neither of us can make promises, Freeman van Rijn." Lennart clipped off each word. "We are simply executives of our corporations." She herself was a vice president of Global Cybernetics. "And in fact, neither the Home Companies nor the Seven form a monolith. They are only tied together by certain business agreements."

The recital of what a schoolboy should know did not insult van Rijn. "Plus interlocking directorates," he added blandly, taking up a tiny sandwich of smoked eel upon cold scrambled egg. "Besides, each of you got more voice in things than you let on, *ja,* you can bellow like wounded blast furnaces any time you want. And those business agreements, what they mean is the Seven is one cartel and the Home Companies another, and got plenty of political flunkies in high places."

"Not us in the Commonwealth," Story said. "That's become your plutocracy, Freelady Lennart, not ours."

Her thin cheeks flushed. "You can say that truly of your poor little puppet states on their poor little planets," she retorted. "As for the Commonwealth, we've now had fifty years of progressive reforms to strengthen democracy."

"By damn," van Rijn muttered, "maybe you really believe that."

"I hope we aren't here to rehearse stale partisan politics," Story said.

"Me too," van Rijn answered. "That is what it will amount to, what the Council will do if we leave it to itself. Members will take their positions and then not be able to get off because they have spread so much manure around. They will quarrel till plaster falls from the sky. And nothing else will happen . . . unless a few leaders agree to let it happen. That is what I want us to wowpow about."

"The issues are simple," Lennart declared. She repeated what she had said more than once at the conference table. "Mirkheim is too valuable, too strategic a resource, to be allowed to fall into the claws of beings that have demonstrated their hostility. I include certain human beings. The Commonwealth has a just title to sovereignty over it, inasmuch as the original discoverers represented no government whereas the Rigassi expedition was composed of our citizens. The Commonwealth likewise has a duty to mankind, to civilization itself, to safeguard that planet. The Home Companies support this. It's a patriotic obligation, and I am frankly surprised that persons of your education don't recognize it."

"My education was in the school of hard knockers," van Rijn replied. "Yours too, I suspect, Freeman Story, ha? You and me should understand each other."

"*I* understand why you change the subject," Lennart flung forth. "A discussion of morals would embarrass you."

"Well, speaking of morals, and immorals too," van Rijn said, "what about those original discoverers of Mirkheim, ha? What rights you think they have?"

"That can be decided in the courts, after Mirkheim is secured."

"*Ja, ja,* in courts whose judges you buy and sell like shares of stock. I hear a background noise already, you whetting your lawyers. That was why the Supermetals Company worked in secret."

Story raised his brows. "Do you expect us to believe, Freeman, that you aided and abetted them for a decade out of an abstract sense of justice?"

"What makes you suppose I was in any plot, a plain old peddler of belly comfort like me?"

"It's not been made public, but Rigassi learned from the workers at Mirkheim that a member of the Polesotechnic League had been helping in their cover-up, ever since he tracked the planet down. They didn't say who he was; they were simply, rather pathetically, trying to seem stronger than they are—"

Lennart drew a sharp breath. "How do you know that?" she exclaimed.

Story grinned. He was not about to reveal whatever espionage system his bloc maintained. He continued addressing van Rijn: "In retrospect, the man has to have been you. And a gorgeous job you did. Especially those hints you let drop, those clues you let be found, indicating an entire civilization more advanced than ours was producing the supermetals. Expeditions going solemnly out in search . . . Surely the most magnificent hoax in history." After a moment: "Do you mind telling us why you did it?"

"Well, you would call me a liar if I said I thought it was the right thing, and could be I would myself." Van Rijn swallowed a confection of Limburger cheese and onion on pumpernickel, tamped his pipe with a horny forefinger, and drank smoke. "I admit, partly I got talked into it by somebody I care about," he went on, between blowing rings. "And partly, for independents like me, is best if supermetals be on a free market. I don't want either of your cartels having the power that a Mirkheim monopoly in your hands would give. The original outfit, it is more reasonable."

That was what he had argued for at the Council: that the Polesotechnic League exert the might it had when it was united, in an effort to have Mirkheim declared a stateless planet under the protection of the League, which Supermetals would join. He knew perfectly well that there was no chance of the resolution being adopted unless a lot of hard minds got changed. The Home Companies insisted that they would support the Commonwealth's cause; the Seven were for the entire League holding clear of any struggle, strictly neutral and prepared to negotiate with whatever party won.

He now pursued the matter. "Story, it does not make sense we should sit by and piddle on our thumbs. Freelady Lennart has right as far as she goes: if Babur takes Mirkheim, is the worst outcome for all of us. And Babur is perhaply better armed than the Commonwealth. It for sure has shorter lines of communication."

"Who brought affairs to this pass?" Lennart's tone grew shrill. "Who first began trading with the Baburites, sold them the technology that got them into space, for a filthy profit? The Seven!"

"We had dealings, yes," Story said mildly. "At the time, that kind of transaction was standard practice, you recall. Nobody objected. Subsequently—well, I admit our companies let trade fall to almost nothing because it was no longer paying very well, not because we foresaw Babur's arming. We didn't. Nobody did. Who would have? Just the research and development necessary—incredible they could do it in so few years.

"But." He made a lecturer's gesture. "But from our earlier experience, we know we can do business with the Baburites. The possibility that we'll have to buy our supermetals from them is no more frightening than the possibility we'll have to buy them from the Home Companies, which is what a Commonwealth takeover would amount to. We'll still have things to exchange that Babur needs."

"Would you not prefer buying at a cheaper price from the present owners, and from other companies that will also work Mirkheim and sell on the open market?" van Rijn asked.

"They won't necessarily be cheaper," Story said. "Oxygen breathers are too apt to be in direct competition with us." He bridged his fingers and looked across them first at Lennart, then at van Rijn. "To be blunt, I think most of the fear of Babur is nothing but a child's fear of the unfamiliar. You never took the trouble to learn about it, when it seemed to be only one more obscure planet off in the fringes of known space. But I happen to be a former xenologist, who specialized in subjovians. I've studied all records the Seven have of their dealings with it. I've been there myself in the past and talked with its leaders. So I tell you—and I'm here to tell the entire Council—Babur's no den of ogres. It's the home of a species as reasonable by their lights as we are by ours."

"Exactly," van Rijn growled. "God help reason, if we and they is the best it can do. But I had a little brush-up with the Baburites myself once. I also have lately been scanning what data on them can be got here in the Solar System. Their lights is very flickery."

"Their claim to Mirkheim is ridiculous," Lennart put in. "Nothing but a slogan for territorial aggression."

"Not in terms of their own dominant culture," Story said.

"Then it isn't a culture we can afford to let become strong. It makes no bones about intending to establish an empire. If that meant only Babur-type worlds, perhaps we could live with it. But as I read their statements and actions to date, they plan to seize hegemony over that entire volume of space. That cannot be tolerated."

"How will you stop it?"

"For a start, by taking appropriate action at Mirkheim. Quickly, decisively. Our intelligence indicates Babur will back down from a *fait accompli.*"

"'Our' intelligence?" Story murmured. "How good are your connections to the Ministry of Defense?"

Van Rijn jetted thick blue clouds. "I think you just answered something I wasn't so sure about, Lennart," he said.

She stared. Apprehension crossed her features. "I didn't—I am only advocating, personally, you realize—"

"I got connections of my own. Not to nothing secret, like you seem to. But so simple a datum as clearances of civilian craft for deep space—suddenly for a while a lot of them got to wait—that kind of thing—*ja,* drop by drop by drop of fact I collect, till I got a full jigsaw puddle. Your way of talking, after these many years I have known you, Lennart, that says much too."

Van Rijn stood up, lightly in the low weight, like a rising moon which eclipsed the radiance of Earth. "Story," he said, "it will not be announced right away, but I bet you rubies to rhubarb the Commonwealth government has already dispatched a task force to Mirkheim. And I am not the least bit sure Babur will take that meekly-weakly." He turned to a little Martian sandroot statuette of St. Dismas that stood on the bar, his traveling companion of a lifetime. "Better get busy and pray for us," he told it.

✧IV✧

Under full hyperdrive, spaceship *Muddlin' Through* fared from the Solar System toward the sun that men had named Mogul. Pulsed Schrödinger waves drove her at a pseudovelocity equivalent to thousands of times the true speed of radiation; and in galactic terms those stars were near neighbors. Yet her clocks would have registered two and a half weeks when she reached her destination. So big is the universe. Sentient beings speak lightly of crossing light-years because they cannot comprehend what they are doing.

David Falkayn, Chee Lan, Adzel, and Muddlehead were in the saloon playing poker. Rather, the first three were. The computer was represented by an audiovisual sensor and a pair of metal arms. It was an advanced model, functioning at consciousness level, very little of its capability needed en route to maintain the systems of the ship. The live travelers had even less to do.

"I'll bet a credit," said Chee. A blue chip clattered to the middle of the table.

"Dear me." Adzel laid down his hand. "Can I fetch more refreshment for anyone?"

"Thanks." Falkayn held out an empty beer mug. "I'll raise." He doubled the bet. After half a minute during which the faint purr of engines and ventilators came through silence: "Hey, Muddlehead, what's keeping you?"

"The probabilities for and against me are calculable as being exactly balanced," said the flat artificial voice. Electronic brooding continued for a few seconds. "Very well," it decided, and matched Falkayn.

"*Ki-yao?*" wondered Chee. Her whiskers dithered, her tail switched the stool on which she sat. "Well, if you insist." She raised back.

Inwardly, the human jubilated. He had a full house. Outwardly, he pretended to ponder before he raised again. Muddlehead saw him. "Are you sure you don't need some readjustment somewhere?" Falkayn asked it.

"Whom the gods would destroy," said Chee smugly. Again she raised back. Meanwhile Adzel, his hoofs thudding on the carpet, returned with Falkayn's beer. The Wodenite himself refrained from drinking it on a voyage—no ship could have carried enough—and instead sipped a martini in a one-liter chillglass.

Falkayn raised another credit. Muddlehead saw. Chee and Falkayn peered its way, as if they could read an expression in the vitryl lens. Slowly, Chee added two chips to the pot. Falkayn suppressed a grin and raised once more. Muddlehead raised back. Chee's fur stood on end. "Damn your mendacious transistors to hell!" she screamed, and threw down her hand.

Falkayn hesitated. Muddlehead *had* implied its cards were mediocre, but—He called. His opponent revealed four queens.

"What the jumping blue blazes?" Falkayn half rose. "You said the probabilities—"

"I referred to the odds in favor of suckering you," explained Muddlehead, and raked in the pot.

"It appears that after our long hiatus, we will have to learn each other's styles of play *ab initio,*" Adzel remarked.

"Well, listen." Chee shuffled the deck. "I'm growing tired of nothing but straight poker. Dealer's choice, right? I say seven card stud, low hole wild."

Falkayn grimaced. "That's a nasty thing to say."

"The odds in wild card games are precisely as determinable as those in the standard versions," declared Muddlehead.

"Yes, but you're a computer," Falkayn grumbled.

"You want to cut?" Chee asked Adzel.

"What?" The dragon blinked. "Oh—oh, my apologies. I was taking the opportunity to meditate." With astonishing delicacy, an enormous hand split the pack.

The beating he took in that round did not seem to disturb his feelings. But when the deal came to him, he announced placidly, "This will be baseball."

"Oh, no!" Falkayn groaned. "What's happened to you two in the past three years?" He soon folded and sat grimly drinking and thinking.

His turn arrived. "I'll show you bastards," he said. "This will be Number One. You know it? Seven card stud, high-low, kings and tens wild for low, sevens and deuces wild for high."

"*Om mani padme hum,*" whispered Adzel shakenly.

Chee arched her back and spat. Settling down again on her cushion, she protested, "Muddlehead could blow a fuse."

"The problem is less complex than computing an entry orbit," the ship reassured her, "though rather more ridiculous."

The game went on, in a weird fashion. Falkayn took the whole pot, largely by default. "I hope we've all learned our lesson," he said. "Your deal, Muddlehead."

"I believe I am also permitted to call an unorthodox game," replied the machine.

Falkayn winced, Chee Lan bottled her tail, but Adzel proposed, "Fair is fair. However, let us thereafter confine ourselves to straight draw and stud."

"My assessment is that this one will confirm you in that desire," Muddlehead told them, shuffling. "It is played like draw except that there is no point in drawing. Players pick up their cards with the backs toward them, so that each can see the hand of everybody but himself."

After a shocked silence, Chee demanded: "What kind of perverts were they that gave you your last overhaul?"

"I am self-programming within the limits of the types of task for which I am built," the computer reminded her. "Thus whenever I am activated but idle, I endeavor to make that idleness creative."

"I think the Manichaean heresy just scored a point," said Adzel. Van Rijn would have understood the reference, but it went by Falkayn, though he was reasonably well-read.

At least play was mercifully short. At its end, the man rose. "Deal me out," he said. "I want to check on dinner." Gourmet cooking was among the hobbies with which he passed the time on voyages, as painting and sculpture were for Chee, music and the study of Terrestrial history for Adzel.

Having basted the roast, he did not immediately return to the saloon but lit his pipe and sought the bridge. His footfalls sounded loud. This was during the period of several hours per twenty-four when the ship's gravity generator was set at fifty-five percent above Earth's pull, to accustom the crew to what they would undergo on Babur if they landed there. An added forty-five kilos of weight did not unduly tire him. It was uniformly distributed over a body in good condition. What he and his mates had to adapt was chiefly their cardiovascular systems. Nonetheless he felt the heaviness in his bones.

On the bridge, optical compensators projected an exact simulacrum of whichever half of the sky they were set to show. Falkayn stopped at the control board. Beyond the glowing instruments, darkness roofed him in, housing a wilderness of stars. They gleamed at him from every side, sword-sharp swarms, the Milky Way an argent cataract, the Magellanic Clouds and the Andromeda galaxy made small and strange by distances he would never see overleaped. As if he felt the elemental cold between them, he cradled the bowl of his pipe in one fist, his campfire symbol. Beneath the susurrus of the ship lay an infinite stillness.

And yet, he thought, yonder suns were not quiet. They were appallingly aflame; and the spaces roiled with matter, seethed with energy, travailed with the birth of new suns and new worlds. Nor was the universe eternal; it had its strange destiny. To look into it was to know the sorrow and glory of being alive.

More than once Coya had gotten her wish that they make love here.

Falkayn's eyes sought in the direction of Sol, though it had long since dwindled from sight. His trained gaze could still find its way among constellations that had changed, some beyond recognition, and were nearly drowned in the number of stars that shone through airlessness. *How are you doing now, darling?* he wondered, knowing full well that "now" was a noise without meaning when cried across the interstellar reaches. *I didn't expect to feel homesick on this trip. I forgot that home is where you are.*

He recognized his regret as being partly guilt. He had not been frank with her. In his judgment, this journey held more dangers than he had admitted. (But then, she had tried to hide from him that she thought the same.) Regardless, when van Rijn broached the idea, the blood had leaped in him, after three staid years. Some lines passed through his head, from the archaic poetry which was a special interest of his:

> "*I am a part of all that I have met;*
> *Yet all experience is an arch wherethro'*
> *Gleams that untravell'd world, whose margin fades*

For ever and for ever when I move.
How dull it is to pause, to make an end,
To rust unburnish'd, not to shine in use!
As though to breathe were life. . . ."

Consoling himself with smoke, he decided he might as well admit that he had a hopeless case of go-fever. Coya and, yes, the kids could come a-roving with him later. Meanwhile

"My mariners,
Souls that have toil'd, and wrought, and thought with me—
That ever with a frolic welcome took
The thunder and the sunshine, and opposed
Free hearts, free foreheads—"

A chuckle interrupted. Neither Adzel nor Chee Lan would take kindly to the idea of manning oars in a Grecian galley. Not but what they hadn't done equally curious things from time to time, and might again. He'd better get back to the game. After dinner, if their mood suited, he'd break out his fiddle and play for them. The sight of those two dancing a jig together never wearied him.

✤ V ✤

The sun of Babur was more than twice as bright as Sol; but the planet was more than six times as far from its luminary as Earth. Thus Mogul stood in the spatial sky as a tiny disc of unbearable brilliance. A moon of Babur's four was close enough to show craters; the rest were like small sharp sickles. The world itself was a tawny globe partly shaded by night, partly veiled by bands and swirls of cloud, white tinged with gold, brown, or pale red. The majesty of the sight gave Falkayn to understand why its human discoverer had named it for a conqueror who went down in the memory of India as the Tiger. *He didn't know how well he chose,* he thought.

The bridge where he sat felt profoundly silent, only a breath from the ventilators to be heard. Hyperdrive was off and *Muddlin' Through* maneuvering on gravs at a true speed of a few kilometers per second. Chee was in the weapons control turret, Adzel in the engine room: their trouble stations. On Falkayn rested the burden of deciding when danger grew so great as to require fight or flight. He doubted that either would be possible here. The two warcraft that had challenged the ship as she approached and escorted her in now flanked and paced her arrowhead hull like wolves herding along a prey. Distance made them tiny until Falkayn magnified their sections of the view; then he saw them the size of a Technic destroyer but much more heavily armed, flying arsenals.

When Muddlehead spoke, he started, fetching up short against the safety web that held him in his seat. "I have commenced analysis of data obtained from neutrino and mass detectors, radar, gravity and hyperdrive pulse registers, and the local interplanetary field. Subject to correction, approximately fifty vessels are in wide orbit around Babur. Only one is of a size to be a possible dreadnought or equivalent thereof. Many of the rest appear to be noncombatant, perhaps groundable transports. More detailed information should be available presently."

"Fifty? Huh?" Falkayn exclaimed. "But we know—Babur put on

that show near Valya—we know its fleet is at least equal to the Commonwealth's. Where are the majority?"

His companions had been listening on the intercom. Adzel's slow basso rolled forth: "It is fruitless to speculate. We lack facts about Babur's plans, or even about the society whose masters have hatched those plans."

Nobody paid attention until too late, Falkayn thought. *Not to hydrogen breathers, who are alien, who can offer us oxygen breathers very little in the way of markets or resources, and by the same token should find nothing to quarrel with us about. There were too many planets which did lure us with treasure, with homesteads, with native beings not hopelessly unlike ourselves. We scarcely remembered that Babur existed—a whole world, as old and many-faced and full of marvels as ever Earth was.*

"I think I know where their missing ships are," Chee said. "They were never intended to orbit idle."

Falkayn's mind paced a rutted track: *How did Babur do it—how build up so great a strength in a mere twenty or thirty years? They couldn't simply put armament on copies of the few merchant vessels they'd produced. Nor could they simply work from plans of human men-of-war. Everything had to be adapted to the peculiar conditions of Babur, the peculiar requirements of its life forms.*

He recalled the shapes of the ships escorting his, bulge-bellied as if pregnant (with what sort of birth to come?). The extra volume housed cryogenic tanks. Air recycling alone was not adequate for hydrogen breathers, whose atmosphere leaked slowly out between the atoms of a hull and must be replenished from liquid gases. A thin plating of a particular supermetal alloy could cure that—but no Baburite knew there was a Mirkheim when the decision was made to found a navy. And the leakage problem was only the most easy and obvious of those the engineers had met.

The research and development effort before manufacture could begin must have been extraordinarily sophisticated. How could the Baburites complete it in the time it had actually taken, they who had never gotten off their home world when men first found them?

Could they have hired outside experts? If so, whose, and how could they pay them?

His repetition of questions which had been raised since the

menace first manifested itself, to no avail, was broken off. Muddlehead was making one of its rare contributions to talk: "Conceivably the Baburites have been anticipating fights with other hydrogen breathers."

"No," Adzel replied. "There aren't any with comparable technology, anywhere in known space, except the Ymirites; and they are as different from the Baburites as they are from us."

"I suggest you write me a program in political science," the computer said.

"Will you two klooshmakers stop snakkering?" Falkayn barked. "The fact is they've got far fewer ships here than we know they own. And I share Chee's foul notion of where the rest of those ships have gone. If we—"

His outercom chimed. He switched it on, and the screen filled with the image of a Baburite.

Around the eldritch caterpillar-centaur-lobster shape, which did not really look like any of those animals, shadowy figures flitted through gloom. Four tiny eyes behind a spongy snout could not make true contact with his. The being hummed its League Latin, noises which a vocalizer transposed into the proper phonemes. "We have notified the Imperial Band of Sisema and you are about to receive your instructions. Stand by." The statement was neither polite nor rude; it announced how things were.

Then the image faded out. For a minute Falkayn sat alone with his thoughts. Again they ran back over what little he knew.

"Sisema" was nothing but the vocalizer's rendition of a sound that in the original was a thin droning. "Imperial Band" was a Baburite attempt, probably suggested by earlier human visitors, to translate a concept that had no counterpart on Earth. Seemingly in Acarro—as the vocalizer called one region on the planet—the unit of society was not individual, family, clan, or tribe. It was an association of beings, tied together by bonds more powerful and pervasive than any that men could experience, involving some mutuality or complementarity of their sexual cycles but extending from this to every aspect of life. Each Band had its own personality, which differed more from that of its fellow Bands than members of any did from each other. Yet informants had told xenologists that every single member was unique, with a special contribution to make; the merging together was not subordination, it was communication (communion?) on a level deeper than consciousness. Telepathy? It was hard to know what such a word might mean on this world, and the informants had been unwilling or unable to speak further. A Baburite did radiate variably at radio frequencies, strongly enough to be detected by a sensitive instrument in the neighborhood. If that was due to neurochemistry(?), perhaps another nervous system(?) could act as a receiver. Perhaps in this way a part of tradition was not oral or written but directly perceived.

Potentially immortal, a Band recruited itself by adoption as much as by reproduction. Cross-adoptions linked various groups as cross-marriages had once allied human families. The Imperial Band seemed to have first choice in such cases, and to that extent was dominant, providing a leadership that had finally brought the entire planet under its sway. Yet it was not a true monarchy or dictatorship. Self-regulating, not given to conflict with their own kind, the Bands needed little government in the Terrestrial sense.

Which made their sudden aggressiveness all the less comprehensible, Falkayn thought. They'd tried some sharp business in this sector thirty years ago, and been worsted by the Solar Spice & Liquors factor—but sunblaze, that was a trivial incident, no cause for them lately to start trumpeting about their "right to control ambient space." Nor did the idea of dividing the stars up into spheres of interest seem like a safe one. The League could not tolerate that, if the League wanted to survive as a set of free-market entrepreneurs. The Commonwealth might accept the principle . . . but not if that involved loss of Mirkheim, the exact explosive issue Babur had chosen for precipitating the crisis.

I suppose even the agents of those companies of the Seven that formerly traded here have been baffled to foresee what minds so strange to us will do next—Hoy!

Again the screen gave him the picture of a Baburite. Though Falkayn was well schooled in noting individual differences between non-humans, he identified this one as new only by the color and cut of robe. The outlandishness of the whole simply drowned every detail in his perception. "You are Captain Ah-kyeh?" the being demanded without preamble. It had not heard his name well enough to hum an accurate equivalent. "This member speaks to you for the Imperial Band of Sisema. You have told our sentinels your purpose in coming. Redescribe it, in exact detail."

The muscles tightened around Falkayn's belly and between his shoulderblades. For an instant he was more conscious of stars, planet, moons, sun in the hemisphere above him than he was of the image he confronted. To go down in death, losing all that splendor, losing Coya and Juanita and the child unborn . . . But those warcraft hemming him in would not wantonly open fire. Would they? The habit of courage took charge of him and he answered steadily:

"Forgive me if I leave off a greeting or similar courtesy. I've been told your people don't employ such phrases, at least not with a foreign species." *Sensible. What rituals could we possibly have in common?* "My partners and I are here not on behalf of any government, but as representatives of a company in the Polesotechnic League, Solar Spice & Liquors. We know you had a dispute with us on the planet we call Suleiman, somewhat more than two of your years ago. We hope this won't prevent you from listening to us now."

He employed a vocalizer himself, not because he knew anything of the other sophont's language, but in order that it might convert his words into sounds that the latter could readily hear. He wondered how badly his meaning got distorted. If the Siseman speech had been tonal like Chinese, little but gibberish would have gotten through. The Baburite was wise to require reiteration.

"We listen," it said.

"I'm afraid I haven't any precise plan to describe. The conflict over Mirkheim disturbs us greatly. By 'us' I mean, here, the company for which my companions and I work. And of course the leaders of associated firms feel the same way. A war would be as disastrous to trade as to everything else. Besides, uh, economic motives, common decency demands we do whatever we can to help prevent it. You doubtless know the Polesotechnic League is not a government, but commands comparable power. It will gladly lend its good offices toward reaching a peaceful agreement."

"You do not speak for the entire League. It no longer has a single voice."

Touché! thought Falkayn, and felt indeed as if a blade had pierced him. *How in cosmos do the Baburites know that? They ought to be as ignorant of the ins and outs of Technic politics as we are of theirs.*

True, if they've been preparing for a long time to fight us, they'd investigate us carefully beforehand. But when did they, and how?

*A Baburite traveling around among us and asking questions would
be too conspicuous for van Rijn not to have heard about. And surely
they couldn't rely on occasional traders from the Seven for such
information, especially after that trade became practically extinct.*

*The fact that they are this well-informed is a flamingly important
datum all by itself. Van Rijn needs to know.*

He had reached his conclusion in a nearly intuitive leap. Best not
to let the officer(?) guess how dismayed he was. "We will be glad to
discuss that with you, and anything else," he temporized. "If we can
give some understanding, and gain some for ourselves, that will
make our journey a success. I'd like to emphasize that we don't
represent the Commonwealth in any way. In fact, none of us three is
a citizen of it. No matter who gets Mirkheim in the end, companies
of the League will be dealing with them," *unless Babur gets it and
then keeps the supermetals exclusively for itself.* "I hope you will
regard us as ambassadors of a sort," *who double in espionage if they
get the chance.* "We're experienced in dealing with different races, so
maybe we have more chance than average of exchanging information
and ideas."

The Baburite fired several disconcertingly shrewd queries, which
Falkayn answered as evasively as he dared. Since the being knew the
League was divided against itself, he strove to give the impression
of a less serious breach than was the case. At last his interrogator
said, "You will be conducted to a landing place on Babur. Earth-
conditioned quarters will be provided."

"Oh, we can quite well stay in our ship, in orbit, and communicate by screen," Falkayn said.

"No. We cannot allow an armed vessel, surely equipped with surveillance devices, to remain loose in local space."

"I can see that, but, um . . . we could set down on a moon."

"No. It will be necessary to study you at length, and you may not
have access to your ship. Else you might try to break away from us if
the process takes an inconvenient turn. A guide vessel is on its way.
Do as its chieftain commands you." The screen blanked.

Falkayn sat still for a while, hearing Chee swear. "Well," he said
at last, "if nothing else, we'll get a close look at the ground. Keep
those surveillance devices busy, Muddlehead."

"They are," the computer assured him. "Data analysis is also proceeding. It has become evident that most of the ships around Babur belong to oxygen breathers."

"Huh?"

"Infrared radiation shows their internal temperatures are too high for denizens of this planet."

"Yes, yes, obviously," Chee's voice came. "But what are the crews? Mercenaries? How in the name of Nick van Rijn's hairy navel did the Baburites contact them, let alone recruit them?"

"I suspect those are questions we are better off not asking," Adzel said. "To be sure, we must try to find the answers."

The guide came in sight, larger than *Muddlin' Through* but with similar streamlining proving that she was groundable. The part of her armament that showed was by itself more than the League ship carried. Falkayn did not propose making a dash for freedom.

Having received his travel orders and turned them over to Muddlehead to execute, he gave his attention to the viewscreen hemisphere. From time to time he rotated the scene or enlarged a part of it. He wanted to see everything he could, and not merely because an item might prove useful. This was a new, utterly strange world on which he was about to tread. A *world*. After all his years of roving, and even today when he fared under guard, the old thrill tingled through him.

Babur swelled in his sight as the ships accelerated inward. The approach curve took him around the globe, and he saw the tiny, fiery sun set in gold and rise in scarlet over an ocean of subtly tinted clouds. Then he was braking heavily and the planet was no longer before him or beside him, it was below. A thin scream of split atmosphere reached his ears. The stars of space vanished in a sky gone purple. Lightning flared across a storm far under this hurtling hull.

The surface came in view. Mountains glimmered blue-white, either sheathed in ice or purely glacial. Here water was a solid mineral. The liquid that took its place was ammonia. Air was hydrogen and helium, with traces of ammonia vapor, methane, and more complex organic compounds. Certain materials had gone on to become alive.

A sea heaved gray beneath rosy clouds. It was small for a body with twelve and a third times the mass of Earth, two and four-fifths times the diameter. Ammonia is less plentiful than water. The interiors of the enormous continents were arid; there the black vegetation grew sparsely, glittering dust scudded across the horizon's vast circle, and never a trace of habitation showed.

A volcano blew flame and smoke on high. It did not erupt like one on Earth; it was melting itself, streams raging forth and congealing into mirror-bright veins and sheets. The very structure of Babur was unearthly, a metallic core overlaid with ice and rocky strata, water in the depths compressed into a hot solid ever ready to expand explosively when that pressure happened to ease. Here there were true Atlantises, lands that sank beneath the waves in a year or less; new countries were upheaved as fast. Falkayn glimpsed such a place, hardly touched as yet by life, raw ranges and plains still ashudder with quakes.

On their downward slant, the ships passed above a second desert and then a fertile seaboard. A forest was squat trees on which long black streamers of leaves were fluttering. Aerial creatures breasted a gale on stubby wings. A leviathan beast wallowed blue in a gray lake beneath a lash of ammonia rain. Wilderness yielded to farms, darkling fields laid out in hexagons, houses built of gleaming ice and anchored with cables against storms. By magnification, Falkayn spied workers and their draft annuals. He could barely tell the species apart. Would a Baburite see as little distinction between a man and a horse?

A city appeared on the shore. Because it could not grow tall, it spread wide, kilometers of domes, cubes, pyramids in murky colors. In what seemed to be a new section, buildings were aerodynamically designed to withstand winds stronger than would ever blow across Earth. Wheeled and tracked vehicles passed among them, aircraft above—but remarkably little traffic for a community this size.

The city went below the curve of the world. "Make for that field," directed the guide. Falkayn saw a stretch of pavement, studded with great circular coamings that were mostly covered by hinged metal discs. A few stood open, revealing hollow cylinders beneath, sunk deep into the ground. It had been explained to him that for safety's sake, spacecraft which landed here were housed in such silos. The guide told him which to take, and Muddlehead eased its hull down.

"Here we are," Falkayn said unnecessarily. The words came dull and loud, now that his view was only of fluoro-lit blankness. "Let's get our suits on pronto. Our hosts might not like to be kept waiting. . . . Muddlehead, hold all systems ready for action. Don't let anybody or anything in except one of us. In case of arguments about that, refer the arguer to us."

"We might want a countersign," came Adzel's voice.

"Good thinking," Falkayn said. "Hm . . . does everybody know this?" He whistled a few bars. "Somehow I doubt the Baburites have ever heard 'One-Ball Riley.'" Beneath his cheerfulness, he thought, *What does it matter? We're totally at their mercy.* And then: *Not necessarily, by God!*

At the main personnel lock, he, Adzel, and Chee donned their spacesuits. They took time for a complete checkout. The walk ahead of them was short, but the least failure would be lethal. "Fare you well, Muddlehead," said Adzel before he closed his faceplate.

"Provided you don't sit here inventing new distortions of poker," Chee added.

"Would backgammon variations interest you?" asked the computer.

"Come on, let's move along, for Job's sake," Falkayn said.

Having completed their preparations, they took each a ready-packed personal kit and cycled through the lock. A platform elevator in a recess in the silo wall, with an up-and-down lever control, bore them to the top. Adzel was forced to use it alone, and at that most of him hung over the edge. Nevertheless, the fact that it could carry him was suggestive. It was meant solely for passengers; elsewhere on the field Falkayn had seen support cradles for ships that were to be loaded or unloaded, and cargo handling equipment. So the Baburites had visitors bigger than themselves often enough to justify a machine like this, did they?

As he emerged, Falkayn paid attention also to the controls of the hatch cover. A wheel steered a small motor which ran the hydraulic system moving the heavy piece of metal up or down.

Heavy . . . Unrelieved by his vessel's interior gee field, weight smote him. Without optical amplification, his eyes saw the world as twilit. Mogul glared low above buildings on his left, near the end of Babur's short day. Clouds hung amber in purple heaven; beneath them blew a ruddy wrack. With three and a third Terrestrial atmospheres of pressure behind it, the wind made motion through it feel like wading a river. Its sound was shrill, as was every noise borne by this air.

Several Baburites met him. They carried energy weapons. Pointing the way to go, they led the newcomers trudging across the expanse. A complex occupied an entire side of it. When close, able to make out details through the dusk, Falkayn recognized the structure. No workshop or warehouse of ice such as shimmered elsewhere, this was a man-made environmental unit, a block fashioned of alloys and plastics chosen for durability, thick-walled, triple-insulated. Light from some of the reinforced windows glowed yellow. Inside, he knew, the air was warm and recycled. As part of that cycle, the hydrogen that seeped through was catalytically treated to make water. The helium that entered took the place of a corresponding amount of nitrogen. A fifth of the gas was oxygen. A grav generator kept weight at Terrestrial standard.

"Our home away from home," he muttered.

Chee's astonishment sounded in his radio earphones: "This large a facility? How many do they house at a time? And why?"

A member of the escort thrummed into a communicator beside an airlock. Evidently it summoned assistance from within, for after a couple of minutes the outer valve swung back. The three from Sol entered the chamber in response to gestures. There was barely room for them. Pumps roared, sucking out Babur's air. Gas from the Interior gushed through a nozzle. The inner valve opened.

Beyond was an entryroom, empty save for a spacesuit locker. Two beings waited. They were lightly clad, but they carried sidearms. One was a Merseian, a biped whose face was roughly manlike but whose green-skinned body, leaning stance, and ponderous tail were not. The other was a human male.

Falkayn stepped out, almost losing his balance as the pull on him dropped. He unlatched his faceplate. "Hello," he heard. "Welcome to the monastery."

"Thanks," he mumbled.

"A word of warning first," the man said. "Don't try making trouble, no matter how husky your Wodenite friend is. The Baburites have armed watchers everywhere. Cooperate with me, and I'll help you settle in. You'll be here for quite a spell."

"Why?"

"You can't expect they'll let you go till the war is over, can you? Or don't you know? The main fleet of Babur is off to grab Mirkheim. And scoutboats have reported human ships on their way there."

✦VI✦

The man, large, heavy-featured, thick-mustached, introduced himself as Sheldon Wyler. "Sure, I'm working for the Baburites," he said almost coolly. "What's the Commonwealth or the League to me? And no, don't bother asking for details, because you won't get them."

He did, though, name his sullenly mute companion, Blyndwyr of the Vach Ruethen. "A fair number of Merseians are enlisted in the navy," he volunteered. "Mostly they belong to the aristocratic party at home and have no love for the League, considering how it shunted their kind aside and dealt instead with the Gethfennu group. You know, not many League people seem to understand what a cosmos of enemies it's made for itself over the years."

After the newcomers had unsuited, he squeezed past Adzel to a phone set in the wall. When he had punched, the screen lit with the likeness of a Baburite. "They're here," he reported in Anglic, and went on to describe the three from *Muddlin' Through*. "We're about to show them their quarters."

"Have you examined their effects for weapons?" asked the vocalizer voice.

"Why, no. What good—Well, all right. Hold on." To the prisoners: "You heard. We've got to check your gear."

"Proceed," Adzel said dully. "*We* are not so foolish as to use firearms inside an environmental unit; so we have brought none."

Wyler laughed. "Blyndwyr and I are good enough shots to blast you without putting a hole anywhere else." He went quickly through the luggage. The Merseian kept hand on gun butt. Chee's whiskers quivered with rage, her fur stood on end, her eyes had gone ice-green. A sickness gripped Falkayn by the throat.

Having verified the bags contained nothing more dangerous than compact tool kits, Wyler blanked the phone and led the way down a corridor. A room opening on it held four bunks and a window rapidly filling with night. "Bath and cleanup yonder," he pointed. "You can cook for yourselves; the kitchen's well stocked. Blyndwyr and me, we don't live here just now, but you'll be seeing a good deal of us, I'll bet. Behave yourselves and you won't be hurt. That includes telling us whatever we want to know."

Adzel brought his forelimbs through the door and the room grew crowded. "Uh, I guess you'd better sleep in the hall, fellow," Wyler said. "Tell you what, we'll go straight on to the mess, where there's space for all of us, and talk."

Falkayn gripped his spirit as if it were a wrestler trying to throw him. As he walked, his neck ached from its own stiffness. *Lead him on,* he thought. *Collect information, no matter how unlikely it is you'll ever bring it to anybody who can use it.* "What's this building for?" he got out in what he attempted to make a level tone.

"Engineering teams used to need it," Wyler said. "Later it housed officers of oxygen-breathing auxiliary forces while they got their indoctrination."

"You speak too freely," Blyndwyr reproved him.

Wyler bit his lip. "Well, I didn't sign on to be a goddamn interrogator—" He relaxed a little. "What the muck, my answer was pretty obvious, wasn't it? And they aren't going anywhere with it, either. . . . Here we are."

The messroom was broad and echoing. Furniture had been stacked against the walls and the air smelled musty, as if no one had adjusted the recyclers for some time. Adzel went motionless, like a statue of an elemental demon. Chee poised at his feet, her tail whipping her flanks and the floor. Falkayn and Wyler drew out a couple of chairs and sat. Blyndwyr stood well aside, ever watchful.

"Suppose you start by telling me exactly who sent you and why," Wyler said. "You've been goddamn vague so far."

Our assignment itself was vague, Falkayn thought. *Van Rijn trusted we'd be able to improvise as we went, as we learned. Instead, we've been captured as casually as fish in a net. And as hopelessly?* Aloud, he dared be defiant: "We might both be more interested in what you're doing. How can you claim it's not treason to your species?"

Wyler scowled. "Are you going to spout a sermon at me, Captain? I don't have to take that." He considered. "But okay, okay, I will explain. What's so evil about the Baburites? Without a navy, they'd never stand a chance. The Commonwealth would grab Mirkheim and the whole goddamn industrial revolution that

Mirkheim means, with crumbs for anybody else. Or the League would. The Baburites think differently. To them, this is no question of profit or loss on a balance tape. No, it's an opportunity for the race. With it, they can buy their way into the front rank—buy ships, mount expeditions, plant colonies, not to speak of all they might do at home—immediately!"

"But Mirkheim was not foreseeable," Falkayn argued. "Before that, why was Babur arming? Why did it plan to fight . . . and whom?"

"The Commonwealth has a navy, doesn't it? And the League companies keep warships too. They've seen use. We never know what we may come up against tomorrow. You of all people should remember the Shenna. Babur has a right of self-defense."

"You talk like a convert."

"You do not talk like a businessman, Captain Falkayn," Wyler said in anger. "I think you're stalling me. And I'm not going to stand for that, you hear? Maybe you imagine being famous will protect you. Well, forget that. You're a long ways off into a territory that doesn't care a good goddamn about your reputation. They don't feel obliged here to send you back undamaged, or send you back at all. If we have to, we'll pump you full of babble juice. And if that doesn't seem to be working so well, we'll go on from there."

He stopped, swallowed, smoothed countenance and tone: "But hey, let's not quarrel. I'm sure you're a reasonable osco. And you say one of your aims is to see what you can dicker out for your employer. Well, I might be able to help you there, if you help me first. Let's brew some coffee and talk sense."

Chee Lan rattled a string of syllables. "What?" Wyler asked.

She spat out words like bullets: "I was making remarks about those refrigerated centipedes of yours that you wouldn't want to translate for them."

Falkayn sat very quiet. His blood made a cataract noise in his ears. Chee had used the Haijakatan language, which they three knew and surely no one else within many light-years. *If we don't escape, we'll die here sooner or later. And even what little we've learned is important to bring home. I think we can take these two, and get Davy back to the ship in disguise.*

"Her comments are, however, quite apposite," the Wodenite put in. "I myself might go so far as to say—" He switched to Haijakatan. "*If you can begin on the greenskin, Chee, I can handle the man.*"

"True and triple true." The Cynthian did not pace, she bounded, back and forth like a cat at play but with her tail bottled to twice its normal size.

Wyler's hand slipped down toward his gun. Blyndwyr drew a hissing breath and backed off, gripping his own blaster in its holster. Falkayn held himself altogether still, believing he saw what his comrades intended but not quite sure, ready only to trust them.

Start by distracting attention. "You can't blame my friends for getting excited," he said. "They're not Commonwealth citizens. Neither am I. And we haven't come on behalf of the League, just of a single company. Nevertheless we're to be interned indefinitely and quizzed under threats, possibly under drugs or torture. The best thing you can do, Wyler, is make the higher-ups of Babur listen to us. They should put away this blind hostility of theirs to the League. Its independent members want it to be in charge of Mirkheim. That'd guarantee everybody access to the supermetals."

"Would it?" Wyler snorted. "The League's split in pieces. And the Baburites know that."

"How? When we're as ignorant about them as we are, how did they get so close an impression of us? Who told them? And what makes them ready to stake their whole future on the word of those persons?"

"I don't know everything," Wyler admitted. "Goddamn, this planet's got eight times the surface of Earth, most of it land surface. Why shouldn't the Imperial Band feel confident?" He thrust out his jaw. "And that will be the last question you get to ask, Falkayn. I'm starting now."

Chee's restlessness had brought her near the Merseian. His alertness had focused itself back on the seated humans. Abruptly she made a final leap, sidewise but straight at him. Landing halfway up his belly, she gripped fast to his garment with her toes while both arms wrapped around his gun hand. He yelled and tried to draw regardless. She was too strong; she clung. He hammered at her with his free fist. Her teeth raked blood from it.

Adzel had taken a single stride. It brought him in reach of Wyler, whom he plucked from the chair, lowered, and bowled backward across the floor. His tail slapped down over the man's midriff to hold him pinioned. Meanwhile Adzel kept moving. He got to Blyndwyr, picked him up by the neck, shook him carefully, and set him down in a stunned condition. Chee hauled the blaster loose and scampered aside. Wyler was struggling to get at his gun. Falkayn arrived and took the weapon from its holster.

Adzel released Wyler and stepped back with his comrades. Wyler lurched to his feet; Blyndwyr sat gasping. "Are you crazy?" the human chattered. "What is this nonsense, you can't—can't—"

"Maybe we can." Glee surged through Falkayn. He knew he should have been more cautious, vetoed the attack, stayed meek lest he get himself killed. *But if none of us three is an Earthling, Coya is; and on the whole, Earth has been good to us too. Besides, ours is Old Nick's single ship in these parts. He sent us mainly to gather information, that he might not have to grope totally blind. And his welfare is also the welfare of thousands of his workers, millions among the planetary peoples who trade with him. . . . To Satan with that. What counts is breaking free!* The fire in his flesh roared too loudly for him to hear any fright.

At the same time, the logical part of him was starkly conscious. "Stay where you are, both of you," he told Wyler and Blyndwyr. "Adzel, Chee, your idea is that I can go out dressed as him, right?"

"Of course." The Cynthian settled down on her haunches and began to groom herself. "One human must look like another to a Baburite."

Adzel cocked his head and rubbed his snout with a loud sandpapering sound. "Perhaps not entirely. Freeman Wyler does have dark hair and a mustache. We must do something about that."

"Meanwhile, Wyler, off with your clothes," Chee ordered. The Merseian, half recovered, made as if to rise. She swung the blaster in his direction. "You stay put," she said in his native Eriau. "I'm not a bad marksman either."

Bloodless in the cheeks, Wyler cried, "You're on collision orbit, I tell you, you can't get away, you'll die for goddamn nothing!"

"Undress, I told you," Chee replied. "Or must Adzel do it?"

Looking at the muzzle of her weapon and the implacable eyes behind, Wyler started to remove his garments. "Falkayn, haven't you any sense?" he pleaded.

The response he got was a thoughtful "Yes. I'm planning how we can take you along to quiz."

Chee lifted her ears. "'We,' Davy?" she asked. "How are Adzel and I going to get out? No, you can ransom us later."

"You two most certainly are coming," Falkayn said. "We don't know how revengeful Baburites are, or their human and Merseian chums."

"But—"

"Besides, I'll need your help with Wyler, not to mention after we're spaceborne."

Adzel returned from the kitchen where he had been rummaging, "Here is the means to provide you with dark hair and mustache," he announced proudly. "A container of chocolate sauce."

It didn't seem like what a really dashing hero would use in a jailbreak, but it would have to do. While he stripped, put on Wyler's garb, and submitted to the anointing, Falkayn exchanged rapid-paced words with his companions. A scheme evolved, not much more precarious than the one which had gotten them this far.

Adzel ripped up Blyndwyr's clothes and tied him securely in place. He and Chee kept Wyler unbound, naked, under guard of her firearm. The Wodenite uttered a benediction, all the goodbye that Falkayn took time for. They three might never fare together again, he might never come back to Coya and Juanita, but he dared not stop to think about that, not now.

The hallway clattered to his footfalls. At the airlock, he punched the number he had seen and stood feeling as if he waited to be shot at in a duel. When the Baburite's four eyes peered out of the screen at him, he couldn't help passing his tongue over dry lips. A sweet taste reminded him of how crude his disguise was.

He spoke without preliminary, as Wyler had done before: "The prisoners seem to have lost morale. They asked me to fetch some medicines and comforts for them from their ship. I think that may make them cooperative."

He was gambling that human psychology would be as little known here as human bodies were.

A heartbeat and a heartbeat went by before the creature answered: "Very well. The guards will be told to expect you." Blankness.

Falkayn found Wyler's spacesuit and its undergarment in a locker.

The suit was distinctively painted; probably every offplanet employee had an individual pattern for identification purposes. So he must adjust it to fit his somewhat taller frame. He could have used help, but didn't dare have anyone else in scanner range of the phone, lest the Baburite call him back.

Cycling through the lock, he emerged into bulldog jaws of gravitation. The field stretched bare before him, pockmarked with hatch covers. Here and there a caterpillar shape crossed it on some unguessable errand. Blue-white lights glared along the fronts of buildings till their ice shimmered like cold made visible. A wind whined and thrust. In darkness overhead, two moons shone dimly, but no stars. The walk was long to his destination.

It seemed impossible that no one challenged him while he opened the silo, stepped onto the elevator, and descended. By the time he had reached the personnel entrance of his ship, his helmet was chokeful of sweat-reek, he could barely whistle the countersign, and superstition rose from the grave of his childhood to croak, *This can't go on. You're overdue for bad luck.*

We've already had it, he defended. *We came too late—after the fleet had left.*

Do you think if it were still here, you would have been this lightly guarded?

The valve turned. Waiting in the chamber for air exchange, Falkayn invoked some of Adzel's Buddhist techniques and regained a measure of calm. "There should be no bow, no arrow, no archer: only the firing."

He left his space armor on inside, though frost was instantly white upon it. A flick of a switch in the heater controls cleared his faceplate, and he hurried to the bridge. Working his awkward bulk into his shockseat, he said via radio, "Muddlehead, we have to break Adzel and Chee loose. I'll steer, because you haven't seen where they are. We'll land in front of an entry lock. Blast it instantly—they won't have time to go through in the regular way—and have the outer valve of the number-two belly entrance open for them. The moment they're aboard, lift for space, taking such evasive maneuvers as your instruments suggest are best. Go into hyperdrive as soon as we're far enough out, and I mean as soon; forget about safety margins. Is this clear?"

"As clear as usual," said the computer.

The power plant came to full, murmurous life. Negafield generators thrust against that fabric of physical relationships which we call space. The ship glided upward.

"Yonder!" Falkayn yelled uselessly. Dancing over the manual pilot console, his fingers were handicapped by their gloves. But if the hull should be seriously holed by an enemy shot, an unprotected oxygen breather would be dead. Air roared outside. He had left the acceleration compensator off, in order that he might have that extra sensory input for this tricky task, and forces yanked at him, threw him against the safety web and then back into the seat. Hai-ah!

The building was straight ahead. He dropped, he hovered. A gun in its turret flung forth a shaped-charge shell. Flame erupted, the outer portal crumpled in wreckage. With surgical delicacy, an energy cannon sent its beam lancing at the inner valve. Metal turned white hot and flowed.

The caterpillar figures dashed about on the field. Had they no ground defenses? Well, who could have anticipated this kind of attack? Wait—above—forms in the moonglow, suddenly diving, aircraft—

The barrier went down. A frost-cloud boiled as Baburite and Terrestrial gases met. Falkayn was fleetingly glad that automatic doors would close off the module where Blyndwyr lay. Doubly gigantic in his spacesuit, Adzel stormed forth. Was he carrying Chee and Wyler? A firebolt spat from above. The spaceship swung her cannon about and threw lightning back. Adzel was out of sight, below the curve of the hull. What had happened, in God's name, what had happened?

"They are aboard," Muddlehead reported, and sent the vessel leaping.

Acceleration jammed Falkayn deep into his chair. "Compensators," he ordered hoarsely. A steady one gee underfoot returned. Split atmosphere raved and the first stars came in sight. Falkayn unlocked his faceplate and reached shakily for the intercom button. "Are you all right?" he called.

A shell exploded close by, flash of light, buffet of noise, trembling of deck. *Muddlin' Through* drove on outward.

Adzel's tones rumbled through the fury round about.

"Essentially we are well, Chee and I. Unfortunately, a shot from an aircraft struck our prisoner, who was under my right arm, penetrated his suit, and killed him instantly. I left the body behind."

There's our bad luck, raged within Falkayn. *I would've put him under narco and maybe learned—Damn, oh, damn!*

"My own suit was damaged, but not too badly for the self-sealing to work, and I suffered no more than a scorched scale," Adzel went on. "Chee was safe on my left side. . . . I would like to say a prayer for Sheldon Wyler."

Steadiness took over in Falkayn. "Later. First we've got to escape. We've surprise and speed on our side, but the alarm must be in space by now. Take battle stations, you two."

He knew as well as they that in a close encounter with any fighter heavier than a corvette, they were done for. They might ward off missiles for a time; but so would the enemy, and meanwhile its energy beams, powered by generators more massive than *Muddlin' Through* could carry, would gnaw through plating much thinner than its own.

The chance of combat was small, however. Probably no Baburite had such a position and velocity at this moment that its grav drive was capable of equalizing vectors, at the same point in space, with the furiously accelerating Solar craft. Nearly all slug-it-out contests took place because opponents had deliberately sought each other.

Target-seeking torpedoes, whose mass was small enough to permit enormous changes in speed and direction, were something else. So were rays that traveled at the speed of light.

The sky of Babur had fallen well aft, the globe was still huge in heaven but dwindling. Stars burned manyfold, some among them the color of blood.

"When can we go hyper, Muddlehead?" Falkayn asked. It shouldn't be long. They were already high in the gravity well of Mogul and climbing upward fast in Babur's. Soon the metric of space would be too flat to interfere unduly with fine-tuned oscillators; and once they were moving at their top faster-than-light pseudovelocity, practically nothing ever built had legs to match theirs.

"One-point-one-six-hour, given our present vector," said the computer. "But I propose to add several minutes to that time by applying transverse thrust to bring us near the satellite called Ayisha. My instruments show a possible anomalous radiation pattern there."

Falkayn hesitated a second. If heavy ground installations were on the moon . . . Decision: "Very well. Carry on."

Time crawled. Twice Chee yelled savagely, when her guns destroyed a missile on its intercept course. Falkayn could only sit and think. Mostly he remembered, in jumbled oddments—wingsailing with Coya at Lunograd, a red sun forever above a desert on Ikrananka, his father's sternness about *noblesse oblige*, fear that he might drop newborn Juanita when she was laid in his arms, *The Flyting of Dunbar and Kennedie*, his first night with Coya and his last, youthful beer hall arguments about God and girls, Rodin's *Burghers of Calais*, a double moonglade on the Auroral Ocean, a firefall between two stars, Coya beside him beholding the crooked towers of a city on a planet which did not yet have a human-bestowed name, his mother using a prism to show him what made the rainbow, Coya and he laughing like children as they had a snowball fight at an Antarctic resort, the splendor of an Ythrian on the wing, Coya bringing him sandwiches and coffee when he sat far into a nightwatch studying the data readouts on a new world the ship was circling, Coya—

The scarred moon-disc grew big in the viewscreen. Falkayn magnified, searched, suddenly found it: a sprawling complex of domes, turrets, ship housings, spacefield, test stands. . . . "Record!" he ordered automatically.

Did Muddlehead sound hurt? Impossible. "Of course. Infrared signs are of beings thermodynamically similar to or identical with humans."

"You mean that stuff's not meant for Baburites? Why, then—"

"*A-yu!*" Chee Lan screamed; and incandescence flared momentarily. "Close, friends, close!"

"I suggest we do not dawdle," Adzel said.

The colony, or whatever it was, reeled out of sight behind a mountain range as the ship sped past Ayisha. "According to my instruments," Muddlehead reported, "if we persevere as at present, surrounding conditions will grow progressively less unsalubrious for us."

That means we're going to get away, Falkayn thought. *We're clear.* The pains and tingles of tension spread upward through his body to the brain.

"Where are we bound, then?" he heard Chee ask.

He forced himself to say, "Mirkheim. We just might arrive ahead of the Baburites, in time to warn those approaching humans, whoever they are, and the workers there."

"I doubt that," the Cynthian replied. "The enemy probably has too big a jump on us. And should we take the risk? Isn't it more important to bring home the information we've collected, that somehow Babur's acquired a substantial corps of military and technical oxygen breathers? A courier torp might not get through."

"No, we must attempt to warn," Adzel said. "It could forestall a battle. One violent death is too much."

Falkayn nodded wearily. His gaze sought back to the uncaring stars. *Poor Wyler,* he thought. *Poor everybody.*

✦ VII ✦

An intercom presented the captain of *Alpha Cygni*. "Madame," he said, "Navigation reports we are one light-year from destination."

"Oh—" Sandra gathered in her wits. So soon? Then how had the trip from Hermes taken so long? *A light-year,* raced through her. *The extreme distance at which the space-pulses from our hyperdrives are detectable. Instantaneously. Now they'll know at the planet that we're coming. And "they" could be an enemy.* "Order all units to prepare for action."

"Yellow alert throughout. Aye, madam." The image disappeared.

Sandra stared about her. Save where viewscreens showed heaven, the admiral's bridge was a narrow and cheerless cave. It throbbed slightly with engine beat; the air blew warm, smelling faintly of oil and chemicals. Abruptly it felt unreal, her naval uniform a costume, the whole proceeding a ridiculous piece of playacting.

Clad in a similar two-toned coverall, which could at need be the underpadding in a spacesuit, Eric gave her a wry look. "Buck fever?" he murmured. "Me too." He could speak candidly, since he was the only other person there.

"I suppose that's what it is." Sandra tried to shape a smile and failed.

"I'm surprised. When you're one of the few people along who have any combat experience."

"Diomedes wasn't like this. That was hand-to-hand warfare. And . . . and anyway, nobody expected me to issue commands."

Why didn't I hire mercenaries, years ago, to form the nucleus of a proper-sized officer corps?

Because it didn't seem that the peace we had always known on Hermes would ever be threatened. Brushfire clashes happened around stars too far off for us to really notice: nothing worse. We were warned of aliens getting into space; but surely they were not too dangerous—not even the Shenna, whom, after all, the League put down before any great harm was done. Double and triple surely, Technic civilization would never know wars among its own member peoples. That was something man had left behind him, like purdah, tyranny, and cannibalism. We kept a few warcraft with minimum crews to act as a police and rescue corps, and as insurance against a contingency we didn't really believe was possible. (Inadequate insurance, I see today.) Their practice with heavy weapons we considered rather a joke, except when taxpayer organizations complained.

"Damn me for letting you come!" she blurted. "You should have stayed behind, in charge of the reserves—"

"We've been over that ground often enough, think you not, Mother?" Eric answered. "No better man than Mike Falkayn could be holding the reins there. What I wish is that I'd had sense to ask for an assignment that'd hold me busy here. Being your executive officer sounded big, but it turns out to be sheer comic opera."

"Well, I'm scant more than a passenger myself till we start negotiating. Pray God I can do that. In history, comic operas have had a way of turning into tragedies."

If only Nadi were along. His company quiets me. But she had sent the chief of the Supermetals patrol on ahead, to ready the entire outfit for cooperation with hers.

About three hours till arrival, at their top pseudospeed . . . She drew several deep breaths. Never mind about a battle. If that came, let her leave it in the hands of her captains, with the skipper of this flagship the coordinator, as had been agreed at the outset. Their purpose then would almost certainly be just to fight free and escape. They had no great strength. Besides *Alpha Cygni,* a light battleship, it was two cruisers, four destroyers, and a carrier for ten Meteor-class pursuers. At that, they had not left much behind to guard their home.

Her job was to prevent a clash, to establish Hermes as an impartial agent intervening to see justice done and order restored. And she did know something about handling people. She settled into her shock-seat, lit a cigar, and began consciously relaxing, muscle by muscle. Eric paced.

"Madame!" The words came harsh and not quite even. "Hyperdrives detected."

Sandra made herself remain seated. "Coming to meet us?"

"No, madam. They're in our fourth quadrant. As near as can be extrapolated, we and they have the same destination."

She twisted her head about, eyes seeking from screen to screen. Darkness still held the sun of Mirkheim. They would have to come almost on top of that dim remnant to see it. The fourth quadrant— She could not identify what she sought there. It was only a small spark at its remove, lost among thousands. But in the fourth quadrant lay Mogul.

Eric smacked fist into palm. "The Baburites!"

"A moment, please, sir," said the captain. "I'm getting a preliminary data analysis. . . . 'Tis a huge force. No details computable yet; but in numbers, at least, 'tis overwhelming."

For a moment Sandra gulped nausea, as if she had been kicked in the gut. Then her mind went into emergency operation. Self-doubt fell away. Decisions snapped forth. "This changes things," she said. "Best we try for a parley. From this ship, since I'm aboard her. Prepare an intercept course for us. The rest of ours—they can reach Mirkheim well ahead of the newcomers, not? . . . Good. Let them continue yonways under leadership of *Achilles,* rendezvous with Nadi, and hold themselves combat ready. But in case of doubt—'fore all, if something appears to have happened to us on *Alpha*—they are to return home at once."

"Aye, madam." In a corner of herself, Sandra felt sorry for the captain. He was a young man, really, striving to be cool and efficient in the face of ruin. He repeated her instructions and his image vanished.

"Oh, no," Eric groaned. "What can we do?"

"Very little, I'm afraid," Sandra admitted. "Let me be, please. I have to think." She leaned back and closed her eyes.

An hour passed. From time to time, relayed information hauled her mind briefly out of the circle around which it struggled. The Baburites were holding course at moderate pseudospeed. Their complacency was almost an insult. Finally one ship left formation and angled off to meet the oncoming Hermetian. A while later, signals began to go back and forth, modulations imposed on hyperdrive oscillations: *We wish to communicate—We will communicate.* The calls were stereotyped, an on-off code, the rate of conveyance of meaning tormentingly slow: for the uncertainty principle is quick to make chaos of space-pulses. Not until vessels are within a few thousand kilometers of each other is there enough coherence for voice transmission. Pictures require more proximity than that.

Which is why we can't send messages directly between the stars, crossed Sandra's head, relic of a lesson in physics when she was young. *Nobody could position that many relay stations. Nor would they stay positioned. So we must use couriers, and hell can come to a boil someplace before we know aught has gone wrong.*

Instruments accumulated ever better data, computers analyzed, until it was clear that the strange craft was approximately the size of *Alpha,* surely as well armed. At last the captain's face reappeared. He was pale. "Madame, we've received a vocal communication. It goes . . . goes . . . quote, 'You will come no nearer, but will match hypervelocity to ours and stand by for orders.' Close quote. That's how it goes."

Eric reddened. Sandra peeled lips back from teeth and said, "We'll go along. However, phrase your acknowledgment, hm, 'We will do as you request.'"

"Thank you, Your Grace!" The captain's whole being registered an appreciation that should spread through the crew . . . though doubtless the Anglic nuance would quite go by the Baburites.

Still the viewscreens held only stars. Sandra could imagine the foreign ship, a spheroid like hers, never meant to land on a planet, studded with gun emplacements, missile launchers, energy projectors, armored in forcefields and steel, magazines bearing the death of half a continent. She would not see it in reality. Even if they fought, she probably never would. The flesh aboard it and the flesh aboard *Alpha* would not touch, would not witness each other's perishing nor hear the anguish of the wounded. The abstractness was nightmarish. Peter Asmundsen, Nicholas van Rijn, she herself had ever been in the middle of their own doings: a danger dared, a blow struck or taken, a word spoken, a hand clasped, all in the living presence of the doers. *Is our time past? Is the whole wild, happy age of the pioneers? Are we today crossing the threshold of the future?*

Preliminaries must have taken place before the captain announced, "Lady Sandra Tamarin-Asmundsen, Grand Duchess of Hermes; the delegate of the Imperial Siseman Naval Command."

The sound of the vocalizer was emotionless and blurred by irregularities in the carrier wave. Yet did a roughness come through? "Greeting, Grand Duchess. Why are you here?"

She dismissed her despair and cast back, "Greeting, Admiral, or whatever you want to be called. We're naturally curious about your purpose, too. You're no nearer home than we are."

"Our mission is to take possession of Mirkheim for the Autarchy of United Babur."

A part of her wished that the ships were close enough together for picture transmission. Somehow it would have helped to look into four little eyes in an unhuman visage. It would have felt less like contending with a ghost,

But the determination is as solid as yonder invisible sun, she thought, *and so are the weapons which back it.* She said with care, "Is't not obvious why we Hermetians have come? Our objective is simply to . . . to take charge, to act as caretakers, while a settlement is worked out. Being neither Commonwealth nor Babur nor League, we hoped we could make all sides stay their hands, think twice, and avoid a war. Admiral, 'tis not too late for that."

"It is," said the artificial voice. When it added its stunning news, was there the least hint of sardonicism? "We do not refer to the fact that the Imperial Band does not desire your interference, but to the fact, established by scouts of ours, that the Commonwealth already has a fleet at Mirkheim. We are coming to oust it. Hermetians will be well advised to withdraw before combat begins."

"Son of a bitch—" she heard Eric gasp, and herself whisper, "Merciful Jesus!"

"Rejoin your flotilla and take it home," said the Baburite. "Once action has commenced, we will attack every human vessel we encounter."

"No, wait, wait!" Sandra cried, half rising. No response came. After a minute her captain told her: "The alien is moving off, madam, back toward its companion units."

"Battle stations," Sandra directed. "Full speed on a course to intercept ours."

Stars streamed across viewscreens as *Alpha* swung about. The pulse of the engines strengthened.

"Was that crawler lying?" Eric roared.

As if in reply, the captain described readings, numerous hyperdrives activated in the neighborhood of the planet. Obviously somebody was present who had now detected the newest invaders. Who could that be but a Solar task force?

"Curse the cosmos, what a kloodge of amateurs we are." Pain stretched Eric's mouth wide as he spoke. "The Baburites kept watch on Mirkheim. They knew when the Earthlings arrived. We, we plowed ahead like a bull with a fever."

"No, remember, we relied on Nadi's patrol to come give us warning of aught untoward," Sandra reminded him mechanically. "No doubt the Earthlings captured them—he had nothing particularly fast or powerful—captured them with some idea of preserving surprise. But meanwhile the Baburites had high-speed observers in the vicinity." She grimaced. "It seems the worst amateurs are in the Commonwealth Admiralty."

They've never had to fight a war. Skills, doctrine, the military style of thinking evaporated generations ago.

Such things must needs be relearned in the time that is upon us.

Tidings continued to arrive. The fleet ahead was leaving Mirkheim, deploying in what looked like combat formation. It was considerably inferior to the armada from Babur. The sensible act would have been to cut and run. But no doubt its commander had his orders from the politicians back home: "Don't give up easily. We're sure those bugs will just attempt a bluff. They can't be serious about fighting *us.*"

They sure can be, Sandra thought. *They are.*

Eric stopped in his tracks. It was as if a flame kindled in him, though he spoke low. "Mother . . . Mother, if we joined the Commonwealthers—our fellow humans, after all—"

She shook her head. "Not. 'Twould make slim difference, save to get Hermetians killed and ships wrecked that we'll want for home defense. I'm about to tell all other units of ours to sheer off and start back immediately."

He divined her intention. "We, though? *Alpha Cygni?*"

"We'll continue to Mirkheim. Belike the whole Solar strength will be gone by the time we get there, off to meet the Baburites. In any event, this is too formidable a craft for anybody to tangle with casually. We do have a duty to help Nadi's folk get free if possible. They're our allies, after a fashion. Including technicians on the ground." Sandra achieved a smile of sorts. "And since the news first broke about it, I've been curious to see Mirkheim."

✵ ✵ ✵

No guard was at the planet. The Supermetals patrol vessels orbited empty. A quick radio exchange confirmed that their crews had been ferried down to the mining base, as deep an oubliette as ever was. The battleship took a circling station of her own. Boats sprang from her sides to evacuate the personnel below. Sandra left a protesting Eric behind, nominally in charge, and herself rode in one of the auxiliaries.

Mirkheim loomed monstrous ahead. The wanly glowing ashes of its sun were unseeable at its distance, and it might almost have been a rogue world which had never belonged to any star, drifting eternally among winter-bright constellations. Almost, not quite. No snows of frozen atmosphere decked it from pole to pole; its gleam was of metal, hard, in places nearly mirrorlike. Mountains and chasms made rough shadows. Regions of dark iron sketched a troll's face.

Soon the boat neared the surface and leveled off. Behind Sandra stretched a plain, on and on to a horizon so far off that a dread of being alone in limitless emptiness awoke in the soul of the onlooker. The ground was not cratered and dust-covered like that of a normal airless body; it was blank, dimly shining, here and there corrugated in fantastic ridges where moltenness had congealed. Its darkness cut sharply across the Milky Way. To right and left, the plain was pocked by digging. Incredibly—no, understandably—work went on; a robot tractor was hauling a train of ore cars. Ahead bulked a scarp, upthrown by some ancient convulsion through the crust of metals left by the supernova, a black wall beneath which the domes and cubes and towers of the compound huddled as if crushed, on whose heights a radio mast seemed to have been spun by spiders.

The scene tilted and appeared to leap upward as the boat descended. Landing jacks made a contact that vibrated through hull and crew. Engine purr died away. Silence pressed inward.

Sandra broke it. "I'm bound out," she said, leaving her seat.

"Madame?" her pilot protested. "But the drag's more than five gees!"

"I'm reasonably strong."

"We—you know, you ordered yourself—we'll simply take them directly aboard and scramble."

"I doubt not we'll hit complications even in that. I want to be on the spot to help cope, not at the end of a phone beam." *And I can hardly say it aloud, but I feel a need to . . . to experience, however briefly, this thing for which so many sacrifices have been made, for which so much blood may soon be spilled. I need for Mirkheim to become real to me.*

A pair of crewmen accompanied her, checking out her spacesuit with more than usual care and flanking her when she cycled through the airlock and stepped forth. That was well. Caught by the gravitation as she left the boat's interior field, she would have crashed to a bone-breaking fall had the men not supported her. The three of them hastily activated their impellers to hold them up, as if suspended in a harness. That let them shuffle forward across the steely soil, forcing leaden ribs to draw air in and out of them, staring past sagging lids with eyeballs whose weight sent blurs and blotches floating across vision. Unseen, unfelt, radioactive emanation sleeted through them, enough to kill in a matter of weeks.

And workers have been coming here for eighteen years, Sandra remembered. *Do I love my own kind that much?*

They were emerging from a dome. Despite their variegated suits, she recognized their races from past contact or from reading and pictures. Nadi the Wodenite led them, of course. Near him came two raven-featured Ikranankans, a four-armed shaggy-headed Gorzuni, a leonine Ivanhoan, a faintly saurian-looking Vanessan, two Cynthians (from societies less advanced than the spacefaring one, which had shown no desire to help them progress), and four humans (from colony planets where existence could become much easier if an adequate capital investment be made; but Technic capital was attracted to more lucrative things). In the middle of barrenness, they were like grotesque symbols of life; Vigeland might have sculptured them.

It was not surprising that they were so few. Environment made short the periods during which any sophont could work here, and forced him to stay mostly indoors. Flesh and blood were present chiefly to perform certain maintenance and communication tasks, and to make decisions which were not routine. Otherwise, machines dwelt on Mirkheim. They prospected, mined, transported, refined, loaded, did the brute labor and most of the delicate. Some were slaved to others which had self-programming computers, while the central computer at the base was of consciousness level. The entire operation was a miracle of technological ingenuity—and still more, Sandra thought, of *sisu, esprit,* indomitability, selflessness.

A man toiled ahead of the rest. The visage behind the vitryl of his helmet was battered and worn. "My lady from Hermes?" he began in accented Anglic. "I'm Henry Kittredge from Vixen, superintendent of this particular gang."

"I'm . . . happy to meet you. . . ." she replied between breaths.

His smile was bleak. "I dunno 'bout that, lady. These aren't exactly happy circumstances, are they? But, uh, I do want to say how grateful we are. We've already overstayed our time, should've been relieved many days ago. If we'd had to stay much longer, working outdoors as often as usual, we'd've gotten a dangerous dosage. After a while, we'd've died."

"Couldn't you have kept indoors?"

"Maybe the Earthlings would've let us. I doubt the Baburites would. Why should they care? And we'd've been wanted to show them how to run these digs."

Sandra nodded, though it was an effort to pull her head back up again. "You've had years of accumulated experience, sometimes at the cost of lives, not?" she said. "That's a good strategic reason for evacuating you. Without your help, anybody else will be a long, expensive time about resuming exploitation. You—you and your co-workers, wherever they live, you might just prove to be a valuable bargaining counter."

"Yes, we've talked about that 'mong ourselves. Listen." Eagerness awoke in the tired voice. "Let's take some of the key equipment with us. Or if you don't want to delay that long, let's sabotage it. Huh?"

Sandra hesitated. She hadn't considered that possibility, and now the choice was thrust upon her. Dared she linger for extra hours?

She did. The fleets would not likely end their strife soon. "We'll remove the stuff," she said, and wondered if she was being wise or merely spiteful.

✤ VIII ✤

"We're too late."

The words seemed to hang for a moment in the murmurous quiet of the bridge. Any of three, Adzel, Chee Lan, David Falkayn, might have spoken them, out of shared pain and anger. All of three stared emptily forth into darkness and uncaring suns. There fire had blossomed, tiny at its remove but still a dreadful glory.

Another spark winked, and another. Nuclear warheads were exploding throughout the space near Mirkheim.

Chee reached for the hyperwave receiver controls. As she turned them past different settings, the speaker buzzed, chattered, crackled, gobbled: coded messages from ship to ship, across distances that light would take hours to bridge. The frontrunners of either fleet had begun engagement—gone into normal state, moving at true speeds of kilometers per second and true accelerations of a few gravities, reaching for each other with missiles, energy beams, shells, meteor boats.

Adzel studied instruments, held a soft colloquy with Muddlehead, and announced: "The battle cannot be very old as yet. Else we would observe more traces of fusion bursts, more complicated neutrino patterns left by engines, than we do. We have missed a beforehand arrival by an ironically small margin."

"I wonder if our warning would have made much difference," Falkayn sighed. "Judging by these data"—he swept his hand across a row of meters—"the Commonwealth fleet came first, defied the Baburites in hopes they'd back down, found that wasn't the case, and will be fighting for bare survival."

"Why doesn't it simply flee?"

Falkayn shrugged, as if the fact were not gall in his throat. "Orders, no doubt—to inflict maximum damage if combat should erupt—orders issued by politicians safe at home, who've always held the theory and practice of war is too wicked a subject for civilized men to study."

89

Fighting could go on for days before the Commonwealth admiral decides he must retreat, he thought. *Ships will accelerate, decelerate, orbit freely over millions of kilometers, seeking an opponent, meeting him, firing in an orgasm of violence, then both of them drawn apart by their velocities till they can come about for a new encounter, probably each with a new foe.*

"We had to try, of course," he went on dully. "The question is what we try next."

They had ransacked their minds for plans, contingency after contingency, while *Muddlin' Through* sped from Babur toward Mirkheim. "Not contact," Adzel said. They might rendezvous with a Solar vessel and, through her, get in touch with the admiral. But they had nothing left to offer him, and the risk involved was considerable.

"Hang around?" Chee asked—wait with power systems throttled down, nearly undetectable, on the fringes of war, till they had seen what happened. But surely survivors would bring that news to Earth.

Yet it was no longer certain, as it once had been, that the Commonwealth government would be frank with the people; and van Rijn needed a full account.

It was not even sure that he would receive the dispatch they had sent him in a courier torpedo after their escape. When the thing entered the Solar System and broadcast its signal, the Space Service that retrieved it might not forward the written contents. Falkayn doubted the cipher could be broken in reasonable time; still, van Rijn would remain in the dark.

Thus the safety of this crew was a prime criterion—not to speak of Coya, Juanita, and the child unborn. Nevertheless, here sentient beings were dead, dying, mutilated, in mortal peril; and the horror would go on. To skulk in the deeps before slinking home had a foul taste.

And—"We haven't accomplished such an everlovin' lot so far, have we?" Falkayn muttered. "Blundered into captivity and out again, getting a man killed in the process."

"Do not feel guilty about that, Davy," Adzel counseled. "It was tragic, true, but Wyler was collaborating with the enemy."

"The uselessness of it, though!" Knuckles stood white on the human's fists.

"You both ought to discipline those consciences of yours," Chee said. "They squeam at you too much." Her carnivore instincts awakened, she bounded onto the console and stood white against blackness, stars, the distant firebursts where ships perished. "We can do active, not passive intelligence collection," she declared eagerly. "Why are we dithering? Let's make for Mirkheim."

"Is there any point in our landing?" Adzel replied. They had talked about the rescue of Supermetals personnel stranded on the planet; but they could only take a few without overloading their life support system.

"Probably not," Chee said. "However, that course will bring us near the thick of action. Who knows what might turn up? Come *on!*"

Inward bound, they received a laser-borne message. That meant it was directed specifically at them; they had been detected. The code was Commonwealth. Falkayn knew this from having compared different signals they acquired. He could not read it, but the meaning was plain: *Identify yourself or we attack.*

Muddlehead reeled off data analysis. The other craft was most likely a Continent-class destroyer. Her position, velocity, and acceleration were more definite. She could not draw near enough on this pass ever to show to the unaided eye as a black blade drawn over the Milky Way. But her weapons could span the gap. And both were too close to the dead sun to enter hyperdrive.

"Evade," Falkayn ordered. He sent back a voice transmission in Anglic: "We are not your enemy, we happen to be here from Earth."

A minute later, Muddlehead reported a missile launched toward him. He was not surprised. The men in yonder hull must be dazed with weariness and strangled terror, stress had worn them down till they were nothing but duty machines, and if he failed to reply in code then he must be a Baburite attempting a ruse.

At such a distance, a ray would be too attenuated to do harm. A ship as small as his could not carry a forcefield generator sufficiently strong to ward off a hard-driven warhead. Nor, despite her low mass, should she have the potential of running from a killer that homed on her engine output.

But *Muddlin' Through* had power for twice her size and spent none of it on energy screens. The heavens wheeled crazily around Falkayn's head as her computer sent her through an arc that would have torn the guts out of an ordinary vessel. Sliding clear of the torpedo, she opened fire on it. It blew apart in a rain of flames and incandescent gobbets. She swung about again and resumed her original course. The Terrestrial ship receded without making a second assault.

Briefly before Falkayn stood the idea of a man aboard that destroyer. He came from—where?—Japan, say, and always in him dwelt a memory of those beautiful islands, old high-curved roofs, cherry trees in bloom under the pure steeps of Fuji, a garden where gardener and bonsai worked together through a lifetime's love, temple bells cool at evening when he walked forth with a certain girl at his side. This day he sat webbed in place before the idiot faces of instruments while engines droned through his bones; thirst thickened his tongue, he had sweated too much in his tension, his garments stank, salt stung his eyes and lay bitter on his lips. Hour crept by hour, the waiting, the waiting, the waiting, until reality shrank to this and home was a half-forgotten fever dream: then alarms yammered, creatures that he had never seen even in his nightmares were somewhere on the far side of a bulkhead, or so the instruments said, and he ordered the launch parameters computed for a missile, sent it forth, sat waiting once more to know if he had slain or they would slay him, hoped wildly that his death would be quick and clean, not a shrieking with his skin seared off and his eyeballs melted, and perhaps through him there flitted a wondering whether those monsters he fired at also remembered a beautiful home.

Where had Sheldon Wyler come from?

Falkayn spoke harshly at the intercom pickup: "We seem to've gone free this time."

The incident would have sent most crews scuttling immediately toward safety. Instead, it hatched a goblin of an idea in Chee. Adzel heard her out, pondered, and agreed the possible gain was worth the hazard. Falkayn argued for a while, then assented, the part of him that was Coya's husband outvoted by a part he had imagined lay buried with his youth.

Not that they had any chance to pull off a swift, gleeful exploit. Time drained away while the ship moved cautiously about, detectors straining, Muddlehead sifting and discarding. Falkayn puffed on his pipe till his raw tongue could not taste the food he made himself swallow. Chee worked on a statuette, attacking the clay as if it threatened her life. Adzel meditated and slept.

Endlessness finally had an end. "A Solar vessel has demolished a Baburite," the computer announced, and recited coordinates.

Falkayn jerked out of half a doze where he sat. "Are you sure?" He sprang to his feet.

"The characteristic flash of a detonation has been followed by a cessation of neutrino emission from one of two sources. The other source is departing, and would be unable to return at any available acceleration for a period of more than a standard day."

"Not that she'll want to—"

"We can lie alongside the wreck in a period I calculate to be three-point-seven hours plus or minus approximately forty minutes."

It thrilled in Falkayn. "And I suppose we've a fifty-fifty chance she'll be Baburite."

"No, that is positive. I have conducted statistical studies of emission patterns from thermonuclear reactors in both fleets. This ship that was defeated showed a distinctly Baburite spectrum."

Falkayn nodded. Fusion engines built to operate under subjovian conditions would not radiate quite like those which worked for oxygen breathers. He'd been aware of that, but had not been aware enough data would come in to make the mathematics reliable. "Bully for you, Muddlehead," he said. "You keep surprising me, the amount of initiative you show."

"I have also invented three new wild card games," the computer told him . . . hopefully?

"Never mind," Chee snapped. "You make for that cockering wreck!"

Drive pulses intensified. "We fared more happily the first time we cruised this part of space," Adzel mused. "But then, we were younger, eighteen Earth-years ago." Was he being tactful? The span was not so great a part of his life expectancy as it was of a human's or a Cynthian's.

"We were proud," Falkayn said. "*Our* discovery, that was going to give a dozen races the chance they needed. Now—" His voice died away.

Adzel laid a hand on his shoulder. He must consciously stiffen himself against the gee-field to support such a weight. "Feel no blame that this is being fought over, Davy," the Wodenite urged. "What we gave was good. It may be yet again."

"We knew the secret couldn't last," Chee added. "It was sheer luck that the first person to repeat our reasoning was Old Nick, and we could talk him into keeping quiet. Sooner or later, a nasty scramble was bound to happen."

"Sure, sure," Falkayn answered. "But war—I'd thought civilization had evolved beyond war."

"The Shenna hadn't, the Baburites haven't," Chee snorted. "You needn't accuse the Technic societies because outsiders have bad manners. That notion of symmetrical sinfulness is a strange tendency in your species."

"Somehow I can't see the cases as being parallel," Falkayn argued. "Damnation, it made a contorted kind of sense for the Shenna to plot an assault on us. But the Baburites—why should they arm as they did, never foreseeing a Mirkheim to fight over? And why should they ever fight, anyway? If they could buy the tools and technology they needed to build the kind of navy they have, why, they could buy all the supermetals they'd require for a fraction of the cost. I have this gnawing notion that something in us, in Technic culture, is responsible."

"Wyler might have given us a hint or three if he'd lived. I wish you'd stop moping about him, Davy. He wasn't a nice man."

"Who can afford to be, these days? . . . Oh, to hell with this." Falkayn flung himself back into his chair.

"Agreed. To hell by express. Me, I'm going to do some more modeling." Chee left the bridge.

"Perhaps I, at least, could play cards with you, Muddlehead, if you want diversion," Adzel offered. "We have little else to occupy us until we arrive."

Except sit and wish nothing we can't handle will home on us, Falkayn thought.

> "*—Fear and trembling Hope,*
> *Silence and Foresight; Death the Skeleton*
> *And Time the Shadow. . . .*"

Spacesuited, he gave himself a touch of impeller thrust and drifted across a hundred meters of void between his own craft and the ruin.

Stars and stillness enfolded him. Here he saw no trace of the battle; all that agony was lost in the hollow reaches of space, save for a twisted shape that tumbled before him among lesser metal shards. He dared not think how many lives were gone—surely Baburites rejoiced to see their sun, even as he did his—but bent his attention wholly, dryly to the task ahead.

The ship had been more or less cruiser size. A missile had gotten past her defenses and shattered her. Without a surrounding atmosphere, concussion had been insufficient to blow her entirely to fragments. Survivors, if any, had found an undamaged lifeboat, in a section built to break away upon impact, and fled. The largest remnant of the hull was bigger than *Muddlin' Through* and ought to contain plenty of apparatus, not too badly damaged for study. A gauge on his wrist told him that the level of radioactivity was tolerable.

He felt and heard the thud as his bootsoles touched plates and gripped fast. Chee poised nearby; Adzel was a gigantic silhouette farther off against heaven. "You two stay put while I take a look around," he directed them, and plodded off. It felt a little like walking upside down, for he was weightless and the dead vessel was slowly spinning. Constellations streamed by, blacknesses flickered around the shapes of turrets and housings. His breath sounded loud in his ears.

When he reached an edge where the hull had been torn apart, he picked his way cautiously through a tangle of projecting, knotted girders. A body was caught between two of them. He stood for a minute gazing at it by the light of his flashlamp. Undiffused in airlessness, a wan puddle of luminance draped itself over a form that was too alien to seem hideous, as human corpses usually did after a violent death; the Baburite looked pitifully small and frail. *I'm wasting time, which I still have though he no longer does,* Falkayn realized, and went onward, around the verge, into the cavity of the derelict.

Star-gleam and his flash picked out surrealistically intricate masses half submerged in darkness. A bleak pleasure jumped in him. *Good luck for us! This seems to've been the main drive room. Which means control units, too, if their craft are laid out along roughly the same lines as ours.*

It could be the fulfillment of the hope which had led to his and his companions' search. So little was known about the race which built the invading armada. Who could tell what clues might lie in their engineering?

Would the Commonwealth admiral get the same thought, and order a salvage operation for intelligence purposes? Probably not. His fleet was too hard pressed. Besides, its entire management bespoke idiocy—well, be charitable and say ignorance—at the highest levels of government.

And assuming that relics nevertheless did get back to Earth, the government would scarcely share them with van Rijn. Falkayn was not simply being loyal to his patron; he feared that the old man was the last competent thinker left in the Solar System. Van Rijn might be able to make something of a bit of evidence that was meaningless to everybody else.

Not that we can do any serious work here, Falkayn knew. *We haven't the facilities. Also, it's too bloody dangerous to linger very long. But we can spend a few hours investigating, and we can carry off selected items for closer examination. Maybe we'll make a marginally useful discovery. Maybe.*

Move! He crept toward the nearest of the forms which towered before him.

❖IX❖

The evening before he left, Bayard Story invited Nicholas van Rijn to join him for dinner. The Council of the League had dissolved in dissonance, and the delegates must now see to their own affairs as best they could.

The Saturn Room of the Hotel Universe was nearly full, though thanks to widely spaced tables and discreet lighting it did not seem so. Perhaps, when rumors of war hissed everywhere about them, friends and lovers were seizing whatever enjoyment they might while the chance lasted; or perhaps not. The Solar System had been without direct experience of armed conflict for so long that it was hard to guess how anybody would behave. Couples held each other close while they moved about on the dance floor. Was there really a wistful note in the music of the live orchestra? Overhead lifted the vast half-circles of the rings, tinted more subtly than rainbows in a violet sky where four moons were presently visible. Sparks of light flickered in the streaming arcs and meteors clove the heavens. Where a tiny sun was setting, dimmed by thick air, clouds lay tawny and rosy.

"The place is more suitable for romance than for a pair of tired businessmen," Story remarked with a slight smile.

"Well, any notion we can agree is plenty romantic," grunted van Rijn from the depths of the menu. His free hand brought to his mouth alternate slurps of akvavit and gulps of beer. Story sipped a champagne and rum. "Let me see—*dood en ondergang,* please to let me see, this place is dim like a bureaucrat's brain!—I begin with a dozen Limfjord oysters, Limfjord, mind you, waiter, the chilled crab legs and asparagus tips, and fifty grams of Strasbourg paté. Then while I eat my appetizer you can fill me a nice bowl of onion soup à la Ansa. You do not want to miss that, Story, it uses spices we maybe do not get any more if comes something as stupid as a war. For a wine with the soup—" He went on for several minutes.

"Oh, bring me the tournedos on the regular dinner, medium

rare," Story laughed. "And, all right, I will have the onion soup, since it's recommended."

"You should pay better attention to what you eat, boy," van Rijn said.

Story shrugged. "I don't make a god of my stomach."

"You think I do, ha? No, by damn, I make my stomach work for me, like a slave it works. My palate, that is what I pay attention to. And what is wrong with that? Who is harmed? The very first miracle Our Lord did was turning water into wine, and a select vintage it was, too." Van Rijn shook his head; the ringlets swirled across his brocade jacket. "The troublemakers, they are those what are not contented with God's gifts of good food, drink, music, women, profit. No, they bring on misery because they must play at being God themselves, they will be our Saviors with a capital ass."

Story grew grave. "Are you sure you're not the self-righteous one? What you were advocating at the Council could have, almost certainly would have gotten the League into war."

Van Rijn's hedge of eyebrows twisted together in a scowl. "I think not. League and Commonwealth together would be too much for Babur. It would retreat."

"Maybe—if the Commonwealth were willing to go along with putting Mirkheim under League administration. But you know the Home Companies would never agree to that. Commonwealth—government—trusteeship will mean that *they* dispose of the supermetals. It'll be their entry into space on a scale of operations grand enough to threaten the Seven and the independents with being driven to the wall."

"So by keeping us deadlocked, you pest-bespattered Seven guaranteed the united League does nothing, does not even exist."

"The League will stay neutral, you mean. Do you actually want an open, irrevocable breach in it? As is, the Seven keeping on reasonably good terms with Babur, whichever side wins, the League as a whole will have a voice. In fact, when I'm back in my headquarters, I'm going to see if the Seven can lend their good offices toward a settlement." Story lifted a finger. "That's why I wanted to see you tonight, Freeman van Rijn. A last appeal. If you'd cooperate with us, and try to get the independents to join you—"

"Cooperate?" Van Rijn took out his snuffbox and brought a

pinch to his nose. "What would that amount to? Doing whatever you tell? *(Hrrromp!)*"

"Well, of course we'd have to have a central strategy. It would involve an embargo, declared or undeclared, on trade with either side. We could plead hazard, to be diplomatic about it. Both would soon start hurting for materials, including military materials, and be more ready to accept League mediation."

"Not the League's," van Rijn said. "Not the whole League's. How would the Home Companies fit in? They and the Commonwealth government is two sides of the same counterfeit coin, by damn. They been that way more and more for—how long?—ever since the Council of Hiawatha, I think."

"I'm not saying anything I haven't often before," Story pursued. "I simply have a—well, I won't call it a prospect of making you see reason. Let's say I feel it my duty to keep trying to persuade you till the last minute."

"My duty is not that I listen. I told you and told you, me, if the independents join up with the Seven, or with the Home Companies either, that is truly the end of the League, because we Independents is the last properly spiritous members of it." Van Rijn leaned back, glass to lips, and gazed at the mighty simulacrum above him. Night had fallen on the scene, the moons hung in frost halos and Saturn's shadow began to creep across the rings. No stars had appeared. He sighed. "We was born too late, though. If I had been at the Council of Hiawatha, what I could have warned them!"

"They made a perfectly logical decision," Story said.

Van Rijn nodded. "*Ja*. That was the deadly part of it."

Not until long afterward would historians appreciate the irony of the meeting having gathered where it did. At the time, if there was any conscious symbolism in the choice of site, it expressed optimism. After all, the O'Neill colonies had not only given man his first dwellings in space, the burgeoning of wholly new industries within them had been of primary importance in a revival of free enterprise. So thoroughgoing did that revival become, in ways of thinking and living as well as in economics, that, together with the alloying of formerly disparate Terrestrial societies, a whole civilization can be thought to have come freshly into existence—the Technic. After the development of the hyperdrive, man's explosive expansion away from Sol made the artificial worldlets obsolete. Yet they continued faithfully orbiting around their Lagrangian points, in Luna's path but sixty degrees ahead or behind, and were not abandoned overnight. In particular, Hiawatha and its companion Minnehaha still housed substantial working populations when the Polesotechnic League called the most fateful of its executive sessions.

The problem it faced was manifold. Quite naturally, most governments resented it. Although its constitution made it simply a mutual-help association, it wielded more strength than any single state. It hampered as well as humiliated governments when it gave them no part in decisions which deeply affected domestic trade; when its hard credit displaced their fiat money; when their attempts at regulation were covertly subverted or openly scorned. Nor was this a mere matter of officialdom hankering for power. Many grudges were genuine. No system that mortals devise is perfect; all break their share of lives. A poor boy or girl or nonhuman might rise to living like a god and controlling forces that would have been beyond the imagination of mythmakers. Efficient underlings could do very well for themselves. But those would always exist who did not have the special abilities or the plain luck. Most were not too unhappy at becoming routineers; some were poisonously embittered. More important, perhaps, was that large percentage of mankind which never really wanted to be free. Of this, a majority yearned for security, which political candidates promised to get for them. A more active minority wanted solidarity behind exciting causes, and thought that everybody else should desire the same thing.

The League had its own troubles. Sheer scale and diversity of undertakings, the overwhelming rate of information flow, were undermining administration of the larger companies. The concept of free contract was being increasingly abused, as in the establishment of indentures. Reckless exploitation of societies and natural resources was waxing. Ominous was the introduction of modern technologies to backward races without careful prior consideration—irresponsibly, for a quick credit, regardless of whether it was desirable to have such cultures loose with things like spaceships and nuclear weapons.

A parliament was finally elected in the Commonwealth that was pledged to thoroughgoing reforms; and its jurisdiction was still the League's greatest market and source of manpower. In the "thousand days" it passed an astonishing number of radical new laws and, what counted, began enforcing them as well as a good many old ones.

Therefore the Polesotechnic League called a Grand Council at Hiawatha to discuss what to do.

It enacted several resolutions which founded more humane and farsighted policies than hitherto. Where it unknowingly came to grief was in the question raised by the measures in the Commonwealth. These included a central banking commission, floors and ceilings on interest rates, income tax, an antitrust rule, compulsory arbitration of certain kinds of disputes, loans by the state to distressed enterprises, subsidies to industries deemed critical, production quotas, and much else.

A few hotheads among the delegates talked about resorting to arms, but were shouted down. While members of the League had occasionally overturned difficult local governments, the League itself was not in the business of government. The decision to be made was: Should it boycott the Commonwealth until the recent legislation was repealed, or should it acquiesce within the Solar System?

Acquiescence won. A boycott would be immensely expensive, would ruin several members if they weren't underwritten and badly hurt the rest. It would also create an unpleasant image of saber-toothed greed versus the altruistic statesman. In vain did some speakers argue that in the long run it is best to stand firm by one's principles, and that the principle which gave the League its sole meaning and justification was liberty. Opponents retorted that liberty demands frequent compromises and, on a less exalted plane, so does common sense; the laws were not totally bad, they actually had various features desirable from a mercantile point of view; and in any case, by remaining on the scene the League companies would stay influential and could work for modifications.

And indeed this proved to be true. Regulatory commissions soon turned into creatures of the industries they regulated—and discouraged (at first) or stifled (later) all new competition. This was much aided by a tax structure heavily weighted against the middle class. After a while, the great bankers were not just handling money, they were creating it, with a vested interest in inflation. Union leaders, with enormous funds to invest, fitted cozily into the system; if you did not enroll, you did not work, and the leaders and the managers between them set the conditions under which you must work. Antitrust actions penalized efficient management to the satisfaction of the less enterprising. Likewise did quotas, tariffs, wage and price limits, preferential contract policies. A set of ineffective but self-perpetuating welfare programs helped produce the votes useful for maintaining the corporate state.

For that is what the Commonwealth became. No longer distinct from politicians or bureaucrats, the magnates of the Home Companies gained a powerful say in decisions about matters far removed from finance or engineering. Their natural allies became the heads of various other constituencies—geographical, cultural, professional—which were thus brought under ever closer governmental control.

Meanwhile, companies which did not have an originally strong position in the Commonwealth found themselves being more and more squeezed out. Accordingly, they concentrated on developing markets beyond its borders. They were involved in the declarations of independence of several colony planets, some of whose politics they then gradually took over. Certain of them began to make cooperative agreements, limiting competition among themselves, to the exclusion of the rest of the League. Thus, by slow stages, were born the Seven In Space.

Lesser companies, fearful of being engulfed, avoided joining either side, and formed no organization of their own. They were the independents.

By no means did the Council of Hiawatha produce these results overnight. In fact, the period which came immediately after seemed, if anything, more dominated by capitalists than before. It was the most expansive, most brilliant time which Technic civilization would ever know. At home, remedies applied to the body politic took hold quite gradually, and their side effects were still slower to become obvious. On the stellar frontier, discovery followed discovery, triumph followed triumph; each year told of an evil conquered, a fortune made; if strife ran high, likewise did hope. The tree was growing, ever leafing, though a snake gnawed its roots. Thus was it often before on Earth, in the age of the Chun-Chiu, the age of the Delian alliance, the age of the Renaissance.

But when a century had passed—

"Well, never mind stale history," Story said. "We're alive now, not then. Will you join the Seven in making a peace effort?"

"Join." Van Rijn tugged his goatee. "You mean take orders from you and not ask rude questions."

"We'll try to consult, of course. But with communications as slow as they are, compared to the speed with which a crisis can build up, we must have a clear chain of command."

Van Rijn shook his head. "No, always I am too hungry for feedback."

Story made a chopping gesture. "Do you want to cut yourself off entirely from whatever congress makes the peace?"

"It is not sure there will be a congress, and double not sure what tune it will dance to. . . . Ah, here comes my appetizers. You will be surprised, Freeman, at how much I can bite all by myself."

X

Sandra Tamarin-Asmundsen was in the Arcadian Hills, hunting, when word reached her. Though she had felt guilty about leaving Starfall at a time of crisis—domestic as well as foreign, with more and more of the Traver class in an uproar—a brief escape from its atmosphere was like spring water going through a dried-out throat.

Her hounds had gotten on the track of a cyanops. Their baying resounded down forest vaults, a savage plainsong in green cathedral dimness. She bounded in pursuit of the noise. Her hands parted branches and scanty underbrush, her feet overleaped fallen trees, her lungs drank breath after sweet-scented breath, her eyes beheld high boles, overarching branches rich with leaves, sunflecks in shadow, the brilliant wings of a nidiflex, her body rejoiced. After her bounded half a dozen men from the ancestral estate at Windy Run. Otherwise the wilderness was hers alone.

She sped up a slope and came out onto a meadow along the top of a cliff. The light of Maia was almost blinding on the low lobate yerb, studded with tiny white wildflowers, that covered this open ground. Beyond, she saw further hills, rank upon arrogant rank, and in the distance the solitary peak of Cloudhelm, its snows veiled in mist. The dogs had the cyanops cornered at the edge. A rangy, heavy-jawed, dun-coated breed raised by folk in these parts, they knew better than to attack iron-gray scales and raking claws. But since they could, together, pull the big herpetoid down if they must, it had lumbered from them. Now it stood its ground and hissed defiance.

"Oh, good!" Sandra exulted. She unslung her rifle and approached with care. A hasty shot might hit a dog or merely madden the beast. It was hard to kill except by a bullet straight through one of those eerily innocent-looking blue eyes.

The portable phone at her belt buzzed.

She stopped dead. The clamor of hounds and men dropped out of her awareness. Via relay satellite, the phone leashed her to the

New Keep and nowhere else. It buzzed again. She unclipped the small flat box and brought it near her face. "Yes?"

A voice rattled forth: "Andrew Baird, Your Grace"—her appointed vice executive whom she had left in charge during her absence. "We have received word from Admiral Michael"—Michael Falkayn, her second in command of the little Hermetian navy. "They've detected a substantial fleet bound this way under hyperdrive, apparently from the general direction of Mogul. Distance is still too great for anything but simple code signals. The strangers have sent none so far, nor responded to any of ours."

It was as if a machine spoke for Sandra, free of the dread that shocked through her: "Get every unit into space that isn't already, and have them report to him for duty. Alert every police and rescue corps. Keep me informed of developments as they occur. 'Twill take me . . . about ninety minutes to reach my car, and another hour to fly to you." Not pausing to hear his goodbye, she put the phone back on her belt and swung about. Her men stood in a bunch; their gaze upon her was troubled. As if sensing something, the hounds grew less noisy.

"I must return immediately." She rinsed her mouth from her canteen before she started down into the forest at a long, energy-conserving lope. Two hunters tarried to call off the pack. The cyanops stared after them, not understanding the fortune which had saved its life.

Sandra's eastbound flight kept her near the Palomino River, which shone like a saber drawn across the lowlands. They were an agrarian property of the Runeberg domain. At the present season, the summer green of pastures was fading; but even from her altitude, the herds that grazed them were majestic. Opulent grainfields mingled with orchards and groves. Houses belonging to Follower families in charge of various sections stood snug beneath their red tiles, amidst their gardens. Afar she glimpsed the mansion of the Runebergs themselves. She had visited there and remembered well its gracious rooms, ancestral portraits, immensity of tradition, and children's laughter for a sign that new life was ever bubbling up from beneath these things.

Not for the first time, a moment's wistfulness touched her. To be born into the Kindred, the thousand families who headed the domains . . . Her descent went back as far as theirs; her forebears had also been among the first passengers from Earth. It was almost an accident that the early Tamarins had not founded a corporation to tame a particular part of this world. Instead, they had mostly been scientists, technicians, consultants, explorers, teachers: free lances.

Too late to change, she thought. When the constitution of an independent Hermes was written, it specified that the chief executives would be of Tamarin birth but that the Tamarins should have no domain: a lonely glory.

I could have refused election, she recalled. *Why didn't I? Well, pride, and . . . and Pete was there, my consort, to help me. But supposing he'd not been . . . well, had I refused, I'd have become like any other Tamarin who's not made Grand Duke or Duchess, I'd have had my living to earn as best I could—a Traver in all but name and, yes, in having a vote.* Defensively, as if an accuser from that class confronted her in yet another public debate: *And what's so bad about Traver status? Comes the word not simply from* travailleur, *worker, descendant of latecomers, a hireling or an unaffiliated businessman?*

I might have joined a family of the Kindred by marrying into it. That would have been best. She could have gotten the in-between degree of Follower in the same way, merging her bloodline with one that held entailed shares making it a junior partner in a domain. But she would always have been embarrassed to address with certain courtesies the high-ranking people who had been her childhood playmates. To be of the Kindred, though—not necessarily serene on a landed estate; quite likely in some other of the industrial, scientific, cultural, or public service undertakings of a corporation—yes, thus she could strike roots deep into her planet, and know how securely her children would belong.

The car phone projected Eric's image. "Mother!" he cried. "You've heard . . . Listen, I just have, and—"

"Get off the circuit," she interrupted. "Baird may be calling me at any minute." Because he was betrothed and she hoped for grandchildren, she took time to add: "You might make sure Lorna gets to a safe place. I daresay you'll insist on being at the Keep."

"Right. I . . . I'll stand by in the Sapphire Office." His countenance vanished.

The wind of her speed roared around the car's canopy. Sandra straightened in her seat. No use wishing she were different from what she was. And did she really wish it, anyway? Somebody had to hold the reins of the state. If only because of experience, she could probably do so better than anyone else. *Hang on,* she thought ahead of her. *I'm coming.*

Starfall appeared on the horizon, at first a darkness along the bright sheet of Daybreak Bay; then as she slipped downward it became the buildings, streets, parks, quays, monuments she had loved of old. Yonder stood the Mayory in red brick dignity, nearby lifted the slim spire of St. Carl's Church, the Hotel Zeus soared above Phoenix Boulevard, flowers flaunted themselves like banners around Elvander's statue in Riverside Common, traffic was dense and terrace cafés busy at Constitution Square, she actually identified Jackboot Lane where stood the Ranger's Roost tavern that had seen her drink and talk and sing in her youth like generations before her. . . . Pilgrim Hill stood ahead. A police car hung above Signal Station. Sandra flashed it her name and made for the ducal parking roof. The thought that all this might go out in a burst of radioactive flame was unendurable.

The Insignia Room was large and austere, ornamented only with the devices of the Kindred on its walls. They were colorful, but a thousand of them crowded together soon became featureless in the mind. On this high floor, windows gave on sky, long evening light, a glimpse of ocean, an ornithoid winging by. Yet as Sandra sat behind her desk, the chamber felt small, warm, dear, against the darkness at its far end.

A three-dimensional comscreen occupied half that wall. It was as if cold radiated from the scene it held, deep into human marrow. The Baburite whose outlines posed before her did not seem dwarfish or bizarre—rather, the eidolon of something gigantic and triumphant. The picture showed a bit of a compartment aboard its ship, which hung in synchronous orbit above the city and sent down a tight beam. The fittings and furnishings were too alien for her fully to see. Behind and around the being loomed reddish dusk wherein dim shapes stirred.

"Hear us well," a vocalizer said for it. "We represent the Imperial Band of Sisema and the united race.

"War is inevitable between the Autarchy of Babur and the Solar Commonwealth. We have intelligence that the Commonwealth will seek to occupy the Maian System. Your resources would obviously be of extreme value to a navy campaigning far from home: especially the terrestroid planet Hermes. There bases are easy to build, repairs and munitions to make, accumulated toxins to flush out of the life support systems of ships; personnel can get rest and hospital care, recruits can possibly be found among the populace. The Imperial Band cannot permit this."

"We're neutral!" Sandra's hands strained together. Their palms were damp, their fingers chill.

"Your neutrality would not be respected," said the Baburite. "It is necessary that the Imperial Band forestall the Commonwealth and establish a protectorate. Hear us well. A fleet detachment, which your admiral will have told you is considerably your superior in strength, is waiting at the outer limits of your planetary system. Its mission is to prevent Commonwealth forces from entering.

"You will cooperate with it. A majority of the crews are oxygen breathers who will be based on Hermes. Their correct behavior is guaranteed; but hostile actions directed at them will be severely punished. You will deal with them, as well as with the Baburite command, through our military authority.

"Conduct yourselves properly, and you need have no fears. The Maian System contains no planet which Baburites could colonize. Their ways and yours are so mutually foreign that interference of one with another is unlikely in the extreme. You should instead fear Commonwealth imperialism, against which you will be shielded."

Sandra half rose. "But we don't want your shielding—" She choked down more words like *you filthy worm.*

"It is necessary that you accept," said the emotionless voice. "Resistance would cost the Imperial Band casualties, but you your entire armed service. Thereafter, Hermes would lie exposed to bombardment from space. Consider the welfare of your people."

Sandra sank back. "When would you come?" she whispered.

"We will move as soon as this conference is over."

"No, wait. You realize not—I can't issue orders to a whole world, I've not dictatorial powers—"

"You will have time to persuade. The ships of the Imperial Band will need it to deploy, since they cannot use hyperdrive within the inner parts of the system. You can be granted as much as four of your planetary rotations before the surrender of your navy and the landing of the first occupation units must be accepted."

There was more: hot protest and frosty demand, plea and refusal, bargaining over detail after detail, wrath and despair met by calm immovability; but the time was far shorter than it would have been between two humans. The Baburite was simply not concerned about honorific formulas, face savings, alternatives, compromises. Conceivably it might have been, had the gulf between the races been less unbridgeably wide. Sandra remembered the cyanops on the cliff edge, hounds and hunters before it.

When at last the screen blanked, she covered her eyes for a little before she summoned her cabinet to come witness the playback and give her what counsel it could.

Up and down Eric Tamarin-Asmundsen paced, from end to end of the living room in his mother's apartment. She had set the lights low and left open the French doors to the balcony, for it was a beautiful night, both moons aloft and nearly full, dew aglimmer on lawns and the crowns of trees, cool air full of the odor of daleflower and the trills of a tilirra. Beyond the garden wall, a modest sky-glow from the city picked out a few steeples. The lamps of cars flitting overhead were like many-colored glowflies.

Eric's boots thudded savagely on the carpet. "We *can't* just give in," he said for the dozenth frantic time. "We'd be slaves forever."

"We're promised internal self-government," Sandra reminded him from the chair where she sat.

"How much is that promise worth?"

She drew heavily on her cigar. The smoke tasted harsh; she'd had too many in the past several hours. "I know not," she admitted in a flat tone. "Still, I can't imagine any interest the Baburites might take in our local politics."

"Intend you to wait with folded hands and find out?"

"We can't fight. Michael sent me his considered opinion that our forces are grossly outnumbered. Why kill and be killed to no good end?"

"We can organize guerrillas."

"They'd spend nigh their whole time surviving." At the present epoch, Hermes had a single continent, Greatland, so enormous that most of its interior was a desert of blazing summers and bitter winters. "Worse, they'd invite reprisals on everybody else. And never could they defeat well-equipped troops on the ground, missile-throwing ships in orbit."

"Oh, we can't free ourselves alone." Eric's arm slashed the air. "But see you not, if we lie down to be walked on—if we actually add our fleet to theirs, let our factories work for them—why should the Commonwealth care what happens to us? It might leave us under Babur as part of a bargain. Whereas if we're its allies, no matter how minor—"

Sandra nodded. "Believe me, the Council and I discussed this at length. I dare not tell Michael to lead our ships off. He'd be intercepted by a squadron of theirs, have to fight his way past them."

Eric stopped in midstride. "Hermes isn't responsible if he and his men disobey your orders, is it?"

Sandra locked her glance with his, for seconds. "The admiral and I have our understanding," she said at last.

"What?" It blazed in Eric.

"No untoward sentence passed between us. I'd better not say more, even to you."

"And you're going, too!" he shouted. "A government in exile, by the whole Trinity, yes!"

"My duty is here."

"No."

Sandra slumped. "Eric, dear, I'm wrung dry. Plague me not. You should go join Lorna."

He gazed at the big woman, who had turned her face outward to the night, until he said, "All right. I see. For your part, will you help Lorna forgive me?"

She nodded wearily. "I expected you'd go, and I'll not plead," she replied low. "You are my son."

"And my father's."

She shook her head. The ghost of a smile crossed her lips. "He'd not hare off to be a dashing warrior. He'd stay put and brew trouble till the Baburites wished they'd never stirred from their planet." Her calm broke. "Oh, Eric!" She dropped her cigar and rose, arms outspread. They embraced hard. Nothing remained to say in words. After a while, he kissed her and departed.

He did not take the ducal space-yacht, but his personal runabout. It barely overhauled the Hermetian ships. They were already accelerating out of the system. Admiral Falkayn did not summon him aboard *Alpha Cygni*, but assigned him to the destroyer *North Atlantis*. That proved to be sound thinking.

Soon afterward, as had been easily predictable, they encountered those units of the Baburite task force which were near enough to intercept them. As yet, they were too deep in Maia's gravitational well to go safely into hyperdrive. "Hold vectors steady," Falkayn ordered them. "We'll not have more than this engagement. Fire at will."

The captain of *North Atlantis* had allowed Eric on the bridge as a courtesy, provided the heir apparent keep absolutely quiet. That was a command more stern than chains. Presently he felt the scourge, as the hostile forces closed.

Around his eyes blazed the stars in their thousands, the Milky Way foamed across the girth of heaven, a nebula shone distance-dimmed bearing new suns and worlds in its womb, the Magellanic Clouds and the Andromeda galaxy glimmered in their mystery. That was one part of reality. The opposite part was the hardness which enclosed him, faint beat of driving energies and mumble of ventilators, men who stood thralls of instruments and controls, the wetness and reek of his own sweat . . . and a muttered "First shot theirs. Must've been a missile from *Caduceus* that stopped it," as flame winked briefly afar.

The kinetic velocities of both groups were too high to match in a single pass. They intermingled, exchanging fire, for minutes; then they were moving out of effective range. Eric saw a ghastly rose unfold, where a weapon from his vessel had tracked down another from the foe. Otherwise the explosions were remote, hundreds of kilometers off, and registered as glints; an energy beam striking a target did not register at all.

Seated like a statue, the destroyer's captain heard the combat analysis officer report in a cracking voice: "Sir, practically every strike of theirs is concentrated on *Alpha Cygni*. They must hope to saturate her defenses."

"I was afraid of that," the captain said dully. "The only capital ship we've got. The Baburites are more interested in stopping her than buzzbugs like this."

"If we accelerated in her direction, sir, we might be able to catch a few of their missiles."

"Our orders are to maintain our vectors." The captain's features remained visor-blank; but he glanced across at Eric. "The important thing is that *some* of us escape."

The officer swallowed. "Aye, sir."

A few minutes later, the information arrived: *Alpha Cygni* had taken a warhead. No further word came from her—but flash after flash of fireball did, for her screens and interceptors were now gone, and even receding, the Baburites could pound her hulk into dust and slag.

The captain of *North Atlantis* looked straight at Eric. "I think you're our new commander, sir," he said.

"C-carry on." The son of the Duchess wrestled down a scream.

Battle faded out. Eventually the Hermetian flotilla dared enter hyperdrive. Detectors declared the enemy was not pursuing. Because they spent their main effort on the battleship, the invaders had taken losses of their own, making theirs temporarily the inferior force. Divisions of their armada elsewhere were too far-flung to have any hope of catching up. Besides, fighting at faster-than-light was a tricky business of drawing alongside and trying to match phase; a kill was too unlikely to make the attempt worthwhile, when Hermes had not yet been brought under the yoke.

Eric rose. Each muscle felt like a separate ache. "Proceed toward Sol at the highest feasible rate," he ordered. "Have everybody stand by for a message from me." His grin was acid. "I'd better give them a talk, not?"

In this wise died Michael Falkayn, older brother of David and, since their father's death a pair of years ago, head of the Falkayn domain.

❖ XI ❖

As swift as any vessel in that near-infinitesimal droplet of the galaxy which we have slightly explored, *Muddlin' Through* reached Earth almost simultaneously with the first messengers from the embattled Mirkheim expedition, whose survivors would not come limping in for two or more weeks. Traffic Control kept her hours in orbit. Her crew did manage to swap a few radioed words with Nicholas van Rijn. "I will meet you at Ronga," the merchant said—and little else, when communication was surely being monitored.

The likelihood of war had evidently thrown the bureaucrats in charge of space safety into a blue funk. But clearance finally came. Ship and pilot were licensed to set down anywhere on the planet that adequate facilities existed. Muddlehead got orders to make for a certain atoll in the South Pacific Ocean.

Approached from above, the scene was impossibly lovely. The waters shone in a thousand shades of blue and green, sunlight sparkling over their wrinkled vastness; breakers burst silvery on the coral necklace of the island, within whose arc a lagoon lay like an amethyst; tall clouds massed in the west, their purity shaded azure, while elsewhere heaven was a dome of light. *We have so few places like this left on Earth,* David Falkayn thought fleetingly. *Is that—not ambition, not adventure, no, the longing for a peace which only our genes remember—is that what really sends us out into the universe?*

Feather-softly, landing jacks touched the surface of a small paved field. The main personnel lock opened and its gangway extruded. Falkayn had been waiting there, but Chee Lan darted between his legs and reached ground first, bounced in the air, sped to the adjacent beach, and rolled on warm white sand. He followed more sedately, until he saw who came to meet him. Then he also ran.

"Davy, oh, Davy!" Coya flung herself at him and they kissed for an unbroken minute or better, while Adzel paraded discreetly by. Waves rushed and murmured, seabirds cried.

"I tried to call you right after the boss," Falkayn stammered. What a poor greeting words gave.

"He'd already contacted me, told me to come here," she said, leaning happily against him.

"How're Juanita and X?" He saw, as he had felt, the growth of the child within her during the weeks of his absence.

"Fat and sassy. Look over yonder. C'mon." She tugged his arm.

Van Rijn stood at the border of the field, holding his great-granddaughter by the hand. As the newcomers reached them, the girl released herself, flew to Daddy to be hugged, then from his embrace looked up at Adzel and chirped, "Ride?"

The dragon set her on his back and all started for the house. Palms soughed in a wind whose salt was sweetened by odors of jasmine; hibiscus and bougainvillea glowed ardent in arbors. "Welcome home, by damn," van Rijn boomed. "Was a poxy long wait, not knowing if you was chopped into cutlets or what."

Falkayn broke stride. A chill blew across his joy. "Then you didn't get our dispatch?" he said. "We sent a torp from the neighborhood of Mogul."

"No, nothings. Our data bank stayed bare as a mermaid's bottom."

Falkayn's grip tightened around Coya's waist. That time had surely been, for her, the frozen ninth circle of hell. "I was afraid you might not," he said slowly.

"You mean somebody snaffled it?" Coya asked.

"*Ja*," van Rijn growled. "The Space Service, who elses? Plain to see, they got secret orders to take anything for me to somebody different."

"But that's illegal!" she protested.

"The Home Companies is behind it, of course, and in a case like this they don't give snot whether it's illegal or well eagle. I hope you used cipher, Davy."

"Yes, naturally," Falkayn said. "I don't think they can have broken it."

"No, but you see, they kept me from getting maybe an advantage in this diarrhea-fluid situation we got. I seven-point-three-tenths expected it. . . . Here we are." The party climbed the steps, crossed a verandah, and entered an airily furnished room where stood a table covered with drinks and snacks.

Chee soared to a chair, crouched on it, and chattered, "You've heard about a battle commencing at Mirkheim, I gather. We were there. Earlier, the *wan-yao jan-gwo chai reng pfs-s-st* Baburites jailed us—" Her native phrase gave a succinct description of their ancestors, morals, personal cleanliness, and fate if she could have her way.

"Oh, no," Coya breathed.

"Hold, hold," van Rijn commanded. "I decree first we snap some schnapps, with a little liter or so of beer in tow and maybe a few herring filets or such for ballast. You do not want your new baby should become an adrenalin addict, ha?"

"Nor this young lady," said Adzel, for Juanita's giggles had given place to a worried silence. He reached around, lifted her off his shoulders, and started juggling her from hand to enormous hand. She squealed in delight. Her parents didn't mind; she was safer with him than with anybody else they knew, including themselves.

"Well—" Falkayn could not quite yield to pleasure. "What's been happening at home?"

"Nothing, except the bomb going ticktacktoe," van Rijn said. "Bayard Story, he made one last try to get me in combination with the Seven, what meant putting me under their orders. I told him to paint it green, and he left the Solar System. Otherwise, only rumors, and news commentators who I would like to do a hysteria-ectomy on."

"Who's Bayard Story?" Chee inquired.

"A director of Galactic Developments, delegate to the meeting at Lunograd," van Rijn told her. "He was pretty much the spokesman for the Seven. In fact, I suspect he was the wheelsman."

"Mmm, yes, I remember now, I happened to see his arrival on a newscast," Falkayn put in. "I admired his skill in giving the reporter a brief, crisp, straightforward statement that didn't say a flinkin' thing." He turned to Coya. "No matter. Haven't you anything special to relate, darling?"

"Oh, I was offered a contract by Danstrup Cargo Carriers," she answered, referring to an independent within the League. Since she stopped trade pioneering, she had worked out of her home as a high-powered free-lance computer programmer. "They wanted an analysis of their best strategy in case of war. Everybody is terrified of war, nobody knows what the consequences would be, nobody wants it, but still we drift and drift. . . . It's horrible, Davy. Can you imagine how horrible?"

Falkayn brushed a kiss across her hair. "Did you take the job?"

"No. How could I, not being sure what had become of you? I've filled in the time with routine-type stuff. And—and I've played a lot of tennis, that sort of thing, to help me sleep." She shared his distrust of chemical consolations.

In a way, van Rijn did too. He used alcohol not as a crutch but as a pogo stick. "Drink, you slobberwits!" he roared. "Or do I have to give it to you with a hypochondriac needle? You got home safe, that's what matters first. So crow about it; then look at this nice table of goodies and raven."

Adzel set Juanita down. "Come," he said, "let us go off in a corner and have a tea party." She paused to pet Chee. The Cynthian submitted, merely switching her tail.

Yet it was impossible to pretend for long that no universe existed beyond the blue overhead. Soon the *Muddlin' Through* trio were relating their experiences. Van Rijn listened intently, interrupting less often than Coya with questions or exclamations.

At the end: "This equipment you salvaged from the warship, did you learn anything about it on your way home?" he asked.

"Very little." Falkayn rubbed the back of his neck. "And damned puzzling. Most of what we saw, as well as what we took away, is modeled on Technic designs, as you'd expect. But certain transistors— we can't figure out how they were manufactured in a hydrogen atmosphere. Hydrogen would poison the semiconductors."

"Maybe they're produced off Babur, like on a satellite," Coya suggested.

"Maybe," Falkayn said. "Though I can't see why. Alternative kinds of transistor exist which don't require going to that much trouble. Then there's a unit which we guess to be a containment field-strength regulator. It involves a rectifier operating at a high temperature. Okay. But this particular rectifier is cupric oxide. Hydrogen reduces that stuff when it's hot; you get copper and water. Oh, yes, the piece is inside an iron shell to protect it. But hydrogen leaks through iron. So what the Baburites have got is a part less reliable, more often in need of replacement, than necessary."

"Bad engineering as a result of haste," Coya offered with a quirked smile. "Not the first time in history."

"True," Falkayn said. "But—Look, the Baburites have had offplanet help. That much was admitted to us; and we identified an oxygen-breather colony on one of their moons, you recall; and there are those foreign mercenaries, also oxygen-breathing. Obviously they hired such outsiders to help them with research, development, and production of their military machine. Why didn't the outsiders do a better job?"

Van Rijn stumped about, worrying his goatee and crunching bites off a Spanish onion. "More interesting is how the Baburites found those people, and how paid them as well as the other costs," he opined. "Babur is not a rich world nor very populous, proportional to its size, even allowing for industrial backwardness. Too much of it is desert, for lack of liquid ammonia. What has it to pay *with?*"

"It did do some interstellar trade in the past," Falkayn reminded. "Possibly somebody made contact or—I don't know. You're right, it's tough to find an economic explanation for everything they've managed to accomplish."

"Or any kind of explanation for their actions, by billy damn. I never sent you off expecting the kind of gumblesnatch you got into. No, I thought sure the Baburites would talk at you, probably not tell you much but anyhows talking. The sensible thing from their viewpoint should be, if they going to butt heads with the Commonwealth, they stay friends with the League, or at least not make it also an activated enemy. *Nie?*"

"They seemed, from what microscopic contact we had with them, they seemed contemptuous of the League. They certainly know it's divided against itself."

"How can they be so cock-a-doodle sure of that? Do we savvy the ins and outs of their politics? And why not try to take advantage of our divisions? For instance, they might get the Seven and the independents bidding competitive for business with them . . . if they treat the representatives halfway decent."

"Could you simply have run into an overzealous official?" Coya wondered.

Falkayn shook his head. "From what smidgen we know of the Baburites, hardly," he replied. "They don't appear to be organized that way. They don't have hierarchies of individuals holding positions. In their dominant culture, if not in all, it's a matter of whole Bands overlapping. So-and-so many single beings may each be responsible for a fraction of a job, and confer about it with their mates; a given being can be on several different teams."

"That makes for fewer contradictions," Adzel added, "though likewise, I suspect, less imagination and a lower speed of reaction to developments."

"Which suggests it was a policy agreed on beforehand, that any strangers who arrived would promptly be thrown in the freezer," Chee said. "Oh, we three have had plenty of time to speculate."

"Have you speculated about companies of the Seven possibly maintaining quiet relationships with Babur?" Coya asked.

"Yes." Falkayn shrugged. "If so, under present circumstances you wouldn't expect them to advertise the fact, would you? They could easily have been kept in the dark for decades about the intentions of the Imperial Band."

"Are you positive, dear?"

"Well, what can such a relationship actually have amounted to? Occasional visits by one or a few agents to a strictly limited region of a planet with more than twenty-two times Earth's area—a much bigger proportion of it dry land, at that."

"Still," Chee murmured, "the section where significant action has been taking place isn't necessarily huge." A phone chimed. "*Kai-yu!* Of every tyranny you humans have ever saddled yourselves with, that thing has got to be the most insolent."

"Nobody knows I am here but my top secretary," said van Rijn. His bare feet slap-slapped across the *tatami* to the instrument. When he pressed accept, it announced, "Edward Garver wishes to speak to you personally, sir. What shall I tell him?"

"What I would like you to tell him is not anatomically possible," van Rijn grunted. "Put him on. Uh, the rest of you stand back from the scanner. No sense handing out free information."

Square shoulders, bald head, and pugdog face sprang into simulacrum. "You're on Ronga, I believe, where your snoopship is," said the Commonwealth's Minister of Security without preamble.

"You got told about her, ha?" van Rijn replied, quiet as the center of a hurricane.

"I issued standing orders the day I learned she'd left." Garver hunched forward, as if to thrust himself past the vitryl. "You've been a special interest of mine for an almighty long while."

Falkayn—still more, perhaps, Adzel, who had once been arrested after a certain incident—remembered. Since the years when he was chief law enforcement officer of the Lunar Federation, Garver had hated van Rijn. His terms in the Commonwealth Parliament had put a fresh edge on that. It was an oddly pure passion. Because of the particular encounters they chanced to have had, he saw the merchant as an archetype of everything he abominated about the Polesotechnic League.

"I want to know where the crew have been, what they've done, and why," he said. "I'm calling personally so you'll know I mean this . . . personally."

"Go ahead and want as much as you feel like." Van Rijn beamed. "Wallow in it. Scrub your tummy with it. Blow bubbles. Try different flavors." Behind his back, he crooked a finger. Falkayn in turn gestured to Chee and Adzel, who went quickly out. The younger man stayed by Coya. His partners could remove the log and Baburite apparatus—to which the health inspector had paid no particular attention prior to their descent—from *Muddlin' Through* before a search party arrived with a warrant.

Another log would remain, which had been faked as a matter of routine. He'd better brief his wife and his grandfather-in-law fast.

"—no more of your apishness," Garver was rasping. "I presume you know about the Baburite attack on our ships. It means war, I guarantee. Parliament will meet, by multiway phone, inside the next hour. And I know what the vote will be."

I do too, Falkayn thought sadly, while silent tears started forth in Coya's eyes. *Not that we should do nothing about the killing of our men. But this haste—? Well, the Home Companies see a vital interest in Mirkheim. Let the Commonwealth possess it, and that will be their foothold in space, against the Seven.*

"And the war will purify us," Garver said.

It will give the government powers over free enterprise that it never had before. You can't consider the Home Companies free enterprises any longer. No, they're part of the power structure. He loathes us because we've never either joined or toadied to the coalition of cartels, politicians, and bureaucrats. To him, we represent Chaos.

Garver checked himself from orating. With iron joy, he went on: "Meanwhile, as of an hour back, the Premier has declared a state of emergency. Under it, my department takes authority over all spacecraft. We'll be commandeering, van Rijn; and no ship will move without our permission. I've called you like this in the faint hope that'll make you comprehend the gravity of the situation, and what'll happen to you if you don't cooperate."

"How sweet of you to tell me," the merchant replied expressionlessly. "Was there more? Hokay, pippity-pip." He switched off.

Turning to the rest, he said, "I would not give him the satisfaction." He jumped up and down. The floor thundered. He pummeled the air with his fists. "*Schijt, pis, en bederf!*" he bellowed. "God throw him in Satan's squatpot! His parents was brothers! May he *wish* to become decent! Make us a four-letter Angular-Saxon language just for him! *Ga-a-a-ah*—"

Adzel, reentering the house, dropped his load to cover Juanita's ears. Chee scuttled past him, carrying the log reel, in search of a good hiding place for it. Coya and Falkayn caught at each other. A whine rose outside as two Central Police vehicles came over the horizon and turned downward for a landing.

✧XII✧

Was this truly Earth?

Eric could sit still no longer. The program he watched was interesting—doubtless banal to a native, but exotic to him. However, he was too restless. He flung himself off the lounger, strode across his room, halted at a window.

Evening was stealing across Rio de Janeiro Integrate. From his high perch his gaze swept over the flowing lines and rich tints of skyscrapers, bold silhouettes of Sugarloaf and Corcovado, bay agleam as if burnished, Niterói bridge an ethereal tracing. Cars torrented along streets and elevated roads below him, wove an intricate dance through the flight lanes above. He touched a button to open the window and filled his lungs with unconditioned moist heat. No traffic noises actually reached him, but he had a sense of them, the unheard throb of a monster machine, almost like the pulse of a spaceship. The sheer existence of such a megalopolis came near being frightening, now that he stood brow to brow with it.

His right hand's grip on his left wrist tightened. *I am not nobody,* he defied the immensity. *I led a score of warcraft here.*

The door chimed. He spun on his heel, heart irrationally jumping. "Come in," he said. The door swung itself wide.

A man, small and dark as most Brazilians apparently were, stood there in a fanciful uniform, holding a package. "This came for you, sir," he announced in accented Anglic. The Hotel Santos-Dumont employed live servitors.

"What?" Puzzled, Eric approached. "Who'd be sending me anything?"

"I don't know, sir. It arrived by conveyor a few minutes ago. We knew you were still here and thought you might like to have it at once."

"Well, uh, uh, thank you." Eric took the parcel. It was in plain packwrap and bore only his name and address. The man remained for a moment, then left. The door shut behind him. *Damn!* Eric thought. *Should I have given him money? Haven't I read about that as a Terrestrial custom?* His face heated.

Well, though . . . He laid his present on a table and tugged the unsealer. Inside were a box and an envelope. The box held a freshly folded suit of clothes. The envelope held two sheets. On the first was written: "To his Excellency Eric Tamarin-Asmundsen, in appreciation of his gallant efforts, from a member of United Humanity."

Who—Wait, it did get mentioned while I was with those politicians and officers yesterday. A mildly racist association, naturally jingoistic about Babur. With the publicity that our escape from Hermes seems to have gotten . . . Hm, a second message. WAIT A GOD-SMITTEN MINUTE!

> My son,
> Read this and destroy. Leave the other note lying about so it may satisfy the curiosity of those who have a watch on you.
>
> I am anxious to meet you, for your own sake but also for the sake of both our planets and perhaps many more. It must be done secretly, or it is useless. I will only say now that you and your men are in danger of being made pawns.
>
> If you possibly can, cancel any appointment you have, wear the enclosed outfit, and at 2000 hours—Earth-clock, not Hermetian—go to the parking roof. Take a taxi numbered 7383 and follow instructions. If you can't tonight, make it the same time tomorrow.
>
> "Long live freedom and damn the ideologies."
>
> > Your father,
> > [seismograph scrawl]
> > N. van Rijn

For a minute that stretched, Eric stood where he was. *Old Nick himself,* hammered through him. *You hear stories about him throughout space as if he were already a myth. Of course I intended to look him up, but—*

His blood began to sing. After the grinding voyage, the wary reception, the strenuous drabness of two conferences with highly placed Earthlings, conferences that were more like interrogations, the interview before a telenews camera, and now this . . . Why not?

He was invited to dinner at the Hermetian ambassador's home in Petrópolis. He might have been housed there, except for lack of guest facilities; the embassy had a very small budget, because hitherto it had had little to do. Hence the Commonwealth government was treating him to these quarters. Quite possibly they were bugged. Certainly he was separated from his crews, who had been sent to dwell in—what was the name?—Cape Verde Base?

Yet why should he suspect the Commonwealth? He had everywhere met politeness, if not effusiveness.

Could be I'll learn tonight. He phoned, pleading fatigue, and postponed his engagement a day. Room service brought him sandwiches and milk. (Earth's food and drink had subtly peculiar tastes.) Afterward he changed into the new garments. They were flamboyant: sheening blue velvyl tunic and culottes, white iridon stockings, scarlet shimmerlyn cloak. Even here, where colorful garb was the rule, he'd stand out. Shouldn't he be inconspicuous instead?

Somehow he outlived the wait. Dusk fell. At the designated time he stepped from a gravshaft out onto the roof. The muggy atmosphere had not lost much heat; the city's horizon-wide shattered rainbow of lights seemed feverish. Several cabs stood in line. Opposite them, a man leaned against the parapet as if admiring the view. *Is he a watcher?* The sleek teardrop vehicles bore numbers on their sides. Eric's was in the middle of the row. *How to take it without making obvious that that's the one I want? . . . Ah, yes, I know. I hope.* He paced back and forth for a bit, cloak aswirl behind him, like a person not sure what to do; then, passing 7383, he feigned the impulse that made him lay a hand on its door.

It opened. He got in. A shadowy shape crouched on the floor. "Quiet," muttered forth. Aloud, to the autopilot: "Palacete de Amor." The car took off vertically, entered the lane assigned it by the traffic monitoring system, and headed west.

The man crawled up. "Now I can sit," he said in Anglic. "They're following us; but that far off, they can't see through our windows." He extended a hand. "I'm honored to meet you, sir. You may as well call me Tom."

Eric accepted the clasp numbly. He was looking at himself.

No, not quite. The clothes were identical, the body similar, the head less closely so though it should pass a cursory inspection.

Tom grinned. "Partly I'm disguised, hair dye, maskflesh here and there, et cetera," he explained. "And a standout costume, which draws attention from me to itself. Gait's important too. Did you know that you Hermetians walk differently from any breed of Earthling? Looser jointed. I've spent the past day in crash-course training."

"You . . . are a man of van Rijn's?" Eric asked. His mouth was somewhat dry.

"Yes, sir. He keeps several like me on tap. Now please listen close. I'll get off at the Palacete while you hunch down the way I was doing. I'll give them a satisfying look at me, hesitating before I go in. Meanwhile you tell the car, 'To the yacht.' It isn't really a cab, it just looks like one. It'll take you to him. At 0600 tomorrow morning, it'll bring you back to me, I'll step in, we'll let you off at your hotel. As far as the Secret Service is concerned, you spent the night at the Palacete."

"What, uh, what am I supposed to be doing there?"

Tom blinked, then guffawed. "Having a glorious time with assorted delicious wenches after your long journey. Don't worry, I'll leave behind me a goodly tale of your prowess. At times like this, I enjoy my work. Nobody will mention it to you; that's bad form on Earth. Just be prepared for a few smirks when you tell people you're tired because you slept poorly."

Eric was spared the need to respond, since Tom said, "Get down" as a garishly lighted façade came in view. A minute later, they landed, Tom got out, the vehicle took off again.

The episode felt unreal. Eric brought his face to a pane and stared. The city fell behind him, the bay, the coast whereon he glimpsed kilometers of magnificent surf. He was over the ocean. Luna stood low ahead, near the full, casting a witchcraft of brilliance across the waves. In its presence, not many stars were visible. Was that bright one Alpha Centauri, the beacon for which men steered when first they departed the Solar System? Were those four the Southern Cross, famous in books he had read as a boy? The constellations were strange. Maia was drowned in distance.

The car canted. Eric saw a watership in the middle of otherwise

empty vastness. She was a windjammer, with three masts rigged fore
and aft though only the mizzen sail and a jib were set to keep her
hove to. He couldn't remember what the type was called; no pleasure
boat on Hermes was that big. Doubtless she had an auxiliary engine.
. . . What a place to meet. The reason was total privacy—nevertheless,
how wildly romantic, here under Earth's moon. Lunatic?

The false taxi came to a hover alongside the starboard rail. Eric
emerged, springing to a deck that thudded beneath his feet. The air
was blessedly cool. A man took his seat and the vehicle flitted off, to
abide somewhere till it must return.

More sailors were in sight, but Eric knew the captain at once, huge
in the pouring pale radiance. He wore simply a blouse, wraparound
skirt, and diamonds glistery on his fingers. "My boy!" he roared, and
stampeded to meet the newcomer. His handshake well-nigh tore an
arm off, his backslap sent the Hermetian staggering. "Ho, ho, welcome,
by damn! For this, you bet I give good St. Dismas candles till he
wonders if maybe he was martyred by a grease fire." He clasped his
son's shoulders. "*Ja,* you got some of your mother in you, even if
mainly you are what they call extinctive-looking like me. What a jolly
roger we raised together, she and me! Often have I wished I was not
too obstreptococcus a bastard for her to live with long. You, now,
you is a fine, upstanding type of bastard, *nie?* Come below and we
talk." He propelled Eric forward.

A lean man in early middle age and a pregnant woman who
looked younger stood at the cabin door. Van Rijn halted. "Here is
David Falkayn, you heard about him after the Shenna affair, also his
wife Coya—Hoy, what's wrong, *jongen?*"

David Falkayn. I should have expected this. Eric bowed in the
manner of kindred among each other. "Well met," he said ritually,
and wondered how he could add what he must.

"Below, below, the akvavit calls," van Rijn urged, less loudly than
before.

The ship's saloon was mahogany and mirrorlike brass.
Refreshments crowded a table. The quartet settled themselves
around it. Van Rijn poured with more skill than was obvious from
his slapdash manner. "How was Lady Sandra when you left her?" he
asked, still quieter.

"Bearing up," Eric said.

"*Proost!*" Van Rijn raised his liquor. The rest imitated him, sending the chilled caraway spirit down their gullets at a gulp, following it with beer. Across his tankard, Eric studied faces. Coya's was delicately molded, though somehow too strong to be merely pretty. David's was rakish in shape, rather grim in mien. *No, hold, I'd better think of him as "Falkayn." Most Earthlings seem to use their surnames with comparative strangers, like Travers, not the first name like Kindred, and he's been long off Hermes.*

Van Rijn's visage—sharply remembered from documentary shows a decade ago following the Shenna business—was the most mobile and least readable of the three. *What do I actually think of him? What should I?*

Sandra had never spoken much of her old liaison. She wasn't regretful, she just didn't care to dwell on the past. And she had married Peter Asmundsen when Eric was four standard years old. The stepfather had won the child's wholehearted love. That was why Eric had never considered seeking out van Rijn, nor given him a great deal of thought until lately. It would have felt almost like disloyalty. But half the genes in yonder gross body were his.

And . . . be damned if he wasn't enjoying this escapade!

Falkayn spoke. Abruptly Eric recalled the tidings he bore, and lost enjoyment. "We'd better get straight to work. No doubt you wonder about the elaborate secrecy. Well, we could have arranged to meet you candidly, but it would've been under covert surveillance—not too fussing covert at that. This way, we keep an option or two open for you."

"I knew you would come," van Rijn said. "Your mother proved it on Diomedes before you was born."

"We're not sure how complete your information is about the Commonwealth," Coya added. She had a lovely low voice. "The fact is, we're in the bad graces of the government."

Let me buy time, while I figure out how to tell Falkayn. "Please say on, my lady," Eric urged.

She glanced back and forth between the men. They signed her to continue. She spoke fast and rather abstractly, perhaps as a shield for nervousness.

"Well, to generalize, for a long time in the Solar System, underneath all catchwords and cross-currents, the issue has been what shall be the final arbiter. The state, which in the last analysis relies on physical coercion; or a changeable group of individuals, whose only power is economic. . . . Oh, I know it's nowhere near that simple. Either kind of leadership might appeal to emotion, for instance—yes, does, in fact, because at bottom the choice between them is a matter of how you feel, how you see the universe. And of course they melt into each other. On Hermes, for instance, you get the interesting situation of a state having essentially risen from private corporations. In the Solar System, on the other hand, the so-called Home Companies have become an unofficial but real component of government. In fact, they've had the most to do with strengthening it, extending its control of everybody's life. And for its part, it protects them from a lot of the competition they used to have, as well as doing them a lot of different favors on request." She frowned at the table. "This didn't happen because of any conspiracy, you realize. It just . . . happened. The Council of Hiawatha—well, never mind."

"You remind me of the final examination in the philosophy class, my dear," van Rijn said. "The single question was: 'Why?' You got an A if you answered, 'Why not?' You got a B if you answered, 'Because.' Any other answer got a C."

Smiles twitched. Coya met Eric's eyes and proceeded. "You must know enough about Solar Spice & Liquors and its fellow independents to understand why we aren't popular in the Capitol. We can't greatly blame them for fearing us. After all, if we claim the right to act freely, we might do anything whatsoever, and simply the claim itself is a threat to the establishment. When Gunung Tuan—Freeman van Rijn—sent my husband off on a private expedition during this crisis, that was the last quantum. Commonwealth agents ransacked his ship after he returned, and sequestered her. They didn't find evidence to convict him; not that David had done anything particularly unlawful. But like everybody else, we're forbidden to leave Earth except on common carriers. And we're incessantly spied on."

Eric stirred. His words came hesitant. "Uh, given the war, aren't your interests the same as the Commonwealth's?"

"If you mean the government of the Commonwealth," Falkayn said, "then no, probably not. Nor are yours necessarily. Don't forget, I'm a Hermetian citizen myself."

And you are now the Falkayn.

"I do have my underblanket connections," van Rijn added. "So I know you is been watched since you arrived. They think: You come for an ally, yes; but how trustworthy is you? Anyways, it is in the nature of governments to be nosy."

"Don't worry," Falkayn advised. "I'm sure you'll be accepted for what you are, and accorded more rank than you maybe want. Nor will we ask any treachery of you. At this minute I'm not sure what we will ask. Maybe only that you use the influence you're going to have—a popular hero, granted special status and so forth—your influence to get us back some mobility. I believe if you think over what we've done in the past, you'll agree we aren't such dreadful villains."

The miners on Mirkheim. Their high-flying hopes. Eric nodded.

"In return," Coya said, "our group may help keep Hermes from becoming a counter in a game. Because Babur and the Commonwealth won't fight till one is crushed. That's hardly possible for them. After they've traded some blows, they'll negotiate, with the upper hand in battle being the upper hand at the conference table. Tonight it looks as if that hand will be a Baburite claw—because everything we've learned indicates their force in being is at least equal to the Commonwealth's, and their lines of communication are short where its are long. For the sake of an annual quota of supermetals, the Commonwealth might well agree to let Hermes remain a so-called protectorate. Certainly the liberation of your planet is not its prime objective."

Lorna. The home we mean to have.

"What I would like to do," van Rijn came in, "is send messages to the heads of independent companies, get them together for some kind of joint action. Right now they got no leadership, and I know them and their fumblydiddles by themselves. If you can arrange for people of ours to go off to them, that will be a real *coup de poing*."

"*Coup de main*," Coya corrected under her breath. "I think."

Van Rijn lifted the akvavit bottle. "Better let me pour you a buckshot more, my son," he invited. "This will be a long night."

Eric accepted, tossed off the fiery swallow, and said, before he should lose all heart for the task: "Yes, we've much to tell, much to talk over, but first—This didn't get into the news, as far as I'm aware, nobody mentioned it while my men and I were being interviewed, because we'd agreed en route to avoid naming names as much as possible for fear of provoking reprisals at home, but—You recall we lost our battleship on the way out. Well, its commander was Michael Falkayn. I understand he was your brother, Captain."

The blond man sat still. His wife seized his arm. "I'm sorry." Eric's tone stumbled. "He was a gallant officer."

"Mike—" Falkayn shook his head. "Excuse me."

"Oh, darling, darling," Coya whispered.

Falkayn's fist smote the tabletop, once. Then he blinked hard, sought van Rijn's eyes, and met them unwaveringly. "You realize what this means, don't you, Gunung Tuan?" he asked, flat-voiced. "I'm the new head of the family and president of the domain. That's where my first duty lies."

✤XIII✤

The telephone image of Irwin Milner said: "Greeting, Your Grace. I hope you are well."

Like death and hell you do, Sandra thought. She jerked a nod in reply, but could not bring herself to wish good health to the commander of planet-based Baburite occupation forces.

Did he stiffen the least bit? She watched his features more narrowly. He was a squat redhead whose gray uniform differed little from that on the lowliest human among his troops. Born on Earth, he retained an accent in his Anglic that she had been told was North American. He was naturalized on Germania, he said; it was a faraway neutral, hence his service with Babur did not make him guilty of any treason.

So he claims.

"What did you wish to discuss, General?" she demanded rather than inquired.

"A necessary change," he replied. "To date, we've been busy getting the protectorate functional, the military side of it, that is."

Warcraft in orbit, whose crews are more alien to man than a shark or a nightshade, ready to hurl their nuclear weapons downward. On the ground, oxygen-breathing mercenaries, human, Merseian, Gorzuni, Donarrian—adventurers, the scourings of space, though thus far they've stayed disciplined. Not that we see much of them. They have taken over our abandoned navy facilities, plus the Hotel Zeus and a few other buildings roundabout in Starfall. He says they will spread out in garrisons, in all the inhabited parts of Hermes. He has given me no satisfactory answer as to why, when it would seem that those circling spacecraft are ample to assure our meek behavior.

"That work will go on," Milner continued. "But we're now ready to start making a sound, uh, infrastructure. I'm sure your people understand they can't have our protection for nothing. They'll need to do their share, producing supplies in their factories, food and raw materials from their lands—you see what I mean, I'm sure, madam."

He scowled. "I told you before, the attack those Hermetian ships made on ours, their defiance of orders . . . Yes, yes, not your fault, madam. But if your navy had that many subversives in it, what about civilians? We might start getting sabotage, espionage, aid and comfort to enemy agents. That has to be guarded against, doesn't it?"

He paused. "Go on," Sandra said. The words sounded remote in her ears. She was tensing to receive a blow.

The first several days of the occupation had gone with eerie smoothness. Were the people stunned, mechanically tracing out routines—or how much ordinary life went on, education, recreation, lovemaking, even laughter? She herself had been astonished to find she could still enjoy a meal, be concerned when her favorite horse developed a limp, take interest in some unusual triviality on the newscast. Of course, no doubt it helped that few dwellers on the planet had glimpsed an invader. And she liked to think that her speeches had had their effect—first, on a conference hookup, to the world legislature, the presidents of the domains; afterward on television to everybody. "We have no other choice but our useless deaths and our children's. . . . We yield under protest, praying for eventual justice. . . . Our forebears entered wildernesses whose very life forms were mostly unknown to them, and many suffered or died, but in the end they overcame. In this hour we must be worthy of them. . . . Prudence. . . . Patience. . . . Endure. . . ."

"We'll have to organize for the long pull," Milner told her. "Now I'm a plain soldier. I don't know the ins and outs of your society here. But I do know there isn't another like it anywhere that humans have settled. So we're bringing in a High Commissioner. He and his staff will work closely with you, to ease the, uh, transition and make what reforms are required. He's Hermetian born, you see, madam, Benoni Strang by name."

Strang? Not one of the Thousand Families. Possibly a Follower, but I doubt it; I'm sure I'd remember. Then he must be—

"He arrived today and would like to meet with you informally as soon as possible," Milner was saying. "You know, get acquainted, let you see that it's his world too and he has its best interests at heart. When would be a convenient time, madam?"

They are very polite to the prisoners, not?

✳ ✳ ✳

Waiting, she wandered alone save for one of her hounds, across the top of Pilgrim Hill to the Old Keep. Its stone massiveness housed nothing these days but records and a museum; nobody else was in the formal gardens surrounding it. The stillness made her footsteps seem loud on the graveled paths.

Flowerbeds and low hedges formed an intricate design anchored to occasional trees. Most blooms were gone; colors other than green were only in crimson daleflower and small whitefoot, in shrubs where skyberries ripened vivid blue, in the first yellow on leaves of birch and purple on leaves of fallaron. Maia shone muted through a hazy sky. The air was mild, with a slight tang. Trekking wings passed overhead. Autumn is gentle around Starfall, despite its latitude; Hermes tilts less on its axis than Earth. Under the hill gleamed the river, the city stretched eastward in roofs and towers to the bay, westward it soon gave place to plowland and pasture and Cloudhelm's ghostly peak. She saw little traffic and heard none. The world might have been keeping a Sabbath.

But nothing ever really stopped work, least of all the forces of disruption. Soon she must go back inside and haggle for the liberties of her people. She remembered that it had been just this season and just this weather when she and Pete rode into the trouble at Whistle Creek. *Pete*—Her mind flew back across twenty-two Hermetian years.

This was awhile after they met. That hour was still in the future when he would ask for marriage, or she would. (They were never quite sure which.) They were, though, seeing a good deal of each other. He had suggested she join him for some outdoor sport. She left Eric in her mother's care and flitted northeast from Windy Rim, across the Apollo Valley, to Brightwater in the foothills of the Thunderhead Mountains.

It did not belong to him. The Asmundsens were Followers of the Runebergs, whose domain had property in these parts as well as on the coastal plain and elsewhere. However, the Asmundsens had been tenants of the estate called Brightwater for generations, managers of the copper mining and refining which were the area's sole industry. Pete was content to let his older brother handle that, while he went into business for himself, exploring the planets of the Maian System and developing their resources. (Naturally the domain took a share of the profits; but then, it had put up the original investment, after he persuaded the president and advisors that his idea was sound.)

The family made Sandra welcome, at first with the formalities due a person of her rank, but soon warmly and merrily. Having seen different cultures in her travels, she noticed what she would earlier have taken for granted, the absolute lack of subservience. If they had by birthright a single vote each in domain affairs while every adult Runeberg had ten, what of it? Their rights were equally inviolable; they enjoyed hereditary privileges, such as this use of a lucrative region; they were spared tedious detail work vis-a-vis neighbor domains; if any of them came to grief, it was the duty of the presidential bloodline to mobilize what resources were necessary to help. Indeed, they stood to the Runebergs much as the Runebergs stood to whatever head of state the legislature elected from the Tamarins. Her awareness growing keener as time passed, Sandra often wondered whether she envied more the Kindred or the Followers.

On the day that she was to recall long afterward, she and Pete took horse for a ride to Whistle Creek, the industrial community. There they would visit the plant and have a late lunch before turning back. The route was lovely, a trail along ridges and down into vales whose forests were beginning to add gold, bronze, turquoise, amethyst, silver to their green, along hasty brooks, across meadows which had heaven for a roof. Mostly they rode in a silence that was more than companionable. But for an hour Pete unburdened himself to her of certain cares. Grand Duke Robert, old and failing, had begun by seeking his opinion on interplanetary development questions, then lately was progressing to a variety of matters. Pete did not want to become a gray eminence. Sandra did her awkward best to assure him that he was simply a valuable counselor. Inwardly she thought that if somehow she *should* be chosen successor, he never would escape the role.

They entered the town in a step, for it had no agricultural hinterland or suburbs. A single paved road to the mine served it; otherwise traffic went by air. Its core was the sleek, largely automated refinery, carefully designed to spare the environment. Round about clustered the shops, homes, and public buildings of a few thousand inhabitants. The streets smelled of woods.

Today they were strangely empty. "What's going on?" Pete asked, and sent his horse clopping ahead. Presently a human noise became audible, the fitful shouting of a crowd. Heading in that direction, the riders rounded a corner and found a small park. Three or four hundred folk stood in it. Mostly they were clad in coveralls without insignia, showing them to be Travers who worked here. Shoulder patches identified Runeberg Followers; these kept apart from the rest and looked unhappy. Followers, too, were the police at the corners of the park. Evidently a disturbance was considered possible.

This was near the end of the midday break. Obviously the meeting would continue into working hours, and the management had decided not to make an issue of that. The arrangers had timed themselves shrewdly; Pete's brother was absent, overseeing the start of a new mine.

A woman stood on the bed of a truck which had set down on the yerb and spoke into an amplifier mike. From newscasts seen at Windy Rim, Sandra recognized her wiry figure, intense dark features, military-style slacksuit—Christa Broderick, Traver born but heiress of a fortune made by her sea-ranching parents. Her words stormed forth.

"—overdue to end the reign of the Thousand Families and their lackeys. What are the domains but closed corporations, whose shares are required by self-serving law to pass from generation to generation? What were those corporations, ever, but the outfits which happened to come here first, and so seized the choicest lands of an entire planet? What was the Declaration of Independence but an attempt to escape the democratization that was stirring in the Commonwealth, an attempt to perpetuate an aristocracy which even stole a medieval title for its new head of state?

"And what are you, the Travers, but workers and businesspeople, excluded from inherited privilege, denied any vote, who nevertheless provide the energy that drives what progress Hermes is making? What are you but the fraction of its population which is not caught in a web of custom and superstition, the part whose vitality would haul this stagnant world into the modern age and the forefront of tomorrow, were you not shackled hand and foot by the ancestor worshipers? What are you but a three-fifths majority?

"Oh, the feudalists are clever, I admit. They hire you, they buy from you and sell to you, they leave your private lives alone, occasionally they adopt one of you into their own ranks, above all they exempt you from taxation. I have heard many a Traver say that he or she is quite happy with things as they are. But ask yourselves: Is this not a subtle slavery in itself? Are you not being denied the right to tax yourselves for public purposes chosen by your democratically elected representatives? Are you content with the do-nothing government of a decadent aristocracy, or would you rather bequeath to your children a state—yes, I will say a commonwealth—to which everything is possible? Answer me!"

A part of the listeners cheered, a part booed, most stood in troubled muteness. Never before had the Liberation Front sent a speaker—its leader, at that—to Whistle Creek. Of course, Sandra realized, those here would have seen rallies and heard speeches made elsewhere, on their telescreens; some would have read the literature; a few might have dropped in on movement headquarters in Starfall. But she felt with shocking suddenness that there was nothing as powerful as a meeting of flesh with eye, voice with ear, body packed close to body. Then the ancient ape awoke. Briefly, sardonically went through her the thought that perhaps this was why Kindred and Followers went in for so much pageantry.

Turning her head, Broderick saw her and Pete in their saddles. They had each gotten a certain amount of publicity; she knew them by sight. At once she pounced. Yet her sarcasm was delicate. "Well, greeting! All of you, look who've come. Peter Asmundsen, brother of your general manager; Sandra Tamarin, possibly your next Grand Duchess. Sir, madam"—and that second title reminded those who knew of Eric that he might in his turn bring foreign blood to the throne—"I hope I've not given offense in proposing some reforms."

"No, no," Pete called. "Sail right ahead."

"Perhaps you would like to reply?"

"'Tis your speech."

Chuckles came from the Followers and half the Travers. Broderick plainly knew the charm was broken. Men and women were beginning to glance at their watches; most of them were skilled technicians who could not be absent too long without problems developing in their departments. She would have to start fresh to rearouse interest.

"I'm glad you're here," she said. "Very few of your class can be bothered to debate the issues the Liberation Front is raising. Thank you for showing public spirit. . . . *Do* you wish to respond?"

Expectant gazes turned toward the pair. Dismayed, Sandra felt her tongue lock tight. The sky pressed down on her. Then Pete brought his horse forward a pace, sat there with light shining on his blond mane and in his blue eyes, and said in a deep drawl that carried from end to end of the park:

"Well, thank you, but we're only visiting. Anybody interested in a thorough discussion of the pros and cons of this subject should fax the Quadro twelfth issue of the *Starfall Weekly Meteor*. After that, you can find any number of books, recorded talks, and what have you.

"I might say this, for whatever 'tis worth. I don't think democracy, or aristocracy, or any other political arrangement should be an end in itself. Such things are simply means to an end, not? All right, then ask yourselves if what we've got isn't at least serving the end of keeping Hermes a pleasant place to live.

"If you're feeling restless—well, belike most of you know I'm in charge of an effort to exploit the other planets, instead of overexploiting this one we inhabit. 'Tis tough and often dangerous work, but if you live, you've a goodly chance of getting rich, and are bound to have the satisfaction of knowing you did what not many persons could have done. We're chronically short of labor. I'll be delighted if you mail me your applications." He paused. "My brother will be less delighted."

"Carry on," he said into their laughter, and led Sandra away.

Later, when having skipped lunch they were riding back through the woods, he apologized: "I'm sorry. We'll have to try another time. I'd no idea this would happen."

"I'm glad it did," she answered. "It was interesting. No, more than that."

I learned a little something, Sandra Tamarin-Asmundsen remembered. *Including, maybe then, maybe a bit later, that I loved you, Pete.*

During the years between, the Liberation Front had gained strength. Much of her reign had gone into a search for compromises. Principally, Travers now had a vote in choosing municipal officers.

Broderick and her kind were still maintaining that this was a mere sop; and they seemed to make ever more converts. *What will Benoni Strang be like?*

Received in her confidential conference room, he proved a surprise. Medium-sized, slim, the rather handsome features of his rectangular face ornamented by a neat mustache and a suntan, his slightly grizzled brown hair sleeked back, he spoke as smoothly as he moved. His clothes were of rich material, soft in hue but cut in the latest Terrestrial mode. He bowed to her as courtesy required a Traver do. (A member of the Kindred would have shaken hands with the Duchess, a Follower would have saluted.) "Good greeting, Your Grace. I thank you for the honor you do me." The words were traditional, though Hermetian intonation had worn away. He must have spent long years separated from the Strangs whom a city directory listed as being of his class.

Her throat tightened as if to keep her heart from jumping out. *Traitor, traitor.* Barely could she make herself say, "Be seated" and take her own carven armchair.

He obeyed. "It's a wonderful feeling to be back, madam. I'd well-nigh forgotten how beautiful this area is."

"Where else were you?" *I must find out everything about him I can. For this purpose, I may have to smile at him.*

"Many places, madam. A checkered career. I'll be glad to reminisce if you wish. However, I suspect today you'd rather get straight to the point."

"Yes. Why are you working for the Baburites?"

"I'm not really, madam. I hope to do my best for Hermes. It was not always kind to me, but it is the world of my fathers."

"Invaded!"

Strang frowned, as if wounded. "I sympathize with your distress, madam. But Babur was forestalling the Commonwealth. Intelligence discovered that the general staff of the enemy had a plan, the preliminaries already in train, to take over this system."

So you say, Sandra thought. Yet she could not help wondering.

"You can hardly blame Babur for acting," Strang continued. "And from your viewpoint, isn't it the lesser of two evils? It doesn't want to rule you; couldn't possibly; the idea is ridiculous. At most, some kind of postwar association for mutual defense and trade may prove desirable. But the Commonwealth has always deplored the fact that several colonies broke loose from it."

True enough. Our forebears did because they were evolving societies, interests, philosophies in their new homes, too strange to Earth, Luna, or Venus to fit in well with laws and usages developed for those worlds. The Commonwealth didn't resist independence by force of arms. But many of its citizens believed that it ought to.

"Madame," Strang said earnestly, "I've been a xenologist, specializing in subjovian planets and Babur in particular. I know that race and its different cultures better than any other human. No boast, a plain statement of fact. In addition, as I said, I'm a Hermetian, yes, a Hermetian patriot. God knows I'm not perfect. But I do think I'm the realistic choice for High Commissioner. That's why I volunteered my services."

"Not on any quick impulse," Sandra scoffed. "This whole operation must have been planned far ahead."

"True, madam. In a way, all my life. Since I was a boy here in Starfall, I was conscious of things deeply wrong, and thinking how the wrong might be set right."

Fear brushed Sandra and made her snap, "I've lost more time out of my own life than I like to reckon up, listening to the self-pity of the Liberation Front. What's your tale?"

Cold anger flared back at her: "If you haven't understood yet, probably you never will. Have you no imagination? Think of yourself as a child, crowded into a public school while Kindred children were getting individual tutoring from the finest teachers on the planet. Think of having dreams of accomplishment, of becoming somebody whose name will survive, and then finding that all the land worth having, all the resources, all the key businesses belong to the domains—to the Kindred and their Followers—who stifle every chance for a change because it might upset their privileges and make them use their brains. Think of a love affair that should have led to marriage, was going to, till her parents stepped in because a Traver son-in-law would hurt their social standing, would keep them from using her to make a fat alliance—"

Strang broke off. Silence filled the room for half a minute. Thereafter he spoke calmly.

"Madame, quite aside from justice, Hermes must be reorganized so it can aid in its own defense. This archaic half-feudal society is flat-out too cumbersome, too unproductive . . . most important, too alienating. The naval mutiny and flight to Earth showed that not even your government is safe from the insolence and insubordination of an officer corps drawn from the aristocrats. You have to win the loyalty of the Traver majority for practical as well as for moral reasons. But why should it care what becomes of Kindred and Followers? What stake has it in the planet as a whole? Production can no longer be divided among domains. It has to be integrated on a global scale. So do distribution, courts, police, education, welfare, everything. For this, the domains have to be dissolved. In their place, we need the entire populace.

"And after the war—it'll be an altogether new universe. The Polesotechnic League won't be dominant anymore. The Commonwealth won't be the most powerful state. Leisured negotiation won't be the single way of settling disputes between nations and races. Hermes will have to adapt or go under. I want the adaptation to start immediately.

"We're going to have a revolution here, madam. I hope you and your upper classes will willingly assist it. But be that as it may, the revolution is going to happen."

✲XIV✲

Hanny Lennart, serving the Commonwealth at a credit a year as Special Assistant Minister of Extrasolar Relations, declared across a continent and an ocean: "You appreciate what a difficult position your coming has put us into, Admiral Tamarin-Asmundsen. We welcome your offer to join your strength to ours. However, you admit that your government, which we still recognize, did not order you here."

"I've been told that a few times," Eric replied to the phone as dryly as he was able. Within him raged, *Will you say something real, you mummy?*

She did, and the end of suspense almost kicked the wind out of him. "I am calling informally to let you know without delay that I've decided to support the position taken by your ambassador. That is, the Hermetian government is under duress and therefore only those of its agents who are at large can properly represent it. I expect this will get Cabinet approval."

"Thank you . . . much," he breathed.

"It will take at least a month," she warned. "The Cabinet has a host of urgent problems. There's no hurry about your case, because our fleet won't move till it has reasonably good intelligence of Baburite forces and their dispositions. We don't want a second Mirkheim!"

"According to the news," Eric ventured, "quite a lot of your citizens don't want the fleet to move at all. They want a negotiated peace."

Lennart's sparse brows drew together. "Yes, the fools. That's the softest name I can give them—fools." She grew brisk again. "Pending acceptance of my proposal concerning you, I have the authority and obligation to rule on your temporary status. Frankly, I'm puzzled why Ambassador Runeberg objects so hard to your being considered internees. It's a mere formality for a short period."

Nicholas van Rijn put him up to it, that's why. The knowledge

140

surged through Eric that he was winning this round. But it wasn't over yet and the fight had many more to go. His mind and tongue began working at full speed.

"I'm sure he's explained to you, Freelady. We will be answerable to our government after the war. Accepting internment would imply that its status was dubious. Nor can we put ourselves under your command till we're fully recognized as allies."

Lennart compressed her lips. "Someday I must study your curious legal system, Admiral. . . . Very well. I trust you're willing to commence unofficially developing plans with us for integrating your flotilla with our navy?"

"Our *fleet* with yours, if you please, Freelady." The tide of confidence rose in Eric. "Yes, certainly, save when I'm looking after the well-being of my men. And about them, they've been effectively interned already. That has to stop. I want a written statement that they're free to travel around on any innocent errands they may have."

The discussion that followed took less time than he had expected. Lennart yielded to his demands. After all, they appeared minor. And the Commonwealth government was new to the business of war, unsure how best to handle its own citizens. It would not gratuitously insult the Hermetian popular heroes of the day. Van Rijn's publicists had done their job well.

In the end, Eric switched off, leaned back, and gusted a sigh which turned into an oath. His look roved from the screen on his desk, across the room to a window beyond which green meadows tilted up toward snows and the sheen of a glacier. His new lodging and headquarters was a chalet in the Southern Alps of New Zealand, into which communication and data equipment had hastily been moved. Given a few precautions, it was spyproof and bugproof. The wealthy "sympathizer" who lent it was a dummy of van Rijn's.

His elation receded before a wave of anger. *Haggling,* he thought. *Scheming. Waiting. Waiting. When do we fight, for God's sake?*

For Lorna's sake. The vision of his betrothed rose before him, sharper than any electronic ghost but powerless to speak. Two hundred and twenty-odd light-years beyond this bland sky, she dwelt beneath the guns of Babur, and he had had no chance to kiss her farewell. A pen snapped between his fingers.

Van Rijn came in from the next room, where he had been listening. "We got what we was after, ha?" His tone was unlightened by the minikin victory. "I would shout hurray and toss my hat in the air, except my heart is not in it. We still need to move fast, *nie?* Let us right away knock up a plan."

Eric wrenched attention to the merchant. "Oh, I've done that," he said.

"Ha?" The little black eyes blinked. "I come so we could be sure we talked safe."

Eric shoved back his frustration. Here was another step he could take toward his desire. "I worked it out while you were on your way. Then Lennart called, as we'd been hoping, right after you arrived.

"You go quietly with your agents to your midocean retreat, Ronga, as if for a few days' relaxation from the harassment the government's doubtless been giving you."

Van Rijn's mustaches vibrated. "Who told you about there?"

Eric felt progressively better as he spoke. "David Falkayn. Remember the night on your yacht, how toward morning, when we seemed pretty well talked out, he and I went topside for a breath of fresh air before the car came for me? He described your various private landing facilities, in case of need, and Ronga seems to me like the best bet."

That wasn't all he told, he thought. *Already then, he knew what he aimed to do and had a fair idea of how to go about it. Today I have been, I still am acting at his behest as much as I am at my own.*

"Well, now," he continued into the prawnlike stare, "each of my cruisers carries a speedster—outfitted for interstellar travel, I mean. I'll personally order one down, to land at Ronga. Some Commonwealth naval functionary will have to grant clearance. I'm wagering he'll just retrieve a listing of Ronga as bearing a civilian field suitable for that kind of vessel, and not check any further, like whose property it is. He won't dare to delay me. I've been acting mighty touchy—you noticed how I snooted Lennart—in hopes that word will go out to handle me with velvyl waldos.

"To avoid phone taps, I suggest you visit my ambassador after you leave here—get him out of bed if necessary—and hand him my commissions of your agents as officers of the Hermetian navy. Then bring to the island, and hand to them, my orders that they're to leave the Solar System according to instructions delivered verbally. They'll take the speedster after she's touched down; you can talk her pilot back to his ship. She carries several weeks' worth of basic supplies. Can you see to it that the nonhumans have along whatever supplementary nutrients they require?

"I don't imagine the boat will meet any problems getting cleared to lift, either. The person in charge will assume I want to visit my ships in their orbits. But once away from Earth, she'll head for the deeps. Space is big enough that it's unlikely she can be intercepted, if your man knows his trade. The Commonwealth navy isn't deployed against possible outward movements, as the Baburites were at Hermes."

A laugh clanked forth. "Oh, yes, I'll get any amount of thunder about this," Eric finished. "I'll enjoy pointing out that I've been entirely within my rights. We are not interned, and as yet we are not under the Commonwealth supreme command. 'Tisn't my fault if their officer took for granted I wanted a jaunt for myself. I'm not obliged to explain any orders I issue to personnel of mine—though as a matter of fact, 'tis quite reasonable that I'd send scouts to see from afar, if they can, how Hermes is doing. Yes, the brouhaha should be the first fun I've had since you smuggled me out of Rio."

Van Rijn stood moveless for seconds. Then: "Oh, ho, ho, ho!" he bellowed. "You is my son for sure, a chip off the old blockhead, *ja,* in you the Mendelian excessives is bred true! Let me find a bottle Genever I said should come with the office gear, and we will drink a wish to the enemy—bottoms up!"

"Later," Eric replied. Warmth touched him. "Yes, I do look forward to getting imperially drunk with you . . . Dad. But right now we've got to keep moving. I'll take your word for it that nobody can have traced you to this place. However, if you're out from under surveillance, if your whereabouts are unknown for long at a time, it could start the watchers speculating, not?"

He reached for writing materials. "Give me again the names of Falkayn's partners," he requested.

Van Rijn started where he stood. "Falkayn's? David? No, no, boy. I got others standing by."

Eric was surprised. "Of course you're reluctant to send him back into danger. But have you anybody more competent?"

"No." Van Rijn began ponderously pacing. "*Ach,* I admit I hate seeing Coya try not to show she grieves while he is gone. Nevertheleast I would send him, except—Well, you heard, that night on the boat. He will not go arrange a getting together of the independent company heads like he is supposed to. He does not lie to me about that. Give him a chance, he goes to Hermes."

"Why, yes. Should I object?"

"Tombs and torment!" van Rijn spluttered. "What can he *do* there? Get himself killed? Then what has all this pile of maneuvers been for?"

"I'm assuming he didn't boast when he told me, that dawn on your yacht, he and his gang can slip down onto the planet unbeknownst," Eric said. "Once there, yes, quite likely he will stay for the duration. That's good from my viewpoint, because his advice and leadership should be valuable. He also said it'd be harder to get a vessel back into space, but his partners have a sporting chance of being able to do it, after they've left him off. They have a record of such stunts. So they'll assemble your entrepreneurs for you. Though frankly, I've no clear idea of what you think those can accomplish."

"Little, maybe," van Rijn conceded. "And yet . . . I got a hunch on my back, son. It says we should work through what is left of the League, and maybe we find out the reasons for Babur's actions and how we can change them. Because on the face of it, they make no sense." He lifted a slab of a hand. "Oh, *ja,* I know, wars often do not. Still, I wonder and wonder what the Babur leaders imagine they can gain by imperialism against us." He knuckled his forehead. "Somewhere in this thick old noggin is fizzling an idea. . . .

"Davy will insist on going first to Hermes. Then could well be that Adzel and Chee never manage to continue. The jeopardy cannot change its spots. Let me send somebody else than them. Please."

That his father should finally use that word to him gave Eric a curious pang. "I'm sorry," he said. "It has to be Falkayn, no matter what terms he sets. You see, I've got to carry a rose in my tail—uh, that's Hermetian—I've got to guard my rear, legally, for the sake of my own men. Falkayn has my nationality. And his partners don't belong to the Commonwealth either, do they? Then I have a right to commission them. Have you any equally qualified spacers on tap that that's true of?"

Suddenly van Rijn looked shrunken. "No," he whispered.

He's old, passed through Eric, *weary, and, here at last, forsaken.* He wanted to clasp the bent shoulders. But he could merely say, "Does it make such a difference? At most, we'll set up a liaison, first with my home, later with your colleagues. We hope 'twill prove useful." He made his next words ring. "The issue, though, will depend on how well we fight."

Van Rijn gave him a long regard. "You do not see, do you, boy?" he asked, low and harshly. "Win, lose, or draw, much more war means the end of the Commonwealth like we has known it, and the League, and Hermes. You beg the saints we do not have to fight to what we call a decision." He was mute for a little. "Maybe we is already too late. Hokay, let us go ahead the way you want."

Burnt orange shading to molten gold and far-flung coral, sunset lay extravagant over the ocean. Light bridged the waters from horizon to surf. High in the west stood Venus. Beneath a lulling of waves, Ronga was wholly quiet. The day's odors of blossoms were fading away as air cooled.

Adzel came along a beach that edged the outside of the atoll. On his left a stand of palms glowed against eastern violet. On his right side, the scales shimmered. Chee Lan rode him; her fur seemed gilded. They were spending their last hour before they returned to space.

She said into a silence that had held them both for a while: "After this is done with, if we're still alive, I'm going back to Cynthia. For aye."

Adzel rumbled an inquiring sound.

"I've been thinking about it since the trouble began," she told him—or did she tell herself? "And tonight . . . the beauty here disturbs me. It's too much like home, and too much unlike. I try to recall the living forests of Dao-lai, malo trees in flower and wings around them, everywhere wings; but all I see is this. I try to remember folk I care about, and all I have left is their names. It's a cold way to be."

"I'm glad your appetite for wealth is sated," Adzel said.

She bristled. "Why in chaos was I confessing to you, you over-grown gruntosaur? You wouldn't know what homesickness is.

You can pursue your silly enlightenment anywhere you may be, till you've run the poor thing ragged."

The great head shook; and that, meaning no, was a gesture learned among humans, not seen in any land on Woden. "I am sorry, Chee. I did not mean to sound smug, simply happy on your account."

She calmed as fast as she had flared and gave him a purr. He continued doggedly, "I thought in my vanity that I was indeed free of birth ties. But this sun is dim, these horizons are narrow, and often in my dreams I gallop again with comrades across a wind-singing plain. And I long for a wife, I who am supposed to have such wishes only when a female is near me in her season. Or is it young that I really want, tumbling about my feet till I gather them up in my arms?"

"Yes, that," Chee murmured. "A lover I can be kind to, for always."

The beach thinned as it bent around a grove. Passing by, he and she came in sight of Falkayn and Coya, who faced each other with hands joined and had no vision of anything else. Adzel did not slacken his steady pace; he and his rider neither watched nor averted their eyes. Of three races and one fellowship, these four had little they need conceal between them.

"Oh, I regret nothing," said the Wodenite. "The years have been good. I will but wish my children have the same fortune I did, to fare among miracles."

"I likewise," Chee answered, "though I'm afraid—I'm afraid we've had the best of what there was. The time that is coming—" Her voice trailed off.

"You are not compelled to endure the future today," Adzel counseled. "Let us savor this final adventure of ours for what it is."

The Cynthian shook herself, as if she had climbed out of a glacial river, and leaped back to her olden style. "Adventure?" she snarled. "Crammed in a hull half the size of *Muddlin' Through*, with none of our pet amusements? Not even a computer that can play poker!"

❖XV❖

At first Hermes was a blue star. It grew to a sapphire disk marbled with white weather, darkened where its single huge continent lay, elsewhere a shining of seas sun-brightened or moon-shimmery. Later it filled half the firmament and was no longer ahead but below.

Here was the danger point. Her crew had ridden *Streak* in on a hyperbolic orbit, entering the Maian System from well off its ecliptic plane, nuclear power plant shut down and life support apparatus running at minimum activity off electric capacitors. Thus if any radar from a guardian Baburite ship fingered her, she would most likely be taken for a meteoroid from interstellar space, a fairly common sort of object. But now, lest she burn in the atmosphere, Falkayn must briefly apply thrust to give her the precise velocity required.

Readouts glided before his eyes, data on air density and its gradient, gravity, altitude, planetary curvature, the boat's ever-changing vectors. A computation flashed forth: in thirty seconds, aerodynamic descent would be feasible, given the correct amount of deceleration, and would bring the speedster down at such-and-such a point. He must decide whether to take advantage of that opportunity or wait for the next. Then less negagrav force would be needed; but the hull would grow hotter and the place of landing would be different. Acting half on reason, half on trained instinct, he pressed the button which elected the immediate option.

With no internal field to compensate, deceleration crammed him forward into his safety web. Weight dragged on his body, darkness went tattered across his vision, thunder sounded through his skull. After minutes the drive cut off and he was flying free on a shallow slant. This high in the stratosphere, stars still shone in a heaven gone blue-black.

"Are you all right back there?" he croaked into the intercom.

"As all right as any other squashed tomato," Chee grumbled from the weapons control turret.

"Oh, I found the maneuver quite refreshing, after so long a time weightless," Adzel said in the engine compartment. "I can't wait to disembark and stretch my legs." Aboard *Streak* he had had no room for anything except isometric exercises and pushups. He must vacate the recreation chamber, the only one in which he could extend himself, whenever his shipmates wanted a workout—either that or risk becoming a backstop for a handball.

"You may get in more jogging than you really want," Chee said dourly, "if somebody's detector registered our power output."

"We were over the middle of the Corybantic Ocean," Falkayn reminded her. "The odds should favor us. . . . Whoops, here we start bouncing."

The boat struck the interface of stratosphere and troposphere at a small, calculated angle. Like a stone skimmed across water, she rebounded from the denser gas. Shock drummed through her structure. For a while she flew on, almost free, rising higher toward space, then curving downward to strike and leap again . . . again . . . again. Each pass was deeper in the atmosphere, at a lower speed. The sky outside turned blue by day, starry only as she rounded the night side. A wail of cloven air swelled to a hurricane roar. Land and sea began to fill more view than heaven did.

At last she was mere kilometers above the surface, acting now as a lifting body. Falkayn tapped a button to demand her geographical coordinates, computed from the continuous signals of navigation satellites. Eagerly he compared a map in his hands. He was over Greatland, bound for a setdown in the Thunderhead Mountains. Below him stretched the sunlit desert of the continental interior, red soil rising in fantastic wind-sculptured yardangs, scantily begrown with yerb, empty of man. If he hadn't been observed yet, he doubted he would be. So he could use the engine to bring the vessel quite near Hornbeck, ancestral home of the Falkayns.

Chee's voice was a swordcut across his hopes. "*Yao leng!* Two aircraft from northeast and southeast, converging on our track."

"You sure?" Falkayn almost shouted.

"Radar and . . . yes, by all doom and hell, neutrino emission, nuclear power plants. I don't think they're spaceable, but they're big, and you can bet they're well heeled."

Oh, no, oh, no, twisted in Falkayn. *We were spotted. How? Well, the occupation force must be bigger and more dispersed than Eric realized, for whatever reason. After all, he was gone before it took over. . . . Somebody noted an energy burst high up, and queried a centrum which said it probably was nothing Baburite, and a widespread detector net got busy, and we were discovered, and the nearest military flyers were scrambled to check on us.*

He shoved out the dismay in him and asked, "Any prospect of shooting them down when they come close?"

"Poor, I'd say," Chee replied.

Falkayn nodded. *Streak* wasn't *Muddlin' Through.* In atmosphere and a strong gravity field, she was much less agile than machines intended for such conditions. She had no forcefield generator capable of stopping a missile, and her unarmored sides were desperately vulnerable to rays. Before she could strike a first-class fighting aircraft, it would likeliest have blown her apart.

To attempt a return to space would be as senseless as to try combat here. Tracking devices already had a lock on her. Warcraft in orbit must already have been alerted.

The three had discussed this, and every other contingency they could think of, during their voyage. "Okay," Falkayn said. "Where'll they meet us, Chee?"

"In about another five hundred kilometers, if everybody keeps his present vector," the Cynthian told him.

"Give thanks for so much luck. We'll be well over the Thunderheads, a section of them that I knew as a boy. I'll land us short of our destination, and we'll bolt into the woods. Maybe we can shake pursuit. You two, leave your posts right away; no further point in your staying on watch. Chee, collect our supplemental rations." They could all eat most of the native life, but it lacked certain vitamins and trace minerals. "Adzel, get the traveling gear." A bundle of that had been prepared in advance, including impellers on which they could fly if they did elude enemy search. "Stand by at the personnel lock, but buckle onto stanchions. I'll be slamming on brakes quite soon."

Trailing a sonic boom that shivered the ground below, *Streak* continued her long descent. The mountains reared ghost-blue over the worldrim, then starkly gray and tawny, then beneath the speedster, rock, crags, talus slopes, eternal snows. Peaks raked at her as she crossed their divide. The eastern heights were gentler, falling in long curves toward the Apollo Valley, beyond which lay the Arcadian Hills, the coastal plain, Starfall, and the Auroral Ocean. In the moister air of this side, clouds drifted, alpine meadows glimmered autumnally pale, the lower slopes lay mantled in forest.

Here we go! Falkayn cut in the drive afresh. With a surge of force, the spaceboat shuddered to a virtual halt, tipped to a vertical position, sank, struck. Her landing jacks bit into topsoil, found solidity, adjusted themselves to hold her steady. By then Falkayn was out of his seat. A dose of equilibrol had compensated his organs of balance for the time under zero gee. He swung himself down a companion, dashed along a corridor, found the airlock open and sped over the gangway after his partners.

They gave him the lead. He pelted across the glade where he had settled, toward the trees that walled it. The bare sky bore death. Between the trunks, shrubs and withes grew thick, stiffly resistant. Old skill came back to him and he parted them with economical movements of arms and shins. Adzel must follow more cautiously, lest he leave a trampled trail; but each of his strides was longer than the man's. Chee traveled easily from branch to branch.

Falkayn guessed they had gone three kilometers when a whistling sounded overhead. Glancing up, he saw one of the vehicles as it moved toward *Streak.* The lean shape belonged to an Avelan, produced for human-occupied planets after the Shenna scare made them arm to some degree, as formidable a war machine as he had feared. The insigne painted upon it was the linked figure eights of united Babur. It and its like had surely been bought through dummies years ago, and put in care of human mercenaries.

Relief fountained in Falkayn when it passed out of sight. It had not spied them.

"Let me take a look," Chee called. Adzel tossed her a pair of binoculars adjustable to her eyes, and she swarmed aloft.

Falkayn felt glad of the halt. He wasn't yet tired. On a clear track he could still run his thirty klicks without breathing unduly hard. But this was a chance to let his senses range around, to become part of the world instead of its being a set of obstacles.

Late afternoon light speared among boles and boughs from a blue in which small clouds wandered. The trees hereabouts were mainly stonebark, now leafless, and rainroof, whose canopies were gone yellow but would provide cover if he picked his way with forethought. The forest floor was less overgrown in this area of summer shade than it had been around his landing spot. Its new-fallen cover scrunched beneath his feet, sending up a rich, damp odor. Ornithoids flitted among bare twigs and buzzbugs danced in the sunbeams like dustmotes. A sudden powerful sense of—not homecoming—longing gripped Falkayn. Was this his country yet, or had he roamed away from it for overly many years?

No time to mope about that. Chee scampered back down. "I saw our bandit descend, and the other's hovering above, evidently at the boat," she reported. "They'll soon find nobody's minding that store."

"We had best move fast," Adzel proposed.

"No," Falkayn decided. "Not till we know how thorough they're going to be. Let's get tucked away while we can, especially you, old bulligator."

Chee returned to her post while Adzel squeezed into a thicket. Falkayn used his blaster to slash bushes and boughs, which he laid across the Wodenite's protruding tail. He himself could more readily hide—

The Cynthian zipped to the ground and across it. "School's out," she snapped. "They're coming on impellers, four men flying a search spiral. What d'you bet they've got a sniffer?"

Falkayn stiffened. Short of a cave, there would be no concealment from an instrument sensitive to the gases of breath and perspiration. Wild animals might cause delays with false alarms, but hardly enough to do the hunted any real good.

This could be the end, after all our years of luck. The thought was strange. Aloud, idiotically, he asked, "How would they happen to have a sniffer?"

"Precaution against guerrillas, or maybe guerrillas already are active," Chee said. "Only one of the flyers seems to've carried any, though. Else they'd have two parties in motion."

"Could we take to the air ourselves?"

"*Chu,* no! Where've your wits gone? We'd be seen for sure, this close to them."

Adzel spoke from the coppice: "I'll register much the most strongly when they come in range. You two proceed. Let me stay and decoy them."

"Have your brains turned to oatmeal too?" Chee snorted.

"Listen, friends, it is impossible in any event for me to escape—"

Intelligence slammed back into Falkayn like sword into sheath. "Sunblaze!" he cried. "Turn that notion inside out. Adzel, you stay put. Chee, come along with me. Guide me on a course that'll make them scent us first."

Her ears lifted. "What have you in mind?"

"Hurry, move, you jittertongue!" Falkayn said. "I'll explain as we run."

He stood beneath a rainroof at the edge of a stand of stonebark, whose limbs and twigs traced a skeletal pattern across what he could see of the sky. It hummed above him, and his hunters glided into view, well clear of the treetops. They were human but didn't seem so, the impellers on their backs like thick, paired fins, the helmets on their heads like naked bone, metal agleam in the level light. Otherwise they wore unfamiliar gray uniforms, and three of them carried energy guns whose long barrels bespoke heavy destructive capacity. The leader, who flew lower than the rest, bore a box with scanners and intake valves on its front, meters on its rear: yes, a sniffer.

That man pointed. A bolt raved from the weapon of another, scything dazzlingly across limbs that fell off and crashed downward in bitter-smelling smoke. An amplified voice boomed in accented Anglic: "Come out in sight or we'll burn the ground you're on!"

Falkayn stepped forth, empty hands raised. He was beyond fear. But every sense was at its keenest pitch, he saw each separate fallen leaf under his boots, heard it rustle, felt it give beneath his tread, he knew how a breeze whispered the sweat away from his cheeks, he drank fragrances of growth and healthy decay, it felt impossible to him that Chee's presence did not shout a warning.

The soldiers paused. "That's right, hold where you are," the voice ordered. The four of them conferred. They would naturally be wary of any ambush. However, their instrument had told of just this single man. . . .

An arboreal animal clinging to a high branch didn't count. It was inconspicuous, its fur gray with black spots, its posture that of a creature frozen into terrified immobility. Chee had rolled in the humus below the dead leaves. And the men were not Hermetians, they knew nothing of the planet's wildlife. Perhaps none of them had even noticed her.

One remained high. His companions came down to take the prisoner. As they passed near the Cynthian, she whipped her blaster from under her belly and opened fire.

The first bolt struck the sniffer, slashed through the cover and in among the circuits. He who bore it screamed and let go. The shot trailed across him, searing shut the mortal wound it made. His body continued down on its impeller, brokenly dangling.

Her second ray missed. It only got her target on the leg. But that put him out of action. He fled straight up, his own shrieks horrible to hear.

The third blazed at Chee. She had already slipped behind the trunk and was on her way groundward, springing from bough to bough across meters of air. He slewed his gun about in search of Falkayn, but Falkayn was back under foliage. Hermetian and Cynthian snapped shots from what shelter they had. The soldier retreated. In blind fury, he and his unhurt companion sent flame after flame. Where those struck, wood burst and soil steamed. Hundreds of wings lifted in panic, till cries well-nigh drowned out the flat thunder.

It was useless. Slipping from cover to cover, Falkayn was out of that area within seconds. Chee had less trouble moving invisibly. When they rejoined Adzel, she went on high and glimpsed no hostiles, apart from the one aircraft at hover. The mercenaries must have helped their wounded mate back.

"And they'll be without a sniffer till somebody brings a replacement," Falkayn said. As he had not been afraid earlier, he was not exultant now; he merely knew what he must do, and momentum carried him headlong. "We've got to be far gone before then. We'll start off now, slowly and ultracautiously. Come nightfall, which thank God is soon, we'll move fast. I mean fast." To the Wodenite: "Never mind any more noble self-sacrifices, huh? You carry me, and Chee on my back, and we *will* have a good speed without needing rest stops." *Yes,* he thought, *the old team is still working rather well,* and pointed to a landmark glimpsed between trees, an unmistakable snowpeak. "Steer yonderward. That way are my people."

❖XVI❖

Hornbeck occupied a plateau jutting from a lower flank of Mount Nivis. North beyond a forest climbed the heights, up to where whiteness forever gleamed. In the west also the horizon was ridged, but to east and south vision met just sky at the end of plowlands. The gray stone manor house stood a little apart from a thorp of lesser dwellings and other buildings. Here was the origin of the Falkayn domain, in timber and iron; though its enterprises had since spread planetwide, here was still its heart.

Walking along a road that wound among the fields, he saw them empty at this season, stubble and bare brown soil except when cattle in pastures cropped the last Earthside grass which autumn had left. The day was clear, windless, and cool; so great a silence filled it that the scrunch of his boots on gravel seemed mysteriously meaningful. Far overhead a steelwing hovered, alert for prey. No cars flew by to trouble it, nor did any move across the ground. The whole settlement had withdrawn: sending few messages to the outside world and those curt; sending few of its members there and those, closemouthed, on the briefest of errands; inviting no visitors—as if in preparation for onslaught.

Which it would soon undergo, in a form more dangerous to it than physical attack, Falkayn thought.

He and his mother had come forth, this morning after his arrival, to talk together away from last night's loving turmoil. But for half an hour they walked speechless. After the years that had passed, he could not be sure what she was thinking. He himself found he could not dwell on plans. His body was too busy remembering.

Athena Falkayn finally took the word. She was a tall woman, still handsome and vigorous, white hair falling thick past her shoulders. Like her son, she wore a coverall ornamented by the family patch; but she had added a necklace of fallaron amber.

"David, dear, I was too happy to see you again, too horrified at the risks you've run and then realizing you did come through them safe—I couldn't say this erenow. Why are you really here?"

"I told you," he answered.

"Yes. To take over from Michael, as is your right."

"And my duty."

"No, David. You know better. John and Vicky"—her remaining two children, living elsewhere—"and their spouses are perfectly competent. For that matter, I was essentially in charge after your father died, Michael being away so much with his naval work. Or have you grown so foreign to us that you don't believe we can cope?"

Falkayn winced and rubbed his face. It was gaunt from days of hard traveling, living off the country; his party had not dared fly. "Never," he replied. "But with my, well, my experience—"

"Could you not have applied that more usefully in space, helping organize the war effort?" The glance she sent on high, where ships patrolled, was like a shaken fist.

"I doubt it," he said roughly. "Do you suppose the Commonwealth government would have any part of me? As for van Rijn—well, maybe I've made a bad mistake. Or maybe not. But . . . look, Hermes has always been at peace. The rough and tumble of history is unreal to you—to everybody living on this planet—no more than a set of names and dates we learn as children, and forget afterward because they mean nothing to us. I, though, I've seen war, tyranny, conquest, upheaval, among scores of races. It made me visit sites on Earth, from Jericho and Thermopylae to Hiroshima and Vladivostok, only there were more of them in between than anybody could have time for. . . . I know something about how these horrors work. Not much—the League's got plenty of people as well informed as I am or better—but I can claim more understanding than most Hermetians."

He gripped her arm. "Before I go on, please let some air into this vacuum I've been talking in," he craved. "Tell me what the situation is. I heard mention of a social revolution sponsored by the occupation authorities, but no details. Everybody yesterday was excited and— Lord, it did get to be one hooraw of a sentimental occasion, didn't it? Plus the cursing of traitors who've stirred up the Travers. It can't be as simple as that."

"No, 'tis not," Athena agreed. "Maybe you can see a pattern, different from what I fear I see."

"Tell me."

"Well, I'm a light-year from having all the facts, and I may be shading those I do have, according to my own biases. You should talk to others, consult news records—"

"Yes, of course." Falkayn laughed sadly. "Mother, I'm fifty years old. Uh, that's forty-five Hermetian."

Her smile responded in the same mood. "And I can't feel, I suppose I can believe but I can't feel it's been that long since the doctor laid you down on my stomach and I heard what a fine pair of lungs you had."

They walked on. The road was interrupted by a plank bridge crossing the Hornbeck itself. They halted at the middle and leaned on the rail, looking down through the water to the stones on the bottom which it made ripply. The current clucked.

"Well," she said in a low monotone, "you know the Baburites came into this system and announced we were their protectorate. They meant to take our few warships, but Michael led those out.

"Michael," she said again after a second, in pride and mourning.

Wyvernflies danced above the brook, golden on gauzy wings.

"I imagine Lady Sandra needed a moonful of nerve then," she continued. "The fleet gone, her oldest son with it—what an excuse to depose her. She must have stood up to those creatures and made them see that she alone could maintain a government, that otherwise they'd inherit anarchy on a planet about which they were nigh totally ignorant. Which was true. Her purpose is to save our lives, our way of living, as many and as much as she can. If she has to compromise, well, I at least will thank her for whatever she can keep."

Falkayn nodded. "You're wise, Mother. Listening to some of those hotheads last night . . . Help me tell them there's nothing romantic about war and politics."

Athena sent her gaze toward a glacier which gleamed under the snows of Mount Nivis. "Soon afterward, the Baburites brought in oxygen-breathing mercenaries, mostly human," she said. "Happens I've a little information about those, because the Duchess asked me to get folk I could trust to make inquiries, since businesses of our domain would inevitably be dealing with the occupiers and Lady Sandra knew I've always been close to our chief Followers.

"The humans and nonhumans are both a motley lot, recruited

over a period of years—from the broken, the embittered, the greedy, the outlawed, the amoral, the heedless adventurous."

Falkayn nodded. Expanding through space with the speed and blindness of a natural force, Technic civilization had bred many such. "Recruitment alone must have required quite an organization, backed by plenty of resources," he said.

"'Tis plain," Athena answered. "I suppose their upper-echelon officers knew part of the truth; but the ranks weren't told. The story *they* were handed was this: A consortium of investors, who wanted to stay anonymous, was quietly preparing a free-lance army, crack troops who'd hire out at high prices wherever they might. That might be on behalf of societies which found themselves meeting a threat like the Shenna; or it might be to assist would-be imperialists venturing outside of known space. There was a strong hint that the Ymirites in particular were interested in that and would find oxygen-breathing auxiliaries useful on smaller worlds—for instance, to exact tribute in the form of articles manufactured to order."

Falkayn let a corner of his mouth bend upward. "I almost have to, no, I do have to admire their audacity," he said. "Ymir was a natural choice, however; it's a favorite object of superstition."

Because we know hardly a byte about it, he recalled. *Our name for a giant planet, dwarfing Babur, whose inhabitants are traveling and colonizing through space but apparently uninterested in any close contact with us—or else have decided we're too hopelessly alien.*

"I wonder why you, the League, got no inkling of all that recruitment," Athena said. "The best estimate I can make, from what reports of conversations I've gathered—and, yes, between us, interrogations of a few kidnapped soldiers—some small guerrilla activity has begun, we disown it publicly but word does filter back to us—" She drew breath. "Never mind. Mainly, my folk have counted the occupying troops as well as possible. They number about a million. Other information suggests that about as many more are being held in reserve."

Falkayn whistled.

And yet—"It's quite understandable why no intelligence of it reached us," he told her. "A couple of million individuals, collected piecemeal in tens of thousands of places on dozens of planets, they don't amount to a particularly noticeable statistic. Intrigues are forever going on anyway.

"Maybe agents of one or two companies did get some intimations. But if so, they or their bosses didn't see fit to pass the information on to the rest of us and push for a full investigation. Communication between members of the League is not what it used to be."

Space is too big, and we too divided.

Athena sighed. "I've gathered that.

"Well. The soldiers were warned they'd be in isolation for years. But the accumulating pay was excellent, and apparently some fairly lavish recreational facilities were provided, everything from beer halls and brothels to multi-sense library service. And of course the planet where they were sent had its natural wonders to explore, grim though 'twas, marginally terrestroid, hot, wet, perpetually clouded."

"Clouds?" Falkayn said. "Oh, yes. So nobody who wasn't cleared for Top Secret could figure out where it is."

"Its name among them was Pharaoh. Conveys that aught to you?"

"No."

"Maybe 'tis outside of known space altogether."

"Hm, I doubt that. Explorers keep expanding known space, and might well come upon it. I'd guess Pharaoh was visited once and is down in the catalogues with a number, not a name, as a not particularly interesting globe, compared to most others. . . . Okay. The army lived and trained there, till lately it shipped out and found it was working for Babur against the Commonwealth and possibly against the League. Has that shaken morale?"

"I really know not. My folk—like all true Hermetians—haven't gotten exactly intimate with them. My impression is that most of them still feel entirely confident. If anything, they're glad to lash out at a Technic civilization that kicked them aside. Surely the Merseians among them are. If any individuals do have qualms, military discipline keeps them quiet. That's a highly disciplined outfit."

Athena bowed her head. "I'm afraid I can't tell you more about them," she finished.

Falkayn laid his hand over hers, where it rested on the rail, and squeezed hard. "Judas priest, Mother, what are you apologizing for? You've missed your career. You should've been in charge of Nick van Rijn's intelligence corps."

Meanwhile he could not help thinking what an epic the gathering of the host was. Somebody very high-powered had been at work.

"Let's go on," Athena said. "I need to exercise the misery out of me."

Falkayn flinched as he matched his pace to hers. "Yes, it must be a foretaste of hell, having to sit helpless day after day while—Am I correct in thinking the Baburites originally promised no interference in our domestic affairs?"

"More or less."

"And then, once they were firmly based here, they reneged; and they've been pouring in additional troops, stationed over the entire planet, to deter revolt."

"Right. They planted a High Commissioner on us who's going ahead mostly as he pleases. If Lady Sandra gives him not a minimum of cooperation, 'tis plain he'll depose her and put us completely under martial law. But the poor brave lass stays on, with Christ knows how many struggles, in hopes of preserving some representation for Kindred, Followers, and loyal Travers . . . some part of our institutions."

"At the same time, by remaining Duchess, she does give a certain cachet of legitimacy to his decrees. . . . Well, who am I to criticize? I'm not there on the throne. Tell me about this High Commissioner."

"Nobody knows much. His name is Benoni Strang. That means naught to you either, not? Well, he claims being Hermetian, Traver born and raised. I did manage to have birth and school records checked, and they bear that out. Bad experiences early in life seem to have turned him into a revolutionary. But instead of becoming a Liberation Fronter, he went offplanet—got a scholarship from Galactic Developments to study Xenology—and nobody here heard a word about him for the next three decades, even his relatives, till suddenly he reappeared among the Baburites. He's very familiar with them, belike as much as is possible for an oxygen breather. But he's also been in topflight human circles; he's sophisticated."

Falkayn frowned across the fields. A loperjack padded from a hedge and over the stubble, small furry shape whose freedom was untouched by ships and soldiers. "And he's taking this chance to get revenge. Or to right old wrongs, he'd say. Same thing. Does the Liberation Front cheer him on?"

"Not really," Athena said. "Their leader, Christa Broderick, made a televised speech after the Commissioner proclaimed his intention of putting through basic social reforms. She welcomed that. Quite a

few Libbies promptly resigned, declaring they're Hermetians first.
And later, he's made no effort to enlist her organization as such; he's
bypassing it entirely. She's grown resentful. Censorship won't allow
her to denounce him openly, but her public silence indicates how she
now stands. His Traver supporters are moving to form a new party."

"I'm not surprised at Strang's action," Falkayn observed. "He
wouldn't want a strong native group for an ally. He'd have to give it
a voice, and the voice wouldn't always echo his. If you plan to
restructure a society, you start by atomizing it."

"He's said, through the throne, there'll be a Grand Assembly to
draft a new constitution—as our present constitution provides
for, you know—as soon as suitable procedures for the election of
delegates can be set up."

"Ye-ih. That means as soon as he can rig it, without being too
blatant about the fact that everything's happening under Baburite
missile launchers. Do you know what changes he plans to make?"

"Naught's been definitely promised yet save 'an end to special
privilege.' But we're hearing so much about one 'proposal' that I'm
sure 'tis scheduled to be enacted. The domains will be 'democratized'
and will conduct all their operations through a central trade authority."

"A good, solid basis for a totalitarian state," Falkayn said.
"Mother, I did do right to come back."

She regarded him for a while before she asked, "What do you
intend?"

"I'll have to learn more and think a lot before I can get specific,"
he replied. "Basically, though, I'll take over the presidency of this
domain as I'm entitled to, and then organize resistance among the
rest."

Appalled, she protested, "You'll be jailed the minute you reveal
yourself!"

"Will I? Unlikely. I'll come onstage with fanfare. What have I
done that was illegal? Nobody can prove how or when I arrived here.
I could have been meditating in a backcountry hermitage since
before the war. And . . . the Shenna episode made me a standard-
model hero. Never mind modesty—the fact has often been a damned
nuisance—but a fact it is. If Strang's proceeding as warily as you tell,
he won't move against me without gross provocation, which I won't
give. I believe I can rally the Kindred and Followers, get them out of

their demoralization, and appeal also to plenty of Travers. When the Grand Assembly is called, we'll pull some weight in it. Probably not much, but some. We may at least be able to preserve elementary civil liberties, and keep Hermes enough of a symbol of that that the Commonwealth can't bargain us away."

"I'm afraid you're overoptimistic, David," Athena warned.

"I know I am," he answered grayly. "At best, I'll hate the next few years, or however long the war lasts—separated from Coya and our kids, with the same emptiness in their lives—

"But I've got to try, don't I? We can only lose all hope by giving up all hope."

Falkayn had left Adzel and Chee in the woods before he hiked the last several kilometers to the manor. Among his earliest concerns was to get them safely tucked away without too many people learning about them, even at Hornbeck.

Athena had been able to arrange it immediately. When the Baburites made known their intention to occupy, Duchess Sandra had distributed among trustworthy households those Supermetals personnel she had evacuated from Mirkheim. Athena took charge of Henry Kittredge, the ground operations chief. She sent him to a hunting lodge off in the wilderness. None but she and a few ultratrusted underlings who brought him his necessities knew he was there. He was delighted when the Wodenite and the Cynthian were guided—on their impellers, after dark—to keep him company.

In the morning, the three of them settled down for intensive talk. Kittredge sat on the porch of the log cabin, Chee perched on a chair beside his, Adzel lay at ease on the ground outside with his head rearing above the rail. Sunlight streamed past surrounding trees, turning vivid what leaves remained, yellow, russet, white, blue. Animal life made occasional remote drummings and flutings that drifted through speckled shadows. Otherwise the air was quiet, pungent, a little chilly.

"Books, music tapes, television," Kittredge said. "Chatter whenever somebody brought me more grub. It got lonesome. Worse, it got boring. I've caught myself wishing something would happen, anything, good or bad."

"Could you not take recreation in the forest?" Adzel asked.

"I've never dared go far. I might get lost, or come to grief in a hundred unpredictable ways. This planet is too unlike mine."

Chee flicked ashes off her cigarette at the end of its holder. "Vixen has a human-habitable hemisphere," she said, "including woodlands."

"But not like these, except in superficial appearance," Kittredge replied. "Hell, you know that, as many worlds as you've seen." Wistfully: "Me, I'd settle for just seeing Vixen again, and never stirring my butt off it anymore."

"Nor the rest of you, I presume," Chee muttered.

"I sympathize," Adzel said gently. "Home is home, no matter how stern."

"Vixen's a better place to live than it was," Kittredge said with an upsurge of pride. "Our share in Supermetals has paid for founding a net of weather stations, which we badly needed, and—Well, we've gained that much, whatever becomes of Mirkheim in the future."

Chee stirred restlessly. "It may make a difference in determining what gets done with Mirkheim if Adzel and I can continue our mission," she declared. "Have you any notion of how we might get a ship?"

Kittredge shrugged. "Sorry, none. No doubt it'll depend on how things are going elsewhere."

"You must have some idea about that," Adzel urged. "You've spent considerable time here watching broadcasts, and must also have talked to Hermetians at length *viva voce.*"

Kittredge raised his brows. "Talked how?"

"Never mind him," Chee advised. "He gets that way occasionally."

"Well, I'm a total foreigner to this planet," Kittredge said. "And you two, what do you know about it, starting with its type of society?"

"A fair amount," Adzel assured him. "David Falkayn discussed it with us, over and over. He had to."

"Yes, I suppose he would," Kittredge said compassionately. "Well, then, as near as I can discover, the Baburites, through their human honcho, intend to mount a revolution on Hermes—from the top, though doubtless they expect to get support from the bottom. The whole scheme of law and property is to be revised, the aristocracy abolished, a 'participatory republic' established, whatever that means."

Adzel straightened his neck and Chee sat stiffly upright with her whiskers dithering. "*Chu-wai?*" she exclaimed. "Why in cosmos would the Baburites care what kind of government Hermes has, as long as they're in control?"

"I think they intend to stay in control," Kittredge answered. "Also after the war—for which purpose they'll have to have a pro-Babur native regime, since otherwise too much of their strength would be tied down here." He tugged his chin. "I figure this takeover of theirs is not just to forestall the Commonwealth's doing the same thing."

"Which was a poison-blooded lie from the first," Chee snapped. "The Commonwealth never had any such intention, and the Baburites can't be too stupid to know that."

"Are you sure?"

"Quite sure. Van Rijn would have gotten at least an intimation, and told us. Besides, we come straight from the Solar System. We've seen what disarray the war effort is in there—military unpreparedness, political uproar, a substantial party howling in terror for peace at whatever cost . . . The Commonwealth is not and never has been in shape to practice imperialism."

"Then why in the name of all that's crazy did the Baburites invade Hermes? And why do they want to keep it in the empire they'd build around Mirkheim?"

"That is a mystery," Adzel said, "among other mysteries, largest of which is the reason for Babur's launching a campaign of conquest in the first place. What does it hope to gain? As a world, a sophont species, it can only suffer a net loss by replacing peaceful trade with armed subjugation. Napoleon himself remarked that one can do everything with bayonets except sit on them. Of course, there may be a small dominant class on Babur which stands to make a profit—*Hro-o-oh!*"

He bounded to his feet. Chee snatched for the blaster she wore holstered. A car had appeared above the trees.

"Easy, easy," Kittredge laughed, getting up himself. "It's lugging in extra supplies to feed you two."

Adzel eased. Chee did so more slowly, as she inquired, "Isn't that a bit risky? An occupation patrol might notice."

"I asked the same question," Kittredge assured her. "The Lady

Falkayn said the family's always let its servants use this lodge when they're off duty if it's not otherwise in demand. Nothing unusual about them flitting here for a few hours."

The car landed in the open before the cabin and the pilot got out. Kittredge recoiled. "I don't know him!" Chee's hand snaked toward her gun.

"I'm a friend," the stranger called. "Lady Athena sent me. I've brought your food." He approached, short, stocky, weatherbeaten, plainly clad, with a slightly rolling gait. "My name's Sam Romney, from Longstrands."

Introductions were made and hands shaken. Kittredge fetched beer and everybody settled down.

"I'm a fisherman," Romney related. "An independent shipowner, but I've done most of my business with the Falkayns, we've gotten pretty close, and in fact, uh, a lad of yours from Mirkheim is currently being supercargo on a herder of mine out at sea. The Hornbeck pantries can't supply a bonzer your size, Adzel, not without making a conspicuous hole on the shelves. So last night Lady Athena sent a messenger asking me to come with a lot, explaining roughly how matters stand. She also thinks, and I believe she's right, she thinks it might be useful, when nobody knows what'll happen next, it might be useful for you to have outside contacts."

"Perhaps," Chee muttered, coiled herself on a cushion, and started a fresh cigarette. Whatever harm had been done, was done.

Adzel gave the newcomer a searching look. "Excuse me," he said, "but are you of the Traver class?"

"Sure am," Romney replied.

"I do not mean to impugn your loyalty, sir, but I had been given to understand that considerable conflict exists on Hermes."

"The Travers on this manor can be trusted," Kittredge pointed out. "Otherwise I'd've been clutched weeks ago."

"Yes, of course, the phenomenon of the faithful retainer is reasonably general," Adzel said. "And obviously Captain Romney is on our side. I merely wonder how many more like him there are."

The seaman spat. "I don't know," he admitted. "That's one hell-wicked thing about having the enemy amongst us, we can't speak our minds out loud any longer. But I can tell you this, plenty Travers never swallowed that Liberation Front crock. Like me.

I begrudge not the Kindred and the Followers an atom. Their ancestors earned it, and if they maintain it not, they can still lose it, fair and square. Besides, once a government starts dividing property up, where does it stop? I worked hard for what I have, and I mean for my youngsters to have it after me—not a cluttle of zeds who can't be bothered to do anything for themselves save fart in unison when their glorious leader says to."

He took out a pipe and tobacco pouch. "Also this," he continued, "several Libbies have told me, because you know people will talk now and then regardless, confidential-like, several Libbies have told me they're not happy either. They want not change pushed down everybody's throats by those creepie-crawlies; and Babur's using a traitor like Strang to do it makes the whole affair stink worse. And they, the Libbies, that is, they've not been invited into any conferences. Strang's given them a glop of praise for the, what's he say, the noble ideals they've long upheld—*ptui!*—he's given them a few fine words, like a bone thrown to a yellow dog, but that's been it."

Having stuffed his pipe, he applied fire before he ended: "Oh, we've got a fair-sized minority of yellow dogs, who're overjoyed at the prospects before 'em. I'll say to her credit, Christa Broderick, the Libbie leader, Christa Broderick's not among those. But what means that, save that the only thing she has left to lead is a powerless rump of the old organization? Maybe the Duchess will keep some small voice when the Grand Assembly gathers. But not Broderick, no, not Broderick."

Adzel met Chee's eyes. "Partner," he said, "I suspect we had better make sure that before he reveals himself or does anything else irrevocable, David talks with Lady Sandra."

✣XVII✣

The image of Benoni Strang stated: "I am calling you about Elvander's Birthday, madam."

For a moment Sandra could not brace herself. She had had to do that too often, until now she sat back and waited in weariness for the next blow. Then thunder resounded outside, she heard anew the trumpet of wind and march of rain, it was as if Pete rode by. She straightened in her chair and replied coldly, "What of it? The date is still a month off."

"We're wisest to be beforehand, madam," Strang said. "My request is that you announce there will be no public celebrations of the holiday this year, in view of the emergency—that demonstrations of any kind are forbidden."

"What? On our planetary day?"

"Exactly, madam. The danger of emotions avalanching is too great. Citizens may quietly observe it at home if they wish; but we can't allow any large private parties either. Churches must be closed."

No real surprise, Sandra thought. Yet her earliest memory was of her father holding her high above a crowd on Riverside Common, to see the fireworks cascade upward off a barge draped in flags. The water was alive with their light. "What if I don't issue your proclamation?" she challenged.

Strang frowned. "You must, madam. For the sake of your people. Riots, which could lead to actual attempts at overthrow . . . the military would have no choice but to open fire." He paused. "If you do not issue the order, I will. That would seriously undermine your authority."

What authority?

Nevertheless, this polite, grisly game we play, you and I, is all that postpones—what?

"A massacre would lose you much of your support," she warned.

His mouth tightened beneath the neat mustache. "Your use of an

166

emotional word like that shows that an incident might necessitate extreme measures on the part of my office, madam."

"Oh, I'll cancel the festivities. Belike nobody would be in a mood for them anyway."

"Thank you, madam. Ah . . . you will consult with me on the wording, won't you?"

"Yes. Good day, Commissioner."

"Good day, Your Grace."

Alone, Sandra rose and sought an open window. She had not turned on fluoros, and the storm made her conference chamber gloomy, a cave wherein only a few visions stood out, shimmer of a polished wood panel, dulled colors of a picture, curve of the Diomedean battle-ax. Freshness blew in, though, loud and raw. Rain struck the garden like spears and hid sight of the world beyond its wall. Lightning flared, making every bare twig on the shrubs leap forth under a sheet-metal sky; thunder rolled across unending reaches while murk returned.

She would not ride forth today. She had been doing that every morning, taking her best-beloved horse over Pilgrim Hill to Riverway, along the Palomino to Silver Street, thence to Olympic Avenue and back, a distance of several kilometers—always alone—to let the people see her, for whatever comfort that might give on either side. Folk often bowed deeply or kissed their hands to her. But too few would be out in this weather to make the gesture worth the effort.

I want to, however, I am parched with wanting. Though not through Starfall. West instead, on Canyon Road into the countryside, at a gallop straight against wind and rain, gallop and gallop without stop, hoofs smashing skulls of Strang and his men, then beyond them into the hills, the mountains, the deserts, a leap off the horizon and out among the stars.

A buzzer sounded. She untied her fists, strode to the intercom, and pressed accept. "Yes?"

"Madame," said the voice of her entrykeeper, "Martin Schuster is waiting to see you."

"What?" She came back to herself. "Oh. Yes. Send him in."

*Whoever he is. I know only that Athena Falkayn sent me a message asking me to receive him in private, which is why I happened to be here when Strang—*her *gullet clenched—called.*

The door opened for him and closed again. He was like her in being tall, blond, and middle-aged. When she looked more closely into the lean countenance, she choked down a cry of startlement and stood rigid.

He bowed. "Good greeting, Your Grace. Thank you for receiving me." He kept a touch of Hermetian accent if not of phrasing, for, as she knew, throughout the years he had not been long at a time on Earth, nor on any other world where Anglic was spoken. "What I have to say is confidential."

"Right." Her heart fluttered. "This room is spyproofed." As he hesitated: "Since the occupation, I've assigned guards and technicians to full-time duty, making sure it stays secure."

"Fine." Their gazes locked. "I think you know me."

"David Falkayn?"

"Yes."

"Why have you come back?"

"To help however I can. I was hoping you, madam, could give me a few ideas about that."

Sandra's gesture was jagged. "Welcome. Sit. Care you for refreshment, a smoke, aught I can offer?"

"Not now, thank you." Falkayn remained standing till she had taken her seat. She fumbled forth a cigar from a humidor beside her chair, bit the end off, and started it going.

"Tell me your story," she said.

"Eric reached Sol unharmed," he began, and continued. She seldom interrupted his succinct narrative with questions.

When he was through, she shook her head and sighed. "I admire your courage and resource, Captain Falkayn, and maybe you can be of help. That's dreadfully far from certain, though. At best, between us we can fight a delaying action, buying temporary concessions from Strang with our cooperation in laying the foundations for his eventual dictatorship. Naught can really save Hermes but the defeat of Babur."

"Which will take years if it's possible at all, and lives and treasure and social disruption beyond reckoning," he said. "The Commonwealth is confused, dismayed, and lacks will. The League is paralyzed by its own feuds. I think after a while the Commonwealth will fight all-out, largely because the Home Companies want that.

They see Mirkheim as their entry into space on a scale that'll make them competitive with the Seven. But they can't conjure up a determined populace and a powerful navy overnight. Meanwhile Babur will—who can tell what? Yes, madam, I doubt we on Hermes can count on rescue from abroad."

"What would you advocate, then?" She drew savagely on her cigar. The smoke bit her tongue.

"Political maneuvers, as you've been carrying out and I may be able to join you in. Simultaneously, covert organization of armed resistance, to operate out of our enormous hinterlands. We just might make the cost of supporting Strang more than it's worth to Babur, which has little to gain here."

"Whatever the real reason was for Babur overrunning us, won't that continue to obtain?" she argued against all her dearest wishes. "And never underestimate Strang. He's surely foreseen that we may try what you suggest, and taken steps. In his evil way—not that he sees himself as evil—he's a genius."

Falkayn stared past her, out the rainful window. "You must know him better than anybody else on this planet," he said.

"That's not well. He's as dedicated as a machine, and no easier to get near. I wonder if he ever sleeps. Why, shortly before you came in, he called me personally about banning public events on Elvander's Birthday. He could have told an aide to make the arrangements, but no, he had to see to it himself."

Falkayn smiled a little. "I must study him, try to get a notion of his style. I'm told he makes no speeches, and hardly ever delivers a statement in his own name."

"True. He's no egotist, I must admit. Or . . . rather . . . he's interested in the substance of power, not the show."

"I don't even know what he looks like."

"Well, I can play back our conversation." Sandra was vaguely relieved to rise, walk across to her phone, and punch the button. She wasn't sure how to respond to this man, home-born but far-faring, famous but a stranger, who had come to her out of the storm.

The screen lit, the familiar, well-hated features appeared, Strang said, "Good morning, Your Grace—"

"*Yaaah!*"

The yell ripped at her eardrums. She whirled and saw Falkayn on his feet, crouched crook-fingered. "Can't be!" he roared. And then, a whisper: "Is."

"I am calling you about Elvander's Birthday, madam," said the recording.

"Turn it off," Falkayn asked hoarsely. "Judas priest." He looked around him, as if seeking among the shadows. "What else can I say? Judas priest."

It was as if a tendril of the lightning ran up Sandra's spine, but cold, cold. She went stiff-legged back to him. "Tell me, David."

"This—" He shook himself violently. "Does Strang have a twin brother, a double, anything of the kind?"

"No." She halted. "No, I'm certain not."

He began to pace, hands wrestling behind his back. "A piece of the puzzle, a keystone, an answer?" he mumbled. "Be quiet. Let me think." Neither of them noticed his breach of manners.

She waited in a chill draught from the window while he prowled the room, his lips shaping unvoiced words or now and then a nonhuman oath. When at last he stopped and regarded her, it was strangely right that he stood beneath the ax.

"This is information that has got to get to Earth," he thrust forth. "To van Rijn. Immediately. And secretly. How can you smuggle a message out?"

She shook her head. "There's no way."

"There must be."

"None. Think you I have not wanted it, have not sat with my officers trying to imagine how we might do it? This planet is meshed in radar sweeps, detectors, and ships. Your friends could never have gotten off it alive. You reached atmosphere by masking yourself as a meteoroid, yes. But you know what happened after that. And . . . meteoroids don't rise."

Falkayn's fist smote the wall. "Listen. What I've learned could determine the whole course of the war. If we get it to van Rijn in time. That's worth virtually any sacrifice we can make."

She took hold of his arm. "Why?"

He told her.

She stood long silent. "You see I don't have a complete solution to the riddle," he added. "I'll leave that for Old Nick to work out. He's good at such things. I could even be wrong, in which case our effort will have gone for zero. But you see why we must make the effort. Don't you?"

"Yes." She nodded blindly. "A wild gamble, though. If aught goes awry, we've lost more than our lives."

"Of course. Nevertheless," he hammered, "we must try. No matter how fantastic our scheme, it's better than nothing.

"Surely communication goes back and forth between Strang and the Baburite high command. If we could hijack one of those boats—"

"Impossible." Sandra walked from him, back to the window. Wind whooped, rain rushed, thunder went like enormous wheels. Winter was on its way to Starfall.

He came up behind her. "You know something," he accused.

"Yes," she answered beneath the noise, not turning her head. "I do. But oh, God, my people—and yours, your mother, brother, sister, spaceship comrades, everybody left behind—"

It was his turn to fall mute, and afterward to force: "Go on."

"I still have the ducal space-yacht," she told him, drop by drop. "Strang has more than once suggested I might like to take a cruise to relax. I've ever answered no. His meaning is obvious. I can flee to Sol. He'll not oppose that."

"No, he wouldn't," Falkayn agreed low. "It'd give him the perfect excuse to seize total control, with the support of the extremist Hermetian Liberation Fronters. 'The Grand Duchess, like her son before her, has defected to the enemy, intending to lead back a foreign force that will crush our glorious revolution.'"

"There'd be no leadership for Kindred, Followers, and loyal Travers. They'd feel I'd betrayed them . . . and erelong they could become the subjects of a reign of terror."

"I see you've read your history, Lady Sandra."

Once more they stood dumb.

"I'd still be here," he said at last. "I'd proclaim myself and do whatever I was able."

She swung about. "Oh, no," she denied. "Oh, no, David. I'd take my entire immediate family, including Eric's fiancée, because this would make it doubly plausible to Strang that I intended to run. But you . . . you'd come along under your false name, substituted for one of my regular crew. I can't leave you."

"Why not?"

"You could stay incognito, useless, when we've need of your talents in space. Or you could invoke your prestige, try to fill my role . . . and provoke the terror for certain. Strang would know we'd conspired. He'd feel he must strike fast and hard. Whereas if you're not on hand, if the aristocrats in fact are leaderless and dismayed, he *may* think it politic to spare them the worst."

"If he doesn't—"

"I said it before, David. Everybody at Hornbeck must remain, save you."

His gaze yielded to hers. After he had long been hypnotized by the floor, she barely heard him: "If we do help short-circuit a total war, we'll save lives in the hundreds of millions. But they'll be lives that we never knew."

He lifted his head. "So be it. Are you game, Sandra?"

An early snow decked the land when the yacht *Castle Catherine* lifted from Williams Field. Beyond ferrocrete, cradles, buildings, and machines, the country lay blue-shadowed white, altogether hushed, rolling away westward to the panther forms of the Arcadian Hills. Above, heaven was unutterably blue. Breath smoked from nostrils, footfalls rang loud.

High Commissioner Benoni Strang had provided Her Grace with an honor guard of his soldiers. They presented arms while she and her crew passed by them. She touched her brow in return salute. All proceedings were correct.

Likewise was the paperwork which had led to this day. Her Grace had expressed a desire to visit the outer planet Chronos, enjoy the beauty of its rings, mountaineer and vac-ski on its moon Ida. Clearance was naturally granted.

She, her children, Lorna Stanton, and her men boarded. Nobody paid the men any special heed, though it was alive on their faces that they knew where they were really going. The gangway retracted behind them, the airlock shut. Soon engines hummed, negagravity took hold, the hull rose like a snowflake borne on a breeze, until it was so high that it gleamed like a star and then blinked out.

Past the guardian vessels *Castle Catherine* accelerated, outward and outward in the ecliptic plane. The sun dwindled, the Milky Way beckoned. At a sufficient distance, she sprang over into hyperdrive and overtook the light that fled from Maia.

There was no pursuit.

When it was clear that she would go free, Sandra sought Falkayn in private, laid her head on his breast, and wept.

✻XVIII✻

Hanny Lennart appeared uncomfortable. Eric suspected that that was less because of having to rebuke him than because of the surroundings where she must do so. Leading the navy of a world which the Commonwealth still recognized as sovereign, he could not well be given a formal reprimand. She had asked him to join her at lunch and he had promptly chosen the Tjina House, off a list that van Rijn had supplied earlier.

The last of twenty-one boys set down his dish of condiment, bowed above hands laid together, and withdrew from the private room. The diners would ring for further service when they desired. It was a lovely day along the Sunda Strait, and a wall had been retracted to let sea-cooled tropical air flow in. Gardens fell in thousand-hued terraces toward the water, palms rustled, bamboo swayed. Out on cobalt blue glided the stately torpedo shape of a cargo carrier and the winging sails of sportcraft. Unseen, a musician drew softness from a wooden flute.

Eric took a long swallow of beer and began slathering his curry. Lennart gave him a disapproving look across the table. "This much luxury feels indecent in wartime," she said.

"What wartime?" he retorted. "If we were bestirring ourselves, I might agree."

"Patience, please, Admiral Tamarin-Asmundsen. But I'm afraid that's a quality you lack. It's what I want to speak to you about."

"Carry on, Freelady." Thought of Lorna, his mother, his planet made the food suddenly ashen. "I'd like to have the Solar strategy explained to me, if any. I don't have to sit here stuffing my gut. Rather would I be out raiding."

"This government cannot condone your acting independently."

"Then let it integrate us with its forces and give us work to do!"

Lennart puckered her lips. "Quite frankly, Admiral, you are responsible for the delay in that. After your connivance at David Falkayn's escape—"

"What escape? I'm tired of repeating that he and his fellows went as commissioned Hermetian officers, on orders from me, to gather intelligence . . . because the Commonwealth has persistently neglected that elementary operation."

Lennart gave way a little. "Let's not quarrel." She constructed a smile of sorts. "I argued on your behalf, argued that you could not really be blamed for wanting news about your home, nor for your now obvious liaison with your father. Yes, I wanted you to become part of a unified command as soon as possible."

To become subordinate, you mean, subject to court martial if I misbehave again, Eric knew.

"Well, Admiral," Lennart proceeded, "what I wish to discuss today is the additional difficulties you have since created for me, for all your friends. Your appearances before civic groups, your speech on the *issues* show—they have alienated high officials. They give the impression of a chronic troublemaker, if you will excuse the language."

"Why, yes, Freelady, I am a troublemaker, or hope to be," he said. "For the Baburites, that is. I've urged that we move. If we're not ready for another pitched battle, we can still make life fairly miserable for the enemy. We can harass his commerce, we can dump megatons on his bases, till he sees 'twill pay him to disgorge Hermes and negotiate an agreement about Mirkheim."

Lennart's expression bleakened. "There can be no compromise. Otherwise Babur has gained by its aggression. It must be made to yield on every point—especially on Mirkheim, which precipitated the whole war. For that purpose, we need to build more strength than we have at present. This cannot be done overnight. Meanwhile we have to keep our forces guarding the Commonwealth against the kind of tactics you describe."

Eric thought of crowds wild with fear, demonstrating in favor of just such a policy, as well as influential commentators, businesspeople, politicians. . . . Pressure on the government, yes. But how much of the pressure was being engineered? The Home Companies had an overriding interest in protecting their properties from attack, in manufacturing unlimited armaments at fat profits, in getting the citizenry into the habit of being closely controlled by a state wherein they exercised much of the power; and the devil might have Hermes for all they cared.

Yet why did Dad talk me into making those speeches, antagonizing those authorities? He had a purpose of his own. At the time, I was too impatient, too angry to probe him. Protest came natural to me. But now I begin to see we'll have to talk further, he and I.

He couldn't continue the minuet. "Freelady," he growled, "these arguments have been batted back and forth till the meaning's knocked out of them; they've become slogans. Let's drop them. Are you and I hopelessly at odds, or can we reach an agreement?"

"You do not put it very diplomatically."

"My food's getting cold." Eric began eating.

Lennart picked at hers. "Well-ll . . . if you insist on being blunt—"

"'Tis why we're here, not? Go ahead."

"Well, then, quite simply, if you will be discreet, refrain from further public statements, prepare yourself and your following to cooperate in our larger mutual purpose—if you will prove you can do that, then I believe, I do not promise but I believe, in due course I can persuade the high command to enlist you on the terms originally proposed."

More delay. Which Dad prodded me into causing. Why?

"What is the alternative?" he asked.

Redness splotched Lennart's skin. "You cannot expect that the Commonwealth will indefinitely grant shelter and assistance to a violator of its hospitality."

Eric scowled. "I'll not take time to analyze that sentence, Freelady. But I will wonder aloud precisely what 'the Commonwealth' is. An individual, receiving another individual as a guest? Or a government? In that case, who makes up the government, the real power, and why have they received us, and why like they not my presenting a different point of view from theirs to the people at large? I thought this was a democracy."

He raised his palm. "Enough," he said. "I don't mean to irritate; and I am prepared to be realistic. You'll admit my first duty is to Hermes, that if the freeing of Hermes isn't going to be an objective, my men and I have no business in your war. But I'm willing to try working for that quietly, laying it before cabinet ministers, corporation chairmen, and union leaders rather than the public."

Lennart relaxed a trifle. "That would probably be acceptable."

"One small thing," Eric continued. "Your navy has sequestered a spacecraft belonging to my father's company. I want her released to me, assigned to my force."

She was surprised. "Why?"

"No great matter. She's my father's, and I feel under some filial obligation to him."

Actually 'twas Coya who begged me to insist on this. Muddlin' Through *isn't really van Rijn's, she's David's.*

Though . . . did Old Nick put her up to that bit of sentimentalism? Muddlin' Through *does have more capabilities than most ships.*

Lennart clutched her fork tightly. "That's another matter you and I must handle today," she said. "We on Earth knew of your parentage, but hoped Freeman van Rijn would have no attraction for you. You had never seen him. At first those hopes seemed fulfilled. But suddenly you were collaborating with him, doubtless after furtive contacts. We are quite disappointed."

"Why? Should I have disowned him? Was I ever required to file reports of all my comings, goings, and meetings? Is he not a citizen in good standing of the Commonwealth?"

"Only technically, Admiral Tamarin-Asmundsen, only technically. His has been a pernicious influence."

Which is to say, he's taken a forefront position in combating the growth of statism. Also, from time to time he's cut the Home Companies out of juicy deals.

"You can explain why at your leisure, Freelady," Eric said, resigning himself. "First, though, what about yon vessel? Blame my request on my primitive colonial hankering for tangibles."

Lennart pondered. "You would have custody, not he?"

"That's right. I'd arrange for her commissioning in the Hermetian navy. Which will bring her under the Commonwealth when our forces are integrated." *If.*

"Hm. . . . I see no major objection. It's not my department, but I could make a recommendation. In return—"

"Yes. I stop stumping." Eric filled his mouth. Now the food tasted good. Lennart would lecture him during the whole meal, but he needn't pay close attention. Instead, he could daydream about bringing Lorna here . . . sometime.

✧ ✧ ✧

Nicholas Falkayn was born in his great-grandfather's mansion in Delfinburg, which was then passing through the Coral Sea above the wrecks of an ancient battle. Labor was long, for he was big and his mother slender. Since her man was away, she denied admittance to everyone save the medics, who noted that she often had half a grin on her face, as if telling the universe to put down its pride.

Afterward she received her new child gladly. She was nursing him when van Rijn hurricaned into her room. "Hallo, hallo, harroo!" the old man boomed. "Congratugoddamnlations! Is that the pup? Ah, a whopper. He has the family looks, I see—never mind which family, Adam's maybe, they are all crumpled red worms at this age. How is you?"

"Restless," Coya complained. "They won't let me out of bed till tomorrow."

"I got some conosolium," van Rijn told her in a stage whisper, and slipped a bottle of brandy from under his jacket.

"Well, I don't know. . . . Oh, he may as well start learning early. Thanks, Gunung Tuan." She took a hearty swig.

He studied her, pale features in which the eyes still seemed too large, dark hair spread across the pillows. "I am sorry I did not come sooner. I could not get free of business."

"It must have been important."

"To the other osco. A little trader what supplies me with a particular offplanet spice. Jula, you ever heard of it? Tastes like chocolate soap to me, but they like it on Cynthia. The war, the ban on travel, he was threatened with bankrupture. I could not just give him a loan over the phone because of the tapioca-brain antitrust laws. Better he should crawl broken to the government and beg for a crust, *nie*? So we met and talked personal; and things is now hunky-dinghy."

"That was good of you."

"No, no, bah, is a bad time, and a worse time coming. If we do not stand together, we will have to stand for anything. Never mind such fumblydiddles. How you do, bellybird?"

She had long ago accepted the fact that he would never stop using the nickname he had bestowed when she was a baby. "I'm fine. My parents called an hour ago. They said to give you their regards."

"Swat my regards straight back at them." Van Rijn took a turn about the chamber. Sunlight, slanting inward, cast wave reflections on the wall behind him. "They is nice people," he said, "but like their whole generation, they do not understand an image is not enough. We is been too intellectual too long, here on Earth."

Coya kept silent. Nicholas tugged lustily at her breast.

"*Ach,* my apologetics," van Rijn said. "I should not have criticized. Everybody does his or her foolish best. But the touch of a hand— especial when Davy is gone from you—" He poked a finger toward the infant, who, temporarily sated, rolled his head that way and blew milk bubbles at him. "Ho, ho, already he has got the art of making political speeches!"

"Davy," Coya whispered. Aloud: "No, I will not bawl, no matter how he's been cheated. But Gunung Tuan, what do you think may be happening to him?"

Van Rijn tugged unmercifully on a ringlet. "How can I tell, a futtersnipe like me? Too many unknowns, darling, too many unknowns."

She half lifted the arm which was not holding her child. "Haven't you thought your way toward any answer? Provisional, yes, yes, but an answer?"

Van Rijn grimaced, banged his great bottom down on a chair, and took a long drag on the bottle he carried, which afterward he offered to Coya. She signed refusal, intently watching him.

"We got a mystery here," he said. "Some parts is plain to see, or ugly to see. Others—" He gave a shrug like a mountain shedding a snowpack. "Others make no sense. We got many paradoxes and no paradoctors. You heard me talk about this."

"Yes, but I've been so concerned about Davy, and later this kid here. . . . Talk. Please. No harm done if you repeat things. I need to be able to imagine I'm somehow working on Davy's behalf."

"Hokay," van Rijn sighed. "We go down the list." He ticked points off on his hairy fingers.

"Item: How did Babur arm for war? And why? Nobody could have foreseen Mirkheim; that was only the trigger to the landslide, what caught Babur splatfooted too and maybe made it act before it had really intended.

"Item: A couple companies of the Seven had been having dealings with Babur over the years. Why did they get no hint of that arming? Oh, *ja,* the dealings was small and unoften, and the planet is huge and strange. But nothingtheless—

"Item: What makes Babur so sure it can win? And why is it been so contemptuous of the League as to arrest your husband when he came peaceful like? Babur is not really such a mighty place. Most of it is desert.

"Item: Looks like Babur has got lots of oxygen-breathing mercenaries. You tell me how hydrogen breathers recruited those, secretly, over the worlds and the years. No, Babur had help—also with research, development, and production for its war machine— but whose, and why?

"Item: What makes Babur think it knows enough about us aliens that it can fight us and, eventfully, negotiate whatever kind of peace? Who's been telling it things?

"Item: Why should Babur occupy a neutral, small-populated, terrestroid planet—"

The phone at the bedside chimed. Coya swore and accepted. The image of van Rijn's executive secretary burst onto the screen. "Sir," he stammered, "sir, news received, a—a—a ship from Hermes, the Grand Duchess aboard, she's broadcast an announcement that she's the Hermetian government in exile . . . and—and David Falkayn is with her!"

Glory exploded in the room.

Later came grimness, as they who were there got to wondering.

XIX

A third of a century had blurred Sandra's memories of Earth. She recalled the hugeness of megalopolitan integrates, but had forgotten how daunting it could be. She had experienced totally synthetic, totally controlled environment, but only now did it come to her that this was in its way more alien than the outer planets of Maia. And in her earlier visit she had been a tourist, free to flit around, available for every adventure that came along; she had not known how heavy were the chains which Earth laid upon the prominent. Each hour was appointed, each meeting a ritual dance of words, each smile measured for its public effect. She was shown some of the remaining natural marvels, but she could only look, she could not scramble down a trail into the Grand Canyon or cast off her clothes and plunge into Lake Baikal. And everywhere, everywhere guards must accompany her.

"Who would want power, here, at this price?" she lamented once.

David Falkayn had grinned wryly and replied, "The politicians don't have that much. They put on a show, but most of the real decisions are made by owners, managers, bureaucrats, union chiefs, people who aren't conspicuous enough to need all that protection or all that secretarial prearrangement of their days. . . . Of course, the politicians think they lead."

So it was immensely good to be back among her own, aboard her flagship, the cruiser *Chronos,* cramped and sterile though the interior was. Orbiting independently around Sol, the Hermetian flotilla counted as Hermetian soil. After an unpleasant argument, she had even gotten the secret service left behind. And the men and women aboard were bred of the same lands as hers, born to the same skies, walking with the easy gait and talking with the slight burr that were hers, standing together in a loneliness that she shared.

Yet her heart stumbled. This day she would again meet Nicholas van Rijn. No matter that that was in her territory—to prevent electronic eavesdropping, if nothing else—she felt half afraid, and raged at herself for it. Eric, waiting beside her, should have been a tall comfort, but was instead almost a stranger, flesh of this stranger she must receive, reluctantly come from Earth and his Lorna. The spacemen in their white dress uniforms, their double line flanking the airlock, had also gone foreign to her; for what were they thinking behind their carefully smoothed-out faces? Ventilation muttered, touching her with a coolness that said her skin was damp.

The inner valve opened. There he stood.

Her first thought was an astonished *How homely he is.* She remembered him bulky and craggy rather than corpulent; and he did not belong in the lace-trimmed sylon blouse, iridon vest, purple culottes he had donned for this occasion. Behind him, in plain gray tunic and slacks, Falkayn was downright cruelly contrasting. *Why, he's old,* Sandra knew, and her embarrassment dropped from her. The stranger was no longer her son but that girl who had once been headstrong.

"Good greeting, gentlemen," she said as if they were anybody with whom she meant to confer.

And then van Rijn, damn his sooty heart, refused to be pitiable but grabbed her hand, bestowed a splashing kiss upon it, and pumped it as if he expected water to gush from her mouth. "Good day, good day," he bawled, "good nights too, cheers and salutations, Your Gracefulness, and may joy puff up your life. Ah, you is a sight for footsore eyes, getting better and better with time like a fine cheese. I could near as damn thank the Baburites for making you come shine at us, except they brought you trouble. For that they will pay through the noses they isn't got but we will make them buy from us at a five hundred percent markup. *Nie?*"

She disengaged herself. Cold with indignation, she presented the captain and ranking officers of the ship. Eric took over the making of formal excuses to them, since they were not invited to the wardroom for drinks before dinner. They had already been apprised of that; van Rijn's message had asked for a conference in secret. Mechanically they accepted the courtesy due them, their attention mainly on the merchant, the living legend. Could *this* be he? And what hope for Hermes might he have in his pocket?

He took Sandra's arm when she led off their son and Falkayn. She resented the familiarity but couldn't think how to break loose without a scene. He dropped his voice: "I would say, '*Weowar arronach,* '"—the phrase from the Lannachska language of Diomedes was one they had made their own during their first year together—"but is long ago too late. Let me only be glad you was happy afterward."

"Thank you." She was caught off balance anew.

They entered the wardroom. It was not large, but was outfitted in stonebark wainscoting and cyanops leather as a sign of home. Faint odors of them lingered. Pictures hung on the bulkheads, Cloudhelm seen from a wooded Arcadian hilltop, dunes in the Rainbow Desert, the South Corybantic Ocean alive with night phosphorescence. A viewscreen gave a wild contrast, the spaces which encompassed this hull, millionfold stars, billionfold Milky Way, Earth a globule almost lost among them, fragile as blue glass. Eric stepped behind the miniature bar. "I'll be your messboy," he said. "What'll you have?"

It broke a certain tension. *Gets he that skill from his father?* flashed in Sandra. *I've never been quick to transform the mood of a group.* Seeing that the men waited for her, she chose an Apollo Valley claret. Van Rijn tried a Hermetian gin and pronounced it scorchful. Falkayn and Eric took Scotch. It struck Sandra as funny—or symbolic, or something—that that should have been hauled the whole way from Edinburgh to Starfall and back.

They settled themselves on the bench which curved around the table: she, Eric, Falkayn, and, to her relief, van Rijn at the far end. But when she took out her cigar case, the trader did likewise, and insisted she have a genuine Havana. She found she had also forgotten how good that was.

Silence fell.

After a minute or two, Eric shifted in his seat, took a gulp from his drink, and said roughly, "Hadn't we better get to our business? We're here because Freeman van Rijn has a word for us. I'm anxious to know what."

Sandra tautened, met the old man's eyes, and felt as if sparks flew. "Yes," she agreed, "we've no right to dawdle. Please tell us." Her look sought Falkayn's. *We know.* And Eric's. *You and I talked about this too, after we had first embraced on Earth.*

Van Rijn streamed smoke from his nostrils. "We ought to put on a scene like from a *roman policier,* where I dump a kilo of clues on the rug and we fit them together in the shape of the villain, us having a guilting bee," he began. "But you has a fair-to-muddling notion of what must be the answer. Mainly we is got to decide what to do.

"Let me lay everything out before us anyways, to make sure we is thinking the same."

For a few breaths he sat quiet. The murmurs of the ship came to Sandra like a single thrum from a plucked string that was stretched close to breaking.

Van Rijn said: "Bayard Story of Galactic Developments, leader of the delegates of the Seven In Space to our council in Lunograd, is Benoni Strang, High Commissioner of Babur on Hermes. There is the fact what makes all the rest tumble into place."

"I suppose not, in spite of the pictures and other evidence Mother brought, I suppose not that could possibly be wrong," Eric ventured with a caution she recognized as new to him.

Van Rijn shook his head. "No. Resemblance is too close. Besides, the identity does explain so much else."

"Especially the help Babur's gotten," Falkayn put in. His tone was that of a judge handing down a sentence. "Armament, military and political intelligence, recruitment of mercenaries, direction of the entire campaign thus far—by the Seven."

"Not as a whole, surely," Eric protested, as if the shock had just now reached him.

"Oh, no," van Rijn said. "That secret could never have kept, it would have spoiled and stunk up the galaxy, did any except a few top managers know—and, of course, the human technicians they engaged and held strictly isolated. Surely, too, not many Baburites is been told."

He laid a fist on the table, big, hairy, knobbly, with power in it to smash. "Makes no difference," he stated. "Policy, orders come from the top down. The Baburites treat the League with contempt because their supreme chiefs know the League is broken from within."

"But what an enormous effort," Eric wondered. "Research, development, construction, decade after decade till a whole giant planet was ready to launch its hordes—how could that ever stay unknown? Why, the cost would show up on the accountants' tapes—"

"You underestimate the size of operations on an interstellar scale," Falkayn told him. "No underling, even a highly placed underling, can keep track of everything a big company does. Spread over several companies, the expense could easily be disguised as statistical fluctuations. It was never overwhelmingly great. Babur undoubtedly supplied most labor. Raw materials came from there as well, and from uninhabited planets and asteroids. Once the basic machine tools were built, comparatively little of the Seven's original capital was tied up. Various persons must have been getting paid fortunes, to get them to live a goodly chunk of their lives cut off from their own civilization. But a fortune to an individual is small change to a major corporation."

He added slowly: "We had an important clue to the whole thing quite some time ago. The Baburite warships seem to have electronic systems certain of whose parts can't be manufactured there, others of which deteriorate in a hydrogen atmosphere. They aren't obliged to; they could do better. We put it down to sloppy engineering, the result of haste, and quite likely the lords of Babur still believe that's the case, if anybody on that planet with scientific training has been given time to stop and think about the matter. But actually . . . the Seven would want to have a hold on their allies, something to keep them subordinate till the objectives of the Seven have been achieved. Why not leave them in chronic need of vital replacement parts which are supplied from outside?"

"The revelation of Mirkheim precipitated action," Sandra said. "'Twas simply too mighty a prize to let slip. But what is the real goal, of Babur and the Seven alike? Why go to war at all? That's what I still can't grasp."

"I am not sure anybody will ever grasp why mortals make war," van Rijn answered somberly. "Maybe someday we will find a sophont species what is not fallen from grace, and they can tell us."

Falkayn addressed the woman: "Well, we can use logic. Successful imperialism does in fact pay off for its leaders, in wealth, power, the sense of glory . . . yes, and often the sense of duty carried out, destiny fulfilled."

"Better we stay with honest greed," van Rijn remarked.

"In the case of the Baburites," Falkayn continued, "we can't be certain till a lot of intensive xenological research has been done— unless we can get hold of Strang's files on them. But we do know they resented being shoved aside in the scramble for a place on the frontier. Influential ones among them may well have decided that nothing but *force majeure* would win their species its due. And don't forget, Babur was united rather recently, by the conquering Imperial Band. I suspect the wish to go on conquering acquired a momentum, as it's done in most human cases. Also, again like human history, I suspect the rulers saw foreign adventures as a way of giving their empire a common purpose, of securing their grip on the lately acquired lands.

"Be that as it may, Babur *was* ripe to be coaxed and helped into overrunning its stellar neighborhood. I wouldn't be surprised but what Benoni Strang was the man to whom the idea first occurred, and who persuaded the masters of the Seven to undertake it. He seems to've started his career as a scientist on the planet."

Sandra nodded. Before her rose a vision of her enemy, the fire beneath his armor of courtliness, the often faraway look in his eyes, and words he had now and then let slip.

"And the motives of the Seven?" she asked, though she and Falkayn had talked this over for hours while they fared Solward.

"I already tried to list a few reasons why humans run amok," he reminded her.

"There is this too," van Rijn added. "The Home Companies is become near as damn the government of the Commonwealth. At least, the government does nothings they don't want, and every-things they do want. I, an independent, see the threat in that; but I am not hungry for power myself, I simply want people should let me be to play my little games.

"The owners of the Seven feel different. Else they would not be organized as they are. They must dread the day when the Home Companies do actively move out into space. Against that, what better than to be operating a strong government of their own? Except nothing exists ready-made out there. So they have to build an empire. Then they can afford to let the whole conspiracy be known."

"In alliance with Babur . . . yes, it makes a creepy kind of sense," Eric said. "The two races would not likely fall out with each other; they don't want the same real estate, save the kind that Mirkheim represents, and they could agree to divvy that up. Meanwhile Hermes, under totalitarian rule, would be the human power base in those parts."

He slammed the table. "No!" he shouted.

"That is agreed," van Rijn said. "What we is here today for is to grind out what we can best do. Is everybody clear on what the situation computes to? Hokay, we roll up our sleeves and get down to the nutty-gutty."

Sandra sipped her claret as if its taste of vanished sunshine could give strength. "You do not want to inform the Commonwealth," she foreknew.

"Positive not," van Rijn replied. "They see the weakness, they strike, they win—and who gets Mirkheim? The Home Companies."

"They'd move to utterly crush the Seven," Falkayn supplied. "I don't believe the empire in space that they'd win would be less vicious . . . or more likely to set Hermes free. Oh, they'd make Babur withdraw. But the temptation to impose a 'caretaker' government which'd build a corporate state in the Commonwealth's image and be properly subservient in its foreign relations—they could scarcely resist that."

Van Rijn turned toward Eric. "That is why I got you to stall the co-option of this force into Sol's," he explained. "I only had a hunch then it was best you keep your freedom of action. Now we know it is."

This too had been in Sandra's mind for endless days. Yet voicing it still felt like stepping onto a bridge which her tread must cause to break behind her. "You propose we leave, to carry out our private campaign."

"*Ja.* Not direct attacks on Babur. We hit holdings of the Seven. They got little defense for those. We can give them choice, either they pull away support from their allies so both must make peace with us, or else we ruin them."

"Let's not be overhasty," Falkayn urged. "For instance, it'd be worthwhile, it'd save lives in the long run, to alert as many independent League members as possible, and get them to join their fighting craft to ours."

"Then they'll want a part in writing the peace," Eric objected.

"Yes," Falkayn said. "Don't you think it's best if they do? That way we might salvage a little stability, a little decency."

In the meantime, Sandra thought, *the agony of Hermes goes on. But I myself dare not speak against it. I've not the wisdom to know a better way.*

Does anybody?

Again they stood in Delfinburg, David and Coya, and from a balcony of van Rijn's house looked across a nighted sea. In the room behind them, their children slept. Before them was a shadowy drop down to the yacht harbor where boats lay phantomlike at piers. Beyond, under a high wind, waves rushed to break in whiteness, rise, and march onward. Above arched a moonless sky where the stars fled among ragged clouds.

"The third time you're going," she said. "Must you really?"

He nodded. "I couldn't leave Adzel and Chee fighting alone on my planet, could I?"

"But you can leave us—" She caught herself. "No. I'm sorry. Forget that ever crossed my mind."

"This time will be the last," he vowed, and drew her toward him. Neither of them spoke: *The last indeed, if one never comes home.*

Instead, she told him, "Right. Because afterward, when and wherever you travel, you're taking me along. Me and the kids."

"If I go anyplace, sweetheart. After all the hooraw, I should be quite content to settle down on Earth and let the tropics toast my bones."

She shook her head so the dark hair swirled. "You won't. Nor will I. If nothing else, it's no world for Juanita and Nicky. You don't imagine the war will cleanse it, do you? No, the rot can only grow worse. We're getting the hell out while we still can."

"Hermes—" He was mute for a while. "Maybe. We'll see. It's a big universe."

The wind whistled cold. Chill also, and bitter, was spindrift cast off the booming waters.

✷XX✷

Abdallah Enterprises, of the Seven In Space, guarded its centrum on Hopewell against possible banditry from without and sabotage from within. But the former seemed so unlikely that a single corvette orbited the planet, whose successive crews had never encountered a worse problem than filling the time until they were relieved.

The destroyer *North Atlantis* sped inward to engage. Despite the risk, Eric found he must beam a warning: "Get out of our way before we attack you." Astounded profanity replied, then a brace of missiles and an energy beam.

The Hermetian vessel glided sidewise on thrust. The torpedoes maneuvered still more agilely, but now she had a good sight on them. A lightning storm of rays struck outward. The missiles disintegrated in fire-fountains, momentarily dazzling athwart the stars and the serene disc of the world. She did not reply in kind, for Eric wanted to conserve munitions not readily replaceable. Instead, he ordered her conned near the foe, until he was in range for energy weapons. "Kill," he said, and nuclear-powered flame leaped forth.

The corvette accelerated to escape. With less mass, she could change velocity faster. *North Atlantis* followed doggedly, smashing or warding off missiles, absorbing blast-cannon shots in armor plate, unleashing fresh bursts of her own whenever the shifting configurations of battle brought her close enough. After hours, the survivors aboard a ruin knew they could not break free, and signaled surrender.

"My compliments on your gallantry," Eric responded, "though you might ask yourselves if your cause was worth it. You may take lifeboats to Hopewell. I advise you do not bring them down at Abdallah City."

He already knew, from communication, what had happened there. Accompanying him on his voyage, *Muddlin' Through* had left him to his warfare and herself entered atmosphere.

Falkayn uttered the broadcast words that he knew would bring him into peril of his life. "Attention, attention. . . . Your owners have conspired with the rulers of Babur to bring war. . . . The Free Hermetian navy is about to demolish your company installations. Evacuate immediately. . . ."

Aerial vehicles swarmed aloft. But *Muddlin' Through* was not the specialized speedster through the void, well-nigh helpless above a planet, which *Streak* had been. Trade pioneers must be prepared for trouble in any environment. The spacecraft descended in great spirals, from which again and again she swooped to dodge a missile or blaze at an opponent.

Before Falkayn, as he sat in the pilot's chair, land and sea revolved crazily, clouds streamed past through day-bright azure, fighting machines flashed across vision like wind-flung raindrops. This was no space combat, which computers alone could direct. Movements were too fast, actions too unforeseeable. He meshed his intuition with Muddlehead's logic, sank his personality into his ship, and steered. Engines growled, air outside shrilled. His nostrils caught a thundery tang of ozone.

"Hoo and ha!" van Rijn's voice bawled from the weapons control turret. Gleefully he tracked, sighted, fired, manning the entire system, sending vessel after vessel to its meteoric grave. "Oh, ho, ho! Casting bull's eyes at me, is you? Smack right back at you with a wet loincloth! Ha-ah, that was a near miss at us, good shooting, boy, only not quite good as this, by damn! Whoo-hoo! Brocken and brimstone, here goes another!"

In the end, *Muddlin' Through* hung alone; and there was silence in heaven about the space of half an hour.

Underneath her stretched a land that had been rich. Miners, builders, industrialists had ripped and befouled it till its river coursed poisoned among dumps and slag heaps, pavements and waste outlets, bearing death to the sea. Few human colonists of Hopewell had protested. This was not Earth, they still had plenty of room, nobody need make his home in the place that ground forth prosperity. Besides, the local government belonged to Abdallah Enterprises. In the middle of the desert it had created, the centrum raised splendid towers above many-colored sleeknesses. Looking down, Falkayn thought, *This was a grand era in its way. I too will miss it.*

Cars fled in flocks. At his height they were like midges. He must make an effort to remember that each one bore fear, bewilderment, crushed hopes, longing for loves who were elsewhere and terror on their behalf. War scrubbed such peculiarities out of consciousness. He had not heart to speak further to this world, but let a recording repeat itself. "Free Hermes is striking at the Seven, Babur's allies. Our campaign will end when the war against the Commonwealth and the occupations of Hermes and Mirkheim do. Convey our message." He reflected that someday his wife and children might be likewise fleeing; for when would civilization in the future know safety?

His time allowance was generous. Nothing had stirred for fifteen minutes when he ordered a torpedo released.

Fifty kilotons sufficed. A fireball blossomed and rifted, smoke and dust roiled after to rise in a monstrous pillar that spread out in an ice-fringed toadstool cap, reverberations toned through the spaceship, and when sight came back, a crater lay in the land, from which a few twisted frameworks lifted like dead men's fingers.

"Take orbit at ten radii," Falkayn directed, "and we'll wait for *North Atlantis* to finish her business."

After Hopewell was once more a blue-and-white loveliness among the stars, he met with his shipmates, van Rijn and engineer Tetsuo Yoshida. The merchant was still gleeful. "Halloo, harroo," he chortled, "how I feel youthed! We had what Aristotle called a cathartic, *ja,* and gives me an abysmal appetite. Suppose I quickroast a nice Virginia ham with sweet potatoes and Caesar salad—and what would you two like for lunch?"

"Later," Falkayn said. "I'm not hungry."

Van Rijn considered him. "Your conscience is panging, ha? But that is silly, boy. We is vented a lot of beast in us by bashing what well deserved bashing. Is it a sin if we enjoy? Me, I wish we could make more raids."

Yoshida lifted his brows. "I would not object personally," he said, "but unless I am mistaken, Freeman van Rijn, you gave your fellow planners a promise to confine yourself to this single action, if they would agree to your doing that much."

He's too valuable to risk, Falkayn remembered: *first as a leader of our overall strategy, afterward as our chief negotiator. My job from here on is to convey him safely to the headquarters he will set up, and then act as his special advisor and deputy.*

Damn him, though, he's right. Being in battle ourselves was something we inwardly needed. Even I, even I.

"*Ja,* is true," van Rijn grumbled. "So we got weeks, maybe months where we do hardly nothing but sit snuggled in our own fat. You got ideas how we can put our minds to some good use in between happenings?"

"Poker," said Muddlehead.

Experts agreed that it would take considerable time and money, and no few lives, to start Mirkheim producing afresh. However, immensely precious stocks of metals and supermetals lay already cast in ingots, awaiting shipment out. The Baburite occupation force received instructions to let the Stellar Metals Corporation have this on a profit-sharing basis. Stellar, in turn, contracted with Interstar Transport to carry it to the numerous markets.

In the deeps of space, ships which had been lurking and watching drew alongside the freighters, matched hyperdrive phase, and signaled a wish to send people aboard. Suspecting no evil, the captains did. But those who entered, grinning, were armored and armed. In each case, they took swift possession.

Crews were sent off in lifeboats, bearing word that Free Hermes was confiscating both cargo and carrier. The losses to Timebinders Insurance were staggering—and also to Stellar and Interstar, for their coverage extended to less than half of these values.

Men landed in wilderness areas of the planet Ramanujan and flitted inconspicuously to rendezvous in the city Maharajah. On an appointed night, they converged on a cluster of towers which were the core of XT Systems. Overpowering the guards, they set explosives to wreck equipment which would take years to replace and destroy data stores which could never be replaced. Prisoners whom they released afterward said they had identified themselves as a commando of Free Hermes.

XT had been at a nexus of the global economy. As such, it had made the government its servant. Now massive unemployment came, bankruptcies, dislocations, civic upheaval. The cry arose for legislators whose loyalty was to Ramanujan itself, and Parliament dissolved on a vote of no confidence.

⁂

Sanchez Engineering was engaged in an ambitious project on barren but mineral-rich St. Jacques, which would make its resources readily available to the humans dwelling on its sister world Esperance. The leaders of the colony, who were nobody's hirelings, had written a stiff penalty for nonfulfillment into the contract.

Suddenly the technicians called a strike, alleging that the war posed too great a hazard. In vain did the directors of Sanchez reveal what detectives learned, that the union bosses had taken a whopping bribe. No legal proof was available, at least not without disastrously prolonged litigation; and if this went against them, the persons accused need only withdraw themselves from Esperancian jurisdiction.

"The answer's easy," said their spokesman around his cigar to the board chairman of Sanchez. "Use your influence to end the fighting."

But at best, the corporation would remain gravely injured.

Galactic Developments owned a moon of Germania, which it had made into an entrepot for that stellar neighborhood. There, after a short, sharp battle, landed ships, whose crews efficiently looted the treasures before lifting back into space and bombarding the installations.

They did not even pretend to be Hermetian. They were from the independents Sindbad Prospecting and the Society of Venturers, out to punish the Seven for an unholy alliance with Babur.

The Germanian space police made no move throughout. Later the government denied complicity, declared it had been taken by surprise, and took charge of the remaining assets which Galactic Developments had in this system "pending an arrangement which, in view of the present emergency, will be more in the public interest."

The Seven struck back. Baburite warships accompanied theirs. The announcement was that Babur thus exercised its right and duty to suppress piracy. Few beings believed it.

Hammer blows fell on bases of the hostile companies. But these, forewarned, had for the most part been abandoned. Damage was thus comparatively small. The character of the typical independent operator—else he would long since have entered one of the great combines—was such that he counted it as an investment. He might go broke; but if not, his gamble should pay off richly. A share in Mirkheim, reduced competition from the Seven, plunder along the way . . . he saw opportunity before him, and jumped.

Privateers and Hermetians alike could resupply on a hundred different worlds, attack wherever they chose, and vanish back into vastness. Babur had no such advantage. Seeing the forces of the Imperial Band dispersed and under fire, the Commonwealth naturally launched probing assaults of its own, which intensified with time and lack of effective response. As for the Seven, the whole intricate structure whereon they had based their might was crumbling. After Timebinders Insurance stopped payment on claims, they knew they must make what terms they could.

Spring was full-blooming in Starfall when the patriot army stormed it. The attack was two-pronged. Christa Broderick's city and farmland followers, who throughout the winter had held themselves to sniping and sabotage while they gathered strength, appeared in the streets. They fell on all the mercenaries they could find, surrounded such strongholds as the Hotel Zeus, and commenced bombardment. Meanwhile the guerrillas whom Adzel and Chee Lan had been leading in the Arcadian Hills and the Thunderhead Mountains entered from the west and moved to take Pilgrim Hill. A wild variety of cars, trucks, and buses had carried them from their fastnesses over the valleys, protected by atmospheric fighters which the ducal navy had sent down. Now that navy was in combat with the enemy's guardian ships—off behind a cruelly soft blue sky—and the fight for the city must be waged on the ground.

Must be. As long as the occupation forces refused to surrender, it was necessary to dig them out, body by body. A nuclear warhead fired from orbit would annihilate them, if the Free Hermetian fleet was victorious, but at cost of the city. The hope that their side would win in space, and thus hold the entire planet hostage, kept Benoni Strang's men in battle—that, and the fear of retaliation among those of them who were native born and had freely served his revolutionary regime.

Adzel trotted along the esplanade. It thudded to his hoofs. In the crook of an arm he carried a blast rifle. Perched on his shoulders, Chee manned a heavier energy weapon. Most of the troop loping wolfishly behind bore slugthrowers, tools for hunting such as every outback household possessed. The artillery that trundled among them—cannon, mortars, rocket launchers—used chemical explosives. It had been furtively made in hundreds of small factories and home workshops, according to plans retrieved from public data banks before the first Baburite soldier landed.

Coordinating the whole effort, across the world and at last with the armed return of Grand Duchess Sandra, had been the truly difficult task. The anger to power it was already there, in many a Traver as well as in Followers and Kindred. Government by terror does not work on people used to liberty, if they have hope of deliverance. And Strang's most rigid censorship could not keep hidden the fact that Babur's cause was waning.

Overhead in sunlight, flyers dueled. Seen from below, they were bright flecks, unreal as stars. Reality was the hardness underfoot, sweat, harshly drawn breath, the taste of the fact that soon one might be dead but there was no way left to turn back. On the right flowed the Palomino, brown and murmurous, its opposite shore rising in green slopes where villas lay scattered and fallaron trees bloomed golden. On the left, older houses stood close-ranked, deserted, their windows blind. Ahead swelled the hill, steeps and terraces, gardens and bough-roofed walks, to the gray bulk of the Old Keep. Beyond it lifted the lattice of Signal Station and a pastel glimpse of the New Keep. Sounds of gunfire drifted from the east.

"You're shivering," Chee said to Adzel.

"Today I must again make myself kill," the Wodenite answered.

John Falkayn quickened his pace and drew alongside. Like the other humans, he was unkempt, grimy, and gaunt, clad in whatever rough clothes he happened to own, his uniform a blue band wrapped around the left biceps. Sewn to it was the insigne of a colonel, cut out of sheet metal. He pointed. "We should turn off up yonder path," he said. "'Twill bring us around to a grove of millionleaf which'll give us some cover."

"Aye." Adzel took that direction.

Bullets began to whinner past, followed by the crack of their rifles. A man in the ranks screamed, clutched his stomach, went to his knees. His fellow irregulars drew further apart and advanced crouched, zigzag, as Chee had drilled them. Several flung themselves prone to return the fire before hurrying on.

It grew heavier when they reached the bosquet, a buzzing that ripped through foliage, thudded into wood and sometimes meat. Energy beams flashed from the Old Keep and back against it, trailing thunder and acridness. Adzel trotted about, calming his men, disposing them in formation. An occasional slug, nearly spent, bounced off his scales. Chee crouched low, a minute target, wasting no shots of her own across this distance.

"The enemy are concentrated in the stout stone building," Adzel said. "Our first move will be to neutralize it."

"Destroy, you mean?" John Falkayn said. "Oh, merciful Christ, no. The records, the mementos—half our past is in there."

"Your whole stinking future is here," Chee snapped.

Positioned, the artillery cut loose. Guns roared, rockets whooshed, explosives detonated in racket, smoke, and flinders. Slowly the Old Keep crumbled. At last from the wreckage stepped a Merseian waving a white flag.

"Kittredge, have your unit secure this place," Adzel said. "The rest of us, on to the New Keep." He lifted his weapon and charged. Men howled as they followed. "*Namu Amida Butsu*," he whispered.

"Ya-ah!" screamed Chee. Her gun began to throw its bolts. They crashed lurid around the barricade which blocked the main door. A cyclic slugthrower hailed forth its reply. Adzel staggered. Chee swiveled her weapon past the right side of his torso and centered her fire. Flame geysered. A burning man climbed over the barricade, mindlessly shrieking, fell on the turf outside and sprattled like an overturned beetle, still burning. Adzel recovered and pounded onward.

He reached the rude fortification. Timbers, tables, sandbags, rocks came apart beneath his flailing hoofs. He leaned across and laid about him with his clubbed blaster. From his back, Chee sent narrow beams, finickily aimed. Surviving defenders broke and fled.

Adzel pursued them down echoing corridors. A squad dashed from a side room. His tail sent them tumbling. "Come on, you sons!" John Falkayn shouted to his troops. "Is he going to do it all?" They entered like a tidal wave.

Grim small battles ramped throughout the edifice. From its rotunda, the attackers recoiled. There every entrance had an obstruction, behind which men crouched shoulder to shoulder, firing—Strang's

Hermetians. Dead lay thick in the halls after that charge; the wounded begged for help which nobody could bring.

In a room where councillors had met, Adzel and Chee gathered their officers. Blood smeared the Wodenite's scales and dripped from between them, scorch marks dulled his flanks, the dragon head was blackened by smoke. "I think we should offer them amnesty if they will lay down their arms," he said.

John Falkayn spat. "When my sister's husband died under their arrest, God knows how? Never."

"Besides," Chee observed, "if I'm not much mistaken about human affairs, you'll have trouble enough after this war without them in your body politic."

Assent rasped forth. "Very well," said Adzel. "However, I refuse to send unsupported infantry again. And if we destroy the structure from outside, as we did the Old Keep, we'll exhaust ammunition that will be needed in the lower city, not to mention killing disabled people of ours. Suggestions?"

Chee bounced in her saddle. "Yes," she said.

The enemy occupied the galleries beneath the dome . . . but not the outside of it. The Cynthian climbed that and planted a shaped charge which blew a hole. Perched on the edge, she sprayed the interior with fire. The soldiers in gray uniforms must seek shelter away from their breastworks. Adzel led a rush across these, and fighting became hand-to-hand.

The Wodenite himself found Benoni Strang dying of a gut shot, recognized him from pictures, and bent down to learn what he could and give what comfort he might. Cradled in those great arms, the man looked dimly upward and gasped, "Listen. Tell them. Why should you not tell them? You're not human, it's nothing to you. I brought everything about . . . I, from the first . . . for the sake of Hermes, only for the sake of Hermes. A new day on this world I love so much . . . Tell them. Don't let them forget. There will be other days."

The ducal navy was victorious in its home space because, while it had considerable help from the independent merchants, Babur had recalled much of its Hermetian force to the sun Mogul. This was after the Seven had—piecemeal, in chaos—withdrawn as allies.

Thereafter the defeat of Babur would have hinged only on time and determination; and the lack of replacements for rapidly deteriorating parts of ships would have made the time fairly short. The Imperial Band did not surprise van Rijn when they declined a finish fight. Thirty years before, they had shown the intelligence to cut their losses on Suleiman. Nevertheless he admitted gaining astonished respect for them when they sent messengers directly to him. Had they all along known that much about Technic civilization?

The meeting took place near Mirkheim, between a pair of ships. *Chronos* came battle-ready from Hermes, bearing him and Sandra. (David Falkayn and Eric Tamarin-Asmundsen stayed behind in command of the united fleet, prepared if need be to exact vengeance.) The Baburite vessel humbly bore no weapons. They orbited amidst uncountable diamond suns while images passed back and forth between them.

The little being stood foursquare before the scanners and spoke into a vocalizer. To Sandra it no longer appeared ugly. And was it just her imagination that found sorrow in the flat syllables?

"—We were used. We understand that we ourselves were among those who used us. . . . Let you and we make peace."

"What of the Commonwealth?" she replied.

"It mounts its onslaught. But as yet it is not strong."

"Hold on," said van Rijn, and switched off sound transmission. He turned to the woman. "The boojer speaks right. The Home Companies would fight a total war if possible, so they may gain what the Seven has lost. But if we, Hermetians and independents, stop fighting, if we use our influence against more war by anybodies, *ja,* hint that we and Babur together will resist—the public wish to go on spending lives and money should puffle away on Earth and Luna till not even the Commonwealth government can continue."

Troubled, she said, "I can't believe in suddenly putting ourselves on the side of these . . . creatures. After what they've done."

His words came whetted. "Can you instead believe in more people killed? And is not a question of getting buttock to buttock with the Baburites, what would freeze ours and sizzle theirs anyway. Is simply a question of we stop hostilities quick, on terms everybody can live with, and then lean on the Commonwealth to squash its 'unconditional surrender' clabberbrains."

Sandra paced around the bridge. How her muscles longed for a horse, a surf, a trail among glaciers. The viewscreen gave her mere immensities. Van Rijn sat like a spider, puffing a churchwarden pipe whose reek stung her nostrils. In the viewscreen frame the nonhuman shape waited patiently.

"What should we propose today?" she asked.

"We is talked about it before often enough," he answered. "Now that we see how anxious Babur is to make a deal with us, I say let's pick these quidbits out of our chaffing.

"The Commonwealth government can never recognize the independents as rightful agents, no more than it could ever really recognize the League. *Hemel!* Something besides another government having the right to decide things? Much too dangerous. Might get folks at home wondering if they do need politicians and bureaucrats on top of themselves.

"So: You, heading the Hermetian state, has got to front for us. Like you originally proposed, Hermes takes over Mirkheim, under a treaty that says you license legitimate companies from everywhere. A reasonable tax on that ought to repay what you lost in the war, plus a little extra for buying offplanet goodies like heavy industrial equipment and Genever. Babur disarms. Its fleet will soon be no use anyways, without supplies from outside; and the Commonwealth would not make peace if Babur was going to reengineer its forces. Hermes, though, will guarantee its safety plus a fair share in Mirkheim." Van Rijn chortled. "Babur becomes your protectorate! Musical chairmanships, *nie?*"

Sandra halted, folded her arms, caught his gaze, and inquired pointedly, "What about yourself? You and your buccaneer companies?" *O Pete, be with me now.*

But he made no demand, he only looked off into the Milky Way and said, rough-toned, "Is not your problem. Give those of us that want, a chance at Mirkheim, and everything else is a bone we gnaw between ourselves. Many bones must go dry before what is dead can rise again."

He smote his knee. "Ready to start bargaining on this basement?" he challenged.

Dumbstruck, she nodded. He swung back to the stranger.

�✸XXI✸

Early during the triumph and toil, reunion and wrangling, merry-making and mourning, there was held a private party at Windy Rim on Hermes. It was to say farewell.

Two of those who came would soon be departing together for Sol aboard *Chronos,* David Falkayn and Eric Tamarin-Asmundsen. However, they had been separated for weeks, each busy with different shards of the huge confusion. This was their first chance to talk at length since shortly after the armistice. Following dinner, they drew apart from the others for a while.

The room they chose was a study, enclosed in wood panels of beautiful grain, shelves of codices in leather bindings, ancestral portraits, a gun rack, a desk whereon many high decisions had been written. A window stood open to the young night. Air drifting in was cool, fragrant with blossoms, alive with the sound of the river in the canyon below.

Falkayn hoisted his tumbler. "Cheers." Rims clinked. The men settled down in deep armchairs and drank, a taste of peat smoke from the birthworld of their race.

"Well," Falkayn said, "so you're the new Hermetian ambassador."

"Oh, no," Eric replied. "By all accounts, Runeberg conducted our affairs very competently throughout the war. We want to keep him on. My title will be special envoy, head of our negotiators with the Commonwealth."

"Why you? No offense, of course, but what experience have you had at that sort of thing?"

Eric grinned crookedly. "I wondered too. In fact, I objected with a deal of noise. But Mother insisted. 'Tis a matter of politics. I *am* the heir apparent, the biggest name Hermes could send save for her, and she's got her hands full and overflowing here. That should carry weight on Earth—a token that we're determined about the peace settlement we want. And, uh, it should help at home likewise, that the Grand Ducal house is still concerning itself with crucial matters."

"I see." Falkayn studied the homely, strong countenance. "Also, and this time no flattery, I think you're a good choice, you'll be much more than a figurehead. The blood of Sandra Tamarin and Nicholas van Rijn . . . yes."

Eric flushed. "Maybe. Still, I'm not trained for diplomacy, I know not the ins and outs and roundabouts. . . . David, friend, will you help me? Can you?"

"How?"

"Oh, advice and—I know not. You do." Eric dropped his glance. "If, uh, if you'll not be too busy yourself."

"I'll have plenty to keep me out of mischief, for certain. In effect, I'll take over the Solar Spice & Liquors Company, try to keep it afloat through all the hooraw to come." Falkayn sipped, set his drink down, and reached for his pipe. "On second thought, that'll keep me in mischief."

Eric stared. "What about Freeman van Rijn?"

"Damn him, he'll be charging around through space, probably for years to come, mending broken fences and, I have no doubt, making new ones out of pieces stolen from the competition. I wish— Ah, well, I can't do that anyway, me a family man." Falkayn loaded tobacco before continuing. "But yes, Eric, I'll find time and energy somewhere to give you what help I can. Your job is more important than mine. In fact, I might not choose to do mine, if I didn't think it had some value to yours—I mean to getting back some stability throughout what we are pleased to call civilization. A strong private company under the right leadership can contribute toward that end." He started fire and puffed smoke. "For a while," he finished.

"What imply you?" Eric asked.

Falkayn shrugged. "I'm coming to share Gunung Tuan's opinion. The wound to the old order of things is too deep, and I don't see anything to replace it that'll be worth having. We can buy time, you and I, maybe as much as a few decades before our splints and bandages give way. Meanwhile you can batten down on Hermes. And I . . . I can look for a place to begin afresh."

"I never knew you so glum, David," Eric said in a distressed voice.

Falkayn smiled, a genuine smile though not that of a young man. "Why, I'm basically optimistic, as you should be. Come the necessity, I expect we and those we care about will respond like survivor types. And until then, we can find a lot of happiness." He leaned forward and lightly punched his companion's shoulder. "Think. You're going to Lorna and marry her. I'm going to Coya and our kids." He raised his glass. "Here's to the lot of them."

"Here indeed," Eric responded with regained eagerness.

"They're what life is all about, right?" said Falkayn, and drank.

Van Rijn and Sandra wandered out onto the terrace. Light fell soft from the house, soon losing itself in clear darkness. Above bulks of trees and hilltops reached a sky full of stars, Milky Way, glimmer of a nebula and of a sister galaxy. They reached the parapet and lingered. Beneath them ran the river, dimly agleam, a breath from it blowing upward. The water belled.

Van Rijn slurped from his beer tankard and threw a sidewise glance at Sandra. She stood tall in a deep blue gown that seemed to make her part of the night. Unbound, her hair flowed below her shoulders and gave back what glow there was. "By damn, but you is a looker yet!" he exclaimed. "You is got too much stuff in you for being just a sovereign."

She evaded his intent by replying, while she gazed outward, "I may not be that much longer."

"I heard you got some shatterbrained list of demands dumped on your head." He was very lately back from Babur, where he had been overseeing the dismantling of the Seven's facilities. She had requested it, knowing how few men would be able to make sure that nothing was kept slyly in reserve, somewhere in an entire planetary system.

"It took the form of a petition. But the real meaning's unmistakable. Christa Broderick's organization has tasted victory, and does have a claim on our gratitude. Also, the revolutionary terror weakened Kindred and Followers, the whole structure of the domains."

"You is still got plenty who is personal loyal to you, *nie?* Including the navy."

"No doubt," she said. "But do I, does anybody in his right mind want to see Hermes a police state ruling a population of helots? The upper classes would have to sacrifice their own freedoms to maintain that, you know.

"Every side will bargain, and maneuver, and orate, and distort the issues beyond telling what shape they ever had. Because more than two sides are involved. I can't guess how many factions will spring up. The quarreling will belike go on for years. In the end, however—Well, it does give me hope that Broderick agrees we can't hold a constitutional convention till we have a firm peace. Then I fear we must. My guess at the moment is that Hermes will nominally still be a duchy, but in practice a republic.

"It may be for the best. Who knows?"

"I doubt it will make much difference in the long running," van Rijn said. "Autocrats, plutocrats, timocrats, bureaucrats, technocrats, democrats, they all tell everybody else at gunpoint what to do. We is bound into an age of crats." He sighed like a receding tide. "Was a good holiday from that while we had it, *nie?* Till mankind went and spoiled things. Back to school, children of Adam. Maybe after a few more whippings you will learn water not only flows downhill, it reaches bottom."

She turned her head toward his promontory of a profile. "Mean you the Polesotechnic League is done for?"

He nodded heavily. "*Ja.* Oh, we will keep the name. That is what I will dash about for, like a toad in a pot, to patch the old garment so it will hold off the coldest winds till those who is close to me has reached a safe port where they won't need so many metaphors. Afterward I suppose will still be held solemn councils of the League for another century, till some Napoleon type without no sense of humor comes along and ends the farce."

Almost of itself, her right hand reached to touch his left, which gripped the parapet. "How can you be sure, Nick?" she asked mutedly. "Yes, the Seven are crippled, they may well go under. But the Home Companies are if anything stronger than ever, and likewise your independents, not?"

He gave her a wry look which lasted. "Where does the strength come from?" he said. "For the Home Companies it is the Commonwealth, which is been kicked into starting a big military establishment and will not forget that kick. The independents, they is allied with *you.*

"In both cases, like what the Seven was trying for, a government.

"Don't you see, the League was once a free association of

entrepreneurs what offered goods and services but did not force them on nobody. It is not private outfits what fights wars and operates concentration camps, it is governments, because governments is those organizations what claims the right to kill whoever will not do what they say. Corporations, unions, political parties, churches, God knows what, it makes no matter who gets hold of the machinery of government, they will use it and use it and use it.

"*Ach,* we mortals is not wise enough to trust with power.

"The League . . . it was split before this trouble came out in the open. Now it is had a civil war. Its first. Strang seduced the Seven into that, but he could not have done it if they had not already had their legs spread. We can temporary fake the shadow of what was, but the body is gone. And the spirit went before then, away back when men who had been free began grabbing for control over other men."

Van Rijn's vision lost itself in the night. "No more important private decisions," he predicted. "Instead, authority takes over. Slogans substitute for thinking, beginning with the intellectuals but soon percolating down to the ordinary working man. Politicians appoint themselves magicians, who by passing laws and jacking up taxes and conjuring money out of thin air can guarantee everybody a soft ride through life. The favored businesses and institutions divide up the territory and strangle out anybody what might have something new. For every shipwreck what government brings about, the cure is more government. Power grows till its appetite is too great for filling on a single planet. Also, maybe troubles at home can be exported on bayonet points. But somehow, the real barbarians is never those that is fought, until too late. . . .

"War. War. War.

"I would advise we pray to the saints, except I wonder if the saints is left us."

He tossed off half the contents of his tankard. "Whoo hoo, but I is been talking! Like yonder stream guggles into the sea, what stays just as salt as it always was, ha?" He laughed. "We should not waste good drinking time God has given us. See, a moon is rising."

Sandra tugged his sleeve till he faced her. "Believe you seriously what you were saying, Nick?"

"Well, might not be too bad on Hermes for the next couple generations, if you can put your new regime on a short leash."

"I mean in general. . . . See you," she forced out, "I've had some-what the same thoughts and—What intend you to do about it?"

"I told you. Patch up how best I can."

"But afterward? If we get an afterward in our lifetimes."

Suddenly, strangely shy, he looked away. "I don't know. I expect the patching will be fun, you understand. Else maybe I would not try, old tired man like I am. Later—is an interesting question. Maybe later Muddlehead and me—I will be using *Muddlin' Through,* and should ought to have many a stiff poker game aboard—maybe we will lead a little expedition quite outside of known space, for whatever we may find."

"I envy you that," she blurted.

He swung back. "Why, by damn, sweetling," he exploded, "why you not come too?"

She raised her hands as if to fend him off. "Oh, no, impossible."

"Bah!" He made a chopping gesture. "How would you violate conservation of energy if you did? Conservation of momentousness, perhaps. But suppose in five, ten years you abdicate. Let Eric take over before time turns him doddery. You take the Long Trail with me!" He drained his tankard, clashed it down, and slapped her bottom. His right hand waved widely across heaven. "A universe where all roads lead to roaming. Life never fails us. We fail it, unless we reach out."

She drew back from him a little while she laughed a little. "No, do stop, Nick. We came not together for discussing absurd plans—or politics or philosophy—only for being together. I need a drink."

"Me too," said van Rijn. "Hokay, we will drink that moon down and the sun up, we will sing rowdy songs and try if we can dance a galliard to a Bach oratorio, we will not be solemn fools but honest ones, only you will remember what we spoke of." He offered his arm. She took it and they returned to the house of her fathers.

Adzel went lurching along a cliffside path to the river, a five-liter mug in his grasp which his freedom fighters had given him. He had repeatedly filled it with martinis. You could hear him singing a kilometer away, "*Baw-aw beedle eet bee dum bee bow,*" like a cheerful thunderstorm. At the water's edge, he saw Chee Lan seated on a rock, and halted. "Ho. I thought I would find you here."

The Cynthian dipped her cigarette holder to him. The glow at its end traced a tiny red comet-streak. "And I took for granted you'd arrive when you'd tanked away enough to get sentimental," she purred. "You big blundlebumber."

Adzel loomed slightly unsteady athwart woods, water, sky. Dawn was close. Overhead, between canyon walls that still were hulks of night, the stars were paling and whiteness mounted to eastward. The stream shone, glinted, swirled over bars and foamed past stones, on its way among boulders and gnarly trees. Its voice clanged laughter-ful from cliff to cliff. He took long breaths of the cold moist air which flowed above, the odors of upland summer.

"Well, our last chance," he said. "Day after this, we embark on our courtesy rides home to our planets. I look forward, yes, obviously . . . but those were good years. Were they not? I will miss my partners. I told Davy so. I got a phone patch through to Muddlehead at Williams Field and told it so too. It answered that it is not programmed to be touched; but I wonder, I wonder. Here comes your turn. No mercy, small person." A hand descended, amply large to close around her. Quadrupedal, holder jaunty between her teeth, she arched her back to receive the caress, which was very gentle. "Come to Woden sometime," he urged. "Your folk have spacecraft. You will be investing in such ventures, and getting hog-rich. Come visit me."

"In that gravity and glare?" she snorted.

"That wild bright openness where the winds run loose, horizons endlessly before us but also flowers underfoot, a land that is the living Nirvana—*Aiyu*, Chee, I know I babble. Yet I would like to share with you as much of it as you can feel."

"Why don't you come to me instead? We could rig a set of impellers for you to get a hint of treetop faring."

"Do you think I can appreciate it?"

"I should hope you'd have that much wit. Light across a sea of leaves, but down below full of shapes and mysteries, a cry of color on wings and petals, a glen where a rill comes joyful—" The Cynthian shook herself. "*Dood en ondergang*, you've got me doing it!"

Adzel smiled around his fangs. "At least we are agreed we should make an occasional rendezvous, to swap lies about bygone times," he said.

Chee discarded her cigarette butt, ground it out on the rock where she sat, and considered whether to add more narcotic to what she had already taken. Emerald in the mask of her face, her eyes went to Adzel's stein; her tail waved away prudence and she recharged the holder from a pouch at her waist.

After she had struck fire, she stated rapidly: "Let's be rational for a moment, if you will pardon the expression. ·I think we will be rejoining forces in years to come, you and I, simply because circumstances won't allow us to enjoy our otium. We can't go home to what we left when we were young; it may still be, but we aren't, nor is the rest of the cosmos. We'll be wealthy, powerful, me more in absolute terms but you more relative to your society . . . while outside, the order of things that the Earthfolk brought goes tumbling down into the Earthfolk's flaming hell.

"Old Nick knows. He'll be doing what he can, maybe just because he never left a game while a chip remained to him, but anyhow doing what he can against the evil days.

"Cynthia, Woden—will we sit by and allow them to become victims after we're snugly dead? Or will we spend our money and knowledge working to make them ready?"

She blew smoke at the huge head. "I don't relish the prospect," she admitted. "Ya-ah, how I curse it, I who imagined I'd retire to domestic comfort and expensive fun! But we'll be conferring, Adzel, for the rest of our days, yes, yes, we will."

A rippling went the length of the dragon. "I fear you are right," he said. "I have had such forebodings myself, though I tried to dismiss them because they bind one to the Wheel. . . . Well, certain things matter more than one's immediate salvation."

Chee grinned, a flash in the strengthening light. "Let's neither play noble," she replied. "We enjoyed the trader game as long as that lasted. The power game is less amusing, and at best it merely serves to hold off what is worse. Regardless, we can enjoy it too. And, who knows, could be that our races will build us a monument after they've started a whole new course of history for all the planets."

"Oh, we'd better keep a sense of proportion," Adzel cautioned. "We may perhaps help them survive. What they do a thousand years hence—return then and see. Reality is more big than we can imagine."

"Of course," Chee Lan said. "And now suppose we drop the subject, go join the rest, and have a last round of jollity before breakfast."

"Excellent thinking, old shipmate," Adzel answered. "Hop aboard." She leaped to his outstretched arm and thence to his back. Above the cliffs, a few eastern clouds turned red.

INTRODUCTION

The rest would appear to be everyone's knowledge: how at last, inevitably, the secret of Mirkheim's existence was ripped asunder; how the contest for its possession brought on the Babur War; how that struggle turned out to be the first civil war in the Commonwealth and gave the Polesotechnic League a mortal wound. The organization would linger on for another hundred Terran years, but waning and disintegrating; in truth, already it had ceased to be what it began as, the proud upbearer of liberty. Eventually the Commonwealth, too, went under. The Troubles were only quelled with the rise and expansion of the Empire—and its interior peace is often bought with foreign violence, as Ythri and Avalon have learned. Honor be forever theirs whose deathpride preserved for us our right to rule ourselves!

Surely much of that spirit flies through time from David and Coya Conyon/Falkayn. When they led to this planet humans who would found new homes, they were doing more than escaping from the chaos they foresaw; they were raising afresh the ancient banner of freedom. When they obtained the protection and cooperation of Ythri, they knew—it is in their writings—how rich and strong a world must come from the dwelling together of two races so unlike.

Thus far the common wisdom. As for the creation and history of our choth upon Avalon, that is in *The Sky Book of Stormgate*.

Yet Hloch has somewhat more to give you before his own purpose is fully served. As you well know, our unique society did not come easily into being. Especially in the early years, misunderstandings, conflicts, bitterness, even enmity would often strike talons into folk.

Have you heard much of this from the human side? Belike not. It is fitting that you learn.

Hloch has therefore chosen two final tales as representative. That they are told from youthful hoverpoints is, in his mind, very right.

The first of them is the last that Judith Dalmady/Lundgren wrote for *Morgana*. Though she was then in her high old age, the memories upon which she was drawing were fresh.

—Hloch of the Stormgate Choth
The Earthbook of Stormgate

WINGLESS

As far as we know—but how much do we really know, in this one corner of this one galaxy which we have somewhat explored?— Avalon was the first planet whereon two different intelligent species founded a joint colony. Thus much was unforeseeable, not only about the globe itself, whose mysteries had barely been skimmed by the original explorers, but about the future of so mixed a people. The settlers began by establishing themselves in the Hesperian Islands, less likely to hold fatal surprises than a continent. And the two races chose different territories.

Relations between them were cordial, of course. Both looked forward to the day when men and Ythrians would take over the mainlands and dwell there together. But at first it seemed wise to avoid possible friction. After all, they had scarcely anything in common except more or less similar biochemistries, warm blood, live birth, and the hope of making a fresh start on an uncorrupted world. Let them get acquainted gradually, let mutuality develop in an unforced way.

Hence Nat Falkayn rarely saw winged folk in the early part of his life. When an Ythrian did, now and then, have business in Chartertown, it was apt to be with his grandfather David, or, presently, his father Nicholas: certainly not with a little boy. Even when an eaglelike being came as a dinner guest, conversation was seldom in Anglic. Annoyed by this, Nat grew downright grindstone about learning the Planha language as his school required. But the effort didn't pay off until he was seventeen Avalonian years old—twelve

211

years of that Mother Earth he had never seen, of which his body bore scarcely an atom.

At that time, the archipelago settlements had grown to a point where leaders felt ready to plant a seed of habitation on the Coronan continent. But much study and planning must go before. Nicholas Falkayn, an engineer, was among those humans who joined Ythrian colleagues in a research and development team. The headquarters of his happened to be at the chief abode of the allied folk, known to its dwellers as Trauvay and to humans as Wingland. He would be working out of there for many cycles of the moon Morgana, each of which equalled not quite half a Lunar month. So he brought his wife and children along.

Nat found himself the only boy around in his own age bracket. However, there was no lack of young Ythrian companions.

"Hyaa-aah!" In a whirl and thunder, Keshchyi left the balcony floor and swung aloft. Sunlight blazed off his feathers. The whistling, trumpeting challenge blew down: "What are you waiting for, you mudfeet?"

Less impetuous than his cousin, Thuriak gave Nat a sharp yellow glance. "Well, are you coming?" he asked.

"I . . . guess so," the human mumbled.

You are troubled, Thuriak said, not with his voice. Infinitely variable, Ythrian plumage can send ripples of expression across the entire body, signs and symbols often more meaningful than words will ever be. Nat had learned some of the conventional attitudes as part of his Planha lessons. But now, during these days of real acquaintance with living creatures, he had come to feel more and more like a deaf-mute.

He could merely say, in clumsy direct speech: "No, I'm fine. Honest I am. Just, uh, well, wondering if I shouldn't at least call my mother and ask—"

His tone trailed off. Thuriak seemed to be registering scorn. And yet this was a gentle, considerate youth, not at all like that overbearing Keshchyi. . . .

If you must, like a nestling. Did that really stand written on the bronze-hued feathers, the black-edged white of crest and tail?

Nat felt very alone. He'd been delighted when these contemporaries of his, with whom he'd talked a bit and played a few games, invited him to spend the Freedom Week vacation at their home. And certainly that whole extended household known as the Weathermaker Choth had shown him politeness, if not intimacy—aside from a few jeering remarks of Keshchyi's, which the fellow probably didn't realize were painful. And his parents had been glad to let him accept. "It's a step toward the future," his father had exclaimed. "Our two kinds are going to have to come to know each other inside out. That's a job for your generation, Nat . . . and here you're beginning on it."

But the Ythrians were alien, and not just in their society. In their bones, their flesh, the inmost molecules of their genes, they were not human. It was no use pretending otherwise.

"Different" did not necessarily mean "inferior." Could it, heart-breakingly, mean "better"? Or "happier"? Had God been in a more joyful mood when He made the Ythrians than when He made man?

Perhaps not. They were pure carnivores, born hunters. Maybe that was the reason why they allowed, yes, encouraged their young to go off and do reckless things, accepting stoically the fact that the unfit and the unlucky would not return alive—

Keshchyi swooped near. Nat felt a gust of air from beneath his wings. "Are you glued in your place?" he shouted. "The tide isn't, I can tell you. If you want to come, then for thunder's sake, move!"

"He's right, you know," said calmer Thuriak. Eagerness quivered across him.

Nat gulped. As if searching for something familiar, anything, his gaze swept around.

He stood on a balcony of that tall stone tower which housed the core families. Below were a paved courtyard and rambling wooden buildings. Meadows where meat animals grazed sloped downhill in Terrestrial grass and clover, Ythrian starbell and wry, Terrestrial oak and pine, Ythrian braidbark and copperwood, until cultivation gave way to the reddish mat of native susin, the scattered intense green of native chasuble bush and delicate blue of janie. The sun Laura stood big and golden-colored at morning, above a distantly glimpsed mercury line of ocean. Elsewhere wandered a few cottony clouds and the pale, sinking ghost of Morgana. A flock of Avalonian draculas passed across view, their leathery wings awkward beside the plumed splendor of Keshchyi's. No adult Ythrians were to be seen; they ranged afar on their business.

Nat, who was short and slender, with rumpled brown hair above thin features, felt dwarfed in immensity.

The wind murmured, caressed his face with coolness, blew him an odor of leaves and distances, a smoky whiff of Thuriak's body.

Though young, that being stood nearly as tall as one full-grown, which meant that he was about Nat's height. What he stood on was his enormous wings, folded downward, claws at their main joints to serve as a kind of feet. What had been the legs and talons of his birdlike ancestors were, on him, arms and hands. His frame had an avian rigidity and jutting keelbone, but his head, borne proudly on a rather long neck, was almost mammalian beneath its crest— streamlined muzzle, tawny eyes, mouth whose lips looked oddly delicate against the fangs, little brow yet the skull bulging backward to hold an excellent brain.

"Are you off, then?" Thuriak demanded while Keshchyi whistled in heaven. "Or would you rather stay here? It might be best for you, at that."

Blood beat in Nat's temples. *I'm not going to let these creatures sneer at humans!* ran through him. At the same time he knew he was being foolish, that he ought to check with his mother—and knew he wasn't going to, that he couldn't help himself. "I'm coming," he snapped.

Good, said Thuriak's plumage. He brought his hands to the floor and stood on them an instant while he spread those wings. Light shining through made his pinions look molten. Beneath them, the gill-like antlibranch slits, the "biological superchargers" which made it possible for an animal this size to fly under Earthlike conditions, gaped briefly, a row of purple mouths. In a rush and roar of his own, Thuriak mounted.

He swung in dizzying circles, up and up toward his hovering cousin. Shouts went between them. An Ythrian in flight burned more food and air than a human; they said he was more alive.

But I am no Ythrian, Nat thought. Tears stung him. He wiped them away, angrily, with the back of a wrist, and sought the controls of his gravbelt.

It encircled his coveralls at the waist. On his back were the two cylinders of its powerpack. He could rise, he could fly for hours. But how wretched a crutch this was!

Leaving the tower, he felt a slight steady vibration from the drive unit, pulsing through his belly. His fingers reached to adjust the controls, level him off and line him out northward. Wind blew, shrill and harsh, lashing his eyes till he must pull down the goggles on his leather helmet. The Ythrians had transparent third lids.

In the last several days, he had had borne in on him—until at night, on the cot set up for him in the young males' nest, he must stifle his sobs lest somebody hear—borne in on him how much these beings owned their unbounded skies, and how his kind did not.

The machine that carried him went drone, drone. He trudged on a straight course through the air, while his companions dipped and soared and reveled in the freedom of heaven which was their birthright.

The north shore curved to form a small bay. Beyond susin and bush and an arc of dunes, its waters glistened clear blue-green; surf roared furious on the reefs across its mouth. A few youngsters kept sailboats here. Keshchyi and Thuriak were among them.

But . . . they had quietly been modifying theirs for use on open sea. Today they proposed to take it out.

Nat felt less miserable when he had landed. On foot, he was the agile one, the Ythrians slow and limited. That was a poor tradeoff, he thought grayly. Still, he could be of help to them. Was that the real reason they had invited him to join this maiden venture?

For *Keshchyi, yes, no doubt,* the boy decided. *Thuriak seems to like me as a person. . . . Seems to.* His look went across that haughty unhuman countenance, and though it was full of expression, he could read nothing more subtle than a natural excitement.

"Come on!" Keshchyi fairly danced in his impatience. "Launch!" To Nat: "You. Haul on the prow. We'll push on the stern. Jump!"

For a moment of anger, Nat considered telling him to go to hell and returning alone. He knew he wasn't supposed to be here anyway, on a dangerous faring, without having so much as told his parents. The whole idea had been presented to him with such beast-of-prey suddenness. . . . *No,* he thought. *I can't let them, believe I, a human, must be a coward. I'll show 'em better.* He seized the stempost, which curved over the bow in a graceful sculpture of vines and leaves. He bent his back and threw his muscles into work.

The boat moved readily from its shelter and across the beach. It was a slim, deckless, nearly flat-bottomed hull, carvel-built, about four meters long. A single mast rested in brackets. Sand, gritty beneath Nat's thin shoesoles, gave way to a swirl of water around his trouser legs. The boat uttered a chuckling sound as it came afloat.

Keshchyi and Thuriak boarded in a single flap. Nat must make an undignified scramble across the gunwale and stand there dripping. Meanwhile the others raised the mast, secured its stays, began unlashing jib and mainsail. It was a curious rig, bearing a flexible gaff almost as long as the boom. The synthetic cloth rose crackling into the breeze.

"Hoy, wait a minute," Nat said. The Ythrians gave him a blank glance and he realized he had spoken in Anglic. Had they never imagined it worth the trouble to learn his language properly, as he had theirs? He shifted to Planha: "I've been sailing myself, around First Island, and know—uh, what is the word?" Flushing in embarrassment, he fumbled for ways to express his idea.

Thuriak helped him. After an effort, they reached understanding. "You see we have neither keel nor centerboard, and wonder how we'll tack," the Ythrian interpreted. "I'm surprised the sportsmen of your race haven't adopted our design." He swiveled a complexly curved board, self-adjusting on its pivot by means of vanes, upward from either rail. "This interacts with the wind to provide lateral resistance. No water drag. Much faster than your craft. We'll actually sail as a hydrofoil."

"Oh, grand!" Nat marvelled.

His pleasure soured when Keshchyi said in a patronizing tone: "Well, of course, knowledge of the ways of air comes natural to us."

"So we're off," Thuriak laughed. He took the tiller in his right hand and jibsheet in his left; wing-claws gripped a perch-bar. The flapping sails drew taut. The boat bounded forward.

Hunkered in the bottom—there were no thwarts—Nat saw the waters swirl, heard them hiss, felt a shiver of speed and tasted salt on his lips. The boat reached planing speed and skimmed surface in a smooth gallop. The shore fell aft, the surf grew huge and loud ahead, dismayingly fast.

Nat gulped. *No, I will not show them any uneasiness.* After all, he still wore his gravbelt. In case of capsizing or—or whatever—he could flit to shore. The Ythrians could too. Was that why they didn't bother to carry lifejackets along?

The reefs were of some dark coraloid. They made a nearly unbroken low wall across the lagoon entrance. Breakers struck green-bright, smashed across those jagged backs, exploded in foam and bone-rattling thunder. Whirlpools seethed. In them, thick brown nets of atlantis weed, torn loose from a greater mass far out to sea, snaked around and around. Squinting through spindrift, Nat barely made out a narrow opening toward which Thuriak steered.

I don't like this, I don't like it one bit, went through him, chill amidst primal bellows and grunts and hungry suckings.

Thuriak put down the helm. The boat came about in a slash of boom and gaff, a snap of sailcloth, sounds that were buried in the tornado racket. On its new tack, it leaped for the passage. Thuriak fluted his joy. Keshchyi spread plumes which shone glorious in sun and scud-blizzard.

The boat dived in among the reefs. An unseen net of weed caught the rudder. A riptide and a flaw of wind grabbed hold. The hull smashed against a ridge. Sharpnesses went like saws through the planks. The surf took the boat and started battering it to death.

Nat was aloft before he knew what had really happened. He hovered on his thrust-fields, above white and green violence, and stared wildly around. There was Thuriak, riding the air currents, dismay on every feather, but alive, safe. . . . Where was Keshchyi?

Nat yelled the question. Faint through the noise there drifted back to him the shriek: "I don't know, I don't see him, did the gaff whip over him—?" and Thuriak swooped about and about, frantic.

A cry tore from him. "Yonder!" And naked grief: "No, no, oh, Keshchyi, my blood-kin, my friend—"

Nat darted to join the Ythrian. Winds clawed at him; the breakers filled his head with their rage. Through a bitter upflung mist he peered. And he saw—

—Keshchyi, one wing tangled in the twining weed, a-thresh in waves that surged across him, bore him under, cast him back for an instant and swept him bloodily along a reefside.

"We can grab him!" Nat called. But he saw what Thuriak had

already seen, that this was useless. The mat which gripped Keshchyi was a dozen meters long and wide. It must weigh a ton or worse. He could not be raised, unless someone got in the water first to free him.

And Ythrians, winged sky-folk, plainly could not swim. It was flat-out impossible for them. At most, help from above would keep the victim alive an extra minute or two.

Nat plunged.

Chaos closed on him. He had taken a full breath, and held it as he was hauled down into ice-pale depths. *Keep calm, keep calm, panic is what kills.* The currents were stronger than he was. But he had a purpose, which they did not. He had the brains to use them. Let them whirl him under—he felt his cheek scraped across a stone—for they would cast him back again and—

Somehow he was by Keshchyi. He was treading water, gulping a lungful when he could, up and down, up and down, away and back, always snatching to untangle those cables around the wing, until after a time beyond time, Keshchyi was loose.

Thuriak extended a hand. Keshchyi took it. Dazed, wounded, plumage soaked, he could not raise himself, nor could Thuriak drag him up alone.

A billow hurled Nat forward. His skull flew at the reef where the boat tossed in shards. Barely soon enough, he touched the controls of his gravbelt and rose.

He grabbed Keshchyi's other arm and switched the power output of his unit to Overload. Between them, he and Thuriak brought their comrade to land.

"My life is yours, Nathaniel Falkayn," said Keshchyi in the house. "I beg your leave to honor you."

"Aye, aye," whispered through the rustling dimness where the Weathermaker Choth had gathered.

"Awww . . ." Nat mumbled. His cheeks felt hot. He wanted to say, "Please, all I ask is, don't tell my parents what kind of trouble I got my silly self into." But that wouldn't be courteous, in this grave ceremony that his friends were holding for him.

It ended at last, however, and he and Thuriak got a chance to slip off by themselves, to the same balcony from which they had started. The short Avalonian day was drawing to a close. Sunbeams lay level across the fields. They shimmered off the sea, beyond which were homes of men. The air was still, and cool, and full of the scent of growing things.

"I have learned much today," Thuriak said seriously.

"Well, I hope you've learned to be more careful in your next boat," Nat tried to laugh. *I wish they'd stop making such a fuss about me,* he thought. *They will in time, and we can relax and enjoy each other. Meanwhile, though—*

"I have learned how good it is that strengths be different, so that they may be shared."

"Well, yes, sure. Wasn't that the whole idea behind this colony?"

And standing there between sky and sea, Nat remembered swimming, diving, surfing, all the years of his life, brightness and laughter of the water that kissed his face and embraced his whole body, the riding on splendid waves and questing into secret twilit depths, the sudden astonishing beauty of a fish or a rippled sandy bottom, sunlight a-dance overhead . . . and he looked at the Ythrian and felt a little sorry for him.

INTRODUCTION

For his last chapter, Hloch returns to A. A. Craig's *Tales of the Great Frontier*. The author was a Terran who traveled widely, gathering material for his historical narratives, during a pause in the Troubles, several lifetimes after the World-Taking. When he visited Avalon, he heard of an incident from the person, then aged, who had experienced it, and made therefrom the story which follows. Though fictionalized, the account is substantially accurate. Though dealing with no large matter, it seems a fitting one wherewith to close.

—Hloch of the Stormgate Choth
The Earthbook of Stormgate

RESCUE ON AVALON

The Ythrian passed overhead in splendor. Sunlight on feathers made bronze out of his six-meter wingspan and the proudly held golden-eyed head. His crest and tail were white as the snowpeaks around, trimmed with black. He rode the wind like its conqueror.

Against his will, Jack Birnam confessed the sight was beautiful. But it was duty which brought up his binoculars. If the being made a gesture of greeting, he owed his own race the courtesy of a return salute; and Ythrians often forgot that human vision was less keen than theirs. *I have to be especially polite when I'm in country that belongs to them,* the boy thought. Bitterness rushed through him. *And this does, now, it does. Oh, curse our bargaining Parliament!*

Under magnification, he clearly saw the arched carnivore muzzle with its oddly delicate lips; the talons which evolution had made into hands; the claws at the "elbows" of the wings, which served as feet on the ground; the gill-like slits in the body, bellows pumped by the flight muscles, a biological supercharger making it possible for a creature that size to get aloft. He could even see by the plumage that this was a middle-aged male, and of some importance to judge by the ornate belt, pouch, and dagger which were all that he wore.

Though the Ythrian had undoubtedly noticed Jack, he gave no sign. That was likely just his custom. Choths differed as much in their ways as human nations did, and Jack remembered hearing that the Stormgate folk, who would be moving into these parts, were quite reserved. Nevertheless the boy muttered at him, "You can call it dignity if you want. I call it snobbery, and I don't like you either."

The being dwindled until he vanished behind a distant ridge. *He's probably bound for Peace Deep on the far side, to hunt,* Jack decided. *And I wanted to visit there. . . . Well, why not, anyway? I'll scarcely meet him; won't be going down into the gorge myself. The mountains have room for both of us—for a while, till his people come and settle them.*

He hung the glasses on his packframe and started walking again through loneliness.

The loftiest heights on the planet Avalon belong to the Andromeda Range. But that is a name bestowed by humans. Not for nothing do the Ythrians who have joined them in their colonizing venture call that region the Weathermother. Almost exactly two days—twenty-two hours—after he had spied the stranger, a hurricane caught Jack Birnam. Born and raised here, he was used to sudden tempests. The rapidly spinning globe was always breeding them. Yet the violence of this one astonished him.

He was in no danger. It had not been foolish to set off by himself on a trip into the wilderness. He would have preferred a companion, of course, but none of his friends happened to be free; and he didn't expect he'd ever have another chance to visit the beloved land. He knew it well. He intended merely to hike, not climb. At age twenty-four (or seventeen, if you counted the years of an Earth where he had never been) he was huskier than many full-grown men. In case of serious difficulty, he need merely send a distress signal by his pocket transceiver. Homing on it, an aircar from the nearest rescue station in the foothills should reach him in minutes.

If the sky was fit to fly in!

When wind lifted and clouds whirled like night out of the north, he made his quick preparations. His sleeping bag, with hood and breathing mask for really foul conditions, would keep him warm at lower temperatures than occurred anywhere on Avalon. Unrolled and erected over it as a kind of pup tent, a sheet of duraplast would stop hailstones or blown debris. The collapsible alloy frame, light but equally sturdy, he secured to four pegs whose explosive heads had driven them immovably into bedrock. This shelter wasn't going anywhere. When he had brought himself and his equipment inside, he had nothing to do but wait out the several shrieking hours which followed.

Nonetheless, he was almost frightened at the fury, and half-stunned by the time it died away.

Crawling forth, he found the sun long set. Morgana, the moon, was full, so radiant that it crowded most stars out of view. Remote snowfields glittered against blue-black heaven; boulders and shrubs on the ridgetop where Jack was camped shone as if turned to silver, while a nearby stream flowed like mercury. The cluck and chuckle of water, the boom of a more distant cataract, were the only sounds. After the wind-howl, this stillness felt almost holy. The air was chill but carried odors of plant life, sharp trefoil, sweet livewell, and janie. Breath smoked ghostly.

After his long lying motionless, he couldn't sleep. He decided to make a fire, cook a snack and coffee, watch dawn when it came. Here above timberline, the low, tough vegetation wasn't much damaged. But he was sure to find plenty of broken-off wood. The trees below must have suffered far worse. He'd see in the morning. At present, to him those depths were one darkness, hoar-frosted by moonlight.

His transceiver beeped. He stiffened. That meant a general broadcast on the emergency band. Drawing the flat object from his coverall, he flipped its switch for two-way. A human voice lifted small: "—Mount Farview area. Andromeda Rescue Station Four calling anyone in the Mount Farview area. Andromeda—"

Jack brought the instrument to his mouth. "Responding," he said. Inside his quilted garment, he shivered with more than cold. "John Birnam responding to ARS Four. I . . . I'm a single party, on foot, but if I can help—"

The man at the other end barked: "Where are you, exactly?"

"It doesn't have a name on the map," Jack replied, "but I'm on the south rim of a big canyon which starts about twenty kilometers east-north-east of Farview's top. I'm roughly above the middle of the gorge, that'd be, uh, say thirty kilometers further east."

It does have a name, though, went through his mind. *I named it Peace Deep, five years ago when I first came on it, because the forest down there is so tall and quiet. Wonder what the Ythrians will call it, after I can't come here anymore?*

"Got you," answered the man. He must have an aerial survey chart before him. "John Birnam, you said? I'm Ivar Holm. Did you come through the storm all right?"

"Yes, thanks, I was well prepared. Are you checking?"

"In a way." Holm spoke grimly. "Look, this whole sector's in bad trouble. The prediction on that devil-wind was totally inadequate, a gross underestimate. Not enough meteorological monitors yet, I suppose. Or maybe the colonies are too young to've learned every trick that Avalon can play. Anyhow, things are torn apart down here in the hills—farms, villages, isolated camps—aircars smashed or crashed, including several that belonged to this corps. In spite of help being rushed in from outside, we'll be days in finding and saving the survivors. Our pilots and medics are going to have to forget there ever was such a thing as sleep."

"I . . . I'm sorry," Jack said lamely.

"I was praying someone would be in your vicinity. You see, an Ythrian appears to have come to grief thereabouts."

"An Ythrian!" Jack whispered.

"Not just any Ythrian, either. Ayan, the Wyvan of Stormgate."

"What?"

"Don't you know about that?" It was very possible. Thus far, the two races hadn't overlapped a great deal. Within the territories they claimed, they had been too busy adapting themselves and their ways to a world that was strange to them both. Jack, whose family were sea ranchers, dwelling on the coast five hundred kilometers westward, had seldom encountered one of the other species. Even a well-educated person might be forgiven for a certain vagueness about details of an entire set of alien societies.

"In the Stormgate choth," Holm said, "'Wyvan' comes as close to meaning 'Chief' or 'President' as you can get in their language. And Stormgate, needing more room as its population grows, has lately acquired this whole part of the Andromedas."

"I know," Jack couldn't help blurting in a refreshed rage. "The Parliament of Man and the Great Khruath of the Ythrians made their nice little deal, and never mind those of us who spent all the time we could up here because we love the country!"

"Huh? What're you talking about? It was a fair exchange. They turned over some mighty good prairie to us. We don't live by hunting and ranching the way they do. We can't use alps for anything except recreation—and not many of us ever did—and why are you and I wasting time, Birnam?"

Jack set his teeth. "Go on, please."

"Well. Ayan went to scout the new land personally, alone. That's Ythrian style. You must be aware what a territorial instinct their race has got. Now I've received a worried call from Stormgate headquarters. His family says he'd have radioed immediately after the blow, if he could, and asked us to relay a message that he wasn't hurt. But he hasn't. Nor did he ever give notice of precisely where he'd be, and no Ythrian on an outing uses enough gear to be readily spotted from the air."

"A low-power sender won't work out of that particular forest," Jack said. "Too much ironleaf growing there."

"Sunblaze!" Holm groaned. "Things never do go wrong one at a time, do they?" He drew breath. "Ordinarily we'd have a fleet of cars out searching, regardless of the difficulty. We can't spare them now, especially since he may well be dead. Nevertheless—You spoke as if you had a clue to his whereabouts."

Jack paused before answering slowly, "Yes, I believe I do."

"What? Quick, for mercy's sake!"

"An Ythrian flew by me a couple of days ago, headed the same way I was. Must've been him. Then when I arrived on this height, down in the canyon I saw smoke rising above the treetops. Doubtless a fire of his. I suppose he'd been hunting and—Well, I didn't pay close attention, but I could point the site out approximately. Why not send a team to where I am?"

Holm kept silent a while. The moonlight seemed to grow more cold and white.

"Weren't you listening, Birnam?" he said at last. "We need every man and every vehicle we can get, every minute they can be in action. According to my map, that gorge is heavily wooded. Do you mean we should tie up two or three men and a car for hours or days, searching for the exact place—when the chances of him being alive look poor, and . . . you're right on the scene?

"Can't you locate him? Find what the situation is, do what you can to help, and call back with precise information. Given that, we can snake him right out of there, without first wasting man-hours that should go to hundreds of people we know we can save. How about it?"

Now Jack had no voice.

"Hello?" Holm's cry was tiny in the night. "Hello?"

Jack gripped the transceiver till his knuckles stood bloodless. "I'm not sure what I can manage," he said.

"How d'you mean?"

"I'm allergic to Ythrians."

"*Huh?*"

"Something about their feathers or—It's gotten extremely bad in the last year or two. If I come near one, soon I can hardly breathe. And I didn't bring my antiallergen, this trip. Never expected to need it."

"Your condition ought to be curable."

"The doctor says it is, but that requires facilities we don't have on Avalon. RNA transformation, you know. My family can't afford to send me to a more developed planet. I just avoid those creatures."

"You can at least go look, can't you?" Holm pleaded. "I appreciate the risk, but if you're extra careful—"

"Oh, yes," Jack said reluctantly. "I can do that."

With the starkness of his folk, Ayan had shut his mind to pain while he waited for rescue or death. From time to time he shrilled forth hunting calls, and these guided Jack to him after the boy reached the general location. They had grown steadily weaker, though.

Far down a steep slope, the Ythrian sprawled rather than lay, resting against a chasuble bush. Everywhere around him were ripped branches and fallen boles, a tangle which had made it a whole day's struggle for Jack to get here. Sky, fading toward sunset, showed through rents in the canopy overhead. Mingled with green and gold of other trees was the shimmering, glittering purple foliage of iron-leaf.

The alatan bone in Ayan's left wing was bent at an ugly angle. That fracture made it alike impossible for him to fly or walk. Gaunt, exhausted, he still brought his crest erect as the human blundered into view. Hoarseness thickened the accent of his Anglic speech: "Welcome indeed!"

Jack stopped three meters off, panting, sweating despite the chill, knees wobbly beneath him. He knew it was idiotic, but could think of nothing else than: "How . . . are you, . . . sir?" *And why call him "sir," this land-robber?*

"In poor case," dragged out of Ayan's throat. "Well it is that you arrived. I would not have lasted a second night. The wind cast a heavy bough against my wing and broke it. My rations and equipment were scattered; I do not think you could find them yourself." The three fingers and two thumbs of a hand gestured at the transceiver clipped on his belt. "Somehow this must also have been disabled. My calls for help have drawn no response."

"They wouldn't, here." Jack pointed to the sinister loveliness which flickered in a breeze above. "Didn't you know? That's called ironleaf. It draws the metal from the soil and concentrates pure particles, to attract pollinating bugs by the sliminess. Absorbs radio waves. Nobody should go into an area like this without a partner."

"I was unaware—even as the weather itself caught me by surprise. The territory is foreign to me."

"It's home country to *me*." Fists clenched till nails bit into palms.

Ayan's stare sharpened upon Jack. Abruptly he realized how peculiar his behavior must seem. The Ythrian needed help, and the human only stood there. Jack couldn't simply leave him untended; he would die.

The boy braced himself and said in a hurry: "Listen. Listen good, because maybe I won't be able to repeat this. I'll have to scramble back up to where I can transmit. Then they'll send a car that I can guide to you. But I can't go till morning. I'd lose my way, or break my neck, groping in the dark through this wreckage the storm's made. First I'll do what's necessary for you. We better plan every move in advance."

"Why?" asked Ayan quietly.

"Because you make me sick! I mean—allergy—I'm going to get asthma and hives, working on you. Unless we minimize my exposure, I may be too ill to travel tomorrow."

"I see." For all his resentment, Jack was awed by the self-control. "Do you perchance carry anagon in your first-aid kit? No? Pity. I believe that is the sole painkiller which works on both our species. *Hrau.* You can toss me your filled canteen and some food immediately. I am near collapse from both thirst and hunger."

"It's human-type stuff, you realize," Jack warned. While men and Ythrians could eat many of the same things, each diet lacked certain essentials of the other. For that matter, native Avalonian life did not hold adequate nutrition for either colonizing race. The need to maintain separate ecologies was a major reason why they tended to live apart. *I can't ever return,* Jack thought. *Even if the new dwellers allowed me to visit, my own body wouldn't.*

"Calories, at least," Ayan reminded him. "Though I have feathers to keep me warmer than your skin would, last night burned most of what energy I had left."

Jack obliged. "Next," he proposed, "I'll start a fire and cut enough wood to last you till morning."

Was Ayan startled? That alien face wasn't readable. It looked as if the Ythrian was about to say something and then changed his mind. The boy went on: "What sort of preliminary care do you yourself need?"

"Considerable, I fear," said Ayan. Jack's heart sank. "Infection is setting in, and I doubt you carry an antibiotic safe for use on me; so my injuries must be thoroughly cleansed. The bone must be set and splinted, however roughly. Otherwise—I do not wish to complain, but the pain at every slightest movement is becoming quite literally unendurable. I barely managed to keep the good wing flapping, thus myself halfway warm, last night. Without support for the broken one, I could not stay conscious to tend the fire."

Jack forgot that he hated this being. "Oh, gosh, no! I wasn't thinking straight. You take my bag. I can, uh, sort of fold you into it."

"Let us see. Best we continue planning and preparations."

Jack nodded jerkily. The time soon came when he must take a breath, hold it as long as possible, and go to the Ythrian.

It was worse than his worst imagining.

At the end, he lay half-strangled, eyes puffed nearly shut, skin one great burning and itch, wheezed, wept, and shuddered. Crouched near the blaze, Ayan looked at him across the meters of cold, thickening dusk which again separated them. He barely heard the nonhuman voice:

"You need that bedroll more than I do, especially so when you must have strength back by dawn to make the return trip. Take your rest."

Jack crept to obey. He was too wretched to realize what the past hour must have been like for Ayan.

✿ ✿ ✿

First light stole bleak between trees. The boy wakened to a ragged call: "*Khrraah, khrraah, khrraah,* human—" For a long while, it seemed, he fought his way through mists and cobwebs. Suddenly, with a gasp, he came to full awareness.

The icy air went into his lungs through a throat much less swollen than before. Bleariness and ache still possessed his head, but he could think, he could see. . . .

Ayan lay by the ashes of the fire. He had raised himself on his hands to croak aloud. His crest drooped, his eyes were glazed. "*Khrraah—*"

Jack writhed from his bag and stumbled to his feet. "What happened?" he cried in horror.

"I . . . fainted . . . only recovered this moment—Pain, weariness, and . . . lack of nourishment—I feared I might collapse but hoped I would not—"

It stabbed through Jack: *Why didn't I stop to think? Night before last, pumping that wing—the biological supercharger kindling his metabolism beyond anything a human can experience—burning not just what fuel his body had left, but vitamins that weren't in the rations I could give him—*

"Why didn't you insist on the bedding?" the human cried in anguish of his own. "I could've stayed awake all right!"

"I was not certain you could," said the harsh whisper. "You appeared terribly ill, and . . . it would have been wrong, that the young die for the old. . . . I know too little about your kind—" The Ythrian crumpled.

"And I about yours." Jack sped to him, took him in his arms, brought him to the warm bag and tucked him in with enormous care. Presently Ayan's eyes fluttered open, and Jack could feed him.

The asthma and eruptions weren't nearly as bad as earlier. Jack hardly noticed, anyway. When he had made sure Ayan was resting comfortably, supplies in easy reach, he himself gulped a bite to eat and started off.

It would be a stiff fight, in his miserable shape, to get past the ironleaf before dark. He'd do it, though. He knew he would.

✿ ✿ ✿

The doctors kept him one day in the hospital. Recovered, he borrowed protective garments and a respirator, and went to the Ythrian ward to say goodbye.

Ayan lay in one of the frames designed for his race. He was alone in his room. Its window stood open to a lawn and tall trees— Avalonian king's-crown, Ythrian windnest, Earthly oak—and a distant view of snowpeaks. Light spilled from heaven. The air sang. Ayan looked wistfully outward.

But he turned his head and, yes, smiled as Jack entered, recognizing him no matter how muffled up he was. "Greeting, galemate," he said.

The boy had spent his own time abed studying usages of Stormgate. He flushed; for he could have been called nothing more tender and honoring than "galemate."

"How are you?" he inquired awkwardly.

"I shall get well, because of you." Ayan grew grave. "Jack," he murmured, "can you come near me?"

"Sure, as long's I'm wearing this." The human approached. Talons reached out to clasp his gloved hand.

"I have been talking with Ivar Holm and others," Ayan said very low. "You resent me, my whole people, do you not?"

"Aw, well—"

"I understand. We were taking from you a place you hold dear. Jack, you, and any guests of yours, will forever be welcome there, to roam as you choose. Indeed, the time is over-past for our two kinds to intermingle freely."

"But . . . I mean, thank you, sir," Jack stammered, "but I can't."

"Your weakness? Yes-s-s." Ayan uttered the musical Ythrian equivalent of a chuckle. "I suspect it is of largely psychosomatic origin, and might fade of itself when your anger does. But naturally, my choth will send you off-planet for a complete cure."

Jack could only stare and stutter.

Ayan lifted his free hand. "Thank us not. We need the closeness of persons like you, who would not abandon even an enemy."

"But you aren't!" burst from Jack. "I'll be proud to call you my friend!"

AFTERWORD

To those who have traveled with him this far, Hloch gives thanks. It is his hope that he has aided you to a little deeper sight, and thereby done what honor he was able to his choth and to the memory of his mother, Rennhi the wise.

Countless are the currents which streamed together at Avalon. Here we have flown upon only a few. Of these, some might well have been better chosen. Yet it seems to Hloch that all, in one way or another, raise a little higher than erstwhile his knowledge of that race with which ours is to share this world until God the Hunter descends upon both. May this be true for you as well, O people.

Now *The Earth Book of Stormgate* is ended. From my tower I see the great white sweep of the snows upon Mount Anrovil. I feel the air blow in and caress my feathers. Yonder sky is calling. I will go.

Fair winds forever.

—Hloch of the Stormgate Choth
The Earthbook of Stormgate

INTRODUCTION

The following is a part, modernized but otherwise authentic, of that curious book found by excavators of the ruins of Sol City, Terra—the Memoirs of Rear Admiral John Henry Reeves, Imperial Solar Navy. Whether or not the script, obviously never published or intended for publication, is a genuine record left by a man with a taste for dramatized reporting, or whether it is pure fiction, remains an open question; but it was undoubtedly written in the early period of the First Empire and as such gives a remarkable picture of the times and especially of the Founder. Actual events may or may not have been exactly as Reeves described, but we cannot doubt that in any case they were closely similar. Read this fifth chapter of the Memoirs as historical fiction if you will, but remember that the author must himself have lived through that great and tragic and triumphant age and that he must have been trying throughout the book to give a true picture of the man who even in his own time had become a legend.

Donvar Ayeghen, President of
the Galactic Archeological
Society

THE STAR PLUNDERER

They were closing in now. The leader was a gray bulk filling my sight scope, and every time I glanced over the wall a spanging sleet of bullets brought my head jerking down again. I had some shelter from behind which to shoot in a fragment of wall looming higher than the rest, like a single tooth left in a dead man's jaw, but I had to squeeze the trigger and then duck fast. Once in awhile one of their slugs would burst on my helmet and the gas would be sickly-sweet in my nostrils. I felt ill and dizzy with it.

Kathryn was reloading her own rifle, I heard her swearing as the cartridge clip jammed in the rusty old weapon. I'd have given her my own, except that it wasn't much better. It's no fun fighting with arms that are likely to blow up in your face but it was all we had—all that poor devastated Terra had after the Baldics had sacked her twice in fifteen years.

I fired a burst and saw the big gray barbarian spin on his heels, stagger and scream with all four hands clutching his belly, and sink slowly to his knees. The creatures behind him howled, but he only let out a deep-throated curse. He'd be a long time dying. I'd blown a hole clear through him, but those Gorzuni were tough.

The slugs wailed around us as I got myself down under the wall, hugging the long grass which had grown up around the shattered fragments of the house. There was a fresh wind blowing, rustling the grass and the big war-scarred trees, sailing clouds across a sunny summer sky, so the gas concentration was never enough to put us out. But Jonsson and Hokusai were sprawled like corpses there against the broken wall. They'd taken direct hits and they'd sleep for hours.

Kathryn knelt beside me, the ragged, dirty coverall like a queen's robe on her tall young form, a few dark curls falling from under her helmet for the wind to play with. "If we get them mad enough," she said, "they'll call for the artillery or send a boat overhead to blow us to the Black Planet."

"Maybe," I grunted. "Though they're usually pretty eager for slaves."

"John—" She crouched there a moment, the tiny frown I knew so well darkening her blue eyes. I watched the way leaf-shadows played across her thin brown face. There was a grease smudge on the snub nose, hiding the little freckles. But she still looked good, really good, she and green Terra and life and freedom and all that I'd never have again.

"John," she said at last, "maybe we should save them the trouble. Maybe we should make our own exit."

"It's a thought," I muttered, risking a glance above the wall.

The Gorzuni were more cautious now, creeping through the trampled gardens toward the shattered outbuilding we defended. Behind them, the main estate, last knot of our unit's resistance, lay smashed and burning. Gorzuni were swarming around us, dragging out such humans as survived and looting whatever treasure was left. I was tempted to shoot at those big furry bodies but I had to save ammunition for the detail closing in on us.

"I don't fancy life as the slave of a barbarian outworlder," I said. "Though humans with technical training are much in demand and usually fairly well treated. But for a woman—" The words trailed off. I couldn't say them.

"I might trade on my own mechanical knowledge," she said. "And then again, I might not. Is it worth the risk, John, my dearest?"

We were both conditioned against suicide, of course. Everyone in the broken Commonwealth navy was, except bearers of secret information. The idea was to sell our lives or liberty as exorbitantly as possible, fighting to the last moment. It was a stupid policy, typical of the blundering leadership that had helped lose us our wars. A human slave with knowledge of science and machinery was worth more to the barbarians than the few extra soldiers he could kill out of their hordes by staying alive till captured.

But the implanted inhibition could be broken by a person of strong will. I looked at Kathryn for a moment, there in the tumbled ruins of the house, and her eyes sought mine and rested, deep-blue and grave with a tremble of tears behind the long silky lashes.

"Well—" I said helplessly, and then I kissed her.

That was our big mistake. The Gorzuni had moved closer than I realized and in Terra's gravity—about half of their home planet's—they could move like a sunbound comet.

One of them came soaring over the wall behind me, landing on his clawed splay feet with a crash that shivered in the ground.

A wild "Whoo-oo-oo-oo!" was hardly out of his mouth before I'd blown the horned head off his shoulders. But there was a gray mass swarming behind him, and Kathryn yelled and fired into the thick of another attack from our rear.

Something stung me, a bright sharp pain and then a bomb exploding in my head and a whirling sick spiral down into blackness. The next thing I saw was Kathryn, caught in the hairy arms of a soldier. He was half again as tall as she, he'd twisted the barrel off her weapon as he wrenched it from her hands, but she was giving him a good fight. A hell of good fight. Then I didn't see anything else for some time.

They herded us aboard a tender after dark. It was like a scene from some ancient hell—night overhead and around, lit by many score of burning houses like uneasy torches out there in the dark, and the long, weary line of humans stumbling toward the tender with kicks and blows from the guards to hurry them along.

One house was aflame not far off, soaring blue and yellow fire glancing off the metal of the ship, picking a haggard face from below, glimmering in human tears and in unhuman eyes. The shadows wove in and out, hiding us from each other save when a gust of wind blew up the fire. Then we felt a puff of heat and looked away from each other's misery.

Kathryn was not to be seen in that weaving line. I groped along with my wrists tied behind me, now and then jarred by a gunbutt as one of the looming figures grew impatient. I could hear the sobbing of women and the groaning of men in the dark, before me, behind me, around me as they forced us into the boat.

"Jimmy. Where are you. Jimmy?"

"They killed him. He's lying there dead in the ruins."

"O God, what have we done?"

"My baby. Has anyone seen my baby? I had a baby and they took him away from me."

"Help, help, help, help, help—"

A mumbled and bitter curse, a scream, a whine, a rattling gasp of breath, and always the slow shuffle of feet and the sobbing of the women and the children.

We were the conquered. They had scattered our armies. They had ravaged our cities. They had hunted us through the streets and the hills and the great deeps of space, and we could only snarl and snap at them and hope that the remnants of our navy might pull a miracle. But miracles are hard to come by.

So far the Baldic League had actually occupied only the outer planets. The inner worlds were nominally under Commonwealth rule but the government was hiding or nonexistent. Only fragments of the navy fought on without authority or plan or hope, and Terra was the happy hunting ground of looters and slave raiders. Before long, I supposed bitterly, the outworlders would come in force, break the last resistance, and incorporate all the Solar System into their savage empire. Then the only free humans would be the extrasolar colonists, and a lot of them were barbaric themselves and had joined the Baldic League against the mother world.

The captives were herded into cells aboard the tender, crammed together till there was barely room to stand. Kathryn wasn't in my cell either. I lapsed into dull apathy.

When everyone was aboard, the deckplates quivered under our feet and acceleration jammed us cruelly against each other. Several humans died in that press. I had all I could do to keep the surging mass from crushing in my chest but of course the Gorzuni didn't care. There were plenty more where we came from.

The boat was an antiquated and rust-eaten wreck, with half its archaic gadgetry broken and useless. They weren't technicians, those Baldics. They were barbarians who had learned too soon how to build and handle spaceships and firearms, and a score of their planets united by a military genius had gone forth to overrun the civilized Commonwealth.

But their knowledge was usually by rote; I have known many a Baldic "engineer" who made sacrifices to his converter, many a general who depended on astrologers or haruspices for major decisions. So trained humans were in considerable demand as slaves. Having a degree in nuclear engineering myself, I could look for a halfway decent berth, though of course there was always the possibility of my being sold to someone who would flay me or blind me or let me break my heart in his mines.

Untrained humans hadn't much chance. They were just flesh-and-blood machines doing work that the barbarians didn't have automatics for, rarely surviving ten years of slavery. Women were the luxury trade, sold at high prices to the human renegades and rebels. I groaned at that thought and tried desperately to assure myself that Kathryn's technical knowledge would keep her in the possession of a nonhuman.

We were taken up to a ship orbiting just above the atmosphere. Airlocks were joined, so I didn't get a look at her from outside, but as soon as we entered I saw that she was a big interstellar transport of the Thurnogan class, used primarily for carrying troops to Sol and slaves back, but armed for bear. A formidable fighting ship when properly handled.

Guards were leaning on their rifles, all of Gorzuni race, their harness worn any way they pleased and no formality between officers and men. The barbarian armies' sloppy discipline had blinded our spit-and-polish command to their reckless courage and their savage gunnery. Now the fine-feathered Commonwealth navy was a ragged handful of hunted, desperate men and the despised outworlders were harrying them through the Galaxy.

This ship was worse than usual, though. I saw rust and mold on the unpainted plates. The fluoros were dim and in places burned out. There was a faint pulse in the gravity generators. They had long ago been stripped and refurnished with skins, stolen hold goods, cooking pots, and weapons. The Gorzuni were all as dirty and unkempt as their ship. They lounged about gnawing chunks of meat, drinking, dicing, and looking up now and then to grin at us.

A barbarian who spoke some Anglic bellowed at us to strip. Those who hesitated were cuffed so the teeth rattled in their heads.

We threw the clothes in a heap and moved forward slowly past a table where a drunken Gorzuni and a very sober human sat. Medical inspection.

The barbarian "doctor" gave each of us the most cursory glance. Most were passed on. Now and then he would look blearily at someone and say, "Sickly. Never make trip alive. Kill."

The man or woman or child would scream as he picked up a sword and chopped off the head with one expert sweep.

The human sat halfway on the table swinging one leg and whistling softly. Now and again the Gorzuni medic would look at him in doubt over some slave. The human would look closer. Usually he shoved them on. One or two he tapped for killing.

I got a close look at him as I walked by. He was below medium height, stockily built, dark and heavy-faced and beak-nosed, but his eyes were large and blue-gray, the coldest eyes I have ever seen on a human. He wore a loose colorful shirt and trousers of rich material probably stolen from some Terran villa.

"You filthy bastard," I muttered.

He shrugged, indicating the iron collar welded about his neck. "I only work here, Lieutenant," he said mildly. He must have noticed my uniform before I shed it.

Beyond the desk, a Gorzuni played a hose on us, washing off blood and grime. And then we were herded down the lone corridors and by way of wooden ladders (the drop-shafts and elevators weren't working, it seemed) to the cells. Here they separated men and women. We went into adjoining compartments, huge echoing caverns of metal with bunks tiered along the wall, food troughs, and sanitary facilities the only furnishings.

Dust was thick on the corroded floor, and the air was cold and had a metallic reek. There must have been about five hundred men swarming hopelessly around after the barred door clanged shut on us.

Windows existed between the two great cells. We made a rush for them, crying out, pushing and crowding and snarling at each other for first chance to see if our women still lived.

I was large and strong. I shouldered my way through the mob up to the nearest window. A man was there already, flattened against the wall by the sweating bodies behind, reaching through the bars to the three hundred women who swarmed on the other side.

"Agnes!" he shrieked. "Agnes, are you there? Are you alive?"

I grabbed his shoulder and pulled him away. He turned with a curse, and I fed him a mouthful of knuckles and sent him lurching back into the uneasy press of men. "Kathryn!" I howled.

The echoes rolled and boomed in the hollow metal caves, crying voices, prayers and curses and sobs of despair thrown back by the sardonic echoes till our heads shivered with it. "Kathryn! Kathryn!"

Somehow she found me. She came to me and the kiss through those bars dissolved ship and slavery and all the world for that moment. "Oh, John, John, John, you're alive, you're here. Oh, my darling—"

And then she looked around the metal-gleaming dimness and said quickly, urgently: "We'll have a riot on our hands, John, if these people don't calm down. See what you can do with the men. I'll tackle the women."

It was like her. She was the most gallant soul that ever walked under Terran skies, and she had a mind which flashed in an instant to that which must be done. I wondered myself what point there was in stopping a murderous panic. Those who were killed would be better off, wouldn't they? But Kathryn never surrendered, so I couldn't either.

We turned back into our crowds, and shouted and pummeled and bullied, and slowly others came to our aid until there was a sobbing quiet in the belly of the slave ship. Then we organized turns at the windows. Kathryn and I both looked away from those reunions, or from the people who found no one. It isn't decent to look at a naked soul.

The engines began to thrum. Under way, outward bound to the ice mountains of Gorzun, no more to see blue skies and green grass, no clean salt smell of ocean and roar of wind in tall trees. Now we were slaves and had nothing to do but wait.

✿ ✿ ✿

There was no time aboard the ship. The few dim fluoros kept our hold forever in its uneasy twilight. The Gorzuni swilled us at such irregular intervals as they thought of it, and we heard only the throb of the engines and the asthmatic sigh of the ventilators. The twice-normal gravity kept most of us too weary even to talk much. But I think it was about forty-eight hours after leaving Terra, when the ship had gone into secondary drive and was leaving the Solar System altogether, that the man with the iron collar came down to us.

He entered with an escort of armed and wary Gorzuni who kept their rifles lifted. We looked up dull-eyed at the short stocky figure. His voice was almost lost in the booming vastness of the hold.

"I'm here to classify you. Come one at a time and tell me your name and training, if any. I warn you that the penalty for claiming training you haven't got is torture, and you'll be tested if you do make such claims."

We shuffled past. A Gorzuni, the drunken doctor, had a tattoo needle set up and scribbled a number on the palm of each man. This went into the human's notebook, together with name, age, and profession. Those without technical skills, by far the majority, were shoved roughly back. The fifty or so who claimed valuable education went over into a corner.

The needle burned my palm and I sucked the breath between my teeth. The impersonal voice was dim in my ears: "Name?"

"John Henry Reeves, age twenty-five, lieutenant in the Commonwealth navy and nuclear engineer before the wars." I snapped the answers out, my throat harsh and a bitter taste in my mouth. The taste of defeat.

"Hmmm." I grew aware that the pale chill eyes were resting on me with an odd regard. Suddenly the man's thick lips twisted in a smile. It was a strangely charming smile, it lit his whole dark face with a brief radiance of merriment. "Oh, yes, I remember you, Lieutenant Reeves. You called me, I believe, a filthy bastard."

"I did," I almost snarled. My hand throbbed and stung. I was unwashed and naked and sick with my own helplessness.

"You may be right at that," he nodded. "But I'm in bad need of a couple of assistants. This ship is a wreck. She may never make Gorzun without someone to nurse the engines. Care to help me?"

"No," I said.

"Be reasonable. By refusing you only get yourself locked in the special cell we're keeping for trained slaves. It'll be a long voyage, the monotony will do more to break your spirit than any number of lashings. As my assistant you'll have proper quarters and a chance to move around and use your hands."

I stood thinking. "Did you say you needed two assistants?" I asked.

"Yes. Two who can do something with this ruin of a ship."

"I'll be one," I said, "if I can name the other."

He scowled. "Getting pretty big for the britches you don't have, aren't you?"

"Take it or leave it," I shrugged. "But this person is a hell of a good technician."

"Well, nominate him, then, and I'll see."

"It's a her. My fiancee, Kathryn O'Donnell."

"No." He shook his dark curly head. "No woman."

"No man, then." I grinned at him without mirth.

Anger flamed coldly in his eyes. "I can't have a woman around my neck like another millstone."

"She'll carry her own weight and more. She was a j.g. in my own ship, and she fought right there beside me till the end."

The temper was gone without leaving a ripple. Not a stir of expression in the strong, ugly, olive-skinned face that looked up at me. His voice was as flat. "Why didn't you say so before? All right, then, Lieutenant. But the gods help you if you aren't both as advertised!"

It was hard to believe it about clothes—the difference they made after being just another penned and naked animal. And a meal of stew and coffee, however ill prepared, scrounged at the galley after the warriors had messed, surged in veins and bellies which had grown used to swilling from a pig trough.

I realized bleakly that the man in the iron collar was right. Not many humans could have remained free of soul on the long, heart-cracking voyage to Gorzun. Add the eternal weariness of double weight, the chill dark grimness of our destination planet, utter remoteness from home, blank hopelessness, perhaps a touch of the whip and branding iron, and men became tame animals trudging meekly at the heels of their masters.

"How long have you been a slave?" I asked our new boss.

He strode beside us as arrogantly as if the ship were his. He was not a tall man, for even Kathryn topped him by perhaps five centimeters, and his round-skulled head barely reached my shoulder. But he had thick muscular arms, a gorilla breadth of chest, and the gravity didn't seem to bother him at all.

"Going on four years," he replied shortly. "My name, by the way, is Manuel Argos, and we might as well be on first name terms from the start."

A couple of Gorzuni came stalking down the corridor, clanking with metal. We stood aside for the giants, of course, but there was no cringing in Manuel's attitude. His strange eyes followed them speculatively.

We had a cabin near the stern, a tiny cubbyhole with four bunks, bleak and bare but its scrubbed cleanliness was like a breath of home after the filth of the cell. Wordlessly, Manuel took one of the sleazy blankets and hung it across a bed as a sort of curtain. "It's the best privacy I can offer you, Kathryn," he said.

"Thank you," she whispered.

He sat down on his own bunk and looked up at us. I loomed over him, a blond giant against his squatness. My family had been old and cultured and wealthy before the wars, and he was the nameless sweeping of a hundred slums and spaceports, but from the first there was never any doubt of who was the leader.

"Here's the story," he said in his curt way. "I knew enough practical engineering in spite of having no formal education to get myself a fairly decent master in whose factories I learned more. Two years ago he sold me to the captain of this ship. I got rid of the so-called chief engineer they had then. It wasn't hard to stir up a murderous quarrel between him and a jealous subordinate. But his successor is a drunken bum one generation removed from the forests.

"In effect, I'm the engineer of this ship. I've also managed to introduce my master, Captain Venjain, to marijuana. It hits a Gorzuni harder than it does a human, and he's a hopeless addict by now. It's partly responsible for the condition of this ship and the laxness among the crew. Poor leadership, poor organization. That's a truism."

I stared at him with a sudden chill along my spine. But it was Kathryn who whispered the question: "Why?"

"Waiting my chance," he snapped. "I'm the one who made junk out of the engines and equipment. I tell them it's old and poorly designed. They think that only my constant work holds the ship together at all; but I could have her humming in a week if I cared to. I can't wait too much longer. Sooner or later someone else is going to look at that machinery and tell them it's been deliberately haywired. So I've been waiting for a couple of assistants with technical training and a will to fight. I hope you two fit the bill. If not—" He shrugged. "Go ahead and tell on me. It won't free you. But if you want to risk lives that won't be very long or pleasant on Gorzun, you can help me take over the ship?"

I stood for some time looking at him. It was uncanny, the way he had sized us up from a glance and a word. Certainly the prospect was frightening. I could feel sweat on my face. My hands were cold. But I'd follow him. Before God, I'd follow him!

Still—"Three of us?" I jeered. "Three of us against a couple of hundred warriors?"

"There'll be more on our side," he said impassively. After a moment's silence he went on: "Naturally, we'll have to watch ourselves. Only two or three of them know Anglic. I'll point them out to you. And of course our work is under surveillance. But the watchers are ignorant. I think you have the brains to fool them."

"I—" Kathryn stood, reaching for words. "I can't believe it," she said at last. "A naval vessel in this condition—"

"Things were better under the old Baldic conquerors," admitted Manuel. "The kings who forged the League out of a hundred planets still in barbaric night, savages who'd learned to build spaceships and man atomblasts and little else. But even they succeeded only because there was no real opposition. The Commonwealth society was rotten, corrupt, torn apart by civil wars, its leadership a petrified bureaucracy, its military forces scattered over a thousand restless planets, its people ready to buy peace rather than fight. No wonder the League drove everything before it!

"But after the first sack of Terra fifteen years ago, the barbarians split up. The forceful early rulers were dead, and their sons were warring over an inheritance they didn't know how to rule. The League is divided into two hostile regions now, and I don't know how many splinter groups. Their old organization is shot to hell.

"Sol didn't rally in time. It was still under the decadent Commonwealth government. So one branch of the Baldics has now managed to conquer our big planets. But the fact that they've been content to raid and loot the inner worlds instead of occupying them and administering them decently shows the decay of their own society. Given the leadership, we could still throw them out of the Solar System and go on to overrun their home territories. Only the leadership hasn't been forthcoming."

It was a harsh, angry lecture, and I winced and felt resentment within myself. "Damn it, we've fought," I said.

"And been driven back and scattered." His heavy mouth lifted in a sneer. "Because there hasn't been a chief who understood strategy and organization, and who could put heart into his men."

"I suppose," I said sarcastically, "that you're that chief."

His answer was flat and calm and utterly assured. "Yes."

In the days that followed I got to know more about Manuel Argos. He was never loath to talk about himself.

His race, I suppose, was primarily Mediterranean-Anatolian, with more than a hint of Negro and Oriental, but I think there must have been some forgotten Nordic ancestor who looked out of those ice-blue eyes. A blend of all humanity, such as was not uncommon these days.

His mother had been a day laborer on Venus. His father, though he was never sure, had been a space prospector who died young and never saw his child. When he was thirteen he shipped out for Sirius and had not been in the Solar System since. Now, at forty, he had been spaceman, miner, dock walloper, soldier in the civil wars and against the Baldics, small-time politician on the colony planets, hunter, machinist, and a number of darker things.

Somewhere along the line, he had found time to do an astonishing amount of varied reading, but his reliance was always more on his own senses and reason and intuition than on books. He had been captured four years ago in a Gorzuni raid on Alpha Centauri, and had set himself to study his captors as cold-bloodedly as he had studied his own race.

Yes, I learned a good deal about him but nothing of him. I don't think any living creature ever did. He was not one to open his heart. He went wrapped in loneliness and dreams all his days. Whether the chill of his manner went into his soul, and the rare warmth was only a mask, or whether he was indeed a yearning tenderness sheathed in armor of indifference, no one will ever be sure. And he made a weapon out of that uncertainty. A man never knew what to await from him and was thus forever strained in his presence, open to his will.

"He's a strange sort," said Kathryn once, when we were alone. "I haven't decided whether he's crazy or a genius."

"Maybe both, darling," I suggested, a little irritably. I didn't like to be dominated.

"Maybe. But what is sanity, then?" She shivered and crept close to me. "I don't want to talk about it."

The ship wallowed on her way, through a bleak glory of stars, alone in light-years of emptiness with her cargo of hate and fear and misery and dreams. We worked, and waited, and the slow days passed.

The laboring old engines had to be fixed. Some show had to be made for the gray-furred giants who watched us in the flickering gloom of the power chambers. We wired and welded and bolted, tested and tore down and rebuilt, sweltering in the heat of bursting atoms that rolled from the radiation shields, deafened by the whine of generators and thud of misadjusted turbines and the deep uneven drone of the great converters. We fixed Manuel's sabotage until the ship ran almost smoothly. Later we would on some pretext throw the whole thing out of kilter again. "Penelope's tapestry," said Manuel, and I wondered that a space tramp could make the classical allusion.

"What are we waiting for?" I asked him once. The din of the generator we were overhauling smothered our words. "When do we start our mutiny?"

He glanced up at me. The light of our trouble lamp gleamed off the sweat on his ugly pockmarked face. "At the proper time," he said coldly. "For one thing, it'll be while the captain is on his next dope jag."

Meanwhile two of the slaves had tried a revolt of their own. When an incautious guard came too near the door of the men's cell one of them reached out and snatched his gun from the holster and shot him down. Then he tried to blast the lock off the bars. When the Gorzuni came down to gas him his fellow battled them with fists and teeth till the rebels were knocked out. Both were flayed living in the presence of the other captives.

Kathryn couldn't help crying after we were back in our cabin. She buried her face against my breast and wept till I thought she would never stop weeping. I held her close and mumbled whatever foolish words came to me.

"They had it coming," said Manuel. There was contempt in his voice. "The fools. The blind stupid fools! They could at least have held the guard as a hostage and tried to bargain. No, they had to be heroes. They had to shoot him down. Now the example has frightened all of the others. Those men deserved being skinned."

After a moment, he added thoughtfully, "Still, if the fear-emotion aroused in these slaves can be turned to hate it may prove useful. The shock has at least jarred them from their apathy."

"You're a heartless bastard," I said tonelessly.

"I have to be, seeing that everyone else chooses to be brainless. These aren't times for the tender-minded, you. This is an age of dissolution and chaos, such as has often happened in history, and only a person who first accepts the realities of the situation can hope to do much about them. We don't live in a cosmos where perfection is possible or even desirable. We have to make our compromises and settle for the goals we have some chance of attaining." To Kathryn, sharply: "Now stop that snuffling. I have to think."

She gave him a wide-eyed tear-blurred look.

"It gives you a hell of an appearance." He grinned nastily. "Nose red, face swollen, a bad case of hiccoughs. Nothing pretty about crying, you."

She drew a shuddering breath and there was anger flushing her cheeks. Gulping back the sobs, she drew away from me and turned her back on him.

"But I stopped her," whispered Manuel to me with a brief impishness.

* * *

The endless, meaningless days had worn into a timelessness where I wondered if this ship were not the Flying Dutchman, outward bound forever with a crew of devils and the damned. It was no use trying to hurry Manuel, I gave that up and slipped into the round of work and waiting. Now I think that part of his delay was on purpose, that he wanted to grind the last hope out of the slaves and leave only a hollow yearning for vengeance. They'd fight better that way.

I hadn't much chance to be alone with Kathryn. A brief stolen kiss, a whispered word in the dimness of the engine room, eyes and hands touching lightly across a rusty, greasy machine. That was all. When we returned to our cabin we were too tired, generally, to do much except sleep.

I did once notice Manuel exchange a few words in the slave pen with Ensign Hokusai, who had been captured with Kathryn and myself. Someone had to lead the humans, and Hokusai was the best man for that job. But how had Manuel known? It was part of his genius for understanding.

The end came suddenly. Manuel shook me awake. I blinked wearily at the hated walls around me, feeling the irregular throb of the gravity field that was misbehaving again. More work for us. "All right, all right," I grumbled. "I'm coming."

When he flicked the curtain from Kathryn's bunk and aroused her, I protested. "We can handle it. Let her rest."

"Not now!" he answered. Teeth gleamed white in the darkness of his face. "The captain's off in never-never land. I heard two of the Gorzuni talking about it."

That brought me bolt awake, sitting up with an eerie chill along my spine. "Now—?"

"Take it easy," said Manuel. "Lots of time."

We threw on our clothes and went down the long corridors. The ship was still. Under the heavy shuddering drone of the engines, there was only the whisper of our shoes and the harsh rasp of the breath in my lungs. Kathryn was white-faced, her eyes enormous in the gloom. But she didn't huddle against me. She walked between the two of us and a remoteness was over her that I couldn't quite understand. Now and then we passed a Gorzuni warrior on some errand of his own, and shrank aside as became slaves. But I saw the bitter triumph in Manuel's gaze as he looked after the titans.

In the power chamber where the machines loomed in a flickering red twilight like heathen gods. We found three Gorzuni standing there, armed engineers who snarled at us. One of them tried to cuff Manuel. He dodged without seeming to notice and bent over the gravity generator and signaled me to help him lift the cover.

I could see that there was a short circuit in one of the field coils, inducing a harmonic that imposed a flutter on the spacewarping current. It wouldn't have taken long to fix. But Manuel scratched his head, and glanced back at the ignorant giants who loomed over our shoulders. He began tracing wires with elaborate puzzlement.

He said to me: "We'll work up to the auxiliary atom-converter. I've fixed that to do what I want."

I knew the Gorzuni couldn't understand us, and that human expressions were meaningless to them, but an uncontrollable shiver ran along my nerves.

Slowly we fumbled to the squat engine which was the power source for the ship's internal machinery. Manuel hooked in an oscilloscope and studied the trace as if it meant something. "Ah-hah!" he said.

We unbolted the antiradiation shield, exposing the outlet valve. I knew that the angry, blood-red light streaming from it was harmless, that baffles cut off most of the radioactivity, but I couldn't help shrinking from it. When a converter is flushed through the valve, you wear armor.

Manuel went over to a workbench and took a gadget from it which he'd made. I knew it was of no use for repair but he'd pretended to make a tool of it in previous jobs. It was a lead-plated flexible hose springing from a magnetronic pump, with a lot of meters and switches haywired on for pure effect. "Give me a hand, John," he said quietly.

We fixed the pump over the outlet valve and hooked up the two or three controls that really meant something. I heard Kathryn gasp behind me, and the dreadful realization burst into my own brain and numbed my hands. There wasn't even a gasket—

The Gorzuni engineer strode up to us, rumbling a question in his harsh language, his fellows behind him. Manuel answered readily, not taking his gaze off the wildly swinging fake meters.

He turned to me, and I saw the dark laughter in his eyes. "I told them the converter is overdue for a flushing out of waste products," he said in Anglic. "As a matter of fact, the whole ship is."

He took the hose in one hand and the other rested on a switch of the engine. "Don't look, Kathryn," he said tonelessly. Then he threw the switch.

I heard the baffle plates clank down. Manuel had shorted out the automatic safety controls which kept them up when the atoms were burning. I threw a hand over my own eyes and crouched.

The flame that sprang forth was like a bit of the sun. It sheeted from the hose and across the room. I felt my skin shriveling from incandescence and heard the roar of cloven air. In less than a second, Manuel had thrown the baffles back into place but his improvised blaster had torn away the heads of the three Gorzuni and melted the farther wall. Metal glowed white as I looked again, and the angry thunders boomed and echoed and shivered deep in my bones till my skull rang with it.

Dropping the hose, Manuel stepped over to the dead giants and yanked the guns from their holsters. "One for each of us," he said.

Turning to Kathryn: "Get on a suit of armor and wait down here. The radioactivity is bad, but I don't think it'll prove harmful in the time we need. Shoot anyone who comes in."

"I—" Her voice was faint and thin under the rolling echoes. "I don't want to hide—"

"Damn it, you'll be our guard. We can't let those monsters recapture the engine room. Now, null gravity!" And Manuel switched off the generator.

Free fall yanked me with a hideous nausea. I fought down my outraged stomach and grabbed a post to get myself back down to the deck. Down—no. There was no up and down now. We were floating free. Manuel had nullified the gravity advantage of the Gorzuni. "All right, John, let's go!" he snapped.

I had time only to clasp Kathryn's hand. Then we were pushing off and soaring out the door and into the corridor beyond. Praise all gods, the Commonwealth navy had at least given its personnel free-fall training. But I wondered how many of the slaves would know how to handle themselves.

The ship roared around us. Two Gorzuni burst from a side cabin, guns in hand. Manuel burned them as they appeared, snatched their weapons, and swung on toward the slave pens.

The lights went out. I swam in a darkness alive with the rage of the enemy. "What the hell—" I gasped.

Manuel's answer came dryly out of blackness: "Kathryn knows what to do. I told her a few days ago."

At the moment I had no time to realize the emptiness within me from knowing that those two had been talking without me. There was too much else to do. The Gorzuni were firing blind. Blaster bolts crashed down the halls. Riot was breaking loose. Twice a lightning flash sizzled within centimeters of me. Manuel fired back at isolated giants, killing them and collecting their guns. Shielded by the dark, we groped our way to the slave pens.

No guards were there. When Manuel began to melt down the locks with low-power blasting I could dimly see the tangle of free-floating naked bodies churning and screaming in the vast gloom. A scene from an ancient hell. The fall of the rebel angels. Man, child of God, had stormed the stars and been condemned to Hell for it.

And now he was going to burst out!

Hokusai's flat eager face pressed against the bars. "Get us out," he muttered fiercely.

"How many can you trust?" asked Manuel.

"About a hundred. They're keeping their heads, see them waiting over there? And maybe fifty of the women."

"All right. Bring out your followers. Let the rest riot for a while. We can't do anything to help them."

The men came out, grimly and silently, hung there while I opened the females' cage. Manuel passed out such few guns as we had. His voice lifted in the pulsing dark.

"All right. We hold the engine room. I want six with guns to go there now and help Kathryn O'Donnell hold it for us. Otherwise the Gorzuni will recapture it. The rest of us will make for the arsenal."

"How about the bridge?" I asked.

"It'll keep. Right now the Gorzuni are panicked. It's part of their nature. They're worse than humans when it comes to mass stampedes. But it won't last and we have to take advantage of it. Come on!"

Hokusai led the engine room party—his naval training told him where the chamber would be—and I followed Manuel, leading the others out. There were only three or four guns between us but at least we knew where we were going. And by now few of the humans expected to live or cared about much of anything except killing Gorzuni. Manuel had timed it right.

We fumbled through a livid darkness, exchanging shots with warriors who prowled the ship firing at everything that moved. We lost men but we gained weapons. Now and again we found dead aliens, killed in the rioting, and stripped them too. We stopped briefly to release the technicians from their special cage and then shoved violently for the arsenal.

The Gorzuni all had private arms, but the ship's collection was not small. A group of sentries remained at the door, defending it against all comers. They had a portable shield against blaster bolts. I saw our flames splatter off it and saw men die as their fire raked back at us.

"We need a direct charge to draw their attention, while a few of us use the zero gravity to soar 'overhead' and come down on them from 'above,'" said Manuel's cold voice. It was clear, even in that wild lightning-cloven gloom. "John, lead the main attack."

"Like hell!" I gasped. It would be murder. We'd be hewed down as a woodsman hews saplings. And Kathryn was waiting—Then I swallowed rage and fear and lifted a shout to the men. I'm no braver than anyone else but there is an exaltation in battle, and Manuel used it as calculatingly as he used everything else.

We poured against them in a wall of flesh, a wall that they ripped apart and sent lurching back in tattered fragments. It was only an instant of flame and thunder, then Manuel's flying attack was on the defenders, burning them down, and it was over. I realized vaguely that I had a seared patch on my leg. It didn't hurt just then, and I wondered at the minor miracle which had kept me alive.

Manuel fused the door and the remnants of us swarmed in and fell on the racked weapons with a terrible fierceness. Before we had them all loaded a Gorzuni party charged us but we beat them off.

There were flashlights too. We had illumination in the seething dark. Manuel's face leaped out of that night as he gave his crisp, swift orders. A gargoyle face, heavy and powerful and ugly, but men jumped at his bidding. A party was assigned to go back to the slave pens and pass out weapons to the other humans and bring them back here.

Reinforcements were sent to the engine room. Mortars and small antigrav cannon were assembled and loaded. The Gorzuni were calming too. Someone had taken charge and was rallying them. We'd have a fight on our hands.

We did!

I don't remember much of those fire-shot hours. We lost heavily in spite of having superior armament. Some three hundred humans survived the battle. Many of them were badly wounded. But we took the ship. We hunted down the last Gorzuni and flamed those who tried to surrender. There was no mercy in us. The Gorzuni had beaten it out, and now they faced the monster they had created. When the lights went on again three hundred weary humans lived and held the ship.

✿ ✿ ✿

We held a conference in the largest room we could find. Everyone was there, packed together in sweaty silence and staring at the man who had freed them. Theoretically it was a democratic assembly called to decide our next move. In practice Manuel Argos gave his orders.

"First, of course," he said, his soft voice somehow carrying through the whole great chamber, "we have to make repairs, both of battle damage and of the deliberately mishandled machinery. It'll take a week, I imagine, but then we'll have us a sweet ship. By that time, too, you'll have shaken down into a crew. Lieutenant Reeves and Ensign Hokusai will give combat instruction. We're not through fighting yet."

"You mean—" A man stood up in the crowd. "You mean, sir, that we'll have opposition on our return to Sol? I should think we could just sneak in. A planet's too big for blockade, you know, even if the Baldics cared to try."

"I mean," said Manuel calmly, "that we're going on to Gorzun."

It would have meant a riot if everyone hadn't been so tired. As it was, the murmur that ran through the assembly was ominous.

"Look, you," said Manuel patiently, "we'll have us a first-class fighting ship by the time we get there, which none of the enemy has. We'll be an expected vessel, one of their own, and in no case do they expect a raid on their home planet. It's a chance to give them a body blow. The Gorzuni don't name their ships, so I propose we christen ours now—the *Revenge*."

It was sheer oratory. His voice was like an organ. His words were those of a wrathful angel. He argued and pleaded and bullied and threatened and then blew the trumpets for us. At the end they stood up and cheered for him. Even my own heart lifted and Kathryn's eyes were wide and shining. Oh, he was cold and harsh and overbearing, but he made us proud to be human.

In the end, it was agreed, and the Solar ship *Revenge*, Captain Manuel Argos, First Mate John Henry Reeves, resumed her way to Gorzun.

In the days and weeks that followed, Manuel talked much of his plans. A devastating raid on Gorzun would shake the barbarian confidence and bring many of their outworld ships swarming back to defend the mother world. Probably the rival half of the Baldic League would seize its chance and fall on a suddenly weakened enemy. The *Revenge* would return to Sol, by that time possessed of the best crew in the known universe, and rally mankind's scattered forces. The war would go on until the System was cleared—

"—and then, of course, continue till all the barbarians have been conquered," said Manuel.

"Why?" I demanded. "Interstellar imperialism can't be made to pay. It does for the barbarians because they haven't the technical facilities to produce at home what they can steal elsewhere. But Sol would only be taking on a burden."

"For defense," said Manuel. "You don't think I'd let a defeated enemy go off to lick his wounds and prepare a new attack, do you? No, everyone but Sol must be disarmed, and the only way to enforce such a peace is for Sol to be the unquestioned ruler." He added thoughtfully: "Oh, the empire won't have to expand forever. Just till it's big enough to defend itself against all comers. And a bit of economic readjustment could make it a paying proposition, too. We could collect tribute, you know."

"An empire—?" asked Kathryn. "But the Commonwealth is democratic—"

"Was democratic!" he snapped. "Now it's rotted away. Too bad, but you can't revive the dead. This is an age in history such as has often occurred before when the enforced peace of Caesarism is the only solution. Maybe not a good solution but better than the devastation we're suffering now. When there's been a long enough period of peace and unity it may be time to think of reinstating the old republicanism. But that time is many centuries in the future, if it ever comes. Just now the socio-economic conditions aren't right for it."

He took a restless turn about the bridge. A million stars of space in the viewport blazed like a chill crown over his head. "It'll be an empire in fact," he said, "and therefore it should be an empire in name. People will fight and sacrifice and die for a gaudy symbol when the demands of reality don't touch them. We need a hereditary aristocracy to put on a good show. It's always effective, and the archaism is especially valuable to Sol just now. It'll recall the good old glamorous days before space travel. It'll be even more of a symbol now than it was in its own age. Yes, an empire, Kathryn, the Empire of Sol. Peace, ye underlings!"

"Aristocracies decay," I argued. "Despotism is all right as long as you have an able despot but sooner or later a meathead will be born—"

"Not if the dynasty starts with strong men and women, and continues to choose good breeding stock, and raises the sons in the same hard school as the fathers. Then it can last for centuries. Especially in these days of gerontology and hundred-year active lifespans."

I laughed at him. "One ship, and you're planning an empire in the Galaxy!" I jeered. "And you yourself, I suppose, will be the first emperor?"

His eyes were expressionless. "Yes," he said. "Unless I find a better man, which I doubt."

Kathryn bit her lip. "I don't like it," she said. "It's—cruel."

"This is a cruel age, my dear," he said gently.

Gorzun rolled black and huge against a wilderness of stars. The redly illuminated hemisphere was like a sickle of blood as we swept out of secondary drive and rode our gravbeams down toward the night side.

Once only were we challenged. A harsh gabble of words came over the transonic communicator. Manuel answered smoothly in the native language, explaining that our vision set was out of order, and gave the recognition signals contained in the codebook. The warship let us pass.

Down and down and down, the darkened surface swelling beneath us, mountains reaching hungry peaks to rip the vessel's belly out, snow and glaciers and a churning sea lit by three hurtling moons. Blackness and cold and desolation.

Manuel's voice rolled over the intercom: "Look below, men of Sol. Look out the viewports. This is where they were taking us!"

A snarl of pure hatred answered him. That crew would have died to the last human if they could drag Gorzun to oblivion with them. God help me, I felt that way myself.

It had been a long, hard voyage even after our liberation, and the weariness in me was only lifted by the prospect of battle. I'd been working around the clock, training men, organizing the hundred units a modern warcraft needs. Manuel, with Kathryn for secretary and general assistant, had been driving himself even more fiercely, but I hadn't seen much of either of them. We'd all been too busy.

Now the three of us sat on the bridge watching Gorzun shrieking up to meet us. Kathryn was white and still, the hand that rested on mine was cold. I felt a tension within myself that thrummed near the breaking point. My orders to my gun crews were strained. Manuel alone seemed as chill and unruffled as always. There was steel in him. I sometimes wondered if he really was human.

Atmosphere screamed and thundered behind us. We roared over the sea, racing the dawn, and under its cold colorless streaks of light we saw Gorzun's capital city rise from the edge of the world.

I had a dizzying glimpse of squat stone towers, narrow canyons of streets, and the gigantic loom of spaceships on the rim of the city. Then Manuel nodded and I gave my firing orders.

Flame and ruin exploded beneath us. Spaceships burst open and toppled to crush buildings under their huge mass. Stone and metal fused, ran in lava between crumbling walls. The ground opened and swallowed half the town, A blue-white hell of atomic fire winked through the sudden roil of smoke. And the city died.

We slewed skyward, every girder protesting, and raced for the next great spaceport. There was a ship riding above it. Perhaps they had been alarmed already. We never knew. We opened up, and she fired back, and while we maneuvered in the heavens the *Revenge* dropped her bombs. We took a pounding, but our forcescreens held and theirs didn't. The burning ship smashed half the city when it fell.

On to the next site shown by our captured maps. This time we met a cloud of space interceptors. Ground missiles went arcing up against us. The *Revenge* shuddered under the blows. I could almost see our gravity generator smoking as it tried to compensate for our crazy spins and twists and lurchings. We fought them, like a bear fighting a dog pack, and scattered them and laid the base waste.

"All right," said Manuel. "Let's get out of here."

Space became a blazing night around us as we climbed above the atmosphere. Warships would be thundering on their way to smash us. But how could they locate a single ship in the enormousness between the worlds? We went into secondary drive, a tricky thing to do so near a sun, but we'd tightened the engines and trained the crew well. In minutes we were at the next planet, also habitable. Only three colonies were there. We smashed them all!

The men were cheering. It was more like the yelp of a wolf pack. The snarl died from my own face and I felt a little sick with the ruin. Our enemies, yes. But there were many dead. Kathryn wept, slow silent tears running down her face, shoulders shaking.

Manuel reached over and took her hand. "It's done, Kathryn," he said quietly. "We can go home now."

He added after a moment, as if to himself: "Hate is a useful means to an end but damned dangerous. We'll have to get the racist complex out of mankind. We can't conquer anyone, even the Gorzuni, and keep them as inferiors and hope to have a stable empire. All races must be equal." He rubbed his strong square chin. "I think I'll borrow a leaf from the old Romans. All worthy individuals, of any race, can become terrestrial citizens. It'll be a stabilizing factor."

"You," I said, with a harshness in my throat, "are a megalomaniac." But I wasn't sure any longer.

It was winter in Earth's northern hemisphere when the *Revenge* came home. I walked out into snow that crunched under my feet and watched my breath smoking white against the clear pale blue of the sky. A few others had come out with me. They fell on their knees in the snow and kissed it. They were a wild-looking gang, clad in whatever tatters of garment they could find, the men bearded and long-haired, but they were the finest, deadliest fighting crew in the Galaxy now. They stood there looking at the gentle sweep of hills, at blue sky and ice-flashing trees and a single crow hovering far overhead, and tears froze in their beards.

Home.

We had signalled other units of the Navy. Some would come along to pick us up soon and guide us to the secret base on Mercury, and there the fight would go on. But now, just now in this eternal instant we were home.

I felt weariness like an ache in my bones. I wanted to crawl bear-like into some cave by a murmuring river, under the dear tall trees of Earth, and sleep till spring woke up the world again. But as I stood there with the thin winter wind like a cleansing bath around me, the tiredness dropped off. My body responded to the world which two billion years of evolution had shaped it for and I laughed aloud with the joy of it.

We couldn't fail. We were the freemen of Terra fighting for our own hearthfires and the deep ancient strength of the planet was in us. Victory and the stars lay in our hands, even now, even now.

I turned and saw Kathryn coming down the airlock gangway. My heart stumbled and then began to race. It had been so long, so terribly long. We'd had so little time but now we were home, and she was singing.

Her face was grave as she approached me. There was something remote about her and a strange blending of pain with the joy that must be in her too. The frost crackled in her dark unbound hair, and when she took my hands her own were cold.

"Kathryn, we're home," I whispered. "We're home, and free, and alive. O Kathryn, I love you!"

She said nothing, but stood looking at me forever and forever until Manuel Argos came to join us. The little stocky man seemed embarrassed—the first and only time I ever saw him quail, even faintly.

"John," he said, "I've got to tell you something."

"It'll keep," I answered. "You're the captain of the ship. You have authority to perform marriages. I want you to marry Kathryn and me, here, now, on Earth."

She looked at me unwaveringly, but her eyes were blind with tears. "That's it, John," she said, so low I could barely hear her. "It won't be. I'm going to marry Manuel."

I stood there, not saying anything, not even feeling it yet.

"It happened on the voyage," she said, tonelessly. "I tried to fight myself, I couldn't. I love him, John. I love him even more than I love you, and I didn't think that was possible."

"She will be the mother of kings," said Manuel, but his arrogant words were almost defensive. "I couldn't have made a better choice."

"Do you love her too," I asked slowly, "or do you consider her good breeding stock?" Then: "Never mind. Your answer would only be the most expedient. We'll never know the truth."

It was instinct, I thought with a great resurgence of weariness. A strong and vital woman would pick the most suitable mate. She couldn't help herself. It was the race within her and there was nothing I could do about it.

"Bless you, my children," I said.

They walked away after awhile, hand in hand under the high trees that glittered with ice and sun. I stood watching them until they were out of sight. Even then, with a long and desperate struggle yet to come, I think I knew that those were the parents of the Empire and the glorious Argolid dynasty, that they carried the future within them.

And I didn't give a damn.

INTRODUCTION

Many scholarly works of varying lengths have been written on both the history and the literature of the early years of the Terran Empire, and the majority completely ignore the piece which follows. The few which do mention it mostly do so only in passing, describing it as "obvious fiction," or even scorn it as a hoax. The eminent Donvar Ayeghen once hastily changed the subject when the present document was brought up in an interview.

One doubter of its authenticity, Winston P. Sanders IX, has listed his objections to the document's authenticity as: (1) How likely is it that only one species in the known galaxy could have developed such mental powers? Telepathic races are rare, but known, but no other such near-supernatural abilities have been reported in any known non-human races. The universe does not favor unique events. (2) The narrative, in third person, is obviously a retelling of an earlier description of the events, yet no other accounts even slightly resembling the events in the piece have ever been unearthed by archaeologists or other researchers. (3) The course of the story, with an enemy of the young Empire gradually becoming one of its supporters, and also helping to defeat a deadly menace to the Empire and its subjects, makes the piece look suspiciously like a work of propaganda, put together to drum up patriotic fervor for the Empire and its controversial annexation policies.

One of the few supporters of the document's being authentic, D. H. Thomas, has not been taken very seriously because of his not-quite-respectable studies of ancient pre-atomic authors of dubious literary merit, such as Lester Dent, Walter B. Gibson, and

Norvell W. Page. Still, Thomas' scholarship, however eccentric, is unquestioned, and he has noted subtle points in the narrative that indicate a close knowledge of technology and customs of the time frame in which the piece is set, arguing that the alleged time of writing rings true.

In any case, once the excavated document had been translated, its story proved popular with the lay public, both in subetheric text form, and in several vidplay versions (all of which, it should be mentioned, take great liberties with the original tale).

Final proof might lie within the "Black Nebula" that is the setting for much of the tale, but the few clues as to the nebula's location use terms—such as the name of stars—which centuries ago fell into disuse, so that even *their* locations are doubtful, let alone the location of the nebula.

There are, as one of the characters says, *many* black nebulae. Someday, an exploring ship might find the bizarre planet described herein. Or, even if that planet exists, it might never be stumbled on, leaving us forever with an undeniably rousing tale whose truth will forever remain unproven.

—Michael Karageorge

SARGASSO OF LOST STARSHIPS

✧ | ✧

Basil Donovan was drunk again.

He sat near the open door of the Golden Planet, boots on the table, chair tilted back, one arm resting on the broad shoulder of Wocha, who sprawled on the floor beside him, the other hand clutching a tankard of ale. The tunic was open above his stained gray shirt, the battered cap was askew on his close-cropped blond hair, and his insignia—the stars of a captain and the silver leaves of an earl on Ansa—were tarnished. There was a deepening flush over his pale gaunt cheeks, and his eyes smoldered with an old rage.

Looking out across the cobbled street, he could see one of the tall, half-timbered houses of Lanstead. It had somehow survived the space bombardment, though its neighbors were rubble, but the tile roof was clumsily patched and there was oiled paper across the broken plastic of the windows. An anachronism, looming over the great bulldozer which was clearing the wreckage next door. The workmen there were mostly Ansans, big men in ragged clothes, but a well-dressed Terran was bossing the job. Donovan cursed wearily and lifted his tankard again.

The long, smoky-raftered taproom was full—stolid burghers and peasants of Lanstead, discharged spacemen still in their worn uniforms, a couple of tailed greenies from the neighbor planet Shalmu. Talk was low and spiritless, and the smoke which drifted from pipes and cigarettes was bitter, cheap tobacco and dried bark. The smell of defeat was thick in the tavern.

265

"May I sit here, sir? The other places are full."

Donovan glanced up. It was a young fellow, peasant written over his sunburned face in spite of the gray uniform and the empty sleeve. Olman—yes, Sam Olman, whose family had been under Donovan fief these two hundred years, "Sure, make yourself at home."

"Thank you, sir. I came in to get some supplies, thought I'd have a beer too. But you can't get anything these days. Not to be had."

Sam's face looked vaguely hopeful as he eyed the noble. "We do need a gas engine bad, sir, for the tractor. Now that the central powercaster is gone, we got to have our own engines. I don't want to presume, sir, but—"

Donovan lifted one corner of his mouth la a tired smile. "I'm sorry," he said. "If I could get one machine for the whole community I'd be satisfied. Can't be done. We're trying to start a small factory of our own up at the manor, but it's slow work."

"I'm sure if anyone can do anything it's you, sir."

Donovan looked quizzically at the open countenance across the table, "Sam," he asked, "why do you people keep turning to the Family? We led you, and it was to defeat. Why do you want anything more to do with nobles? We're not even that, any longer. We've been stripped of our titles. We're just plain citizens of the Empire now like you, and the new rulers are Terran. Why do you still think of us as your leaders?"

"But you are, sir! You've always been. It wasn't the king's fault, or his men's, that Terra had so much more'n we did. We gave 'em a fight they won't forget in a hurry!"

"You were in my squadron, weren't you?"

"Yes, sir. CPO on the *Ansa Lancer*, I was with you at the Battle of Luga." The deep-set eyes glowed. "We hit 'em there, didn't we, sir?"

"So we did." Donovan couldn't suppress the sudden fierce memory. Outnumbered, outgunned, half its ships shot to pieces and half the crews down with Sirius fever, the Royal Lansteaders had still made naval history and sent the Imperial Fleet kiyoodling back to Sol. Naval historians would be scratching their heads over that battle for the next five centuries. Before God, they'd fought!

He began to sing the old war-song, softly at first, louder as Sam joined him—

✣ ✣ ✣

Comrades, hear the battle tiding,
hear the ships that rise and yell
faring outward, standard riding—
Kick the Terrans back to hell!

The others were listening, men raised weary heads, an old light burned in their eyes and tankards clashed together. They stood up to roar out the chorus till the walls shook.

Lift your glasses high,
kiss the girls good-bye,
(Live well; my friend, live well, live you well)
for we're riding,
for we're riding,
for we're riding out to Terran sky! Terran sky! Terran sky!
We have shaken loose our thunder
where the planets have their way,
and the starry deeps of wonder
saw the Impies in dismay.
Lift your glasses high,
kiss the girls good-bye—

The workmen in the street heard it and stopped where they were. Some began to sing. The Imperial superintendent yelled, and an Ansan turned to flash him a wolfish grin. A squad of blue-uniformed Solarian marines coming toward the inn went on the double.

Oh, the Emp'ror sent his battle
ships against us in a mass,
but we shook them like a rattle
and we crammed them—

"Hi, there! Stop that!"

The song died, slowly and stubbornly, the men stood where they were and hands clenched into hard-knuckled fists. Someone shouted an obscenity.

The Terran sergeant was very young, and he felt unsure before those steady, hating eyes. He lifted his voice all the louder: "That will be enough of that. Any more and I'll run you all in for *lèse majesté*. Haven't you drunken bums anything better to do than sit around swilling beer?"

A big Ansan smith laughed with calculated raucousness.

The sergeant looked around, trying to ignore him. "I'm here for Captain Donovan—Earl Basil, if you prefer. They said he'd be here. I've got an Imperial summons for him."

The noble stretched out a hand. "This is he. Let's have that paper."

"It's just the formal order," said the sergeant. "You're to come at once."

"Commoners," said Donovan mildly, "address me as 'sir.'"

"You're a commoner with the rest of 'em now." The sergeant's voice wavered just a little.

"I really must demand a little respect," said Donovan with drunken precision. There was an unholy gleam in his eyes. "It's a mere formality, I know, but after all my family can trace itself farther back than the Empire, whereas you couldn't name your father."

Sam Olman snickered.

"Well, sir—" The sergeant tried elaborate sarcasm. "If you, sir, will please be so good as to pick your high-bred tail off that chair, sir, I'm sure the Imperium would be mostly deeply grateful to you, sir."

"I'll have to do without its gratitude, I'm afraid." Donovan folded the summons without looking at it and put it in his tunic pocket. "But thanks for the paper. I'll keep it in my bathroom."

"You're under arrest!"

Donovan stood slowly up, unfolding his sheer two meters of slender, wiry height. "All right, Wocha," he said. "Let's show them that Ansa hasn't surrendered yet."

He threw the tankard into the sergeant's face, followed it with the table against the two marines beside him, and vaulted over the sudden ruckus to drive a fist into the jaw of the man beyond.

Wocha rose and his booming cry trembled in the walls. He'd been a slave of Donovan's since he was a cub and the man a child, and if someone had liberated him he wouldn't have known what to do. As batman and irregular groundtrooper he'd followed his master to the wars, and the prospect of new skull-breaking lit his eyes with glee.

For an instant there was tableau, Terrans and Ansans rigid,

staring at the monster which suddenly stood behind the earl. The natives of Donarr have the not uncommon centauroid form, but their bodies are more like that of a rhinoceros than of a horse, hairless and slaty blue and enormously massive. The gorilla-armed torso ended in a round, muzzled, ape-like face, long-eared, heavy-jawed, with canine tusks hanging over the great gash of a mouth. A chair splintered under his feet, and he grinned.

"Paraguns—" cried the sergeant.

All hell let out for noon. Some of the customers huddled back into the corners, but the rest smashed the ends off bottles and threw themselves against the Terrans. Sam Olman's remaining arm yanked a marine to him and bashed his face against the wall. Donovan's fist traveled a jolting arc to the nearest belly and he snatched a rifle loose and crunched it against the man's jaw. A marine seized him from behind, he twisted in the grip and kicked savagely, whirled around and drove the rifle butt into the larynx.

"Kill the bluebellies! Kill the Impies! Hail, Ansa!"

Wocha charged into the squad, grabbed a hapless Terran in his four-fingered hands, and swung the man like a club. Someone drew his bayonet to stab the slave, it glanced off the thick skin and Wocha roared and sent him reeling. The riot blazed around the room, trampling men underfoot, shouting and cursing and swinging.

"Donovan, Donovan!" shouted Sam Olman. He charged the nearest Impy and got a bayonet in the stomach. He fell down, holding his hand to his wound, screaming.

The door was suddenly full of Terrans, marines arriving to help their comrades. Paraguns began to sizzle, men fell stunned before the supersonic beams and the fight broke up. Wocha charged the rescuers and a barrage sent his giant form crashing to the floor.

They herded the Ansans toward the city jail. Donovan, stirring on the ground as consciousness returned, felt handcuffs snap on his wrists.

Imperial summonses being what they were, he was bundled into a grounder and taken under heavy guard toward the ordered place. He leaned wearily back, watching the streets blur past. Once a group of children threw stones at the vehicle. "How about a cigarette?" he said.

"Shut up."

To his mild surprise, they did not halt at the military government headquarters—the old Hall of Justice where the Donovans had presided before the war—but went on toward the suburbs, the space-port being still radioactive. They must be going to the emergency field outside the city. Hm. He tried to relax. His head ached from the stunbeam.

A light cruiser had come in a couple of days before, H.M. *Ganymede.* It loomed enormous over the green rolling fields and the distance-blued hills and forests, a lance of bright metal and energy pointed into the clear sky of Ansa, blinding in the sun. A couple of spacemen on sentry at the gangway halted as the car stopped before them. "This man is going to Commander Jansky."

"Aye, aye. Proceed."

Through the massive airlock, down the mirror-polished companionway, into an elevator and up toward the bridge—Donovan looked about him with a professional eye. The Impies kept a clean, tight ship, he had to admit.

He wondered if he would be shot or merely imprisoned. He doubted if he'd committed an enslaving offense. Well, it had been fun, and there hadn't been a hell of a lot to live for anyway. Maybe his friends could spring him, if and when they got some kind of underground organized.

He was ushered into the captain's cabin. The ensign with him saluted. "Donovan as per orders, ma'm."

"Very good. But why is he in irons?"

"Resisted orders, ma'm. Started a riot. Bloody business."

"I—see." She nodded her dark head. "Losses?"

"I don't know, ma'm, but we had several wounded at least. A couple of Ansans were killed, I think."

"Well, leave him here. You may go."

"But—ma'm, he's dangerous!"

"I have a gun, and there's a man just outside the door. You may go, ensign."

Donovan swayed a little on his feet, trying to pull himself erect, wishing he weren't so dirty and bloody and generally messed up. You look like a tramp, man, he thought. Keep up appearances. Don't let them outdo us, even in spit and polish.

"Sit down, Captain Donovan," said the woman.

He lowered himself to a chair, raking her with deliberately insolent eyes. She was young to be wearing a commander's twin planets—young and trim and nice looking. Tall body, sturdy but graceful, well filled out in the blue uniform and red cloak; raven-black hair falling to her shoulders; strong blunt-fingered hands, one of them resting close to her sidearm. Her face was interesting, broad and cleanly molded, high cheekbones, wide full mouth, stubborn chin, snub nose, storm-gray eyes set far apart under heavy dark brows. A superior peasant type, he decided, and felt more at ease in the armor of his inbred haughtiness. He leaned back and crossed his legs.

"I am Helena Jansky, in command of this vessel," she said. Her voice was low and resonant, the note of strength in it. "I need you for a certain purpose. Why did you resist the Imperial summons?"

Donovan shrugged. "Let's say that I'm used to giving orders, not receiving them."

"Ah—yes." She ruffled the papers on her desk. "You were the Earl of Lanstead, weren't you?"

"After my father and older brother were killed in the war, yes." He lifted his head. "I am still the Earl."

She studied him with a dispassionate gaze that he found strangely uncomfortable. "I must say that you are a curious sort of leader." she murmured. "One who spends his time in a tavern getting drunk, and who on a whim provokes a disorder in which many of his innocent followers are hurt or killed, in which property difficult to replace is smashed—yes, I think it was about time that Ansa had a change of leadership."

Donovan's face was hot. Hell take it, what right had she to tell him what to do? What right had the whole damned Empire to come barging in where it wasn't wanted? "The Families, under the king, have governed Ansa since it was colonized," he said stiffly. "If it had been such a misrule as you seem to think, would the commons have fought for us as they did?"

❖❚❖

Again that thoughtful stare. She saw a tall young man, badly disarrayed, blood and dirt streaking his long, thin-carved, curve-nosed features, an old scar jagging across his high narrow forehead. The hair was yellow, the eyes were blue, the whole look that of an old and settled aristocracy. His bitter voice lashed at her: "We ruled Ansa well because we were part of it, we grew up with the planet and we understood our folk and men were free under us. That's something which no upstart Solar Empire can have, not for centuries, not ever to judge by the stock they use for nobility. When peasants command spaceships—"

Her face grew a little pale, but she smiled and replied evenly, "I am the Lady Jansky of Torgandale on Valor—Sirius A IV—and you are now a commoner. Please remember that."

"All the papers in the Galaxy won't change the fact that your grandfather was a dirt farmer on Valor."

"He was an atomjack, and I'm proud of it. I suggest further that an aristocrat who has nothing to trade on but his pedigree is very ragged indeed. Now, enough of that." Her crisp tones snapped forth. "You've committed a serious offense, especially since this is still occupied territory. If you wish to cooperate with me, I can arrange for a pardon—also for your brawling friends. If not, the whole bunch of you can go to the mines."

Donovan shook his head, trying to clear it of alcohol and weariness and the ringing left by the parabeam. "Go on," he said, a little thickly. "I'll listen, anyway."

"What do you know of the Black Nebula?"

She must have seen his muscles jerk. For an instant he sat fighting himself, grasping at rigidity with all the strength that was in him, and the memory was a blaze and a shout and a stab of pure fear.

Valduma, Valduma!

The sudden thudding of his heart was loud in his ears, and he could feel the fine beads of sweat starting forth on his skin. He made a wrenching effort and pulled his mouth into a lopsided grin, but his voice wavered: "Which black nebula? There are a lot of them."

"Don't try to bait me." Her eyes were narrowed on him, and the fingers of one hand drummed the desktop. "You know I mean *the* Black Nebula. Nobody in this Galactic sector speaks of any other."

"Why—well—" Donovan lowered his face to hide it till he could stiffen the mask, rubbing his temples with manacled hands. "It's just a nebula. A roughly spherical dustcloud, maybe a light-year in diameter, about ten parsecs from Ansa toward Sagittari. A few colonized stars on its fringes, nothing inside it as far as anyone knows. It has a bad name for some reason. The superstitious say it's haunted, and you hear stories of ships disappearing—Well, it gets a pretty wide berth. Not much out there anyway."

His mind was racing, he thought he could almost hear it click and whirr as it spewed forth idea after idea, memory after memory. *Valduma and the blackness and they who laughed. The Nebula is pure poison, and now the Empire is getting interested. By God, it might poison them! Only would it stop there? This time they might decide to go on, to come out of the blackness.*

Jansky's voice seemed to come from very far away: "You know more than that, Donovan. Intelligence has been sifting Ansan records. You were the farthest-ranging space raider your planet had, and you had a base on Heim, at the very edge of the Nebula. Among your reports, there is an account of your men's unease, of the disappearance of small ships which cut through the Nebula on their missions, of ghostly things seen aboard other vessels and men who went mad. Your last report on the subject says that you investigated personally, that most of your crew went more or less crazy while in the Nebula, and that you barely got free. You recommend the abandonment of Heim and the suspension of operations in that territory. This was done, the region being of no great strategic importance anyway."

"Very well." The voice held a whipcrack undertone. "What do you know about the Black Nebula?"

Donovan had fought his way back to impassivity. "You have about the whole story already," he said. "There were all sorts of illusions as we penetrated, whisperings and glimpses of impossible things and so on. It didn't affect me much, but it drove many toward insanity and some died. There was also very real and unexplainable trouble—engines, lights, and so on. My guess is that there's some sort of radiation in the Nebula which makes atoms and electrons misbehave; that'd affect the human nervous system too, of course. If you're thinking of entering it yourself, my only advice is—don't."

"Hm." She cupped her chin in one hand and looked down at the papers. "Frankly, we know very little about this Galactic sector. Very few Terrans were ever here before the war, and previous intercourse on your part with Sol was even slighter. However, Intelligence has learned that the natives of almost every inhabited planet on the fringes of the Nebula worship it or at least regard it as the home of the gods."

"Well, it is a conspicuous object in their skies," said Donovan. He added truthfully enough: "I only know about Heim, where the native religion in the area of our base was a sort of devil-worship centered around the Nebula. They made big sacrifices—foodstuffs, furs, tools, every conceivable item of use or luxury—which they claimed the devil-gods came and took. Some of the colonists thought there was something behind the legends, but I have my doubts." He shrugged. "Will that do?"

"For the time being." Jansky smiled with a certain bleak humor. "You can write a detailed report later on, and I strongly advise you not to mislead me. Because you're going there with us."

Donovan accepted the news coldly, but he thought the knocking of his heart must shake his whole body. His hands felt chilly and wet. "As you wish. Though what I can do—"

"You've been there before and know what to expect. Furthermore, you know the astrogation of that region; our charts are worse than sketchy, and even the Ansan tables have too many blank spots."

"Well—" Donovan got the words out slowly. "If I don't have to enlist. I will not take an oath to your Emperor."

"You needn't. Your status will be that of a civilian under Imperial command, directly responsible to me. You will have a cabin of your own, but no compensation except the abandonment of criminal proceedings against you." Jansky relaxed and her voice grew gentler. "However, if you serve well I'll see what I can do about pay. I daresay you could use some extra money."

"Thank you," said Donovan formally. He entered the first phase of the inchoate plan which was taking cloudy shape in his hammering brain: "May I have my personal slave with me? He's nonhuman, but he can eat Terran food."

Jansky smiled. There was sudden warmth in that smile, it made her human and beautiful. "As you wish, if he doesn't have fleas. I'll write you an order for his embarkation." She'd hit the ceiling when she found what kind of passenger she'd agreed to, thought Donovan.

But by then it would be too late. *And, with Wocha to help me, and the ship blundering blind into the Nebula—Valduma, Valduma, I'm coming back! And this time will you kiss me or kill me?*

The *Ganymede* lifted gravs and put the Ansa sun behind her. Much farther behind was Sol, an insignificant mote fifty light-years away, lost in the thronging glory of stars. Ahead lay Sagittari, Galactic center and the Black Nebula.

Space burned and blazed with a million bitter-bright suns, keen cold unwinking flames strewn across the utter dark of space, flashing and flashing over the hollow gulf of the leagues and the years. The Milky Way foamed in curdled silver around that enormous night, a shining girdle jeweled with the constellations. Far and far away wheeled the mysterious green and blue-white of the other galaxies, sparks of a guttering fire with a reeling immensity between. Looking toward the bows, one saw the great star-clusters of Sagittari, the thronging host of suns burning and thundering at the heart of the Galaxy. *And what have we done?* thought Basil Donovan. *What is man and all his proud achievements? Our home star is a dwarf on the lonely fringe of the Galaxy, out where the stars thin away toward the great emptiness. We've ranged maybe two hundred light-years from it in all directions and it's thirty thousand to the Center! Night and mystery and nameless immensities around us, our day of glory the briefest flicker on the edge of nowhere, then oblivion forever—and we won't be forgotten, because we'll never have been noticed. The Black Nebula is only the least and outermost of the great clouds which thicken toward the Center and hide its ultimate heart from us, it is nothing even as we, and yet it holds a power older than the human race and a terror that may whelm it.*

He felt again the old quailing funk, fear crawled along his spine and will drained out of his soul. He wanted to run, escape, huddle under the sky of Ansa to hide from the naked blaze of the universe, live out his day and forget that he had seen the scornful face of God. But there was no turning back, not now, the ship was already outpacing light on her secondary drive and he was half a prisoner aboard. He squared his shoulders and walked away from the viewplate, back toward his cabin.

Wocha was sprawled on a heap of blankets, covering the floor with his bulk. He was turning the brightly colored pages of a child's picture book. "Boss," he asked, "when do we kill 'em?"

"The Impies? Not yet, Wocha. Maybe not at all." Donovan stepped over the monster and lay down on his bunk, hands behind his head. He could feel the thrum of the driving engines, quivering in the ship and his bones. "The Nebula may do that for us."

"We go back there?" Wocha stirred uneasily. "I don't like, boss. It's *toombar*. Bad."

"Yeah, so it is."

"Better we stay home. Manor needs repair. Peasants need our help. I need beer."

"So do I. I'll see if we can't promote some from the quartermaster. Old John can look after the estate while we're away, and the peasants will just have to look after themselves. Maybe it's time they learned how." At a knock on the door: "Come in."

Tetsuo Takahashi, the ship's exec, brought his small sturdy form around Wocha and sat down on the edge of the bunk. "Your slave has the Old Lady hopping mad," he grinned. "He'll eat six times a man's ration."

"And drink it." Donovan smiled back; he couldn't help liking the cocky little Terran. Then, with a sudden renewed bitterness: "And he's worth it. I couldn't be without him. He may not be so terribly bright, but he's my only proof that loyalty and decency aren't extinct."

Takahashi gave him a puzzled look. "Why do you hate us so much?" he asked.

"You came in where you weren't asked. Ansa was free, and now it's just another province of your damned Empire."

"Maybe so. But you were a backwater, an underpopulated agricultural planet which nobody had ever heard of, exposed to barbarian raids and perhaps to nonhuman conquest. You're safe now, and you're part of a great social-economic system which can do more than all those squabbling little kingdoms and republics and theocracies and God knows what else put together could ever dream of."

"Who said we wanted to be safe? Our ancestors came to Ansa to be free. We fought Shalmu when the greenies wanted to take what we'd built, and then we made friends with them. We had elbow room and a way of life that was our own. Now you'll bring in your surplus population to fill our green lands with yelling cities and squalling people. You'll tear down the culture we evolved so painfully and make us just another bunch of kowtowing Imperial citizens."

"Frankly, Donovan, I don't think it was much of a culture. It sat in its comfortable rut and admired the achievements of its ancestors. What did your precious Families do but hunt and loaf and throw big parties? Maybe they did fulfill a magisterial function—so what? Any elected yut could do the same in that simple a society." Takahashi fixed his eyes on Donovan's. "But rights and wrongs aside, the Empire had to annex Ansa, and when you wouldn't come in peaceably you had to be dragged in."

"Yeah. A dumping ground for people who were too stupid not to control their own breeding."

"Your Ansan peasants, my friend, have about twice the Terran birth rate. It's merely that there are more Terrans to start with—and Sirians and Centaurians and all the old settled planets. No, it was more than that. It was a question of military necessity."

"Uh-huh. Sure."

"Read your history sometime. When the Commonwealth broke up in civil wars two hundred years ago it was hell between the stars. Half savage peoples who never should have left their planets had learned how to build spaceships and were going out to raid and conquer. A dozen would-be overlords scorched whole worlds with their battles. You can't have anarchy on an interstellar scale. Too many people suffer. Old Manuel I had the guts to proclaim himself Emperor of Sol—no pretty euphemisms for him, an empire was needed and an empire was what he built. He kicked the barbarians out of the Solar System and went on to conquer their home territories and civilize them. That meant he had to subjugate stars closer to home, to protect his lines of communication. This led to further trouble elsewhere. Oh, yes, a lot of it was greed, but the planets which were conquered for their wealth would have been sucked in anyway by sheer economics. The second Argolid carried on, and now his son, Manuel II, is finishing the job. We've very nearly attained what we must have—an empire large enough to be socio-economically self-sufficient and defend itself against all comers, of which there are many, without being too large for control. You should visit the inner

Empire sometime, Donovan, and see how many social evils it's been possible to wipe out because of security and central power. But we need this sector to protect our Sagittarian flank, so we're taking it. Fifty years from now you'll be glad we did."

Donovan looked sourly up at him.

"Why are you feeding me that?" he asked. "I've heard it before."

"We're going to survey a dangerous region, and you're our guide. The captain and I think there's more than a new radiation in the Black Nebula. I'd like to think we could trust you."

"Think so if you wish."

"We could use a hypnoprobe on you, you know. We'd squeeze your skull dry of everything it contained. But we'd rather spare you that indignity."

"And you might need me when you get there, and I'd still be only half conscious. Quit playing the great altruist, Takahashi."

The exec shook his head. "There's something wrong inside you, Donovan," he murmured. "You aren't the man who licked us at Luga."

"Luga!" Donovan's eyes flashed. "Were you there?"

"Sure. Destroyer *North Africa*, just come back from the Zarune front—Cigarette?"

They fell to yarning and passed a pleasant hour. Donovan could not suppress a vague regret when Takahashi left. *They aren't such bad fellows, those Impies, They were brave and honorable enemies, and they've been lenient conquerors as such things go. But when we hit the Black Nebula—*

He shuddered. "Wocha, get that whiskey out of my trunk."

"You not going to get drunk again, boss?" The Donarrian's voice rumbled disappointment.

"I am. And I'm going to try to stay drunk the whole damn voyage. You just don't know what we're heading for, Wocha."

Stranger, go back.
Spaceman, go home. Turn back, adventurer.
It is death. Return, human.

The darkness whispered. Voices ran down the length of the ship, blending with the unending murmur of the drive, urging, commanding, whispering so low that it seemed to be within men's skulls.

Basil Donovan lay in darkness. His mouth tasted foul, and there was a throb in his temples and a wretchedness in his throat. He lay and listened to the voice which had wakened him.

Go home, wanderer. You will die, your ship will plunge through the hollow dark till the stars grow cold. Turn home, human.

"Boss. I hear them, boss. I'm scared."

"How long have we been under weigh? When did we leave Ansa?"

"A week ago, boss, maybe more. You been drunk. Wake up, boss, turn on the light. They're whispering in the dark, and I'm scared."

"We must be getting close."

Return. Go home. First comes madness and then comes death and then comes the spinning outward forever. Turn back, spaceman.

Bodiless whisper out of the thick thrumming dark, sourceless all-pervading susurration, and it mocked, there was the cruel cynical scorn of the outer vastness running up and down the laughing voice. It murmured, it jeered, it ran along nerves with little icy feet and flowed through the brain, it called and gibed and hungered. It warned them to go back, and it knew they wouldn't and railed its mockery at them for it. Demon whisper, there in the huge cold loneliness, sneering and grinning and waiting.

Donovan sat up and groped for the light switch. "We're close enough," he said tonelessly. "We're in their range now."

Footsteps racketed in the corridor outside. A sharp rap on his door. "Come in. Come in and enjoy yourself."

❈ III ❈

Donovan hadn't found the switch before the door was open and light spilled in from the hallway fluorotubes. Cold white light, a shaft of it picking out Wocha's monstrous form and throwing grotesque shadows on the walls. Commander Jansky was there, in full uniform, and Ensign Jeanne Scoresby, her aide. The younger girl's face was white, her eyes enormous, but Jansky wore grimness like an armor.

"All right, Donovan," she said. "You've had your binge, and now the trouble is starting. You didn't say they were voices."

"They could be anything," he answered, climbing out of the bunk and steadying himself with one hand. His head swam a little. The corners of the room were thick with shadow.

Back, spaceman. Turn home, human.

"Delusions?" The man laughed unpleasantly. His face was pale and gaunt, unshaven in the bleak radiance. "When you start going crazy, I imagine you always hear voices."

There was contempt in the gray eyes that raked him. "Donovan, I put a technician to work on it when the noises began a few hours ago. He recorded them. They're very faint, and they seem to originate just outside the ear of anyone who hears them, but they're real enough. Radiations don't speak in human Anglic with an accent such as I never heard before. Not unless they're carrier waves for a message. Donovan, who or what is inside the Black Nebula?"

The Ansan's laugh jarred out again. "Who or what is inside this ship?" he challenged. "Our great human science has no way of making the air vibrate by itself. Maybe there are ghosts, standing invisible just beside us and whispering in our ears."

"We could detect nothing, no radiations, no energy-fields, nothing but the sounds themselves. I refuse to believe that matter can be set in motion without some kind of physical force being applied." Jansky clapped a hand to her sidearm. "You know what is waiting for us. You know how they do it."

"Go ahead. Hypnoprobe me. Lay me out helpless for a week. Or shoot me if you like. You'll be just as dead whatever you do."

Her tones were cold and sharp. "Get on your clothes and come up to the bridge."

He shrugged, picked up his uniform, and began to shuck his pajamas. The women looked away.

Human, go back. You will go mad and die.

Valduma, he thought, with a wrenching deep inside him. *Valduma, I've returned.*

He stepped over to the mirror. The Ansan uniform was a gesture of defiance, and it occurred to him that he should shave if he wore it in front of these Terrans. He ran the electric razor over cheeks and chin, pulled his tunic straight, and turned back. "All right."

They went out into the hallway. A spaceman went by on some errand. His eyes were strained wide, staring at blankness, and his lips moved. The voices were speaking to him.

"It's demoralizing the crew," said Jansky. "It has to stop."

"Go ahead and stop it," jeered Donovan. "Aren't you the representative of the almighty Empire of Sol? Command them in the name of His Majesty to stop."

"The crew, I mean," she said impatiently. "They've got no business being frightened by a local phenomenon."

"Any human would be," answered Donovan. "You are, though you won't admit it. I am. We can't help ourselves. It's instinct."

"Instinct?" Her clear eyes were a little surprised.

"Sure." Donovan halted before a viewscreen. Space blazed and roiled against the reaching darkness. "Just look out there. It's the primeval night, it's the blind unknown where unimaginable inhuman Powers are abroad. We're still the old half-ape, crouched over his fire and trembling while the night roars around us. Our lighted, heated, metal-armored ship is still the lonely cave-fire, the hearth with steel and stone laid at the door to keep out the gods. When the Wild Hunt breaks through and shouts at us, we must be frightened, it's the primitive fear of the dark. It's part of us."

She swept on, her cloak a scarlet wing flapping behind her. They took the elevator to the bridge.

Donovan had not watched the Black Nebula grow over the days, swell to a monstrous thing that blotted out half the sky, lightlessness fringed with the cold glory of the stars. Now that the ship was entering its tenuous outer fringes, the heavens on either side were blurring and dimming, and the blackness yawned before. Even the densest nebula is a hard vacuum; but tons upon incredible tons of cosmic dust and gas, reaching planetary and interstellar distances on every hand, will blot out the sky. It was like rushing into an endless, bottomless hole, the ship was falling and falling into the pit of Hell.

"I noticed you never looked bow-wards on the trip," said Jansky. There was steel in her voice. "Why did you lock yourself in your cabin and drink like a sponge?"

"I was bored," he replied sullenly.

"You were afraid!" she snapped contemptuously. "You didn't dare watch the Nebula growing. Something happened the last time you were here which sucked the guts out of you."

"Didn't your Intelligence talk to the men who were with me?"

"Yes, of course. None of them would say more than you've said.

They all wanted us to come here, but blind and unprepared. Well, Mister Donovan, we're going in!"

The floorplates shook under Wocha's tread. "You not talk to boss that way," he rumbled.

"Let be, Wocha," said Donovan. "It doesn't matter how she talks."

He looked ahead, and the old yearning came alive in him, the fear and the memory, but he had not thought that it would shiver with such a strange gladness.

And—who knew? A bargain—

Valduma, come back to me!

Jansky's gaze on him narrowed, but her voice was suddenly low and puzzled. "You're smiling," she whispered.

He turned from the viewscreen and his laugh was ragged. "Maybe I'm looking forward to this visit, Helena."

"My name," she said stiffly, "is Commander Jansky."

"Out there, maybe. But in here there is no rank, no Empire, no mission. We're all humans, frightened little humans huddling together against the dark." Donovan's smile softened. "You know, Helena, you have very beautiful eyes."

The slow flush crept up her high smooth cheeks. "I want a full report of what happened to you last time," she said. "Now. Or you go under the probe."

Wanderer, it is a long way home. Spaceman, spaceman, your sun is very far away.

"Why, certainly." Donovan leaned against the wall and grinned at her. "Glad to. Only you won't believe me."

She made no reply, but folded her arms and waited. The ship trembled with its forward thrust. Sweat beaded the forehead of the watch officer and he glared around him.

"We're entering the home of all lawlessness," said Donovan. "The realm of magic, the outlaw world of werebeasts and night-gangers. Can't you hear the wings outside? These ghosts are only the first sign. We'll have a plague of witches soon."

"Get out!" she said.

He shrugged. "All right, Helena. I told you you wouldn't believe me." He turned and walked slowly from the bridge.

✳ ✳ ✳

Outside was starless, lightless, infinite black. The ship crept forward, straining her detectors, groping into the blind dark while her crew went mad.

Spaceman, it is too late. You will never find your way home again. You are dead men on a ghost ship, and you will fall forever into the Night.

"I saw him, Wong, I saw him down in Section Three, tall and thin and black. He laughed at me, and then there wasn't anything there."

Sound of great wings beating somewhere outside the hull.

Mother, can I have him? Can I have his skull to play with?

Not yet, child. Soon. Soon.

Wicked rain of laughter and the sound of clawed feet running.

No one went alone. Spacemen First Class Gottfried and Martinez went down a starboard companionway and saw the hooded black form waiting for them. Gottfried pulled out his blaster and fired. The ravening beam sprang backward and consumed him. Martinez lay mumbling in psychobay.

The lights went out. After an hour they flickered back on again, but men had rioted and killed each other in the dark.

Commander Jansky recalled all personal weapons on the grounds that the crew could no longer be trusted with them. The men drew up a petition to get them back. When it was refused, there was muttering of revolt.

Spacemen, you have wandered too far. You have wandered beyond the edge of creation, and now there is only death.

The hours dragged into days. When the ship's timepieces started disagreeing, time ceased to have meaning.

Basil Donovan sat in his cabin. There was a bottle in his hand, but he tried to go slow. He was waiting.

When the knock came, he leaped from his seat and every nerve tightened up and screamed. He swore at himself. They wouldn't knock when they came for him. "Go on, enter—" His voice wavered.

Helena Jansky stepped inside, closing the door after her. She had thinned, and there was darkness in her eyes, but she still bore herself erect. Donovan had to salute the stubborn courage that was in her. The unimaginative peasant blood—no, it was more than that, she was as intelligent as he, but there was a deep strength in that tall form, a quiet vitality which had perhaps been bred out of the Families of Ansa. "Sit down," he invited.

She sighed and ran a hand through her dark hair. "Thanks."

"Drink?"

"No. Not on duty."

"And the captain is always on duty. Well, let it go." Donovan lowered himself to the bunk beside her, resting his feet on Wocha's columnar leg. The Donarrian muttered and whimpered in his sleep. "What can I do for you?"

Her gaze was steady and grave. "You can tell me the truth."

"About the Nebula? Why should I? Give me one good reason why an Ansan should care what happens to a Solarian ship."

"Perhaps only that we're all human beings here, that those boys have earth and rain and sunlight and wives waiting for them."

And Valduma—no, she isn't human. Fire and ice and storming madness, but not human. Too beautiful to be flesh.

"This trip was your idea," he said defensively.

"Donovan, you wouldn't have played such a foul trick and made such a weak, self-righteous excuse in the old days."

He looked away, feeling his cheeks hot. "Well," he mumbled, "why not turn around, get out of the Nebula if you can, and maybe come back later with a task force?"

"And lead them all into this trap? Our subtronics are out, you know. We can't send information back, so we'll just go on and learn a little more and then try to fight our way home."

His smile was crooked. "I may have been baiting you, Helena. But if I told you everything I know, it wouldn't help. There isn't enough."

Her hand fell strong and urgent on his. "Tell me, then! Tell me anyway."

"But there is so little. There's a planet somewhere in the Nebula, and it has inhabitants with powers I don't begin to understand. But among other things, they can project themselves hyperwise, just like a spaceship, without needing engines to do it. And they have a certain control over matter and energy."

"The fringe stars—these beings in the Nebula really have been their 'gods'?"

"Yes. They've projected themselves, terrorized the natives for centuries, and carry home the sacrificial materials for their own use. They're doubtless responsible for all the ships around here that never came home. They don't like visitors." Donovan saw her smile, and his own lips twitched. "But they did, I suppose, take some prisoners, to learn our language and anything else they could about us."

She nodded. "I'd conjectured as much. If you don't accept theories involving the supernatural, and I don't, it follows almost necessarily. If a few of them projected themselves aboard and hid somewhere, they could manipulate air molecules from a distance so as to produce the whisperings—" She smiled afresh, but the hollowness was still in her. "When you call it a new sort of ventriloquism, it doesn't sound nearly so bad, does it?"

Fiercely, the woman turned on him. "And what have you had to do with them? How are you so sure?"

"I—talked with one of them," he replied slowly. "You might say we struck up a friendship of sorts. But I learned nothing, and the only benefit I got was escaping. I've no useful information." His voice sharpened. "And that's all I have to say."

"Well, we're going on!" Her head lifted pridefully.

Donovan's smile was a crooked grimace. He took her hand, and it lay unresisting between his fingers. "Helena," he said, "you've been trying to psychoanalyze me this whole trip. Maybe it's my turn now. You're not so hard as you tell yourself."

"I am an officer of the Imperial Navy." Her haughtiness didn't quite come off.

"Sure, sure. A hard-shelled career girl. Only you're also a healthy human being. Down underneath, you want a home and kids and quiet green hills. Don't lie to yourself, that wouldn't be fitting to the Lady Jansky of Torgandale, would it? You went into service because it was the thing to do. And you're just a scared kid, my dear." Donovan shook his head. "But a very nice-looking kid."

Tears glimmered on her lashes. "Stop it," she whispered desperately. "Don't say it."

He kissed her, a long slow kiss with her mouth trembling under his and her body shivering ever so faintly. The second time she responded, shy as a child, hardly aware of the sudden hunger.

She pulled free then, sat with eyes wide and wild, one hand lifted to her mouth. "No," she said, so quietly he could scarce hear. "No, not now—"

Suddenly she got up and almost fled. Donovan sighed.

Why did I do that? To stop her inquiring too closely? Or just because she's honest and human, and Valduma isn't? Or—

Darkness swirled before his eyes. Wocha came awake and shrank against the farther wall, terror rattling in his throat. "Boss—boss, she's here again—"

Donovan sat unstirring, elbows on knees, hands hanging empty, and looked at the two who had come. "Hello, Valduma," he said.

"Basil—" Her voice sang against him, rippling, lilting, the unending sharp laughter beneath its surprise. "Basil, you have come back."

"Uh-huh." He nodded at the other. "You're Morzach, aren't you? Sit down. Have a drink. Old home week."

The creature from Arzun remained erect. He looked human on the outside, tall and gaunt in a black cape which glistened with tiny points of starlight, the hood thrown back so that his red hair fell free to his shoulders. The face was long and thin, chiseled to an ultimate refinement of classical beauty, white and cold. Cold as space-tempered steel, in spite of the smile on the pale lips, in spite of the dark mirth in the slant green eyes. One hand rested on the jeweled hilt of a sword.

Valduma stood beside Morzach for an instant, and Donovan watched her with the old sick wildness rising and clamoring in him.

You are the fairest thing which ever was between the stars, you are ice and flame and living fury, stronger and weaker than man, cruel and sweet as a child a thousand years old, and I love you. But you are not human, Valduma.

She was tall, and her grace was a lithe rippling flow, wind and fire and music made flesh, a burning glory of hair rushing past her black-caped shoulders, hands slim and beautiful, the strange clean-molded face white as polished ivory, the mouth red and laughing, the eyes long and oblique and gold-flecked green. When she spoke, it was like singing in Heaven and laughter in Hell. Donovan looked at her, not moving.

"Basil, you came back to me?"

"He came because he had to." Morzach of Arzun folded his arms, eyes smoldering in anger. "Best we kill him now."

"Later, perhaps later, but not now." Valduma laughed aloud.

Suddenly she was in Donovan's arms. Her kisses were a rain of fire. There was thunder and darkness and dancing stars. He was aware of nothing else, not for a long, long time.

She leaned back in his grasp, smiling up at him, stroking his hair with one slender hand.

His cheek was bloody where she had scratched him. He looked back into her eyes—they were cat's eyes, split-pupiled, all gold and emerald without the human white. She laughed very softly. "Shall I kill you now?" she whispered. "Or drive you mad first? Or let you go again? What would be most amusing, Basil?"

"This is no time for your pranks," said Morzach sharply. "We have to deal with this ship. It's getting dangerously close to Arzun, and we've been unable yet to break the morale and discipline of the crew. I think the only way is to wreck the ship."

"Wreck it on Arzun, yes!" Valduma's laughter pulsed and throbbed. "Bring them to their goal. Help them along, even. Oh, yes, Morzach, it is a good thought!"

"We'll need your help," said the creature-man to Donovan. "I take it that you're guiding them. You must encourage them to offer no resistance when we take over the controls. Our powers won't stand too long against atomic energy."

"Why should I help you?" Donovan's tones were hoarse. "What can you give me?"

"If you live," said Valduma, "and can make your way to Drogobych, I might give you much." She laughed again, maniac laughter which did not lose its music. "That would be diverting!"

"I don't know," he groaned. "I don't know—I thought a bargain could be made, but now I wonder."

"I leave him to you," said Morzach sardonically, and vanished.

"Basil," whispered Valduma. "Basil, I have—sometimes—missed you."

"Get out, Wocha," said Donovan,

"Boss—she's toombar—"

"Get out!"

Wocha lumbered slowly from the cabin. There were tears in his eyes.

✧IV✧

The *Ganymede*'s engines rose to full power and the pilot controls spun over without a hand on them.

"Engine room! Engine room! Stop that nonsense down there!"

"We can't—they're frozen—the converter has gone into full without us—"

"Sir, I can't budge this stick. It's locked somehow."

The lights went out. Men screamed.

"Get me a flashlight!" snapped Takahashi in the dark. "I'll take this damned panel apart myself."

The beam etched his features against night. "Who goes?" he cried.

"It's I." Jansky appeared in the dim reflected glow. "Never mind, Takahashi. Let the ship have her way."

"But ma'm, we could crash—"

"I've finally gotten Donovan to talk. He says we're in the grip of some kind of powerbeam. They'll pull us to one of their space stations and then maybe we can negotiate—or fight. Come on, we've got to quiet the men."

The flashlight went out. Takahashi's laugh was shrill. "Better quiet me first, Captain."

Her hand was on his arm, steadying, strengthening. "Don't fail me, Tetsuo. You're the last one I've got. I just had to paralyze Scoresby."

"Thanks—thanks, chief. I'm all right now. Let's go."

They fumbled through blindness. The engines roared, full speed ahead with a ghost on the bridge. Men were stumbling and cursing and screaming in the dark. Someone switched on the battle-stations siren, and its howl was the last voice of insanity.

Struggle in the dark, wrestling, paralyzing the berserk, calling on all the iron will which had lifted humankind to the stars—slow restoration of order, men creeping to general quarters, breathing heavily in the guttering light of paper torches.

The engines cut off and the ship snapped into normal matter state. Helena Jansky saw blood-red sunlight through the viewport. There was no time to sound the alarm before the ship crashed.

"A hundred men. No more than a hundred men alive."

She wrapped her cloak tight about her against the wind and stood looking across the camp. The streaming firelight touched her face with red, limning it against the utter dark of the night heavens, sheening faintly in the hair that blew wildly around her strong bitter countenance. Beyond, other fires danced and flickered in the gloom, men huddled around them while the cold seeped slowly to their bones. Here and there an injured human moaned.

Across the ragged spine of bare black hills they could still see the molten glow of the wreck. When it hit, the atomic converters had run wild and begun devouring the hull. There had barely been time for the survivors to drag themselves and some of the cripples free, and to put the rocky barrier between them and the mounting radioactivity. During the slow red sunset, they had gathered wood, hewing with knives at the distorted scrub trees reaching above the shale and snow of the valley. Now they sat waiting out the night.

Takahashi shuddered. "God, it's cold!"

"It'll get colder," said Donovan tonelessly. "This is an old planet of an old red dwarf sun. Its rotation has slowed. The nights are long."

"How do you know?" Lieutenant Elijah Cohen glared at him out of a crudely bandaged face. The firelight made his eyes gleam red. "How do you know unless you're in with them? Unless you arranged this yourself?"

Wocha reached forth a massive fist. "You shut up," he rumbled.

"Never mind," said Donovan. "I just thought some things would be obvious. You saw the star, so you should know it's the type of a burned-out dwarf. Since planets are formed at an early stage of a star's evolution, this world must be old too. Look at these rocks— citrified, back when the stellar energy output got really high just before the final collapse; and nevertheless eroded down to bare snags. That takes millions of years."

He reflected that his reasoning, while sound enough, was based on foreknown conclusions. *Cohen's right. I have betrayed them. It was Valduma, watching over me, who brought Wocha and myself unhurt through the crash. I saw, Valduma, I saw you with your hair flying in the chaos, riding witch-like through sundering ruin, and you were laughing. Laughing!* He felt ill.

"Nevertheless, the planet has a thin but breathable atmosphere, frozen water, and vegetable life," said Takahashi. "Such things don't survive the final hot stage of a sun without artificial help. This planet has natives. Since we were deliberately crashed here, I daresay the natives are our earlier friends." He turned dark accusing eyes on the Ansan. "How about it, Donovan?"

"I suppose you're right," he answered. "I knew there was a planet in the Nebula, the natives had told me that in my previous trip. This star lies near the center, in a 'hollow' region where there isn't enough dust to force the planet into its primary, and shares a common velocity with the Nebula. It stays here, in other words."

"You told me—" Helena Jansky bit her lip, then slowly forced the words out: "You told me, and I believed you, that there was nothing immediately to fear when the Nebulites took over our controls. So we didn't fight them; we didn't try to overcome their forces with our own engines. And it cost us the ship and over half her crew."

"I told you what happened to me last time," he lied steadfastly. "I can't help it if things were different this trip."

She turned her back. The wind blew a thin hissing veil of dry snow across her ankles. A wounded man suddenly screamed out there in the dark.

How does it feel, Donovan? You made her trust you and then betrayed her for a thing that isn't even human. How does it feel to be a Judas?

"Never mind recriminations," said Takahashi. "This isn't the time to hold trials. We've got to decide what to do."

"They have a city on this planet," said Donovan. "Drogobych, they call it, and the planet's name is Arzun. It lies somewhere near the equator, they told me once. If they meant us to make our own way to it—and it would be like them—then it may well be due south. We can march that way, assuming that the sun set in the west."

"Nothing to lose," shrugged the Terran. "But we haven't many weapons, a few assorted sidearms is all, and they aren't much use against these creatures anyway."

Something howled out in the darkness. The ground quivered, ever so faintly, to the pounding of heavy feet.

"Wild animals yet!" Cohen grinned humorlessly. "Better sound battle stations, Captain."

"Yes, yes, I suppose so." She blew her whistle, a thin shrilling in the windy dark. As she turned around, Donovan saw a gleam running along her cheek. Tears?

The noise came closer. They heard the rattle of claws on stone. The Terrans moved together, guns in front, clubs and rocks and bare hands behind. They have guts, thought Donovan. God, but they have guts!

"Food would be scarce on a barren planet like this," said Ensign Chundra Dass. "We seem to be elected."

The hollow roar sounded, echoing between the hills and caught up by the thin harrying wind. "Hold fire," said Helena. Her voice was clear and steady. "Don't waste charges. Wait—"

The thing leaped out of darkness, a ten-meter length of gaunt scaled body and steel-hard claws and whipping tail, soaring through the snow-streaked air and caught in the vague uneasy firelight, Helena's blaster crashed, a lightning bolt sizzled against the armored head.

The monster screamed. Its body tumbled shatteringly among the humans, it seized a man in its jaws and shook him and trampled another underfoot. Takahashi stepped forward and shot again at its dripping wound. The blaster bolt zigzagged wildly off the muzzle of his gun.

Even the animals can do it—!

"I'll get him, boss!" Wocha reared on his hind legs, came down again with a thud, and charged. Stones flew from beneath his feet. The monster's tail swept out, a man tumbled before it with his ribs caved in, and Wocha staggered as he caught the blow. Still he rushed in, clutching the barbed end of the tail to his breast. The monster writhed, bellowing. Another blaster bolt hit it from the rear. It turned, and a shot at its eyes veered away.

Wocha hit it with all the furious momentum he had. He rammed its spearlike tail down the open jaws and blood spurted. "Ho, Donovan!" he shouted. As the thing screamed and snapped at him, he caught its jaws in his hands.

"Wocha!" yelled Donovan. "Wocha!" He ran wildly toward the fight.

The Donarrian's great back arched with strain. It was as if they could hear his muscles crack. Slowly, slowly, he forced the jaws wider. The monster lashed its body, pulling him to his knees, dragging him over the ground, and still he fought.

"Damn you," he roared in the whirling dust and snow, "hold still!"

The jaws broke. And the monster screamed once more, and then it wasn't there. Wocha tumbled over.

Donovan fell across him, sobbing, laughing, cursing. Wocha picked him up. "You all right, boss?" he asked. "You well?"

"Yes—yes—oh, you blind bloody fool! You stupid, blundering ass!" Donovan hugged him.

"Gone," said Helena. "It vanished."

They picked up their dead and wounded and returned to the fires. The cold bit deep. Something else hooted out in the night.

It was a long time before Takahashi spoke. "You might expect it," he said. "These parapsychical powers don't come from nowhere. The intelligent race, our enemies of Drogobych, simply have them highly developed; the animals do to a lesser extent. I think it's a matter of life being linked to the primary atomic probabilities, the psi functions which give the continuous-field distribution of matter-energy in space-time. In a word, control of external matter and energy by conscious will acting through the unified field which is space-time. Telekinesis."

"Uh-huh," said Dass wearily. "Even some humans have a slight para power. Control dice or electron beams or what have you. But why aren't the—what did you call them?—Arzunians overrunning the Galaxy?"

"They can only operate over a certain range, which happens to be about the distance to the fringe stars," said Donovan. "Beyond that distance, dispersion limits them, plus the fact that differences of potential energy must be made up from their own metabolism. The animals, of course, have very limited range, a few kilometers perhaps. The Arzunians use telekinesis to control matter and energy, and the same subspatial principles as our ships to go faster than light. Only since they aren't lugging around a lot of hull and passengers and assorted machinery—just themselves and a little air and maybe an armful of sacrificial goods from a fringe planet, they don't need atomic engines.

"They aren't interested in conquering the Galaxy. Why should they be? They can get all their needs and luxuries from the peoples to whom they are gods. An old race, very old, decadent if you will. But they don't like interference."

Takahashi looked at him sharply. "I glimpsed one of them on the ship," he said. "He carried a spear."

"Yeah. Another reason why they aren't conquerors. They have no sense for mechanics at all. Never had any reason to evolve one when they could manipulate matter directly without more than the simplest tools. They're probably more intelligent than humans in an all-around way, but they don't have the type of brain and the concentration needed to learn physics and chemistry. Aren't interested, either."

"So, swords against guns—We may have a chance!"

"They can turn your missiles, remember. Guns are little use, you have to distract them so they don't notice your shot till too late. But they can't control you. They aren't telepaths and their type of matter-control is heterodyned by living nerve currents. You could kill one of them with a sword where a gun would most likely kill you."

"I—see—" Helena looked strangely at him. "You're becoming very vocal all of a sudden."

Donovan rubbed his eyes and shivered in the cold. "What of it? You wanted the truth. You're getting it."

Why am I telling them? Why am I not just leading them to the slaughter as Valduma wanted? Is it that I can't stand the thought of Helena being hunted like a beast?

Whose side am I on? he thought wildly.

Takahashi gestured and his voice came eager. "That's it. That's it! The ship scattered assorted metal and plastic over twenty hectares as she fell. Safe for us to gather up tomorrow. We can use our blaster flames to shape weapons. Swords, axes, spears. By the Galaxy, we'll arm ourselves and then we'll march on Drogobych!"

❖**V**❖

It was a strange little army, thought Donovan, as strange as any the Galaxy had ever seen.

He looked back. The old ruined highway went down a narrow valley between sheer cliffs of eroded black stone reaching up toward the deep purplish heaven. The sun was wheeling westerly, a dull red ember throwing light like clotted blood on the dreariness of rock and ice and gaunt gray trees; a few snowflakes, borne on a thin dull wind, drifted across the path of march. A lonely bird, cruel-beaked and watchful, hovered on great black wings far overhead, waiting for them to die.

The men of the Imperial Solar Navy walked close together. They

were haggard and dirty and bearded, clad in such ragged articles as they
had been able to salvage, armed with the crudely forged weapons of a
vanished age, carrying their sick and wounded on rude litters. Ghost
world, ghost army, marching through an echoing windy solitude to its
unknown weird—but men's faces were still brave, and one of them was
singing. The sunburst banner of the Empire flapped above them, the
one splash of color in the great murky landscape.

Luck had been with them, of a sort. Game animals had appeared
in more abundance than one would have thought the region could
support, deer-like things which they shot for meat to supplement
their iron rations. They had stumbled on the old highway and
followed its arrow-straight course southward. Many days and many
tumbled hollow ruins of great cities lay behind them, and still they
trudged on.

Luck? wondered Donovan. *I think it was intentional. I think the
Arzunians want us to reach Drogobych.*

He heard the scrape of boots on the slanting hillside behind him,
and turned around to face Helena. He stopped and smiled. There had
been a slow unspoken intimacy growing between them as they
worked and struggled together. Not many words, but the eyes of each
would often stray to the other, and a hand would brush over a hand
as if by accident. Tired and hungry and road-stained, cap set askew
on tangled hair, skin reddened by wind and blued with cold, she was
still good to look on.

"Why are you walking so far from the road?" she asked.

"Oh serving as outrider, maybe," he said, resuming his stride. She
fell into step beside him. "Up here you get a wider view."

"Do you think we have much further to go, Basil?"

He shrugged.

"We'd never have come this far without you," she said, looking
down at her scuffed boots. "You and Wocha and Takahashi."

"Maybe the Empire will send a rescue mission when we don't
come back," he suggested.

"No doubt they will. But they can't find one little star in this
immensity. Even thermocouples won't help, the Nebula diffuses
radiation too much. And they'd be blundering into the same trap as we."
Helena looked up. "No, Basil, we've got to fight our way clear alone."

There was a long stretch of thicket growing on the hillside.

Donovan went along the right of it, cutting off view of the army. "You know," he said, "you and those boys down there make me feel a lot kinder toward the Empire."

"Thank you. Thank you. We—" She took his arm. "It's a question of unifying the human race, ultimately this whole region of stars, and—*Oh!*"

The beasts were suddenly there in front of them, lean black things which snarled with mouths of hunger. One of them circled toward the humans' flank, the other crouched. Donovan yanked his sword clear.

"Get behind me," he snapped, turning to face the approaching hunter.

"No—back to back—" Helena's own blade rasped from its sheath. She lifted a shout for help.

The nearest animal sprang for her throat. She hacked wildly, the blade twisted in her hand and scraped the muzzled face. Jaws clamped on the edged steel and let go with a bloody howl. Donovan swung at the other beast, the blow shuddered home and it screamed and writhed and snapped at his ankles.

Whirling, he turned on the thing which had launched itself at Helena. He hewed, and the animal wasn't there, his blade rang on naked stone. A weight crashed against his back, he went down and the teeth clamped on his shoulder.

Helena swung. The carnivore raised its head to snarl at her, and she gripped the sword in both hands and stabbed. It threshed wildly, dying, spewing blood over the hillside. The other, wounded creature disappeared.

Helena bent over Donovan, held him close, her eyes wild. "Are you hurt? Basil. Oh Basil, are you hurt?"

"No," he muttered. "The teeth didn't have time to work through this heavy jacket." He pulled her head down against his.

"Basil, Basil!"

He rose, still holding her to him. Her arms locked about his neck, and there were tears and laughter in her voice. "Oh, Basil, my darling."

"Helena," he murmured. "I love you, Helena."

"When we get home—I'm due for furlough, I'll retire instead—your house on Ansa—Oh, Basil, I never thought I could be so glad!"

The massive thunder of feet brought them apart. Wocha burst around the thicket, swinging his giant ax in both hands. "Are you all right, boss?" he roared.

"Yes, yes, we're all right. A couple of those damned wolf-like things which've been plaguing us the whole march. Go on back, Wocha, we'll join you soon."

The Donarrian's ape-face split in a vast grin. "So you take a female, boss?" he cried. "Good, good, we need lots of little Donovans at home!"

"Get on back, you old busybody, and keep that gossiping mouth shut!"

Hours later, Helena returned to the army where it was making camp. Donovan stayed where he was, looking down at the men where they moved about gathering wood and digging fire-pits. The blazes were a note of cheer in the thickening murk.

Helena, he thought. *Helena. She's a fine girl, wonderful girl, she's what the thinning Family blood and I, myself, need. But why did I do it? Why did I talk that way to her? Just then, in the strain and fear and loneliness, it seemed as if I cared. But I don't. She just another woman. She's not Valduma.*

The twilight murmured, and he saw the dim sheen of metal beside him. The men of Drogobych were gathering.

They stood tall and godlike in helmet and ring-mail and night-black cloaks, leaning on swords and spears, death-white faces cold with an ancient scorn as they looked down on the human camp. Their eyes were phosphorescent green in the dark.

Donovan nodded, without fear or surprise or anything but a sudden great weariness. He remembered some of them from the days when he had been alone in the bows of the ship with the invaders while his men cowered and rioted and went crazy in the stern sectors. "Hello, Morzach, Uboda, Zegoian, Korstuzan, Davleka," he said. "Welcome back again."

Valduma walked out of the blood-hued twilight, and he took her in his arms and held her for a long fierce time. Her kiss was as cruel as a swooping hawk. She bit his lips and he tasted blood warm and salt where she had been. Afterward she turned in the circle of his arm and they faced the silent men of Drogobych.

"You are getting near the city," said Morzach. His tones were deep, with the chill ringing of struck steel in them. "It is time for the next stage."

"I thought you saved some of us deliberately," said Donovan.

"*Us?*" Valduma's lips caressed his cheek. "Them, Basil, them. You don't belong there, you are with Arzun and me."

"You must have projected that game where we could spot it," went on Donovan, shakily. "You've kept us—them—alive and enabled us to march on your city—on the last inhabited city left to your race. You could have hunted them down as you did all the others, made sport of them with wild animals and falling rocks and missiles shooting out of nowhere, but instead you want them for something else. What is it?"

"You should have guessed," said Morzach. "We want to leave Arzun."

"Leave it? You can do so any time, by yourselves. You've done it for millennia."

"We can only go to the barbarian fringe stars. Beyond them it is a greater distance to the next suns than we can cross unaided. Yet though we have captured many spaceships and have them intact at Drogobych, we cannot operate them. The principles learned from the humans don't make sense! When we have tired to pilot them, it has only brought disaster."

"But why do you want to leave?"

"It is a recent decision, precipitated by your arrival, but it has been considered for a long while. This sun is old, this planet exhausted, and the lives of we few remnants of a great race flicker in a hideous circumscribed drabness. Sooner or later, the humans will fight their way here in strength too great for us. Before then we must be gone."

"So—" Donovan spoke softly, and the wind whimpered under his voice. "So your plan is to capture this group of spacemen and make them your slaves, to carry you—where?"

"Out. Away." Valduma's clear lovely laughter rang in the night. "To seize another planet and build our strength afresh." She gripped his waist and he saw the white gleam of her teeth out of shadow. "To build a great army of obedient spacegoing warriors—and then out to hunt between the stars!"

"Hunt—"

"Look here." Morzach edged closer, his eyes a green glow, the vague sheen of naked steel in his hand. "I've been polite long enough. You have your chance, to rise above the human scum that spawned you and be one of us. Help us now and you can be with us till you die. Otherwise, we'll take that crew anyway, and you'll be hounded across the face of this planet."

"Aye—aye—welcome back, Basil Donovan, welcome back to the old king-race . . . Come with us, come with us, lead the humans into our ambush and be the lord of stars . . ."

They circled about him, tall and mailed and beautiful in the shadow-light, luring whispering voices, ripple of dark laughter, the hunters playing with their quarry and taming it. Donovan remembered them, remembered the days when he had talked and smiled and drunk and sung with them, the Lucifer-like intoxication of their dancing darting minds, a wildness of magic and mystery and reckless wizard sport, a glory which had taken something from his soul and left an emptiness within him. Morzach, Marovech, Uboda, Zegoian, for a time he had been the consort of the gods.

"Basil." Valduma laid sharp-nailed fingers in his hair and pulled his lips to hers. "Basil, I want you back."

He held her close, feeling the lithe savage strength of her, recalling the flame-like beauty and the nights of love such as no human could ever give. His whisper was thick: "You got bored last time and sent me back. How long will I last now?"

"As long as you wish, Basil. Forever and forever." He knew she lied, and he didn't care.

"This is what you must do, Donovan." said Morzach.

He listened with half his mind. It was a question of guiding the army into a narrow cul-de-sac where the Arzunians could perform the delicate short-range work of causing chains to bind around them. For the rest, he was thinking.

They hunt. They intrigue, and they whittle down their last few remnants with fighting among themselves, and they prey on the fringe stars, and they capture living humans to hunt down for sport. They haven't done anything new for ten thousand years, creativeness has withered from them, and all they will do if they escape the Nebula is carry ruin between the stars. They're mad.

Yes—a whole society of psychopaths, gone crazy with the long racial dying. That's the real reason they can't handle machines, that's why they don't think of friendship but only of war, that's why they carry doom within them.

But I love you, I love you, I love you, O Valduma the fair.

He drew her to him, kissed her with a terrible intensity, and she laughed in the dark. Looking up, he faced the blaze that was Morzach.

"All right," he said. "I understand. Tomorrow."

"Aye—good, good, well done!"

"Oh, Basil, Basil!" whispered Valduma. "Come, come away with me, now."

"No. They'd suspect. I have to go down to them or they'll come looking for me."

"Good night, Basil, my darling, my vorza. Until tomorrow!"

He went slowly down the hillside, drawing his shoulders together against the cold, not looking back. Helena rose when he approached her campfire, and the glimmering light made her seem pale and unreal.

"Where have you been, Basil? You look so tired."

"Just walking around. I'm all right." He spread his couch of stiff and stinking animal hides. "We'd better turn in, eh?"

But he slept little.

✣VI✣

The highway curved between great looming walls of cragged old rock, a shadow tunnel with the wind yowling far overhead and the sun a disc of blood. Men's footfalls echoed from the cracked paving blocks to boom hollowly off time-gnawed cliffs and ring faintly in the ice. It was cold, their breath smoked from them and they shivered and cursed and stamped their feet.

Donovan walked beside Helena, who was riding Wocha. His eyes narrowed against the searching wind, looking ahead and around, looking for the side track where the ambush waited. Drogobych was very near.

Something moved up on the ridge, a flapping black thing which was instantly lost to sight. The Arzunians were watching.

There—up ahead—the solitary tree they had spoken of, growing out between age-crumbled fragments of the road. The highway swung west around a pinnacle of rock, but here there was a branch road running straight south into a narrow ravine. *All I have to do is suggest we take it. They won't know till too late that it leads up a blind canyon.*

Helena leaned over toward him, so that the long wind-whipped hair blew against his cheek. "Which way should we go?" she asked. One hand rested on his shoulder.

He didn't slacken his stride, but his voice was low under the whine of bitter air: "To the right, Helena, and on the double. The Arzunians are waiting up the other road, but Drogobych is just beyond that crag."

"Basil! How do you know—"

Wocha's long hairy ears cocked attentively, and the little eyes under the heavy bone ridges were suddenly sharp on his master.

"They wanted me to mislead you. I didn't say anything before for fear they'd be listening, somehow."

Because I hadn't decided, he thought grayly. *Because Valduma is mad, and I love her.*

Helena turned and lifted her arm, voice ringing out to rattle in jeering echoes: "Column right! Forward—charge!"

Wocha broke into a trot, the ground booming and shivering under his huge feet. Donovan paced beside, drawing his sword and swinging it naked in one hand, his eyes turned to the canyon and the rocks above it. The humans fell into a jogging run.

They swept past the ambush road, and suddenly Valduma was on the ridge above them, tall and slim and beautiful, the hair like a blowing flame under her helmet. "Basil!" she screamed. "Basil, you triple traitor—"

The others were there with her, men of Drogobych standing on the heights and howling their fury. They had chains in their hands, and suddenly the air was thick with flying links.

One of them smashed against Donovan and curled itself snake-like around his waist. He dropped his sword and tugged at the cold iron, feeling the breath strained out of him, cursing with the pain of it. Wocha reached down a hand and peeled the chain off, snapping it in two and hurling it back at the Arzunians. It whipped in the air, lashing itself across his face, and he bellowed.

The men of Sol were weltering in a fight with the flying chains, beating them off, stamping the writhing lengths underfoot, yelling as the things cracked against their heads. "Forward!" cried Helena. "Charge—get out of here—forward, Empire!"

A chain whistled viciously for her face. She struck at it with her sword, tangling it on the blade, metal clashing on metal. Takahashi had his blaster out, its few remaining charges thundering to fuse the missiles. Other flames roared at the Arzunians, driving them back, forcing them to drop control of the chains to defend their lives.

"Run! Forward!"

The column shouted and plunged down the highway. Valduma was suddenly before them, her face distorted in fury, stabbing a spear at Donovan's breast. The man parried the thrust and hewed at her— she was gone, and the Terrans rushed ahead.

The rocks groaned. Donovan saw them shuddering above him, saw the first hail of gravel and heard the huge grinding of strata. "They're trying to bury us!" he yelled. "We've got to get clear!"

Wocha stooped, snatched him up under one arm, and galloped. A boulder whizzed by his head, smashing against the farther wall and spraying him with hot chips of stone. Now the boom of the landslide filled their world, rolling and roaring between the high cliffs. Cracks zigzagged across the worn black heights, the crags shivered and toppled, dust boiled across the road.

"Basil!"

Donovan saw Valduma again, dancing and leaping between the boulders, raising a scream of wrath and laughter. Morzach was there, standing on a jut of rock, watching the hillside fall.

Wocha burst around the sentinel peak. A line of Arzunians stood barring the way to Drogobych, the sunlight flaming off their metal. Wocha dropped Donovan, hefted his ax in both hands, and charged them.

Donovan picked himself up and scrambled in the wake of his slave. Behind him, the Terrans were streaming from the collapsing dale, out over open ground to strike the enemy. The rocks bounded and howled, a man screamed as he was pinned, there were a dozen buried under the landslide.

Wocha hit the Arzunian line. His ax blazed, shearing off an arm, whirling up again to crumple a helmet and cleave the skull beneath.

Rearing, he knocked down two of them and trampled them underfoot. A warrior smote at his flank. Helena, gripping one mighty shoulder, engaged him with her free hand, her blade whistling around his ears. They fell away from that pair, and the Terrans attacked them.

Donovan crossed swords with one he knew—Marovech, the laughing half-devil whose words he had so much enjoyed in earlier days. The Arzunian grinned at him across a web of flying steel. His blade stabbed in, past the Ansan's awkward guard, reaching for his guts. Donovan retreated, abandoning the science he didn't know for a wild whirling and hacking, his iron battering at the bright weapon before him. Clash and clang of edged metal, leaping and dancing, Marovech's red hair wild in the rising wind and his eyes alight with laughter.

Donovan felt his backward step halted, he was against the high stone pillar and could not run. He braced his feet and hewed out, a scream of cloven air and outraged steel. Marovech's sword went spinning from his hand.

It hit the ground and bounced up toward the Arzunian's clutch. Donovan smote again, and the shock of iron in flesh jarred him where he stood. Marovech fell in a rush of blood.

For an instant Donovan stood swaying over the Arzunian, looking stupidly at the blood on his own hands, hearing the clamor of his heartbeat and sucking a dry gasp into his lungs. Then he picked up the fallen being's glaive. It was a better weapon.

Turning, he saw that the fight had become a riot, knots of men and un-men snarling and hacking in a craziness of death. No room or time here for wizard stunts, it was blood and bone and nerve against its kind. The Terrans fought without much skill in the use of their archaic equipment but they had the cold courage blended of training and desperation. And they knew better how to cooperate. They battled a way to each other and stood back to back against all comers.

Wocha raged and trampled, smashing with ax and fist and feet and hurled stones, his war-cry bellowing and shuddering in the hills. An Arzunian vanished from in front of him and appeared behind with spear poised. The Donarrian suddenly backed up, catching the assailant and smashing him under his hind feet while he dueled another from the front. Helena's arm never rested, she swung to right and left, guarding his flanks, yelling as her blade drove home.

Donovan shook himself and trotted warily over to where a tide of Arzunians raged about a closely-drawn ring of Impies. The humans were standing firm, driving each charge back in a rush of blood, heaping the dead before them. But now spears were beginning to fall out of the sky, driven by no hand but stabbing for the throats and eyes and bellies of men. Donovan loped for the sharp edge of the hills, where they toppled to the open country in which the fight went on.

He scrambled up a rubbled slope and gripped a thin pinnacle to swing himself higher. She was there.

She stood on a ledge, the heap of spears at her feet, looking down over the battle and chanting as she sent forth the flying death. He noticed even then how her hair was a red glory about the fine white loveliness of her head.

"Valduma," he whispered, as he struck at her.

She was not there, she sat on a higher ledge and jeered at him. "Come and get me, Basil, darling, darling. Come up here and talk to me!"

He looked at her as Lucifer must have looked back to Heaven. "Let us go," he said. "Give us a ship and send us home,"

"And have you bring our overlords back in?" She laughed aloud.

"They aren't so bad, Valduma. The Empire means peace and justice for all races."

"Who speaks?" Her scorn flamed at him. "You don't believe that."

He stood there for a moment. "No," he whispered. "No, I don't."

Stooping, he picked up the sheaf of spears and began to crawl back down the rocks. Valduma cursed him from the heights.

There was a break in the combat around the hard-pressed Terran ring as the Arzunians drew back to pant and glare. Donovan ran through and flung his load clashing at the feet of Takahashi.

"Good work," said the officer. "We need these things. Here, get into the formation. Here we go again!"

The Arzunians charged in a wedge to gather momentum. Donovan braced himself and lifted his sword. The Terrans in the inner ring slanted their spears between the men of the outer defense. For a very long half minute, they stood waiting.

The enemy hit! Donovan hewed at the nearest, drove the probing sword back and hammered against the guard. Then the whirl of battle swept his antagonist away, someone else was there, he traded blows and the howl of men and metal lifted skyward.

The Terrans had staggered a little from the massive assault, but it spitted itself on the inner pikes and then swords and axes went to work. Ha, clang, through the skull and give it to 'em! Hai, Empire! Ansa, Ansa! Clatter and yell and deep-throated roar, the Arzunians boiling around the Solar line, leaping and howling and whipping out of sight—a habit which saved their lives but blunted their attack, thought Donovan in a moment's pause.

Wocha smashed the last few who had been standing before him, looked around to the major struggle, and pawed the ground. "Ready, lady?" he rumbled.

"Aye, ready, Wocha. Let's go!"

The Donarrian backed up to get a long running space. "Hang on tight," he warned. "Never mind fighting, lady. All right!"

He broke into a trot, a canter, and then a full gallop. The earth trembled under his mass. "Hoooo!" he screamed. "Here we come!"

Helena threw both arms around his corded neck. When they hit it was like a nuclear bomb going off.

In a few seconds of murder, Wocha had strewn the ground with smashed corpses, whirled, and begun cutting his way into the disordered main group of the Arzunians. They didn't stand before him. Suddenly they were gone, all of them, except for the dead.

Donovan looked over the field. The dead were thick, thick. He estimated that half the little Terran force was slain or out of action. But they must have taken three or four times their number of Arzunians to the Black Planet with them. The stony ground was pooled and steaming with blood. Carrion birds stooped low, screaming.

Helena fell from Wocha's back into Donovan's arms. He comforted her wild sobbing, holding her to him and murmuring in her ear and kissing the wet cheeks and lips. "It's over, dear, it's over for now. We drove them away."

She recovered herself in a while and stood up, straightening her torn disarray, the mask of command clamping back over her face. To Takahashi: "How are our casualties?"

He reported. It was much as Donovan had guessed. "But we gave 'em hell for it, didn't we?"

"How is that?" wondered Cohen. He leaned against Wocha, not showing the pain that jagged through him as they bandaged his wounded foot except by an occasional sharp breath. "They're more at home with this cutlery than we, and they have those damned parapsych talents too."

"They're not quite sane," replied Donovan tonelessly. "Whether you call it a cultural trait or a madness which has spread in the whole population, they're a wild bloodthirsty crew, two-legged weasels, and with a superiority complex which wouldn't have let them be very careful in dealing with us. No discipline, no real plan of action." He looked south over the rolling moorland. "Those things count. They may know better next time."

"Next time? Fifty or sixty men can't defeat a planet, Donovan," said Takahashi.

"No. Though this is an old dying race, their whole population in the city ahead, and most of it will flee in panic and take no part in any fighting. They aren't used to victims that fight back. If we can slug our way through to the spaceships they have there—"

"*Spaceships!*" The eyes stared at him, wild with a sudden blaze of hope, men crowding close and leaning on their reddened weapons and raising a babble of voices. "*Spaceships, spaceships—home!*"

"Yeah." Donovan ran a hand through his yellow hair. The fingers trembled just a bit. "Some ships, the first ones, they merely destroyed by causing the engines to run loose; but others they brought here, I suppose, by inducing the crew to land and parley. Only they killed the crews and can't handle the machines themselves."

"If they captured ships," said Helena slowly, "then they captured weapons too, and even they can squeeze a trigger."

"Sure. But you didn't see them shooting at us just now, did you? They used all the charges to hunt or duel. So if we can break through and escape—"

"They could still follow us and wreck our engines," said Takahashi.

"Not if we take a small ship, as we'd have to anyway, and mount guard over the vital spots. An Arzunian would have to be close at

hand and using all his energies to misdirect atomic flows. He could
be killed before any mischief was done. I doubt if they'd even try.

"Besides," went on Donovan, his voice dry and toneless as a
lecturing professor's, "they can only do so much at a time. I don't
know where they get the power for some of their feats, such as leaving
this planet's gravitational well. It can't be from their own metabolisms,
it must be some unknown cosmic energy source. They don't know
how it works themselves, it's an instinctive ability. But it takes a lot
of nervous energy to direct that flow, and I found last time I was here
that they have to rest quite a while after some strenuous deed. So if
we can get them tired enough—and the fight is likely to wear both
sides down—they won't be able to chase us till we're out of their
range."

Takahashi looked oddly at him. "You know a lot," he murmured.

"Yeah, maybe I do."

"Well, if the city is close as you say, we'd better march right away
before our wounds stiffen, and before the natives get a chance to
organize."

"Rig up carrying devices for those too badly hurt to move," said
Helena. "The walking wounded can tote them, and the rest of us
form a protective square."

"Won't that slow us and handicap us?" asked Donovan.

Her head lifted, the dark hair blowing about her proud features
in the thin whimpering wind. "As long as it's humanly possible we're
going to look after our men. What's the Imperium for if it can't protect its own?"

"Yeah. Yeah, I suppose so."

Donovan slouched off to join the salvaging party that was stripping
the fallen Arzunians of arms and armor for Terran use. He rolled
over a corpse to unbuckle the helmet and looked at the blood-
masked face of Korstuzan who had been his friend once, very long
ago. He closed the staring eyes, and his own were blind with tears.

Wocha came to join him. The Donarrian didn't seem to notice
the gashes in his hide, but he was equipped with a shield now and
had a couple of extra swords slung from his shoulders. "You got a
good lady, boss," he said. "She fights hard. She will bear you strong
sons."

"Uh-huh."

Valduma could never bear my children. Different species can't breed. And she is the outlaw darkness, the last despairing return to primeval chaos, she is the enemy of all which is honest and good. But she is very fair.

Slowly, the humans reformed their army, a tight ring about their wounded, and set off down the road. The dim sun wheeled horizonward.

✧VII✧

Drogobych lay before them.

The city stood on the open gray moor, and it had once been large. But its outer structures were long crumbled to ruin, heaps and shards of stone riven by ages of frost, fallen and covered by the creeping dust. Here and there a squared monolith remained like the last snag in a rotted jaw, dark against the windy sky. It was quiet. Nothing stirred in all the sweeping immensity of hill and moor and ruin and loneliness.

Helena pointed from her seat on Wocha, and a lilt of hope was eager in the tired voice: "See—a ship—ahead there!"

They stared, and someone raised a ragged cheer, Over the black square-built houses of the inner city they could make out the metal nose of a freighter. Takahashi squinted. "It's Denebian, I think," he said. "Looks as if man isn't the only race which has suffered from these scum."

"All right, boys," said Helena, "Let's go in and get it."

They went down a long empty avenue which ran spear-straight for the center. The porticoed houses gaped with wells of blackness at their passage, looming in cracked and crazily leaning massiveness on either side, throwing back the hollow slam of their boots. Donovan heard the uneasy mutter of voices to his rear: *Don't like this place . . . Haunted . . . They could be waiting anywhere for us . . .*

The wind blew a whirl of snow across their path.

Basil. Basil, my dear.

Donovan's head jerked around, and he felt his throat tighten. Nothing. No movement, no sound, emptiness.

Basil, I am calling you. No one else can hear.

Why are you with these creatures, Basil? Why are you marching with the oppressors of your planet? We could free Ansa, Basil, given time to raise our armies. We could sweep the Terrans before us and hound them down the ways of night, and yet you march against us.

"Valduma," he whispered.

Basil, you were very dear to me. You were something new and strong and of the future, come to our weary old world, and I think I loved you.

I could still love you, Basil. I could hold you forever, if you would let me.

"Valduma—have done!"

A mocking ripple of laughter, sweet as rain in springtime, the gallantry of a race which was old and sick and doomed and could still know mirth. Donovan shook his head and stared rigidly before him. It was as if he had laid hands on that piece of his soul which had been lost, and she was trying to wrench it from him again. Only he wanted her to win.

Go home, Basil. Go home with this female of yours. Breed your cubs, fill the house with brats, and try to think your little round of days means something. Strut about under the blue skies, growing fat and gray, bragging of what a great fellow you used to be and disapproving of the younger generation. As you like, Basil. But don't go out to space again. Don't look at the naked stars. You won't dare.

"No," he whispered.

She laughed, a harsh bell of mockery ringing in his brain. "*You could have been a god—or a devil. But you would rather be a pot-bellied Imperial magistrate. Go home, Basil Donovan, take your female home, and when you are wakened at night by her—shall we say her breathing?—do not remember me.*

The Terrans slogged on down the street, filthy with dust and grease and blood, uncouth shamblers, apes in the somber ruin of the gods. Donovan thought he had a glimpse of Valduma standing on a rooftop, the clean lithe fire of her, silken flame of her hair and the green unhuman eyes which had lighted in the dark at his side. She had been a living blaze, an unending trumpet and challenge, and when she broke with him it had been quick and dean, no soddenness of age and custom and—and, damn it, all the little things which made humanness.

All right, Valduma. We're monkeys. We're noisy and self-important, compromisers and trimmers and petty cheats, we huddle away from the greatness we could have, our edifices are laid brick by brick with endless futile squabbling over each one—and yet, Valduma, there is something in man which you don't have. There's something by which these men have fought their way through everything you could loose on them, helping each other, going forward under a ridiculous rag of colored cloth and singing as they went.

Fine words, added his mind. *Too bad you don't really believe them.*

He grew aware of Helena's anxious eyes on him. "What's the matter, darling?" she asked gently. "You look ill."

"Tired," he said. "But we can't have so very far to go now—"

"*Look out!*"

Whirling, he saw the pillars of the house to the right buckle, saw the huge stone slabs of the roof come thundering over the top and streetward. For a blinding instant he saw Valduma, riding the slab down, yelling and laughing, and then she was gone and the stone struck.

They were already running, dropping their burden of the hurt and fleeing for safety. Another house groaned and rumbled. The ground shook, flying shards stung Donovan's back, echoes rolled down the ways of Drogobych. Someone was screaming, far and faint under the grinding racket.

"Forward. Forward!" Helena's voice whipped back to him, she led the rush while the city thundered about her. Then a veil of rising dust blotted her out, he groped ahead, stumbling over fallen pillars and cornices, hearing the boom around him, running and running.

Valduma laughed, a red flame through the whirling dust. Her spear gleamed for his breast, he grabbed it with one hand and hacked at her with his sword. She was gone, and he raced ahead, not stopping to think, not daring.

They came out on a great open plaza. Once there had been a park here, and carved fountains, but nothing remained save a few leafless trees and broken pieces. And the spaceships.

The spaceships, a loom of metal against the dark stone beyond, half a dozen standing there and waiting—spaceships, spaceships, the most beautiful sight in the cosmos! Helena and Wocha were halted near a small fast Comet-class scoutboat. The surviving Terrans ran toward them. Few, thought Donovan sickly, few—perhaps a score left, bleeding from the cuts of flying stone, gray with dust and fear. The city had been a trap.

"Come on!" yelled the woman. "Over here and off this planet!"

The men of Drogobych were suddenly there, a ring about the ship and another about the whole plaza, crouched with their weapons and their cat's eyes aflame. A score of hurt starvelings and half a thousand un-men.

A trumpet blew its high note into the dusking heavens. The Arzunians rested arms, expressionless. Donovan and the other humans continued their pace, forming a battle square.

Morzach stood forth in front of the scoutship. "You have no further chance to escape," he called. "But we want your services, not your lives, and the service will be well rewarded. Lay down your weapons."

Wocha's arm straightened. His ax flew like a thunderbolt, and Morzach's head burst open. The Donarrian roared and went against the enemy line.

They edged away, fearfully, and the Terrans followed him in a trotting wedge. Donovan moved up on Wocha's right side, sword hammering at the thrusts for his ribs.

An Arzunian yelled an order which must have meant "Stop them!" Donovan saw the outer line break into a run, converging on the knot of struggle. No flying spears this time, he reflected in a moment's bleak satisfaction—tearing down those walls must have exhausted most of their directing energies.

A native rushed at him, sword whistling from behind a black shield. Donovan caught the blow on his own plundered scute, feeling it ring in the bones of his arm, and hewed back. His blade screamed close to the white teeth-bared face, and he called a panting salutation: "Try again, Davleka!"

"I will!"

The blows rained on his shield, sang viciously low to cut at his legs, clattering and clanging, whistle of air and howl of iron under the westering sun. He backed up against Wocha's side, where the Donarrian and the woman smote against the airlock's defenders, and braced himself and struck out.

Davleka snarled and hacked at Donovan's spread leg. The Ansan's glaive snaked forth against his unshielded neck. Davleka's sword clashed to earth and he sprawled against the human. Raising his bloody face, he drew a knife, lifted it, and tried to thrust upward. Donovan, already crossing blades with Uboda, stamped on his hand. Davleka grinned, a rueful crooked grin through the streaming blood, and died.

Uboda pressed close, working up against Donovan's shield. He had none himself, but there was a dirk in his left hand. His sword locked with Donovan's, strained it aside, and his knife clattered swiftly for an opening.

Helena turned about and struck from her seat. Uboda's head rolled against Donovan's shield and left a red splash down it. The man retched.

Wocha, swinging one of his swords, pushed ahead into the Arzunians, crowding them aside by his sheer mass, beating down a guard and the helmet or armor beyond it. "Clear!" he bellowed. "I got the way clear, lady!"

Helena sprang to the ground and into the lock. "Takahashi, Cohen, Basil, Wang-ki, come in and help me start the engines. The rest of you hold them off. Don't give them time to exert what collective para power they have left and ruin something. Make them think!"

"Think about their lives, huh?" Wocha squared off in front of the airlock and raised his sword. "All right, boys, here they come. Let 'em have what they want."

Donovan halted in the airlock. Valduma was there, her fiery head whirling in the rush of black-clad warriors. He leaned over and grabbed a spaceman's arm. "Ben Ali, go in and help start this crate. I have to stay here."

"But—"

Donovan shoved him in, stood beside Takahashi, and braced himself to meet the Arzunian charge.

They rushed in, knowing that they had to kill the humans before there was an escape, swinging their weapons and howling. The shock of the assault threw men back, pressed them to the ship and jammed weapons close to breasts. The Terrans cursed and began to use fists and feet, clearing a space to fight in.

Donovan's sword clashed against a shield, drove off another blade, stabbed for a face, and then it was all lost in the crazed maelstrom, hack and thrust and take the blows they give, hew, sword, hew!

They raged against Wocha, careless now of their lives, thundering blows against his shield, slashing and stabbing and using their last wizard strength to fill the air with blades. He roared and stood his ground, the sword leaped in his hand, metal clove in thunder. The shield was crumpled, falling apart—he tossed it with rib-cracking force against the nearest Arzunian. His nicked and blunted sword burst against a helmet, and he drew the other.

The ship trembled, thutter of engines warming up, the eager promise of sky and stars and green Terra again. "Get in!" bawled Donovan. "Get in! We'll hold them!"

He stood by Wocha as the last crewmen entered, stood barring the airlock with a wall of blood and iron. Through a blurring vision, he saw Valduma approach.

She smiled at him, one slim hand running through the copper hair, the other held out in sign of peace. Tall and gracious and lovely beyond his knowing, she moved up toward Donovan, and her clear voice rang in his darkening mind.

Basil—you, at least, could stay. You could guide us out to the stars.

"You go away," groaned Wocha.

The devil's rage flamed in her face. She yelled, and a lance whistled from the sky and buried itself in the great breast.

"Wocha!" yelled Donovan.

The Donarrian snarled and snapped off the shaft that stood between his ribs. He whirled it over his head, and Valduma's green eyes widened in fear.

"Donovan!" roared Wocha, and let it fly.

It smashed home, and the Ansan dropped his sword and swayed on his feet. He couldn't look on the broken thing which had been Valduma.

"Boss, you go home now."

Wocha laid him in the airlock and slammed the outer valve shut. Turning, he faced the Arzunians. He couldn't see very well—one eye was gone, and there was a ragged darkness before the other. The sword felt heavy in his hand. But—

"Hooo!" he roared and charged them.

He spitted one and trampled another and tossed a third into the air. Whirling, he clove a head and smashed a rib-cage with his fist and chopped another across. His sword broke, and he grabbed two Arzunians and cracked their skulls together.

They ran, then turned and fled from him. And he stood watching them go and laughed. His laughter filled the city, rolling from its walls, drowning the whistle of the ship's takeoff and bringing blood to his lips. He wiped his mouth with the back of one hand, spat, and lay down.

"We're clear, Basil." Helena clung to him, shivering in his arms, and he didn't know if it was a laugh or a sob in her throat. "We're away, safe, we'll carry word back to Sol and they'll clear the Black Nebula for good."

"Yeah." He rubbed his eyes. "Though I doubt the Navy will find anything. If those Arzunians have any sense, they'll project to various fringe planets, scatter, and try to pass as harmless humanoids. But it doesn't matter, I suppose. Their power is broken."

"And we'll go back to your home, Basil, and bring Ansa and Terra together and have a dozen children and—"

He nodded. "Sure. Sure."

But he wouldn't forget. In the winter nights, when the stars were sharp and cold in a sky of ringing crystal black, he would—go out and watch them? Or pull his roof over him and wait for dawn? He didn't know yet.

Still—even if this was a long ways from being the best of all possible universes, it had enough in it to make a man glad of his day.

He whistled softly, feeling the words ran through his head:

> *Lift your glasses high,*
> *kiss the girls good-bye,*
> *(Live well, my friend, live well, live you well)*
> *for we're riding,*
> *for we're riding,*
> *for we're riding out to Terran sky! Terran sky! Terran sky!*

The thought came all at once that it could be a song of comradeship, too.

THE PEOPLE OF THE WIND

❀|❀

"You can't leave now," Daniel Holm told his son. "Any day we may be at war. We may already be."

"That's just why I have to go," the young man answered. "They're calling Khruaths about it around the curve of the planet. Where else should I fare than to my choth?"

When he spoke thus, more than his wording became bird. The very accent changed. He was no longer using the Planha-influenced Anglic of Avalon—pure vowels, r's trilled, m's and n's and ng's almost hummed, speech deepened and slowed and strongly cadenced; rather, it was as if he were trying to translate for a human listener the thought of an Ythrian brain.

The man whose image occupied the phone screen did not retort, "You might consider staying with your own family," as once he would have. Instead Daniel Holm nodded, and said quietly, "I see. You're not Chris now, you're Arinnian," and all at once looked old.

That wrenched at the young man. He reached forth, but his fingers were stopped by the screen. "I'm always Chris, Dad," he blurted. "It's only that I'm Arinnian too. And, and, well, if war comes, the choths will need to be prepared for it, won't they? I'm going to help—shouldn't be gone long, really."

"Sure. Good voyage."

"Give Mother and everybody my love."

"Why not call her yourself?"

"Well, uh, I do have to hurry . . . and it's not as if this were any-thing unusual, my heading off to the mountains, and—oh—"

"Sure," said Daniel Holm. "I'll tell them. And you give my regards to your mates." The Second Marchwarden of the Lauran System blanked off.

Arinnian turned from the instrument. For a moment he winced and bit his lip. He hated hurting people who cared about him. But why couldn't they understand? Their kind called it "going bird," being received into a choth, as if in some fashion those who did were renouncing the race that begot them. He couldn't count how many hours he had tried to make his parents—make any number of orthohumans—see that he was widening and purifying his humanity.

A bit of dialogue ran through memory: "Dad, look, two species can't inhabit the same globe for generations without pretty deep mutual consequences. Why do you go sky-hunting? Why does Ferune serve wine at his table? And these're the most superficial symptoms."

"I know that much. Credit me with some fair-mindedness, hm? Thing is, you're making a quantum jump."

"Because I'm to be a member of Stormgate? Listen, the choths have been accepting humans for the past hundred years."

"Not in such flocks as lately. And my son wasn't one of them. I'd've . . . liked to see you carry on *our* traditions."

"Who says I won't?"

"To start with, you'll not be under human law any more, you'll be under choth law and custom. . . . Hold on. That's fine, if you're an Ythrian. Chris, you haven't got the chromosomes. Those who've pretended they did, never fitted well into either race, ever again."

"Damnation, I'm not pretending—!"

Arinnian thrust the scene from him as if it were a physical thing. He was grateful for the prosaic necessities of preparation. To reach Lythran's aerie before dark, he must start soon. Of course, a car would cover the distance in less than an hour; but who wanted to fly caged in metal and plastic?

He was nude. More and more, those who lived like him were tending to discard clothes altogether and use skin paint for dress-up. But everybody sometimes needed garments. An Ythrian, too, was seldom without a belt and pouch. This trip would get chilly, and he lacked feathers. He crossed the tiny apartment to fetch cover-all and boots.

Passing, he glanced at the desk whereon lay papers of his work and, in a heap, the texts and references he was currently employing, printouts from Library Central. *Blast!* he thought. *I loathe quitting when I've nearly seen how to prove that theorem.*

In mathematics he could soar. He often imagined that then his mind knew the same clean ecstasy an Ythrian, aloft alone, must know in the flesh. Thus he had been willing to accept the compromise which reconciled him and his father. He would continue his studies, maintain his goal of becoming a professional mathematician. To this end, he would accept some financial help, though he would no longer be expected to live at home. The rest of what little income he required he would earn himself, as herdsman and hunter when he went off to be among the Ythrians.

Daniel Holm had growled, through the hint of a grin, "You own a good mind, son. I didn't want to see it go to waste. At the same time, it's too good. If 'tweren't for your birding, you'd be so netted in your books, when you aren't drawing a picture or writing a poem, you'd never get any exercise; at last your bottom would grow fast to your chair, and you'd hardly notice. I s'pose I should feel a little grateful to your friends for making their kind of athlete out of you."

"My chothmates," Arinnian corrected him. He had just been given his new name and was full of glory and earnestness. That was four years ago; today he could smile at himself. The guv'nor had not been altogether wrong.

Thus at thirty—Avalonian reckoning—Christopher Holm was tall, slender, but wide-shouldered. In features as well as build, he took after his mother: long head, narrow face, thin nose and lips, blue eyes, mahogany hair (worn short in the style of those who do much gravbelt flying), and as yet not enough beard to be worth anything except regular applications of antigrowth enzyme. His complexion, naturally fair, was darkened by exposure. Laura, a G_5 star, has only 72 percent the luminosity of Sol and less ultraviolet light in proportion; but Avalon, orbiting at a mean distance of 0.81 astro-nomical unit in a period of 0.724 Terran, gets 10 percent more total irradiation than man evolved under.

He made the customary part-by-part inspection of his unit

before he put arms through straps and secured buckle at waist. The twin cone-pointed cylinders on his back had better have fully charged accumulators and fully operating circuits. If not, he was dead. One Ythrian couldn't hold back a human from toppling out of the sky. A couple of times, several together had effected a rescue; but those were herders, carrying lassos which they could cast around their comrade and pull on without getting in each other's way. You dared not count on such luck. O God, to have real wings!

He donned a leather helmet and lowered the goggles which were his poor substitute for a nictitating membrane. He sheathed knife and slugthrower at his hips. There would be nothing of danger—no chance of a duel being provoked, since a Khruath was peace-holy— not that deathpride quarrels ever happened often—but the Stormgate folk were mostly hunters and didn't leave their tools behind. He had no need to carry provisions. Those would be supplied from the family stores, to which he contributed his regular share, and ferried to the rendezvous on a gravsled.

Going out the door, he found himself on ground level. Humans had ample room on Avalon—about ten million of them; four million Ythrians—and even here in Gray, the planet's closest approximation to a real city, they built low and widespread. A couple of highrises sufficed for resident or visiting ornithoids.

Arinnian flicked controls. Negaforce thrust him gently, swiftly upward. Leveling off, he spent a minute savoring the view.

The town sprawled across hills green with trees and susin, color-patched with gardens, that ringed Falkayn Bay. Upon the water skimmed boats; being for pleasure, they were principally sail-driven hydrofoils. A few cargo vessels, long shapes of functional grace, lay at the docks, loaded and unloaded by assorted robots. One was coming in, from Brendan's Islands to judge by the course, and one was standing out to the Hesperian Sea, which flared silver where the sun struck it and, elsewhere, ran sapphire till it purpled on northern and southern horizons. Laura hung low in the empty west, deeper aureate than at midday. The sky was a slowly darkening blue; streaks of high cirrus clouds, which Arinnian thought of as breastfeathers, promised fair weather would continue. A salt breeze whispered and cooled his cheeks.

Air traffic was scant. Several Ythrians passed by, wings gleaming bronze and amber. A couple of humans made beltflights like Arinnian; distant, they were hardly to be told from a flock of slim leathery draculas which evening had drawn out of some cave. More humans rode in cars, horizontal raindrops that flung back the light with inanimate fierceness. Two or three vans lumbered along and an intercontinental liner was settling toward the airport. But Gray was never wildly busy.

High up, however, paced shapes that had not been seen here since the end of the Troubles: warcraft on patrol.

War against the Terran Empire—Shivering, Arinnian lined out eastward, inland.

Already he could see his destination, far off beyond the coastal range and the central valley, like a cloudbank on worldedge, those peaks which were the highest in Corona, on all Avalon if you didn't count Oronesia. Men called them the Andromedas, but in his Anglic Arinnian had also taken to using the Planha name, Weathermother.

Ranchland rolled beneath him. Here around Gray, the mainly Ythrian settlements northward merged with the mainly human south; both ecologies blent with Avalon's own, and the country became a checkerboard. Man's grainfields, ripening as summer waned, lay tawny amidst huge green pastures where Ythrians grazed their maukh and mayaw. Stands of timberwood, oak or pine, windnest or hammerbranch, encroached on nearly treeless reaches of berylline native susin where you might still glimpse an occasional barysauroid. The rush of his passage blew away fretfulness. Let the Empire attack the Domain . . . if it dared! Meanwhile he, Arinnian, was bound for Eyath—for his whole choth, of course, and oneness with it, but chiefly he would see Eyath again.

Across the dignity of the dining hall, a look passed between them. *Shall we wander outside and be ourselves?* She asked permission to leave of her father Lythran and her mother Blawsa; although she was their dependent, that was mere ritual, yet rituals mattered greatly. In like fashion Arinnian told the younger persons among whom he was benched that he had the wish of being unaccompanied. He and Eyath left side by side. It caused no break in the slow, silence-punctuated conversation wherein everyone else took part. Their closeness went back to their childhood and was fully accepted.

The compound stood on a plateau of Mount Farview. At the middle lifted the old stone tower which housed the senior members of the family and their children. Lower wooden structures, on whose sod roofs bloomed amberdragon and starbells, were for the unwed and for retainers and their kin. Further down a slope lay sheds, barns, and mews. The whole could not be seen at once from the ground, because Ythrian trees grew among the buildings: braidbark, copperwood, gaunt lightningrod, jewelleaf which sheened beneath the moon and by day would shimmer iridescent. The flowerbeds held natives, more highly evolved than anything from offplanet— sweet small janie, pungent livewell, graceful trefoil and Buddha's cup, a harp vine which the breeze brought ever so faintly to singing. Otherwise the night was quiet and, at this altitude, cold. Breath smoked white.

Eyath spread her wings. They were more slender than average, though spanning close to six meters. This naturally forced her to rest on hands and tail. "Br-r-r!" she laughed. "Hoarfrost. Let's lift." In a crack and whirl of air, she rose.

"You forgot," he called. "I've taken off my belt." She settled on a platform built near the top of a copperwood. Ythrians made few redundant noises; obviously he could climb. He thought she overrated his skill, merely because he was better at it than she. A misstep in that murky foliage could bring a nasty fall. But he couldn't refuse the implicit challenge and keep her respect. He gripped a branch, chinned himself up, and groped and rustled his way.

Ahead, he heard her murmur to the uhoth which had fluttered along behind her. It brought down game with admirable efficiency, but he felt she made too much fuss over it. Well, no denying she was husband-high. He didn't quite like admitting that to himself. *(Why?* he wondered fleetingly.)

When he reached the platform, he saw her at rest on feet and alatans, the uhoth on her right wrist while her left hand stroked it. Morgana, almost full, stood dazzling white over the eastward sierra and made the plumes of Eyath glow. Her crest was silhouetted against the Milky Way. Despite the moon, constellations glistered through upland air, Wheel, Swords, Zirraukh, vast sprawling Ship. . . .

He sat down beside her, hugging his knees. She made the small ululation which expressed her gladness at his presence. He responded as best he could. Above the clean curve of her muzzle, the great eyes glimmered.

Abruptly she broke off. He followed her gaze and saw a new star swing into heaven. "A guardian satellite?" she asked. Her tone wavered the least bit.

"What else?" he replied. "I think it must be the latest one they've orbited."

"How many by now?"

"They're not announcing that," he reminded her. Ythrians always had trouble grasping the idea of government secrets. Of government in any normal human sense, for that matter. Marchwardens Ferune and Holm had been spending more energy in getting the choths to cooperate than in actual defense preparations. "My father doesn't believe we can have too many."

"The wasted wealth—"

"Well, if the Terrans come—"

"Do you expect they will?"

The trouble he heard brought his hand to squeeze her, very gently, on the neck, and afterward run fingers along her crest. Her feathers were warm, smooth and yet infinitely textured. "I don't know," he said. "Maybe they can settle the border question peacefully. Let's hope." The last two words were perforce in Anglic rather than Planha. Ythrians had never beseeched the future. She too was bilingual, like every educated colonist.

His look went back skyward. Sol lay . . . yonder in the Maukh, about where four stars formed the horns . . . how far? Oh, yes, 205 light-years. He recalled reading that, from there, Quetlan and Laura were in a constellation called the Lupus. None of the three suns had naked-eye visibility across such an abyss. They were mere G-type dwarfs; they merely happened to be circled by some motes which had fermented till there were chemistries that named those motes Terra, Ythri, Avalon, and loved them.

"Lupus," he mused. "An irony."

Eyath whistled: "?"

He explained, adding: "The lupus is, or was, a beast of prey on Terra. And to us, Sol lies in the sign of a big, tame herd animal. But who's attacking whom?"

"I haven't followed the news much," she said, low and not quite steadily. "It seemed a fog only, to me or mine. What need we reck if others clashed? Then all of a sudden—Might we have caused some of the trouble, Arinnian? Could folk of ours have been too rash, too rigid?"

Her mood was so uncharacteristic, not just of Ythrian temperament in general but of her usually sunny self, that astonishment jerked his head around. "What's made you this anxious?" he asked.

Her lips nuzzled the uhoth, as if seeking consolation that he thought he could better give. Its beak preened her. He barely heard: "Vodan."

"What? Oh! Are you betrothed to Vodan?"

His voice had cracked. *Why am I shaken?* he wondered. *He's a fine fellow. And of this same choth, too; no problems of changed law and custom, culture shock, homesickness*—Arinnian's glance swept over the Stormgate country. Above valleys steep-walled, dark and fragrant with woods, snowpeaks lifted. Closer was a mountainside down which a waterfall stood pillarlike under the moon. A night-flying bugler sounded its haunting note through stillness. On the Plains of Long Reach, in arctic marshes, halfway around the planet on a scorching New Gaiilan savannah, amidst the uncounted islands that made up most of what dry land Avalon had—how might she come to miss the realm of her choth?

No, wait, I'm thinking like a human. Ythrians get around more. Eyath's own mother is from the Sagittarius basin, often goes back to visit. . . . Why shouldn't I think like a human? I am one. I've found wisdom, rightness, happiness of a sort in certain Ythrian ways; but no use pretending I'll ever be an Ythrian, ever wed a winged girl and dwell in our own aerie.

She was saying: "Well, no, not exactly. Galemate, do you believe I wouldn't tell you of my betrothal or invite you to my wedding feast? But he is a . . . a person I've grown very fond of. You know I planned on staying single till my studies were finished." She wanted the difficult, honored calling of musician. "Lately . . . well, I thought about it a lot during my last lovetime. I grew hotter then than ever before, and I kept imagining Vodan." Arinnian felt himself flush. He stared at the remote gleam of a glacier. She shouldn't tell him such things. It wasn't decent. An unmarried female Ythrian, or one whose husband was absent, was supposed to stay isolated from males when the heat came upon her; but she was also supposed to spend the energy it raised in work, or study, or meditation, or—

Eyath sensed his embarrassment. Her laughter rippled and she laid a hand over his. The slim fingers, the sharp claws gripped him tenderly. "Why, I declare you're shocked! What for?"

"You wouldn't talk like that to—your father, a brother—" *And you shouldn't feel that way, either. Never. Estrus or no. Lonely, maybe; dreamy, yes; but not like some sweating trull in the bed of some cheap hotel room. Not you, Eyath.*

"True, it'd be improper talk in Stormgate. I used to wonder if I shouldn't marry into a less strict choth. Vodan, though—Anyhow, Arinnian, dear, I can tell you anything. Can't I?"

"Yes." *After all, I'm not really an Ythrian.*

"We discussed it later, he and I," she said. "Marriage, I mean. No use denying, children would be a terrible handicap at this stage. But we fly well together; and our parents have been nudging us for a long time, it'd be so good an alliance between houses. We've wondered if, maybe, if we stayed hriccal the first few years—"

"That doesn't work too well, does it?" he said as her voice trailed off, through the bloodbeat in his ears. "That is, uh, continual sex relations may not be how Ythrians reinforce pair bonds, but that doesn't mean sex has no importance. If you separate every lovetime, you, you, well, you're rejecting each other, aren't you? Why not, uh, contraception?"

"No."

He knew why her race, almost if not quite uniformly, spurned that. Children—the strong parental instinct of both mates—were what kept them together. If small wings closed around you and a small head snuggled down alongside your keelbone, you forgot the inevitable tensions and frustrations of marriage as much as if you were a human who had just happily coupled.

"We could postpone things till I've finished my studies and his business is on the wing," Eyath said. Arinnian remembered that Vodan, in partnership with various youths from Stormgate, Many Thermals, and The Tarns, had launched a silvicultural engineering firm. "But if war comes—kaah, he's in the naval reserve—"

Her free arm went around his shoulder, a blind gesture. He

leaned his weight on an elbow so he could reach beneath the wings to embrace her stiff body. And he murmured to her, his sister since they both were children, what comfort he was able.

In the morning they felt more cheerful. It was not in Ythrian nature to brood—not even as a bad pun, they giving live birth—and bird-humans had tried to educate themselves out of the habit. Today, apart from a few retainers on maintenance duty, Lythran's household would fly to that mountain where the regional Khruath met. On the way they would be joined by other Stormgate families; arrived, they would find other choths entirely. However bleak the occasion of this gathering was, some of the color, excitement, private business, and private fun would be there that pervaded the regular assemblies.

And the dawn was clear and a tailwind streamed.

A trumpet called. Lythran swung from the top of his tower. Folk lifted their wings until the antlibranch slits beneath stood agape, purple from blood under the oxygen-drinking tissues. The wings clapped back down, and back on high; the Ythrians thundered off the ground, caught an updraft, and rode it into formation. Then they flew eastward over the crags.

Arinnian steered close to Eyath. She flashed him a smile and broke into song. She had a beautiful voice—it could nearly be named soprano—which turned the skirls and gutturals of Planha into a lilt. What she cataracted forth on the air was a traditional carol, but it was for Arinnian because he had rendered it into Anglic, though he always felt that his tricks of language had failed to convey either the rapture or the vision.

> "Light that leaps from a sun still sunken
> hails the hunter at hover,
> washes his wings in molten morning,
> startles the stars to cover.
> Blue is the bell of hollow heaven,
> rung by a risen blowing.
> Wide lie woodlands and mountain meadows,
> great and green with their growing.
>   But—look, oh, look!—
>   a red ray struck

through tattered mist.
A broadhorn buck
stands traitor-kissed.
The talons crook.

"Tilt through tumult of wakened wind-noise,
whining, whickering, whirly;
slip down a slantwise course of currents.
Ha, but the hunt comes early!
Poise on the pinions, take the target
there in the then of swooping—
Thrust on through by a wind-wild wingbeat,
stark the stabber comes stooping.
    The buck may pose
    for one short breath
    before it runs
    from whistling death.
    The hammer stuns.
    The talons close.

"Broad and bright is the nearing noontide.
Drawn to dreamily drowsing,
shut-eyed in shade he sits now, sated.
Suddenly sounds his rousing.
Cool as the kiss of a ghost, then gusty,
rinsed by the rainfall after,
breezes brawl, and their forest fleetness
lives in leafage like laughter.
    Among the trees
    the branches shout
    and groan and throw
    themselves about.
    It's time to go.
    The talons ease.

"Beat from boughs up to row through rainstreams
Thickly thutters the thunder.
Hailwinds harried by lash of lightning

roar as they rise from under.
Blind in the black of clawing cloudbanks,
wins he his way, though slowly,
breaks their barrier, soars in sunlight.
High is heaven and holy.
> The glow slants gold
> caressingly
> across and through
> immensity
> of silent blue.
> The talons fold."

✧ ❙❙ ✧

Avalon rotates in 11 hours, 22 minutes, 12 seconds, on an axis tilted 21° from the normal to the orbital plane. Thus Gray, at about 43° N., knows short nights always; in summer the darkness seems scarcely a blink. Daniel Holm wondered if that was a root of his weariness.

Probably not. He was born here. His ancestors had lived here for centuries; they arrived with Falkayn. If individuals could change their circadian rhythms—as he'd had to do plenty often in his spacefaring days—surely a race could. The medics said that settling down in a gravity field only 80 percent of Terra's made more severe demands than that on the organism; its whole fluid balance and kinesthesia must readjust. Besides, what humans underwent was trivial compared to what their fellow colonists did. The Ythrians had had to shift a whole breeding cycle to a different day, year, weight, climate, diet, world. No wonder their first several generations had been of low fertility. Nevertheless, they survived; in the end, they flourished.

Therefore it was nonsense to suppose a man got tired from anything except overwork—and, yes, age, in spite of antisenescence. Or was it? Really? As you grew old, as you neared your dead and all who had gone before them, might your being not yearn back to its earliest beginnings, to a manhome you had never seen but somehow remembered?

Crock! Come off that! Who said eighty-four is old? Holm yanked a cigar from his pocket and snapped off the end. The inhalation which lit it was unnecessarily hard.

He was of medium height, and stocky in the olive tunic and baggy trousers worn by human members of the Ythrian armed services. The mongoloid side of his descent showed in round head, wide face, high cheekbones, a fullness about the lips and the blunt nose; the caucasoid was revealed in gray eyes, a skin that would have been pale did he not spend his free time outdoors hunting or gardening, and the hair that was grizzled on his scalp but remained crisp and black on his chest. Like most men on the planet, he suppressed his beard.

He was wading into the latest spate of communications his aides had passed on to him, when the intercom buzzed and said: "First Marchwarden Ferune wishes discussion."

"Sure!" Holm's superior was newly back from Ythri. The man reached for a two-way plate, withdrew his hand, and said, "Why not in the flesh? I'll be right there."

He stumped from his office. The corridor beyond hummed and bustled—naval personnel, civilian employees of the Lauran admiralty—and overloaded the building's air system till the odors of both species were noticeable, slightly acrid human and slightly smoky Ythrian. The latter beings were more numerous, in reversal of population figures for Avalon. But then, a number were here from elsewhere in the Domain, especially from the mother world, trying to help this frontier make ready in the crisis.

Holm forced himself to call greetings right and left as he went. His affability had become a trademark whose value he recognized. *At first it was genuine,* he thought.

The honor guard saluted and admitted him to Ferune's presence. (Holm did not tolerate time-wasting ceremoniousness in his department, but he admitted its importance to Ythrians.) The inner room was typical: spacious and sparsely furnished, a few austere decorations, bench and desk and office machinery adapted to ornithoid requirements. Rather than a transparency in the wall, there was a genuine huge window, open on garden-scented breezes and a downhill view of Gray and the waters aglitter beyond.

Ferune had added various offplanet souvenirs and a bookshelf loaded with folio copies of the Terran classics that he read, in three original languages, for enjoyment. A smallish, tan-feathered male, he was a bit of an iconoclast. His choth, Mistwood, had always been one of the most progressive on Avalon, mechanized as much as a human community and, in consequence, large and prosperous. He had scant patience to spare for tradition, religion, any conservatism. He endured a minimum of formalities because he must, but never claimed to like them.

Bouncing from his perch, he scuttled across the floor and shook hands Terran style. "Khr-r-r, good to see you, old rascal!" He spoke Planha; Ythrian throats are less versatile than human (though of course no human can ever get the sounds quite right) and he wanted neither the nuisance of wearing a vocalizer nor the grotesquerie of an accent.

"How'd it go?" Holm asked.

Ferune grimaced. But that is the wrong word. His feathers were not simply more intricate than those of Terran birds, they were more closely connected to muscles and nerve endings, and their movements constituted a whole universe of expression forever denied to man. Irritation, fret, underlying anger and dismay, rippled across his body.

"Huh." Holm found a chair designed for him, sank down, and drew tobacco pungency over his tongue. "Tell."

Foot-claws clicked on lovely-grained wood. Back and forth Ferune paced. "I'll be dictating a full report," he said. "In brief, worse than I feared. Yes, they're scrambling to establish a unified command and shove the idea of action under doctrine into every captain. But they've no dustiest notion of how to go about it."

"God on a stick," Holm exclaimed, "we've been telling them for the past five years! I thought—oh, bugger, communication's so vague in this so-called navy, I'd nothing to go on but impressions, and I guess I got the wrong ones—but you know I thought, we thought a halfway sensible reorganization was in progress."

"It was, but it moulted. Overweening pride, bickering, haggling about details. We Ythrians—our dominant culture, at least—don't fit well into anything tightly centralized." Ferune paused. "In fact," he went on, "the most influential argument against trading our separate, loosely coordinated planetary commands for a Terran-model hierarchy has been that Terra may have vastly greater forces, but these need to control a vastly greater volume of space than the Domain; and if they fight us, they'll be at the end of such a long line of communication that unified action is self-defeating."

"Huh! Hasn't it occurred to those mudbrains on Ythri, the Imperium isn't stupid? If Terra hits, it won't run the war from Terra, but from a sector close to our borders."

"We've found little sign of strength being marshaled in nearby systems."

"Certainly not!" Holm slammed a fist on the arm of his chair. "Would they give their preparations away like that? Would you? They'll assemble in space, parsecs from any star. Minimal traffic between the gathering fleet and whatever planets our scouts can sneak close to. In a few cubic light-years, they can hide power to blow us out of the plenum."

"You've told me this a few times," Ferune said dryly. "I've passed it on. To scant avail." He stopped pacing. For a while, silence dwelt in the room. The yellow light of Laura cast leaf shadows on the floor. They quivered.

"After all," Ferune said, "our methods did save us during the Troubles."

"You can't compare war lords, pirates, petty conquerors, barbarians who'd never have gotten past their stratospheres if they hadn't happened to've acquired practically self-operating ships—you can't compare that bloody-clawed rabble to Imperial Terra."

"I know," Ferune replied. "The point is, Ythrian methods served us well because they accord with Ythrian nature. I've begun to wonder, during this last trip, if an attempt to become poor copies of our rivals may not be foredoomed. The attempt's being made, understand— you'll get details till they run back out of your gorge—but could be that all we'll gain is confusion. I've decided that while Avalon must make every effort to cooperate, Avalon must at the same time expect small help from outside."

Again fell stillness. Holm looked at his superior, associate, friend of years; and not for the first time, it came to him what strangers they two were.

He found himself regarding Ferune as if he had never met an Ythrian before.

✳ ✳ ✳

Standing, the Marchwarden was about 120 centimeters high from feet to top of crest; a tall person would have gone to 140 or so, say up to the mid-breast of Holm. Since the body tilted forward, its actual length from muzzle through tail was somewhat more. It massed perhaps 20 kilos; the maximum for the species was under 30.

The head looked sculptured. It bulged back from a low brow to hold the brain. A bony ridge arched down in front to a pair of nostrils, nearly hidden by feathers, which stood above a flexible mouth full of sharp white fangs and a purple tongue. The jaw, underslung and rather delicate, merged with a strong neck. That face was dominated by its eyes, big and amber, and by the dense, scalloped feather-crest that rose from the brow, lifted over the head, and ran half the length of the neck: partly for aerodynamic purposes, partly as a helmet on the thin skull.

The torso thrust outward in a great keelbone, which at its lower end was flanked by the arms. These were not unlike the arms of a skinny human in size and appearance; they lacked plumage, and the hide was dark yellow on Ferune's, brown or black in other Ythrian subspecies. The hands were less manlike. Each bore three fingers between two thumbs; each digit possessed one more joint than its Terran equivalent and a nail that might better be called a talon. The wrist sprouted a dew claw on its inner surface. Those hands were large in proportion to the arms, and muscles played snakishly across them; they had evolved as ripping tools, to help the teeth. The body ended in a fan-shaped tail of feathers, rigid enough to help support it when desired.

At present, though, the tremendous wings were folded down to work as legs. In the middle of either leading edge, a "knee" joint bent in reverse; those bones would lock together in flight. From the "ankle," three forward toes and one rearward extended to make a foot; aloft, they curled around the wing to strengthen and add sensitivity. The remaining three digits of the ancestral ornithoid had fused to produce the alatan bone which swept backward for more than a meter. The skin over its front half was bare, calloused, another surface to rest on.

Ferune being male, his crest rose higher than a female's, and it and the tail were white with black trim; on her they would have been of uniform dark lustrousness. The remainder of him was lighter-colored than average for his species, which ranged from gray-brown through black.

"Khr-r-r-r." The throat-noise yanked Holm out of his reverie. "You stare."

"Oh. Sorry." To a true-born carnivore, that was more rude than it was among omnivorous humans. "My mind wandered."

"Whither?" Ferune asked, mild again.

"M-m-m . . . well—well, all right. I got to thinking how little my breed really counts for in the Domain. I figure maybe we'd better assume everything's bound to be done Ythrian-style, and make the best of that."

Ferune uttered a warbling "reminder" note and quirked certain feathers. This had no exact Anglic equivalent, but the intent could be translated as: "Your sort aren't the only non-Ythrians under our hegemony. You aren't the only ones technologically up to date." Planha was in fact not as laconic as its verbal conventions made it seem.

"N-no," Holm mumbled. "But we . . . in the Empire, we're the leaders. Sure, Greater Terra includes quite a few home worlds and colonies of nonhumans; and a lot of individuals from elsewhere have gotten Terran citizenship; sure. But more humans are in key positions of every kind than members of any other race—fireflare, probably of all the other races put together." He sighed and stared at the glowing end of his cigar. "Here in the Domain, what are men? A handful on this single ball. Oh, we get around, we do well for ourselves, but the fact won't go away that we're a not terribly significant minority in a whole clutch of minorities."

"Do you regret that?" Ferune asked quite softly.

"Huh? No. No. I only meant, well, probably the Domain has too few humans to explain and administer a human-type naval organization. So better we adjust to you than you to us. It's unavoidable anyhow. Even on Avalon, where there're more of us, it's unavoidable."

"I hear a barrenness in your tone and see it in your eyes," Ferune said, more gently than was his wont. "Again you think of your son who has gone bird, true? You fear his younger brothers and sisters will fare off as he did."

Holm gathered strength to answer. "You know I respect your

ways. Always have, always will. Nor am I about to forget how Ythri
took my people in when Terra had rotted away beneath them. It's
just . . . just . . . we rate respect too. Don't we?"

Ferune moved forward until he could lay a hand on Holm's
thigh. He understood the need of humans to speak their griefs.

"When he—Chris—when he first started running around, flying
around, with Ythrians, why, I was glad," the man slogged on. He held
his gaze out the window. From time to time he dragged at his cigar,
but the gesture was mechanical, unnoticed. "He'd always been too
bookish, too alone. So his Stormgate friends, his visits there—Later,
when he and Eyath and their gang were knocking around in odd
corners of the planet—well, that seemed like he was doing over what
I did at his age, except he'd have somebody to guard his back if a
situation got sharp. I thought maybe he also would end enlisting in
the navy—" Holm shook his head. "I didn't see till too late, what'd
gotten in him was not old-fashioned fiddlefootedness. Then when I
did wake up, and we quarreled about it, and he ran off and hid in the
Shielding Islands for a year, with Eyath's help—But no point in my
going on, is there?"

Ferune gestured negative. After Daniel Holm went raging to
Lythran's house, accusations exploding out of him, it had been all the
First Marchwarden could do to intervene, calm both parties and pre-
vent a duel.

"No, I shouldn't have said anything today," Holm continued.
"It's only—last night Rowena was crying. That he went off and did-
n't say goodbye to her. Mainly, she worries about what's happening
to him, inside, since he joined the choth. Can he ever make a normal
marriage, for instance? Ordinary girls aren't his type any more; and
bird girls—And, right, our younger kids. Tommy's completely in
orbit around Ythrian subjects. The school monitor had to come in
person and tell us how he'd been neglecting to screen the material or
submit the work or see the consultants he was supposed to. And
Jeanne's found a couple of Ythrian playmates—"

"As far as I know," Ferune said, "humans who entered choths
have as a rule had satisfactory lives. Problems, of course. But what life
can have none? Besides, the difficulties ought to become less as the
number of such persons grows."

"Look," Holm floundered, "I'm not against your folk. Break my bones if ever I was! Never once did I say or think there was anything dishonorable about what Chris was doing, any more than I would've said or thought it if, oh, if he'd joined some celibate order of priests. But I'd not have liked that either. It's no more natural for a man. And I've studied everything I could find about bird people. Sure, most of them have claimed they were happy. Probably most of them believed it. I can't help thinking they never realized what they'd missed."

"Walkers," Ferune said. In Planha, that sufficed. In Anglic he would have had to state something like: "We've lost our share, those who left the choths to become human-fashion atomic individuals within a global human community."

"Influence," he added, which conveyed: "Over the centuries on Avalon, no few of our kind have grown bitter at what your precept and example were doing to the choths themselves. Many still are. I suspect that's a major reason why several such groups have become more reactionary than any on the mother world."

Holm responded, "Wasn't the whole idea of this colony that both races should grant each other the right to be what they were?"

"That was written into the Compact and remains there," Ferune said in two syllables and three expressions. "Nobody has been compelled. But living together, how can we help changing?"

"Uh-huh. Because Ythri in general and Mistwood in particular have made a success of adopting and adapting Terran technology, you believe nothing's involved except a common-sense swap of ideas. It's not that simple, though."

"I didn't claim it is," Ferune said, "only that we don't catch time in any net."

"Yeh. I'm sorry if I—Well, I didn't mean to maunder on, especially when you've heard me often enough before. These just happen to be thin days at home." The man left his chair, strode past the Ythrian, and halted by the window, where he looked out through a veil of smoke.

"Let's get to real work," he said. "I'd like to ask specific questions about the overall state of Domain preparedness. And you'd better listen to me about what's been going on here while you were away—through the whole bloody-be-flensed Lauran System, in fact. That's none too good either."

✳ ✳ ✳

✧❙❙❙✧

The car identified its destination and moved down. Its initial altitude was such that the rider inside glimpsed a dozen specks of ground strewn over shining waters. But when he approached they had all fallen beneath the horizon. Only the rugged cone of St. Li was now visible to him.

With an equatorial diameter of a mere 11,308 kilometers, Avalon has a molten core smaller in proportion than Terra's; a mass of 0.635 cannot store as much heat. Thus the forces are weak that thrust land upward. At the same time, erosion proceeds fast. The atmospheric pressure at sea level is similar to the Terrestrial—and drops off more slowly with height, because of the gravity gradient—and rapid rotation makes for violent weather. In consequence, the surface is generally low, the highest peak in the Andromedas rising no more than 4500 meters. Nor does the land occur in great masses. Corona, capping the north pole and extending down past the Tropic of Swords, covers barely eight million square kilometers, about the size of Australia. In the opposite hemisphere, Equatoria, New Africa, and New Gaiila could better be called large islands than minor continents. All else consists of far smaller islands.

Yet one feature is gigantic. Some 2000 kilometers due west of Gray begins that drowned range whose peaks, thrusting into air, are known as Oronesia. Southward it runs, crosses the Tropic of Spears, trails off at last not far from the Antarctic Circle. Thus it forms a true, hydrological boundary; its western side marks off the Middle Ocean, its eastern the Hesperian Sea in the northern hemisphere and the South Ocean beyond the equator. It supports a distinct ecology, incredibly rich. And thereby, after the colonization, it became a sociological phenomenon. Any eccentrics, human or Ythrian, could go off, readily transform one or a few isles, and make their own undisturbed existence.

The mainland choths were diverse in size as well as in organization and tradition. But whether they be roughly analogous to clans, tribes, baronies, religious communes, republics, or whatever, they counted their members in the thousands at least. In Oronesia there were single households which bore the name; grown and married, the younger children were expected to found new, independent societies.

Naturally, this extremism was exceptional. The Highsky folk in particular were numerous, controlling the fisheries around latitude 30° N. and occupying quite a stretch of the archipelago. And they were fairly conventional, insofar as that word has any meaning when applied to Ythrians.

The aircar landed on the beach below a compound. He who stepped out was tall, with dark-red hair, clad in sandals, kilt, and weapons.

Tabitha Falkayn had seen the vehicle descending and walked forth to meet it "Hello, Christopher Holm," she said in Anglic.

"I come as Arinnian," he answered in Planha. "Luck fare beside you, Hrill."

She smiled. "Excuse me if I don't elaborate the occasion." Shrewdly: "You called ahead that you wanted to see me on a public matter. That must have to do with the border crisis. I daresay your Khruath decided that western Corona and northern Oronesia must work out a means of defending the Hesperian Sea."

He nodded awkwardly, and his eyes sought refuge from her amusement.

Enormous overhead, sunshine brilliant off cumulus banks, arched heaven. A sailor winged yonder, scouting for schools of piscoid; a flock of Ythrian shuas flapped by under the control of a herder and his uhoths; native pteropleuron lumbered around a reef rookery. The sea rolled indigo, curled in translucent green breakers, and exploded in foam on sands nearly as white. Trawlers plied it, kilometers out. Inland the ground rose steep. The upper slopes still bore a pale emerald mat of susin; only a few kinds of shrub were able to grow past those interlocking roots. But further down the hills had been plowed. There Ythrian clustergrain rustled red, for ground cover and to feed the shuas, while groves of coconut palm, mango, orange, and pumpernickel plant lifted above to nourish the human members of Highsky. A wind blew, warm but fresh, full of salt and iodine and fragrances.

"I suppose it was felt bird-to-bird conferences would be a good idea," Tabitha went on. "You mountaineers will have ample trouble understanding us pelagics, and vice versa, without the handicap of differing species. Ornithoids will meet likewise, hm?" Her manner turned thoughtful: "You had to be a delegate, of course. Your area has so few of your kind. But why come in person? Not that you aren't welcome. Still, a phone call—"

"We . . . we may have to talk at length," he said. "For days, off and on." He took for granted he would receive hospitality; all choths held that a guest was sacred.

"Why me, though? I'm only a local."

"You're a descendant of David Falkayn."

"That doesn't mean much."

"It does where I live. Besides—well, we've met before, now and then, at the larger Khruaths and on visits to each other's home areas and—We're acquainted a little. I'd not know where to begin among total strangers. If nothing else, you . . . you can advise me whom to consult, and introduce me. Can't you?"

"Certainly." Tabitha took both his hands. "Besides, I'm glad to see you, Chris."

His heart knocked. He struggled not to squirm. *What makes me this shy before her?* God knew she was attractive. A few years older than he, big, strongly built, full-breasted and long of leg, she showed to advantage in a short sleeveless tunic. Her face was snubnosed, wide of mouth, its green eyes set far apart under heavy brows; she had never bothered to remove the white scar on her right cheekbone. Her hair, cropped beneath the ears, was bleached flaxen. It blew like banners over the brown, slightly freckled skin.

He wondered if she went as casually to bed as the Coronan bird girls—never with a male counterpart; always a hearty, husky, not overintelligent worker type—or if she was a virgin. That seemed unlikely. What human, perpetually in a low-grade lovetime, could match the purity of an Eyath? Yet Highsky wasn't Stormgate or The Tarns—he didn't know—Tabitha had no companions of her own species here where she dwelt—however, she traveled often and widely. . . . He cast the speculation from him.

"Hoy, you're blushing," she laughed. "Did I violate one of your precious mores?" She released him. "If so, I apologize. But you always take these things too seriously. Relax. A social rite or a social gaffe isn't a deathpride matter."

Easy for her, I suppose, he thought. *Her grandparents were received into this choth. Her parents and their children grew up in it. A fourth of the membership must be human by now. And they've influenced it—like this commercial fishery she and Draun have started, a strictly private enterprise—*

"I'm afraid we've no time for gaiety," he got out. "We've walking weather ahead."

"Indeed?"

"The Empire's about to expand our way."

"C'mon to the house." Tabitha took his arm and urged him toward the compound. Its thatch-roofed timber dwellings were built lower than most Ythrian homes and were sturdier than they seemed; for here was scant protection from Avalon's hurricanes. "Oh, yes," she said, "the empire's been growing vigorously since Manuel the First. But I've read its history. How has the territory been brought under control? Some by simple partnership—civilized nonhumans like the Cynthians found it advantageous. Some by purchase or exchange. Some by conquest, yes—but always of primitives, or at most of people whose strength in space was ridiculously less than Greater Terra's. We're a harder gale to buck."

"Are we? My father says—"

"Uh-huh. The Empire's sphere approaches 400 light-years across, ours about 80. Out of all the systems in its volume, the Empire's got a degree of direct contact with several thousand, we with barely 250. But don't you see, Chris, we know our planets better? We're more compact. Our total resources are less but our technology's every bit as good. And then, we're distant from Terra. Why should they attack us? We don't threaten them, we merely claim our rights along the border. If they want more realm, they can find plenty closer to home, suns they've never visited, and easier to acquire than from a proud, well-armed Domain."

"My father says we're weak and unready."

"Do you think we would lose a war?"

He fell silent until they both noticed, through the soughing ahead, how sand scrunched beneath their feet. At last: "Well, I don't imagine anybody goes into a war expecting to lose."

"I don't believe they'll fight," Tabitha said. "I believe the Imperium has better sense."

"Regardless, we'd better take precautions. Home defense is among them."

"Yes. Won't be easy to organize, among a hundred or more sovereign choths."

"That's where we birds come in, maybe," he ventured. "Long established ones in particular, like your family."

"I'm honored to help," she told him. "And in fact I don't imagine the choths will cooperate too badly—" she tossed her head in haughtiness—"when it's a matter of showing the Empire who flies highest!"

Eyath and Vodan winged together. They made a handsome pair, both golden of eyes and arms, he ocher-brown and she deep bronze. Beneath them reached the Stormgate lands, forest-darkened valleys, crags and cliffs, peaks where snowfields lingered to dapple blue-gray rock, swordblade of a waterfall and remote blink of a glacier. A wind sang *whoo* and drove clouds, which Laura tinged gold, through otherwise brilliant air; their shadows raced and rippled across the world. The Ythrians drank of the wind's cold and swam in its swirling, thrusting, flowing strength. It stroked their feathers till they felt the barbs of the great outer pinions shiver.

He said: "If we were of Arinnian's kind, I would surely wed you, now, before I go to my ship. But you won't be in lovetime for months, and by then I might be dead. I would not bind you to that sorrow for nothing."

"Do you think I would grieve less if I had not the name of widow?" she answered. "I'd want the right to lead your memorial dance. For I know what parts of these skies you like best."

"Still, you would have to lift some awkward questions, obligation toward my blood and so on. No. Shall our friendship be less because, for a while, you have not the name of wife?"

"Friendship—" she murmured. Impulsively: "I dreamt last night that we were indeed like humans."

"What, forever in rut?"

"Forever in love."

"Kh-h'ng, I've naught against Arinnian, but sometimes I wonder if you've not been too much with him, for too many years since you both were small. Had Lythran not taken you along when he had

business in Gray—" Vodan saw her crest rise, broke off and added in
haste: "Yes, he's your galemate. That makes him mine too. I only
wanted to warn you . . . don't try, don't wish to be human."

"No, no." Eyath felt a downdraft slide by. She slanted herself to
catch it, a throb of wings and then the long wild glide, peaks leaping
nearer, glimpse through trees of a pool ashine where a feral stallion
drank, song and rush and caress of cloven air, till she checked herself
and flew back upward, breasting a torrent, every muscle at full
aliveness—traced a thermal by the tiny trembling of a mountain
seen through it, won there, spread her wings and let heaven carry
her hovering while she laughed.

Vodan beat near. "Would I trade this?" she called joyously. "Or
you?"

Ekrem Saracoglu, Imperial governor of Sector Pacis, had hinted
for a while that he would like to meet the daughter of Fleet Admiral
Juan de Jesús Cajal y Palomares. She had come from Nuevo México
to be official hostess and feminine majordomo for her widowed
father, after he transferred his headquarters to Esperance and rented
a house in Fleurville. The date kept being postponed. It was not that
the admiral disliked the governor—they got along well—nor distrusted
his intentions, no matter how notorious a womanizer he was. Luisa
had been raised among folk who, if strict out of necessity on their dry
world, were rich in honor and bore a hair-trigger pride. It was merely
that both men were overwhelmed by work.

At last their undertakings seemed fairly well along, and Cajal
invited Sarocoglu to dinner. A ridiculous last-minute contretemps
occurred. The admiral phoned home that he would be detained at
the office a couple of hours. The governor was already on his way.

"Thus you, Donna, have been told to keep me happy in the teeth
of a postponed meal," Saracoglu purred over the hand he kissed. "I
assure you, that will not be in the least difficult." Though small, she
had a lively figure and a darkly pretty face. And he soon learned that,
albeit solemn, she knew how to listen to a man and, rarer yet, ask him
stimulating questions.

By then they were strolling in the garden. Rosebushes and cherry
trees might almost have been growing on Terra; Esperance was a
prize among colony planets. The sun Pax was still above the horizon,

now at midsummer, but leveled mellow beams across an old brick wall. The air was warm, blithe with birdsong, sweet with green odors that drifted in from the countryside. A car or two caught the light, high above; but Fleurville was not big enough for its traffic noise to be heard this far from the centrum.

Saracoglu and Luisa paced along graveled paths and talked. They were guarded, which is to say discreetly chaperoned. However, no duenna followed several paces behind, but a huge four-armed Gorzunian mercenary on whom the nuances of a flirtation would be lost.

The trouble is, thought the governor, *she's begun conversing in earnest.*

It had been quite pleasant at first. She encouraged him to speak of himself. "—yes, the Earl of Anatolia, that's me. Frankly, even if it is on Terra, a minor peerage. . . . Career bureaucrat. Might rather've been an artist—I dabble in oils and clays—maybe you'd care to see. . . . Alas, you know how such things go. Imperial nobles are expected to serve the Imperium. Had I but been born in a decadent era! Eh? Unfortunately, the Empire's not run out of momentum—"

Inwardly, he grinned at his own performance. He, fifty-three standard years of age, squat, running to fat, totally bald, little eyes set close to a giant nose, and two expensive mistresses in his palace— acting the role of a boy who acted the role of an *homme du monde!* Well, he enjoyed that once in a while, as he enjoyed gaudy clothes and jewels. They were a relaxation from the wry realism which had never allowed him to improve his appearance through biosculp.

But at this point she asked, "Are we really going to attack the Ythrians?"

"Heh?" The distress in her tone brought his head swinging sharply around to stare at her. "Why, negotiations are stalled, but—"

"Who stalled them?" She kept her own gaze straight ahead. Her voice had risen a note and the slight Espanyol accent had intensified.

"Who started most of the violent incidents?" he countered. "Ythrians. Not that they're monsters, understand. But they are predators by nature. And they've no strong authority—no proper government at all—to control the impulses of groups. That's been a major stumbling block in the effort to reach an accommodation."

"How genuine was the effort—on our side?" she demanded, still refusing to look at him. "How long have you planned to fall on them? My father won't tell me anything, but it's obvious, it's been obvious ever since he moved here—how often are naval and civilian headquarters on the same planet?—it's obvious something is b-b-being readied."

"Donna," Saracoglu said gravely, "when a fleet of spacecraft can turn whole worlds into tombs, one prepares against the worst and one clamps down security regulations." He paused. "One also discovers it is unwise to let spheres interpenetrate, as Empire and Domain have. I daresay you, young, away off in a relatively isolated system . . . I daresay you got an idea the Imperium is provoking war in order to swallow the whole Ythrian Domain. That is not true."

"What is true?" she replied bitterly.

"That there have been bloody clashes over disputed territories and conflicting interests."

"Yes. Our traders are losing potential profits."

"Would that were the only friction. Commercial disputes are always negotiable. Political and military rivalries are harder. For example, which of us shall absorb the Antoranite-Kraokan complex around Beta Centauri? One of us is bound to, and those resources would greatly strengthen Terra. The Ythrians have already gained more power, by bringing Dathyna under them, than we like a potentially hostile race to have.

"Furthermore, by rectifying this messy frontier, we can armor ourselves against a Merseian flank attack." Saracoglu lifted a hand to forestall her protest. "Indeed, Donna, the Roidhunate is far off and not very big. But it's growing at an alarming rate, and aggressive acquisitiveness is built into its ideology. The duty of an empire is to provide for the great-grandchildren."

"Why can't we simply write a treaty, give a *quid pro quo,* divide things in a fair and reasonable manner?" Luisa asked.

Saracoglu sighed. "The populations of the planets would object to being treated like inanimate property. No government which took that attitude would long survive." He gestured aloft. "Furthermore, the universe holds too many unknowns. We have traveled hundreds—in earlier days, thousands—of light-years to especially interesting stars. But what myriads have we bypassed? What may turn up when we do seek them out? No responsible authority, human or Ythrian, will blindly hand over such possibilities to an alien.

"No, Donna, this is no problem capable of neat, final solutions. We just have to do our fumbling best. Which does *not* include subjugating Ythri. I'm the first to grant Ythri's right to exist, go its own way, even keep offplanet possessions. But this frontier must be stabilized."

"We—interpenetrate—with others—and have no trouble."

"Of course. Why should we fight hydrogen breathers, for example? They're so exotic we can barely communicate with them. The trouble is, the Ythrians are too like us. As an old, old saying goes, two tough, smart races want the same real estate."

"We can live with them! Humans are doing it. They have for generations."

"Do you mean Avalon?"

She nodded.

Saracoglu saw a chance to divert the conversation back into easier channels. "Well, there's an interesting case, certainly," he smiled. "How much do you know about it?"

"Very little," she admitted, subdued. "A few mentions here and there, since I came to Esperance. The galaxy's so huge, this tiny fleck of it we've explored. . . ."

"You might get to see Avalon," he said. "Not far off, ten or twelve light-years. I'd like that myself. The society does appear to be unusual, if not absolutely unique."

"Don't you understand? If humans and Ythrians can share a single planet—"

"That's different. Allow me to give you some background. I've never been there either, but I've studied material on it since getting this appointment."

Saracoglu drew breath. "Avalon was discovered five hundred years ago, by the same Grand Survey ship that came on Ythri," he said. "It was noted as a potential colony, but was so remote from Terra that nobody was interested then; the very name wasn't bestowed till long afterward. Ythri was forty light-years further, true, but much more attractive, a rich planet full of people vigorously entering the modern era who had a considerable deal to trade.

"About three and a half centuries back, a human company made the Ythrians a proposal. The Polesotechnic League wasn't going to collapse for another fifty years, but already anybody who had a functional brain could read what a cutthroat period lay ahead. These humans, a mixed lot under the leadership of an old trade pioneer, wanted to safeguard the future of their families by settling on out-of-the-way Avalon—under the suzerainty, the protection, of an Ythri that was not corrupted as Technic civilization was. The Ythrians agreed, and naturally some of them joined the settlement.

"Well, the Troubles came, and Ythri was not spared. The eventual results were similar—Terra enforced peace by the Empire, Ythri by the Domain. In the meantime, standing together, bearing the brunt of chaos, the Avalonians had been welded into one.

"Nothing like that applies today."

They had stopped by a vine-covered trellis. He plucked a grape and offered it to her. She shook her head. He ate it himself. The taste held a slight, sweet strangeness; Esperancian soil was not, after all, identical with that of Home. The sun was now gone from sight, shadows welled in the garden, an evening star blossomed.

"I suppose . . . your plans for 'rectification' . . . include bringing Avalon into the Empire," Luisa said.

"Yes. Consider its position." Saracoglu shrugged. "Besides, the humans there form a large majority. I rather imagine they'll be glad to join us, and Ythri won't mind getting rid of them."

"Must we fight?"

Saracoglu smiled. "It's never too late for peace." He took her arm. "Shall we go indoors? I expect your father will be here soon. We ought to have the sherry set out for him."

He'd not spoil the occasion, which was still salvageable, by telling her that weeks had passed since a courier ship brought what he requested: an Imperial rescript declaring war on Ythri, to be made public whenever governor and admiral felt ready to act.

❖IV❖

A campaign against Ythri would demand an enormous fleet, gathered from everywhere in the Empire. No such thing had been publicly seen or heard of, though rumors flew. But of course units guarding the border systems had been openly reinforced as the crisis sharpened, and drills and practice maneuvers went on apace.

Orbiting Pax at ten astronomical units, the Planet-class cruisers *Thor* and *Ansa* flung blank shells and torpedoes at each other's force screens, pierced these latter with laser beams that tried to hold on a single spot of hull for as long as an energy blast would have taken to gnaw through armor, exploded magnesium flares whose brilliance represented lethal radiation, dodged about on grav thrust, wove in and out of hyperdrive phase, used every trick in the book and a few which the high command hoped had not yet gotten into Ythrian books. Meanwhile the Comet- and Meteor-class boats they mothered were similarly busy.

To stimulate effort, a prize had been announced. That vessel the computers judged victorious would proceed with her auxiliaries to Esperance, where the crew would get a week's liberty.

Ansa won. She broadcast a jubilant recall. Half a million kilometers away, an engine awoke in the Meteor which her captain had dubbed *Hooting Star.*

"Resurrected at last!" Lieutenant (j.g.) Philippe Rochefort exulted. "And in glory at that."

"And unearned." The fire control officer, CPO Wa Chaou of Cynthia, grinned. His small white-furred body crouched on the table he had been cleaning after a meal; his bushy tail quivered like the whiskers around his blue-masked muzzle.

"What the muck you mean, 'unearned'?" the engineer-computer-man, CPO Abdullah Helu, grumbled: a lean, middle-aged careerist from Huy Braseal. "Playing dead for three mortal days is beyond the call of duty." The boat had theoretically been destroyed in a dogfight and drifting free, as a real wreck would, to complicate life for detector technicians.

"Especially when the poker game cleaned and reamed you, eh?" Wa Chaou gibed.

"I won't play with you again, sir," Helu said to the captain-pilot. "No offense. You're just too mucking talented."

"Only luck," Rochefort answered. "Same as it was only luck that threw such odds against us. The boat acquitted herself well. As you did afterward, over the chips. Better luck to both next time."

She was his first, new and shiny command—he having recently

been promoted from ensign for audacity in a rescue operation—and he was anxious for her to make a good showing. No matter how inevitable under the circumstances, defeat had hurt.

But they were on the top team; and they'd accounted for two opposition craft, plus tying up three more for a while that must have been used to advantage elsewhere; and now they were bound back to *Ansa* and thence to Esperance, where he knew enough girls that dates were a statistical certainty.

The little cabin trembled and hummed with driving energies. Air gusted from ventilators, smelling of oil and of recycling chemicals. A Meteor was designed for high acceleration under both relativistic and hyperdrive conditions; for accurate placement of nuclear-headed torpedoes; and for no more comfort than minimally essential to the continued efficiency of personnel.

Yet space lay around the viewports in a glory of stars, diamond-keen, unwinking, many-colored, crowding an infinitely clear blackness till they merged in the argent torrent of the Milky Way or the dim mysterious cloudlets which were sister galaxies. Rochefort wanted to sit, look, let soul follow gaze outward into God's temple the universe. He could have done so, too; the boat was running on full automatic. But better demonstrate to the others that he was a conscientious as well as an easy-going officer. He turned the viewer back on which he had been using when the message came.

A canned lecture was barely under way. A human xenologist stood in the screen and intoned:

"Warm-blooded, feathered, and flying, the Ythrians are not birds; they bring their young forth viviparously after a gestation of four and a half months; they do not have beaks, but lips and teeth. Nor are they mammals; they grow no hair and secrete no milk; those lips have developed for parents to feed infants by regurgitation. And while the antlibranchs might suggest fish gills, they are not meant for water but for—"

"Oh, no!" Helu exclaimed. "Sir, won't you have time to study later? Devil knows how many more weeks we'll lie in orbit doing nothing."

"War may erupt at any minute," Wa Chaou said.

"And if and when, who cares how the enemy looks or what his love life is? His ships are about like ours, and that's all we're ever likely to see."

"Oh, you have a direct line to the future?" the Cynthian murmured.

Rochefort stopped the tape and snapped, "I'll put the sound on tight beam if you want. But a knowledge of the enemy's nature might make the quantum of difference that saves us when the real thing happens. I suggest you watch too."

"Er, I think I should check out Number Three oscillator, long's we're not traveling faster-than-light," Helu said, and withdrew into the engine room. Wa Chaou settled down by Rochefort.

The lieutenant smiled. He refrained from telling the Cynthian, *You're a good little chap. Did you enlist to get away from the domination of irascible females on your home planet?*

His thought went on: *The reproductive pattern—sexual characteristics, requirements of the young—does seem to determine most of the basics in any intelligent species. As if the cynic's remark were true, that an organism is simply a DNA molecule's way of making more DNA molecules. Or whatever the chemicals of heredity may be on a given world. . . . But no, a Jerusalem Catholic can't believe that. Biological evolution inclines, it does not compel.*

"Let's see how the Ythrians work," he said aloud, reaching for the switch.

"Don't you already know, sir?" Wa Chaou asked.

"Not really. So many sophont races, in that bit of space we've sort of explored. And I've been busy familiarizing myself with my new duties." Rochefort chuckled. "And, be it admitted, enjoying what leaves I could get."

He reactivated the screen. It showed an Ythrian walking on the feet that grew from his wings: a comparatively slow, jerky gait, no good for real distances. The being stopped, lowered hands to ground, and stood on them. He lifted his wings, and suddenly he was splendid.

Beneath, on either side, were slits in column. As the wings rose, the feathery operculum-like flaps which protected them were drawn back. The slits widened until, at full extension, they gaped like purple mouths. The view became a closeup. Thin-skinned tissues, intricately wrinkled, lay behind a curtain of cilia which must be for screening out dust.

When the wings lowered, the slits were forced shut again, bellows fashion. The lecturer's voice said: "This is what allows so heavy a body, under Terra-type weight and gas density, to fly. Ythrians attain more than twice the mass of the largest possible airborne creature on similar planets elsewhere. The antlibranchs, pumped by the wing-strokes, take in oxygen under pressure to feed it directly to the bloodstream. Thus they supplement lungs which themselves more or less resemble those of ordinary land animals. The Ythrian acquires the power needed to get aloft and, indeed, fly with rapidity and grace."

The view drew back. The creature in the holograph flapped strongly and rocketed upward.

"Of course," the dry voice said, "this energy must come from a correspondingly accelerated metabolism. Unless prevented from flying, the Ythrian is a voracious eater. Aside from certain sweet fruits, he is strictly carnivorous. His appetite has doubtless reinforced the usual carnivore tendency to live in small, well-separated groups, each occupying a wide territory which instinct makes it defend against all intruders.

"In fact, the Ythrian can best be understood in terms of what we know or conjecture about the evolution of his race."

"Conjecture more than know, I suspect," Rochefort remarked. But he found himself fascinated.

"We believe that homeothermic—roughly speaking, warm-blooded— life on Ythri did not come from a reptilian or reptiloid form, but directly from an amphibian, conceivably even from something corresponding to a lungfish. At any rate, it retained a kind of gill. Those species which were most successful on land eventually lost this feature. More primitive animals kept it. Among these was that small, probably swamp-dwelling thing which became the ancestor of the sophont. Taking to the treetops, it may have developed a membrane on which to glide from bough to bough. This finally turned into a wing. Meanwhile the gills were modified for aerial use, into superchargers."

"As usual," Wa Chaou observed. "The failures at one stage beget the successes of the next."

"Of course, the Ythrian can soar and even hover," the speaker said, "but it is the tremendous wing area which makes this possible, and the antlibranchs are what make it possible to operate those wings.

"Otherwise the pre-Ythrian must have appeared fairly similar to Terran birds." Pictures of various hypothetical extinct creatures went by. "It developed an analogous water-hoarding system—no separate urination—which saved weight as well as compensating for evaporative losses from the antlibranchs. It likewise developed light bones, though these are more intricate than avian bones, built of a marvelously strong two-phase material whose organic component is not collagen but a substance carrying out the functions of Terra-mammalian marrow. The animal did not, however, further ease its burdens by trading teeth for a beak. Many Ythrian ornithoids have done so, for example the uhoth, hawklike in appearance, doglike in service. But the pre-sophont remained an unspecialized dweller in wet jungles.

"The fact that the young were born tiny and helpless—since the female could not fly long distances while carrying a heavy fetus—is probably responsible for the retention and elaboration of the digits on the wings. The cub could cling to either parent in turn while these cruised after food; before it was able to fly, it could save itself from enemies by clambering up a tree. Meanwhile the feet acquired more and more ability to seize prey and manipulate objects.

"Incidentally, the short gestation period does not mean that the Ythrian is born with a poorly developed nervous system. The rapid metabolism of flight affects the rate of fetal cell division. This process concentrates on laying down a body pattern rather than on increasing the size. Nevertheless, an infant Ythrian needs more care, and more food, than an infant human. The parents must cooperate in providing this as well as in carrying their young about. Here we may have the root cause of the sexual equality or near equality found in all Ythrian cultures.

"Likewise, a rapid succession of infants would be impossible to keep alive under primitive conditions. This may be a reason why the female only ovulates at intervals of a year—Ythri's is about half of Terra's—and not for about two years after giving birth. Sexuality does not come overtly into play except at these times. Then it is almost uncontrollably strong in male and female alike. This may well have given the territorial instinct a cultural reinforcement after intelligence evolved. Parents wish to keep their nubile daughters isolated from chance-met males while in heat. Furthermore, husband and wife do not wish to waste a rich, rare experience on any outsider.

"The sexual cycle is not totally rigid. In particular, grief often brings on estrus. Doubtless this was originally a provision of nature for rapid replacement of losses. It seems to have brought about a partial fusion of Eros and Thanatos in the Ythrian psyche which makes much of the race's art, and doubtless thought, incomprehensible to man. An occasional female can ovulate at will, though this is considered an abnormality; in olden days she would be killed, now she is generally shunned, out of dread of her power. A favorite villain in Ythrian story is the male who, by hypnosis or otherwise, can induce the state. Of course, the most important manifestation of a degree of flexibility is the fact that Ythrians have successfully adapted their reproductive pattern, like everything else, to a variety of colonized planets."

"Me, I think it's more fun being human," Rochefort said.

"I don't know, sir," Wa Chaou replied. "Superficially the relationship between the sexes looks simpler than in your race or mine; you're either in the mood or you're not, and that's that. I wonder, though, if it may not really be more subtle and complicated than ours, even more basic to the whole psychology."

"But to return to evolution," the lecturer was saying. "It seems that a major part of Ythri underwent something like the great Pliocene drought in Terra's Africa. The ornithoids were forced out of dwindling forests onto growing savannahs. There they evolved from carrion eaters to big-game hunters in a manner analogous to pre-man. The original feet became hands, which eventually started making tools. To support the body and provide locomotion on the ground, the original elbow claws turned into feet, the wings that bore them became convertible to legs of a sort.

"Still, the intelligent Ythrian remained a pure carnivore, and one which was awkward on land. Typically, primitive hunters struck from above, with spears, arrows, axes. Thus only a few were needed to bring down the largest beasts. There was no necessity to cooperate in digging pits for elephants or standing shoulder to shoulder against a charging lion. Society remained divided into families or clans, which seldom fought wars but which, on the other hand, did not have much contact of any sort.

"The revolution which ended the Stone Age did not involve agriculture from the beginning, as in the case of man. It came from the systematic herding, at last the domestication, of big ground animals like the maukh, smaller ones like the long-haired mayaw. This stimulated the invention of skids, wheels, and the like, enabling the Ythrian to get about more readily on the surface. Agriculture was invented as an ancillary to ranching, an efficient means of providing fodder. The food surplus allowed leisure for travel, trade, and wide-spread cultural intercourse. Hence larger, complex social units arose.

"They cannot be called civilizations in a strict sense, because Ythri has never known true cities. The mobility of being winged left no necessity for crowding together in order to maintain close relationships. Granted, sedentary centers did appear—for mining, metallurgy, and other industry; for trade and religion; for defense in case the group was defeated by another in aerial battle. But these have always been small and their populations mostly floating. Apart from their barons and garrisons, their permanent inhabitants were formerly, for the main part, wing-clipped slaves—today, automated machines. Clipping was an easy method of making a person controllable; yet since the feathers could grow back, the common practice of promising manumission after a certain period of diligent service tended to make prisoners docile. Hence slavery became so basic to pre-industrial Ythrian society that to this day it has not entirely disappeared."

Well, we're reviving it in the Empire, Rochefort thought. *For terms and under conditions limited by law; as a punishment, in order to get some social utility out of the criminal; nevertheless, we're bringing back a thing the Ythrians are letting die. How more moral are we than they? How much more right do we have?*

He straightened in his chair. *Man is my race.*

A willowy blonde with the old-fashioned Esperancian taste for simplicity in clothes, Eve Davisson made a pleasing contrast to Philippe Rochefort, as both were well aware. He was a tall, rather slender young man, his bearing athletic, his features broad-nosed, full-lipped, and regular, his hair kinking itself into a lustrous black coif over the deep-brown skin. And he stretched to the limit the tolerance granted officers as regards their dress uniforms—rakishly tilted bonnet bearing the sunburst of Empire, gold-trimmed blue tunic, scarlet sash and cloak, snowy trousers tucked into low boots of authentic Terran beef-leather.

They sat in an intimate restaurant of Fleurville, by a window opening on gardens and stars. A live sonorist played something old and sentimental; perfumed, slightly intoxicant vapors drifted about; they toyed with hors d'oeuvres and paid more serious attention to their champagne. Nonetheless she was not smiling.

"This world was settled by people who believed in peace," she said. Her tone mourned rather than accused. "For generations they kept no armed forces, they relied on the good will of others whom they helped."

"That good will didn't outlive the Troubles," Rochefort said.

"I know, I know. I shan't join the demonstrators, whatever some of my friends may say when they learn I've been out with an Imperial officer. But Phil—the star named Pax, the planet named Esperance are being geared for war. It hurts."

"It'd hurt worse if you were attacked. Avalon isn't far, and they've built a lot of power there."

Her fingers tightened on the stem of her glass. "Attack from Avalon? But I've *met* those people, both races. They've come here on trade or tour or—I made a tour there myself, not long ago. I went because it's picturesque, but was so graciously treated I didn't want to leave."

"I daresay Ythrian manners have rubbed off on their human fellows." Rochefort let a draft go over his palate, hoping it would tingle away his irritation. This wasn't supposed to be a political evening. "Likewise less pleasant features of the Ythrian personality."

She studied him through the soft light before she said low, "I get an impression you disapprove of a mixed colony."

"Well . . . in a way, yes." He could have dissembled, facilely agreed to everything she maintained, and thus improved his chances of bedding her later on. But he'd never operated thus; and he never would, especially when he liked this girl just as a person. "I believe in being what you are and standing by your own."

"You talk almost like a human supremacist," she said, though mildly.

"To the extent that man is the leading race—furnishes most of the leaders—in Technic civilization, yes, I suppose you'd have to call me a human supremacist," he admitted. "It doesn't mean we aren't chronically sinful and stupid, nor does it mean we have any right to oppress others. Why, my sort of people are the xenosophont's best friend. We simply don't want to imitate him."

"Do you believe the Terran Empire is a force for good?"

"On balance, yes. It commits evil. But nothing mortal can avoid that. Our duty is to correct the wrongs . . . and also to recognize the values that the Empire does, in fact, preserve."

"You may have encountered too little of the evil."

"Because I'm from Terra itself?" Rochefort chuckled. "My dear, you're too bright to imagine the mother system is inhabited exclusively by aristocrats. My father is a minor functionary in the Sociodynamic Service. His job caused us to move around a lot. I was born in Selenopolis, which is a spaceport and manufacturing center. I spent several impressionable years on Venus, in the crime and poverty of a planet whose terraforming never had been quite satisfactory. I joined the navy as an enlisted rating—not out of chauvinism, merely a boyish wish to see the universe—and wasn't tapped for pilot school for two-three years; meanwhile, I saw the grim side of more than one world. Sure, there's a cosmos of room for improvement. Well, let's improve, not tear down. And let's defend!"

He stepped. "Damn," he said frankly. "I'd hoped to lure you out of your seriousness, and fell into it myself."

Now the girl laughed, and raised her glass. "Let's help each other climb out, then," she suggested.

They did. Rochefort's liberty became highly enjoyable. And that was fortunate, because two weeks after he reported back from it, *Ansa* was ordered into deep space. Light-years from Pax, she joined the fleet that had been using immensity as a mask for its marshaling; and ships by the hundreds hurled toward the Domain of Ythri.

❖V❖

The conference was by phone. Most were, these days. It went against old Avalonian courtliness but saved time—and time was getting in mighty short supply, Daniel Holm thought.

Anger crackled through clearly enough. Two of the three holographs on the com board before him seemed about to climb out of their screens and into his office. No doubt he gave their originals the same impression.

Matthew Vickery, President of the Parliament of Man, wagged his forefinger and both plump jowls and said, "We are not under a military regime, may I remind you in case you have forgotten. We, the proper civil government, approved your defense measures of the past several years, though you are aware that I myself have always considered them excessive. When I think of the prosperity that tax money, those resources, could have brought, left in private hands— or the social good it could have done in the public sector—Give you military your heads, and you'd build bases in the fourth dimension to protect us against an invasion from the future."

"We are always being invaded by the future," Ferune said. "The next part of it to arrive will not be pleasant."

Holm crossed his legs, leaned back, blew cigar smoke at Vickery's image, and drawled, "Spare us the oratory. You're not campaigning for re-election here. What's made you demand this four-way?"

"Your entire high-handedness," Vickery declared. "The overflow quantum was that last order, barring non-Ythrian ships from the Lauran System. Do you realize what a trade we do . . . not merely with the Empire, though that supports many livelihoods, but with unaffiliated civilizations like the Kraokan?"

"Do *you* realize how easy it'd be for the Terrans to get a robotic job, disguised, into low orbit around Avalon?" Holm retorted. "Several thousand megatons, touched off at that height when skies are clear, would set about half of Corona afire. Or it might be so sophisticated it could land like a peaceful merchantman. Consciousness-level computers aren't used much any more, when little new exploration's going on, but they could be built, including a suicide imperative. That explosion would be inside a city's force shields; it'd take out the generators, leaving what was left of the city defenseless; fallout from a dirty warhead would poison the whole hinterland. And you, Vickery, helped block half the appropriation we wanted for adequate shelters."

"Hysteria," the president said. "What could Terra gain from a one-shot atrocity? Not that I expect war, if only we can curb our own hotheads. But—well, take this ludicrous home-guard program you've instigated." His glance went toward Ferune and Liaw. "Oh, it gives a lot of young folk a fine excuse to swagger around, getting in people's way, ordering them arrogantly about, feeling important, and never mind the social as well as the fiscal cost of it. But if this navy we've been building and manning at your loud urging, by straining our production facilities and gutting our resources, if this navy is as advertised, the Terrans can never come near us. If not, who has been derelict in his duty?"

"We are near their sector capital," Ferune reminded him. "They may strike us first, overwhelmingly."

"I've heard that till I'm taped for it. I prefer to program myself, thank you." Vickery paused. "See here," he continued in a leveled tone, "I agree the situation is critical. We're all Avalonians together. If I feel certain of your proposals are unwise, I tell this to the public and the Parliament. But in the end we compromise like reasonable beings."

Ferune's face rippled. It was as well that Vickery didn't notice or wasn't able to read the meaning. Liaw of The Tarns remained expressionless. Holm grunted, "Go on."

"I must protest both your proceedings and the manner of them," Vickery said. "We are not under martial law, and indeed the Compact makes no provision for declaring it."

"Wasn't needed in the old days," Holm said. "The danger was clear and present. I didn't think it'd be needed now. The Admiralty is responsible for local defense and liaison with armed forces elsewhere in the Domain—"

"Which does *not* authorize you to stop trade, or raise a tin militia, or anything cutting that deeply into normal Avalonian life. My colleagues and I have endured it thus far, recognizing the necessity of at least some things. But today the necessity is to remind you that you are the servants of the people, not the masters. If the people want your policies executed, they will so instruct their legislative representatives."

"The Khruaths did call for a home guard and for giving the Admiralty broad discretion," Liaw of The Tarns said in his rustling voice. He was old, had frost in his feathers; but he sat huge in his castle, and the screen gave a background image of crags and a glacier.

"Parliament—"

"Is still debating," Holm interrupted to finish. "The Terran

Imperium has no such handicap. If you want a legal formula, well, consider us to be acting under choth law."

"The choths have no government," Vickery said, reddening.

"What is a government?" asked Liaw, Wyvan of the High Khruath—how softly!

"Why . . . well, legitimate authority—"

"Yes. The legitimacy derives, ultimately, no matter by what formula, from tradition. The authority derives, no matter by what formula, from armed force. Government is that institution which is legitimized in its use of physical coercion on the people. Have I read your human philosophers and history aright, President Vickery?"

"Well . . . yes . . . but—"

"You seem to have forgotten for the moment that the choths have been no more unanimous than your human factions," Liaw said. "Believe me, they have been divided and they are. Though a majority voted for the latest defense measures, a vocal minority has opposed: feeling, as you do, President Vickery, that the danger has been exaggerated and does not justify lifting that great a load."

Liaw sat silent for a space, during which the rest of them heard wind whistle behind him and saw a pair of his grandsons fly past. One bore the naked sword which went from house to house as a summons to war, the other a blast rifle.

The High Wyvan said: "Three choths refused to make their gift. My fellows and I threatened to call Oherran on them. Had they not yielded, we would have done so. We consider the situation to be that grave."

Holm choked. *He never told me before!—Of course he wouldn't have.* Ferune grew nearly as still on his bench as Liaw. Vickery drew breath; sweat broke out on his smoothness; he dabbed at it.

I can almost sympathize, Holm thought. *Suddenly getting bashed with reality like that.*

Matthew Vickery should have stayed a credit analyst instead of going into politics (Holm's mind rambled on, at the back of its own shocked alertness). Then he'd have been harmless, in fact useful; interspecies economics is often a wonderland in need of all the study anyone can give it. The trouble was, on a thinly settled globe like Avalon, government never had been too important aside from basic issues of ecology and defense. In recent decades its functions had dwindled still further, as human society changed under Ythrian influence. (A twinge of pain.) Voting was light for offices that looked merely managerial. Hence the more reactionary humans were able to elect Vickery, who viewed with alarm the trend toward Ythrianization. (Was no alarm justified?) He had nothing else to offer, in these darkening times.

"You understand this is confidential," Liaw said. "If word got about, the choths in question would have to consider it a deathpride matter."

"Yes," Vickery whispered.

Another silence. Holm's cigar had burned short, was scorching his fingers. He stubbed it out. It stank. He started a new one. *I smoke too much,* he thought. *Drink too much also, maybe, of late. But the work's getting done, as far as circumstance allows.*

Vickery wet his lips. "This puts . . . another complexion on affairs, doesn't it?" he said. "May I speak plainly? I must know if this is a hint that . . . you may come to feel yourselves compelled to a *coup d'etat.*"

"We have better uses for our energies," Liaw told him. "Your efforts in Parliament could be helpful."

"Well—you realize I can't surrender my principles. I must be free to speak."

"It is written in the Compact," Ferune said, and his quotation did not seem superfluous even by Ythrian standards, "'Humans inhabiting Avalon have the deathpride right of free speech, publication, and broadcast, limited only by the deathpride rights of privacy and honor and by the requirements of protection against foreign enemies.'"

"I meant—" Vickery swallowed. But he had not been years in politics for nothing. "I meant simply that friendly criticism and suggestions will always be in order," he said with most of his accustomed ease. "However, we certainly cannot risk a civil war. Shall we discuss details of a policy of nonpartisan cooperation?"

Behind the ready words, fear could still be sensed. Holm imagined he could almost read Vickery's mind, reviewing the full significance of what Liaw had said.

How shall a fierce, haughty, intensely clannish and territorial race regulate its public business?

Just as on Terra, different cultures on Ythri at different periods in their histories have given a variety of answers, none wholly satisfactory or permanently enduring. The Planha speakers happened to be the most wealthy and progressive when the first explorers arrived; one is tempted to call them "Hellenistic." Eagerly adopting modern technology, they soon absorbed others into their system while modifying it to suit changed conditions.

This was the easier because the system did not require uniformity. Within its possessions—whether these were scattered or a single block of land or sea—a choth was independent. Tradition determined what constituted a choth, though this was a tradition which slowly changed itself, as every living usage must. Tribe, anarchism, despotism, loose federation, theocracy, clan, extended family, corporation, on and on through concepts for which there are no human words, a choth ran itself.

Mostly, internal ordering was by custom and public opinion rather than by prescription and force. After all, families rarely lived close together; hence friction was minimal. The commonest sanction was a kind of weregild, the most extreme was enslavement. In between was outlawry; for some specified period, which might run as high as life, the wrongdoer could be killed by anyone without penalty, and to aid him was to incur the same punishment. Another possible sentence was exile, with outlawry automatic in case of return before the term was up. This was harsh to an Ythrian. On the other hand, the really disaffected could easily leave home (how do you fence in the sky?) and apply for membership in a choth more to their taste.

Now of course some recognized body had to try cases and hand down judgments. It must likewise settle inter-choth disputes and establish policies and undertakings for the common weal. Thus in ancient times arose the Khruath, a periodic gathering of all free adults in a given territory who cared to come. It had judicial and limited legislative authority, but no administrative. The winners of lawsuits, the successful promoters of schemes and ordinances, must depend on willingness to comply or on what strength they could muster to enforce.

As Planha society expanded, regional meetings like this began to elect delegates to Year-Khruaths, which drew on larger territories.

Finally these, in turn, sent their representatives to the High Khruath of the whole planet, which met every six years plus on extraordinary occasions. On each level, a set of presiding officers, the Wyvans, were chosen. These were entrusted with explication of the laws (i.e. customs, precedents, decisions) and with trial of as many suits as possible. It was not quite a soviet organization, because any free adult could attend a Khruath on any level he wished.

The arrangement would not have worked on Terra—where a version of it appeared once, long ago, and failed bloodily. But Ythrians are less talkative, less busybody, less submissive to bullies, and less chronically crowded than man. Modern communications, computers, information retrieval, and educational techniques helped the system spread planetwide, ultimately Domain-wide.

Before it reached that scale, it had had to face the problem of administration. Necessary public works must be funded; in theory the choths made free gifts to this end, in practice the cost required allocation. Behavior grossly harmful to the physical or social environment must be enjoined, however much certain choths might profit by it or regard it as being of their special heritage. Yet no machinery existed for compulsion, nor would Ythrians have imagined establishing any—as such.

Instead, it came slowly about that when a noncompliance looked important, the Wyvans of the appropriate Khruath cried Oherran on the offenders. This, carried out after much soul-searching and with the gravest ceremonies, was a summons to everyone in the territory: that for the sake of their own interests and especially their honor, they attack the defiers of the court.

In early times, an Oherran on a whole choth meant the end of it—enslavement of whoever had not been slaughtered, division of holdings among the victors. Later it might amount to as little as the arrest and exile of named leaders. But always it fell under the concept of deathpride. If the call to Oherran was rejected, as had happened when the offense was not deemed sufficient to justify the monstrosity of invasion, then the Wyvans who cried it had no acceptable alternative to suicide.

Given the Ythrian character, Oherran works about as well as police do among men. If your society has not lost morale, human, how often must you call the police?

None who knew Liaw of The Tarns imagined he would untruthfully say that he had threatened to rip Avalon asunder.

✣VI✣

Where the mighty Sagittarius flows into the Gulf of Centaurs, Avalon's second city—the only one besides Gray which rated the name—had arisen as riverport, seaport, spaceport, industrial center, and mart. Thus Centauri was predominantly a human town, akin to many in the Empire, thronged, bustling, noisy, cheerfully corrupt, occasionally dangerous. When he went there, Arinnian most of the time had to be Christopher Holm, in behavior as well as name.

Defense business now required it. He was not astonished at becoming a top officer of the West Coronan home guard, after that took its loose shape—not in a society where nepotism was the norm. It did surprise him that he seemed to be doing rather well, even enjoying himself in a grim fashion, he who had always scoffed at the "herd man." In a matter of weeks he got large-scale drills going throughout his district and was well along on the development of doctrine, communications, and supply. (Of course, it helped that most Avalonians were enthusiastic hunters, often in large groups on battues; and that the Troubles had left a military tradition not difficult to revive; and that old Daniel was on hand to advise.) Similar organizations had sprung up everywhere else. They needed to coordinate their efforts with the measures being taken by the Seamen's Brotherhood. A conference was called. It worked hard and accomplished as many of its purposes as one could reasonably hope.

Afterward Arinnian said, "Hrill, would you like to go out and celebrate? W-we may not have a lot more chances." He did not speak on impulse. He had debated it for the past couple of days.

Tabitha Falkayn smiled. "Sure, Chris. Everybody else will be."

They walked down Livewell Street. Her arm was in his; in the subtropical heat he was aware of how their skins traded sweat. "I . . . well, why do you generally call me by my human name?" he asked. "And talk Anglic to me?"

"We are humans, you and I. We haven't the feathers to use Planha as it ought to be used. Why do you mind?"

For a moment he floundered. *That personal a question . . . an insult, except between the closest friends, when it becomes an endearment. . . . No, I suppose she's just thinking human again.* He halted and swept his free hand around. "Look at that and stop wondering," he said. Instantly he feared he had been too curt.

But the big blond girl obeyed. This part of the street ran along a canal, which was oily and littered with refuse, burdened with barges, walled in by buildings jammed together, whose dingy façades reared ten or twelve stories into night heaven. Stars and the white half-disk of Morgana were lost behind the glare, blink, leap and worm-crawl of raw-colored signs. (GROG HARBOR, DANCE, EAT, GENUINE TERRAN SENSIES, FUN HOUSE, SWITCH TO MARIA JUANAS, GAMBLING, NAKED GIRLS, LOANS, BUY . . . BUY . . . BUY . . .) Groundbugs filled the roadway, pedestrians the sidewalks, a sailor, a pilot, a raftman, a fisher, a hunter, a farmer, a whore, a secretary, a drunk about to collapse, another drunk getting belligerent at a monitor, a man gaunt and hairy and ragged who stood on a corner and shouted of some obscure salvation, endless human seething, shrilling, chattering, through engine rumble, foot shuffle, raucousness blared out of loudspeakers. The air stank, dirt, smoke, oil, sewage, flesh, a breath from surrounding swamplands which would there have been a clean rotting but here was somehow made nasty.

Tabitha smiled at him anew. "Why, I call this fun, Chris," she said. "What else've we come for?"

"You wouldn't—" he stammered. "I mean, somebody like you?"

He realized he was gaping at her. Both wore thin short-sleeved blouses, kilts, and sandals; garments clung to wet bodies. But despite the sheen of moisture and the odor of female warmth that he couldn't help noticing, she stood as a creature of sea and open skies.

"Sure, what's wrong with once-in-a-while vulgarity?" she said, still amiable. "You're too puritan, Chris."

"No, no," he protested, now afraid she would think him naive. "Fastidious, maybe. But I've often been here and, uh, enjoyed myself. What I was trying to explain was, uh, I, I'm proud to belong to a choth and not proud that members of my race elect to live in a sty. Don't you see, this is the old way, that the pioneers wanted to escape."

Tabitha said a word. He was staggered. Eyath would never have spoken thus. The girl grinned. "Or, if you prefer, 'nonsense,'" she continued. "I've read Falkayn's writings. He and his followers wanted not one thing except unmolested elbow room." Her touch nudged him along. "How about that dinner we were aimed at?" Numbly, he moved.

He recovered somewhat in the respectable dimness of the Phoenix House. Among other reasons, he admitted to himself, the room was cool and her clothes didn't emphasize her shape as they did outside.

The place had live service. She ordered a catflower cocktail. He didn't. "C'mon," she said. "Unbuckle your shell."

"No, thanks, really." He found words. "Why dull my perceptions at a happy moment?"

"Seems I've heard that line before. A Stormgate saying?"

"Yes. Though I didn't think they used drugs much in Highsky either."

"They don't. Barring the sacred revels. Most of us keep to the Old Faith, you know." Tabitha regarded him awhile. "Your trouble, Chris, is you try too hard. Relax. Be more among your own species. How many humans do you have any closeness to? Bloody-gut few, I'll bet."

He bridled. "I've seen plenty of late."

"Yeh. And emergency or no, doesn't it feel good? I wouldn't try to steer somebody else's life, of course, nor am I hinting it's true of you—but fact is, a man or woman who tries to be an Ythrian is a rattlewing."

"Well, after three generations you may be restless in your choth," he said, gauging his level of sarcasm as carefully as he was able. "You've knocked around quite a bit in human country, haven't you?"

She nodded. "Several years. Itinerant huntress, trapper, sailor, prospector, over most of Avalon. I got the main piece of my share in the stake that started Draun and me in business—I got that at assorted poker tables." She laughed. "Damn, sometimes it is easier to say things in Planha!" Serious: "But remember, I was young when my parents were lost at sea. An Ythrian family adopted me. They encouraged me to take a wandertime; that's Highsky custom. If anything, my loyalty and gratitude to the choth were strengthened. I simply, well, I recognize I'm a member who happens to be human.

As such, I've things to offer which—" She broke off and turned her head. "Ah, here comes my drink. Let's talk trivia. I do get starved for that on St. Li."

"I believe I will have a drink too," Arinnian said.

He found it helpful. Soon they were cheerily exchanging reminiscences. While she had doubtless led a more adventurous life than he, his had not been dull. On occasion, such as when he hid from his parents in the surf-besieged Shielding Islands, or when he had to meet a spathodont on the ground with no more than a spear because his companion lay wing-broken, he may have been in worse danger than any she had met. But he found she was most taken by his quieter memories. She had never been offplanet, except for one vacation trip to Morgana. He, son of a naval officer, had had ample chances to see the whole Lauran System from sun-wracked Elysium, through the multiple moons of Camelot, out to dark, comet-haunted Utgard. Speaking of the frigid blue peace of Phaeacia, he chanced to quote some Homeric lines, and she was delighted and wanted more and asked what else this Homer fellow had written, and the conversation turned to books. . . .

The meal was mixed, as cuisine of both races tended increasingly to be: piscoid-and-tomato chowder, beef-and-shua pie, salad of clustergrain leaf, pears, coffee spiced with witchroot. A bottle of vintage dago gave merriment. At the end, having seen her indulge the vice before, Arinnian was not shocked when Tabitha lit her pipe. "What say we look in on the Nest?" she proposed. "Might find Draun." Her partner was her superior in the guard; she was in Centauri as his aide. But the choth concept of rank was at once more complex and more flexible than the Technic.

"Well . . . all right," Arinnian answered.

She cocked her head. "Reluctant? I'd've guessed you'd prefer the Ythrian hangout to anyplace else in town." It included the sole public house especially for ornithoids, they being infrequent here.

He frowned. "I can't help feeling that tavern is wrong. For them," he added in haste. "I'm no prude, understand."

"Yet you don't mind when humans imitate Ythrians. Uh-uh. Can't have it on both wings, son." She stood. "Let's take a glance into the Nest boozeria, a drink if we meet a friend or a good bard is reciting. Afterward a dance club, hm?"

He nodded, glad—amidst an accelerating pulse—that her mood remained light. While no machinery would let them take part in the Ythrian aerial dances, moving across a floor in the arms of another bird was nearly as fine, perhaps. And, while that was as far as such contact had ever gone for him, maybe Tabitha—for she was indeed Tabitha on this steamy night, not Hrill of the skies—

He had heard various muscular oafs talk of encounters with bird girls, less boastfully than in awe. To Arinnian and his kind, their female counterparts were comrades, sisters. But Tabitha kept emphasizing his and her humanness.

They took a taxibug to the Nest, which was the tallest building in the city, and a gravshaft to its rooftop since neither had brought flying gear. Unwalled, the tavern was protected from rain by a vitryl canopy through which, at this height, stars could be seen regardless of the electric lunacy below. Morgana was sinking toward the western bottomlands, though it still silvered river and Gulf. Thunderheads piled in the east, and a rank breeze carried the mutter of the lightning that shivered in them. Insectoids circled the dim fluoroglobe set on every table. Business was sparse, a few shadowy forms perched on stools before glasses or narcobraziers, a service robot trundling about, the recorded twangs of a steel harp.

"Scum-dull," Tabitha said, disappointed. "But we can make a circuit."

They threaded among the tables until Arinnian halted and exclaimed, "Hoy-ah! Vodan, ekh-hirr."

His chothmate looked up, plainly taken aback. He was seated at drink beside a shabby-plumed female, who gave the newcomers a sullen stare.

"Good flight to you," Arinnian greeted in Planha; but what followed, however automatic, was too obvious for anything save Anglic. "I didn't expect to find you here."

"And to you, good landing," Vodan replied. "I report to my ship within hours. My transport leaves from Halcyon Island base. I came early so as not to risk being detained by a storm; we've had three whirldevils in a row near home."

"You are yare for battle, hunter," said Tabitha at her most carefully courteous.

That's true, Arinnian thought. *He's ablaze to fight. Only . . . if he couldn't stay with Eyath till the last minute, at least I'd've supposed he'd've been in flight-under-moon, meditating—or, anyhow, at carouse among friends*—He made introductions.

Vodan jerked a claw at his attendant. "Quenna," he said. His informality was a casual insult. She hunched between her wings, feathers erected in forlorn self-assertion.

Arinnian could think of no excuse not to join the party. He and the girl seated themselves as best they could. When the robot rolled up, they ordered thick, strong New African beer.

"How blows your wind?" Tabitha asked, puffing hard on her pipe.

"Well; as I would like for you," Vodan answered correctly. He turned to Arinnian and, if his enthusiasm was a touch forced, it was nonetheless real. "You doubtless know I've been on training maneuvers these past weeks."

Yes. Eyath told me more than once.

"This was a short leave. My craft demands skill. Let me tell you about her. One of the new torpedo launchers, rather like a Terran Meteor, hai, a beauty, a spear! Proud I was to emblazon her hull with three golden stars."

"Eyath" means "Third Star."

Vodan went on. Arinnian glanced at Tabitha. She and Quenna had locked their gazes. Expressions billowed and jerked across the feathers; even he could read most of the unspoken half-language.

Yes, m' sweet, you long yellow Walker born, Quenna is what she is and who're you to look down that jutting snout of yours? What else could I be, since I, growing from cub to maiden, found my lovetimes coming on whenever I thought about 'em and knew there'd never be any decent place for me in the whole universe? Oh, yes, yes, I've heard it before, don't bother: "medical treatment; counseling."—Well, flabbyflesh, for your information, the choths don't often keep a weakling, and I'll not whine for help. Quenna'll lay her own course, better'n you, who're really like me . . . aren't you, now, she-human?

Tabitha leaned forward, patted one of those arms with no heed for the talons, smiled into the reddened eyes and murmured, "Good weather for you, lass."

Astounded, Quenna reared back. For an instant she seemed about to fly at the girl, and Arinnian's hand dropped to his knife. Then she addressed Vodan: "Better we be going."

"Not yet." The Ythrian had fairly well overcome his embarrassment. "The clouds alone will decide when I see my brother again."

"We better go," she said lower. Arinnian caught the first slight
musky odor. At the next table, another male raised his crest and
swiveled his head in their direction.

Arinnian could imagine the conflict in Vodan—dismiss her, defy
her, strike her; no killing, she being unarmed—and yet that would be
a surrender in itself, less to tradition than to mere conventionality—
"We'll have to leave, ourselves, soon's we finish these beers," the man
said. "Glad to've come on you. Fair winds forever."

Vodan's relief was unmistakable. He mumbled through the
courtesies and flapped off with Quenna. The city swallowed them.

Arinnian wondered what to say. He was grateful for the dull
light; his face felt hotter than the air. He stared outward.

Tabitha said at length, softly, "That poor lost soul."

"Who, the nightflyer?" All at once he was furious. "I've met her
sort before. Degenerates, petty criminals. Pray Vodan doesn't get his
throat cut in whatever filthy crib she's taking him to. I know what
must've happened here. He was wandering around lonely, at loose
ends, a mountaineer who'd probably never come on one like her. She
zeroed in, hit him with enough pheromone to excite—ugh!"

"Why should you care? I mean, of course he's a friend of yours,
but I hardly believe that pathetic creature will dare try more than
wheedling a tip out of him." Tabitha drank smoke. "You know," she
said thoughtfully, "here's a case of Ythrian cultural lag. They've been
affected by human ideas to the point where they don't give their
abnormals a quick death. But they're still not interested in sponsoring
rehabilitation or research on cures, or in simple charity. Someday—"

He scarcely heard the last remark. "Vodan's to marry Eyath," he
said through the interior grip on his gullet.

Tabitha raised her brows. "Oh? That one you mentioned to me?
Well, don't you suppose, if she heard, she'd be glad he's gotten a bit
of unimportant fun and forgetting?"

"It's not right! She's too clean. She—" Arinnian gulped. Abruptly
he thought: *So why not take the risk? Now I need forgetting myself.* "Is
the matter small to you?" he blurted. "In that case, let's us do the
same."

"Hm?" She considered him for a while that grew. Lightning

moved closer on heavy gusts. His rage ebbed and he must fight not to lower his eyes, not to cringe.

At last: "You are bitter for certain, aren't you, Chris?" A chuckle. "But likewise you're hopeful."

"I'm sorry," he got out. "I n-n-never meant disrespect. I wanted to give you a, an imaginary example—make you understand why I'm upset."

"I might resent your calling it imaginary," she smiled, though her tone had become more compassionate than teasing, "except I assume it wasn't really. The answer is no, thanks."

"I expected that. We birds—" He couldn't finish, but stared down into his mug until he lifted it for a quick, deep draft.

"What d'you mean, 'we'?" she challenged.

"Why, we . . . our generation, at least—"

When she nodded, her locks caught what illumination there was. "I know," she said gravely. "That behavior pattern, promiscuous as kakkelaks provided they don't much respect their partners, but hardly able to touch birds of the opposite sex. You're a bright lad, Chris; Avalonians aren't given to introspection, but you must have some idea of the cause. Don't you want a wife and children, ever?"

"Of course. I—of course. I will."

"Most of them will, I'm sure. Most of the earlier ones did eventually, when they'd come to terms with themselves. Besides, the situation's not universal. We birds do have this in common, that we tolerate less prying than the average human. So comparative statistics aren't available. Also, the problem has gotten conspicuous these days for no deeper reason than that the movement into the choths has begun snowballing. And, finally, Chris, your experience is limited. How many out of thousands do you know well enough to describe their private lives? You'd naturally tend to be best acquainted with your own sort, especially since we birds have gotten pretty good at picking up face and body cues."

Tabitha's pipe had gone out. She emptied it and finished: "I tell you, your case isn't near as typical as you think, nor near as serious. But I do wish that going bird didn't make otherwise sensible people lose years in thwarting themselves."

Anger pricked him again. What call had she to act superior? "Now wait—" he began.

Tabitha knocked back her beer and rose. "I'm headed for my hotel," she said.

He stared up at her. "What?"

She ruffled his hair. "I'm sorry. But I'm afraid if we continue tonight, we'll brew one cyclone of a squabble. I think too well of you to want that. We'll take another evening soon if you like. Now I aim to get into bed and have Library Central screen me some of that Homer stuff."

He couldn't dissuade her. Perhaps he took most umbrage at how calm his arguments left her. When he had bidden her a chill goodnight, he slouched to the nearest phoneboard.

The first woman he called was at work. Defense production was running at seven hours on, fifteen and the odd minutes off, plus overtime. The second female acquaintance said frantically that her husband was home if that was the party he wanted; he apologized for punching a wrong number. The third was available. She was overly plump, chattered without cease, and had the brains of a barysauroid. But what the chaos?

—He awoke about the following sunset. She was sweating in her sleep, breath stale from alcohol. He wondered why the air had gone hot and sticky. Breakdown in the conditioner? Or, hm, it'd been announced that if force screens must be raised, the power drain would require Environmental Control to shut off—

Force screens!

Arinnian jumped from bed. Rain had given way to low overcast, but he glimpsed shimmers across that slatiness. He groped through the dusty clutter in the room and snapped on the holovid.

A recording played, over and over, a man's voice high-pitched and his face stretched out of shape: "—war declared. A courier from Ythri has delivered the news in Gray, that Terra has served notice of war."

✧VII✧

"Our basic strategy is simple," Admiral Cajal had explained. "I would prefer a simpler one yet: pitched battle between massed fleets, winner takes all."

"But the Ythrians will scarcely be that obliging," Governor Saracoglu remarked.

"No. They aren't well organized for it, in the first place. Not in character for them to centralize operations. Besides, they must know they're foredoomed to lose any standup fight. They lack the sheer numerical strength. I expect they'll try to maintain hedgehog positions. From those they'd make sallies, harass, annihilate what smaller units of ours they found, prey on our supply lines. We can't drive straight into the Domain with that sort of menace at our rear. Prohibitively costly. We could suffer actual disaster if we let ourselves get caught between their inner and outer forces."

"Ergo, we start by capturing their advanced bases."

"The major ones. We needn't worry about tiny new colonies or backward allies, keeping a few ships per planet." Cajal gestured with a flashbeam. It probed into the darkness of a display tank, wherein gleamed points of luminance that represented the stars of this region. They crowded by thousands across those few scaled-down parsecs, a fire-swarm out of which not many men could have picked an individual. Cajal realized his talent for doing this had small intrinsic value. The storage and processing of such data were for computers. But it was an outward sign of an inner gift.

"Laura the nearest," he said. "Hru and Khrau further on, forming a triangle with it. Give me those, and I'll undertake to proceed directly against Quetlan. That should force them to call in everything they have, to protect the home star! And, since my rear and my lines will then be reasonably secure, I'll get the decisive battle I want."

"Um-m-m." Saracoglu rubbed his massive chin. Bristles made a scratchy sound; as hard as he had been at work, he kept forgetting to put on fresh inhibitor after a depilation. "You'll hit Laura first?"

"Yes, of course. Not with the whole armada. We'll split, approximately into thirds. The detached sections will proceed slowly toward Hru and Khrau, but not attack until Laura has been reduced. The force should be ample in all three systems, but I want to get the feel of Ythrian tactics—and, too, make sure they haven't some unpleasant surprise tucked under their tailfeathers."

"They might," Saracoglu said. "You know our intelligence on them leaves much to be desired. The problems of spying on nonhumans—And Ythrian traitors are almost impossible to find, competent ones completely impossible."

"I still don't see why you couldn't get agents into that mostly human settlement at Laura."

"We did, Admiral, we did. But in a set of small, close-knit communities they could accomplish nothing except report what was publicly available to see. You must realize, Avalonian humans no longer think, talk, even walk quite like any Imperial humans. Imitating them isn't feasible. And, again, deplorably few can be bought. Furthermore, the Avalonian Admiralty is excellent on security measures. The second in command, chap named Holm, seems to have made several extended trips through the Empire, official and unofficial, in earlier days. I understand he did advanced study at one of our academies. He knows our methods."

"*I* understand he's caused not just the Lauran fleet but the planetary defenses to be enormously increased, these past years," Cajal said. "Yes, we must certainly take care of him first."

—That had been weeks ago. On this day (clock concept in unending starry night) the Terrans neared their enemy.

Cajal sat alone in the middle of the superdreadnaught *Valenderay*. Communication screens surrounded him, and humming silence, and radial kilometers of metal, machinery, weapons, armor, energies, through which passed several thousand living beings. But he was, for this moment, conscious only of what lay outside. A viewscreen showed him: darkness, diamond hordes, and Laura, tiny at nineteen astronomical units' remove but gold and shining, shining.

The ships had gone out of hyperdrive and were accelerating sunward on gravity thrust. Most were far ahead of the flag vessel. A meeting with the defenders could be looked for at any minute.

Cajal's mouth tightened downward at the right corner. He was a tall man, gaunt, blade-nosed, his widow's peak hair and pointed beard black though he neared his sixties. His uniform was as plain as his rank allowed.

He had been chain-smoking. Now he pulled the latest cigarette from a scorched mouth and ground it out as if it were vermin. *Why can't I endure these final waits?* he thought *Because I will be safe while I send men to war?*

His glance turned to a picture of his dead wife, standing before their house among the high trees of Vera Fé. He moved to animate but, instead, switched on a recorder.

Music awoke, a piece he and she had loved, well-nigh forgotten on Terra but ageless in its triumphant serenity, Bach's Passacaglia. He leaned back, closed his eyes and let it heal him. *Man's duty in this life,* he thought, *is to choose the lesser evil.*

A buzz snapped him to alertness. The features of his chief executive captain filled a screen and stated, "Sir, we have received and confirmed a report of initial hostilities from Vanguard Squadron Three. No details."

"Very good, Citizen Feinberg," Cajal said. "Let me have any hard information immediately."

It would soon come flooding in, beyond the capacity of a live brain. Then it must be filtered through an intricate complex of subordinates and their computers, and he could merely hope the digests which reached him bore some significant relationship to reality. But those earliest direct accounts were always subtly helpful, as if the tone of a battle were set at its beginning.

"Aye, sir." The screen blanked.

Cajal turned off the music. "Farewell for now," he whispered, and rose. There was one other personal item in the room, a crucifix. He removed his bonnet, knelt, and signed himself. "Father, forgive us what we are about to do," he begged. "Father, have mercy on all who die. All."

"Word received, Marchwarden," the Ythrian voice announced. "Contact with Terrans, about 12 a.u. out, direction of the Spears. Firing commenced on both sides, but seemingly no losses yet."

"My thanks. Please keep me informed." Daniel Holm turned off the intercom.

"As if it were any use for me to know!" he groaned.

His mind ran through the calculation. Light, radio, neutrinos take about eight minutes to cross an astronomical unit. The news was more than an hour and a half old. That initial, exploratory fire-touch of a few small craft might well be ended already, the fragments of the vanquished whirling away on crazy orbits while the victors burned fuel as if their engines held miniature suns, trying to regain a kinetic velocity that would let them regroup. Or if other units on either side were not too distant, they might have joined in, sowing warheads wider and wider across space.

He spoke an obscenity and beat fist on palm. "If we could hyper-communicate—" But that wasn't practical. The "instantaneous" pulses of a vessel quantum-jumping around nature's speed limit could be modulated to send a message a light-year or so—however, not this deep in a star's distorting gravitational field, where you risked annihilation if you tried to travel nonrelativistically—of course, you could get away with it if you were absolutely sure of your tuning, but nobody was in wartime—and anyhow, given that capability, the Terrans would be a still worse foe, fighting them would be hopeless rather than half hopeless—*why am I rehearsing this muck?*

"And Ferune's there and I'm here!"

He sprang from his desk, stamped to the window and stood staring. A cigar fumed volcanic between his teeth. The day beyond was insultingly beautiful. An autumn breeze carried odors of salt up from the bay, which glittered and danced under Laura and heaven; and it bore scents from the gardens it passed, brilliant around their houses. North-shore hills lay in a blue haze of distance. Overhead skimmed wings. He didn't notice.

Rowena came to him. "You knew you had to stay, dear," she said. She was still auburn-maned, still slim and erect in her coverall.

"Yeh. Backup. Logistic, computer, communications support. And maybe Ferune understands space warfare better, but I'm the one who really built the planetary defense. We agreed, months back. No dishonor to me, that I do the sensible thing." Holm swung toward his wife. He caught her around the waist. "But oh, God, Ro, I didn't think it'd be this hard!"

She drew his head down onto her shoulder and stroked the grizzled hair.

Ferune of Mistwood had planned to bring his own mate along. Wharr had traveled beside him throughout a long naval career, birthed and raised their children on the homeships that accompanied every Ythrian fleet, drilled and led gun crews. But she fell sick and the medics weren't quite able to ram her through to recovery before the onslaught came. You grow old, puzzlingly so. He missed her sternness.

But he was too busy to dwell on their goodbyes. More and more reports were arriving at his flagship. A pattern was beginning to emerge.

"Observe," he said. The computers had just corrected the display tank according to the latest data. It indicated sun, planets, and color-coded sparks which stood for ships. "Combats here, here, here. Elsewhere, neutrino emissions reaching our detectors, cross-correlations getting made, fixes being obtained."

"Foully thin information," said the feathers and attitude of his aide.

"Thus far, aye, across interplanetary distances. However, we can fill in certain gaps with reason, if we assume their admiral is competent. I feel moderately sure that his pincer has but two claws, coming in almost diametrically opposite, from well north and south of the ecliptic plane . . . so." Ferune pointed. "Now he must have reserves further out. To avoid making a wide circuit with consequent risk of premature detection, these must have run fairly straight from the general direction of Pax. And were I in charge, I would have them near the ecliptic. Hence we look for their assault, as the pincers close, from here." He indicated the region.

They stood alone in the command bridge, broad though the chamber was. Ythrians wanted room to stretch their wings. Yet they were wholly linked to the ship by her intercoms, calculators, officers, crewfolk, more tenuously linked to that magnificence which darkened and bejeweled a viewscreen, where the killing had begun. Clangor and clatter of activity came faint to them, through a deep susurrus of power. The air blew warm, ruffling their plumes a little, scented with perfume of cinnamon bush and amberdragon. Blood odors would not be ordered unless and until the vessel got into actual combat; the crew would soon be worn out if stimulated too intensely.

Ferune's plan did not call for hazarding the superdreadnaught this early. Her power belonged in his end game. At that time he intended to show the Terrans why she was called after the site of an ancient battle on Ythri. He had had the Anglic translation of the name painted broad on the sides: *Hell Rock.*

A new cluster of motes appeared in the tank. Their brightnesses indicated ship types, as accurately as analysis of their neutrino emanations could suggest. The aide started. His crest bristled. "That many more hostiles, so soon? Uncle, the odds look bad."

"We knew they would. Don't let this toy hypnotize you. I've been through worse. Half of me is regenerated tissue after combat wounds. And I'm still skyborne."

"Forgive me, Uncle, but most of your fights were police actions inside the Domain. This is the *Empire* coming."

Ferune expressed: "I am not unaware of that. And I too have studied advanced militechnics, both practical and theoretical." Aloud he said, "Computers, robots, machines are only half the makers of a war-weird. There are also brains and hearts."

Claws clacked on the deck as he walked to the viewscreen and peered forth. His experienced eye picked out a glint among the stars, one ship. Otherwise his fleet was lost to vision in the immensity through which it fanned.

"A new engagement commencing," said the intercom.

Ferune waited motionless for details. Through his mind passed words from one of the old Terran books it pleasured him to read. *The fear of a king is as the roaring of a lion: whoso provoketh him to anger sinneth against his own soul.*

Hours built into days while the fleets, in their hugely scattered divisions, felt for and sought each other's throats.

Consider: at a linear acceleration of one Terran gravity, a vessel can, from a "standing start," cover one astronomical unit—about 149 million kilometers—in a bit under fifty hours. At the end of that period, she has gained 1060 kilometers per second of velocity. In twice the time, she will move at twice the speed and will have spanned four times the distance. No matter what power is conferred by thermonuclear engines, no matter what maneuverability comes from a gravity thrust which reacts directly against that fabric of relationships we call space, one does not quickly alter quantities on this order of magnitude.

Then, too, there is the sheer vastness of even interplanetary reaches. A sphere one a.u. in radius has the volume of some thirteen million million Terras; to multiply this radius by ten is to multiply the volume by a thousand. No matter how sensitive the instruments, one does not quickly scan those deeps, nor ever do it with much accuracy beyond one's immediate neighborhood, nor know where a detached object is *now* if signals are limited to light speed. As the maddeningly incomplete hoard of data grows, not just the parameters of battle calculations change; the equations do. One discovers he has lost hours in travel which has turned out to be useless or worse, and must lose hours or days more in trying to remedy matters. But then, explosively fast, will come a near enough approach at nearly enough matched velocities for a combat which may well be finished in seconds.

"Number Seven, launch!" warned the dispatcher robot, and flung *Hooting Star* out to battle.

Her engines took hold. A thrum went through the bones of Philippe Rochefort where he sat harnessed in the pilot chair. Above his instrument panel, over his helmet and past either shoulder, viewscreens filled a quarter globe with suns. Laura, radiance stopped down lest it blind him, shone among them as a minikin disk between two nacreous wings of zodiacal light.

His radar alarm whistled and lit up, swiveling an arrow inside a clear ball. His heart sprang. He couldn't help glancing that way. And he caught a glimpse of the cylinder which hurtled toward *Ansa*'s great flank.

During a launch, the negagrav screen in that area of the mother vessel is necessarily turned off. Nothing is there to repulse a torpedo. If the thing makes contact and detonates—In vacuum, several kilotons are not quite so appallingly destructive as in air or water; and a capital ship is armored and compartmented against concussion and heat, thickly shielded to cut down what hard radiation gets inside. Nevertheless she will be badly hurt, perhaps crippled, and men will be blown apart, cooked alive, shrieking their wish to die.

An energy beam flashed. An instant's incandescence followed. Sensors gave their findings to the appropriate computer. Within a millisecond of the burst, a "Cleared" note warbled. One of Wa Chaou's guns had caught the torpedo square on.

"Well done!" Rochefort cried over the intercom. "Good show, Watch Out!" He rotated his detectors in search of the boat which must have been sufficiently close to loose that missile.

Registry. Lockon. *Hooting Star* surged forward. *Ansa* dwindled among the constellations. "Give me an estimated time to come in range, Abdullah," Rochefort said.

"He seems aware of us," Helu's voice answered, stone-calm. "Depends on whether he'll try to get away or close in. . . . Um-m, yes, he's skiting for cover." (*I would too, for fair,* Rochefort thought, *when a heavy cruiser's spitting boats. That's a brave skipper who sneaked this near.*) "We can intercept in about ten minutes, assuming he's at his top acceleration. But I don't think anybody else will be able to help us, and if we wait for them, he'll escape."

"We're not waiting," Rochefort decided. He lasered his intentions back to the squadron control office aboard ship and got an okay. Meanwhile he wished his sweat were not breaking out wet and sour. He wasn't afraid, though; his pulse beat high but steady and never before had he seen the stars with such clarity and exactness. It was good to know he had the inborn courage for Academy psychtraining to develop.

"If you win," SC said, "make for—" a string of numbers which the machines memorized—"and act at discretion. We've identified a light battleship there. We and *Ganymede* between us will try saturating its defenses. Good luck."

The voice clipped off. The boat ran, faster every second until the ballistics meters advised deceleration. Rochefort heeded and tapped out the needful orders. Utterly irrelevant passed through his head the memory of an instructor's lecture. "Living pilots, gunners, all personnel, are meant to make decisions. Machines execute most of those decisions, set and steer courses, lay and fire guns, faster and more precisely than nerve or muscle. Machines, consciousness-level computers, could also be built to decide. They have been, in the past. But while their logical abilities might be far in excess of yours and mine, they always lacked a certain totality, call it intuition or insight or what you will. Furthermore, they were too expensive to use in war in any numbers. You, gentlemen, are multipurpose computers who have a *reason* to fight and survive. Your kind is abundantly available and, apart from programming, can be produced in nine months by unskilled labor." Rochefort remembered telling lower classmen that it was three demerits if you didn't laugh at the hoary joke.

"Range," Helu said.

Energy beams stabbed. The scattered, wasted photons which burned along their paths were the barest fraction of the power within.

One touched *Hooting Star*. The boat's automata veered her before it could penetrate her thin plating. That was a roar of sidewise thrust. The interior fields couldn't entirely compensate for the sudden high acceleration. Rochefort was crammed back against his harness till it creaked, while weight underfoot shifted dizzyingly.

It passed. Normal one-gee-down returned. They were alive. They didn't even seem to need a patchplate; if they had been pierced, the hole was small enough for self-sealing. And yonder in naked-eye sight was the enemy!

With hands and voice, Rochefort told his boat to drive straight at that shark shape. It swelled monstrously fast. Two beams lanced from it and struck. Rochefort held his vector constant. He was hoping Wa Chaou would thus be able to get a fix on their sources and knock them out before they could do serious damage. *Flash! Flash!* Brightness blanked. "Oh, glorious! Ready torps."

The Ythrian drew nearer till the human could see a painted insigne, a wheel whose spokes were flower petals. *That's right, they put personal badges on their lesser craft, same as we give unofficial names. Wonder what that'n means.* He'd been told that some of their speedsters carried ball guns. But hard objects cast in your path weren't too dangerous till relative velocities got into the tens of KPS.

She fired a torpedo. Wa Chaou wrecked it almost in its tube. *Hooting Star*'s slammed home.

The explosion was at such close quarters that its fiery gases filled the Terran's screen. A fragment struck her. She shivered and belled. Then she was past, alone in clean space. Her opponent was a cloud which puffed outward till it grew invisible, a few seared chunks of metal and possibly bone cooling off to become meteoroids, falling away aft, gone from sight in seconds.

"If you will pardon the expression," Rochefort said shakily, "yahoo!"

"That was a near one," Helu said. "We'd better ask for antirad boosters when we get back."

"Uh-huh. Right now, though, we've unfinished business." Rochefort instructed the boat to change vectors. "No fears, after the way you chaps conducted yourselves." They were not yet at the scene when joyful broadcasts and another brief blossoming told them that a hornet swarm of boats and missiles had stung the enemy battleship to death.

✧VIII✧

Slowly those volumes of space wherein the war was being fought contracted and neared each other. At no time were vessels ranked. Besides being unfeasible to maintain, formations tight and rigid would have invited a nuclear barrage. At most, a squadron of small craft might travel in loose echelon for a while. If two major units of a flotilla came within a hundred kilometers, it was reckoned close. However, the time lag of communication dropped toward zero, the reliability of detection swooped upward, deadly encounters grew ever more frequent.

It became possible to know fairly well what the opponent had in play and where. It became possible to devise and guide a campaign.

Cajal remarked in a tape report to Saracoglu: "If every Ythrian system were as strong as Laura, we might need the whole Imperial Navy to break them. Here they possess, or did possess, approximately half the number of hulls that I do—which is to say, a sixth the number we deemed adequate for handling the entire Domain. Of course, that doesn't mean their actual strength is in proportion. By our standards, they are weak in heavy craft. But their destroyers, still more their corvettes and torpedo boats, make an astonishing total. I am very glad that no other enemy sun, besides Quetlan itself, remotely compares with Laura!

"Nevertheless, we are making satisfactory progress. In groundling language—a technical summary will be appended for you—we can say that about half of what remains to them is falling back on Avalon. We intend to follow them there, dispose of them, and thus have the planet at our mercy.

"The rest of their fleet is disengaging, piecemeal, and retreating spaceward. Doubtless they mean to scatter themselves throughout the uninhabitable planets, moons, and asteroids of the system, where they must have bases, and carry on hit-and-run war. This should prove more nuisance than menace, and once we are in occupation their government will recall them. Probably larger vessels, which have hyperdrive, will seek to go reinforce elsewhere: again, not unduly important.

"I am not underestimating these people. They fight skillfully and doggedly. They must expect to use planetary defenses in conjunction with those ships moving toward the home world. God grant, more for their sakes than ours, most especially for the sakes of innocent females and children of both races, God grant their leaders see reason and capitulate before we hurt them too badly."

The half disk of Avalon shone sapphire swirled with silver, small and dear among the stars. Morgana was coming around the dark side. Ferune remembered night flights beneath it with Wharr, and murmured, "*O moon of my delight that knows no wane—*"

"Hoy?" said Daniel Holm's face in the screen.

"Nothing. My mind drifted." Ferune drew breath. "We've skimpy time. They're coming in fast. I want to make certain you've found no serious objection to the battle plan as detailed."

The laser beam took a few seconds to flicker between flagship and headquarters. Ferune went back to his memories.

"I bugger well do!" Holm growled. "I already told you. You've brought *Hell Rock* too close in. Prime target."

"And I told you," Ferune answered, "we no longer need her command capabilities." *I wish we did, but our losses have been too cruel.* "We do need her firepower and, yes, her attraction for the enemy. That's why I never counted on getting her away to Quetlan. There she'd be just one more unit. Here she's the keystone of our configuration. If things break well, she will survive. I know the scheme is not guaranteed, but it was the best my staff, computers, and self could produce on what you also knew beforehand would be short notice. To argue, or modify much, at this late hour is to deserve disaster."

Silence. Morgana rose further from Avalon as the ship moved.

"Well . . ." Holm slumped. He had lost weight till his cheekbones stood forth like ridges in upland desert. "I s'pose."

"Uncle, a report of initial contact," Ferune's aide said.

"Already?" The First Marchwarden of Avalon turned to the

comscreen. "You heard, Daniel Holm? Fair winds forever." He cut the circuit before the man could reply. "Now," he told the aide, "I want a recomputation of the optimum orbit for this ship. Project the Terran's best moves . . . from their viewpoint, in the light of what information we have . . . and adjust ours accordingly."

Space sparkled with fireworks. Not every explosion, nor most, signified a hit; but they were thickening.

Three Stars slammed from her cruiser. At once her detectors reported an object. Analysis followed within seconds—a Terran Meteor, possible to intercept, no nearby companions. "Quarry!" Vodan sang out. "Five minutes to range."

A yell went through the hull. Two weeks and worse of maneuver, cooped in metal save for rare, short hours when the flotilla dipped into combat, had been heavy chains to lift.

His new vector pointed straight at Avalon. The planet waxed; he flew toward Eyath. He had no doubts about his victory. *Three Stars* was well blooded. She was necessarily larger than her Imperial counterpart—Ythrian requirements for room—and therefore had a trifle less acceleration. But her firepower could on that account be made greater, and had been.

Vodan took feet off perch and hung in his harness. He spread his wings. Slowly he beat them, pumping his blood full of oxygen, his body full of strength and swiftness. It tingled, it sang. He heard a rustling aft as his four crewfolk did likewise. Stars gleamed above and around him.

Three representations occupied Daniel Holm's office and, now, his mind. A map of Avalon indicated the ground installations. The majority were camouflaged and, he hoped, he would have prayed if he believed, were unknown to the enemy. Around a holographic world globe, variegated motes swung in multitudinous orbits. Many stations had been established a few days ago, after being transported to their launch sites from underground automated factories which were also supposed to be secret. Finally a display tank indicated what was known of the shifting ships out yonder.

Holm longed for a cigar, but his mouth was too withered by too much smoke in the near past. *Crock, how I could use a drink!* he thought. Neither might that be; the sole allowable drugs were those which kept him alert without exacting too high a metabolic price.

He stared at the tank. *Yeh. They're sure anxious to nail our flagship. Really converging on her.*

He sought the window. While Gray still lay shadowy, the first dawnlight was picking out houses and making the waters sheen. Above, the sky arched purple, its stars blurred by the negagrav screens. They had to keep changing pattern, to give adequate coverage while allowing air circulation. That stirred up restless little winds, cold and a bit damp. But on the whole the country reached serene. The storms were beyond the sky and inside the flesh.

Holm was alone, more alone than ever in his life, though the forces of a world awaited his bidding. It would have to be his; the computers could merely advise. He guessed that he felt like an infantryman preparing to charge.

"There!" Rochefort shouted.

He saw a moving point of light in a viewscreen set to top magnification. It grew as he watched, a needle, a spindle, a toy, a lean sharp-snouted hunter on whose flank shone three golden stars.

The vectors were almost identical. The boats neared more slowly than they rushed toward the planet. *Odd,* Rochefort thought, *how close Ansa's come without meeting any opposition. Are they just going to offer token resistance? I'd hate to kill somebody for a token.* Avalon was utterly beautiful. He was approaching in such wise that on his left the great disk had full daylight—azure, turquoise, indigo, a thousand different blues beneath the intercurving purity of cloud, a land mass glimpsed green and brown and tawny. On his right was darkness, but moonlight shimmered mysteriously across oceans and weather.

Wa Chaou sent a probe of lightning. No result showed. The range was extreme. It wouldn't stay thus for long. Now Rochefort needed no magnification to see the hostile hull. In those screens it was as yet a glint. But it slid across the stellar background, and it was more constant than the fireballs twinkling around.

Space blazed for a thousand kilometers around that giant spheroid which was *Hell Rock.* She did not try to dodge; given her mass, that was futile. She orbited her world. The enemy ships plunged in, shot, went by and maneuvered to return. They were many, she was one, save for a cloud of attendant Meteors and Comets. Her firepower, though, was awesome; still more were her instrumental and computer capabilities. She had not been damaged. When a section of screen must be turned off to launch a pack of missiles, auxiliary energy weapons intercepted whatever was directed at the vulnerable spot.

Rays had smitten. But none could be held steady through an interval sufficient to get past those heavy plates. Bombs whose yield was lethal radiation exploded along the limits of her defense. But the gamma quanta and neutrons were drunk down by layer upon layer of interior shielding. The last of them, straggling to those deep inner sections where organic creatures toiled, were so few that ordinary medication nullified their effects.

She had been built in space and would never touch ground. A planetoid in her own right, she blasted ship after ship that dared come against her.

Cajal's Supernova was stronger. But *Valenderay* must not be risked. The whole purpose of all that armament and armor was to protect the command of a fleet. When word reached him, he studied the display tank. "We're wasting lesser craft. She eats them," he said, chiefly to himself. "I hate to send capital vessels in. The enemy seems to have much more defensive stuff than we looked for, and it's bound to open up on us soon. But that close, speed and maneuverability don't count for what they should. We must have sheer force to take that monster out; and we must do that before we can pose any serious threat to the planet." He tugged his beard. "S-s-so . . . between them, *Persei, Ursa Minor, Regulus, Jupiter,* and attendants should be able to do the job . . . fast enough and at enough of a distance that they can also cope with whatever the planet may throw."

Tactical computers ratified and expanded his decision. He issued the orders.

Vodan saw a torpedo go past. "Hai, good!" he cried. Had he applied a few megadynes less of decelerative force, that warhead would have connected. The missile braked and came about, tracking, but one of his gunners destroyed it.

The Terran boat crawled ahead, off on the left and low. Vodan's instruments reported she was exerting more sideways than forward thrust. The pilot must mean to cross the Ythrian bows, bare kilometers ahead, loose a cloud of radar window, and hope the concerted fire of his beam guns would penetrate before the other could range him. Since Ythrians, unlike Terrans, did not fight wearing spacesuits—how could anybody not go insane after more than a few hours in those vile, confining things?—a large hole in a compartment killed them.

The son-of-a-zirraukh was good, Vodan acknowledged happily. Lumbering and awkward as most space engagements were, this felt almost like being back in air. The duel had lasted until Avalon stood enormous in the bow screens. In fact, they were closer to atmosphere than was prudent at their velocity. They'd better end the affair.

Vodan saw how.

He went on slowing at a uniform rate, as if he intended presently to slant off. He thought the Terran would think: *He sees what I plan. When I blind his radar, he will sheer from my fire in an unpredictable direction. Ah, but we're not under hyperdrive. He can't move at anything like the speed of energy beams. Mine can cover the entire cone of his possible instantaneous positions.*

For that, however, the gun platform needed a constant vector. Otherwise too many unknowns entered the equations and the target had an excellent chance of escaping. For part of a minute, if Vodan had guessed right, the Meteor would forego its advantage of superior mobility. And . . . he had superior weapons.

The Terran might well expect a torpedo and figure he could readily dispose of the thing. He might not appreciate how very great a concentration of energy his opponent could bring to bear for a short while, when all projectors were run at overload.

Vodan made his calculations. The gunners made their settings.

The Meteor passed ahead, dwarfish upon luminous Avalon. A sudden, glittering fog sprang from her. At explosive speed, it spread to make a curtain. And it hid one ship as well as the other.

Rays sliced through, seeking. Vodan knew exactly where to aim his. They raged for 30 seconds.

The metal dust scattered. Avalon again shone enormous and calm. Vodan ceased fire before his projectors should burn out.

Nothing came from the Meteor. He used magnification, and saw the hole which gaped astern by her drive cones. Air gushed forth, water condensing ghost-white until it vanished into void. Acceleration had ended entirely.

Joy lofted in Vodan. "We've struck him!" he shouted.

"He could launch his torps in a flock," the engineer worried.

"No. Come look if you wish. His powerplant took that hit. He has nothing left except his capacitor bank. If he can use that to full effect, which I doubt, he still can't give any object enough initial velocity to worry us."

"Kh'hng. Shall we finish him off?"

"Let's see if he'll surrender. Standard band. . . . Calling Imperial Meteor. Calling Imperial Meteor."

One more trophy for you, Eyath!

Hell Rock shuddered and toned. Roarings rolled inward. Air drifted bitter with smoke, loud with screams and bawled commands, running feet and threshing wings. Compartment after compartment was burst open to space. Bulkheads slid to seal twisted metal and tattered bodies off from the living.

She fought. She could fight on under what was left of her automata, well after the last of the crew were gone whose retreat she was covering.

Those were Ferune, his immediate staff, and a few ratings from Mistwood who had been promised the right to abide by their Wyvan. They made their way down quaking, tolling corridors. Sections lay dark where fluoropanels and facings were peeled back from the mighty skeleton.

"How long till they beat her asunder?" asked one at Ferune's back.

"An hour, maybe," he guessed. "They wrought well who built her. Of course, Avalon will strike before then."

"At what minute?"

"Daniel Holm must gauge that."

They crowded into their lifeboat. Ferune took the controls. The craft lifted against interior fields; valves swung ponderously aside; she came forth to sight of stars and streaked for home.

He glanced behind. The flagship was ragged, crumpled, cratered.

In places metal had run molten till it congealed into ugliness, in other places it glowed. Had the bombardment been able to concentrate on those sites where defenses were down, a megaton warhead or two would have scattered the vessel in gas and ashes. But the likelihood of a precise hit at medium range was too slim to risk a supermissile against her remaining interception capability. Better to hold well off and gnaw with lesser blasts.

"Fare gladly into the winds," Ferune whispered. In this moment he put aside his new ways, his alien ways, and was of Ythri, Mistwood, Wharr, the ancestors and the children.

Avalon struck. The boat reeled. Under an intolerable load of light, viewscreens blanked. Briefly, illumination went out. The flyers crouched, packed together, in bellowing, heat, and blindness.

It passed. The boat had not been severely damaged. Backup systems cut in. Vision returned, inside and outside. Aft, *Hell Rock* was silhouetted against the waning luridness of a fireball that spread across half heaven.

A rating breathed, "How . . . many . . . megatons?"

"I don't know," Ferune said. "Presumably ample to dispose of those Imperials we sucked into attacking us."

"A wonder we came through," said his aide. Every feather stood erect on him and shivered.

"The gases diffused across kilometers," Ferune reminded. "We've no screen field generator here, true. But by the time the front reached us, even a velocity equivalent of several million degrees could not raise our temperature much."

Silence clapped down, while smaller detonations glittered and faded in deeper distances and energy swords lunged. Eyes sought eyes. The brains behind were technically trained.

Ferune spoke it for them. "Ionizing radiation, primary and secondary. I cannot tell how big a dose we got. The meter went off scale. But we can probably report back, at least."

He gave himself to his piloting. Wharr waited.

Rochefort groped through the hull of *Hooting Star*. Interior grav generation had been knocked out; freefalling, they were now weight-less. And airless beyond the enclosing armor. Stillness pressed inward till he heard his heart as strongly as he felt it. Beads of sweat broke off brow, nose, cheeks, and danced between eyes and faceplate, catching light in oily gleams. That light fell queerly across vacuum, undiffused, sharp-shadowed.

"Watch Out!" he croaked into his radio. "Watch Out, are you there?"

"I'm afraid not," said Helu's voice in his earplugs, from the engine room.

Rochefort found the little body afloat behind a panel cut half loose from its moorings. The same ray had burned through suit and flesh and out through the suit, cauterizing as it went so that only a few bloodgouts drifted around. "Wa Chaou bought it?" asked Helu.

"Yes." Rochefort hugged the Cynthian to his breast and fought not to weep.

"Any fire control left?"

"No."

"Well, I think I can squeeze capacitor power into the drive units. We can't escape the planet on that, but maybe we can land without vaporizing in transit. It'll take a pretty fabulous pilot. Better get back to your post, skipper."

Rochefort opened the helmet in order to close the bulged-out eyes, but the lids wouldn't go over them. He secured the corpse in a bight of loose wire and returned forward to harness himself in.

The call light was blinking. Mechanically, conscious mainly of grief, he plugged a jack into his suit unit and pressed the Accept button.

Anglic, accented, somehow both guttural and ringing: "—Imperial Meteor. Are you alive? This is the Avalonian. Acknowledge or we shoot."

"Ack . . . ack—" Before the noise in his throat could turn to sobbing, Rochefort said, "Yes, captain here."

"We will take you aboard if you wish."

Rochefort clung to the seatback, legs trailing aft. It hummed and crackled in his ears.

"Ythri abides by the conventions of war," said the unhuman voice. "You will be interrogated but not mistreated. If you refuse, we must take the precaution of destroying you."

Kh-h-h-h . . . m-m-m-m. . . .

"Answer at once! We are already too nigh Avalon. The danger of being caught in crossfire grows by the minute."

"Yes," Rochefort heard himself say. "Of course. We surrender."

"Good. I observe you have not restarted your engine. Do not. We are matching velocities. Link yourselves and jump off into space. We will lay a tractor beam on you and bring you in as soon as may be. Understood? Repeat."

Rochefort did.

"You fought well," said the Ythrian. "You showed deathpride. I shall be honored to welcome you aboard." And silence.

Rochefort called Helu. The men bent the ends of a cable around their waists, cracked the personnel lock, and prepared to tumble free. Kilometers off they saw the vessel that bore three stars, coming like an eagle.

The skies erupted in radiance.

When ragged red dazzlement had cleared from their vision, Helu choked, "*Ullah akbar, Ullah akbar. . . .* They're gone. What *was* it?"

"Direct hit," Rochefort said. Shock had blown some opening in him for numbness to drain out of. He felt strength rising in its wake. His mind flashed, fast as those war lightnings yonder but altogether cool. "They knew we were helpless and had no friends nearby. But in spite of a remark the captain made, they must've forgotten to look out for their own friends. The planet-based weapons have started shooting. I imagine the missiles include a lot of tracker torpedoes. Our engines were dead. His weren't. A torp homed on the emissions."

"What, no recognition circuits?"

"Evidently not. To lash out on the scale they seem to be doing, the Avalonians would've had to sacrifice quality for quantity, and rely on knowing the dispositions of units. It was not reasonable to expect any this close in. The fighting's further out. I daresay that torp was bound there, against some particular Imperial concentration, when it happened to pass near us."

"Um." They hung between darkness and glitter, breathing. "We've lost our ride," Helu said.

"Got to make do, then," Rochefort answered. "Come."

Beneath his regained calm, he was shaken at what appeared to be the magnitude of the Avalonian response.

✣IX✣

When the boat had come to rest, thundering and shuddering ended, only bake-oven heat and scorched smells remaining, Rochefort let go of awareness.

He swam up from the nothing some minutes later. Helu stood over him. "Are you okay, skipper?" At first the engineer's voice seemed to come across a whining distance, and the sweat and soot on his face blurred into the haze which grayed all vision.

"Okay," Rochefort mumbled. "Get me . . . 'nother stimpill. . . ."

Helu did, with a glass of water that wrought a miracle on wooden tongue and parchment palate. "Hand of Fatima, what a ride!" he said unevenly. "I thought for certain we were finished. How did you ever get us down?"

"I don't remember," Rochefort answered.

The drug took hold, giving him back clarity of mind and senses, plus a measure of energy. He could reconstruct what he must have done in those last wild minutes. The ergs stored in the capacitors had not been adequate to kill the boat's entire velocity relative to the planetary surface. He had used them for control, for keeping the hull from being boiled off by the atmospheric friction that braked it. *Hooting Star* had skipped halfway around the globe on the tropopause, as a stone may be skipped over a lake, then screamed down on a long slant which would have ended in drowning—for the hole aft could not be patched, and a sealed-off engine room would have weighed too much when flooded—except that somehow he, Philippe Rochefort, had spotted (he recollected now) a chain of islands and achieved a crash landing on one. . . .

He spent a while in the awe of being alive. Afterward he unharnessed, and in their separate fashions he and Helu gave thanks; and they added a wish for the soul of Wa Chaou. By that time the hull had cooled to a point where they dared touch the lock. They found its outer valve had been torn loose when the boat plowed across ground.

"Good air," Helu said.

Rochefort inhaled gratefully. It was not just that the cabin was hot and stinking. No regeneration system on any spacecraft could do the entire work of a living world. This atmosphere that streamed to meet him smelled of ozone, iodine, greenery, flower fragrances; it was mild but brisk with breezes.

"Must be about Terran standard pressure," Helu went on. "How does a planet like this keep so much gas?"

"Surely you've met the type before," Rochefort said.

"Yes, but never stopped to wonder. Now that I've had the universe given back to me, I'd, uh, I'd like to know it better."

"Well, magnetism helps," Rochefort explained absently. "The core is small, but on the other hand the rotation is rapid, making for a reasonable value of H. Besides, the field has fewer charged particles to keep off, therefore fewer get by it to bounce off gas molecules. Likewise, the total ultraviolet and X radiation received is less. That sun's fairly close—we're getting about 10 percent more illumination than Terra does—but it's cooler than Sol. The energy distribution curve peaks at a lower frequency and the stellar wind is weak."

Meanwhile he sensed the gravity. His weight was four-fifths what it had been when the boat's interior field was set at standard pull. When you dropped sixteen kilos you noticed it at first—a bounciness, an exuberance of the body which the loss of a friend and the likelihood of captivity did not entirely quench—though you soon came to take the feeling for granted.

He stepped forth and looked around. Those viewscreens which remained functional had shown him this area was unpeopled. Inland it rose steeply. On the other side it sloped down to a beach where surf tumbled in a white violence whose noise reached him across more than a kilometer. Beyond, a syenite sea rolled to a horizon which, in spite of Avalon's radius, did not seem appreciably nearer than on Terra or Esperance. The sky above was a blue more bright and deep than he was used to. The sun was low, sinking twice as fast as on man's home. Its disk showed a bit larger, its hue was tinged golden. A sickle moon trailed, a fourth again the angular diameter of Luna seen from the ground. Rochefort knew it was actually smaller but, being close, raised twice the tides.

Occasional sparks and streaks blinked up there—monstrous explosions in space. Rochefort turned his mind from them. For him the war was presumably over. Let it be over for everybody, soon, before more consciousnesses died.

He gave his attention to the life encircling him. His vessel had gouged and charred through a dense mat of low-growing, beryl-green stuff which covered the island. "I suppose this explains why the planet has no native forests," he murmured, "which may in turn help explain why animal life is underevolved."

"Dinosaur stage?" Helu asked, watching a flock of clumsy winged creatures go by. They each had four legs; the basic vertebrate design on Avalon was hexapodal.

"Well, reptiloid, though some have developed features like hair or an efficient heart. By and large, they don't stand a chance against mammalian or avian life forms. The colonists had to do quite a lot of work to establish a stable mixed colony, and they keep a good deal of land reserved, including the whole equatorial continent."

"You've really studied them up, haven't you?"

"I was interested. And . . . seemed wrong to let them be only my targets. Seemed as if I ought to have some reality on the people I was going to fight."

Helu peered inland. Scattered shrubs and trees did exist. The latter were either low and thick or slim and supple, to survive the high winds that rapid rotation must often create. Autumn or no, many flowers continued in bloom, flamboyant scarlets and yellows and purples. Fruits clustered thick on several other kinds of plant.

"Can we eat local food?" Helu asked.

"Yes, of course," Rochefort said. "They'd never have made the success they did, colonizing, in the time they've had, if they couldn't draw on native resources. Some essentials are missing, assorted vitamins and whatnot. Imported domestic animals had to be revamped genetically on that account. We'd come down with deficiency diseases if we tried to eat Avalonian material exclusively. However, that wouldn't happen fast, and I've read that much of it is tasty. Unfortunately, I've read that much is poisonous, too, and I don't know which is which."

"Hm." Helu tugged his mustache and scowled. "We'd better call for somebody to come get us."

"No rush," said Rochefort. "Let's first learn what we can. The boat has supplies for weeks, remember. We just might be able to—" He stopped. Knowledge stung him. "Right now we've a duty."

Perforce they began by making a spade and pick out of scrap; and then the plant cover was tough and the soil beneath a stubborn clay. Sunset had perished in flame before they got Wa Chaou buried.

A full moon would have cast ample light; higher albedo as well as angular size and illumination gave it more than thrice the brilliance of Luna. Tonight's thin crescent was soon down. But the service could be read by two lamp-white companion planets and numberless stars. Most of their constellations were the same as those Rochefort had shared with Eve Davisson on Esperance. Three or four parsecs hardly count in the galaxy.

Does a life? I must believe so. "—Father, unto You in what form he did dream You, we commit this being our comrade; and we pray that You grant him rest, even as we pray for ourselves. Lord have mercy, Lord have mercy, Lord have mercy."

The gruesome little flashes overhead were dying away.

"Disengage," Cajal said. "Withdraw. Regroup in wide orbits."

"But, but, Admiral," protested a captain of his staff, "their ships—they'll use the chance to escape—disappear into deep space."

Cajal's glance traveled from screen to screen on the comboard. Faces looked out, some human, some nonhuman, but each belonging to an officer of Imperial Terra. He found it hard to meet those eyes.

"We shall have to accept that," he told them. "What we cannot accept is our present rate of losses. Laura is only a prologue. If the cost of its capture proves such that we have to wait for reinforcements, giving Ythri time to reorganize, there goes our entire strategy. The whole war will become long and expensive."

He sighed. "Let us be frank, citizens," he said. "Our intelligence about this system was very bad. We had no idea what fortifications had been created for Avalon—"

In orbit, automated stations by the hundreds, whose powerplants fed no engines but, exclusively, defensive screens and offensive projectors; thus mortally dangerous to come in range of. Shuttling between them and the planet, hence guarded by them, a host of supply craft, bringing whatever might be needed to keep the robots shooting.

On the surface, and on the moon, a global grid of detectors, launch tubes, energy weapons too immense for spaceships to carry;

some buried deep in rock or on the ocean beds, some aboveground or afloat. The chance of a vessel or missile getting through from space, unintercepted, small indeed; and negafields shielding every vital spot.

In the air, a wasp swarm of pursuit craft on patrol, ready to streak by scores against any who was so rash as to intrude.

"—and the defenders used our ignorance brilliantly. They lured us into configurations that allowed those instrumentalities to inflict staggering damage. We're mouse-trapped between the planet and their ships. Inferior though the enemy fleet is, under present circumstances it's disproportionately effective.

"We have no choice. We must change the circumstances, fast. If we pull beyond reach of the defenses, their fleet will again be outmatched and, I'm sure, will withdraw to the outer parts of this system as Captain K'thak has said."

"Then, sir?" asked a man. "What do we do then?"

"We make a reassessment," Cajal told him.

"Can we saturate their capabilities with what we've got on hand?" wondered another.

"I do not know," Cajal admitted.

"How could they do this?" cried a man from behind the bandages that masked him. His ship had been among those smashed. "A wretched colony—what's the population, fourteen million, mostly ranchers?—how was it possible?"

"You should understand that," Cajal reproved, though gently because he knew drugs were dulling brain as well as pain. "Given abundant nuclear energy, ample natural resources, sophisticated automatic technology, one needs nothing else except the will. Machines produce machines, exponentially. In a few years one has full production under way, limited only by available minerals; and an underpopulated, largely rural world like Avalon will have a good supply of those.

"I imagine," he mused aloud—because any thought was better than thought of what the navy had suffered this day—"that same pastoral economy simplified the job of keeping secret how great an effort was being mounted. A more developed society would have called on its existing industry, which is out in the open. The Avalonian leadership, once granted *carte blanche* by the electorate, made most of its facilities from zero, in regions where no one lives." He nodded. "Yes, citizens, let us confess we have been taken." Straightening: "Now we salvage what we can."

Discussion turned to ways and means. Battered, more than decimated, the Terran force was still gigantic. It was strewn through corresponding volumes of space, its units never motionless. Arranging for an orderly retreat was a major operation in itself. And there would be the uncertainties, imponderables, and inevitable unforeseen catastrophes of battle. And the Avalonian space captains must be presented with obvious chances to quit the fight—not mere tactical openings, but a clear demonstration that their withdrawal would not betray their folk—lest they carry on to the death and bring too many Imperials with them.

But at last the computers and underlings were at work on details, the first moves of disengagement were started. Cajal could be alone.

Or can I be? he thought *Ever again? The ghosts are crowding around.*

No. This debacle wasn't his fault. He had acted on wrong information. Saracoglu—No, the governor was a civilian who was, at most, peripherally involved in fact-gathering and had worked conscientiously to help prepare. Naval Intelligence itself—but Saracoglu had spoken sooth. Real espionage against Ythri was impossible. Besides, Intelligence . . . the whole navy, the whole Empire . . . was spread too thin across a reach too vast, inhuman, hostile; in the end, perhaps all striving to keep the Peace of Man was barren.

You did what you could. Cajal realized he had not done badly. These events should not be called a debacle, simply a disappointment. Thanks to discipline and leadership, his fleet had taken far fewer losses than it might have; it remained overwhelmingly powerful; he had learned lessons that he would use later on in the war.

Nevertheless the ghosts would not go away.

Cajal knelt. *Christ, who forgave the soldiers, help me forgive myself. Saints, stand by me till my work is done.* His look went from crucifix to picture. *Before everyone, you, Elena who in Heaven must love me yet, since none were ever too lowly for your love, Elena, watch over me. Hold my hand.*

❉ ❉ ❉

Beneath the flyers, the Middle Ocean rolled luminous black. Above them were stars and a Milky Way whose frostiness cut through the air's warmth. Ahead rose the thundercloud mass of an island. Tabitha heard surf on its beaches, a drumfire in the murmur across her face.

"Are they sure the thing landed here?" asked one of the half-dozen Ythrians who followed her and Draun,

"Either here or in the sea," growled her partner. "What's the home guard for if not to check out detector findings? Now be quiet. And wary. If that was an Imperial boat—"

"They're marooned," Tabitha finished for him. "Helpless."

"Then why've they not called to be fetched?"

"Maybe their transmitter is ruined."

"And maybe they have a little scheme. I'd like that. We've many new-made dead this night. The more Terrans for hell-wind to blow ahead of them, the better."

"Follow your own orders and shut up," Tabitha snapped.

Sometimes she seriously considered dissolving her association with Draun. She had come to see over the years that he didn't really believe in the gods of the Old Faith, nor carry out their rites from traditionalism like most Highsky folk; no, he enjoyed those slaughterous sacrifices. And he had killed in duello more than once, on his own challenge, however much trouble he might have afterward in scraping together winner's gild for the bereaved. And while he seldom abused his slaves, he kept some, which she felt was the fundamental abuse.

Still—he was loyal and, in his arrogant way, generous to friends; his seamanship combined superbly with her managerial talents; he could be good company when he chose; his wife was sweet; his youngest cubs were irresistible, and loved their Kin-She Hrill who took them in her arms. . . .

I'm perfect? Not by a fertilizing long shot, considering how I let my mind meander!

They winged, she thrust above the strand and high over the island. Photoamplifier goggles showed it silver-gray, here and there speckled with taller growth; on boulders, dew had begun to catch starlight. (*How goes it yonder? The news said the enemy's been thrown back, but—*) She wished she were flying nude in this stroking, giddily perfumed air. But her business demanded coveralls, cuirass, helmet, boots. That which had been detected coming down might be a crippled Avalonian, but might equally well be—*Hoy!*

"Look." She pointed. "A fresh track." They swung about, crossed a ridge, and the wreck lay under them.

"Terran indeed," Draun said. She saw his crest and tail-feathers quiver in eagerness. He wheeled, holding a magnifier to his eyes. "Two outside. Hya-a-a-a-ah!"

"Stop!" Tabitha yelled, but he was already stooping.

She cursed the awkwardness of gravbelts, set controls and flung herself after him. Behind came the other Ythrians, blasters clutched to breasts while wings hastened their bodies. Draun had left his gun sheathed, had taken out instead the half-meter-long, heavy, crooked Fao knife.

"Stop!" Tabitha screamed into the whistle of split air. "Give them a chance to surrender!"

The humans, standing by a patch of freshly turned earth, heard. Their glances lifted. Draun howled his battle cry. One man yanked at a holstered sidearm. Then the hurricane was on him. Wings snapped around so it roared in the pinions. Two meters from ground, Draun turned his fall into an upward rush. His right arm swept the blade in a short arc; his left hand, on the back of it, urged it along. The Terran's head flew off the neck, hit the susin and horribly bounced. The body stood an instant, geysering blood, before it collapsed like a puppet on which the strings have been slashed.

"Hya-a-a-a-ah!" Draun shrieked. "Hell-winds blow you before my chothmates! Tell Illarian they are coming!"

The other Terran stumbled back. His own sidearm was out. He fired, a flash and boom in blackness.

Before they kill him too—Tabitha had no time for planning. She was in the van of her squad. The man's crazed gaze and snap shot were aimed at Draun, whose broad-winged shadow had not yet come about for a second pass. She dived from the rear, tackled him low, and rolled over, gripping fast. They tumbled; the belt wasn't able to lift both of them. She felt her brow slammed against a root, her cheek dragged abradingly over the susin.

His threshings stopped. She turned off her unit and crouched beside him. Pain and dizziness and the laboring of her lungs were remote. He wasn't dead, she saw, merely half stunned from his temple striking a rock. Blood oozed in the kinky black hair, but he stirred and his eyeballs were filled with starlight. He was tall, swarthy by Avalonian measure . . . people with such chromosomes generally settled beneath stronger suns than Laura. . . .

The Ythrians swooped near. Wind rushed in their quills. Tabitha scrambled to her feet. She bestrode the Terran. Gun in hand, she gasped, "No. Hold back. No more killing. He's mine."

❖X❖

Ferune of Mistwood reported in at Gray, arranged his affairs and said his goodbyes within a few days.

To Daniel Holm: "Luck be your friend, First Marchwarden."

The man's mouth was stretched and unsteady. "You must have more time than—than—"

Ferune shook his head. The crest drooped ragged; most feathers that remained to him were lusterless white; he spoke in a mutter. His grin had not changed. "No, I'm afraid the medics can't stimulate regeneration in this case. Not when every last cell got blasted. Pity the Imperials didn't try shooting us full of mercury vapor. But you'd find that inconvenient."

Yes, you've more tolerance for heavy metals than humans do, went uselessly through Holm, *but less for hard radiation.* The voice trudged on: "As is, I am held together by drugs and baling wire. Most of those who were with me are already dead, I hear. But I had to get my powers and knowledge transferred to you, didn't I, before I rest?"

"To me?" the man suddenly couldn't hold back. "Me who killed you?"

Ferune stiffened. "Come off that perch, Daniel Holm. If I thought you really blame yourself, I would not have left you in office—probably not alive; anyone that stupid would be dangerous. You were executing my plan, and bloody-gut well it worked too, kh'hng?"

Holm knelt and laid his head on the keelbone. It was sharp, when flesh had melted from above, and the skin was fever-hot and he could feel how the heart stammered. Ferune shifted to handstance. Wings enfolded the man and lips kissed him. "I flew higher because of you," Ferune said. "If war allows, honor us by coming to my rite. Fair winds forever."

He left. An adjutant helped him into a car and took him northward, to the woodlands of his choth and to Wharr who awaited him.

"Permit me to introduce myself. I am Juan de Jesús Cajal y Palomares of Nuevo México, commanding His Imperial Majesty's naval forces in the present campaign. You have my word as a Terran officer that the beam is tight, the relays are automatic, this conversation will be recorded but not monitored, and the tape will be classified secret."

The two who looked out of the screens were silent, until Cajal grew overaware of the metal which enclosed him, background pulse of machinery and slight chemical taint in the air blown from ventilators. He wondered what impression he was making on them. There was no way to tell from the old Ythrian—Liaw? Yes, Liaw—who evidently represented civil authority. That being sat like a statue of grimness, except for the smoldering yellow eyes. Daniel Holm kept moving, cigar in and out of his mouth, fingers drumming desktop, tic in the left cheek. He was haggard, unkempt, stubbly, grimy, no hint of Imperial neatness about him. But he scarcely seemed humble.

He it was who asked at length: "Why?"

"*¿Por qué?*" responded Cajal in surprise. "Why I had a signal shot down to you proposing a conference? To discuss terms, of course."

"No, this secrecy. Not that I believe you about it, or anything else."

Cajal felt his cheeks redden. *I must not grow angry.* "As you wish, Admiral Holm. However, please credit me with some common sense. Quite apart from the morality of letting the slaughter and waste of wealth proceed, you must see that I would prefer to avoid further losses. That is why we're orbiting Avalon and Morgana at a distance and have made no aggressive move since battle tapered off last week. Now that we've evaluated our options, I am ready to talk; and I hope you've likewise done some hard thinking. I am not interested in pomp or publicity. Such things only get in the way of reaching practical solutions. Therefore the confidential nature of our parley. I hope you'll take the chance to speak as frankly as I mean to, knowing your words need not commit you."

"Our word does," Holm said.

"Please," Cajal urged. "You're angry, you'd kill me were you able, nevertheless you're a fellow professional. We both have our duties, however distasteful certain of them may be."

"Well, get on with it, then. What d'you want?"

"To discuss terms, I said. I realize we three alone can't authorize or arrange the surrender, but—"

"I think you can," Liaw interrupted: a low, dry, harshly accented Anglic. "If you fear court-martial afterward, we will grant you asylum."

Cajal's mouth fell open. "What are you saying?"

"We must be sure this is no ruse. I suggest you bring your ships one at a time into close orbit, for boarding. Transportation home for the crews will be made available later."

"Do you . . . do you—" Cajal swallowed. "Sir, I'm told your proper title translates more or less into 'Judge' or 'Lawspeaker.' Judge, this is no time for humor."

"If you don't want to give in," Holm said, "what's to discuss?"

"Your capitulation, *por Díos!*" Cajal's fist smote the arm of his chair. "I'm not going to play word games. You've delayed us too long already. But your fleet has been smashed. Its fragments are scattered. A minor detachment from our force can hunt them down at leisure. We control all space around you. You've no possibility of outside help. Whatever might recklessly be sent from other systems would be annihilated in detail; and the admiralties there know it. If they go anywhere with what pitiful strength they have, it'll be to Quetlan." He leaned forward. "We'd hate to bombard your planet. Please don't compel us to."

"Go right ahead," Holm answered. "Our interceptor crews would enjoy the practice."

"But—are you expecting blockade runners to—to—Oh, I know how big a planet is. I know an occasional small craft could sneak past our detector grids, our patrols and stations. But I also know how very small such craft must be, and how very occasional their success."

Holm drew savagely on his cigar before he stabbed it into its smoke. "Yes, sure," he snapped. "Standard technique. Eliminate a space fleet, and its planet has to yield or you'll pound it into radioactive slag. Nice work for a man, that, hunh? Well, my colleagues and I saw this war coming years back. We knew we'd never have much of a navy by comparison, if only because you bastards have so much more population and area behind you. But defense—Admiral, you're at the end of a long line of communication and supply. The border worlds aren't geared to produce anything like the amount of stuff you require; it has to come from deeper in the Empire. We're *here,* set up to make everything necessary as fast as necessary. We can't come after you. But we can bugger well swamp whatever you throw at us."

"Absolutely?"

"Okay, once in a great while, by sheer luck, you doubtless could land a warhead, and it might be big and dirty. We'd weather that, and the home guard has decontamination teams. Chances of its hitting anything important are about like drawing three for a royal flush. No ship of yours can get close enough with an energy projector husky enough to pinken a baby's bottom. But there're no size and mass limits on our ground-based photon weapons; we can use whole rivers to cool their generators while their snouts whiff you out of our sky. Now tell me why in flaming chaos we should surrender."

Cajal sat back. He felt as if struck from behind. "No harm in learning what conditions you meant to offer," Liaw said, toneless.

Face saving? Those Ythrians are supposed to be satanically proud, but not to the point of lunacy. Hope knocked in Cajal. "Honorable terms, of course," he said. "Your ships must be sequestered, but they will not be used against Ythri and personnel may go home, officers to keep their sidearms. Likewise for your defensive facilities. You must accept occupation and cooperate with the military government, but every effort will be made to respect your laws and customs, individuals will have the right to petition for redress of grievances, and Terran violators of the statutes will be punished as severely as Avalonian. Actually, if the population behaves correctly, I doubt if a large percentage will ever even see an Imperial marine."

"And after the war?"

"Why, that's for the Crown to decide, but I presume you'll be included in a reorganized Sector Pacis, and you must know Governor Saracoglu is efficient and humane. Insofar as possible, the Empire allows home rule and the continuation of local ways of life."

"Allows. The operative word. But let it pass. Let us assume a degree of democracy. Could we stop immigrants from coming until they outvoted us?"

"Well . . . well, no. Citizens are guaranteed freedom of movement. That's one of the things the Empire is for. Confound it, you can't selfishly block progress just because you prefer archaism."

"There is no more to discuss. Good day, Admiral."

"No, wait! Wait! You can't—condemn your whole people to war by yourselves!"

"If the Khruaths and the Parliament change their views, you will be informed."

"But listen, you're letting them die for nothing," Cajal said frantically. "This frontier is going to be straightened out. You, the whole Domain of Ythri have no power to stop that. You can only prolong the murderous, maiming farce. And you'll be punished by worse peace terms than you could have had. Listen, it's not one-sided. You're coming into the Empire. You'll get trade, contact, protection. Cooperate now and I swear you'll start out as a chartered client state, with all the privileges that means. Within years, individuals will be getting Terran citizenship. Eventually the whole of Avalon could become part of Greater Terra. For the love of God, be realistic!"

"We are," said Liaw.

Holm leered. Both screens blanked.

Cajal sat for minutes, staring. *They can't have been serious. They can't.* Twice he reached toward his intercom. Have them called; maybe this was some childish insistence that the Empire beg them to negotiate. . . .

His hand drew back. *No. I am responsible for our own dignity.*

Decision came. Let Plan Two be set in train. Leave the calculated strength here to invest Avalon. Comparatively little would be required. The sole real purpose was to keep this world's considerable resources from flowing to Ythri and these bases from menacing Cajal's lines back to the Empire. Siege would tie up more men and vessels than occupation would have done, but he could spare them.

The important thing was not to lose momentum. Rather, his freed ships must be off immediately to help in simultaneous assaults on Khrau and Hru. He'd direct the former himself, his second in command the latter. What they had learned here would be quite helpful.

And he was sure of quick victories yonder. Intelligence had failed to learn the extent of Avalonian arming, but not to discover the fact itself; that could not be concealed. By the same token, he knew that no other planet of the Domain had had a Daniel Holm nagging it over the years to build against this storm. He knew that the other Ythrian colonial fleets were small and poorly coordinated, the worlds unarmed.

Quetlan, the home sun, was more formidable. But let him rip spectacularly enough through the spaces between, and he dared hope his enemies would have the wisdom to capitulate before he stabbed them in the heart.

And afterward a few distorted molecules, recording the armistice, will give us Avalon. Very well. Better than fighting. . . . Do they know this? Do they merely want to keep, for a few weeks more, the illusion of freedom? Well, I hope the price they'll be charged for that—levies, restrictions, revisions of their whole society, that might otherwise have been deemed unnecessary—I hope they won't find the price unendurably steep—because endure it they must.

Before sunrise, Ferune departed Mistwood.

That day his home country bore its name well. Fog blew cold, wet, and blinding off the sea. Smokiness prowled the glooms around thick boles of hammerbranch, soaring trunks of lightningrod; moisture dripped from boughs onto fallen leaves, and where it struck a pool which had formed among the ringed stems of a sword-of-sorrow, it made a tiny glass chiming. But deeper inland, where Old Avalon remained, a boomer tree frightened beasts that might have grazed on it, and this noise rolled beneath the house of Ferune and echoed off the hanging shields of his ancestors.

Wings gathered. A trumpet sounded through night. Forth came his sons to meet their chothmates. They carried the body on a litter between them. His uhoths fluttered about, puzzled at his quietness. His widow led the way. Flanking were his daughters, their husbands and grown children, who bore lit torches.

Wings beat. The flight cut upward. When it rose past the fog, this was turned to blue-shadowed white under an ice-pale eastern lightening. Westward over sea, the last stars glimmered in royal purple.

Still the folk mounted, until they were near the top of what unaided flesh could reach. Here the airs whittered thin and chill; but on the rim of a twilit world, the snowpeaks of the Weathermother were kindled by a yet hidden sun.

All this while the flight beat north. Daniel Holm and his family, following in heavy garments and breathing masks, saw wings glow across heaven in one tremendous spearhead. They could barely make out the torchflames which streamed at its point, as sparks like the waning stars. More clearly came the throb from under those pinions. Apart from that, silence was total.

They reached wilderness, a land of crags, boulders, and swift-running streams. There the sons of Ferune stopped. Wings outspread, they hovered on the first faint warmth of morning, their mother before them. Around circled their near kin; and in a wheel, the choth surrounded these. And the sun broke over the mountains.

To Ferune came the new Wyvan of Mistwood. Once more he blew the horn, and thrice he called the name of the dead. Wharr swept by, to kiss farewell. Then the Wyvan spoke the words of the New Faith, which was two thousand years old.

"High flew your spirit on many winds; but downward upon you at last came winging God the Hunter. You met Him pride, you fought Him well, from you He has honor. Go hence now, that which the talons left, be water and leaves, arise in the wind; and spirit, be always remembered."

His sons tilted the litter. The body fell, and after it the torches.

Wharr slanted off in the beginning measures of the sky dance. A hundred followed her.

Hanging afar, between emptiness and immensity, Daniel Holm said to Christopher: "And that Terran thought we'd surrender."

✤**XI**✤

Liaw of The Tarns spoke. "We are met in the Great Khruath of Avalon, that free folk may choose their way. Our enemy has taken elsewhere most of the might which he brought against us. This is no victory, since those vessels will make war upon the rest of the Domain. Meanwhile he has left sufficient ships to hold us cut off. They are unlikely to attack our world. But they will seek to find and root out our bases among the sister planets and the few warcraft of ours that are left in space. Save for what harassment our brethren aboard can contrive, we have no means of taking the offensive. Our defenses we can maintain indefinitely. Yet no pledge can be given that great harm will not be wrought on Avalon, should the foe launch a determined effort. He has declared that in the end we are sure to be subjugated. This is possibly true. He has then declared that we can expect better treatment if we yield now than if we fight on, though at best we will come under Imperial law and custom. This is certainly true.

"They who speak for you rejected the demand, as was their duty until you could be summoned to decide. I remind you of the hazards of continued war and the threat of a harsh peace should we lose. I remind you furthermore that if we do resist, the free folk of Avalon must give up many of their rights and submit to the dictation of military leaders for as long as the strife may last.

"What say the choths?"

He and his colleagues stood on the olden site, First Island in the Hesperian Sea. At their backs rose the house of David Falkayn; before them greensward slanted toward beach and surf. But no booths or tents had been raised, no ships lay at anchor, no swarms of delegates flew down to form ranks beneath the trees. Time was lacking for ceremonious assemblies. Those elected at regional meetings, and those individuals who signified a wish to speak, were present electronically.

A computer-equipped staff worked hard inside the house. However taciturn the average Ythrian was, however unwilling to make a fool of himself by declaiming the obvious, still, when some two million enfranchised adults were hooked into a matter of as great moment as this, the questions and comments that arrived must be filtered. Those chosen to be heard must wait their turns.

Arinnian knew he would be called. He sat by Eyath before an outsize screen. They were alone on the front, hence lowest bench. At their backs the tiers rose, the household of Lythran and Blawsa crowded thereon, to the seat of the master and his lady. Liaw's slow words only deepened the quiet in that broad, dark, weapon-hung chamber; and so did the rustle of feathers, the scrape of claws or ala-tans, when someone shifted a little. The air was filled with the woodsmoke odor of Ythrian bodies. A breeze, gusting in from a window open on rain, added smells of damp earth and stirred the banners that hung from high rafters.

"—report on facts concerning—"

The image in the screen became that of a rancher. Behind him could be seen the North Coronan prairie, a distant herd, a string of quadrupedal burden-bearing zirraukhs led by a flapping youth, a more up-to-date truck which passed overhead. He stated, "Food production throughout the Plains of Long Reach has been satisfactory this year. The forecasts for next season are optimistic. We have achieved 75 percent storage of preserved meat in bunkers proofed against radioactive contamination, and expect to complete this task by midwinter. Details are filed in Library Central. Finished." The scan returned to the High Wyvans, who promptly called on another area representative.

Eyath caught Arinnian's arm. He felt the pulse in her fingers, and the claws on the two encircling thumbs bit him. He looked at her. The bronze-brown crest was stiffly raised, the amber eyes like lanterns. Fangs gleamed between her lips. "Must they drone on till eternity molders?" she breathed.

"They need truth before they decide," he whispered back, and felt the disapproving stares between his shoulderblades.

"What's to decide—when Vodan's in space?"

"You help him best by patience." He wondered who he was to give counsel. Well, Eyath was young (*me too, but this day I feel old*) and it was cruel that she could hope for no word of her betrothed until, probably, war's end. No mothership could venture in beaming range of beleaguered Avalon.

At least it was known that Vodan's had been among those which escaped. Too many orbited in wreck. More Terrans had been destroyed, of course, thanks to the trap that Ferune and Holm sprang. But one Ythrian slain was too many, Arinnian thought, and a million Terrans were too few.

"—call on the chief of the West Coronan guard."

He scrambled to his feet, realized that was unnecessary, and opined that he'd better remain standing than compound his gaucherie by sitting down again before he had spoken. "Uh, Arinnian of Stormgate. We're in good shape, equipping, training, and assigning recruits as fast as they come in. But we want more. Uh, since nobody has mentioned it, I'd like to remind people that except for ranking officers, home-guard service is part-time and the volunteer's schedule can be set to minimize interference with his ordinary work. Our section's cooperation with the North Oronesians is now being extended through the entire archipelago, and we aim to do likewise in southerly and easterly directions till, uh, we've an integrated command for the Brendan's, Fiery, and Shielding Islands as well, to protect the whole perimeter of Corona.

"Uh, on behalf of my father, the First Marchwarden, I want to point out a considerable hole in Avalon's defense, namely the absence of a guard for Equatoria, nothing there except some projector and missile launching sites. True, the continent's uninhabited, but the Terrans know that, and if they consider an invasion, they aren't likely to care about preserving a piece of native ecology intact. I, uh, will receive suggestions about this and pass them along the proper channels." His tongue was dry. "Finished."

He lowered himself. Eyath took his hand, gentler this time. Thank fortune, no one wanted to question him. He could be crisp in discussing strictly technical problems with a few knowledgeable persons, but two million were a bit much for a man without political instincts.

The talk seemed interminable. And yet, at the end, when the vote was called, when Liaw made his matter-of-fact announcement that the data bank recorded 83 percent in favor of continued resistance, scarcely six hours had passed. Humans couldn't have done it.

"Well," Arinnian said into the noise of cramped wings being stretched, "no surprises."

Eyath tugged at him. "Come," she said. "Get your belt. I want to use my muscles before dinner."

Rain beat through dusk, cold and tasting of sky. When they came above the clouds, he and she turned east to get away from their chothmates who also sought exercise. Snowpeaks and glaciers thrust out of whiteness, into a blue-black where gleamed the early stars and a few moving sparks which were orbital fortresses.

They fared awhile in silence, until she said: "I'd like to join the guard."

"Hm? Ah. Yes; welcome."

"But not fly patrol. That's essential, I know, and pleasant if the weather's halfway good; but I don't want a lot of pleasure. Look, see Camelot rising yonder. Vodan may be huddled inside a dead moon of it, waiting and waiting for a chance to hazard his life."

"What would you prefer?" he asked.

Her wings beat more steadily than her voice. "You must be caught in a hurricane of work, which is bound to stiffen. Surely your staff's too small, else why would you be so tired? Can't I help?"

"M-m . . . well—"

"Your assistant, your fetch-and-carry lass, even your personal secretary? I can take an electro-cram in the knowledge and skills, and be ready to start inside a few days."

"No. That's rough."

"I'll survive. Try me. Fire me if I can't grip the task, and we'll stay friends. I believe I can, though. Maybe better than someone who hasn't known you all these years, and who can be given another job. I'm bright and energetic. Am I not? And . . . Arinnian, I so much need to be with you, till this cripplewing time is outlived."

She reached toward him. He caught her hand. "Very well, galemate." In the wan light she flew as beautiful as ever beneath sun or moon.

"Yes, I'll call for a vote tomorrow," Matthew Vickery said.

"How d'you expect it'll go?" Daniel Holm asked.

The President sighed. "How do you think? Oh, the war faction won't bring in quite the majority of Parliament that it did of the Khruath. A few members will vote their convictions rather than their mail. But I've seen the analysis of that mail, and of the phone calls and—Yes, you'll get your damned resolution to carry on. You'll get your emergency powers, the virtual suspension of civilian government you've been demanding. I do wish you'd read some of those letters or watch some of those tapes. The fanaticism might frighten you as it does me. I never imagined we had that much latent insanity in our midst."

"It's insane to fight for your home?"

Vickery bit his lip. "Yes, when nothing can be gained."

"I'd say we gain quite a chunk. We kicked a sizable hole in the Terran armada. We're tying up a still bigger part, that was originally supposed to be off to Ythri."

"Do you actually believe the Domain can beat the Empire? Holm, the Empire can't *afford* to compromise. Take its viewpoint for a minute if you can. The solitary keeper of the peace among thousands of wildly diverse peoples; the solitary guardian of the borders against the barbarian and the civilized predatory alien, who carry nuclear weapons. The Empire has to be more than almighty. It must maintain credibility, universal belief that it's irresistible, or hell's kettle boils over."

"My nose bleeds for the Empire," Holm said, "but His Majesty will have to solve his problems at somebody else's expense. He gets no free rides from us. Besides, you'll note the Terrans didn't keep throwing themselves at Avalon."

"They had no need to," Vickery replied. "If the need does arise, they'll be back in force. Meanwhile we're contained." He filled his lungs. "I admit your gamble paid off extraordinarily—"

"Please. 'Investment.' And not mine. Ours."

"But don't you see, now there's nothing further we can use it for except a bargaining counter? We can get excellent terms, and I've dealt with Governor Saracoglu, I know he'll see to it that agreements are honored. Rationally considered, what's so dreadful about coming under the Empire?"

"Well, we'd begin by breaking our oath to Ythri. Sony, chum. Deathpride doesn't allow."

"You sit here mouthing obsolete words, but I tell you, the winds of change are blowing."

"I understand that's a mighty old phrase too," Holm said. "Ferune had one still older that he liked to quote. How'd it go? '—their finest hour—'"

Tabitha Falkayn shoved off from the dock and hauled on two lines in quick succession. Jib and mainsail crackled, caught the breeze, and bellied taut. The light, open boat heeled till foam hissed along the starboard rail, and accelerated outward. Once past the breakwater, on open sea, she began to ride waves.

"We're planing!" Philippe Rochefort cried.

"Of course," Tabitha answered. "This is a hydrofoil. 'Ware boom." She put the helm down. The yard swung, the hull skipped onto the other tack.

"No keel? What do you do for lateral resistance?"

She gestured at the oddly curved boards which lifted above either rail, pivoting in response to vanes upon them. "Those. The design's Ythrian. They know more about the ways of wind than men and men's computers can imagine."

Rochefort settled down to admire the view. It was superb. Billows marched as far as he could see, blue streaked with violet and green, strewn with sun-glitter, intricately white-foamed. They rumbled and whooshed. Fine spindrift blew off them, salty on the lips, spurring the blood where it struck bare skin. The air was cool, not cold, and singingly alive. Aft, the emerald heights of St. Li dwindled at an astonishing speed.

He had to admit the best part was the big, tawny girl who stood, pipe in teeth, hawklike pet on shoulder, bleached locks flying, at the tiller. She wore nothing but a kilt, which the wind molded to her loins, and—to be sure—her knife and blaster.

"How far did you say?" he asked.

"'Bout thirty-five kilometers. A couple of hours at this rate. We needn't start back till sundown, plenty of starlight to steer by, so you'll have time for poking around."

"You're too kind, Donna," he said carefully.

She laughed. "No, I'm grateful for an excuse to take an outing. Especially since those patches of atlantis weed fascinate me. Entire ecologies, in areas that may get bigger'n the average island. And the fisher scout told me he'd seen a kraken grazing the fringes of this one. Hope we find him. They're a rare sight. Peaceful, though we dare not come too near something that huge."

"I meant more than this excursion," Rochefort said. "You receive me, a prisoner of war, as your house guest."

Tabitha shrugged. "Why not? We don't bother stockading what few people we've taken. They aren't going anywhere." Her eyes rested candidly on him. "Besides, I want to know you."

He wondered, with an inward thump, how well.

Somberness crossed her. "And," she said, "I hope to . . . make up for what happened. You've got to see that Draun didn't wantonly murder your friend. He's, well, impetuous; and a gun was being pulled; and it is wartime."

He ventured a smile. "Won't always be, Donna."

"Tabitha's the name, Philippe; or Hrill when I talk Planha. You don't, of course. . . . That's right. When you go home, I'd like you to realize we Ythrians aren't monsters."

"Ythrians? You?" He raised his brows.

"What else? Avalon belongs to the Domain."

"It won't for much longer," Rochefort said. In haste: "Against that day, I'll do what I can to show you we Terrans aren't monsters either."

He could not understand how she was able to grin so lightheartedly. "If it amuses you to think that, you're welcome. I'm afraid you'll find amusement in rather short supply here. Swimming, fishing, boating, hiking . . . and, yes, reading; I'm addicted to mystery stories and have a hefty stack, some straight from Terra. But that's just about the list. I'm the sole human permanently resident on St. Li, and between them, my business and my duties as a home-guard officer will keep me away a lot."

"I'll manage," he said.

"Sure, for a while," she replied. "The true Ythrians aren't hostile to you. They mostly look on war as an impersonal thing, like a famine where you might have to kill somebody to feed him to your young but don't hate him on that account. They don't go in for chitchat, but if you play chess you'll find several opponents."

Tabitha shortened the mainsheet and left it in a snap cleat. "Still," she said, "Avalonians of either kind don't mass-produce entertainment, the way I hear people do in the Empire. You won't find much on the screens except news, sleepifyingly earnest educational programs, and classic dramas which probably won't mean a thing to you. So . . . when you get bored, tell me and I'll arrange for your quartering in a town like Gray or Centauri."

"I don't expect to be," he said, and added in measured softness, "Tabitha." Nonetheless he spoke honestly when he shook his head, stared over the waters, and continued: "No, I feel guilty at not grieving more, at being as conscious as I am of my fantastic good luck."

"Ha!" she chuckled. "Someday I'll count up the different ways you were lucky. That was an unconverted island you were on, lad, pure Old Avalonian, including a fair sample of the nastier species."

"Need an armed man, who stays alert, fear any animals here?"

"Well, no doubt you could shoot a spathodont dead before it

fanged you, though reptiloids don't kill easy. I wouldn't give odds on you against a pack of lycosauroids, however; and if a kakkelak swarm started running up your trousers—" Tabitha grimaced. "But these're tropical mainland beasties. You'd have had your troubles from the plants, which're wider distributed. Suppose a gust stirred the limbs of a surgeon tree as you walked by. Or . . . right across the ridge from where you were, I noticed a hollow full of hell shrub. You're no Ythrian, to breathe those vapors and live."

"Brrr!" he said. "What incurable romantic named this planet?"

"David Falkayn's granddaughter, when he'd decided this was the place to go," she answered, grave again. "And they were right, both of them. If anything, the problem was to give native life its chance. Like the centaurs, who're a main reason for declaring Equatoria off limits, because they use bits of stone and bone in tool fashion and maybe in a million years they could become intelligent. And by the way, their protection was something Ythri insisted on, hunter Ythri, not the human pioneers."

She gestured. "Look around you," she said. "This is our world. It's going to stay ours."

No, he thought, and the day was dulled for him, *you're wrong, Tabitha-Hrill. My admiral is going to hammer your Ythrians until they have no choice but to hand you over to my Emperor.*

✧XII✧

Week after fire-filled week, the Terran armada advanced.

Cajal realized that despite its inauspicious start, his campaign would become a textbook classic. In fact, his decision about Avalon typified it. Any fool could smash through with power like his. As predicted, no other colonial system possessed armament remotely comparable to what he had encountered around Laura. What existed was handled with acceptable skill, but simply had no possibility of winning.

So any butcher could have spent lives and ships, and milled his opposition to dust in the course of months. Intelligence data and Cajal's own estimate had shown that this was the approach his enemies expected him to take. They in their turn would fight delaying actions, send raiders into the Empire, seek to stir up third parties such as Merseia, and in general make the war sufficiently costly for Terra that a negotiated peace would become preferable.

Cajal doubted this would work, even under the most favorable circumstances. He knew the men who sat on the Policy Board. Nevertheless he felt his duty was to avoid victory by attrition—his duty to both realms. Thus he had planned, not a cautious advance where every gain was consolidated before the next was made, but a swordstroke.

Khrau and Hru fell within days of the Terrans' crossing their outermost planetary orbits. Cajal left a few ships in either system and a few occupation troops, mostly technicians, on the habitable worlds.

These forces looked ludicrously small. Marchwarden Rusa collected a superior one and sought to recapture Khrau. The Terrans sent word and hung on. A detachment of the main fleet came back, bewilderingly soon, and annihilated Rusa's command.

On Hru III the choths rose in revolt. They massacred part of the garrison. Then the missiles struck from space. Not many were needed before the siege of the Imperials was called off. The Wyvans were rounded up and shot. This was done with proper respect for their dignity. Some of them, in final statements, urged their people to cooperate with relief teams being rushed from Esperance to the smitten areas.

Meanwhile the invaders advanced on Quetlan. From their main body, tentacles reached out to grab system after system in passing. Most of these Cajal did not bother to occupy. He was content to shatter their navies and go on. After six weeks, the sun of Ythri was englobed by lost positions.

Now the armada was deep into the Domain, more than 50 light-years from the nearest old-established Imperial base. The ornithoids would never have a better chance of cutting it off. If they gathered everything they had for a decisive combat—not a standup slugging match, of course; a running fight that might last weeks—they would still be somewhat outmatched in numbers. But they would have a continuing supply of munitions, which the Imperials would not.

Cajal gave them every opportunity. They obliged.

The Battle of Yarro Cluster took eight standard days, from the first engagement to the escape of the last lonely Ythrian survivors.

But the first two of these days were preliminary and the final three were scarcely more than a mopping up. Details are for the texts. In essence, Cajal made use of two basic advantages. The first was surprise; he had taken pains to keep secret the large number of ammunition carriers with him. The second was organization; he could play his fleet like an instrument, luring and jockeying the ill-coordinated enemy units into death after death.

Perhaps he also possessed a third advantage, genius. When that thought crossed his mind, he set himself a penance.

The remnants of Domain power reeled back toward Quetlan. Cajal followed leisurely.

Ythri was somewhat smaller than Avalon, somewhat drier, the cloud cover more thin and hence the land masses showing more clearly from space, tawny and rusty in hue, under the light of a sun more cool and yellow than Laura. Yet it was very lovely, floating among the stars. Cajal left that viewscreen on and from time to time glanced thither, away from the face in his comboard.

The High Wyvan Trauvay said, "You are bold to enter our home." His Anglic was fluent, and he employed a vocalizer for total clarity of pronunciation.

Cajal met the unblinking yellow eyes and answered, "You agreed to a parley. I trust your honor." *I put faith in my Supernova and her escort, too. Better remind him.* "This war is a sorrow to me. I would hate to blacken any part of your world or take any further lives of your gallant folk."

"That might not be simple to do, Admiral," Trauvay said slowly. "We have defenses."

"Observed. Wyvan, may I employ blunt speech?"

"Yes. Particularly since this is, you understand, not a binding discussion."

No, but half a billion Ythrians are tuned in, Cajal thought. *I wish they weren't. It's as if I could feel them.*

What kind of government is this? Not exactly democratic—you can't hang any Terran label on it, not even "government," really. Might we humans have something to learn here? Everything we try seems to break down at last, and the only answer to that which we ever seem to find is the brute simplicity of Caesar.

Stop, Juan! You're an officer of the Imperium.

"I thank the Wyvan," Cajal said, "and request him and his people to believe we will not attack them further unless forced or ordered to do so. At present we have no reason for it. Our objectives have been achieved. We can now make good our rightful claims along the border. Any resistance must be sporadic and, if you will pardon the word, pathetic. A comparatively minor force can blockade Quetlan. Yes, naturally individual ships can steal past now and then. But to all intents and purposes, you will be isolated from your extrasystemic possessions, allies, and associates. Please consider how long the Domain can survive as a political entity under such conditions.

"Please consider, likewise, how your holding out will be an endless expense, an endless irritation to the Imperium. Sooner or later, it will decide to eliminate the nuisance. I do not say this is just, I say merely it is true. I myself would appeal an order to open fire. Were it too draconian, I would resign. But His Majesty has many admirals."

Stillness murmured around crucified Christ. Finally Trauvay asked, "Do you call for our surrender?"

"For an armistice," Cajal said.

"On what conditions?"

"A mutual cease-fire, of course . . . by definition! Captured ships and other military facilities will be retained by Terra, but prisoners will be repatriated on both sides. We will remain in occupation of systems we have entered, and will occupy those worlds claimed by the Imperium which have not already been taken. Local authorities and populaces will submit to the military officers stationed among them. For our part, we pledge respect for law and custom, rights of nonseditious free speech and petition, interim economic assistance, resumption of normal trade as soon as possible, and the freedom of any individual who so desires to sell his property on the open market and leave. Certain units of this fleet will stay near Quetlan and frequently pass through the system on surveillance; but they will not land unless invited, nor interfere with commerce, except that they reserve the right of inspection to verify that no troops or munitions are being sent."

Waves passed over the feathers. Cajal wished he knew how to read them. The tone stayed flat: "You do demand surrender."

The man shook his head. "No, sir, I do not, and in fact that would exceed my orders. The eventual terms of peace are a matter for diplomacy."

"What hope have we if defeat be admitted beforehand?"

"Much." Cajal made ready his lungs. "I respectfully suggest you consult your students of human sociodynamics. To put it crudely, you have two influences to exert, one negative, one positive. The negative one is your potentiality of renewing the fight. Recall that most of your industry remains intact in your hands, that you have ships left which are bravely and ably manned, and that your home star is heavily defended and would cost us dearly to reduce.

"Wyvan, people of Ythri, I give you my most solemn assurance the Empire does not want to overrun you. Why should we take on the burden? Worse than the direct expense and danger would be the loss of a high civilization. We desire, we need your friendship. If anything, this war has been fought to remove certain causes of friction. Now let us go on together.

"True, I cannot predict the form of the eventual peace treaty. But I call your attention to numerous public statements by the Imperium. They are quite explicit. And they are quite sincere, for it is obviously to the best interest of the Imperium that its word be kept credible.

"The Domain must yield various territories. But compensations can be agreed on. And, after all, everywhere that your borders do not march with ours, there is waiting for you a whole universe."

Cajal prayed he was reciting well. His speeches had been composed by specialists, and he had spent hours in rehearsal. But if the experts had misjudged or he had bungled—

O God, let the slaughter end . . . and forgive me that the back of my mind is fascinated by the technical problem of capturing that planet.

Trauvay sat moveless for minutes before he said, "This shall be considered. Please hold yourself in the vicinity for consultations." Elsewhere in the ship, a xenologist who had made Ythrians his lifetime work leaped out of his chair, laughing and weeping, to shout, "The war's over! The war's over!"

Bells rang through Fleurville, from the cathedral a great bronze striding, from lesser steeples a frolic. Rockets cataracted upward to explode softly against the stars of summer. Crowds roiled in the streets, drunk more on happiness than on any liquor; they blew horns, they shouted, and every woman was kissed by a hundred strange men who suddenly loved her. In daylight, Imperial marines paraded to trumpets and squadrons of aircraft or small spacecraft roared recklessly low. But to the capital of Esperance and Sector Pacis, joy had come by night.

High on a hill, in the conservatory of the gubernatorial palace, Ekrem Saracoglu looked out over the galaxy of the city. He knew why it surged so mightily—the noise reached him as a distant wavebeat— and shone so brilliantly. The pacifist heritage of the colonists was a partial cause; now they could stop hating those brothers who wore the Emperor's uniform. *Although,* his mind murmured, *I suspect plain animal relief speaks louder. The smell of fear has been on this planet since the first border incidents, thick since war officially began. An Ythrian raid, breaking through our surprised cordons—a sky momentarily incandescent—*

"Peace," Luisa said. "I have trouble believing."

Saracoglu glanced at the petite shape beside him. Luisa Carmen Cajal y Gomez had not dressed gaily after accepting his invitation to dinner. Her gown was correct as to length and pattern, but plain gray velvyl. Apart from a tiny gold cross between the breasts, her jewelry was a few synthetic diamonds in her hair. They glistened among high-piled black tresses like the night suns shining through the transparency overhead, or like the tears that stood on her lashes.

The governor, who had covered his portliness with lace, ruffles, tiger-patterned arcton waistcoat, green iridon culottes, snowy shimmerlyn stockings, and gems wherever he could find a place, ventured to pat her hand. "You are afraid the fighting may resume? No. Impossible. The Ythrians are not insane. By taking our armistice terms, they acknowledged defeat to themselves even more than to us. Your father should be home soon. His work is done." He sighed, trusting it wasn't too theatrically. "Mine, of course, will get rougher."

"Because of the negotiations?" she asked.

"Yes. Not that I'll have plenipotentiary status. However, I will be a ranking Terran representative, and the Imperium will rely heavily on the advice of my staff and myself. After all, this sector will continue to border on the Domain, and will incorporate the new worlds."

Her look was disconcertingly weighing from eyes that young. "You'll become quite an important man, won't you, Your Excellency?" Her tone was, if not chilly, cool.

Saracoglu got busy pinching withered petals off a fuchsia. Beside it a cinnamon bush—Ythrian plant—filled the air with fragrance. "Well, yes," he said. "I would not be false to you, Donna, including false modesty."

"The sector expanded and reorganized. You probably getting an elevation in the peerage, maybe a knighthood. At last, pretty likely, called Home and offered a Lord Advisorship."

"One is permitted to daydream."

"You promoted this war, Governor."

Saracoglu ran a palm over his bare scalp. *All right,* he decided. *If she can't see or doesn't care that it was on her account I sent Helga and Georgette packing (surely, by now, the gossip about that has reached her, though she's said no word, given no sign), well, I can probably get them back; or if they won't, there's no dearth of others. No doubt this particular daydream of mine is simply man's eternal silly refusal to admit he's growing old and fat. I've learned what the best condiments are when one must eat disappointment.*

But how vivid she is among the flowers.

"I promoted action to end a bad state of affairs before it got worse," he told her. "The Ythrians are no martyred saints. They advanced their interests every bit as ruthlessly as their resources allowed. Human beings were killed. Donna, my oath is to Terra."

Still her eyes dwelt on him. "Nevertheless you must have known what this would do for your career," she said, still quiet.

He nodded. "Certainly. Will you believe that that did not simplify, it vastly complicated things for me? I *thought* I thought this border rectification would be for the best. And, yes, I think I can do a better than average job, first in rebuilding out here, not least in building a reconciliation with Ythri; later, if I'm lucky, on the Policy Board, where I can instigate a number of reforms. Ought I to lay down this work in order that my conscience may feel smug? Am I wicked to enjoy the work?"

Saracoglu reached in a pocket for his cigarette case. "Perhaps the answer to those questions is yes," he finished. "How can a mortal man be sure?"

Luisa took a pair of steps in his direction. Amidst the skips of his heart he remembered to maintain his rueful half-smile. "Oh, Ekrem—" She stopped. "I'm sorry, Your Excellency."

"No, I am honored, Donna," he said.

She didn't invite him to use her given name, but she did say, smiling through tears, "I'm sorry, too, for what I hinted. I didn't mean it. I'd never have come tonight if I hadn't gotten to know you for a . . . a decent man."

"I hardly dared hope you would accept," he told her, reasonably truthfully. "You could be celebrating with people your age."

The diamonds threw scintillations when she shook her head. "No, not for something like this. Have you heard I was engaged to be married once? He was killed in action two years ago. Preventive action, it was called—putting down some tribes that had refused to follow the 'advice' of an Imperial resident—Well." She drew breath. "Tonight I couldn't find words to thank God. Peace was too big a gift for words."

"You're the Admiral's daughter," he said. "You know peace is never a free gift."

"Do wars come undeserved?"

A discreet cough interrupted. Saracoglu turned. He was expecting his butler to announce cocktails, and the sight of a naval uniform annoyed him. "Yes?" he snapped.

"If you please, sir," the officer said nervously.

"Pray excuse me, Donna." Saracoglu bowed over Luisa's wonderfully slim hand and followed the man out into the hall.

"Well?" he demanded.

"Courier from our forces at Laura, sir." The officer shivered and was pale. "You know, that border planet Avalon."

"I do know." Saracoglu braced himself.

"Well, sir, they got word of the armistice all right. Only they reject it. They insist they'll keep on fighting."

✧XIII✧

The bony, bearded face in the screen said, on a note close to desperation, "Sirs, you are . . . are behaving as if you were mad."

"We've got company," Daniel Holm replied.

"Do you then propose to secede from the Domain?" Admiral Cajal exclaimed.

"No. The idea is to stay in it. We're happy there. No Imperial bureaucrats need apply."

"But the armistice agreement—"

"Sure, let's keep the present cease-fire. Avalon doesn't want to hurt anybody."

Cajal's mouth stiffened. "You cannot pick and choose among clauses. Your government has declared the Empire may occupy this system pending the final peace settlement."

Liaw of The Tarns thrust his frosty head toward the scanner that sent his image to Holm's office and Cajal's orbiting warcraft. "Ythrian practice is not Terran," he said. "The worlds of the Domain are tied to each other principally by vows of mutual fidelity. That our fellows are no longer able to help us does not give them the right to order that we cease defending ourselves. If anything, deathpride requires that we continue the fight for what help it may afford them."

Cajal lifted a fist into view. "Sirs," he rasped, "you seem to think this is the era of the Troubles and your opponents are barbarians who'll lose purpose and organization and go away if they're stalled for a while. The truth is, you're up against Imperial Terra, which thinks in terms of centuries and reigns over thousands of planets. Not that any such time or power must be spent on you. Practically the entire force that broke the Domain can now be brought to bear on your single globe. And it will be, sirs. If you compel the outcome, it will be."

His gaze smoldered upon them. "You have strong defenses," he said, "but you must understand how they can be swamped. Resistance will buy you nothing except the devastation of your homes, the death of thousands or millions. Have *they* been consulted?"

"Yes," Liaw replied. "Between the news of Ythri's capitulation and your own arrival, Khruath and Parliament voted again. A majority favors holding on."

"How big a majority this time?" Cajal asked shrewdly. He saw feathers stir and facial muscles twitch, and nodded. "I do not like the idea of making war on potentially valuable subjects of His Majesty," he said, "most especially not on women and children."

Holm swallowed. "Uh, Admiral. How about . . . evacuating everybody that shouldn't stay or doesn't want to . . . before we start fighting again?"

Cajal sat motionless. His features congealed. When he spoke, it was as if his throat pained him. "No. I may not help an enemy rid himself of his liabilities."

"Are you bound to wage war?" Liaw inquired. "Cannot the cease-fire continue until a peace treaty has been signed?"

"If that treaty gives Avalon to the Empire, will you obey?" Cajal retorted.

"Perhaps."

"Unacceptable. Best to end this affair at once." Cajal hesitated. "Of course, it will take time to set things in order everywhere else and marshal the armada here. The *de jure* cease-fire ends when my ship has returned to the agreed-on distance. But obviously the war will remain in *status quo,* including the *de facto* cease-fire with respect to Avalon and Morgana, for a short period. I shall confer with Governor Saracoglu. I beseech you and all Avalonians to confer likewise with each other and use this respite to reach the only wise decision. Should you have any word for us, you need but broadcast a request for a parley. The sooner we hear, the milder—the more honorable—treatment you can expect."

"Observed," Liaw said. There followed ritual courtesies, and the screen blanked which had shown Cajal.

Holm and Liaw traded a look across the kilometers between them. At the rear of the man's office, Arinnian stirred uneasily.

"He means it," Holm said.

"How correct is his assessment of relative capabilities?" the Wyvan asked.

"Fairly good. We couldn't block a full-out move to wreck us. Given as many ships as he can whistle up, bombarding, ample stuff would be sure to get past our interception. We depend on the Empire's reluctance to ruin a lot of first-class real estate . . . and, yes, on that man's personal distaste for megadeaths."

"You told me earlier that you had a scheme."

"My son and I are working on it. If it shows any promise, you and the other appropriate people will hear. Meanwhile, I imagine you're as busy as me. Fair winds, Liaw."

"Fly high, Daniel Holm." And that screen blanked.

The Marchwarden kindled a cigar and sat scowling, until he rose and went to the window. Outside was a clear winter's day. Gray did not get the snowfall of the mountains or the northern territories, and the susin stayed green on its hills the year around. But wind whooped, cold and exultant, whitecaps danced on a gunmetal bay, cloaks streamed and fluttered about walking humans, Ythrians overhead swooped through changeable torrents of air.

Arinnian joined him, but had to wet his lips before he could speak. "Dad, do we have a chance?"

"Well, we don't have a choice," Holm said.

"We do. We can swallow our damned pride and tell the people the war's lost."

"They'd replace us, Chris. You know that. Ythri could surrender because Ythri isn't being given away. The other colonies can accept occupation because it's unmistakable to everybody that they couldn't now lick a sick kitten. We're different on both counts." Holm squinted at his son through rank blue clouds of smoke. "You're not scared, are you?"

"Not for myself, I hope. For Avalon—All that rhetoric you hear about staying free. How free are corpses in a charred desert?"

"We're not preparing for destruction," Holm said. "We're preparing to risk destruction, which is something else again. The idea is to make ourselves too expensive an acquisition."

"If Avalon went to the Empire, and we didn't like the conditions, we could emigrate to the Domain."

The Marchwarden's finger traced an arc before the window. "Where would we find a mate to that? And what'd be left of this special society we, our ancestors and us, we built?"

He puffed for a minute before musing aloud: "I read a book once, on the history of colonization. The author made an interesting point. He said you've got to leave most of the surface under plant cover, rooted vegetation and phytoplankton and whatever else there may be. You need it to maintain the atmosphere. And these plants are part of an ecology, so you have to keep many animals too, and soil bacteria and so forth. Well, as long as you must have a biosphere, it's cheaper—easier, more productive—to make it supply most of your food and such, than to synthesize. That's why colonists on terrestroid worlds are nearly always farmers, ranchers, foresters, et cetera, as well as miners and manufacturers."

"So?" his son asked.

"So you grow into your world, generation by generation. It's not walls and machinery, it's a live nature, it's this tree you climbed when you were little and that field your grandfather cleared and yonder hilltop where you kissed your first girl. Your poets have sung it, your artists have drawn it, your history has happened on it, your forebears returned their bones to its earth and you will too, you will too. It is you and you are it. You can no more give it away, freely, than you could cut the heart out of your breast."

Again Holm regarded his son. "I should think you'd feel this stronger than me, Arinnian," he said. "What's got into you?"

"That man," the other mumbled. "He didn't threaten terrible things, he warned, he pleaded. That brought them home to me. I saw . . . Mother, the kids, you, my chothmates—"

Eyath. Hrill. Hrill who is Tabitha. In these weeks we have worked together, she and Eyath and I. . . . Three days ago I flew between them, off to inspect that submarine missile base. Shining bronze wings, blowing fair hair; eyes golden, eyes green; austere jut of keelbone, heavy curve of breasts. . . . She is pure. I know she is. I make too many excuses to see her, be with her. But that damned glib Terran she keeps in her house, his tinsel cosmopolitan glamour, he hears her husky-voiced merriment oftener than I do.

"Grant them their deathpride," Holm said.

Eyath will die before she yields. Arinnian straightened his shoulders. "Yes. Of course, Dad."

Holm smiled the least bit. "After all," he pointed out, "you got the first germ of this ver-r-ry intriguing notion we have to discuss."

"Actually, it . . . wasn't entirely original with me. I got talking to, uh, Tabitha Falkayn, you know her? She dropped the remark, half joking. Thinking about it later, I wondered if—well, anyhow."

"Hm. Quite a girl, seems. Especially if she can stay cheerful these days." Holm appeared to have noticed the intensity of his stare, because he turned his head quickly and said, "Let's get to work. We'll project a map first, hm?"

His thoughts could be guessed. The lift in his tone, the crinkles around his eyes betrayed them. *Well, well. Chris has finally met a*

*woman who's not just a sex machine or a she-Ythrian to him. Dare I
tell Ro, yet?—I do dare tell her that our son and I are back together.*

Around St. Li, winter meant rains. They rushed, they shouted,
they washed and caressed, it was good to be out in them unclad, and
when for a while they sparkled away, they left rainbows behind them.

Still, one did spend a lot of time indoors, talking or sharing
music. A clear evening was not to be wasted.

Tabitha and Rochefort walked along the beach. Their fingers
were linked. The air being soft, he wore simply the kilt and dagger
she had given him, which matched hers.

A full Morgana lifted from eastward waters. Its almost unblemished
shield dazzled the vision with whiteness, so that what stars could
be seen shone small and tender. That light ran in a quaking glade
from horizon to outermost breakers, whose heads it turned into
wan fire; the dunes glowed beneath it, the tops of the trees which
made a shadow-wall to left became hoar. There was no wind and the
surf boomed steadily and inwardly, like a heartbeat. Odors of leaf
and soil overlay a breath of sea. The sands gave back the day's
warmth and gritted a little as they molded themselves sensuously to
the bare foot.

Rochefort said in anguish, "This to be destroyed? Burned,
poisoned, ripped to flinders? And you!"

"We suppose it won't happen," Tabitha replied.

"I tell you, I *know* what's to come."

"Is the enemy certain to bombard?"

"Not willingly. But if you Avalonians, in your insane arrogance,
leave no alternative—" Rochefort broke off. "Forgive me. I shouldn't
have said that. It's just that the news cuts too close."

Her hand tightened on his. "I understand, Phil. You're not the
enemy."

"What's bad about joining the Empire?" He waved at the sky.
"Look. Sun after sun after sun. They could be yours."

She sighed. "I wish—"

She had listened in utter bewitchment to his tales of those
myriad worlds.

Abruptly she smiled, a flash in the moonglow that clad her. "No,
I won't wish," she said; "I'll hold you to your promise to show me

Terra, Ansa, Hopewell, Cynthia, Woden, Diomedes, Vixen, every last marvel you've been regaling me with, once peace has come."

"If we're still able."

"We will be. This night's too lovely for believing anything else."

"I'm afraid I can't share your Ythrian attitude," he said slowly. "And that hurts also."

"Can't you? I mean, you're brave, I know you are, and I know you can enjoy life as it happens." Her voice and her lashes dropped. "How much you can."

He halted his stride, swung about, and caught her other hand. They stood wordlessly looking.

"I'll try," he said, "because of you. Will you help me?"

"I'll help you with anything, Phil," she answered.

They had kissed before, at first playfully as they came to feel at ease beside each other, of late more intensely. Tonight she did not stop his hands, nor her own.

"Phil and Hrill," she whispered at last, against him. "Phil and Hrill. Darling, I know a headland, a couple of kilometers further on. The trees shelter it, but you can see moon and water between them and the grass is thick and soft, the Terran grass—"

He followed her lead, hardly able to comprehend his fortune.

She laughed, a catch deep in her breast. "Yes, I planned this," she sang. "I've watched my chance for days. Mind being seduced? We may have little time in fact."

"A lifetime with you is too little," he faltered.

"Now you'll have to help me, my love, my love," she told him. "You're my first. I was always waiting for you."

✦XIV✦

From the ground, Arinnian hailed Eyath. "Hoy-ah! Come on down and get inside." He grinned as he added in Anglic, "We Important Executives can't stall around."

She wheeled once more. Sunlight from behind turned her wings to a bronze fringed by golden haze. *She could be the sun itself,* he thought, *or the wind, or everything wild and beautiful above this ferroconcrete desert.* Then she darted at the flitter, braked in a brawl of air, and stood before him.

Her gaze fell troubled on the torpedo shape looming at his back. "Must we travel in that?" she asked.

"When we have to bounce around half a planet, yes," he replied. "You'll find it isn't bad. Especially since the hops don't take long. Less than an hour to St. Li." *To Tabby.* "Here, give me your hand."

She did. The fingers, whose talons could flay him, were slim and warm, resting trustfully between his. He led her up the gangway. She had flown in vehicles often before, of course, but always "eyeball" cars, frail and slow for the sake of allowing the cabins to be vitryl bubbles.

"This is a problem the choths like Stormgate, members mostly hunters, are going to have to overcome," he said. "Claustrophobia. You limit your travel capabilities too much when you insist on being surrounded by transparency."

Her head lifted. "If Vodan can suffer worse, I am ashamed I hung back, Arinnian."

"Actually, I hope you'll come to see what Vodan sees. He loves it in space, doesn't he?"

"Y-yes. He's told me that. Not to make a career of, but we do want to visit other planets after the war."

"Let's try today to convince you the journey as well as the goal is something special. . . . M-m-m, do you know, Eyath, two congenial couples traveling together—Well. Here we are."

He assisted her into harness in the copilot's seat, though she was his passenger. "Ordinarily this wouldn't be needful," he explained. "The flitter's spaceable—you could reach Morgana easily, the nearer planets if necessary—so it has counter-acceleration fields available, besides interior weight under free fall. But we'll be flying high, in the fringes of atmosphere, not to create a sonic boom. And while nothing much seems to be going on right now in the war, and we'll have a canopy of fortress orbits above us, nevertheless—"

She brushed her crest across his shoulder. "Of course, Arinnian," she murmured.

He secured himself, checked instruments, received clearance, and lifted. The initial stages were under remote control, to get him past that dance of negagrav projections which guarded the spaceport.

Beyond, he climbed as fast as the law allowed, till in the upper stratosphere he fed his boat the power calculated to minimize his passage time.

"O-o-o-oh," Eyath breathed.

They were running quietly. The viewscreens gave outlooks in several directions. Below, Avalon was silver ocean. Around were purple twilight, sun, moon, a few stars: immensity, cold and serene.

"You must've seen pictures," Arinnian said.

"Yes. They're not the same." Eyath gripped his arm. "Thank you, dear galemate."

And I'm bound for Tabby, to tell of a battle plan that may well work, that'll require we work together. How dare I be this happy?

They flew on in the Ythrian silence which could be so much more companionable than human chatter.

There was an overcast at their destination; but when they had pierced its fog they found the sky pearl-gray, the waters white-laced indigo, the island soft green. The landing field was small, carved on the mountainside a few kilometers from the compound where Tabitha dwelt. When Chris called ahead she had promised to meet him.

He unharnessed with fingers that shook a little. Not stopping to help Eyath, he hastened to the airlock. It had opened and the gangway had extruded. A breeze ruffled his hair, warm, damp, perfumed by the janie planted around the field. Tabitha stood near, waving at him.

That was her left hand. Her right clasped the Terran's.

After half a minute she called, "Do you figure to stand there all day, Chris?"

He came down. They two released each other and extended their hands, human fashion. Meanwhile her foot caressed Rochefort's. She was wearing nothing but a few designs in body paint. They included the joyous banality of a heart pierced by an arrow.

Arinnian bowed. "We have an urgent matter to discuss," he said in Planha. "Best we flit straight to Draun's house."

As a matter of fact, Tabitha's partner and superior officer was waiting in her home. "Too many youngsters and retainers at mine," he grunted. "Secrecy must be important, or you'd simply have phoned—though we do see a rattlewing lot of you."

"These are always my welcome guests," the woman said stiffly.

Arinnian wondered if the tension he felt was in the atmosphere or his solitary mind. Draun, lean, scarred, had not erected feathers; but he sat back on tail and alatans in a manner suggesting surliness, and kept stroking a dirk he wore. Tabitha's look seemed to dwell upon Rochefort less meltingly than it had done at the field, more in appeal.

Glancing around, Arinnian found the living room little changed. Hitherto it had pleased him. She had designed the house herself. The ceiling, a fluoropanel, was low by Ythrian standards, to make the overall proportions harmonious. A few susin mats lay on a floor of polished oak, between large-windowed copperwood walls, beneath several loungers, end tables, a stone urn full of blossoms. While everything was clean-scrubbed, her usual homely clutter was strewn about, here a pipe rack and tobacco jar, there a book, yonder a ship model she was building.

Today, however, he saw texts to inform a stranger about Avalon, and a guitar which must have been lately ordered since she didn't play that instrument. The curtain had not been drawn across the doorway to her sleeping room; Arinnian glimpsed a new wood-and-leather-frame bed, double width.

Eyath's wing touched him. She didn't like Draun. He felt the warmth that radiated from her.

"Yes," he said. "We do have to keep the matter below ground." His gaze clanged on Rochefort's. "I understand you've been studying Planha. How far along are you?"

The Terran's smile was oddly shy for an offplanet enemy who had bedazzled a girl sometimes named Hrill. "Not very," he admitted. "I'd try a few words except you'd find my accent too atrocious."

"He's doing damn well," Tabitha said, and snuggled.

His arm about her waist, Rochefort declared: "I've no chance of passing your plans on to my side, if that's what's worrying you, Citizen—uh, I mean Christopher Holm. But I'd better make my position clear. The Empire *is* my side. When I accepted my commission, I took an oath, and right now I've no way to resign that commission."

"Well said," Eyath told him. "So would my betrothed avow."

"What's honor to a Terran?" Draun snorted. Tabitha gave him a furious look. Before she could reply, Rochefort, who had evidently not followed the Planha, was proceeding:

"As you can see, I . . . expect I'll settle on Avalon after the war. Whichever way the war goes. But I do believe it can only go one way. Christopher Holm, besides falling in love with this lady, I have with her planet. Could I possibly make you consider accepting the inevitable before the horror comes down on Tabby and Avalon?"

"No," Arinnian answered.

"I thought not." Rochefort sighed. "Okay, I'll take a walk. Will an hour be long enough?"

"Oh, yes," Eyath said in Anglic.

Rochefort smiled. "I love your whole people."

Eyath nudged Arinnian. "Do you need me?" she asked. "You're going to explain the general idea. I've heard that." She made a whistling noise found solely in the Avalonian dialect of Planha—a giggle. "You know how wives flee from their husbands' jokes."

"Hm?" he said. "What'll you do?"

"Wander about with Ph . . . Phee-leep Hroash For. He has been where Vodan is."

You too? Arinnian thought.

"And he is the mate of Hrill, our friend," Eyath added.

"Go if you wish," Arinnian said.

"An hour, then." Claws ticked, feathers rustled as Eyath crossed the floor to the Terran. She reached up and took his arm. "Come; we have much to trade," she said in her lilting Anglic.

He smiled again, brushed his lips across Tabitha's, and escorted the Ythrian away. Silence lingered behind them, save for a soughing in the trees outside. Arinnian stood where he was. Draun fleered. Tabitha sought her pipes, chose one and began stuffing it. Her eyes held very closely on that task.

"Blame not me," Draun said. "I'd have halved him like his bald-skin fellow, if Hrill hadn't objected. Do you know she wouldn't let me make a goblet from the skull?" Tabitha stiffened.

"Well, tell me when you tire of his bouncing you," Draun continued. "I'll open his belly on Illarian's altar."

She swung to confront him. The scar on her cheek stood bonelike over the skin. "Are you asking me to end our partnership?" tore from her. "Or to challenge you?"

"Tabitha Falkayn may regulate her own life, Draun," Arinnian said.

"Ar-r-rkh, could be I uttered what I shouldn't," the other male growled. His plumage ruffled, his teeth flashed forth. "Yet how long must we sit in this cage of Terran ships?"

"As long as need be," Tabitha snapped, still pale and shivering. "Do you want to charge out and die for naught, witless as any saga hero? Or invite the warheads that kindle firestorms across a whole continent?"

"Why not? All dies at last." Draun grinned. "What glorious pyrotechnics to go out in! Better to throw Terra onto hell-wind, alight; but since we can't do that, unfortunately—"

"I'd sooner lose the war than kill a planet, any planet," Tabitha said. "As many times sooner as it has living creatures. And I'd sooner lose this planet than see it killed." She leveled her voice and looked straight at the Ythrian. "Your trouble is, the Old Faith reinforces every wish to kill that war has roused in you—and you've no way to do it."

Draun's expression said, *Maybe. At least I don't rut with the enemy.* He kept mute, though, and Tabitha chose not to watch him. Instead she turned to Arinnian. "Can you change that situation?" she asked. Her smile was almost timid.

He did not return it. "Yes," he answered. "Let me explain what we have in mind."

Since the ornithoids did not care to walk any considerable distance, and extended conversation was impossible in flight, Eyath first led Rochefort to the stables. After repeated visits in recent weeks she knew her way about. A few zirraukhs were kept there, and a horse for Tabitha. The former were smaller than the latter and resembled it only in being warm-blooded quadrupeds—they weren't mammals, strictly speaking—but served an identical purpose. "Can you outfit your beast?" she inquired.

"Yes, now I've lived here awhile. Before, I don't remember ever even seeing a horse outside of a zoo." His chuckle was perfunctory. "Uh, shouldn't we have asked permission?"

"Why? Chothfolk are supposed to observe the customs of their guests, and in Stormgate you don't ask to borrow when you're among friends."

"How I wish we really were."

She braced a hand against a stall in order to reach out a wing and gently stroke the pinions down his cheek.

They saddled up and rode side by side along a trail through the groves. Leaves rustled to the sea breeze, silvery-hued in that clear shadowless light. Hoofs plopped, but the damp air kept dust from rising.

"You're kind, Eyath," Rochefort said at last, awkwardly. "Most of the people have been. More, I'm afraid, than a nonhuman prisoner of war would meet on a human planet."

Eyath sought words. She was using Anglic, for the practice as much as the courtesy. But her problem here was to find concepts. The single phrase which came to her seemed a mere tautology: "One need not hate to fight."

"It helps. If you're human, anyway," he said wryly. "And that Draun—"

"Oh, he doesn't hate you. He's always thus. I feel . . . pity? . . . for his wife. No, not pity. That would mean I think her inferior, would it not? And she endures."

"Why does she stay with him?"

"The children, of course. And perhaps she is not unhappy. Draun must have his good points, since he keeps Hrill in partnership. Still, I will be much luckier in my marriage."

"Hrill—" Rochefort shook his head. "I fear I've earned the hate of your, uh, brother Christopher Holm."

Eyath trilled. "Clear to see, you're where he especially wanted to go. He bleeds so you can hear the splashes."

"You don't mind? Considering how close you two are."

"Well, I do not watch his pain gladly. But he will master it. Besides, I wondered if she might not bind him too closely." *Sheer off from there, lass.* Eyath regarded the man. "We gabble of what does not concern us. I would ask you about the stars you have been at, the spaces you have crossed, and what it is like to be a warrior yonder."

"I don't know," Tabitha said. "Sounds damned iffy."

"Show me the stratagem that never was," Arinnian replied. "Thing is, whether or not it succeeds, we'll have changed the terms of the fight. The Imperials will have no reason to bombard, good reason not to, and Avalon is spared." He glanced at Draun.

The fisher laughed. "Whether I wish that or not, akh?" he said. "Well, I think any scheme's a fine one which lets us kill Terrans personally."

"Are you sure they'll land where they're supposed to?" Tabitha wondered.

"No, of course we're not sure," Arinnian barked. "We'll do whatever we can to make that area their logical choice. Among other moves, we're arranging a few defections. The Terrans oughtn't to suspect they're due to us, because in fact it is not hard to get off this planet. Its defenses aren't set against objects traveling outward."

"Hm." Tabitha stroked her chin . . . big well-formed hand over square jaw, beneath heavy mouth. . . . "If *I* were a Terran intelligence officer and someone who claimed to have fled from Avalon brought me such a story, I'd put him under—what do they call that obscene gadget?—a hypnoprobe."

"No doubt." Arinnian's nod was jerky. "But these will be genuine defectors. My father has assigned shrewd men to take care of that. I don't know the details, but I can guess. We do have people who're panicked, or who want us to surrender because they're convinced we'll lose regardless. And we have more who feel that way in lesser degree, whom the first kind will trust. Suppose—well, suppose, for instance, we get President Vickery to call a potential traitor in for a secret discussion. Vickery explains that he himself wants to quit, it's political suicide for him to act openly, but he can help by arranging for certain persons to carry certain suggestions to the Terrans. Do you see? I'm not saying that's how it will be done—I really don't know how far we can trust Vickery—but we can leave the specifics to my father's men."

"And likewise the military dispositions which will make the yarn look plausible. Fine, fine," Draun gloated.

"That's what I came about," Arinnian said. "My mission's to brief the various home-guard leaders and get their efforts coordinated."

Rising from his chair, he started pacing, back and forth in front of Tabitha and never looking at her. "An extra item in your case," he went on, staccato. "It'd help tremendously if one of their own brought them the same general information."

Breath hissed between her teeth. Draun rocked forward, off his alatans, onto his toes.

"Yes," Arinnian said. "Your dear Philippe Rochefort. You tell him I'm here because I'm worried about Equatoria." He gave details. "Then I find some business in the neighbor islands and belt-flit with Eyath. Our boat stays behind, carelessly unguarded. You let him stroll freely around, don't you? His action is obvious."

Tabitha's pipestem broke in her grasp. She didn't notice the bowl fall, scattering ash and coals. "No," she said.

Arinnian found he needn't force himself to stop and glare at her as he did. "He's more to you than your world?"

"God stoop on me if ever I make use of him," she said.

"Well, if his noble spirit wouldn't dream of abusing your trust, what have you to fear?"

"I will not make my honor unworthy of his," said Hrill.

"That dungheart?" Draun gibed.

Her eyes went to him, her hand to a table beside her whereon lay a knife.

He took a backward step. "Enough," he muttered. It was a relief when the following stillness was broken. Someone banged on the door. Arinnian, being nearest, opened it. Rochefort stood there. Behind him were a horse and a zirraukh. He breathed unevenly and blood had retreated from under his dark skin.

"You were not to come back yet," Arinnian told him.

"Eyath—" Rochefort began.

"What?" Arinnian grabbed him by the shoulders. "Where is she?"

"I don't know. I . . . we were riding, talking. . . . Suddenly she screamed. Christ, I can't get that shriek out of my head. And she took off, her wings stormed, she disappeared past the treetops before I could call to her. I . . . I waited, till—"

Tabitha joined them. She started to push Arinnian aside, noticed his stance and how his fingers dug into Rochefort's flesh, and refrained. "Phil," she said low. "Darling, think. She must've heard something terrible. What was it?"

"I can't imagine." The Terran winced under Arinnian's grip but stayed where he was. "She'd asked me to, well, describe the space war. My experiences. I was telling her of the last fight before we crash-landed. You remember. I've told you the same."

"An item I didn't ask about?"

"Well, I, I did happen to mention noticing the insigne on the Avalonian boat, and she asked how it looked."

"And?"

"I told her. Shouldn't I have?"

"What was it?"

"Three gilt stars placed along a hyperbolic curve."

Arinnian let go of Rochefort. His fist smashed into the man's face. Rochefort lurched backward and fell to the ground. Arinnian drew his knife, started to pursue, curbed himself. Rochefort sat up, bewildered, bleeding at the mouth.

Tabitha knelt beside him. "You couldn't know, my dear," she said. Her own control was close to breaking. "What you told her was that her lover is dead."

✤XV✤

Night brought rising wind. The clouds broke apart into ragged masses, their blue-black tinged by the humpbacked Morgana which fled among them. A few stars blinked hazily in and out of sight. Surf threshed in darkness beyond the beach and trees roared in darkness ashore. The chill made humans go fully clothed.

Rochefort and Tabitha paced along the dunes. "Where *is* she?" His voice was raw.

"Alone," she answered.

"In this weather? When it's likely to worsen? Look, if Holm can go out searching, at least we—"

"They can both take care of themselves." Tabitha drew her cloak tight. "I don't think Chris really expects to find her, unless she wants to be found, and that's doubtful. He simply must do something. And he has to be away from us for a while. Her grief grieves him. It's typical Ythrian to do your first mourning by yourself."

"Saints! I've bugged things good, haven't I?"

He was a tall shadow at her side. She reached through an arm-slit, groped for and found the reality of his hand. "I tell you again, you couldn't know," she said. "Anyhow, best she learn like this, instead of dragging out more weeks or months, then never being sure he didn't die in some ghastly fashion. Now she knows he went out cleanly, too fast to feel, right after he'd won over a brave foe." She hesitated. "Besides, you didn't kill him. Our own attack did. You might say the war did, like an avalanche or a lightning stroke."

"The filthy war," he grated. "Haven't we had a gutful yet?"

Rage flared. She released him. "Your precious Empire can end it any time, you know."

"It has ended, except for Avalon. What's the sense of hanging on? You'll force them to bombard you into submission."

"Showing the rest of known space what kind of thing the Empire is. That could cost them a great deal in the long run." Tabitha's anger ebbed. *O Phil, my only!* "You know we're banking on their not being monsters, and on their having a measure of enlightened self-interest. Let's not talk about it more."

"I've got to. Tabby, you and Holm—but it's old Holm, of course, and a few other old men and Ythrians, who don't care how many young die as long as they're spared confessing their own stupid, senile willfulness—"

"Stop. Please."

"I can't. You're mounting some crazy new plan you think'll let your one little colony hold off all those stars. I say to the extent it works, it'll be a disaster. Because it may prolong the fight, sharpen it—No, I can't stand idly by and let you do that to yourself."

She halted. He did likewise. They peered at each other through the unrestful wan light. "Don't worry," she said. "We know what we're about."

"Do you? What is your plan?"

"I mustn't tell you that, darling."

"No," he said bitterly, "but you can let me lie awake nights, you can poison my days, with fear for you. Listen, I know a fair amount about war. And about the psychology of the Imperial high command. I could give you a pretty good guess at how they'd react to whatever you tried."

Tabitha shook her head. She hoped he didn't see her teeth catching her lip.

"Tell me," he insisted. "What harm can I do? And my advice— Or maybe you don't propose anything too reckless. If I could be sure of that—"

She could barely pronounce it: "Please. Please."

He laid hands on her shoulders. Moonlight fell into his eyes, making them blank pools. "If you love me, you will," he said.

She stood in the middle of the wind. *I can't lie to him. Can I? But I can't break my oath either. Can I?*

What Arinnian wanted me to tell him—

But I'm not testing you, Phil, Phil. I'm . . . choosing the lesser evil . . . because you wouldn't want your woman to break her oath, would you? I'm giving you what short-lived happiness I can, by an untruth that won't make any difference to your behavior. Afterward, when you learn, I'll kneel to ask your forgiveness.

She was appalled to hear from her throat: "Do we have your parole?"

"Not to use the information against you?" His voice checked for a fractional second. Waves hissed at his back. "Yes."

"Oh, no!" She reached for him. "I never meant—"

"Well, you have my word, sweetheart mine."

In that case—she thought. *But no, I couldn't tell him the truth before I'd consulted Arinnian, who'd be sure to say no, and anyhow Phil would be miserable, in terror for me and, yes, for his friends in their navy, whom honor would not let him try to warn.*

She clenched her fists, beneath the flapping cloak, and said hurriedly: "Well, in fact it's nothing fundamental. You know about Equatoria, the uninhabited continent. Nothing's there except a few thinly scattered emplacements and a skeleton guard. They mostly sit in barracks, because that few trying to patrol that much territory is pointless. Chris has been worried."

"Hm, yes, I've overheard him mention it to you."

"He's gotten his father to agree the defenses are inadequate. In particular, making a close study, they found the Scorpeluna tableland's wide open. Surrounding mountains, air turbulence, and so forth isolate it. An enemy who concentrated on breaking through the orbital fortresses and coming down fast—as soon as he was below fifty kilometers, he'd be shielded from what few rays we can project, and he could doubtless handle what few missiles and aircraft we could send in time. Once on the ground, dug in—you savvy? Bridgehead. We want to strengthen the area. That's all."

She stopped. Dizziness grabbed her. *Did I talk on a single breath?*

"I see," he responded after a while. "Thank you, dearest."

She came to him and kissed him, tenderly because of his hurt mouth.

Later that night the wind dropped, the clouds regathered, and rain fell, slow as tears. By dawn it was used up. Laura rose blindingly out of great waters, into utter blue, and every leaf and blade on the island was jeweled.

Eyath left the crag whereon she had perched the last few hours, after she could breast the weather no more. She was cold, wet, stiff at first. But the air blew keen into nostrils and antlibranchs, blood awoke, soon muscles were athrob.

Rising, rising, she thought, and lifted herself in huge upward spirals. The sea laughed but the island dreamed, and her only sound was the rush which quivered her pinions.

At your death, Vodan, you too were a sun.

Despair was gone, burned out by the straining of her wings, buffeted out by winds and washed out by rain, as he would have demanded of her. She knew the pain would be less quickly healed; but it was nothing she could not master. Already beneath it she felt the sorrow, like a hearthfire at which to warm her hands. Let a trace remain while she lived; let Vodan dwell on in her after she had come to care for another and give that later love his high-heartedness.

She tilted about. From this height she saw more than one island, strewn across the mercury curve of the world. *I don't want to return yet. Arinnian can await me till . . . dusk?* Hunger boiled in her. She had consumed a great deal of tissue. *Bless the pangs, bless this need to hunt—bless the chance, ha!*

Far below, specks, a flock of pteropleuron left their reef and scattered in search of piscoids near the water surface. Eyath chose her prey, aimed and launched herself. When she drew the membranes across her eyes to ward them, the world blurred and dimmed somewhat; but she grew the more aware of a cloven sky streaming and whistling around her; claws which gripped the bend of either wing came alive to every shift of angle, speed, and power.

Her body knew when to fold those wings and fall—when to open them again, brake in thunder, whip on upward—when and how her hands must strike. Her dagger was not needed. The reptiloid's neck snapped at the sheer violence of that meeting.

Vodan, you'd have joyed!

Her burden was handicapping; not heavy, it had nonetheless required wide foils to upbear it. She settled on an offshore rock, butchered the meat and ate. Raw, it had a mild, almost humble flavor. Surf shouted and spouted around her.

Afterward she flew inland, slowly now. She would seek the upper plantations and rest among trees and flowers, in sun-speckled shade; later she would go back aloft; and all the time she would remember Vodan. Since they had not been wedded, she could not lead his funeral dance; so today she would give him her own, their own.

She skimmed low above an orchard. Water, steaming off leaves and ground, made small white mists across the green, beneath the sun. Upwelling currents stroked her. She drank the strong odors of living earth through antlibranchs as well as lungs, until they made her lightheaded and started a singing in her blood. *Vodan,* she dreamed, *were you here beside me, we would flit off, none save us. We would find a place for you to hood me in your wings.*

It was as if he were. The beating that closed in from behind and above, the air suddenly full of maleness. Her mind spun. *Am I about to faint? I'd better set down.* She sloped unevenly and landed hard.

Orange trees stood around, not tall nor closely spaced, but golden lanterns glowed mysteriously in the deeps of their leafage. The soil was newly weeded and cultivated, bare to the sky. Its brown softness embraced her feet, damp, warmed by the sun that dazzled her. Light torrented down, musk and sweetness up, and roared.

Pinions blotted out Laura for a moment. The other descended. She knew Draun.

His crest stood stiff. Every quill around the grinning mouth said: *I hoped I might find you like this, after what's happened.*

"No," she whimpered, and spread her wings to fly.

Draun advanced stiffly over the ground, arms held wide and crook-fingered. "Beautiful, beautiful," he hawked. "Khr-r-r-r."

Her wings slapped. The inrush of air brought strength, but not her own strength. It was a different force that shook her as she might shake a prey.

"Vodan!" she yelled, and somehow flapped off the whirling earth. The lift was slow and clumsy. Draun reached up, hooked foot-claws around an alatan of hers; they tumbled together.

She scratched at his face and groped for her knife. He captured both wrists and hauled her against him. "You don't really want that, you she," his breath gusted in her ear. "Do you now?" He brought her arms around his neck and he himself hugged her. Spread, his wings again shut out the sun, before their plumes came over her eyes.

Her clasp held him close, her wings wrapped below his. She pressed her lids together so hard that dark was full of dancing formless lights. *Vodan,* passed somewhere amidst the noise, *I'll pretend he's you.*

But Vodan would not have gone away afterward, leaving her clawed, bitten, and battered for Arinnian to find.

Tabby was still asleep, Holm still looking for his poor friend, Draun lately departed with a remark about seeing if he couldn't help the retainers and fishers off on their various businesses. The compound lay quiet under the morning.

Rochefort stole back into the bedroom. She was among the few women he'd known who looked good at this hour. The tall body, the brown skin were too firm to sag or puff; the short fair locks tangled in a way that begged his fingers to play games. She breathed deeply, steadily, no snoring though the lips were a little parted over the whiteness beneath. When he bent above her, through bars of light and shade cast by the blind, she had no smell of sourness, just of girl. He saw a trace of dried tears.

His mouth twisted. The broken lip twinged less than his heart. She'd cried on *his* account, after they came home. "Of course you can't tonight, darling," she'd whispered, leaning over him on an elbow and running the other hand down cheek and breast and flank. "With this trouble, and you pulled ninety different ways, and everything. You'd be damned callous if you could, how 'bout that? Don't you cry. You don't know how, you make it too rough on yourself. Wait till tomorrow or the next night, Phil, beloved. We've got a lifetime."

A large subdivision of my hell was that I couldn't tell you why I was taking it so hard, he thought.

If I kiss you ... but you might wake and—O all you saints, St. Joan who burned for her people, help me!

The knowledge came that if he dithered too long, she would

indeed wake. He gave himself a slow count of one hundred before he slipped back out.

The roofs of the buildings, the peak beyond them, stood in impossible clarity against a sky which a pair of distant wings shared with the sun. The softest greens and umbers shone no less than the most brilliant red. The air was drenched in fragrances of growth and of the sea which tumbled beyond the breakwater. *No. This much beauty is unendurable.* Rochefort walked fast from the area, onto a trail among the orchards. Soon it would join the main road to the landing field.

I can't succeed. Someone'll be on guard; or I'll be unable to get in; or something'll happen and I'll simply have been out for a stroll. No harm in looking, is there?

Merely looking and returning for breakfast. No harm in that, except for letting her Avalonians be killed, maybe by millions, maybe including her—and, yes, my shipmates dying too—uselessly, for no reason whatsoever except pride—when maybe they can be saved. When maybe she'll see that I did what I did to end the war quickly that she might live.

The country lay hushed. Nobody had work on the plantations this time of year.

The landing field was deserted. For as scanty traffic as St. Li got, automated ground control sufficed.

The space flitter stood closed. Rochefort strangled on relief till he remembered: *Could be against no more than weather. They have no worries about thieves here.*

How about curious children?

If somebody comes along and sees me, I can explain I got worried about that. Tabby will believe me.

He wheeled a portable ramp, used for unloading cargo carriers, to the sleek hull. Mounting, his boots went knock . . . knock . . . knock. The entrance was similar to kinds he had known and he found immediately a plate which must cover an exterior manual control. It was not secured, it slid easily aside, and behind was nothing keyed to any individual or signal, only a button. He pressed it. The outer valve purred open and a gangway came forth like a licking tongue.

Father, show me Your will. Rochefort stepped across and inside.

The Ythrian vessel was quite similar to her Terran counterparts. No surprise, when you considered that the flying race learned spaceflight from man, and that on Avalon their craft must often carry humans. In the pilot room, seats and controls were adjustable for either species. The legends were in Planha, but Rochefort puzzled them out. After five minutes he knew he could lift and navigate this boat.

He smote palm into fist, once. Then he buckled down to work.

❖ XVI ❖

Arinnian carried Eyath back to the compound on foot. His gravbelt wouldn't safely raise them both and he left it behind. Twice she told him she could fly, or walk at any rate, but in such a weak whisper that he said, "No." Otherwise they did not speak, after the few words she had coughed against his breast while he knelt to hold her.

He couldn't carry that mass long in his arms. Instead, she clung to him, keelbone alongside his back, foot-claws curved over his shoulders, hugging his waist, like a small Ythrian child except that he must help her against the heaviness of the planet by his clasp on her alatans. He had cut his shirt into rags to sponge her hurts with rainwater off the leaves, and into bandages to stop further bleeding. The injuries weren't clinically serious, but it gave him something to use his knife on. Thus the warmth (the heat) and silk featheriness of her lay upon his skin; and the smell of her lovetime, like heavy perfume, was around him and in him.

That's the worst, he kept thinking. *The condition'll last for days—a couple of weeks, given reinforcement. If she encounters him again—*

Is she remorseful? How can she be, for a thing she couldn't halt? She's stunned, of course, harmed, dazed; but does she feel mortally befouled? Ought she to?

Suddenly I don't understand my galemate.

He trudged on. There had been scant rest for him during his search. He ached, his mouth was dry, his brain seemed full of sand. The world was a path he had to walk, so-and-so many kilometers long, except that the kilometers kept stretching. This naturally thinned the path still more, until the world had no room left for anything but a row of betrayals. He tried to shut out consciousness of them by reciting a childish chant in his head for the benefit of his feet. "You *pick* 'em *up* an' *lay* 'em *down*. You *pick* 'em *up*—" But this made him too aware of feet, how they hurt, knees, how they shivered, arms, how they burned, and perforce he went back to the betrayals. Terra-Ythri. Ythri-Avalon. Tabitha-Rochefort. Eyath-Draun, no, Draun-Eyath . . . Vodan-whatsername, that horrible creature in Centauri, yes, Quenna . . . Eyath-anybody, because right now she was anybody's . . . no, a person had self-control, forethought, a person could stay chaste if not preserve that wind-virginity which had been hers. . . . Those hands clasped on his belly, which had lain in his, had lately strained to pull Draun closer; that voice which had sung to him, and was now stilled, had moaned like the voice of any slut— *Stop that! Stop, I say!*

Sight of the compound jarred him back to a sort of reality. No one seemed about. Luck. He'd get Eyath safely put away. Ythrian chemists had developed an aerosol which effectively nullified the pheromones, and doubtless some could be borrowed from a neighbor. It'd keep the local males from strutting and gawking outside her room, till she'd rested enough to fly with him to the boat and thence home to Stormgate.

Tabitha's house stood open. She must have heard his footsteps and breath, for she came to the door. "Hullo," she called. "You found her? . . . Hoy!" She ran. He supposed once he would have appreciated the sight. "She okay?"

"No." He plodded inside. The coolness and shade belonged to a different planet.

Tabitha padded after. "This way," she suggested. "My bed."

"No!" Arinnian stopped. He would have shrugged if he weren't burdened. "Why not?"

Eyath lay down, one wing folded under her, the other spread wide so the pinions trailed onto the floor. The nictitating membranes made her appear blind. "Thank you." She could barely be heard.

"What happened?" Tabitha bent to see. The odor that a male Ythrian could catch across kilometers reached her. "Oh." She straightened. Her jaw set. "Yeh."

Arinnian sought the bathroom, drank glass after glass of cold water, showered beneath the iciest of the needlespray settings. That and a stimpill brought him back to alertness. Meanwhile Tabitha went in and out, fetching supplies for Eyath's care.

When they were both finished, they met in the living room. She put her lips close to his ear—he felt the tiny puffs of her words—to say very low, "I gave her a sedative. She'll be asleep in a few minutes."

"Good," he answered out of his hatred. "Where's Draun?"

Tabitha stepped back. The green gaze widened. "Why?"

"Can't you guess? Where is he?"

"Why do you want Draun?"

"To kill him."

"You won't!" she cried. "Chris, if it was him, they couldn't help themselves. Neither could. You know that. Shock and grief brought on premature ovulation, and then he chanced by—"

"He didn't chance by, that slime," Arinnian said. "Or if he did, he could've veered off from the first faint whiff he got, like any decent male. He most certainly didn't have to brutalize her. Where is he?"

Tabitha moved sidewise, in front of the phone. She had gone paler than when Draun mocked her. He shoved her out of his way. She resisted a moment, but while she was strong, she couldn't match him. "At home, you've guessed," Arinnian said. "A bunch of friends to hand, armed."

"To keep you from trying anything reckless, surely, surely," Tabitha pleaded. "Chris, we've a war. He's too important in the guard. We—If Phil were here you'd never—Must I go after a gun?"

He sat down. "Your stud couldn't prevent me calling from a different place," he snapped. She recoiled. "Nor could your silly gun. Be quiet."

He knew the number and stabbed it out. The screen came to life: Draun and, yes, a couple more in the background, blasters at their sides. The Ythrian spoke at once: "I expected this. Will you hear me? Done's done, and no harm in it. Choth law says not, in cases like this, save that a gild may be asked for wounded pride and any child must be provided for. There'll hardly be a brat, from this early in her season, and as for pride, she enjoyed herself." He grinned and stared past the man. "Didn't you, pretty-tail?"

Arinnian craned his neck around. Eyath staggered from the bedroom. Her eyes were fully open but glazed by the drug which had

her already half unconscious. Her arms reached toward the image in the screen. "Yes. Come," she croaked. "No. Help me, Arinnian. Help."

He couldn't move. It was Tabitha who went to her and led her back out of sight.

"You see?" Draun said. "No harm. Why, you humans can force your females, and often do, I've heard. I'm not built for that. Anyhow, what's one bit of other folk's sport to you, alongside your hundred or more each year?"

Arinnian had kept down his vomit. It left a burning in his gullet. His words fell dull and, in his ears, remote, though every remaining sense had become preternaturally sharp. "I saw her condition."

"Well, maybe I did get a bit excited. Your fault, really, you humans. We Ythrians watch your ways and begin to wonder. You grip my meaning? All right, I'll offer gild for any injuries, as certified by a medic. I'll even discuss a possible pride-payment, with her parents, that is. Are you satisfied?"

"No."

Draun bristled his crest a little. "You'd better be. By law and custom, you've no further rights in the matter."

"I'm going to kill you," Arinnian said.

"What? Wait a wingbeat! Murder—"

"Duel. We've witnesses here. I challenge you."

"You've no cause, I say!"

Arinnian could shrug, this time. "Then you challenge me."

"What for?"

The man sighed. "Need we plod through the formalities? Let me see, what deadly insults would fit? The vulgarism about what I can do when flying above you? No, too much a cliche. I'm practically compelled to present a simple factual description of your character, Draun. Thereto I will add that Highsky Choth is a clot of dung, since it contains such a maggot."

"Enough," the Ythrian said, just as quietly though his feathers stood up and his wings shuddered. "You are challenged. Before my gods, your gods, the memory of all our forebears and the hope of all our descent, I, Draun of Highsky, put you, Christopher Holm, called Arinnian of Stormgate, upon your deathpride to meet me in combat from which no more than one shall go alive. In the presence and honor of these witnesses whom I name—"

Tabitha came from behind. By force and surprise, she hauled Arinnian off his chair. He fell to the floor, bounced erect, and found her between him and the screen. Her left hand fended him off, her right was held as if likewise to keep away his enemy, her partner.

"Are you both insane?" she nearly screamed.

"The words have been uttered." Draun peeled his fangs. "Unless he beg grace of me."

"I would not accept a plea for grace from him," Arinnian said.

She stood panting, swinging her head from each to each. The tears poured down her face; she didn't appear to notice. After some seconds her arms dropped, her neck drooped.

"Will you hear me, then?" she asked hoarsely. They held still. Arinnian had begun to tremble under a skin turning cold. Tabitha's fists closed where they hung. "It's not to your honor that you let th-th-those persons your choths . . . Avalon . . . needs . . . be killed or, or crippled. Wait till war's end. I challenge you to do that."

"Well, aye, if I needn't meet nor talk to the Walker," Draun agreed reluctantly.

"If you mean we must cooperate as before," Arinnian said to Tabitha, "you'll have to be our go-between."

"How can she?" Draun jeered. "After the way you bespoke her choth."

"I think I can, somehow," Hrill sighed.

She stood back. The formula was completed. The screen blanked.

Strength poured from Arinnian. He turned to the girl and said, contrite, "I didn't mean that last. Of you I beg grace, to you I offer gild."

She didn't look his way, but sought the door and stared outward. *Toward her lover,* he thought vaguely. *I'll find a tree to rest beneath till Eyath rouses and I can transport her to the flitter.*

A crash rolled down the mountainside and rattled the windows. Tabitha grew rigid. The noise toned away, more and more faint as the thunderbolt fled upward. She ran into the court. "Phil!" she shouted. *Ah,* Arinnian thought. *Indeed. The next betrayal.*

"At ease, Lieutenant. Sit down."

The dark, good-looking young man stayed tense in the chair. Juan Cajal dropped gaze back to desk and rattled the papers in his hands. Silence brimmed his office cabin. *Valenderay* swung in orbit around

Pax at a distance which made that sun no more than the brightest of the stars, whose glare curtained Esperance where Luisa waited.

"I have read this report on you, including the transcription of your statements, with care, Lieutenant Rochefort," Cajal said finally, "long though it be. That's why I had you sent here by speedster."

"What can I add, sir?" The newcomer's voice was stiff as his body. However, when Cajal raised his look to meet those eyes again, he remembered a gentle beast he had once seen on Nuevo México, in the Sierra de los Bosques Secos, caught at the end of a canyon and waiting for the hunters.

"First," the admiral said, "I want to tender my personal apology for the hypnoprobing to which you were subjected when you rejoined our fleet. It was no way to treat a loyal officer."

"I understand, sir," Rochefort said. "I wasn't surprised, and the interrogators were courteous. You had to be sure I wasn't lying." Briefly, something nickered behind the mask. "To you."

"M-m, yes, the hypnoprobe evokes every last detail, doesn't it? The story will go no further, son. You saw a higher duty and followed."

"Why fetch me in person, sir? What little I had to tell must be in that report."

Cajal leaned back. He constructed a friendly smile. "You'll find out. First I need a bit of extra information. What do you drink?"

Rochefort started. "Sir?"

"Scotch, bourbon, rye, gin, tequila, vodka, akvavit, et cetera, including miscellaneous extraterrestrial bottles. What mixes and chasers? I believe we've a reasonably well-stocked cabinet aboard." When Rochefort sat dumb, Cajal finished: "I like a martini before dinner myself. We're dining together, you realize."

"I am? The, the admiral is most kind. Yes. A martini. Thanks."

Cajal called in the order. Actually he took a small sherry, on the rare occasions when he chose anything; and he suspected Rochefort likewise had a different preference. But it was important to get the boy relaxed.

"Smoke?" he invited. "I don't, but I don't mind either, and the governor gave me those cigars. He's a noted gourmet."

"Uh . . . thank you . . . not till after eating, sir."

"Evidently you're another." Cajal guided the chitchat till the cocktails arrived. They were large and cold. He lifted his. "*A vuestra salud, mi amigo.*"

"Your health—" The embryo of a smile lived half a second in Rochefort's countenance. "*Bonne santé, Monsieur l'Amiral.*"

They sipped. "Go ahead, enjoy," Cajal urged. "A man of your proven courage isn't afraid of his supreme boss. Your immediate captain, yes, conceivably; but not me. Besides, I'm issuing you no orders. Rather, I asked for what help and advice you care to give."

Rochefort had gotten over being surprised. "I can't imagine what, sir." Cajal set him an example by taking a fresh sip. Cajal's, in a glass that bore his crest, had been watered.

Not that he wanted Rochefort drunk. He did want him loosened and hopeful.

"I suppose you know you're the single prisoner to escape," the admiral said. "Understandable. They probably hold no more than a dozen or two, from boats disabled like yours, and you were fabulously lucky. Still, you may not know that we've been getting other people from Avalon."

"Defectors, sir? I heard about discontent."

Cajal nodded. "And fear, and greed, and also more praiseworthy motives, a desire to make the best of a hopeless situation and avoid further havoc. They've been slipping off to us, one by one, a few score total. Naturally, all were quizzed, even more thoroughly than you. Your psychoprofile was on record; Intelligence need merely establish it hadn't been tampered with."

"They wouldn't do that, sir," Rochefort said. Color returned to his speech. "About the worst immorality you can commit on Avalon is stripping someone else of his basic honor. That costs you yours." He sank back and took a quick swallow. "Sorry, sir."

"Don't apologize. You spoke in precisely the vein I wish. Let me go on, though. The first fugitives hadn't much of interest to tell. Of late—Well, no need for lectures. One typical case will serve. A city merchant, grown rich on trade with nearby Imperial worlds. *He* won't mind us taking over his planet, as long as the war doesn't ruin his property and the aftermath cost him extra taxes. Despicable, or realistic? No matter. The point is, he possessed certain information, and had certain other information given him to pass on, by quite highly placed officials who're secretly of the peace group."

Rochefort watched Cajal over the rim of his glass. "You fear a trap, sir?"

Cajal spread his palms. "The fugitives' sincerity is beyond doubt. But were they fed false data before they left? Your story is an important confirmation of theirs."

"About the Equatorian continent?" Rochefort said. "No use insulting the admiral's intelligence, I probably would not have tried to get away if I didn't believe what I'd heard might be critical. However, I know very little."

Cajal tugged his beard. "You know more than you think, son. For instance, our analysis of enemy fire patterns, as recorded at the first battle of Avalon, does indicate Equatoria is a weak spot. Now you were on the scene for months. You heard them talk. You watched their faces, faces of people you'd come to know. How concerned would you say they really were?"

"Um-m-m. . . ." Rochefort drank anew. Cajal unobtrusively pressed a button which signaled the demand for a refill for him. "Well, sir, the, the lady I was with, Equatoria was out of her department." He hastened onward: "Christopher Holm, oldest son of their top commander, yes, I'd say he worried about it a lot."

"What's the place like? Especially this, ah, Scorpeluna region. We're collecting what information we can, but with so many worlds around, who that doesn't live on them cares about their desert areas?"

Rochefort recommended a couple of books. Cajal didn't remind him that Intelligence's computers must have retrieved these from the libraries days or weeks ago. "Nothing too specific," the lieutenant went on. "I've gathered it's a large, arid plateau, surrounded by mountains they call high on Avalon, near the middle of the continent, which the admiral knows isn't big. Some wild game, perhaps, but no real hope of living off the country." He stopped for emphasis. "Counterattackers couldn't either."

"And they, who have oceans to cross, would actually be further from home than our people from our ships," Cajal murmured.

"A dangerous way down, sir."

"Not after we'd knocked out the local emplacements. And those lovely, sheltering mountains—"

"I thought along the same lines, sir. From what I know of, uh, available production and transportation facilities, and the generally sloppy Ythrian organization, they can't put strong reinforcements there fast. Whether or not my escape alarms them."

Cajal leaned over his desk. "Suppose we did it," he said. "Suppose we established a base for aircraft and ground-to-ground missiles. What do you think the Avalonians would do?"

"They'd have to surrender, sir," Rochefort answered promptly. "They . . . I don't pretend to understand the Ythrians, but the human majority—well, my impression is that they'll steer closer to a *Götterdämmerung* than we would, but they aren't crazy. If we're there, on land, if we can shoot at everything they have, not in an indiscriminate ruin of their beloved planet—that prospect is what keeps them at fighting pitch—but if we can do it selectively, laying our own bodies on the line—" He shook his head. "My apologies. That got tangled. Besides, I could be wrong."

"Your impressions bear out every xenological study I've seen," Cajal told him. "Furthermore, yours come from a unique experience." The new drink arrived. Rochefort demurred. Cajal said: "Please do take it. I want your free-wheeling memories, your total awareness of that society and environment. This is no easy decision. What you can tell me certainly won't make up my mind by itself. However, any fragment of fact I can get, I must."

Rochefort regarded him closely. "You want to invade, don't you, sir?" he asked.

"Of course. I'm not a murder machine. Neither are my superiors."

"I want us to. Body of Christ"—Rochefort signed himself before the crucifix—"how I want it!" He let his glass stand while he added: "One request, sir. I'll pass on everything I can. But if you do elect this operation, may I be in the first assault group? You'll need some Meteors."

"That's the most dangerous, Lieutenant," Cajal warned. "We won't be sure they have no hidden reserves. Therefore we can't commit much at the start. You've earned better."

Rochefort took the glass, and had it been literally that instead of vitryl, his clasp would have broken it. "I request precisely what I've earned, sir."

❖XVII❖

The Imperial armada englobed Avalon and the onslaught commenced.

Once more ships and missiles hurtled, energy arrows flew,

fireballs raged and died, across multiple thousands of kilometers. This time watchers on the ground saw those sparks brighten, hour by hour, until at last they hurt the eyes, turned the world momentarily livid and cast stark shadows. The fight was moving inward.

Nonetheless it went at a measured pace. Cajal had hastened his decision and brought in his power as fast as militarily possible—within days—lest the enemy get time to strengthen that vulnerable country of theirs. But now that he was here, he took no needless risks. Few were called for. This situation was altogether different from the last. He had well-nigh thrice his former might at hand, and no worries about what relics of the Avalonian navy might still skulk through the dark reaches of the Lauran System. Patrols reported instrumental indications that these were gathering at distances of one or two astronomical units. Since they showed no obvious intention of casting themselves into the furnace, he saw no reason to send weapons after them.

He did not even order the final demolition of Ferune's flagship, when the robots within knew their foe and opened fire. She was floating too distantly, she had too little ammunition or range left her, to be worth the trouble. It was easier to bypass the poor old hulk and the bones which manned her.

Instead he concentrated on methodically reducing the planetary defense. Its outer shell was the fortresses, some great, most small, on sentry-go in hundreds of orbits canted at as many angles to the ecliptic. They had their advantages *vis-a-vis* spaceships. They could be continually resupplied from below. Nearly all of them wholly automated, they were less versatile but likewise less fragile than flesh and nerve. A number of the least had gone undetected until their chance came to lash out at a passing Terran.

That, though, had been at the first battle. Subsequently the besieging sub-fleet had charted each, destroyed no few and fore-stalled attempts at replacement. Nor could the launching of salvos from the ground be again a surprise. And ships in space had their own advantages, e.g., mobility.

Cajal's general technique was to send squadrons by at high velocity and acceleration. As they entered range of a target they unleashed what they had and immediately applied unpredictable vectors to escape return fire. If the first pass failed, a second quickly followed, a third, a fourth . . . until defense was saturated and the station exploded in vapor and shards. Having no cause now to protect his rear or his supply lines, Cajal could be lavish with munitions, and was.

Spacecraft in that kind of motion were virtually hopeless goals for missiles which must rise through atmosphere, against surface gravity, from zero initial speed. The Avalonians soon realized as much and desisted for the time being.

Cajal's plan did not require the preliminary destruction of every orbital unit. That would have been so expensive that he would have had to hang back and wait for more stocks from the Empire; and he was in a hurry. He did decide it was necessary to neutralize the moon, and for a while Morgana was surrounded and struck by such furies that mountains crumbled and valleys ran molten.

Otherwise, on the whole, the Imperials went after those fortresses which, in their ever-changing configurations, would menace his first landing force on the date set by his tactical scheme. In thus limiting his objective, he was enabled to focus his full energies sharply. Those incandescent hours, running into a pair of Avalonian days, were the swiftest penetration ever made of defenses that strong.

Inevitably, he took losses. The rate grew when his ships started passing so close above the atmosphere that ground-based projectors and missile sites became effective. The next step was to nullify certain of these, together with certain other installations.

Captain Ion Munteanu, commanding fire control aboard H.M.S. *Phobos,* briefed his officers while the ship rushed forward.

"Ours is a special mission, as you must have guessed from this class of vessel being sent. We aren't just going to plaster a spot that's been annoying the boys. We're after a city. I see a hand. Question, Ensign Ozumi?"

"Yes, sir. Two. How and why? We can loose enough torps and decoys, sophisticated enough, that if we keep it up long enough, a few are bound to duck in and around the negafields and burst where they'll do some good. That's against a military target. But surely they've given their cities better protection than that."

"I remind you about eggs and grandmothers, Ensign. Of course they have. Powerful, complicated set-ups, plus rings of exterior surface-to-space launchers. We'll be firing our biggest and best, programmed for detonation at high substratospheric altitude. The pattern I'm about to diagram should allow one, at least, to reach that level before it's intercepted. If not, we start over."

"Sir! You don't mean a continent buster!"

"No, no. Calm down. Remember this ship couldn't accommodate any. We have no orders to damage His Majesty's real estate beyond repair. Ours will be heavy brutes, true, but clean, and shaped to discharge their output straight ahead, mainly in the form of radiation. Blast wouldn't help much against the negafields. We'll whiff the central part of town, and Intelligence tells me the fringes are quite flammable."

"Sir, I don't want to annoy you, but why do we do it?"

"Not wantonly, Ozumi. A landing is to be made. Planetside warfare may go on for a while. This particular town, Centauri they call it, is their chief seaport and industrial capital. We are not going to leave it to send stuff against our friends."

Sweat stood on Ozumi's brow. "Women and children—"

"If the enemy has any sense, he evacuated nonessential persons long ago," Munteanu snapped. "Frankly, I don't give a curse. I lost a brother here, last time around. If you're through sniveling, let's get to work."

Quenna flapped slowly above the Livewell Street canal. Night had fallen, a clear night unlike most in the Delta's muggy winters. Because of that and the blackout, she could see stars. They frightened her. Too many of the cold, nasty little things. And they weren't only that, she was told. They were suns. War came from them, war that screwed up the world.

Fine at first, lots of Ythrians passing through, jingle in their purses, moments when she forgot all except the beauty of the male and her love for him; in between, she could afford booze and dope to keep her happy, especially at parties. Parties were a human idea, she'd heard. (Who was it had told her? She tried to remember the face, the body. She would be able to, if they didn't blur off into the voices and music and happy-making smoke.) A good idea. Like war had seemed. Love, love, love, laugh, laugh, laugh, sleep, sleep, sleep, and if you wake with your tongue tasting bad and needles in your head, a few pills will soon put you right.

Except it went sour. No more navy folk. The Nest empty, a cave, night after night after night, till a lass was ready to scream except that the taped music did that for her. Most humans moving out, too, and those who stayed—she'd even have welcomed human company—keeping underground. The black, quiet nights, the buzzing aloneness by day, the money bleeding off till she could barely buy food, let alone a bottle or a pill to hold off the bad dreams.

Flap, flap. Somebody must be in town and lonesome, now the fighting had started again. "I'm lonesome too," she called. "Whoever you are, I love you." Her voice sounded too loud in this unmoving warm air, above these oily waters and dead pavements, between those shadowy walls and beneath those terrible little stars.

"Vodan?" she called more softly. She remembered him best of the navy folk, almost as well as the first few who had used her, more years back than she cared to count. He'd been gentle and bothered about his lass at home, as if that dragglewing deserved him. But she was being silly, Quenna was. No doubt the stars had eaten Vodan.

She raised her crest. She had her deathpride. She would not be frightened in the midnight streets. Soon dawn would break and she could dare sleep.

The sun came very fast.

She had an instant when it filled the sky. Night caught her then, as her eyeballs melted. She did not know this, because her plumage was on fire. Her scream drowned out the following boom, when superfast molecules of air slipped by the negafields, and she did not notice how it ruptured eardrums and smashed capillaries. In her delirium of pain, there was nothing except the canal. She threw herself toward it, missed, and fell into a house which stood in one blaze. That made no difference, since the canal waters were boiling.

Apart from factors of morale and war potential, the strike at Centauri must commit a large amount of Avalonian resources to rescue and relief. It had been well timed. A mere three hours later, the slot which had been prepared in the defenses completed itself and the first wave of invasion passed through.

Rochefort was in the van. He and his hastily assembled crew had

had small chance to practice, but they were capable men and the Meteor carried out her assignment with an *elan* he wished he could feel. They ran interference for the lumbering gunships till these were below the dangerous altitude. En route, they stopped a pair of enemy missiles. Though no spacecraft was really good in atmosphere, a torpedo boat combined acceptable maneuverability, ample firepower, and more than ample wits aboard. Machines guided by simple robots were no match.

Having seen his charges close to ground, Rochefort took his vessel, as per assignment, against the source of the missiles. It lay beyond the mountains, in the intensely green gorge of a river. The Terran boats roared one after the next, launched beams and torpedoes against negafields and bunkers, stood on their tails and sprang to the stratosphere, swept about and returned for the second pass. No third was needed. A set of craters gaped between cliffs which sonic booms had brought down in rubble. Rochefort wished he could forget how fair that canyon had been.

Returning to Scorpeluna, he found the whole convoy landed. Marines and engineers were swarming from personnel transports, machines from the freighters. Overhead, patrol craft darkened heaven. They were a frantic few days that followed. Hysteria was never far below the skin of purposeful activity. Who knew for certain what the enemy had?

Nothing came. The screen generators were assembled and started. Defensive projectors and missiles were positioned. Sheds were put together for equipment, afterward for men. And no counterattack was made.

Airborne scouts and spaceborne instruments reported considerable enemy activity on the other continents and across the islands. Doubtless something was being readied. But it didn't appear to pose any immediate threat.

The second slot opened. The second wave flowed down, entirely unopposed. Scorpeluna Base spread like an ink-blot.

His intention now being obvious, Cajal had various other orbital fortresses destroyed, in order that slots come more frequently. Thereafter he pulled his main fleet back a ways. From it he poured men and equipment groundward.

The last Avalonian ships edged nearer, fled from sorties,

returned to slink about, wolves too starveling to be a menace. No serious effort was wasted on them. The essential was to exploit this tacit cease-fire while it lasted. On that account, the Imperials everywhere refrained from offensive action. They worked at digging in where they were and at building up their conquest until it could not merely defend itself, it could lift an irresistible fist above all Avalon.

Because he was known to have the favor of the grand admiral, Lieutenant Philippe Rochefort (newly senior grade) got his application for continued planetside duty approved. Since there was no further call for a space torpedo craft, he found himself flying aerial patrol in a two-man skimmer, a glorified gravsled.

His assigned partner was a marine corporal, Ahmed Nasution, nineteen standard years old, fresh off New Djawa and into the corps. "You know, sir, everybody told me this planet was a delight," he said, exaggerating his ruefulness to make sure his superior got the point. "Join the navy and see the universe, eh?"

"This area isn't typical," Rochefort answered shortly.

"What is," he added, "on an entire world?"

The skimmer flew low above the Scorpelunan plateau. The canopy was shut against broiling air. A Hilsch tube arrangement and self-darkening vitryl did their inadequate best to combat that heat, brazen sky, bloated and glaring sun. The only noises were hum of engine, whirr of passage. Around the horizon stood mountain peaks, dim blue and unreal. Between reached emptiness. Bushes, the same low, reddish-leaved, medicinal-smelling species wherever you looked, grew widely apart on hard red earth. The land was not really flat. It raised itself in gnarly mesas and buttes, it opened in great dry gashes. At a distance could be seen a few six-legged beasts, grazing in the shade of their parasol membranes. Otherwise nothing stirred save heat shimmers and dust devils.

"Any idea when we'll push out of here?" Nasution asked, reaching for a water bottle.

"When we're ready," Rochefort told him. "Easy on the drink. We've several hours to go, you and I."

"Why doesn't the enemy give in, sir? A bunch of us in my tent caught a 'cast of theirs—no orders not to, are there?—a 'cast in Anglic. I couldn't understand it too well, their funny accent and, uh, phrases like 'the Imperials have no more than a footgrip,' you have to stop and figure them out and meanwhile the talking goes on. But Gehenna, sir, we don't *want* to hurt them. Can't they be reasonable and—"

"Sh!" Rochefort lifted an arm. His monitoring radio identified a call. He switched to that band.

"*Help! O God, help!*—Engineer Group Three . . . wild animals . . . estimate thirty-four kilometers north-northwest of camp—*Help!*"

Rochefort slewed the skimmer about.

He arrived in minutes. The detail, ten men in a groundcar, had been running geological survey to determine the feasibility of blasting and fuse-lining a large missile silo. They were armed, but had looked for no troubles except discomfort. The pack of dog-sized hexapodal lopers found them several hundred meters from their vehicle.

Two men were down and being devoured. Three had scattered in terror, seeking to reach the car, and been individually surrounded. Rochefort and Nasution saw one overwhelmed. The rest stood firm, back to back, and maintained steady fire. Yet those scaly-bristly shapes seemed almost impossible to kill. Mutilated, they dragged their jaws onward.

Rochefort yelled into his transmitter for assistance, swooped, and cut loose. Nasution wept but did good work at his gun. Nevertheless, two more humans were lost before the lycosauroids had been slain.

After that, every group leaving camp got an aerial escort, which slowed operations elsewhere.

"No, Doctor, I've stopped believing it's psychogenic." The major glanced out of the dispensary shack window, to an unnaturally swift sunset which a dust storm made the color of clotted blood. Night would bring relief from the horrible heat . . . in the form of inward-gnawing chill. "I was ready to believe that at first. Your psychodrugs aren't helping any longer, though. And more and more men are developing the symptoms, as you must know better than I. Bellyache, diarrhea, muscle pains, more thirst than this damned dryness will account for. Above all, tremors and fuzzy-headedness. I hate to tell you how necessary a job I botched today."

"I'm having my own troubles thinking." The medical officer

passed a hand across his temple. It left a streak of grime, despite the furnace air sucking away sweat before that could form drops. "Frequent, blurred vision too? Yes."

"Have you considered a poison in the environment?"

"Certainly. You weren't in the first wave, Major. I was. Intelligence, as well as history, assured us Avalon is acceptably safe. Still, take my word, we'd scarcely established camp when the scientific team was checking."

"How about quizzing Avalonian prisoners?"

"I'm assured this was done. In fact, there've been subsequent commando operations just to collect more for that purpose. But how likely are any except a few specialists to know details about the most forbidding part of a whole continent that nobody inhabits?"

"And of course the Avalonians would have all those experts safely tucked out of reach." The major gusted a weary breath. "So what did your team find?"

The medical officer groped for a stimpill out of the open box on his desk. "There is a, ah, high concentration of heavy metals in local soil. But nothing to worry about. You could breathe the dust for years before you'd require treatment. The shrubs around use those elements in their metabolism, as you'd expect, and we've warned against chewing or burning any part of them. No organic compounds test out as allergens. Look, human and Ythrian biochemistries are so similar the races can eat most of each other's food. If this area held something spectacularly deadly, don't you imagine the average colonist would have heard of it, at least? I'm from Terra—middle west coast of North America—oh, Lord—" For a while his gaze was gone from Scorpeluna. He shook himself. "We lived among oleanders. We cultivated them for their flowers. Oleanders are poisonous. You just need to be sensible about them."

"This has got to have some cause," the major insisted.

"We're investigating," the medic said. "If anyone had foreseen this planet would amount to anything militarily—it'd have been studied before ever we let a war happen, so thoroughly—Too late."

Occasional small boats from the Avalonian remnants slipped among the Terran blockaders at high velocity and maximum variable acceleration. About half were destroyed; the rest got through and returned spaceward. It was known that they exchanged messages with the ground. Given suitable encoding and laser beams, a huge amount of information can be passed in a second or two.

"Obviously they're discussing a move," Cajal snarled at his staff. "Equally obviously, if we try to hunt them, they'll scatter and vanish in sheer distance, sheer numbers of asteroids and moons, same's they did before. And they'll have contingency plans. I do not propose to be diverted, gentlemen. We shall keep our full strength here."

For a growing body of observations indicated that, on land and sea, under sea and in their skies, the colonists were at last making ready to strike back.

Rochefort heard the shrieking for the better part of a minute before it registered on him. *Dear Jesus,* dragged through his dullness, *what ails me?* His muscles protested bringing the skimmer around. His fingers were sausages on the control board. Beside him, Nasution slumped mute, as the boy had been these past days (weeks? years?). The soft cheeks had collapsed and were untidily covered by black down.

Still, Rochefort's craft arrived to help those which had been floating above a ground patrol. The trouble was, it could then do no more than they. Energy weapons incinerated at a flash hundreds of the cockroach-like things, twenty centimeters long, whose throngs blackened the ground between shrubs. They could not save the men whom these bugs had already reached and were feasting on. Rochefort carefully refrained from noting which skimmer pilots gave, from above, a *coup de grace.* He himself hovered low and hauled survivors aboard. After what he had seen, in his present physical shape, Nasution was too sick to be of use.

Having evidently gotten wind of meat in this hungry land, the kakkelaks swarmed toward the main base. They couldn't fly, but they clattered along astonishingly fast. Every effort must go to flaming a cordon against them.

Meanwhile the Avalonians landed throughout Equatoria. They deployed so quickly and widely—being very lightly equipped—that bombardment would have been futile. All who entered Scorpeluna were Ythrian.

✲ ✲ ✲

The chief officers of medicine and planetology confronted their commandant. Outside, an equinoctial gale bellowed and rang through starless night; dust scoured over shuddering metal walls. The heat seemed to come in enormous dry blasts.

"Yes, sir," the medical chief said. Being regular navy rather than marine, he held rear admiral's rank. "We've proven it beyond reasonable doubt." He sighed, a sound lost in the noise. "If we'd had better equipment, more staff—Well, I'll save that for the board of inquiry, or the court-martial. The fact is, poor information got us sucked into a death trap."

"Too many worlds." The civilian planetologist shook his gaunt head. "Each too big. Who can know?"

"While you gabble," the commandant said, "men lie in delirium and convulsions. More every day. Talk." His voice was rough with anger and incomplete weeping.

"We suspected heavy-metal poisoning, of course," the medical officer said, "We made repeated tests. The concentration always seemed within allowable limits. Then overnight—"

"Never mind that," the planetologist interrupted. "Here are the results. These bushes growing everywhere around . . . we knew they take up elements like arsenic and mercury. And the literature has described the hell shrub, with pictures, as giving off dangerous vapors. What we did not know is that here *is* a species of hell shrub. It looks entirely unlike its relatives. Think of roses and apples. Besides, we'd no idea how the toxin of the reported kind works, let alone these. That must have been determined after the original descriptions were published, when a purely organic compound was assumed. The volume of information in every science, swamping—" His words limped to a halt.

The commandant waited.

The medical officer took the tale: "The vapors carry the metals in loose combination with a . . . a set of molecules, unheard of by any authority I've read. Their action is, well, they block certain enzymes. In effect, the body's protections are canceled. No metal atoms whatsoever are excreted. Every microgram goes to the vital organs. Meanwhile the patient is additionally weakened by the fact that parts of his protein chemistry aren't working right. The effects are synergistic and exponential. Suddenly one crosses a threshold."

"I . . . see . . ." the commandant said.

"We top officers aren't in too bad a condition yet," the planetologist told him. "Nor are our staffs. We spend most of our time indoors. The men, though—" He rubbed his eyes. "Not that I'd call myself a well man," he mumbled.

"What do you recommend?" the commandant asked.

"Evacuation," the medical chief said. "And I don't recommend it, I tell you we have no alternative. Our people must get immediate proper care."

The commandant nodded. Himself sick, monstrously tired, he had expected some such answer days ago and started his quiet preparations.

"We can't lift off tomorrow," he said in his dragging tones. "We haven't the bottom; most's gone back to space. Besides, a panicky flight would make us a shooting gallery for the Avalonians. But we'll organize to raise the worst cases, while we recall everybody to the main camp. We'll have more ships brought down, in orderly fashion." He could not control the twitch in his upper lip.

As the Imperials retreated, their enemies struck.

They fired no ground-to-ground missiles. Rather, their human contingents went about the construction of bases which had this capability, at chosen spots throughout the Equatorian continent. It was not difficult. They were only interested in short-range weapons, which needed little more than launch racks, and in aircraft, which needed little more than maintenance shacks for themselves and their crews. The largest undertaking was the assembly of massive energy projectors in the peaks overlooking Scorpeluna.

Meanwhile the Ythrians waged guerrilla warfare on the plateau. They, far less vulnerable to the toxicant peculiar to it, were in full health and unburdened by the spacesuits, respirators, handkerchiefs which men frantically donned. Already winged, they need not sit in machines which radar, gravar, magnetoscopes could spot across kilometers. Instead they could dart from what cover the ground afforded, spray a trudging column with fire and metal, toss grenades at a vehicle, sleet bullets through any skimmers, and be gone before effective reaction was possible.

Inevitably, they had their losses.

"Hya-a-a-ah!" yelled Draun of Highsky, and swooped from a crag down across the sun-blaze. At the bottom of a dry ravine, a Terran column stumbled toward camp from a half-finished emplacement. Dust turned every man more anonymous than what was left of his uniform. A few armored groundcars trundled among them, a few aircraft above. A gravsled bore rapidly mummifying corpses, stacked.

"Cast them onto hell-wind!" The slugthrower stuttered in Draun's grasp. Recoil kept trying to hurl him off balance, amidst these wild thermals. He gloried that his wings were too strong and deft for that.

The Ythrians swept low, shooting, and onward. Draun saw men fall like emptied sacks. Wheeling beyond range, he saw their comrades form a square, anchored by its cars and artillery, helmeted by its flyers. *They're still brave,* he thought, and wondered if they hadn't best be left alone. But the idea had been to push them into close formation, then on the second pass drop a tordenite bomb among them. "Follow me!"

The rush, the bullets and energy bolts, the appallingly known wail at his back. Draun braked, came about, saw Nyesslan, his oldest son, the hope of his house, spiral to ground on a wing and a half. The Ythrian squadron rushed by. "*I'm coming, lad!*" Draun glided down beside him. Nyesslan lay unconscious. His blood purpled the dust. The second attack failed, broke up in confusion before it won near to the square. True to doctrine, that they should hoard their numbers, the Ythrians beat back out of sight. A platoon trotted toward Draun. He stood above Nyesslan and fired as long as he was able.

"Take out everything they have remaining in orbit," Cajal said. "We need freedom to move our transports continuously."

His chief of staff cleared throat. "Hr-r-rm, the admiral knows about the hostile ships?"

"Yes. They're accelerating inward. It's fairly clear that all which can make planetfall hope to do so; the rest are running interference."

"Shouldn't we organize an interception?"

"We can't spare the strength. Clearing away those forts will empty most of our magazines. Our prime duty is to pull our men out of that mess we . . . I . . . sent them into." Cajal stiffened himself. "If any units can reasonably be spared from the orbital work, yes, let them collect what Avalonians they can, provided they conserve munitions to the utmost and rely mainly on energy weapons. I doubt they'll get many. The rest we'll have to let go their ways, perhaps to our sorrow." His chuckle clanked. "As old Professor Wu-Tai was forever saying at the Academy—remember, Jim?—'The best foundation that a decision is ever allowed is our fallible assessment of the probabilities.'"

The tropical storms of Avalon were more furious than one who came from a planet of less irradiation and slower spin could well have imagined. For a day and a night, the embarkation of the sickest men was postponed. Besides the chance of losing a carrier, there was a certainty that those flensing rains would kill some of the patients as they were borne from shacks to gangways.

The more or less hale, recently landed, battled to erect levees. Reports, dim and crackling through radio static, were of flash floods leaping down every arroyo.

Neither of these situations concerned Rochefort. He was in an intermediate class, too ill for work, too well for immediate removal. He huddled on a chair among a hundred of his fellows, in a stinking, steaming bunker, tried to control the chills and nausea that went ebb-and-flow through him, and sometimes thought blurrily of Tabitha Falkayn and sometimes of Ahmed Nasution, who had died three days before.

What Avalonian spacecraft ran the gauntlet descended to Equatoria, where home-guard officers assigned them their places.

The storm raged to its end. The first Imperial vessels lifted from the wrecked base. They were warships, probing a way for the crammed, improvised hospital hulls which were to follow. Sister fighters moved in from orbit to join them.

Avalon's ground and air defenses opened crossfire. Her space force entered battle.

Daniel Holm sat before a scanner. It gave his words and his skull visage to the planet's most powerful linked transmitters, a broadcast which could not fail to be heard:

"—we're interdicting their escape route. You can't blast us in time to save what we estimate as a quarter million men. Even if we didn't resist, maybe half of them would never last till you brought them to adequate care. And I hate to think about the rest—organ, nerve, brain damage beyond the power of regenerative techniques to heal.

"*We* can save them. We of Avalon. We have the facilities prepared, clear around our planet. Beds, nursing staffs, diagnostic equipment, chelating drugs, supportive treatments. We'd welcome your inspection teams and medical personnel. Our wish is not to play political games with living people. The minute you agree to renew the ceasefire and to draw your fleet far enough back that we can count on early warning, that same minute our rescue groups will take flight for Scorpeluna."

✸XVIII✸

The ward was clean and well-run, but forty men must be crowded into it and there was no screen—not that local programs would have interested most of them. Hence they had no entertainment except reading and bitching. A majority preferred the latter. Before long, Rochefort asked for earcups in order that he might be able to use the books lent him. He wore them pretty much around the clock.

Thus he did not hear the lickerish chorus. His first knowledge came from a touch on his shoulder. *Huh?* he thought. *Lunch already?* He raised his eyes from *The Gaiila Folk* and saw Tabitha.

The heart sprang in him and raced. His hands shook so he could barely remove the cups.

She stood athwart the noisy, antiseptic-smelling room as if her only frame were a window behind, open to the blue and blossoms of springtime. A plain coverall disguised the curves and straightness of her. He saw in the countenance that she had lost weight. Bones stood forth still more strongly than erstwhile, under a skin more darkened and hair more whitened by a stronger sun than shone over Gray.

"Tabby," he whispered, and reached.

She took his hands, not pressing them nor smiling much. "Hullo, Phil," said the remembered throaty voice. "You're looking better'n I expected, when they told me you'd three tubes in you."

"You should have seen me at the beginning." He heard his words waver. "How've you been? How's everybody?"

"I'm all right. Most of those you knew are. Draun and Nyesslan bought it."

"I'm sorry," he lied.

Tabitha released him. "I'd have come sooner," she said, "but had to wait for furlough, and then it took time to get a data scan on those long lists of patients and time to get transportation here. We've a lot of shortages and disorganization yet." Her regard was green and grave. "I did feel sure you'd be on Avalon, dead or alive. Good to learn it was alive."

"How could I stay away . . . from you?"

She dropped her lids. "What is your health situation? The staff's too busy to give details."

"Well, when I'm stronger they want to ship me to a regular Imperial navy hospital, take out my liver and grow me a new one. I may need a year, Terran, to recover completely. They promise me I will."

"Splendid." Her tone was dutiful. "You being well treated here?"

"As well as possible, considering. But, uh, my roommates aren't exactly my type and the medics and helpers, both Imperial and Avalonian, can't stop their work for conversation. It's been damned lonesome, Tabby, till you came."

"I'll try to visit you again. You realize I'm on active duty, and most of what leave I'm granted has to be spent at St. Li, keeping the business in shape."

Weakness washed through him. He leaned back into the pillows and let his arms fall on the blanket. "Tabby . . . would you consider waiting . . . that year?"

She shook her head, slowly, and again met his stare. "Maybe I ought to pretend till you're more healed, Phil. But I'm no good at pretending, and besides, you rate better."

"After what I did—"

"And what I did." She leaned down and felt past the tubes to lay palms on his shoulders. "No, we've never hated on that account, have we, either of us?"

"Then can't we both forgive?"

"I believe we've already done it. Don't you see, though? When the hurting had died down to where I could think, I saw there wasn't anything left. Oh, friendship, respect, memories to cherish. And that's all."

"It isn't enough . . . to rebuild on?"

"No, Phil. I understand myself better than I did before. If we tried, I know what sooner or later I'd be doing to you. And I won't. What we had, I want to keep clean."

She kissed him gently and raised herself.

They talked awhile longer, embarrassed, until he could dismiss her on the plea, not entirely untruthful, that he needed rest. When she was gone he did close his eyes, after donning the earcups which shut out the Terran voices.

She's right, probably, he thought. *And my life isn't blighted. I'll get over this one too, I suppose.* He recalled a girl in Fleurville and hoped he would be transferred to an Esperancian hospital, when or if the cease-fire became a peace.

Outside, Tabitha stopped to put on the gravbelt she had retrieved from the checkroom. The building had been hastily erected on the outskirts of Gray. (She remembered the protests when Marchwarden Holm diverted industrial capacity from war production to medical facilities, at a time when renewed combat seemed imminent. Commentators pointed out that what he had ordered was too little for the casualties of extensive bombardment, too much for those of any plausible lesser-scale affray. He had growled, "We do what we can," and rammed the project through. It helped that the principal home-guard officers urged obedience to him. They knew what he really had in mind—these men whose pain kept the weapons uneasily silent.) Where she stood, a hillside sloped downward, decked with smaragdine susin, starred with chasuble bush and Buddha's cup, to the strewn and begardened city, the huge curve of uprising shoreline, the glitter on Falkayn Bay. Small cottony clouds sauntered before the wind, which murmured and smelled of livewell.

She inhaled that coolness. After Equatoria, it was intoxicating. Or it ought to be. She felt curiously empty.

Wings boomed. An Ythrian landed before her. "Good flight to you, Hrill," the female greeted.

Tabitha blinked. Who—? Recognition came. "Eyath! To you,

good landing." *How dull her tone, how sheenless her plumes. I haven't seen her since that day on the island. . . .* Tabitha caught a taloned hand in both of hers. "This is wonderful, dear. Have you been well?"

Eyath's stance and feathers and membranes drawn over her eyes gave answer. Tabitha hunkered down and embraced her.

"I sought you," Eyath mumbled. "I spent the battle at home; afterward too, herding, because I needed aloneness and they told me the planet needs meat." Her head lay in Tabitha's bosom. "Lately I've been freed of that and came to seek—"

Tabitha stroked her back, over and over.

"I learned where you were posted and that you'd mentioned you would stop in Gray on your furlough," Eyath went on. "I waited. I asked of the hotels. Today one said you had arrived and gone out soon after. I thought you might have come here, and trying was better than more waiting."

"What little I can do for you, galemate, tell me."

"It is hard." Eyath clutched Tabitha's arms, painfully, without raising her head. "Arinnian is here too. He has been for some while, working on his father's staff. I sought him and—" A strangled sound, though Ythrians do not weep.

Tabitha foresaw: "He avoids you."

"Yes. He tries to be kind. That is the worst, that he must try."

"After what happened—"

"Ka-a-a-ah. I am no more the same to him." Eyath gathered her will. "Nor to myself. But I hoped Arinnian would understand better than I do."

"Is he the solitary one who can help? What of your parents, siblings, chothmates?"

"They have not changed toward me. Why should they? In Stormgate a, a misfortune like mine is reckoned as that, a misfortune, no disgrace, no impairment. They cannot grasp what I feel."

"And you feel it because of Arinnian. I see." Tabitha looked across the outrageously lovely day. "What can I do?"

"I don't know. Maybe nothing. Yet if you could speak to him— explain—beg grace of him for me—"

Anger lifted. "*Beg* him? Where is he?"

"At work, I, I suppose. His home—"

"I know the address." Tabitha released her and stood up.

"Come, lass. No more talk. We're off for a good hard flight in this magnificent weather, and I'll take advantage of being machine-powered to wear you out, and at day's end we'll go to wherever you're staying and I'll see you asleep."

—Twilight fell, saffron hues over silver waters, elsewhere deep blue and the earliest stars. Tabitha landed before Arinnian's door. His windows glowed. She didn't touch the chime plate, she slammed a panel with her fist.

He opened. She saw he had also grown thin, mahogany hair tangled above tired features and disheveled clothes. "Hrill!" he exclaimed. "Why . . . I never—Come in, come in."

She brushed past him and whirled about. The chamber was in disarray, obviously used only for sleeping and bolted meals. He moved uncertainly toward her. Their contacts had been brief, correct, and by phone until the fighting began. Afterward they verified each other's survival, and that was that.

"I'm, I'm glad to see you, Hrill," he stammered.

"I don't know as I feel the same," she rapped. "Sit down. I've got things to rub your nose in, you sanctimonious mudbrain."

He stood a moment, then obeyed. She saw the strickenness upon him and abruptly had no words. They looked, silent, for minutes.

Daniel Holm sat before the screens which held Liaw of The Tarns, Matthew Vickery of the Parliament, and Juan Cajal of the Empire. A fourth had just darkened. It had carried a taped plea from Trauvay, High Wyvan of Ythri, that Avalon yield before worse should befall and a harsher peace be dictated to the whole Domain.

"You have heard, sirs?" Cajal asked.

"We have heard," Liaw answered.

Holm felt the pulse in his breast and temples, not much quickened but a hard, steady slugging. He longed for a cigar—unavailable—or a drink—unadvisable—or a year of sleep—unbroken. *At that,* crossed his mind, *we're in better shape than the admiral. If ever I saw a death's head, it rides his shoulderboards.*

"What say you?" Cajal went on like an old man.

"We have no wish for combat," Liaw declared, "or to deepen the suffering of our brethren. Yet we cannot give away what our folk so dearly bought for us."

"Marchwarden Holm?"

"You won't renew the attack while we've got your people here," the human said roughly. "Not that we'll hold them forever. I told you before, we don't make bargaining counters out of thinking beings. Still, the time and circumstances of their release have to be negotiated."

Cajal's glance shifted to the next screen. "President Vickery?"

A politician's smile accompanied the response: "Events have compelled me to change my opinion as regards the strategic picture, Admiral. I remain firm in my opposition to absolutist attitudes. My esteemed colleague, Governor Saracoglu, has always impressed me as being similarly reasonable. You have lately returned from a prolonged conference with him. Doubtless many intelligent, well-informed persons took part. Did no possibility of compromise emerge?"

Cajal sagged. "I could argue and dicker for days," he said. "What's the use? I'll exercise my discretionary powers and lay before you at once the maximum I'm authorized to offer."

Holm gripped the arms of his chair.

"The governor pointed out that Avalon can be considered as having already met most terms of the armistice," crawled from Cajal. "Its orbital fortifications no longer exist. Its fleet is a fragment whose sequestration, as required, would make no real difference to you. Most important, Imperial units *are* now on your planet.

"Nothing is left save a few technicalities. Our wounded and our medics must be given the acknowledged name of occupation forces. A command must be established over your military facilities; one or two men per station will satisfy that requirement while posing no threat of takeover should the truce come apart. Et cetera. You see the general idea."

"The saving of face," Holm grunted. "Uh-huh. Why not? But how about afterward?"

"The peace treaty remains to be formulated," said the drained voice. "I can tell you in strict confidence, Governor Saracoglu has sent to the Imperium his strongest recommendation that Avalon not be annexed."

Vickery started babbling. Liaw held stiff. Holm gusted a breath and sat back.

They'd done it. They really had.

The talk would go on, of course. And on and on and on, along with infinite petty particulars and endless niggling. No matter. Avalon would stay Ythrian—stay free.

I ought to whoop, he thought. *Maybe later. Too tired now.*

His immediate happiness, quiet and deep, was at knowing that tonight he could go home to Rowena.

✷XIX✷

There were no instant insights, no dramatic revelations and reconciliations. But Arinnian was to remember a certain hour.

His work for his father had stopped being very demanding. He realized he should use the free time he had regained to phase back into his studies. Then he decided that nothing was more impractical than misplaced practicality. Tabitha agreed. She got herself put on inactive duty. Eventually, however, she must return to her island and set her affairs in order, if only for the sake of her partner's family. Meanwhile he was still confined to Gray.

He phoned Eyath at her rented room: "Uh, would you, uh, care to go for a sail?"

Yes, she said with every quill.

Conditions were less than perfect. As the boat left the bay, rain came walking. The hull skipped over choppy olive-dark waves, tackle athrum; water slanted from hidden heaven, long spears which broke on the skin and ran down in cool splinters, rushing where they entered the sea.

"Shall we keep on?" he asked.

"I would like to." Her gaze sought land, a shadow aft. No other vessels were abroad, nor any flyers. "It's restful to be this alone."

He nodded. He had stripped, and the cleanness dwelt in his hair and sluiced over his flesh.

She regarded him from her perch on the cabin top, across the cockpit which separated them. "You had something to tell me," she said with two words and her body.

"Yes." The tiller thrilled between his fingers. "Last night, before she left—" In Planha he need speak no further.

"Galemate, galemate," she breathed. "I rejoice." She half extended her wings toward him, winced, and withdrew them.

"For always," he said in awe.

"I could have wished none better than Hrill, for you," Eyath replied. Scanning him closer: "You remain in fret."

He bit his lip.

Eyath waited.

"Tell me," he forced forth, staring at the deck. "You see us from outside. Am I able to be what she deserves?"

She did not answer at once. Startled not to receive the immediate yea he had expected, Arinnian lifted his eyes to her silence. He dared not interrupt her thought. Waves boomed, rain laughed.

Finally she said, "I believe she is able to make you able."

He nursed the wound. Eyath began to apologize, summoned resolution and did not. "I have long felt," she told him, "that you needed someone like Hrill to show you that—show you how—what is wrong for my folk is right, is the end and meaning of life, for yours."

He mustered his own courage to say, "I knew the second part of that in theory. Now she comes as the glorious fact. Oh, I was jealous before. I still am, maybe I will be till I die, unable to help myself. She, though, she's worth anything it costs. What I am learning, Eyath, my sister, is that she is not you and you are not her, and it is good that you both are what you are."

"She has given you wisdom." The Ythrian hunched up against the rain.

Arinnian saw her grief and exclaimed, "Let me pass the gift on. What befell you—"

She raised her head to look wildly upon him.

"Was that worse than what befell her?" he challenged. "I don't ask for pity"—human word—"because of past foolishness, but I do think my lot was more hard than either of yours, the years I wasted imagining bodily love can ever be bad, imagining it has any real difference from the kind of love I bear to you, Eyath. Now we'll have to right each other. I want you to share my hopes."

She sprang down from the cabin, stumbled to him and folded him in her wings. Her head she laid murmuring against his shoulder. Raindrops glistened within the crest like jewels of a crown.

✿ ✿ ✿

The treaty was signed at Fleurville on a day of late winter. Little ceremony was involved and the Ythrian delegates left almost at once. "Not in very deep anger," Ekrem Saracoglu explained to Luisa Cajal, who had declined his invitation to attend. "By and large, they take their loss philosophically. But we couldn't well ask them to sit through our rituals." He drew on his cigarette. "Frankly, I too was glad to get off that particular hook."

He had, in fact, simply made a televised statement and avoided the solemnities afterward. A society like Esperance's was bound to mark the formal end of hostilities by slow marches and slower thanksgiving services.

That was yesterday. The weather continued mild on this following afternoon, and Luisa agreed to come to dinner. She said her father felt unwell, which, regardless of his liking and respect for the man, did not totally displease Saracoglu.

They walked in the garden, she and he, as often before. Around paths which had been cleared, snow decked the beds, the bushes and boughs, the top of the wall, still white although it was melting, here and there making thin chimes and gurgles as the water ran. No flowers were left outdoors, the air held only dampness, and the sky was an even dove-gray. Stillness lay beneath it, so that footfalls scrunched loud on gravel.

"Besides," he added, "it was a relief to see the spokesman for Avalon and his cohorts board their ship. The secret-service men I'd assigned to guard them were downright ecstatic."

"Really?" She glanced up, which gave him a chance to dwell on luminous eyes, tip-tilted nose, lips always parted as if in a child's eagerness. But she spoke earnestly—too earnestly, too much of the time, damn it. "I knew there had been some idiot anonymous death threats against them. Were you that worried?"

He nodded. "I've come to know my dear Esperancians. When Avalon dashed their original jubilation—well, you've seen and heard the stuff about 'intransigent militarists.'" He wondered if his fur cap hid his baldness or reminded her of it. Maybe he should break down and get a scalp job.

Troubled, she asked, "Will they ever forget . . . both sides?"

"No," he said. "I do expect grudges will fade. We've too many mutual interests, Terra and Ythri, to make a family fight into a blood feud. I hope."

"We *were* more generous than we had to be. Weren't we? Like letting them keep Avalon. Won't that count?"

"It should." Saracoglu grinned on the left side of his mouth, took a final acrid puff and tossed his cigarette away. "Though everybody sees the practical politics involved. Avalon proved itself indigestible. Annexation would have spelled endless trouble, whereas Avalon as a mere enclave poses no obvious difficulties such as the war was fought to terminate. Furthermore, by this concession, the Empire won some valuable points with respect to trade that might otherwise not have been feasible to insist on."

"I know," she said, a bit impatiently.

He chuckled. "You also know I like to hear myself talk."

She grew wistful. "I'd love to visit Avalon."

"Me too. Especially for the sociological interest. I wonder if that planet doesn't foreshadow the distant future."

"How?"

He kept his slow pace and did not forget her arm resting on his; but he squinted before him and said out of his most serious thought, "The biracial culture they're creating. Or that's creating itself; you can't plan or direct a new current in history. I wonder if that wasn't the source of their resistance—like an alloy or a two-phase material, many times stronger than either part that went into it. We've a galaxy, a cosmos to fill—"

My, what a mixed bag of metaphors, including this one, gibed his mind. He laughed inwardly, shrugged outwardly, and finished: "Well, I don't expect to be around for that. I don't even suppose I'll have to meet the knottier consequences of leaving Avalon with Ythri."

"What could those be?" Luisa wondered. "You just said it was the only thing to do."

"Indeed. I may be expressing no more than the natural pessimism of a man whose lunch at Government House was less than satisfactory. Still, one can imagine. The Avalonians, both races, are going to feel themselves more Ythrian than the Ythrians. I anticipate future generations of theirs will supply the Domain with an abnormal share, possibly most of its admirals. Let us hope they do not in addition supply it with revanchism. And under pacific conditions, Avalon, a unique world uniquely situated, is sure to draw more than its share of trade—more important, brains, which follow opportunity. The effects of that are beyond foreseeing."

Her clasp tightened on his sleeve. "You make me glad I'm not a statesman."

"Not half as glad as I am that you're not a statesman," he said, emphasizing the last syllable. "Come, let's drop these dismal important matters. Let's discuss—for example, your tour of Avalon. I'm sure it can be arranged, a few months hence."

She turned her face from him. When the muteness had lasted a minute, he stopped, as did she. "What's the matter?" he asked, frightened.

"I'm leaving, Ekrem," she said. "Soon. Permanently."

"What?" He restrained himself from seizing her.

"Father. He sent in his resignation today."

"I know he . . . has been plagued by malicious accusations. You recall I wrote to Admiralty Center."

"Yes. That was nice of you." She met his eyes again.

"No more than my duty, Luisa." The fear would not leave him, but he was pleased to note that he spoke firmly and maintained his second-best smile. "The Empire needs good men. No one could have predicted the Scorpeluna disaster, nor done more after the thing happened than Juan Cajal did. Blaming him, calling for court-martial, is wizened spite, and I assure you nothing will come of it."

"But he blames himself," she cried low.

I have no answer to that, he thought.

"We're going back to Nuevo México," she said.

"I realize," he attempted, "these scenes may be unduly painful to him. Need you leave, however?"

"Who else has he?"

"Me. I, ah, will presumably get an eventual summons to Terra—"

"I'm sorry, Ekrem." Her lashes dropped over the delicate cheekbones. "Terra would be no good either. I won't let him gnaw away his heart alone. At home, among his own kind, it will be better." She smiled, not quite steadily, and tossed her head. "*Our* kind. I admit a little homesickness myself. Come visit us sometime." She chose her words: "No doubt I'll be getting married. I think, if you don't mind, I think I'd like to name a boy for you."

"Why, I would be honored beyond anything the Emperor could hang on this downward-slipping chest of mine," he said automatically. "Shall we go inside? The hour's a trifle early for drinks, perhaps; on the other hand, this is a special occasion."

Ah, well, he thought above the pain, *the daydream was a pleasant guest, but now I am freed from the obligations of a host. I can relax and enjoy the games of governor, knight, elevated noble, Lord Advisor, retired statesman dictating interminable and mendacious memoirs.*

Tomorrow I must investigate the local possibilities with respect to bouncy and obliging ladies. After all, we are only middle-aged once.

Summer dwelt in Gray when word reached Avalon. There had been some tension—who could really trust the Empire?—and thus joy amid the human population exploded in festival.

Bird, Christopher Holm and Tabitha Falkayn soon left the merriment. Announcements, ceremonies, feasts could wait; they had decided that the night of final peace would be their wedding night.

Nonetheless they felt no need of haste. That was not the way of the choths. Rather, two sought to become one with their world, their destiny, and their dead—whether in waiting for lovetime or in love itself—until all trouble had been mastered and they could freely become one with each other.

Beyond the northern headland, the hills were as yet uninhabited, though plants whose ancestral seeds arrived with the pioneers had here long ceased to be foreign. Chris and Tabby landed in a sunset whose red and gold ran berserk above a quiet sea. They pitched camp, ate, drank a small glass of wine and a long kiss; afterward, hand in hand, they walked a trail which followed the ridge.

On their left, as daylight smoldered away, grasses wherein clustered trefoil and sword-of-sorrow fell steeply down to the waters. These glimmered immense, out to a horizon which lost itself in a sky deepening from violet to crystalline black. The evening star stood as a candle among the awakening constellations. On their right was forest, darkling, still sweet from odors of pine. A warm small breeze made harp vines ring and brightness twinkle among the jewelleafs.

"Eyath?" she asked once.

"Homebound," he answered.

That, and his tone and the passage of his mouth across her dimly seen hair, said: *In showing me I must heal her, and how, you healed me, my darling.*

Her fingertips, touching his cheek, said: *To my own gladness, which grew and grew.*

Nevertheless he sensed a question in her. He thought he knew what it was. It had often risen in him; but he, the reader, philosopher, poet, could inquire of the centuries better than she, whose gift was to understand the now.

He did not press her to voice it. Enough for this hour, that she was here and his.

Morgana rose, full, murky-spotted and less bright than formerly. So much had it been scarred. Tabby halted.

"Was it worth it?" she said. He heard the lingering anguish.

"The war, you mean?" he prompted.

"Yes." Her free arm rose. "Look there. Look everywhere—around this globe, out to those suns—death, maiming, agony, mourning, ruin—losses like that yonder, things we've cheated our children of—to make a political point!"

"I've wondered too," he confessed. "Remember, though, we did keep something for the children that they'd otherwise have lost. We kept their right to be themselves."

"You mean to be what we are. Suppose we'd been defeated. We nearly were. The next generation would have grown up as reasonably contented Imperial subjects. Wouldn't they have? So had we the right in the first place to do what we did?"

"I've decided yes," he said. "Not that any simple principle exists, and not that I couldn't be wrong. But it seems to me—well, that which we are, our society or culture or what you want to name it, has a life and a right of its own."

He drew breath. "Best beloved," he said, "if communities didn't resist encroachments, they'd soon be swallowed by the biggest and greediest. Wouldn't they? In the end, dead sameness. No challenges, no inspirations from somebody else's way. What service is it to life if we let that happen?

"And, you know, enmities needn't be eternal. I daresay, oh, for instance, Governor Saracoglu and Admiral Cajal had ancestors on opposite sides at Lepanto." He saw that she didn't grasp his reference. No matter, she followed his drift. "The point is, both strove, both resisted, both survived to give something to the race, something special that none else could have given. Can't you believe that here on Avalon we've saved part of the future?"

"Bloodstained," she said.

"That wasn't needful," he agreed. "And yet, we sophonts being what we are, it was unavoidable. Maybe someday there'll be something better. Maybe, even, this thing of ours, winged and wingless together, will help. We have to keep trying, of course."

"And we do have peace for a while," she whispered.

"Can't we be happy in that?" he asked.

Then she smiled through moonlit tears and said, "Yes, Arinnian, Chris, dearest of all," and sought him.

Eyath left Gray before dawn.

At that hour, after the night's revel, she had the sky to herself. Rising, she captured a wind and rode it further aloft. It flowed, it sang. The last stars, the sinking moon turned sea and land into mystery; ahead, sharp across whiteness, lifted the mountains of home.

It was cold, but that sent the blood storming within her.

She thought: *He who cared for me and he who got me share the same honor. Enough.*

Muscles danced, wings beat, alive to the outermost pinion. The planet spun toward morning. *My brother, my sister have found their joy. Let me go seek my own.*

Snowpeaks flamed. The sun stood up in a shout of light.

High is heaven and holy.

CHRONOLOGY OF TECHIC CIVILIZATION

✻COMPILED BY SANDRA MIESEL✻

The Technic Civilization series sweeps across five millennia and hundreds of light-years of space to chronicle three cycles of history shaping both human and non-human life in our corner of the universe. It begins in the twenty-first century, with recovery from a violent period of global unrest known as the Chaos. New space technologies ease Earth's demand for resources and energy permitting exploration of the Solar system.

ca. 2055 "The Saturn Game" (*Analog Science Fiction*, hereafter *ASF*, February, 1981)

22nd C The discovery of hyperdrive makes interstellar travel feasible early in the twenty-second century. The Breakup sends humans off to colonize the stars, often to preserve cultural identity or to try a social experiment. A loose government called the Solar Commonwealth is established. Hermes is colonized.

2150 "Wings of Victory" (*ASF*, April, 1972)
The Grand Survey from Earth discovers alien races on Yithri, Merseia, and many other planets.

23rd C The Polesetechnic League is founded as a mutual protection association of space-faring merchants. Colonization of Aeneas and Altai.

24ᵗʰ C "The Problem of Pain" (*Fantasy and Science Fiction*, February, 1973)

2376 Nicholas van Rijn born poor on Earth
Colonization of Vixen.

2400 Council of Hiawatha, a futile attempt
to reform the League
Colonization of Dennitza.

2406 David Falkayn born noble on Hermes,
a breakaway human grand duchy.

2416 "Margin of Profit" (*ASF*, September, 1956) [van Rijn]
"How to Be Ethnic in One Easy Lesson" (in *Future Quest*, ed. Roger Elwood, Avon Books, 1974)

✿ ✿ ✿

2423 "The Three-Cornered Wheel" (*ASF*, April, 1963)
[Falkayn]

✿ ✿ ✿

stories overlap
2420s "A Sun Invisible" (*ASF*, April, 1966) [Falkayn]
"The Season of Forgiveness" (*Boy's Life*, December, 1973) [set on same planet as "The Three-Cornered Wheel"]

The Man Who Counts (Ace Books, 1978 as *War of the Wing-Men*, Ace Books, 1958 from "The Man Who Counts," *ASF*, February-April,1958) [van Rijn]

"Esau" (as "Birthright," *ASF* February, 1970) [van Rijn]

"Hiding Place" (*ASF*, March, 1961) [van Rijn]

✿ ✿ ✿

stories overlap
2430s "Territory" (*ASF*, June, 1963) [van Rijn]
"The Trouble Twisters" (as "Trader Team,"
ASF, July-August, 1971) [Falkayn]

"Day of Burning" (as "Supernova," *ASF* January, 1967) [Falkayn]
Falkayn saves civilization on Merseia, mankind's future foe.
"The Master Key" (*ASF* August, 1971) [van Rijn]

Satan's World (Doubleday, 1969 from *ASF*, May-August, 1968) [van Rijn and Falkayn]

"A Little Knowledge" (*ASF*, August, 1971)

The League has become a set of ruthless cartels.

✿ ✿ ✿

2446	"Lodestar" (in *Astounding: The John W. Campbell Memorial Anthology*. ed. Harry Harrison. Random House, 1973) [van Rijn and Falkayn] Rivalries and greed are tearing the League apart. Falkayn marries van Rijn's favorite granddaughter.
2456	*Mirkheim* (Putnam Books, 1977) [van Rijn and Falkayn] The Babur War involving Hermes gravely wounds the League. Dark days loom.
late 25th C	Falkayn founds a joint human-Ythrian colony on Avalon ruled by the Domain of Ythri. [same planet—renamed—as "The Problem of Pain"]
26th C	"Wingless" (as "Wingless on Avalon," *Boy's Life*, July, 1973) [Falkayn's grandson] "Rescue on Avalon" (in *Children of Infinity*, ed. Roger Elwood. Franklin Watts, 1973) Colonization of Nyanza.
2550	Dissolution of the Polesotechnic League.
27th C	The Time of Troubles brings down the Commonwealth. Earth is sacked twice and left prey to barbarian slave raiders.
ca. 2700	"The Star Plunderer" (*Planet Stories*, hereafter *PS*, September, 1952) Manuel Argos proclaims the Terran Empire with citizenship open to all intelligent species. The Principate phase of the Imperium ultimately brings peace to 100,000 inhabited worlds within a sphere of stars 400 light-years in diameter.
28th C	Colonization of Unan Besar. "Sargasso of Lost Starships" (*PS*, January, 1952) The Empire annexes old colony on Ansa by force.

29th C   *The People of the Wind* (New American Library
              from *ASF*, February-April, 1973)
              The Empire's war on another civilized imperium
              starts its slide towards decadence. A descendant of
              Falkayn and an ancestor of Flandry cross paths.

30th C   The Covenant of Alfazar, an attempt at détente
              between Terra and Merseia, fails to achieve peace.

3000   Dominic Flandry born on Earth, illegitimate son of a
              an opera diva and an aristocratic space captain.

3019   *Ensign Flandry* (Chilton, 1966 from shorter version
              in *Amazing,* hereafter *AMZ*, October, 1966)
              Flandry's first collision with the Merseians.

3021   *A Circus of Hells* (New American Library, 1970,
              incorporates "The White King's War," *Galaxy*,
              hereafter *Gal*, October, 1969,
              Flandry is a Lieutenant (j.g.).

3022   Degenerate Emperor Josip succeeds weak old
              Emperor Georgios.

3025   *The Rebel Worlds* (New American Library, 1969)
              A military revolt on the frontier world of Aeneas
              almost starts an age of Barracks Emperors.
              Flandry is a Lt. Commander,
              then promoted to Commander.

3027   "Outpost of Empire" (*Gal*, December, 1967)
              [not Flandry]
              The misgoverned Empire continues
              fraying at its borders.

3028   *The Day of Their Return* (New American Library,
              1973) [Aycharaych but not Flandry]
              Aftermath of the rebellion on Aeneas.

3032   "Tiger by the Tail" (*PS*, January, 1951) [Flandry]
              Flandry is a Captain and averts a barbarian invasion.

3033   "Honorable Enemies" (*Future Combined
              with Science Fiction Stories,*
              May, 1951) [Flandry]
              Captain Flandry's first brush with
              enemy agent Aycharaych.

3035   "The Game of Glory" (*Venture*, March, 1958) [Flandry]
Set on Nyanza, Flandry has been knighted.

3037   "A Message in Secret" (as *Mayday Orbit*,
Ace Books, 1961 from shorter version,
"A Message in Secret," *Fantastic*, December, 1959)
[Flandry]
Set on Altai.

3038   "The Plague of Masters" (as *Earthman, Go Home!*,
Ace Books, 1961 from "A Plague of Masters,"
Fantastic, December, 1960-January, 1961.) [Flandry]
Set on Unan Besar.

3040   "Hunters of the Sky Cave" (as *We Claim These Stars!*,
Ace Books, 1959 from shorter version,
"A Handful of Stars, *Amz*, June, 1959)
[Flandry and Aycharaych]
Set on Vixen.

3041   Interregnum: Josip dies. After three years of civil war,
Hans Molitor will rule as sole emperor.

3042   "The Warriors from Nowhere"
(as "The Ambassadors of Flesh," *PS*, Summer, 1954.)
Snapshot of disorders in the war-torn Empire.

3047   *A Knight of Ghosts and Shadows* (New American
Library, 1975 from *Gal* September/October-
November/December, 1974) [Flandry]
Set on Dennitza, Flandry meets his illegitimate son
and has a final tragic confrontation with Aycharaych.

3054   Emperor Hans dies and is succeeded by his sons,
first Dietrich, then Gerhart.

3061   *A Stone in Heaven* (Ace Books, 1979) [Flandry]
Admiral Flandry pairs off with the daughter of his
first mentor from *Ensign Flandry*.

3064   *The Game of Empire* (Baen Books, 1985) [Flandry]
Flandry is a Fleet Admiral, meets his illegitimate
daughter Diana.

early 4ᵗʰ
millennium The Terran Empire becomes more rigid and
tyrannical in its Dominate phase. The Empire and
Merseia wear each other out.

mid 4th

millennium The Long Night follows the Fall of the Terran Empire.
War, piracy, economic collapse, and isolation
devastate countless worlds.

3600 "A Tragedy of Errors" (*Gal*, February, 1968)
Further fragmentation among surviving human worlds.

3900 "The Night Face" (Ace Books, 1978. as *Let the
Spacemen Beware!*, Ace Books, 1963 from shorter
version "A Twelvemonth and a Day," *Fantastic
Universe*, January, 1960)
Biological and psychological divergence among
surviving humans.

4000 "The Sharing of Flesh" (*Gal*, December, 1968)
Human explorers heal genetic defects and
uplift savagery.

7100 "Starfog" (*ASF*, August. 1967)
Revived civilization is expanding. A New Vixen man
from the libertarian Commonalty meets descendants
of the rebels from Aeneas.

Although Technic Civilization is extinct, another—and perhaps better—turn on the Wheel of Time has begun for our galaxy. The Commonalty must inevitably decline just as the League and Empire did before it. But the Wheel will go on turning as long as there are thinking minds to wonder at the stars.

✧ ✧ ✧

Poul Anderson was consulted about this chart
but any errors are my own.